MW01067505

HALLOWEEN

ALSO EDITED BY PAULA GURAN

Embraces
Best New Paranormal Romance
Best New Romantic Fantasy 2
Zombies: The Recent Dead
The Year's Best Dark Fantasy & Horror: 2010
Vampires: The Recent Undead
The Year's Best Dark Fantasy & Horror: 2011
New Cthulhu: The Recent Weird

HALLOWEEN

EDITED BY

PAULA GURAN

PRIME BOOKS

HALLOWEEN

Copyright © 2011 by Paula Guran.
Cover art by Andrey Kiselev (Fotolia).
Cover design by Telegraphy Harness.

All stories are copyrighted to their respective authors,
and used here with their permission. An extension of this
copyright page can be found on pages 527-528.

Prime Books
www.prime-books.com

Publisher's Note:
No portion of this book may be reproduced by any means, mechanical,
electronic, or otherwise, without first obtaining the permission of the
copyright holder.

For more information, contact Prime Books:
prime@prime-books.com

ISBN: 978-1-60701-283-2

For My Kids

*May the magic of Halloween
always be part of your lives.*

CONTENTS

~ CONTENTS ~

AN INTRODUCTION TO HALLOWEEN

Paula Guran

The farther we've gotten from the magic and mystery of our past, the more we've come to need Halloween. It's a festival of fantasy, a celebration of otherness, the one time each year when the mundane is overturned in favor of the bizarre, and everyone can become anyone or anything they wish. At its core, Halloween is a chance to confront our most primal fear—death—and attempt to control it or, at the very least, mock it. Ancient beliefs, religious meanings, a multitude of ethnic heritages, diverse occult traditions, and the continual influence of popular culture have combined to make Halloween a beloved holiday as well as a booming commercial industry.

Festivals emphasizing the supernatural and death are common in almost all cultures and probably date back to prehistory. The first recorded festivals for the dead were those of the ancient Egyptians. Egyptians had no fear of the deceased, no concept of appeasing unquiet spirits. They offered love, respect, and rites for the continuance of a happy afterlife; they communed with dead ancestors and loved ones. Their rituals included bringing food to tombs and sharing it with the deceased. One of the oldest festivals (there were several) was Wag, celebrated on the first month of the first season of the year, the month of Akhet—meaning "inundation"—the season of the Nile's annual flood. (Various sources disagree on Akhet's correspondence to our calendar; dates very from as early as June 19 to as late as mid-August.) Wag evidently including colorful processions, music, offerings of food and drink for the dead, and hearty feasting and drinking for the living. References are made to "shouts of joy" raised at the Wag festival

Modern Halloween is highly influenced by and probably originated with the ancient Celtic festival of Samhain. About 500–1000 BCE, the Celts—who at the time populated Ireland, Scotland, Wales, England,

Brittany, and northern France—celebrated the first day of winter as their New Year. Winter began, in the climate of Northern Europe, in November. The end of summer marked radical change in the daily life of the pastoral Celts. The herds were brought down from the summer pastures in the hills, the best animals put to shelter, and the rest slaughtered. For the Celts, the period we now consider the end of October and start of November was a time of preparation, festival, and plenty before the coming of the long dark winter.

As agriculture became a part of their lives, harvest time became a seasonal activity. The communal celebration became known as *Samhain* (there are a number of variant spellings, including *Samfuin, Samhuinn, Samain*). Linguistically, the word evidently simply combines the Gaelic words *sam* for "end" and *fuin* for "summer"—End of Summer. Samhain may have just been one night—October 31—or it may have stretched out over three days—October 31, November 1, and November 2.

How Samhain was actually celebrated is unknown. Since the Celts left no written records, what we do know of it comes from secondary sources. Our conjectures are, at best, relatively educated guesses, but they still inform much of our modern Halloween mythos.

Although the bounty of nature and the natural change of seasons were important aspects of Samhain, it was also a festival of the supernatural. Samhain was the turning point of the year for a people who believed that even minor "turning points"—the change from one day to the next, the meeting of sea and shore—were magical. The turning of the year, leaving the season of sunshine and light and entering the darkness of winter, was the most powerful and sacred of such junctures. The worlds of the living and of the dead were very close to one another at Samhain, the veil between the two at its thinnest. The living could communicate with those who had gone beyond; the dead could visit the living. In Celtic times, the dead were not considered evil or particularly dreaded so much as consulted and honored as ancestral spirits and guardians of the wisdom of the tribe. Celtic priests, the Druids, contacted the dead in order to divine the future and make predictions for the community.

[In Halloween lore of the last two centuries or so, references are made to Samhain as a deity or Celtic "Lord of the Dead." There is no evidence for such a god. The fallacy seems to have arisen in the 1770s before improved translation of Celtic literary work and modern archeology. It can be traced to the writings of a Col. Charles Vallency (who, for some reason, was trying to prove that the Irish originally came from Armenia) and then was later perpetuated by Lady Jane Francesca Wilde (Oscar's mum) in her mid-nineteenth century book *Irish Cures, Mystic Charms and Superstitions*. It has gone on to be unquestioningly and inaccurately repeated in many sources over the years.]

Although possibly later developed as post-Christian mythology, the Celts may have believed in faeries or similar magical creatures. They did not believe in demons or devils, but they may well have had these not-so-nice entities to deal with. Resentful of humans taking over the world, the faerie-folk were often thought to be hostile and dangerous. During the magical time of Samhain the faeries were even more powerful than usual. Humans might be lured astray by faeries. These unfortunates would then be lost in the fairy mounds and trapped forever.

Faeries and their kin weren't the only ones causing mischief. The yearly turning point was also seen as a suspension of ordinary space and time. For order and structure to be maintained for the rest of the year, chaos would reign during Samhain. Humans supposedly indulged in cross-gender dressing, tricks, and highjinks. On the practical side, such behavior was an outlet for high spirits before the confining winter came.

We know very little of Druidic religious rituals, but we do know Samhain was one of four "Fire Festivals" of the Celts. Hearth fires were extinguished to symbolize the coming "dark half" of the year, then re-lit from Druidic fires to signify the return and continuance of life. Bonfires were also part of this observance.

Halloween can't really be considered a direct outgrowth of ancient Celtic practices. Other cultural elements—including various harvest festivals—eventually became part of Halloween customs. Over the centuries traditions have been both correctly and incorrectly attributed to the Celts. Sometimes this has been done with an appreciation of the ancient ways. More often, cultural-centrism and historic revisionism so colored thinking that the past was unfairly interpreted.

Early Christian missionaries intentionally identified contact with the supernatural as experiences originating with the Devil and inherently evil. The Druids, since they adhered to "false gods" were, therefore, worshippers of Satan. Later religious prejudice also lumped pagans in with Satan-worship and the resulting misinformation has been further propitiated. (For that matter, as we shall see, animosity between Catholics and Protestants resulted in the alteration of some Halloween lore.)

As with other pre-Christian practices, Samhain was eventually absorbed by the Church. In AD 609 or 610, May 13 was designated as a day to honor the Virgin Mary and the martyred saints. In the eighth century, Pope Gregory III (731-741) fixed November 1 as the anniversary for all saints (including the martyrs). October 31 became All Hallows' Eve [Hallowmas or Halloween], the evening before All Hallows Day [All Saints Day] on November 1. (The word "hallow" was used in the Middle Ages as a synonym for "saint.") Gregory IV (827-844) extended the celebration of All Hallows Day to the entire Church.

The old beliefs did not die out so easily and just honoring saints was not enough to replace the notion of a time of year when the dead could travel the earth. A more abstract holiday commemorating all the faithful departed on November 2 began to be marked as early as the ninth century. Although Odilo, Abbot of Cluny (c. 962-1048), actually instituted the date. By the end of the thirteenth century, it was accepted by the entire Church.

Not only did the Church give the holiday its popular name, it also sanctified the custom of remembering the dead on the eve of November 1. Other pagan traditions and religious practices were adapted by the Church and readapted by the people. "Soul cakes" were baked and given to the town's poor in exchange for their prayers to help the dead in Purgatory enter heaven more quickly. Eventually young men and boys went "souling" from house to house, singing and asking for food, ale, and money rather than cakes.

European beliefs began mixing this type of concern for the spirits of the dead and traditions of welcoming the dear departed with a fear of malevolent otherworldly manifestations. The Church associated anything supernatural with evil and the devil, so it became something to fear. Gifts of food and drink might welcome the dead, but they were also offered to keep less friendly ghosts and whatever else might be unnaturally walking in our world at bay; bonfires were now lit to frighten the Devil away.

On October 31, 1517 Martin Luther, intending to stir debate, posted his Ninety-five Theses on the door of the Wittenberg Castle Church. (An occasion still marked in Lutheran churches as Reformation Sunday.) The religious reformation he sparked eventually did away with the celebration of Halloween for many Europeans. Reformation Protestants did away with the observance of saints' days and without the "hallows" one can not have All Hallows' Eve.

The English, however, managed to preserve some of the secular traditions of the holiday with Guy Fawkes Day. (In 1605 a group of English Roman Catholics conspired to blow up Parliament, King James I, and his heir on November 5. They evidently hoped that in the confusion following, the English Catholics could take over the country. What came to be known as the Gunpowder Plot was foiled and in January 1606 Parliament established November 5 as a day of public thanksgiving. The day became known as Guy Fawkes Day for a conspirator who was arrested and, under torture, revealed the names of the other plotters.) Guy Fawkes Day borrowed a great many of the traditions used to mark Halloween that had fallen just six days before. Bonfires, pranks, begging, and dressing in costume became part of the occasion. In some parts of England, the festivities were virulently anti-Catholic.

In the seventeenth century, immigrants brought a variety of traditions, beliefs, customs, and superstitions to what would later become the United States of America. The Puritan influence in New England left little room for any form of Halloween. Guy Fawkes Day (and its attendant anti-Catholicism), however, was celebrated until the Revolution. The Puritans also brought their fear of witchcraft and a history of persecuting witches to the colonies. Anglican settlers in Virginia brought not only commemoration of saints days, but a typically seventeenth century English belief in the occult. Many Germans who settled in the tolerant Quaker-run state of Pennsylvania had pronounced supernatural beliefs and mystical ideas. Catholics in Maryland and other colonies retained their Halloween-connected religious traditions. Spanish Catholic influence was felt in Florida. African slaves imported a belief in an active spirit world into the southern colonies Post-revolutionary America saw the popularization of harvest "play parties." These community get-togethers were non-religious and—unlike other fall gatherings which were task-oriented for sorghum-making, corn husking, apple picking and paring, and the like—were just for fun. The early autumn parties often featured feasting on and fortune-telling games played with apples, pumpkins, and nuts (all seasonally plentiful) and the telling of spooky tales. A tradition of mischief-making on the night of October 31 was common in some communities as well.

African beliefs and customs were imported with slaves beginning in the seventeenth century, but in the early nineteenth century, Haitians and others fleeing unrest in the Caribbean strengthened the Voudoun culture in the South and mixed new mythologies of the dead, witchcraft, and divination into the Halloween cauldron.

Almost 7.4 million new immigrants from all over the world came to the United States between 1820 and 1870 and each nationality brought its own traditions and customs. Spanish and Mexican Catholic traditions of *el Día de los Muertos* (the Day of the Dead) were strong in the Southwest. But the Irish had the greatest influence on the overall celebration of American Halloween. (From 1825 to 1845, Irish famines drove 700,000 Irish Catholics to the U.S. Another 300,000 entered between 1847 and 1854.)

In County Cork, All Hallows was marked with a mummers' procession of young men claiming to be followers of Muck Olla (a boar from Irish folk tales). Led by Lair Bhain (White Mare) who wore a horse's head and white robes, the group went from house to house noisily beseeching householders to impart food, drink, or money in return for a promise of prosperity in the coming year. Similar masquerades were popular in other Irish locales.

Young Irish women and girls marked the night with various methods of telling the future. The divinations most commonly foretold the identity of future spouses or one's destiny in love.

Although the jack o' lantern did not start out as a lantern at all, the Irish were instrumental in the evolution into this now-quintessential symbol of the season. "Jack o' lanterns," like "will-o'-the-wisps," was originally a name for the flickering light produced by ignition of swamp gas, the gaseous product of decomposing organic matter consisting of methane and phosphine (or possibly piezoelectricity generated by tectonic strain). "Jack o' lantern" was also used in a folktale—with many variations in many cultures—as the name of a man with a lantern who tricks the Devil.

Irish villagers have used carved-out turnips and occasionally beets— abundant in late autumn—to make cheap lanterns with which to light their way as the evenings darkened toward winter. (The term "jack o' lantern" first appeared in print in 1750. The reference was to a night watchman or a man carrying a lantern. The meaning applied to carved pumpkins is first attested, in the U.S., in 1837.) Some say these vegetable lights were carved or painted with scary faces to frighten the spirits away on Halloween. In the U.S. the pumpkin supposedly took the place of the turnip, but the abundant squash may have, at first, merely been a seasonally convenient way to used short candle stubs.

Halloween pranking may also have been an Irish import. Probably originally an outlet for mischief that could be blamed on supernatural entities, the pranks were primarily only slightly bothersome—a cabbage tossed down a chimney or knocking on doors and running away. American pranking evolved into slightly more troublesome endeavors such as moving gates or tying them shut, disassembling a wagon or carriage on a barn roof, soaping windows, stealing doormats, overturning outhouses, blocking roads with bales of hay, and "egging" houses.

Pranksters aside, by the 1880s upper and middle class Americans thought of Halloween as a quaint holiday brought to America by genteel English people. This seems to have been the result of the popular fiction and articles in children's and ladies' periodicals of the day. They down-played Irish Catholic connections and provided social tips on entertaining with parties for children, young adults or both. Parlor games (such as bobbing for apples and jumping over candlesticks) were popular. And although death and magic were de-emphasized, divination—especially that involving romance—was a major part of the revelry. Halloween was seen as much of an occasion for matchmaking as for mild fright. Ghost stories in the ladies' magazines became less involved with ghosts and more inclined to be tales of love with mildly Gothic trappings.

By the beginning of the twentieth century, middle-class Halloween became more of a children's holiday full of harmless amusements. Parties, scavenger hunts, and other games became the focus. Scary and eerie elements were sanitized into safe, folkloric fun.

Among the lower classes, however, Halloween remained a night of rough mischief. It became an increasingly destructive way to for poor city dwellers to vent their frustrations. By the 1920s vandalism was no longer confined to tipping over outhouses and soaping windows. Severe property damage, fires, and cruelty to animals and people became all too common. Local civic groups mobilized to deal with the "Halloween problem." Various charitable and community activities—raking leaves, neighborhood clean-ups, property improvements—were organized with young participants treated to parties as a reward. Children were encouraged to go door to door and receive treats instead of making trouble. By the 1930s these "beggar's nights" were starting to be practiced all over U.S. The term "trick or treat" first appeared in print in 1934.

But vandalism and destruction—particularly in crowded urban areas like Detroit, Chicago, and New York—continued to grow. In 1933 and 1934—probably not coincidentally in the dire economic depths of the Great Depression—boys and young men wrought great destruction, even rioting. Arson, overturning cars, sawing down telephone poles, flooding from opened hydrants, blocking thoroughfares, breaking street lights, and other vandalism brought official community encouragement of organized social activities and contests.

World War II made pranking even more seriously frowned upon, even unpatriotic. The Chicago City Council banned Halloween for the duration of the war, substituting "Conservation Day" in its stead. Single-minded community intolerance of wasteful destruction and vigilance curtailed vandalism in other communities. Although some communities did away with officially sanctioning Halloween, most saw the holiday as an opportunity for morale building. Even though some festivities were altered due to war shortages, substitutions and innovation made for adequate wartime Halloween celebrating.

After the war, civic leaders continued their campaigns for "safe and sane" Halloween activities. Halloween became, more and more during the 1940s and 1950s, a holiday for children to enjoy rather than one for pranksters. In the fifties, the impetus moved back to school and family activities. Trick or treating became a firmly entrenched nationwide custom. Its implied threat became less and less a reality in most communities; in others the "tricks" were relegated to a Mischief Night and the "treats" to Halloween itself.

By the 1960s, when most Americans were no longer particularly frightened by supernatural entities, a new element arose: the fear of sadistic or deranged adults intent on harming children. These "urban legends" were originally given impetus by incidents with some truth, but no real malicious intent. In the mid-sixties, the fear was of poisoned candy. In 1967 the focus became the threat of razors and sharp objects hidden in apples (and later candy). In 1973-74, completely unfounded rumors of a Satanic cults plotting to kidnap and sacrifice children on Halloween arose. These new legends altered Halloween celebrations. Trick or treat was banned entirely in some areas; safety factors and "safe" festivities were stressed.

Some conservative fundamentalist Christian groups also began to come out against celebrating Halloween in the 1970s. Many churches, including fundamentalist denominations, had previously sponsored "wholesome" community Halloween activities. Some of the anti-Halloween propaganda from these groups also tended toward anti-Catholicism. In the 1990s some public schools reacted to parental concerns about Halloween—sometimes linked to promoting violence and violent images—by substituting "Harvest Festivals" for Halloween celebrations.

In some parts of the world, All Saints Day and All Souls Day are still important days of religious observance, and in the U.S. there is still a Christian religious aspect to the holiday as marked by Roman Catholics, Anglicans, and Episcopalians. Modern Wiccans and other neopagans consider Samhain a major holiday. But Halloween as we now know it is a secular holiday with no religious significance for most. In the late nineties, there were even some unsuccessful organized efforts made to change the celebration of Halloween to the last Saturday in October, citing practical, safety, and merchandising advantages.

In many ways, modern Halloween has actually become two separate celebrations. One is for adults, the other is child-oriented. For both, Halloween is often celebrated more than just one night. The entire month of October is now full of events and entertainment.

For grown-ups, Halloween is now the third biggest "party day" (after New Year's and Super Bowl Sunday) of the year. According to the National Retail Federation, young adults (age 18-24 years) are more likely than any other age group to throw or attend a party (55.4%). Halloween marketing began to shift toward adults in the seventies. By 1980, a quarter of adults aged 18 to 40 wore some form of costume; by 1986, it was around 60%. In 2010, Americans spent an estimated $800 million on costumes for children, $1 billion on costumes for adults. Adults celebrate not only at home, but at work; nightclubs, restaurants, and bars host Halloween events. Haunted attractions—from local charity-run haunted locations to more extravagant for-profit attractions and major commercial theme parks—now number in the thousands. The commercial enterprises have become a multi-million dollar industry. Although some cater to youngsters, most are aimed at scaring teens and young adults.

The kids' version of Halloween evolves around masquerade, parties, family-oriented events (hayrides, not-very-scary haunted houses, and pumpkin patches), and trick or treating—even if the latter is sometimes restricted, adult-controlled, and made entirely "safe." At the same time, many of the negative myths that arose in the previous three decades were, by the end of the nineties, beginning to be debunked by the media.

A fairly recent innovation, Halloween-themed "agritainment" and has helped offset the loss of traditional farm income, often in a big way. Offering far more than a simple hayride through harvested fields, there are now "fall family adventure farms," complicated corn mazes, pick-it-yourself pumpkin fields, haunted barns and stables, and usually plenty of tasty edibles.

"Educational" events with a Halloween theme abound. Parks, zoos, museums, and nature study facilities teach both adults and children about traditionally scary creatures likes owls, spiders, snakes and bats. There are ghost-tours related to historic locations and events; some older cemeteries even use Halloween as an excuse to nurture an appreciation of history.

"Trick or Treat for UNICEF" is no longer the only charitable event using Halloween for a good cause. There are blood drives with vampires, programs to collect used costumes to allow homeless and disadvantaged children to dress up for the holiday, balls to raise funds for AIDS research, and more.

Halloween remains a predominately North American holiday. It is popular in England: By 2010, the British grocery chain Tesco estimated its Halloween sales had almost tripled—to £55 million—since 2005. (In 2010, they sold 1.4 million pumpkins.) In terms of retail sales, only Christmas and Easter are bigger. Ghost walks, pumpkin carving, dance parties, club nights, and similar events are common. Trick or treating was once widespread, but the last few years have seen its decline. Blame for this new dislike may lie with parental disdain for teaching children the rude behavior of "begging" and what appears to be a rise in egging, flour bombs, and other "anti-social" behavior. "No Trick or Treat Here" posters have been made widely available in many communities. Evidently British youths have put the "tricks" back into the custom.

The Japanese are now starting to celebrate Halloween to some extent. Halloween bento—a meal served in a box—can be bought along with seasonal pumpkin-flavored chocolate and cookies featuring pictures of koalas dressed in Halloween costumes. Trick or treating is not commonplace, but dressing up in costumes for parades is popular.

In Romania, where Dracula has become a tourist industry, adult nightclubs throw parties with bat and vampire themes.

In the mid-1990s, Halloween seemed to be catching on in France. American companies like McDonald's, and Disneyland Paris had Halloween themes; some nightclubs and bars had events. But, from the beginning, French media denounced Halloween as an American marketing gimmick. In 2006, the newspaper *Le Monde* pronounced Halloween "more or less buried" in France.

In the last few years, Halloween has been creeping into Austria, Belgium, Germany, Italy, Norway, Sweden, and Italy, but is not widely celebrated. There has been some backlash in Europe against what is seen as yet another example of crass American commercialism undermining traditional culture and, in some cases, religion. Similarly, Halloween seems to have little chance to take hold "Down Under." A 2009 survey by News.com.au asked: "Should Australia ditch Halloween as an event on the calendar?" More than 77% of the respondents replied, "Yes, It's totally irrelevant."

For Americans, Halloween has manifested itself as an important—if still unofficial—holiday. We are just now beginning to seriously investigate its history and antecedents even as we adapt it to an ever-changing society and devise new traditions and customs with which to celebrate. What we do at Halloween—and what it does for us—varies from individual to individual and group to group depending on our beliefs, backgrounds, sexual orientation, even employment.

There are certain rites of passage associated with Halloween as well. As we progress through different stages in life, we relate to Halloween in different ways. The day comes when we are "too old" for trick or treat, but that may mean we are ready for more adult activities. Young adults often mix the modern equivalent of "matchmaking" with Halloween celebrations. As we become parents ourselves, we pass on traditions, give out the treats, and make the costumes: we become responsible for supplying some of the magic ourselves. At the same time, we discover we still have a need to be, for just one night, something other than what we usually are. Instead of becoming gatekeepers for a new generation, some adults extend the fantasy of Halloween far past the perimeters of age.

Whatever its history, Halloween is anything but a dead tradition. It is, perhaps, more alive and more meaningful now than ever before.

This essay has been updated and considerably modified from an earlier version that appeared as "A Short History of Halloween" in *October Dreams: A Celebration of Halloween*, edited by Richard Chizmar and Robert Morrish, published by Cemetery Dance Publications in 2000.

If you are interested in learning more about the history of Halloween, I recommend only a handful of books . . . and avoiding a great deal of what you will find online. First and foremost is *The Halloween Encyclopedia* (Second Edition) by Lisa Morton (McFarland, 2011). I wish I'd had the first edition (2003) when I wrote "A Short History of Halloween"! Also by Morton: *A Hallowe'en Anthology* (McFarland, 2008). Full of original source materials, it may not appeal to the casual reader, but if you are a true Halloween enthusiast it is full of goodies. *Halloween: An American Holiday, an American History* (Pelican, 1999) and *Halloween Nation: Behind the Scenes of America's Fright Night* (Pelican, 2011), both by Lesley Pratt Bannatyne are also recommended. Ballatyne's *A Halloween Reader: Poems, Stories, and Plays from Halloween Past* (Pelican, 2004) will, like Morton's *Anthology*, appeal to dedicated Halloweenists.

Paula Guran

June 2011

A NOTE ON SPELLING: *Halloween* or *Hallowe'en*? Personally I prefer the latter as closer to the original meaning of the word, but the holiday is now so thoroughly "Americanized" the version without the apostrophe is probably more widely used. For this anthology, I've employed *Halloween* in my own comments, but adhered to whichever spelling was preferred by the authors—so you'll find both. However, I conformed stylistically to *jack o' lantern*, *All Hallows*, *All Souls*, *All Saints*, and *trick or treat* (and variants) with no hyphenation (unless the term is used as an adjective modifying a noun).

CONVERSATIONS IN A DEAD LANGUAGE

Thomas Ligotti

Thomas Ligotti's postal protagonist is both disturbing and disturbed. This elegantly sinister, highly suspenseful story combines both modern non-supernatural horror and the traditionally supernatural.

The idea of an evil human preying on the innocent at Halloween is a fairly recent inclusion in the mythos. The fearful aspects of the holiday are more rooted in uncertainty of the coming dark season, the possibility of being trapped outside normality, or dealing with an unappeased spirit, witch, or malicious trickster. At worst some otherworldly monster might enter our world or the Devil attempt to make a bargain. But by the time Jon Carpenter's 1978 film Halloween *introduced the masses to the idea of a maniacal killer on the loose—or perhaps its sociological reflection of our culture—we were thinking more about frightful humans than placating the supernatural. Ligotti gives us both to consider.*

After changing out of his uniform, he went downstairs to search the kitchen drawers, rattling his way through cutlery and cooking utensils. Finally he found what he wanted. A carving knife, a holiday knife, the traditional blade he'd used over the years. Knifey-wifey.

First he carved out an eye, spearing the triangle with the point of his knife and neatly drawing the pulpy thing from its socket. Pinching the blade, he slid his two fingers along the blunt edge, pushing the eye onto the newspaper he'd carefully placed next to the sink. Another eye, a nose, a howling oval mouth. Done. Except for manually scooping out the seedy and stringy entrails and supplanting them with a squat little candle of the vigil type. Guide them, holy lantern, through darkness and disaster. To me. To meezy-weezy.

He dumped several bags of candy into a large potato chip bowl, fingering pieces here and there: the plump caramels, the tarty sour balls, the chocolate kisses for the kids. A few were test-chewed for taste and texture. A few more. Not too many, for some of his co-workers already called him Fatass, almost behind his back. And he would spoil the holiday dinner he had struggled to prepare in the little time left before dark. Tomorrow he'd start his diet and begin making more austere meals for himself.

At dark he brought the pumpkin out to the porch, placing it on a small but lofty table over which he'd draped a bedsheet no longer in normal use. He scanned the old neighborhood. Beyond the railings of other porches and in picture windows up and down the street glowed a race of new faces in the suburb. Holiday visitors come to stay the night, without a hope of surviving till the next day. All Souls Day. Father Mickiewicz was saying an early morning mass, which there would be just enough time to attend before going to work.

No kids yet. Wait. There we go, bobbing down the street: a scarecrow, a robot, and—what is it?—oh, a white-faced clown. Not the skull-faced thing he'd at first thought it was, pale and hollow-eyed as the moon shining frostily on one of the clearest nights he'd ever seen. The stars were a frozen effervescence.

Better get inside. They'll be coming soon. Waiting behind the glass of the front door with the bowl of candy under his arm, he nervously grabbed up palmsful of the sweets and let them fall piece by piece back into the bowl, a buccaneer reveling in his loot . . . a grizzled-faced pirate, eye-patch over an empty socket, a Jolly Roger on his cap with *X* marking the spot in bones, running up the front walk, charging up the wooden stairs of the porch, rubber cutlass stuffed in his pants.

"Trick or treat."

"Well, well, well," he said, his voice rising in pitch with each successive "well." "If it isn't Blackbeard. Or is it Bluebeard, I always forget. But you don't have a beard at all, do you?" The pirate shook his head shyly to say "no." "Maybe we should call you Nobeard, then, at least until you start shaving."

"I have a moustache. Trick or treat, mister," the boy said, impatiently holding up an empty pillowcase.

"You do have a nice moustache at that. Here you go, then," he said, tossing a handful of candy into the sack. "And cut a few throats for me," he shouted as the boy turned and ran off.

He didn't have to say those last words so loudly. Neighbors. No, no one heard. The streets are filled with shouters tonight, one the same as another. Listen to the voices all over the neighborhood, music against the sounding board of silence and the chill infinity of autumn.

Here come some more. Goody.

Trick or treat: an obese skeleton, meat bulging under its painted-costume bones. How unfortunate, especially at his age. Fatass of the boneyard and the schoolyard. Give him an extra handful of candy. "Thanks a *lot*, mister," "Here, have more." Then the skeleton waddled down the porch steps, its image thinning out into the nullity of the darkness, candy-filled paper bag rattling away to a whisper.

Trick or treat: an overgrown baby, bibbed and bootied, with a complexion problem erupting on its pre-adolescent face. "Well, cootchie coo," he said to the infant as he showered its open bunting with candy. Baby sneered as it toddled off, pouchy diapers slipping down its backside, disappearing once again into the black from which it had momentarily emerged.

Trick or treat: midget vampire, couldn't be more than six years old. Wave to Mom waiting on the sidewalk. "Very scary. Your parents must he proud. Did you do all that makeup work yourself?" he whispered. The little thing mutely gazed up, its eyes underlined with kohl-dark smudges. It then used a tiny finger, pointy nail painted black, to indicate the guardian figure near the street. "Mom, huh? Does she like sourballs? Sure she does. Here's some for Mom and some more for yourself, nice red ones to suck on. That's what you scary vampires like, eh?" he finished, winking. Cautiously descending the stairs, the child of the night returned to its parent, and both proceeded to the next house, joining the anonymous ranks of their predecessors.

Others came and went. An extraterrestrial with a runny nose, a smelly pair of ghosts, an asthmatic tube of toothpaste. The parade thickened as the night wore on. The wind picked up and a torn kite struggled to free itself from the clutches of an elm across the street. Above the trees the October sky remained lucid, as if a glossy veneer had been applied across the night. The moon brightened to a teary gleam, while voices below waned. Fewer and fewer disguises perpetrated deception in the neighborhood. These'll probably be the last ones coming up the porch. Almost out of candy anyway.

Trick or treat. Trick or treat.

Remarkable, these two. Obviously brother and sister, maybe twins. No, the girl looks older. A winning couple, especially the bride. "Well, congratulations to the gride and broom. I know I said it backwards. That's because you're backwards, aren't you? Whose idea was that?" he asked, tossing candy like rice into the bag of the tuxedoed groom. What faces, so clear. Shining stars.

"Hey, you're the mailman," said the boy.

"Very observant. You're marrying a smart one here," he said to the groom.

"I saw you were too," she replied.

"'Course you did. You're sharp kids, both of you. Hey, you guys must be tired, walking around all night." The kids shrugged, unaware of the meaning of fatigue. "I know I am after delivering mail up and down these streets. And I do that every day, except Sunday of course. Then I go to church. You kids go to church?" It seemed they did; wrong one, though. "You know, at our church we have outings and stuff like that for kids. Hey, I got an idea—"

A car slowed down on the street, its constabulary spotlight scanning between houses on the opposite side. Some missing Halloweeners maybe.

"Never mind my idea, kids. Trick or treat," he said abruptly, lavishing candy on the groom, who immediately strode off. Then he turned to the bride, on whom he bestowed the entire remaining contents of the large howl, conveying a scrupulously neutral expression as he did so. Was the kid blushing, or was it just the light from the jack o' lantern?

"C'mon, Charlie," his sister called from the sidewalk.

"Happy Halloween, Charlie. See you next year." Maybe around the i ighborhood.

His thoughts drifted off for a moment. When he regained control the kids were gone, all of them. Except for imaginary ones, ideals of their type. Like that boy and his sister.

He left the candle burning in the jack o' lantern. Let it make the most of "its brief life. Tomorrow it would be defunct and placed out with the other refuse, an extinguished shell pressed affectionately against a garbage bag. Tomorrow . . . All Souls Day. Pick up Mother for church in the morning. Could count it as a weekly visit, holy day of obligation. Also have to remember to talk to Father M. about taking that kiddie group to the football game.

The kids. Their annual performance was now over, the makeup wiped away and all the costumes back in their boxes. After he turned off the lights downstairs and upstairs, and was lying in bed, he still heard "trick or treat" and saw their faces in the darkness. And when they tried to dissolve into the background of his sleepy mind . . . he brought them back.

II

"Ttrrrick or ttrrreat," chattered a trio of hacking, sniffing hoboes. It was much colder this year, and he was wearing the bluish-gray wool overcoat he delivered the mail in. "Some for you, you, and you," he said in a merely efficient tone of voice. The bums were not overly grateful for the handouts. They don't appreciate anything the way they used to. Things change so fast. Forget it, close the door, icy blasts.

Weeks ago the elms and red maples in the neighborhood had been assaulted by unseasonable frigidity and stripped to the bone. Clouds now clotted up the sky, a murky purple ceiling through which no star shone. Snow was imminent.

Fewer kids observed the holiday this year, and of the ones who did a good number of them evidently took little pride in the imagination or lavishness of their disguises. Many were content to rub a little burnt cork on their faces and go out begging in their everyday clothes.

So much seemed to have changed. The whole world had become jaded, an inexorable machine of cynicism. Your mother dies unexpectedly, and they give you two days leave from your job. When you get back, people want to have even less to do with you than before. Strange how you can feel the loss of something that never seemed to be there in the first place. A dwarfish, cranky old woman dies . . . and all of a sudden there's a royal absence, as if a queen had cruelly vacated her throne. It was the difference between a night with a single fibrillating star in it and one without anything but smothering darkness.

But remember those times when she used to . . . No, *nihil nisi bonum*. Let the dead, et cetera, et cetera. Father M. had conducted an excellent service at the funeral home, and there was little point in ruining that perfect sense of finality the priest had managed to convey regarding the earthly phase of his mother's existence. So why bring her now into his thoughts? Night of the Dead, he remembered.

There were no longer very many emissaries of the deceased roaming he streets of the neighborhood. They had gone home, the ones who had left it in the first place. Might as well close up till next year, he thought. No, wait.

Here they are again, coming late in the evening as they did last year. Take off the coat, a sudden flash of warmth. The warming stars had returned, shining their true light once more. How they beamed, those two little points in the blackness. Their stellar intensity went right into him, a bright tightness. He was now grateful for the predominant gloom of this year's Halloween, which only exacerbated his present state of delight. That they were wearing the same costumes as last year was more than he could have hoped.

"Trick or treat," they said from afar, repeating the invocation when the man standing behind the glass door didn't respond and merely stood staring at them. Then he opened the door wide.

"Hello, happy couple. Nice to see you again. You remember me, the mailman?"

The children exchanged glances, and the boy said: "Yeah, sure." The girl antiphonied with a giggle, enhancing his delight in the situation.

"Well, here we are one year later and you two are still dressed and waiting for the wedding to start. Or did it just get over with? At this rate you won't make any progress at all. What about next year? And the next? You'll never get any older, know what I mean? Nothing'll change. Is it okay with you?"

The children tried for comprehending nods but only achieved movements and facial expressions of polite bewilderment.

"Well, it's okay with me too. Confidentially, I wish things had stopped changing for me a long time ago. Anyway, how about some candy?" The candy was proffered, the children saying "thaaank yooou" in the same way they said it at dozens of other houses. But just before they were allowed to continue on their way . . . he demanded their attention once more.

"Hey, I think I saw you two playing outside your house one day when I came by with the mail. It's a big white house over on Pine Court, isn't it?"

"Nope," said the boy as he carefully inched his way down the porch stairs, trying not to trip over his costume. His sister had impatiently made it to the sidewalk already. "It's red with black shutters. On Ash." Without waiting for a reaction to his answer he joined his sister, and side by side the bride and groom walked far down the street, for there didn't seem to be any other houses open for business nearby. He watched them become tiny in the distance, eventually disappear into the dark.

Cold out here, shut the door. There was nothing more to see; he had successfully photographed the encounter for the family album of his imagination. If anything, their faces glowed even brighter and clearer this year. Perhaps they really hadn't changed and never would. No, he thought in the darkness of his bedroom. Everything changes and always for the worst. But they wouldn't make any sudden transformations now, not in his thoughts. Again and again he brought them back to make sure they were the same.

He set his alarm clock to wake himself for early mass the next day. There was no one who would be accompanying him to church this year. He'd have to go alone.

Alone.

III

Next Halloween there was a premature appearance of snow, a thin foundation of whiteness that clung to the earth and trees, putting a pallid face on the suburb. In the moonlight it glittered, a frosty spume. This sparkling below was mirrored by the stars positioned tenuously in the night above. A monstrous mass of snowclouds to the west threatened to intervene, cutting off the reflection from its source and turning everything into a dull emptiness. All sounds were hollowed by the cold, made into the cries of migrating birds in a vacant November dusk.

Not even November yet and look at it, he thought as he stared through the glass of his front door. Very few were out tonight, and the ones who were found fewer houses open to them, closed doors and extinguished porchlights turning them away to roam blindly through the streets. He had lost much of the spirit himself, had not even set out a jack o' lantern to signal his harbor in the night.

Then again, how would he have carried around such a weighty object with his leg the way it was now? One good fall down the stairs and he started collecting disability pay from the government, laid up for months in the solitude of his home.

He had prayed for punishment and his prayers had been answered. Not the leg itself, which only offered physical pain and inconvenience, but the other punishment, the solitude. This was the way he remembered being corrected as a child: sent into the basement, exiled to the cold stone cellar without the relief of light, save for that which hazed in through a dusty window-well in the corner. In that corner he stood, near as he could to the light. It was there that he once saw a fly twitching in a spider web. He watched and watched and eventually the spider came out to begin feasting on its prey. He watched it all, dazed with horror and sickness. When it was over he wanted to do something. He did. With a predatory stealth he managed to pinch up the little spider and pull it off its web. It tasted like nothing at all really, except a momentary tickle on his dry tongue.

"Trick or treat," he heard. And he almost got up to arduously cane his way to the door. But the Halloween slogan had been spoken somewhere in the distance. Why did it sound so close for a moment? Crescendoing echoes of the imagination, where far is near, up is down, pain pleasure. Maybe he should close up for the night. There seemed to be only a few kids playing the game this year. Only the most desultory stragglers remained at this point. Well, there was one now.

"Trick or treat," said a mild, failing little voice. Standing on the other side of the door was an elaborately garbed witch, complete with a warm black shawl and black gloves in addition to her black gown. An old broom was held in one hand, a bag in the other.

"You'll have to wait just a moment," he called through the door as he struggled to get up from the sofa with the aid of his cane. Pain. Good, good. He picked up a full bag of candy from the coffee table and was quite prepared to bestow its entire contents on the little lady in black. But then he recognized who it was behind the cadaver-yellow makeup. Watch it. Wouldn't want to do anything unusual. Play you don't know who it is. And do not say anything concerning red houses with black shutters. Nothing about Ash Street.

To make matters worse, there was the outline of a parent standing on the sidewalk. Insure the safety of the last living child, he thought. But maybe there were others, though he'd only seen the brother and sister. Careful. Pretend she's unfamiliar; after all, she's wearing a different get-up from the one she wore the past two years. Above all don't say a word about you know who.

And what if he would innocently ask where was her little brother this year? Would she say: "He was killed," or maybe, "He's dead," or perhaps just, "He's gone," depending on how the parents handled the whole affair. With any luck, he would not have to find out.

He opened the door just far enough to hand out the candy and in a bland voice said: "Here you go, my little witch." That last part just slipped out somehow.

"Thank you," she said under her breath, under a thousand breaths of fear and experience. So did it seem.

She turned away, and as she descended the porch steps her broom clunked along one step behind her. An old, frayed, throwaway broom. Perfect for witches. And the kind perfect for keeping a child in line. An ugly old thing kept in a corner, an instrument of discipline always within easy reach, always within a child's sight until the thing became a dream-haunting image. Mother's broom.

After the girl and her mother were out of sight, he closed the door on the world and, having survived a tense episode, was actually grateful for the solitude that only minutes ago was the object of his dread.

Darkness. Bed.

But he could not sleep, not to say he did not dream. Hypnagogic horrors settled into his mind, a grotesque succession of images resembling lurid frames from old comic strips. Impossibly distorted faces painted in garish colors frolicked before his mental eye, all entirely beyond his control. These were accompanied by a series of funhouse noises which seemed to emanate from some zone located between his brain and the moonlit bedroom around him. A drone of half-thrilled, half-horrified voices filled the background of his imagination, punctuated by super-distinct shouts which used his name as an excuse for sound. It was in abstract version of his mother's voice, now robbed of any sensual quality to identify it as such, remaining only a pure idea. The voice called out his name from a distant room in his memory. *Sam-u-el*, it shouted with a terrible urgency of obscure origin. Then suddenly—*trick or treat*. The words echoed, changing in sense as they faded into silence: *trick or treat—down the street—we will meet—ashes, ashes.* No, not ashes but other trees. The boy walked behind some big maples, was eclipsed by them. Did he know a car was following him that night? Panic. Don't lose him now. Don't lose him. Ah, there he was on the other side. Nice trees. Good old trees. The boy turned around, and in his hand was a tangled web of strings whose ends extended up to the stars which he began working like kites or toy airplanes or flying puppets, staring up at the night and screaming for the help that never came. Mother's voice started shouting again; then the other voices mixed in, becoming a foul babbling unity of dead voices chattering away. Night of the Dead. All the dead conversed with him in a single voicey-woicey.

Trick or treat, it said.

But this didn't sound as if it were part of his delirium. The words seemed to originate from outside him, for their utterance served to disturb his half-sleep and free him of its terrible weight. Instinctively cautious of his lame leg, he managed to wrest himself from sweaty bedcovers and place both feet on the solid floor. This felt reassuring. But then:

Trick or treat.

It was outside. Someone on the front porch. "I'm coming," he called into the darkness, the sound of his own voice awakening him to the absurdity of what it had said. Had the months of solitude finally exacted their strange price from his sanity? Listen closely. Maybe it won't happen again.

Trick or treat. Trick or treat.

Trick, he thought. But he'd have to go downstairs to be sure. He imagined seeing a playfully laughing shape or shapes scurrying off into the darkness the moment he opened the door. He'd have to hurry, though, it he was to catch them at it. Damn leg, where's that cane. He next found his bathrobe in the darkness and draped it over his underclothed body. Now to negotiate those wicked stairs. Turn on the hallway light. No, that would alert them to his coming. Smart.

He was making it down the stairs in good time, considering the gloomy conditions he was working under. Neither this nor that nor gloom oF night. Gloom of night. Dead of night. Night of the Dead.

With that odd sprightliness of cripples he ambled his way down the stairs, his cane always remaining a step ahead for support. Concentrate, he told his mind, which was starting to wander into strange places in the darkness. Watch out! Almost took a tumble that time. Finally he made it to the very bottom. A sound came through the wall from out on the front porch, a soft explosion it seemed. Good, they were still there. He could catch them and reassure his mind regarding the source of its fancies. The labor of walking down the stairs had left him rather hyperventilated and unsure about everything.

Trying to affect the shortest possible interval between the two operations, he turned the lock above the handle and pulled back the door as suddenly as he was able. A cold wind seeped in around the edges of the outer door, prowling its way past him and into the house. Out on the porch there was no sign of a boyish trickster. Wait, yes there was.

He had to turn on the porchlight to see it. Directly in front of the door a jack o' lantern had been heaved forcefully down onto the cement, caving in its pulpy shell which had exploded into fragments lying here and there on the porch. He opened the outer door for a closer look, and a swift wind invaded the house, flying past his head on frigid wings. What a blast, close the door. Close the door!

"Little buggers," he said very clearly, an attempt to relieve his sense of disorder and delirium.

"Who, meezy-weezy?" said the voice behind him.

At the top of the stairs. A dwarfish silhouette, seemingly with something in its hand. A weapon. Well, he had his cane at least.

"How did you get in here, child?" he asked without being sure it really was a child, considering its strangely hybrid voice.

"Child yourself, sonny. No such things where I come from. No Sammy-Wammies either. I'm just a disguise."

"How did you get in?" he repeated, still hoping to establish a rational manner of entry.

"In? I was already in."

"Here?" he asked.

"No, not here. There-dee-dare." The figure was pointing out the window at the top of the stairs, out at the kaleidoscopic sky. "Isn't it a beauty? No children, no anything."

"What do you mean?" he inquired with oneiric inspiration, the normalcy of dream being the only thing that kept his mind together at this stage.

"Mean? I don't mean nothing, you meany."

Double negative, he thought, relieved to have retained contact with a real world of grammatical propriety. Double negative: two empty mirrors reflecting each other's emptiness to infinite powers, nothing canceling out nothing.

"Nothing?" he echoed with an interrogative inflection.

"Yup, that's where you're going."

"How am I supposed to do that?" he asked, gripping his cane tightly, sensing a climax to this confrontation.

"How? Don't worry. You already made sure of how-wow-wow . . . TRICK OR TREAT!"

And suddenly the thing came gliding down through the darkness.

IV

He was found the next day by Father Mickiewicz, who had telephoned earlier after failing to see this clockwork parishioner appear as usual for early mass on All Souls Day. The door was wide open, and the priest discovered his body at the bottom of the stairs, its bathrobe and under-clothes grotesquely disarranged. The poor man seemed to have taken another fall, a fatal one this time. Aimless life, aimless death: *Thus was his death in keeping with his life*, as Ovid wrote. So ran the priest's ad hoc eulogy, though not the one he would deliver at the deceased's funeral.

But why was the door open if he fell down the stairs? Father M. came to ask himself. The police answered this question with theories about an intruder or intruders unknown. Given the nature of the crime, they speculated on a revenge motive, which the priest's informal testimony was quick to contradict. The idea of revenge against such a man was far-fetched, if not totally meaningless. Yes, meaningless. Nevertheless, the motive was not robbery and the man seemed to have been beaten to death, possibly with his own cane. Later evidence showed that the corpse had been violated, but with an object much longer and more coarse than the cane originally supposed. They were now looking for something with the dimensions of a broomstick, probably a very old thing, splintered and decayed. But they would never find it in the places they were searching.

MONSTERS
Stewart O'Nan

Some fundamentalist Christians have made Halloween into an opportunity for evangelism: dropping tracts into trick-or-treat bags and staging "Hell Houses" in which displays of sins and their horrifying consequences are supposed to scare visitors into redemption. But Father Don's congregation in "Monsters" obviously enjoys Halloween as family event, and this church's spooky displays are all in fun and for fund raising.

There's no hint of the fantastic or supernatural in "Monsters," nothing truly shocking. It's just a quietly brilliant story with its own singular darkness. It is a slice of everyday life. But it's also, among other things, about learning there are "real things to be afraid of" and that no one's life is entirely ordinary or free of shadows.

They were going to be monsters, for the church—Creatures from the Black Lagoon. Mark wanted to be Dracula, but Father Don said only one person could, and Derek convinced him it would be more fun. You got to wear a suit with a zipper up the back and a head that fit like a diving helmet. They could scare the little kids and gross out the girls. No one would know who they were.

"Plus it's boring by yourself," Derek said. "You just sit there."

"Yeah," Mark said, partly because he was secretly afraid of being in there by himself in the dark. "Do we get fangs?"

"You don't need fangs," Derek said. "There's already teeth in the head."

It was Mark's only argument. It was like that with Derek, he was always in charge, which was all right, because Mark was shy and terribly aware and ashamed of it. Plus Derek never ditched him like Peter did. Peter was his brother; he was only two years older than Mark. They'd always played together, ever since they were little, but since Peter started at the high school this fall, he was never home after school. At dinner when Mark brought it up, his father just sighed. "Why don't you go next door?" he said. "You and Derek should be able to find *something* to do."

That's what they were doing, just messing around. It was a Thursday after school and there was nothing to do, so Derek brought out his Daisy and they took turns plinking the same six pop bottles off some old railroad ties Derek's stepfather had piled in the back lot. The gun was so weak they didn't even fall over sometimes, just tinked and wobbled.

It was Derek's idea to play Shooting Gallery. One of them hid behind the ties and then popped up and you had to shoot him. You only pumped the gun once, and they had their jackets on; it only stung if it hit bare skin. You crawled around behind the ties and then popped up and the other person tried to shoot you.

They did that for ten minutes but it was boring. Then Mark came up with Moving Target. In this one, you jumped up and ran and then dove behind the ties. This was even more boring because no one got shot.

Then Derek made up Ambush. The guy with the gun hid somewhere behind the piles of woodchips and gravel, and the guy who popped up threw hand grenades—just round stones Derek's stepfather used to edge the little goldfish ponds he built.

Mark had the gun. He pumped it once and crouched behind a sharp pallet of bricks, waiting for Derek to lob one of the stones. They were a little smaller than baseballs, and he didn't want to get hit with one. He peeked around the corner and saw Derek start to pop up and toss the grenade like a soldier, like a hook shot—saw the stone leave his hand and arc towards him.

He'd have time to think about this later: how impossible it all was. He saw the stone was going to miss, so he ducked around the corner, firing without even bringing the gun up. From the hip, just like in the movies.

He expected Derek to run but he was watching the grenade like it might really explode.

It was just one shot, from the hip.

Derek grabbed his face and bent over, holding it.

Mark thought he was faking. He loved death scenes on TV, dropping to the carpet in their rec room, one hand clutching his heart as he gasped out his last words, the other reaching for Mark's sneaker. But then he was screaming—high and loud and over and over—and walking fast toward his back door, his hand still there, as if he were trying to keep the eye in.

Mark dropped the gun and ran over and walked along with him. "Are you okay?"

"No."

"Let me see."

"No." He was walking slower now, and Mark could have stopped him, but there was blood coming out between his fingers and Mark couldn't think. He went up the porch stairs in front of him and opened the storm door. He saw his own hands were empty, and thought: I shouldn't leave the gun out there.

"Sarah!" he called inside, because Derek's sister was the only one home. He went through the kitchen into the front hall and called her, and she came running down, asking what had happened. When she saw the blood she grabbed Derek and hauled him to the sink and started running water. Mark had a crush on her—her lip gloss, her purple scrunchy, the way she bowed down and then reared up and flung her hair over her head—and her taking charge made her seem heroic, older, even more unreachable.

"What happened?" she asked.

"It was my fault," Mark said. "We were playing with the gun—"

"God damn it," she said. "I can't believe it, you're so stupid, both of you."

Sarah ran some water on a dishcloth and got right up next to Derek. She told him it was okay, everything was okay. They needed to see how bad it was. Derek wasn't screaming anymore, it was more like crying, trying to breathe in too fast. She had her arm over his shoulders, her face so close they could have been kissing. "Yeah, I know," she said, "it's all right, we just need to see."

He nodded and Sarah took his hand away from his eye.

"Oh my God," she said, "Go get your mom," and Mark ran.

There was a path worn between their back doors. He dodged the kitchen table, gave it the same move he did when Peter was chasing him in from something. "Mom!" he called, "Mom!"

She was upstairs sewing costumes for the haunted house, pins between her teeth. She was so used to him screaming she didn't even get up. She talked out of the side of her mouth. "What is it now?"

"I shot him," Mark said, and tried to explain, but suddenly he couldn't talk, and then he was crying just like Derek, trying to get enough air.

His mother spit the pins out and grabbed his arm, dragged him along behind her as she ran down the stairs. He couldn't believe she was so fast, banging out the storm door and flying across the yard and into the Rotas'.

Derek was sitting at the kitchen table with Sarah holding a baggie of ice on his eye. He still had his jacket on. He wasn't crying, just hunched over, rocking back and forth, saying, "Ow, ow, ow."

"Is he all right?" Mark's mom asked.

"No," Sarah said. "It's his eye. I called 911, they said they'd send an ambulance."

"Let me take a look at it." His mother plucked the bag away and put it back fast. "When did they say they'd get here?"

"Five minutes."

His mother sat down, then got up again and walked around the room, biting her thumbnail and looking out the windows.

"I'm sorry," Mark said, and again he began to cry, right in front of Sarah.

"It was an accident," his mom said.

"It's okay," Derek said, but this only made it worse, and Mark ran out into the yard and didn't stop until he reached the back lot.

There was the gun next to the pallet of bricks, and there on a yellow leaf was a dark spot of blood, and another.

"Mark," his mom called. "Mark, get in here now!"

He picked up the gun and the BBs shifted and clicked in the barrel. He loved the Daisy, the afternoons they spent winging cans and bottles and old archery targets Derek's stepfather kept in the shed, but now as he walked across the yard, he promised—honestly, to God—that this was the last time he'd ever touch a gun.

It wasn't even a real gun.

"Give me that," his mom said on the porch, and snatched it by the barrel, something you weren't supposed to do. He knew to just keep quiet.

The kitchen was empty. They'd moved Derek to the front porch to wait for the ambulance. He sat on the glider, still nodding and rocking, making it move. "It hurts," he said.

"I know," Mark's mom said. "It'll be here soon." To Mark, she said, "I'm not mad at you, no one's mad at you, just don't run off like that."

"I'm sorry," Mark said.

"We know you are," she said. "It was an accident, everyone knows that, now just calm down."

"Here it comes," Sarah said, pointing at the ambulance.

It didn't even have its lights on, or its siren. It pulled into the drive and the EMTs jumped out. One looked at Derek while the other talked with Mark's mom. The one with Derek knelt down by the glider and pulled out a mini-flashlight and waved it in front of his face.

"Can you see it now?"

"No," Derek said.

"How about over here?'

"Yeah."

The EMT stood up and told Mark's mom they were taking him to Butler Memorial and that she should contact his parents.

"I already have," his mom said.

They put him in the back, and the one got in with him.

"You can follow us if you want," the other one said.

The nurse at the emergency room said Mark's mom could go in with Derek but Mark and Sarah would have to wait outside. Sarah lost herself in *Cosmopolitan* and Mark got up and looked at everything in the vending machines. The hospital had taped up the same cardboard decorations his Sunday school class had—the same pickle-nosed witches and rearing black cats and ogling, wide-eyed pumpkins. Mark tried to read a *Sports Illustrated* but it was too old. The last time he'd been here was when he broke his wrist trying a grind on a concrete bench in the back lot, and now he wondered if he was bad luck, if the rest of his life would be like this. It would be okay, he thought.

Derek's stepfather showed up first, his work gloves stuffed in his back pockets. He was small but he had a huge mustache; he wore his Steeler cap everywhere except church, where he played guitar up front with Mark's dad.

Mark stood up but he went straight to Sarah.

"They were messing around with the BB gun," she said, pointing to Mark.

"Is that right?"

"Yes sir."

"I thought I showed you two how to handle that thing."

Mark just nodded.

"Well, accidents will happen, I guess. Are you all right?"

"Yeah," Mark said.

"Okay," he said, and put his hand on Mark's shoulder and gave it a squeeze before he went off to find the nurse.

Ten minutes later, Derek's mom ran through the electric doors. She was dressed for the mill, still wearing her clip-on nametag, and she smelled like pencil lead. She had steeltoed boots like Mark's father and a line of grease across the front of her uniform. It looked like a costume on her.

"How is he?" she asked Sarah, and when she didn't like her answer, stalked right past Mark to the nurse.

Mark's mom came out after a while and said the doctors weren't sure. He might lose the eye or it might get better, only time would tell. He'd probably have to stay in the hospital for a day or two, they'd see. While she was explaining everything to them, Mark's dad walked in.

The first thing he did was sit down. It was a thing he had; anytime they had to discuss something serious, he made everyone sit down. His other rule was no shouting, no matter how angry you were. His mom told him the whole thing, and then he stood up and took Mark's hand and then his mom's and then Sarah joined the circle and they all bowed their heads and they prayed.

"Amen," his father said, and gave a little squeeze which Mark returned out of habit.

Sarah suddenly broke into tears, and his mom held her for a while, and then Derek's stepfather came back out and gave his father a hug. Derek was resting, they'd given him something; Derek's mom would stay with him tonight. Meanwhile it was probably best if they all went home.

"Can we visit him later?" Mark asked.

"Tomorrow," his mom said.

It was night out now, the moon almost full. In the parking lot they split up. "Why don't you go with dad?" his mom said, so Mark climbed into the pick-up and buckled himself in.

His dad would tell him a story, Mark knew that. It would be something from the Bible, a parable Mark could learn from, and he waited for it as they got on the highway and headed out of town. It wasn't until they passed the salvage yard by the firehouse that his dad cleared his throat and said, "You know something?"

"What?" Mark said.

"It could have just as easily been you. You know that."

"Yeah."

"Do you remember what it says in John about the two farmers?"

"No," Mark said, because he never knew what the Bible said. In Sunday school they read stories together that everyone had heard before, but his father knew all of it, pulled it out like a favorite wrench.

"There were two farmers who lived next to each other, and one day a plague, of locusts came along, so thick they could hardly see. When the locusts flew off, the one farmer's crop was all gone, bitten down to the roots. But the other farmer's crop wasn't touched at all. It was like a sign, people said." His dad looked to him, and Mark said, "Uh-huh."

"The farmer who lost his crop thought it was the work of sorcery. The farmer whose crop wasn't touched thought it was the hand of God. The two of them accused each other of being in league with the devil. Each of them set about to prove it in the courts. In the meantime no one was tending the fields and it was high summer. And you know what happened?"

"What?" Mark said.

"The whole crop burned up and was lost."

His dad looked to him again as if to make sure he understood, and then they drove along, nothing but the truck's engine and the tires whining over the road.

It was past supper so Mark's mom heated up some lasagna from yesterday. Peter was home, and they had to tell him what happened.

"Your brother and Derek were playing around out back," his mom said. "And somehow . . . "

Every time Mark heard someone tell it, he could feel them blaming him. That was fine, it was his fault; he just wondered if it would get better. He hoped so.

Peter washed while he dried and put the dishes away.

"You weren't trying to hit him," Peter asked

"No," Mark said, angry at him. But was that really true?

It was just a game. Now the crop was gone, the fields burnt.

"He'll be okay," Peter said. "Plus he's still got the other one, it's not like he's blind."

"Shut up."

"I'm just saying," he said.

It was a school night, and they had homework to do, and then when they were done they were allowed an hour of TV. His dad went over to the Rotas' during *Seinfeld* and came back during *Suddenly Susan*. Nothing had changed; Derek's mom was still at the hospital. Maybe they'd know something in the morning.

In bed, Mark pictured the celebration they'd have when they found out Derek was okay. His dad would call for a prayer circle and they'd bow their heads and all of them—Mark, especially—would thank God.

But in the morning Derek's stepfather said the doctors still couldn't say one way or the other. Derek's mom was taking the day off to stay with him. Peter and Sarah walked together to the bus stop; the grass was frosted and they left footprints. Mark's bus came later. He scuffed through the drifted leaves, his backpack a load on his shoulder. It was the last stop on the route, which was good in the morning but bad after school. On a regular day, he and Derek would jag around, maybe play kill-the-man-with-the-ball until the bus came. Today it was just him, and he waited outside the shelter, kicking stones across the road and thinking how impossible the shot was, the terrible odds of it, and how unlucky it was that the person firing the rifle had been him. Sometimes he couldn't believe it was real, he could pretend it never happened. But it did.

In school he didn't mention it.

"Is Derek sick, do you know?" Mrs. Albright asked him, and he said yes.

After school he had haunted house practice, but his mom called Father Don, who said it was okay if he missed it to visit the hospital. The Creature from the Black Lagoon suits weren't in yet anyway, and they knew what to do, they didn't have to practice being monsters.

"Do you not want to go?" his mom said in the car.

"No, I do"

"He's not going to be mad at you, if that's what you're worried about."

"I know," Mark said but he was thinking about the farmer who'd lost his crop. How could you not be angry?

Derek's room was on a floor just for children; the halls were crowded with parents, and the decorations were the same as downstairs. The shades were down and Derek was asleep. His stepfather and mom were both there. His roommate had just been released, so there was an empty bed next to his. Derek's mom took them out in the hall to talk to them.

"They say the eye itself isn't as bad as they thought, but the thing is lodged in there. They're going to try to get it out but they say there's a chance the retina might detach."

"Is there any way to reattach it?" Mark's mom asked.

"No, if it detaches you lose the eye."

The surgery was scheduled for tomorrow morning. That night they prayed for him, Mark's father talking about the mystery of God's purpose and their acceptance of His will. Mark thought it was wrong, that there must be something they could do to fix things. It felt like giving up to him.

And then after the surgery they still had to wait another day to see if it worked. The doctors said everything went well but with something like this there was no guarantee.

Sunday before church Derek's mom came over; she was in the same clothes as yesterday and said she hadn't slept. They weren't going to be there, so she wanted Mark to say Derek's name during the Prayers for the People. Everyone thought it was a good idea, and Mark did too. Maybe this would help a little. He'd already planned what he was going to say during the Confession. It would be like an offering. He didn't think it would change anything, but still, it was something.

His mom laid out his good white shirt and Mark buttoned it till it pinched his neck. His hair was still wet; it combed down dark in the mirror so you wouldn't know he was blond. He fixed his part and leaned close to his own reflection, looking at his eyes, one and then the other. The black part and the green around it and then the white was like a bullseye, three rings. He put his hand over his right eye and everything off to that side disappeared.

It wasn't that much different, was it?

But he could always take his hand away, he thought. Derek couldn't.

His mom drove and he and Peter sat in the back, his dad's guitar case across their laps. Even the new part of the parking lot was full; Mr. Jenner waved people in with a blaze orange vest and parked them on the grass. Mark waited for his dad to slide his guitar out, then followed him around the car to where Peter and his mom were waiting. He saw the Tates across the lot, all dressed up, and Mrs. Lerner in her white gloves, carrying a lily in purple foil. The bells were playing from the loudspeakers above the front doors, and everyone was headed for them. It wouldn't be hard, Mark thought. All he had to do was stand up and say Derek's name.

Inside, it was warm with voices. Since Derek's stepfather wasn't there, Charlie Wycoff was up front tuning up, and Mark's dad needed to go over some changes with him.

"Play well," his mom said, and gave him a kiss.

She let Mark into the pew first and sat down with Peter on the other side of her, on the aisle. They shared the pew with the Rotas, and Mark wasn't used to all the space. His slacks slid on the wood, and he pushed himself side to side like a goalie fixing his crease, his feet on the kneeler. "Stop," his mom said, a hand on his leg. "Now are you all set with what you're going to say?"

"Yes."

"Here." She had her prayer book open to where they said it. "Right after Father Don says this here."

She marked the place with a white ribbon and gave him the book.

His dad and Charlie Wycoff started playing and people stopped talking. Father Don came out in his robes with his old Bible and raised his arms to welcome everyone, and Mark wondered what Father Don would say to him. It wouldn't be like his dad and his farmer story, it would be different. If Derek's eye was all right, then it was a chance for Mark to learn something. In school, Mrs. Albright drew a minus sign on the board, then waited a second till they all saw it and made it into a plus. "Make a positive," she said, "out of a negative." Now Mark wondered how that fit with the two farmers. What could you make from a burnt up field?

Not much.

It was just a story, it wasn't something that actually happened.

They stood to sing and knelt to pray, and he read the whole program, seeing who donated the flowers for the altar this week, whose birthday was coming up. During the announcements before the sermon, Father Don reminded everyone that there would be a sneak preview of the haunted house this Wednesday for church members only, so it would be a good time to beat the lines. Last year they raised over five thousand dollars, so how about a big hand for all those folks who helped put it together?

"That's us," Mark's mom said as they clapped.

And then the sermon, which seemed long, and the offering, and another hymn, until finally Father Don raised his arms and said, "Let us pray," and lowered them for everyone to kneel down.

Mark had the book turned to the right page. They prayed for the president and they prayed for the bishop and for Father Don. They prayed for all those struggling against injustice and oppression and for the poor and the unfortunate. And then they prayed for the sick and infirm, and Father Don asked God to especially keep in mind those members of the congregation in special need of His healing

It was quiet then, and Mark's mom touched his arm. He stood up.

The church was a field of heads bent down, and he was taller than all of them, except Father Don, who turned to look at him, as if he expected this.

"Derek Rota," Mark said, and Father Don nodded.

He wasn't loud enough, he thought, but it was too late and he knelt dawn again.

"Eileen Covington," someone else said, and then it was quiet.

"Gertrude Wheeler."

"Jan Tomczak."

It went on for eight names. Mark thought it was a lot, all of those people in the hospital, and all their families worried about them. Some of them were probably going to die. He'd barely noticed this part of the service before, and now it seemed terrible to him, proof of something gone wrong.

But none of the other people had shot anyone, had they?

They finished and everyone sat up with a rumble of kneelers. "You did very well," his mom said, and then his dad stepped to the center and played and they all stood up to watch the altar boys take the cross away.

In the receiving line, Father Don shook his hand in both of his. "Are you ready to be the Creature?" he said, because the suits had come in yesterday.

"Sure."

He'd have to come by and try it on tomorrow. Mark's mom said it wasn't a problem.

Outside, the little kids were running around on the new sod, one girl crying because she'd gotten grass stains on her white dress. They waited for Mark's dad, who had to pack up his stuff. When he came out he was still talking with Charlie Wycoff.

"He's pretty good," Mark's dad said in the car. "He's really been practicing a lot."

"I thought Mark did a nice job too," his mom said.

"I heard. Good projection."

In the back seat, Peter made a face, and Mark elbowed him, and Peter went to hit him but stopped short just to make him flinch.

Outside the fields went by, long harvested, the stubble white and bent down by the reaper. He could smell someone burning leaves; you weren't supposed to but people still did.

Nothing had changed, Mark thought. Nothing had happened. He'd just said his name, that was all.

But what if saying his name saved his eye? That was possible, wasn't it? That's what faith was. If the two farmers had had faith—was that the meaning of it? He wanted to ask his dad: What were the farmers supposed to do?

It was dumb thinking about it; it was just made-up.

At home they changed clothes and ate lunch and put on the Steeler game. It was dumb; they were beating up on Houston. Mark was thinking about going out and raking the yard when Derek's stepfather came over.

Mark answered the door. Usually he'd just let him in, but Derek's stepfather asked if his dad was around.

"I'll go get him," Mark said.

His dad was lying on the couch with the football in his lap. He looked surprised and got up and handed off to Peter, and Mark knew not to follow him.

His dad didn't come right back. He closed the door and went upstairs where his mom was working on the costumes, and then in a while the two of them came down together. Peter looked at Mark like this was about him.

His dad clicked the set off and had everyone sit down.

"Take hands," he said, and they did.

"Mrs. Rota just called. The doctors said Derek's eye was just too badly damaged."

He went on, but Mark had stopped listening, concentrating on the shot, that one stupid moment with the gun. It was Derek who made up the game, it was Derek's rifle. Derek had shot at him a million times, even shooting one of his mom's cigarettes out of his mouth on three tries. But none of that mattered. Now, bending his head in prayer again, his dad's hand strong in his, all that mattered was that one shot. It was his fault, and he was sorry, but that wasn't enough.

"Amen," his dad said, and there was the squeeze, like a reminder.

Later he went out and raked the yard by himself until he saw his mom at her sewing room window looking down at him. She'd bought a huge trash bag that looked like a pumpkin, and he stuffed it with leaves and faced it toward the road so you could see it when you came around the curve. Then he went in and watched the late game, or sat there not watching, startled when Peter called out, "Nice! Nice!"

No one told him it wasn't his fault. After the dishes, his mom took him into the living room and said he hadn't meant for this to happen. Tucking him in, his dad told him he shouldn't blame himself, that what was done was done. He was a good guy, everyone knew that. Derek knew that, Derek's parents knew it. Okay?

"Okay," Mark said.

His door closed, blocking out the hall light, leaving him alone. He wondered if Derek was awake in the hospital, if he'd gotten a new roommate.

He closed both his eyes and tried to see. Blue dots floated, then shifted when he tried to look at them, drifted like galaxies, little soft stars. He opened his eyes and the room grew back. No, he thought, that wasn't what it was like at all.

It was just one, he still had the other. Peter said that to be mean, but it was true too.

The wind was in the trees. It was only two weeks till Halloween; his mom had already bought candy and hid it where his dad couldn't get at it, set out bowls of candy corn around the house. Would Derek be able to be a Creature? Mark wanted to see him, to say he was sorry to his face. He couldn't remember if he did when he shot him. It was funny: he thought he would never forget it, but already, like his part in the service this morning, the Steeler game, the leaves, the two farmers—like the blue stars under his eyelids, it was all fading away.

The next day his mom picked him up after school and drove him over to church. Father Don had the two suits hung over folding chairs in the parish hall. They were greenish-black, the color of snakes, and sagged like empty skins. They were so fake it made Mark want to laugh. Their claws came to sharp points. On the table sat the two heads, the eyes bugged out under angry brows, flipperlike gills behind the jaw.

"You look out of the mouth," Father Don explained, and fit it over his head.

"Can you see?" his mom asked.

He could, but just a wedge between two even rows of ridiculous fangs. He'd have to remember to tell Derek.

"Okay," Father Don said, "take that off and let's try the body."

It was heavy, and the webbed hands went on separately, like rubber gloves. The feet went over his shoes, kept on with a gumband. It was like wearing armor, he thought, everything covered up.

"How does it feel?" Father Don asked him.

"Good," Mark said.

They had him move around some; it wasn't easy.

"Okay," Father Don said, "get that off and try on the other one. They're supposed to be the same size but it never hurts to check."

So then Derek was going to do it. For some reason, it made Mark afraid the suit wouldn't fit.

It did. Father Don zipped him up, and Mark put the head on and stumped around.

"Growl," his mother said. "Look like you're going to drag someone overboard and take them to your secret cave."

"Graaaahhhh," Mark tried, claws raised, and his mother screamed like she was the girl in the movie. Father Don stepped between them to protect her, and he knocked him aside with one blow.

"Very convincing," Father Don said. "Okay, let's get it off."

Mark wondered if Dracula would have been better. Probably not. It all seemed cheesy now, dumb.

After that they visited Derek. He was awake, drinking ginger ale through a straw. He smiled when he saw Mark. He had a patch over the eye, otherwise he was fine. He turned so his good one was aimed at him. It was brown; Mark hadn't noticed it before.

"Hey," he said.

"Hey," Mark said. "How's it going?"

"All right. Got to miss school. It would have been great but they don't have cable, just the regular stations."

Mark didn't have anything else to say.

"Randy took the gun apart," Derek said. "Did you know that?"

"No."

"He unscrewed all the parts and put them in this plastic bag. He says I can have it back when I'm fifteen."

"Wow."

"Yeah. That's all right, he said we might get a Nintendo 64 for my birthday."

"Cool," Mark said. It was good to hear Derek talk like he always did. It was only bad when he looked at the patch. "Hey, I'm sorry."

"That's okay," Derek said. "Did you know there's a club for people with one eye? Yeah, it's called Singular Vision. A lot of famous people are in it, like Wesley Walker, the receiver for the Jets."

Mark didn't mention that he was retired; Derek knew that. He thought he should say he was sorry again. It was like saying his name; he expected it to do something, but it didn't.

Derek was coming home tomorrow. He could have come home today but they had to fit him with a prosthetic eye.

"It's not glass," Derek insisted. "It's a special kind of plastic they did experiments with on the Space Shuttle. You can drop it fifty feet onto concrete and it won't chip."

"Huh," Mark said.

It was dinner time; a man with a hairnet was rolling a cart down the hall, bringing trays into the rooms. Derek's had plastic wrap over some kind of chicken. Derek's mom peeled the plastic off and steam came up.

"I guess we ought to be heading out," Mark's mom said, and Derek's mom walked them out into the hall. "We'll see you tomorrow, I guess."

"Oh yeah," Derek's mom said. "We're having a little welcome home party for him."

"We'll be there."

"Thanks for coming," Derek's mom said to Mark.

"Sure," Mark said. Because what else was he supposed to say? You're welcome?

He thought about all this in bed—which was dumb, he thought. There was nothing he could do about it then.

Tuesday after school Mark helped his mom hang a banner from the porch. It was one she rented out. It said WELCOME HOME and then had a patch where you spelled out the name of the person. Mark handed her the scratchy, Velcro-backed letters from the plastic bin and then held the ladder.

They were all waiting on the porch for him, and then when the Rotas' truck pulled into the drive they all ran down to the yard. Derek was sitting in the passenger seat; he waited until his stepfather came around to open the door for him.

The patch was gone. At first Mark couldn't see because his mom was hugging him, and then Sarah, her hair pulled back in a black velvet scrunchy. Derek's mom was crying a little, and trying to laugh at how sappy she was, and then Derek turned to get a hug from Mark's dad and Mark could see the eye.

It seemed big, maybe because the lid was puffed-up, and Mark tried not to watch for it to move. It couldn't, he thought, but he couldn't be sure, and he didn't want Derek to catch him staring. But it didn't look right.

No, because inside when they sat down to have cake, they sat Mark right beside him, on that side. It was like they did it on purpose, so he had to see what he'd done, and so close it was impossible not to see the eye was plastic, and stuck looking straight ahead, no matter who Derek was talking to. To talk to Mark he had to twist around in his chair and look at him over his nose.

"Good cake, huh?"

"Great," Mark said.

"My mom said you tried on the costumes."

"Yeah."

"So, are they like amazing?"

"They have teeth just like you said."

"Cool."

"Are you boys ready for the big night?" Mark's dad asked. "You got your act down?"

"Oh, forget it," Derek's mom joked. "I'm not going anywhere near that place. I've had my scare for the year, thank you."

They all laughed and pitched in to convince her.

"All right," she said, "but just once."

It was decided; Mark's mom would drop them off and then the rest of them would all go together, even Peter and Sarah.

The next morning Derek and Mark got on the bus together. Derek's eye wasn't as puffed up, but Philip Dawkins across the aisle wouldn't stop looking at him.

"What are you staring at?" Derek said.

"You. Your eye."

And before he knew what he was doing, Mark shot across the aisle and was smashing Philip Dawkins in the face, driving his fist in again and again and growling as Philip's friends tried to drag him off.

"I'll kill you," Philip was saying, but now everyone was staring at him, then looking away, embarrassed for him because blood was coming from his lip and he was crying, even his ears red.

Mark sat rigid in his seat, ready to hit him again if he didn't shut up. He wouldn't say anything, he'd just hit him. And when Philip said it again, Mark did. And then no one would look at him.

"What are you doing?" Derek asked.

"He was looking at you."

"Yeah, so? People are gonna look."

"I didn't like what he said either."

"You didn't have to hit him again," Derek said, and the rest of the way they didn't talk.

"What's this I hear about a fight on the bus?" his mom said when he got home.

"Nothing," Mark said. "Someone was making fun of Derek."

"So you split his lip, is that right?"

"We got in a fight."

"That's not the way I heard it. The way I heard it it sounds like you attacked him."

"It was a fight," Mark said.

"You make it sound like you've been in fights before. Have you?"

"No."

"Then why now?"

"I don't know."

"Well," his mom said, "why don't you go up to your room and think about it, and I'll think about whether you should do your haunted house tonight."

He didn't argue, he just went up and closed the door. It was starting to get dark, the sun behind the trees, turning the sky orange. He thought of the gun in pieces in Derek's basement, in a plastic bag. He still wanted to hit Philip Dawkins, and he would tomorrow if he said anything, he didn't care.

"Well, have you thought about it?" his mom said when she looked in.

"Yes."

"And?"

"And I'm sorry," he said, and this really was a lie.

"You should be," his mom said, "and if you think you're sorry now, you just wait till your father hears about this." She told him to get ready, they were leaving in five minutes.

Derek must have told on him, but on the way over neither of them mentioned the fight. They talked about the Ghost Mine at Kennywood and all the things that jumped out at you, the hiss of air that made your hair stand up just before the end. This was going to be better, Derek said, because there it was the same ride every time; here things could jump out at you from anywhere. Mark was on the side with his good eye but couldn't stop thinking of the other, the wall of black there, not even blue stars, just nothing.

The haunted house used to be the main building of the old hospital. There was already a long line outside, teenagers and parents with little kids. The fence around the parking lot was covered with giant spiders Mark's mom made from black garbage bags and old socks. From the trees in front hung ghosts and grinning skeletons. The porch was done up in cobwebs, and speakers on the roof blasted out eerie laughter. Mr. Jenner waved them through to the back lot with a flashlight. Father Don's mini-van was there, and a bunch of other cars. Mark's mom got out and came in with them to check on her work.

The hallways were wide but the ceilings were low, and they'd crammed in as much as they could. There were bats that flittered on nylon fishing line, and zombies that peered at you from the rooms, and a mummy who swung down from the ceiling. "Whoa!" Derek said. "Man!" There was an operating room in the real operating room where the doctor cut off the patient's head, and a torture chamber with an iron maiden and a victim stretched hideously on the rack—all his mom's work. She bent over the displays, straightening things, touching up. Right now it looked stupid, but in the dark with the dry ice fog sliding along the floor it would be scary, or that was the idea. Last year when they went through, Mark had stayed close to his dad, hoping he wouldn't notice. None of it was really scary, it was all fake; it was just that he didn't like being frightened. It was stupid to be frightened of that stuff, he thought; there were real things to be afraid of.

Father Don was putting on his costume—the lab coat and wire glasses of Dr. Frankenstein. Mark's mom told him everything looked okay and that she'd see them later and left them with him.

"Let me show you where you are," Father Don said, and took them upstairs.

They had a room of their own, made up to look like the ocean, the walls covered in wavy, mirrored paper with a blue light shining on it, an inflatable shark in one corner, fake sea- weed and cardboard starfish everywhere. There were mossy papier-mâché rocks with a crack you had to squeeze through to get to the next room; that's where they'd scare people.

"Cool," Derek said when he saw the suits, and Mark wished he'd stop being so stupid.

"Okay, I'll let you two get settled. We should be starting in about ten minutes. They'll be an announcement on the PA."

"Wow," Derek said, and looked around the room, turning in a circle. The foil and the blue light made the room seem bigger. He went to the stairs and then came back. "Check this out," he whispered, and pulled a small white tube from his pocket and handed it to Mark.

It was Vampire Blood, Mark had seen some in the novelty shop downtown, thin runny stuff the color of maraschino cherries.

"What are you going to do with it?" Mark asked.

"We'll put it on, it'll be scarier."

"You shouldn't put it on the costumes."

"Look," Derek said, and pointed to where it said Does Not Stain Clothing. "Okay?"

"Whatever."

"Whatever," Derek echoed him.

"Shut up," Mark said, and threw the tube at him.

As soon as it left his hand, he was sure it would hit him in the other eye. He didn't mean it; he didn't know why he was angry. Everything.

The tube flew past Derek and skittered under the shark.

"What was that for?" Derek said.

"Nothing. I'm sorry."

"You should be," Derek said, and retrieved it.

They didn't say anything while they hauled their suits on.

"Here," Mark said, and zipped him up, helped him settle the head.

"It's heavy," Derek said. "Can you see anything?"

"Not much."

The announcement came over the PA and someone's dad ran up the stairs and left a bucket with a chunk of dry ice steaming in the corner. Derek held up the Vampire Blood.

"You want some?"

"Sure," Mark said, more to be nice than anything. It would probably look cheesy; all that stuff did.

Derek held the front of the mask and for a minute all Mark could see were his hands and the tube. The lights flickered and finally stayed on, but just barely. With the blue light it almost looked liked they were underwater.

"How about your claws?"

"Why not," Mark said, and held out his arms. He waited inside the suit and then Derek let go of one hand and took the other.

"Well," Mark said, "how's it look?"

"See for yourself." Derek led him forward a few steps and then turned him toward the wall.

There in the wavy mirror stood the Creature from the Black Lagoon, its lips bright with blood. Mark raised his claws and growled, then did it again, leaning closer, and again, till he was inches from it, his breath coming back off the wall. The foil distorted his face, made the Creature's eyes bulge and slither, his fangs grow. Mark tilted his chin until he could see himself inside the mouth, his eyes looking back at the monster that had devoured him. In the mirror, in the dim light, with the fog rolling all around him, Mark thought it looked very real.

THE HALLOWEEN MAN

William F. Nolan

In his introduction to this story in his Dark Universe *collection, William
F. Nolan writes: "One of my earliest creative endeavors was a poem about
Halloween, written when I was twelve. I've always looked forward to this
holiday, with its ghosts-and-goblins tradition and its celebration of Dark and
Terrible Things. And what could be more terrible than a demon-creature on
the hunt—each Halloween night—for children's souls?*

*"When I finished this one, I realized that the Halloween Man might exist
only in the mind of my character; maybe he was no more than a projection
of Katie's inflamed fears. But then again, maybe not. He might be as real
and terrible as she believes him to be. Thus, the story can be read on two
levels: Does he exist, or doesn't he?"*

Oh, Katie believed in him for sure, the Halloween Man. Him with his long
skinny-spindly arms and sharp-toothed mouth and eyes sunk deep in
skull sockets like softly glowing embers, charcoal red. Him with his long
coat of tatters, smelling of tombstones and grave dirt. All spider-hairy he
was, the Halloween Man.

"You made him up!" said Jan the first time Katie told her about him.
Jan was nine, a year younger than Katie, but she could run faster and jump
higher. "He isn't real."

"Is so," said Katie.

"Is not."

"Is."

"Isn't!"

Jan slapped Katie. Hard. Hard enough to make her eyes sting.

"You're just mean," Jan declared. "Going around telling lies and scaring
people."

"It's true," said Katie, trying not to cry. "He's real and he could be coming here on Halloween night—right to this town. This could be the year he comes here."

The town was Center City, a small farming community in the Missouri heartland, brightened by fire-colored October trees, with a high courthouse clock (Little Ben) to chime the hour, with plowed fields to the east and a sweep of sun-glittered lake to the west.

A neat little jewel of a town by day. By night, when the big oaks and maples bulked dark and the oozy lake water was tar-black and brooding, Center City could be scary for a ten-year-old who believed in demons.

Especially on Halloween night.

All month at school, all through October, Katie had been thinking about the Halloween Man, about what Todd Pepper had told her about him. Todd was very mature and very wise. And a lot older, too. Todd was thirteen. He came from a really big city, Cleveland, and knew a lot of things that only big-city kids know.

He was visiting his grandparents for the summer (old Mr. and Mrs. Willard) and Katie met him in the town library late in August when he was looking through a book on demons.

They got to talking, and Katie asked him if he'd ever seen a demon. He had narrow features with squinty eyes and a crooked grin that tucked up the left side of his face.

"Sure, I seen one," said Todd Pepper. "The old Halloween Man, I seen him. Wears a big pissy-smelling hat and carries a bag over one shoulder, like Santa. But he's got no toys in it, no sir. Not in *that* bag!"

"What's he got in it?"

"Souls. That's what he collects. Human souls."

Katie swallowed. "Where . . . where does he get them from?"

"From kids. Little kids. On Halloween night."

They were sitting at one of the big wooden library tables, and now he leaned across it, getting his narrow face closer to hers.

"That's the only time you'll see him. It's the only night he's got power." And he gave her his crooked grin. "He comes slidin' along, in his rotty tattered coat, like a big scarecrow come alive, with those glowy red eyes of his, and the bag all ready. Steppin' along the sidewalk in the dark easy as you please, the old Halloween Man."

"How does he do it?" Katie wanted to know. "How does he get a kid's soul?"

"Puts his big hairy hands on both sides of the kid's head and gives it a terrible shake. Out pops the soul, like a cork out of a bottle. Bingo! And into the sack it goes."

Katie felt hot and excited. And shaky-scared. But she couldn't stop asking questions. "What does he do with all the kids' souls after he's collected them?"

Another crooked grin. "*Eats 'em*," said Todd. "They're his food for the year. Then, come Halloween, he gets hungry again and slinks out to collect a new batch—like a squirrel collecting nuts for the winter."

"And you—you saw him? Really *saw* him?"

"Sure did. The old Halloween Man, he chased me once when I was your age. In Haversham, Texas. Little bitty town, like this one. He likes small towns."

"How come?"

"Nowhere for kids to hide in a small town. Everything out in the open. He stays clear of the big cities."

Katie shifted on her chair. She bit her lower lip. "Did he catch you—that time in Texas?"

"No sir, not me." Todd squinched his eyes. "If he had of, I'd be dead—with my soul in his bag."

"How'd you get away?"

"Outran him. He was pretty quick, ran like a big lizard he did, but I was quicker. Once I got shut of him, I hid out. Till after midnight. That's when he loses his power. After midnight he's just gone—like a puff of smoke."

"Well, *I've* never seen him, I know," said Katie softly. "I'd remember if I'd seen him."

"You bet," said Todd Pepper, nodding vigorously. "But then, he isn't always so easy to spot."

"What d'ya mean?"

"Magical, that old Halloween Man is. Can take over people. Big people, I mean. Just climbs right inside 'em, like steppin' into another room. One step, and he's inside lookin' out."

"Then how can you tell if it's *him*?" Katie asked.

"Can't," said Todd Pepper. "Not till he jumps at you. But if you're lookin' sharp for him, and you know he's around, then you can kind of spot him by instinct."

"What's that?"

"It's like an animal's got in the jungle when a hunter is after him. The animal gets an instinct about the hunter and knows when to run. It's that way with the ole Halloween Man—you can sort of sniff him out when you're sharp enough. He can't fool you then. Not if you're really concentrating. Then your instinct takes over."

"Is there a picture of him in that book?"

Todd riffled the pages casually. "Nope. No kid's ever lived long enough to take a picture of the Halloween Man. But I've described him to you—and unless he climbs inside somebody you'll be able to spot him easy."

"Thanks," said Katie. "I appreciate that." She looked pensive. "But maybe he'll never come to Center City."

"Maybe not." Todd shut the book of demons with a snap. "Then again, you never know. Like I said, he favors small towns. If you want my opinion, I'd say he's overdue in this one."

And that was the only talk she'd had with Todd Pepper. At summer's end he went back to Cleveland to school, and Katie was left in Center City with a head full of new thoughts. About the Halloween Man.

And then it was October, with the leaves blowing orange and yellow and red-gold over her shoes when she walked to school, and the lake getting colder and darker off beyond the trees, and the gusting wind tugging at her coat and fingering her hair. Sometimes it rained, a chill October drizzle that gave the streets a wet-cat shine and made the sodden leaves stick to her clothes like dead skin.

Katie had never liked October, but this year was the worst, knowing about the Halloween Man, knowing that he could be walking through her town come Halloween night, with his grimy soul-bag over one shoulder and his red-coal eyes penetrating the dark.

Through the whole past week at school that was all Katie could think about and Miss Prentiss, her teacher, finally sent Katie home. With a note to her father that read:

> *Katie is not her normal self. She is listless and inattentive in class. She does not respond to lessons, nor will she answer questions related to them. She has not been completing her homework. Since Katie is one of our brightest children, I suggest you have her examined for possible illness.*

"Are you sick, sugar?" her father had asked her. Her mother was dead and had been for as long as Katie could remember.

"I don't think so," Katie had replied. "But I feel kind of funny. I'll be all right after Halloween. I want to stay home from school till after Halloween."

Her father had been puzzled by this attitude. Katie had always loved

Halloween. It had been her favorite holiday. Out trick or treating soon as it got dark with her best friend Jan. Now Jan never called the house anymore. Katie's father wondered why.

"I don't like her," Katie declared firmly. "She slapped me."

"Hey, that's not nice," said Katie's father. "Why did she do that?"

"She said I lied to her."

"About what?"

"I can't tell you." Katie looked down at her hands.

"Why not, sugar?"

"Cuz."

"Cuz why?"

"Cuz it's something too scary to talk about."

"Are you sure you can't tell your ole Daddy?"

She looked up at him. "Maybe after Halloween. *Then* I'll tell you."

"Okay, it's a deal. Halloween's just a few days off. So I guess I won't have long to wait."

And he smiled, ruffling her hair.

And now it was Halloween day and when it got dark it would be Halloween night.

Katie had a sure feeling that *this* year he'd show up in Center City. Somehow, she knew this would be the year.

That afternoon Katie moved through the town square in a kind of dazed fever. Her father had sent her downtown for some groceries and she had taken a long time getting them. It was so hard to remember what he wanted her to bring home. She had to keep checking the list in her purse. She just couldn't keep her mind on shopping.

Jan was on the street outside when Katie left Mr. Hakim's grocery store. They glared at each other.

"Do you take back what you said?" asked Jan, sullen and pouting. "About that awful, smelly man."

"No, I don't," said Katie. Her lips were tight.

"You lied!"

"I told the truth," declared Katie. "But you're just scared to believe it. And if you try to slap me again I'll kick your shins!"

Jan stepped back. "You're the meanest person I know!"

"Listen, you'd better stay home tonight," warned Katie. "That is, if you don't want the Halloween Man to pop out your soul and eat it."

Jan blinked at this, frowning.

"I figure he'll be out tonight," nodded Katie. "He's due."

"You're crazy! I'm going Trick or treating, like always."

"Well, don't say I didn't warn you," Katie told her. "When he grabs you just remember what I said."

"I *hate* you!" Jan cried, and turned away.

Katie started home.

It was later than she thought. Katie had spent so much time shopping she'd lost track of the day. It had just slipped past.

Now it was almost dark.

God!

Almost dark.

The brightness had drained from the sky, and the westering sun was buried in thick-massed clouds. A thin rain was beginning to dampen the streets.

Katie shifted the heavy bag of groceries and began to walk faster. Only two miles and she'd be home. Just twenty blocks.

A rising wind had joined the rain, driving wet leaves against her face, whipping her coat.

Not many kids will be going out tonight, Katie thought. Not in this kind of weather. Which meant lean pickings for the Halloween Man. If he shows up there won't be many souls to bag. Meaning he'll grab any kid he finds on the street. No pick and choose for him.

I'm all right, Katie told herself. I've still got time to make it home before it gets really dark . . .

But the clouds were thickening rapidly, drawing a heavy gray blanket across the sky.

It was getting dark.

Katie hurried. An orange fell from the top of the rain-damp sack, plopped to the walk. Katie stopped to pick it up.

And saw him.

Coming along the walk under the blowing trees, tall and skeleton-gaunt, with his rotted coat flapping in tatters around his stick-thin legs, and with his sack slung over one bony shoulder.

The red of his deep-sunk eyes burned under a big wide-brimmed slouch hat.

He saw Katie.

The Halloween Man smiled.

She whirled around with an insucked cry, the soggy paper sack ripping, slipping from her fingers, the groceries tumbling to the sidewalk, cans rolling, split milk cartons spitting white foam across the dark concrete.

Katie ran.

Not looking back, heart hammer-thumping her chest, she flung her body forward in strangled panic.

Where? Where to go? He was between her and home; she'd have to go back into the heart of town, run across the square and try to reach her house by another route.

But could she run that far? Jan was the runner; she could do it, she was faster and stronger. Already Katie felt a rising weakness in her legs. Terror was constricting her muscles, numbing her reflexes.

He could run like a lizard. That's what Todd had said, and lizards are fast. She didn't want to look back, didn't want to turn to see him, but she had to know how much distance she'd put between them. *Where was he?*

With a low moan, Katie swung her head around. And suddenly stopped running.

He was gone.

The long wet street stretched empty behind her, char black at its far end—just the wind-lashed trees, the gusting leaves, the blowing curtain of rain silvering the dark pavement. There was no sign of the Halloween Man.

He'd outfoxed her. He'd guessed her intention about doubling back and had cut across the square ahead of her. And he'd done the final demon-clever thing to trap her. He'd climbed inside.

But inside *who?* And *where?*

Concentrate, she told herself. Remember what Todd Pepper said about trusting your instinct. Oh, I'll know him when I see him!

Now Katie was in the middle of the town square. No matter which route she took home she had to pass several stores and shops—and he could be waiting in any doorway, ready to pounce.

She drew a long, shuddering breath, steeling herself for survival. Her head ached; she felt dizzy, but she was prepared to run.

Then, suddenly, horribly, a hand tugged at her shoulder!

Katie flinched like a dog under the whip, looked up in drymouthed terror—into the calm, smiling face of Dr. Peter Osgood.

"Your father tells me you've been ill, young lady," he said in his smooth doctor's voice. "Just step into my office and we'll find out what's wrong."

Step into my parlor said the spider to the fly.

Katie backed away from him. "No . . . No. Nothing's wrong. I'm fine."

"Your face looks flushed. You may have a touch of fever, Katie. Now I really think we should—"

"Get away from me!" she screamed. "I'm not going anywhere with you. I know who you are—you're *him!*"

And she broke into a pounding run.

Past Mr. Thurtle's candy shop: *Him,* waving from the window at her, with his red eyes shining . . .

Past the drug store: *Him,* standing at the door inside Mr. Joergens, smiling with his shark's teeth. "In a big rush today, Katie?"

Yes, away from you! A big rush.

Across the street on the red light. *Him,* in a dirty Ford pickup, jamming on the brakes, poking his head out the window: "Watch where you're running, you stupid little bitch!"

Oh, she knew the Halloween Man.

When Katie reached her house, on Oakvale, she fell to her knees on the cold wooden porch, gasping, eyes full of tears, ears ringing. Her head felt like a balloon about to burst, and she was hot and woozy and sick to her stomach.

But she was safe. She'd made it; he hadn't caught her.

Katie stood up shakily, got the door open and crossed the living room to the big rose sofa, dropped into it with a heavy, exhausted sigh.

Outside, a car pulled to the curb. She could see it through the window. A dark blue Chevy! *Dr. Osgood's car!*

"No!" screamed Katie, running back to the front door and throwing the bolt.

Her father came downstairs, looking confused. "What's wrong, sugar?"

Katie faced him, panting, her back tight against the bolted door. "We can't let him in. He's gonna steal my soul!"

"It's just Dr. Osgood, Katie. I asked him to drop by and see you."

"No, it *isn't*, Daddy. He's not Dr. Osgood. He's *him!*"

"Him?"

"The Halloween Man. He can get into big people's bodies. And he's inside Dr. Osgood right now."

Her father smiled gently, then moved to unlock the door. "I think you've been watching too many movies. You don't have to be afraid of—"

But Katie didn't wait for him to finish. She rushed up the stairs, ran to her room at the end of the hall, hurried inside, and slammed the door.

Panic. There was no lock on her door, no way to keep him out. She ran to the bed, jumping under the covers the way she used to do when she was little and things frightened her in the dark.

Below, muted sounds of greeting. Male voices. Daddy talking to him.

Then footsteps.

Coming up the stairs.

Katie leaped from the bed in a sudden frenzy, tipped over the tall wooden bookcase near her closet, dragged it against the door. *It probably wouldn't hold him, but . . .*

A rapping at the door. Rap-rap-rap. Rap-rap-rap.

"Katie!"

"Go way!" she yelled.

"Katie, open the door." It was Daddy's voice.

"No. You've got him with you. I know he's right there with you."

"Go to the window," her father told her. "See for yourself."

She ran across the room, stumbling over spilled books, and looked out. Dr. Osgood was just driving away through the misting rain in his blue Chevy.

Which meant that her *father* could now be—

He pushed the door open. Katie swung around to face him. "Oh, no!" She was trembling.

"It's true! Now *you're* him!"

Katie's father reached out, put a big hand on each side of her face. "Happy Halloween, sugar!" he said.

And gave her head a terrible shake.

THE YOUNG TAMLANE

Sir Walter Scott

According to Lisa Morton "Tamlane" is "one of the first works to make use of Halloween" rather than the earlier holiday of Samhain. The ballad form is known to have existed in the Scottish Borders for centuries. Sir Walter Scott included "The Young Tamlane" is his Minstrelsy of the Scottish Border, Volume II, *published in 1802. The version here, however, comes from the second edition, published in 1803 after Scott made alterations. Many other versions exist and the story continues to be rewritten, renewed, and retold by modern authors.*

There are many traditions connecting Celtic fairy lore to Halloween and the story of Tamlane (or Tam Lin or a number of other variants) involves one of them: mortals held captive by fairies can be rescued on this night. Here, the brave and defiant Janet (or Margaret) rescues her true love and the father of her unborn child from the Queen of the Fairies on Halloween. Not that "Tamlane" is a fairy tale suitable for children. It involves sex, the possibility of abortion or infanticide, the threat of human sacrifice, horrific transformations, and a truly vicious fairy queen.

(Interpolations are taken from Scott's footnotes and other sources.)

O I forbid ye, maidens a',
    That wear gowd on your hair,
To come or gae by Carterhaugh;
    For young Tamlane is there.

There's nane, that gaes by Carterhaugh,
    But maun leave him a wad *(something valuable)*;
Either goud rings or green mantles,
    Or else their maidenheid.

Now, gowd rings ye may buy, maidens,
    Green mantles ye may spin;
But, gin ye lose your maidenheid,
    Ye'll ne'er get that agen.

But up then spak her, fair Janet,
    The fairest o' a' her kin;
"I'll cum and gang to Carterhaugh,
    "And ask nae leave o' him."

Janet has kilted her green kirtle,
    A little abune her knee;
And she has braided her yellow hair,
    A little abune her bree *(brow)*.

And when she cam to Carterhaugh,
    She gaed beside the well;
And there she fand his steed standing,
    But away was himsell.

She hadna pu'd a red red rose,
    A rose but barely three;
Till up and starts a wee wee man,
    At Lady Janet's knee.

Says—"Why pu' ye the rose, Janet?
    "What gars ye break the tree?
"Or why come ye to Carterhaugh,
    "Withoutten leave o' me?"

Says—"Carterhaugh it is mine ain;
    "My daddie gave it me;
"I'll come and gang to Carterhaugh,
    "And ask nae leave o' thee."

He's ta'en her by the milk-white hand,
    Amang the leaves sae green;
And what they did I cannot tell—
    The green leaves were between.

He's ta'en her by the milk-white hand,
    Amang the roses red;
And what they did I cannot say—
    She ne'er returned a maid.

When she cam to her father's ha',
    She looked pale and wan;
They thought she'd dried some sair sickness,
    Or been wi' some leman. *(lover)*

She didna comb her yellow hair,
    Nor make meikle *(much)* o' her heid;
And ilka thing, that lady took,
    Was like to be her deid.

Its four and twenty ladies fair
    Were playing at the ba' *(ball)*;
Janet, the wightest of them anes,
    Was faintest o' them a'.

Four and twenty ladies fair
    Were playing at the chess;
And out there came the fair Janet,
    As green as any grass.

Out and spak an auld gray-headed knight,
    Lay o'er the castle wa'—
"And ever alas! for thee, Janet,
    "But we'll be blamed a'!"

"Now haud your tongue, ye auld gray knight!
    And an ill deid may ye die!
"Father my bairn on whom I will,
    "I'll father nane on thee."

Out then spak her father dear,
    And he spak meik and mild—
"And ever alas! my sweet Janet,
    "I fear ye gae with child."

"And, if I be with child, father,
   "Mysell maun bear the blame;
"There's ne'er a knight about your ha'
   "Shall hae the bairnie's name.

"And if I be with child, father,
   "Twill prove a wondrous birth;
"For well I swear I'm not wi' bairn
   "To any man on earth.

"If my love were an earthly knight,
   "As he's an elfin grey,
"I wadna gie my ain true love
   "For nae lord that ye hae."

She princked hersell and prinn'd hersell,
   By the ae light of the moon,
And she's away to Carterhaugh,
   To speak wi' young Tamlane.

And when she cam to Carterhaugh,
   She gaed beside the well;
And there she saw the steed standing,
   But away was himsell.

She hadna pu'd a double rose,
   A rose but only twae,
When up and started young Tamlane,
   Says—"Lady, thou pu's nae mae!

"Why pu' ye the rose, Janet,
   "Within this garden grene, "
And a' to kill the bonny babe,
   "That we got us between?"

"The truth ye'll tell to me, Tamlane;
   "A word ye mauna lie;
"Gin ye're ye was in haly chapel,
   "Or sained [hallowed] in Christentie."

"The truth I'll tell to thee, Janet,
   "A word I winna lie;
"A knight me got, and a lady me bore,
   "As well as they did thee.

"Randolph, Earl Murray, was my sire,
   "Dunbar, Earl March, is thine;
"We loved when we were children small,
   "Which yet you well may mind.

"When I was a boy just turned of nine,
   "My uncle sent for me,
"To hunt, and hawk, and ride with him,
   "And keep him cumpanie.

"There came a wind out of the north,
   "A sharp wind and a snell;
"And a dead sleep came over me,
   "And frae my horse I fell.

"The Queen of Fairies keppit me,
   "In yon green hill to dwell;
"And I'm a Fairy, lyth and limb;
   "Fair ladye, view me well.

"But we, that live in Fairy-land,
   "No sickness know, nor pain;
"I quit my body when I will,
   "And take to it again.

"I quit my body when I please,
   "Or unto it repair;
"We can inhabit, at our ease,
   "In either earth or air.

"Our shapes and size we can convert,
   "To either large or small;
"An old nut-shell's the same to us,
   "As is the lofty hall.

"We sleep in rose-buds, soft and sweet,
  "We revel in the stream;
"We wanton lightly on the wind,
  "Or glide on a sunbeam.

"And all our wants are well supplied,
  "From every rich man's store,
"Who thankless sins the gifts he gets,
  "And vainly grasps for more.

"Then would I never tire, Janet,
  "In elfish land to dwell;
"But aye at every seven years,
  "They pay the teind *(tithe)* to hell;

"And I am sae fat, and fair of flesh,
  "I fear 'twill be mysell.
"This night is Hallowe'en, Janet,
  "The morn is Hallowday;
"And, gin ye dare your true love win,
  "Ye hae na time to stay.

"The night it is good Hallowe'en,
  "When fairy folk will ride;
"And they, that wad their true love win,
  "At Miles Cross they maun bide."

"But how shall I thee ken, Tamlane?
  "Or how shall I thee knaw,
"Amang so many unearthly knights,
  "The like I never saw?"

"The first company, that passes by, "
  Say na, and let them gae;
"The next company, that passes by, "
  Say na, and do right sae;
"The third company, that passes by,
  "Than I'll be ane o' thae.

"First let pass the black, Janet,
  "And syne *(then)* let pass the brown;
"But grip ye to the milk-white steed,
  "And pu' the rider down.

"For I ride on the milk-white steed,
  "And ay nearest the town;
"Because I was a christened knight,
  "They gave me that renown.

"My right hand will be gloved, Janet,
  "My left hand will be bare;
"And these the tokens I gie thee,
  "Nae doubt I will be there.

"They'll turn me in your arms, Janet,
  "An adder and a snake;
"But had me fast, let me not pass,
  "Gin ye wad be my maik. *(mate, match)*

"They'll turn me in your arms, Janet,
  "An adder and an ask;
"They'll turn me in your arms, Janet,
  "A bale *(bundle of sticks)* that burns fast.

"They'll turn me in your arms, Janet,
  "A red-hot gad *(rod)* o' aim *(iron)*;
"But had me fast, let me not pass,
  "For I'll do you no harm.

"First, dip me in a stand o' milk,
  "And then in a stand o' water;
"But had me fast, let me not pass—
  "I'll be your bairn's father.

"And, next, they'll shape me in your arms,
  "A toad, but and an eel;
"But had me fast, nor let me gang,
  "As you do love me weel.

"They'll shape me in your arms, Janet,
    "A dove, but and a swan;
"And, last, they'll shape me in your arms,
    "A mother-naked man:
"Cast your green mantle over me—
    "I'll be mysell again."

Gloomy, gloomy, was the night,
    And eiry was the way,
As fair Janet, in her green mantle,
    To Miles Cross she did gae.

The heavens were black, the night was dark,
    And dreary was the place;
But Janet stood, with eager wish,
    Her lover to embrace.

Betwixt the hours of twelve and one,
    A north wind tore the bent;
And straight she heard strange elritch sounds
    Upon that wind which went.

About the dead hour o' the night,
    She heard the bridles ring (*fairy bridles have bells*);
And Janet was as glad o' that,
    As any earthly thing!

Their oaten pipes blew wondrous shrill,
    The hemlock small blew clear;
And louder notes from hemlock large,
    And bog-reed struck the ear;
But solemn sounds, or sober thoughts,
    The Fairies cannot bear.

They sing, inspired with love and joy,
    Like sky-larks in the air;
Of solid sense, or thought that's grave,
    You'll find no traces there.

Fair Janet stood, with mind unmoved,
    The dreary heath upon;
And louder, louder, wax'd the sound,
    As they came riding on.

Will o' Wisp before them went,
    Sent forth a twinkling light;
And soon she saw the Fairy bands
    All riding in her sight.

And first gaed by the black black steed,
    And then gaed by the brown;
But fast she gript the milk-white steed,
    And pu'd the rider down.

She pu'd him frae the milk-white steed,
    And loot the bridle fa';
And up there raise an erlish *(eldritch)* cry—
    "He's won amang us a'!"

They shaped him in fair Janet's arms,
    An esk *[newt]*, but and an adder;

She held him fast in every shape—
    To be her bairn's father.

They shaped him in her arms at last,
    A mother-naked man;
She wrapt him in her green mantle,
    And sae her true love wan.

Up then spake the Queen o' Fairies,
    Out o' a bush o' broom—
"She that has borrowed young Tamlane,
    Has gotten a stately groom."

Up then spake the Queen of Fairies,
    Out o' a bush of rye—
"She's ta'en awa the bonniest knight
    In a' my cumpanie.

"But had I kenn'd, Tamlane," she says,
  "A lady wad borrowed thee—
"I wad ta'en out thy twa gray een,
  "Put in twa een o' tree.

"Had I but kenn'd, Tamlane," she says,
  "Before ye came frae hame—
"I wad tane out your heart o' flesh,
  "Put in a heart o' stane.

"Had I but had the wit yestreen,
  "That I hae coft [bought] the day—
"I'd paid my kane seven times to hell,
  "Ere you'd been won away!"

PORK PIE HAT
Peter Straub

As Hat says: "Most people will tell you growing up means you stop believing in Halloween things—I'm telling you the reverse. You start to grow up when you understand that the stuff that scares you is part of the air you breathe."

This exquisite novella is a story about a story, a mystery about a mystery. In an interview with David Mathew, Peter Straub said his inspiration came from watching a video of "The Sound of Jazz," a live television broadcast from the late 1950s: "Lester Young wandered into view . . . Someone had to give him a push in the back to get him on his feet and moving toward the microphone. You can see him lick his reed and settle the horn in his mouth. What he plays is one uncomplicated chorus of the blues that moves from phrase to phrase with a kind of otherworldly majesty. Sorrow, heartbreak, and what I can only call wisdom take place through the mechanism of following one note, usually a whole note, with another one, slowly. There he is, this stupendous musician who had once transformed everything about him by the grace of his genius, this present shambles, this human wreckage, hardly able to play at all, delivering a statement that becomes more and more perfect, more and more profound as it advances from step to step . . . Eventually, I wondered: what could lead a person to a place like that, what brought him there? That was the origin of Pork Pie Hat.*"*

PART ONE

1

If you know jazz, you know about him, and the title of this memoir tells you who he is. If you don't know the music, his name doesn't matter. I'll call him Hat. What does matter is what he meant. I don't mean what he meant to people who were touched by what he said through his horn. (His horn was an old Selmer Balanced Action tenor saxophone, most of its lacquer worn off.) I'm talking about the whole long curve of his life, and the way that what appeared to be a long slide from joyous mastery to outright exhaustion can be seen in another way altogether.

Hat did slide into alcoholism and depression. The last ten years of his life amounted to suicide by malnutrition, and he was almost transparent by the time he died in the hotel room where I met him. Yet he was able to play until nearly the end. When he was working, he would wake up around seven in the evening, listen to Frank Sinatra or Billie Holiday records while he dressed, get to the club by nine, play three sets, come back to his room sometime after three, drink and listen to more records (he was on a lot of those records), and finally go back to bed around the time day people begin thinking about lunch. When he wasn't working, he got into bed about an hour earlier, woke up about five or six, and listened to records and drank through his long upside-down day.

It sounds like a miserable life, but it was just an unhappy one. The unhappiness came from a deep, irreversible sadness. Sadness is different from misery, at least Hat's was. His sadness seemed impersonal—it did not disfigure him, as misery can do. Hat's sadness seemed to be for the universe, or to be a larger than usual personal share of a sadness already existing in the universe. Inside it, Hat was unfailingly gentle, kind, even funny. His sadness seemed merely the opposite face of the equally impersonal happiness that shone through his earlier work.

In Hat's later years, his music thickened, and sorrow spoke through the phrases. In his last years, what he played often sounded like heartbreak itself. He was like someone who had passed through a great mystery, who was passing through a great mystery, and had to speak of what had seen, what he was seeing.

2

I brought two boxes of records with me when I first came to New York from Evanston, Illinois, where I'd earned a B.A. in English at Northwestern, and the first thing I set up in my shoebox at the top of John Jay Hall in Columbia University was my portable record player. I did everything to music in those days, and I supplied the rest of my unpacking with a soundtrack provided by Hat's disciples. The kind of music I most liked when I was twenty-one was called "cool" jazz, but my respect for Hat, the progenitor of this movement, was almost entirely abstract. I didn't know his earliest records, and all I'd heard of his later style was one track on a Verve sampler album. I thought he must almost certainly be dead, and I imagined that if by some miracle he was still alive, he would have been in his early seventies, like Louis Armstrong. In fact, the man who seemed a virtual ancient to me was a few months short of his fiftieth birthday.

In my first weeks at Columbia I almost never left the campus. I was taking five courses, also a seminar that was intended to lead me to a Master's thesis, and when I was not in lecture halls or my room, I was in the library. But by the end of September, feeling less overwhelmed, I began to go downtown to Greenwich Village. The IRT, the only subway line I actually understood, described a straight north-south axis which allowed you to get on at 116th Street and get off at Sheridan Square. From Sheridan Square radiated out an unimaginable wealth (unimaginable if you'd spent the previous four years in Evanston, Illinois) of cafes, bars, restaurants, record shops, bookstores, and jazz clubs. I'd come to New York to get a M.A. in English, but I'd also come for this.

I learned that Hat was still alive about seven o'clock in the evening on the first Saturday in October when I saw a poster bearing his name on the window of a storefront jazz club near St. Mark's Place. My conviction that Hat was dead was so strong that I first saw the poster as an advertisement of past glory. I stopped to gaze longer at this relic of a historical period. Hat had been playing with a quartet including a bassist and drummer of his own era, musicians long associated with him. But the piano player had been John Hawes, one of my musicians—John Hawes was on half a dozen of the records back in John Jay Hall. He must have been about twenty at the time, I thought, convinced that the poster had been preserved as memorabilia. Maybe Hawes' first job had been with Hat—anyhow, Hat's quartet must have been one of Hawes' first stops on the way to fame. John Hawes was a great figure to me, and the thought of him playing with a back number like Hat a disturbance in the texture of reality. I looked down at the date on the poster, and my snobbish and rule-bound version of reality shuddered under another assault of the unthinkable. Hat's engagement had begun on the Tuesday of this week—the first Tuesday in October, and its last night took place on the Sunday after next—the Sunday before Halloween. Hat was still alive, and John Hawes was playing with him. I couldn't have told you which half of this proposition was the more surprising.

To make sure, I went inside and asked the short, impassive man behind the bar if John Hawes were really playing there tonight. "He'd better be, if he wants to get paid," the man said.

"So Hat is still alive," I said.

"Put it this way," he said. "If it was you, you probably wouldn't be."

3

Two hours and twenty minutes later, Hat came through the front door, and I saw what he meant. Maybe a third of the tables between the door and the bandstand were filled with people listening to the piano trio. This was what I'd come for, and I thought that the evening was perfect. I hoped that Hat would stay away. All he could accomplish by showing up would be to steal soloing time from Hawes, who, apart from seeming a bit disengaged, was playing wonderfully. Maybe Hawes always seemed a bit disengaged. That was fine with me. Hawes was *supposed* to be cool. Then the bass player looked toward the door and smiled, and the drummer grinned and knocked one stick against the side of his snare drum in a rhythmic figure that managed both to suit what the trio was playing and serve as a half-comic, half-respectful greeting. I turned away from the trio and looked back toward the door. The bent figure of a light-skinned black man in a long, drooping, dark coat was carrying a tenor saxophone case into the club. Layers of airline stickers covered the case, and a black porkpie hat concealed most of the man's face. As soon as he got past the door, he fell into a chair next to an empty table—really fell, as if he would need a wheelchair to get any farther.

Most of the people who had watched him enter turned back to John Hawes and the trio, who were beginning the last few choruses of "Love Walked In." The old man laboriously unbuttoned his coat and let it fall off his shoulders onto the back of the chair. Then, with the same painful slowness, he lifted the hat off his head and lowered it to the table beside him. A brimming shot glass had appeared between himself and the hat, though I hadn't noticed any of the waiters or waitresses put it there. Hat picked up the glass and poured its entire contents into his mouth. Before he swallowed, he let himself take in the room, moving his eyes without changing the position of his head. He was wearing a dark gray suit, a blue shirt with a tight tab collar, and a black knit tie. His face looked soft and worn with drink, and his eyes were of no real color at all, as if not merely washed out but washed clean. He bent over, unlocked the case, and began assembling his horn. As soon as "Love Walked In" ended, he was on his feet, clipping the horn to his strap and walking toward the bandstand. There was some quiet applause.

Hat stepped neatly up onto the bandstand, acknowledged us with a nod, and whispered something to John Hawes, who raised his hands to the keyboard. The drummer was still grinning, and the bassist had closed his eyes. Hat tilted his horn to one side, examined the mouthpiece, and slid it a tiny distance down the cork. He licked the reed, tapped his foot twice, and put his lips around the mouthpiece.

What happened next changed my life—changed me, anyhow. It was like discovering that some vital, even necessary substance had all along been missing from my life. Anyone who hears a great musician for the first time knows the feeling that the universe has just expanded. In fact, all that happened was that Hat had started playing "Too Marvelous For Words," one of the twenty-odd songs that were his entire repertoire at the time. Actually, he was playing some oblique, one-time-only melody of his own that floated above "Too Marvelous For Words," and this spontaneous melody seemed to me to comment affectionately on the song while utterly transcending it—to turn a nice little song into something profound. I forgot to breathe for a little while, and goosebumps came up on my arms. Halfway through Hat's solo, I saw John Hawes watching him and realized that Hawes, whom I all but revered, revered *him*. But by that time, I did, too.

I stayed for all three sets, and after my seminar the next day, I went down to Sam Goody's and bought five of Hat's records, all I could afford. That night, I went back to the club and took a table right in front of the bandstand. For the next two weeks, I occupied the same table every night I could persuade myself that I did not have to study—eight or nine, out of the twelve nights Hat worked. Every night was like the first: the same things, in the same order, happened. Halfway through the first set, Hat turned up and collapsed into the nearest chair. Unobtrusively, a waiter put a drink beside him. Off went the pork pie and the long coat, and out from its case came the horn. The waiter carried the case, pork pie, and coat into a back room while Hat drifted toward the bandstand, often still fitting the pieces of his saxophone together. He stood straighter, seemed almost to grow taller, as he got on the stand. A nod to his audience, an inaudible word to John Hawes. And then that sense of passing over the border between very good, even excellent music and majestic, mysterious art. Between songs, Hat sipped from a glass placed beside his left foot. Three forty-five minute sets. Two half-hour breaks, during which Hat disappeared through a door behind the bandstand. The same twenty or so songs, recycled again and again. Ecstasy, as if I were hearing *Mozart* play Mozart.

One afternoon toward the end of the second week, I stood up from a library book I was trying to stuff whole into my brain—*Modern Approaches to Milton*—and walked out of my carrel to find whatever I could that had been written about Hat. I'd been hearing the sound of Hat's tenor in my head ever since I'd gotten out of bed. And in those days, I was a sort of apprentice scholar: I thought that real answers in the form of interpretations could be found in the pages of scholarly journals. If there were at least a thousand, maybe two thousand, articles concerning John Milton in Low Library, shouldn't there be at least a hundred about Hat? And out of the hundred shouldn't a dozen or so at least begin to explain what happened to me when I heard him play? I was looking for *close readings* of his solos, for analyses that would explain Hat's effects in terms of subdivided rhythms, alternate chords, and note choices, in the way that poetry critics parsed diction levels, inversions of meter, and permutations of imagery.

Of course I did not find a dozen articles that applied a musicological version of the New Criticism to Hat's recorded solos. I found six old concert write-ups in the *New York Times*, maybe as many record reviews in jazz magazines, and a couple of chapters in jazz histories. Hat had been born in Mississippi, played in his family band, left after a mysterious disagreement at the time they were becoming a successful "territory" band, then joined a famous jazz band in its infancy and quit, again mysteriously, just after its breakthrough into nationwide success. After that, he went out on his own. It seemed that if you wanted to know about him, you had to go straight to the music: there was virtually nowhere else to go.

I wandered back from the catalogues to my carrel, closed the door on the outer world, and went back to stuffing *Modern Approaches to Milton* into my brain. Around six o'clock, I opened the carrel door and realized that *I* could write about Hat. Given the paucity of criticism of his work—given the virtual absence of information about the man himself—I virtually had to write something. The only drawback to this inspiration was that I knew nothing about music. I could not write the sort of article I had wished to read. What I could do, however, would be to interview the man. Potentially, an interview would be more valuable than analysis. I could fill in the dark places, answer the unanswered questions—why had he left both bands just as they began to do well? I wondered if he'd had problems with his father, and then transferred these problems to his next bandleader. There had to be some kind of story. Any band within smelling distance of its first success would be more than reluctant to lose its star soloist—wouldn't they beg him, bribe him, to stay? I could think of other questions no one had ever asked: who had influenced him? What did he think of all those tenor players whom he had influenced? Was he friendly with any of his artistic children? Did they come to his house and talk about music?

Above all, I was curious about the texture of his life—I wondered what his life, the life of a genius, tasted like. If I could have put my half-formed fantasies into words, I would have described my naive, uninformed conceptions of Leonard Bernstein's surroundings. Mentally, I equipped Hat with a big apartment, handsome furniture, advanced stereo equipment, a good but not flashy car, paintings . . . the surroundings of a famous American artist, at least by the standards of John Jay Hall and Evanston, Illinois. The difference between Bernstein and Hat was that the conductor probably lived on Fifth Avenue, and the tenor player in the Village.

I walked out of the library humming "Love Walked In."

4

The dictionary-sized Manhattan telephone directory chained to the shelf beneath the pay telephone on the ground floor of John Jay Hall failed to provide Hat's number. Moments later, I met similar failure back in the library after having consulted the equally impressive directories for Brooklyn, Queens, and the Bronx, as well as the much smaller volume for Staten Island. But of course Hat lived in New York: where else would he live? Like other celebrities, he avoided the unwelcome intrusions of strangers by going unlisted. I could not explain his absence from the city's five telephone books in any other way. Of course Hat lived in the Village—that was what the Village was *for.*

Yet even then, remembering the unhealthy-looking man who each night entered the club to drop into the nearest chair, I experienced a wobble of doubt. Maybe the great man's life was nothing like my imaginings. Hat wore decent clothes, but did not seem rich—he seemed to exist at the same oblique angle to worldly success that his nightly variations on "Too Marvelous For Words" bore to the original melody. For a moment, I pictured my genius in a slum apartment where roaches scuttled across a bare floor and water dripped from a rip in the ceiling. I had no idea of how jazz musicians actually lived. Hollywood, unafraid of cliche, surrounded them with squalor. On the rare moments when literature stooped to consider jazz people, it, too, served up an ambiance of broken bedsprings and peeling walls. And literature's bohemians—Rimbaud, Jack London, Kerouac, Hart Crane, William Burroughs—had often inhabited mean, unhappy rooms. It was possible that the great man was not listed in the city's directories because he could not afford a telephone.

This notion was unacceptable. There was another explanation—Hat could not live in a tenement room without a telephone. The man still possessed the elegance of his generation of jazz musicians, the generation that wore good suits and highly polished shoes, played in big bands, and lived on buses and in hotel rooms.

And there, I thought, was my answer. It was a comedown from the apartment in the Village with which I had supplied him, but a room in some "artistic" hotel like the Chelsea would suit him just as well, and probably cost a lot less in rent. Feeling inspired, I looked up the Chelsea's number on the spot, dialed, and asked for Hat's room. The clerk told me that he wasn't registered in the hotel. "But you know who he is," I said. "Sure," said the clerk. "Guitar, right? I know he was in one of those San Francisco bands, but I can't remember which one."

I hung up without replying, realizing that the only way I was going to discover Hat's telephone number, short of calling every hotel in New York, was by asking him for it.

5

This was on a Monday, and the jazz clubs were closed. On Tuesday, Professor Marcus told us to read all of *Vanity Fair* by Friday; on Wednesday, after I'd spent a nearly sleepless night with Thackeray, my seminar leader asked me to prepare a paper on James Joyce's "Two Gallants" for the Friday class. Wednesday and Thursday nights I spent in the library. On Friday I listened to Professor Marcus being brilliant about *Vanity Fair* and read my laborious and dimwitted Joyce paper, on each of the five pages of which the word "epiphany" appeared at least twice, to my fellow-scholars. The seminar leader smiled and nodded throughout my performance and when I sat down metaphorically picked up my little paper between thumb and forefinger and slit its throat. "Some of you students are so *certain* about things," he said. The rest of his remarks disappeared into a vast, horrifying sense of shame. I returned to my room, intending to lie down for an hour or two, and woke up ravenous ten hours later, when even the West End bar, even the local Chock Full O' Nuts, were shut for the night.

On Saturday night, I took my usual table in front of the bandstand and sat expectantly through the piano trio's usual three numbers. In the middle of "Love Walked In" I looked around with an insider's foreknowledge to enjoy Hat's dramatic entrance, but he did not appear, and the number ended without him. John Hawes and the other two musicians seemed untroubled by this break in the routine, and went on to play "Too Marvelous For Words" without their leader. During the next three songs, I kept turning around to look for Hat, but the set ended without him. Hawes announced a short break, and the musicians stood up and moved toward the bar. I fidgeted at my table, nursing my second beer of the night and anxiously checking the door. The minutes trudged by. I feared he would never show up. He had passed out in his room. He'd been hit by a cab, he'd had a stroke, he was already lying dead in a hospital room—just when I was going to write the article that would finally do him justice!

Half an hour later, still without their leader, John Hawes and other sidemen went back on the stand. No one but me seemed to have noticed that Hat was not present. The other customers talked and smoked—this was in the days when people still smoked—and gave the music the intermittent and sometimes ostentatious attention they allowed it even when Hat was on the stand. By now, Hat was an hour and a half late, and I could see the gangsterish man behind the bar, the owner of the club, scowling as he checked his wristwatch. Hawes played two originals I particularly liked, favorites of mine from his Contemporary records, but in my mingled anxiety and irritation I scarcely heard them.

Toward the end of the second of these songs, Hat entered the club and fell into his customary seat a little more heavily than usual. The owner motioned away the waiter, who had begun moving toward him with the customary shot glass. Hat dropped the porkpie on the table and struggled with his coat buttons. When he heard what Hawes was playing, he sat listening with his hands still on a coat button, and I listened, too—the music had a tighter, harder, more modern feel, like Hawes' records. Hat nodded to himself, got his coat off, and struggled with the snaps on his saxophone case. The audience gave Hawes unusually appreciative applause. It took Hat longer than usual to fit the horn together, and by the time he was up on his feet, Hawes and the other two musicians had turned around to watch his progress as if they feared he would not make it all the way to the bandstand. Hat wound through the tables with his head tilted back, smiling to himself. When he got close to the stand, I saw that he was walking on his toes like a small child. The owner crossed his arms over his chest and glared. Hat seemed almost to float onto the stand. He licked his reed. Then he lowered his horn and, with his mouth open, stared out at us for a moment. "Ladies, ladies," he said in a soft, high voice. These were the first words I had ever heard him speak. "Thank you for your appreciation of our pianist, Mr. Hawes. And now I must explain my absence during the first set. My son passed away this afternoon, and I have been . . . busy . . . with details. Thank you."

With that, he spoke a single word to Hawes, put his horn back in his mouth, and began to play a blues called "Hat Jumped Up," one of his twenty songs. The audience sat motionless with shock. Hawes, the bassist, and the drummer played on as if nothing unusual had happened—they must have known about his son, I thought. Or maybe they knew that he had no son, and had invented a grotesque excuse for turning up ninety minutes late. The club owner bit his lower lip and looked unusually introspective. Hat played one familiar, uncomplicated figure after another, his tone rough, almost coarse. At the end of his solo, he repeated one note for an entire chorus, fingering the key while staring out toward the back of the club, Maybe he was watching the customers leave—three couples and a couple of single people walked out while he was playing. But I don't think he saw anything at all. When the song was over, Hat leaned over to whisper to Hawes, and the piano player announced a short break. The second set was over.

Hat put his tenor on top of the piano and stepped down off the band-stand, pursing his mouth with concentration. The owner had come out from behind the bar and moved up in front of him as Hat tip-toed around the stand. The owner spoke a few quiet words. Hat answered. From behind, he looked slumped and tired, and his hair curled far over the back of his collar. Whatever he had said only partially satisfied the owner, who spoke again before leaving him. Hat stood in place for a moment, perhaps not noticing that the owner had gone, and resumed his tip-toe glide toward the door. Looking at his back, I think I took in for the first time how genuinely strange he was. Floating through the door in his gray flannel suit, hair dangling in ringlet-like strands past his collar, leaving in the air behind him the announcement about a dead son, he seemed absolutely separate from the rest of humankind, a species of one.

I turned as if for guidance to the musicians at the bar. Talking, smiling, greeting a few fans and friends, they behaved just as they did on every other night. Could Hat really have lost a son earlier today? Maybe this was the jazz way of facing grief—to come back to work, to carry on. Still it seemed the worst of all times to approach Hat with my offer. His playing was a drunken parody of itself. He would forget anything he said to me; I was wasting MY time.

On that thought, I stood up and walked past the bandstand and opened the door—if I was wasting my time, it didn't matter what I did.

He was leaning against a brick wall about ten feet up the alleyway from the club's back door. The door clicked shut behind me, but Hat did not open his eyes. His face tilted up, and a sweetness that might have been sleep lay over his features. He looked exhausted and insubstantial, too frail to move. I would have gone back inside the club if he had not produced a cigarette from a pack in his shirt pocket, lit it with a match, and then flicked the match away, all without opening his eyes. At least he was awake. I stepped toward him, and his eyes opened. He glanced at me and blew out white smoke. "Taste?" he said.

I had no idea what he meant. "Can I talk to you for a minute, sir?" I asked.

He put his hand into one of his jacket pockets and pulled out a half-pint bottle. "Have a taste." Hat broke the seal on the cap, tilted it into his mouth, and drank. Then he held the bottle out toward me.

I took it. "I've been coming here as often as I can."

"Me, too," he said. "Go on, do it."

I took a sip from the bottle—gin. "I'm sorry about your son."

"Son?" He looked upward, as if trying to work out my meaning. "I got a son—out on Long Island. With his momma." He drank again and checked the level of the bottle.

"He's not dead, then."

He spoke the next words slowly, almost wonderingly. "Nobody-told-me-if-he-is." He shook his head and drank another mouthful of gin. "Damn. Wouldn't that be something, boy dies and nobody tells me? I'd have to think about that, you know, have to really *think* about that one."

"I'm just talking about what you said on stage."

He cocked his head and seemed to examine an empty place in the dark air about three feet from his face. "Uh huh. That's right. I did say that. Son of mine passed."

It was like dealing with a sphinx. All I could do was plunge in. "Well, sir, actually there's a reason I came out here," I said. "I'd like to interview you. Do you think that might be possible? You're a great artist, and there's very little about you in print. Do you think we could set up a time when I could talk to you?"

He looked at me with his bleary, colorless eyes, and I wondered if he could see me at all. And then I felt that, despite his drunkenness, he saw everything—that he saw things about me that I couldn't see.

"You a jazz writer?" he asked.

"No, I'm a graduate student. I'd just like to do it. I think it would be important."

"Important." He took another swallow from the half pint and slid the bottle back into his pocket. "Be nice, doing an important interview."

He stood leaning against the wall, moving further into outer space with every word. Only because I had started, I pressed on: I was already losing faith in this project. The reason Hat had never been interviewed was that ordinary American English was a foreign language to him. "Could we do the interview after you finish up at this club? I could meet you anywhere you like." Even as I said these words, I despaired. Hat was in no shape to know what he had to do after this engagement finished. I was surprised he could make it back to Long Island every night.

Hat rubbed his face, sighed, and restored my faith in him. "It'll have to wait a little while. Night after I finish here, I go to Toronto for two nights. Then I got something in Hartford on the thirtieth. You come see me after that."

"On the thirty-first?" I asked.

"Around nine, ten, something like that. Be nice if you brought some refreshments."

"Fine, great," I said, wondering if I would be able to take a late train back from wherever he lived. "But where on Long Island should I go?"

His eyes widened in mock-horror. "Don't go nowhere on Long Island. You come see me. In the Albert Hotel, Forty-Ninth and Eighth. Room 821."

I smiled at him—I had guessed right about one thing, anyhow.

Hat did not live in the Village, but he did live in a Manhattan hotel. I asked him for his phone number, and wrote it down, along with the other information, on a napkin from the club. After I folded the napkin into my jacket pocket, I thanked him and turned toward the door.

"Important as a motherfucker," he said in his high, soft, slurry voice.

I turned around in alarm, but he had tilted his head toward the sky again, and his eyes were closed.

"Indiana," he said. His voice made the word seem sung. "Moonlight in Vermont. I Thought About You. Flamingo."

He was deciding what to play during his next set. I went back inside, where twenty or thirty new arrivals, more people than I had ever seen in the club, waited for the music to start. Hat soon reappeared through the door, the other musicians left the bar, and the third set began. Hat played all four of the songs he had named, interspersing them through his standard repertoire during the course of an unusually long set. He was playing as well as I'd ever heard him, maybe better than I'd heard on all the other nights I had come to the club. The Saturday night crowd applauded explosively after every solo. I didn't know if what I was seeing was genius or desperation.

An obituary in the Sunday *New York Times*, which I read over breakfast the next morning in the John Jay cafeteria, explained some of what had happened. Early Saturday morning, a thirty-eight year old tenor saxophone player named Grant Kilbert had been killed in an automobile accident. One of the most successful jazz musicians in the world, one of the few jazz musicians, known outside of the immediate circle of fans, Kilbert had probably been Hat's most prominent disciple. He had certainly been one of my favorite musicians. More importantly, from his first record, *Cool Breeze*, Kilbert had excited respect and admiration. I looked at the photograph of the handsome young man beaming out over the neck of his saxophone and realized that the first four songs on *Cool Breeze* were "Indiana," "Moonlight in Vermont," "I Thought About You," and "Flamingo." Sometime late Saturday afternoon, someone had called up Hat to tell him about Kilbert. What I had seen had not merely been alcoholic eccentricity, it had been grief for a lost son. And when I thought about it, I was sure that the lost son, not himself, had been the important motherfucker he'd apothesized. What I had taken for spaciness and disconnection had all along been irony.

PART TWO
1

On the 31st of October, after calling to make sure he remembered our appointment, I did go to the Albert Hotel, room 821, and interview Hat. That is, I asked him questions and listened to the long, rambling, often obscene responses he gave them. During the long night I spent in his room, he drank the fifth of Gordon's gin, the "refreshments" I brought with me—all of It, an entire bottle of gin, without tonic, ice, or other dilutants. He just poured it into a tumbler and drank, as if it were water. (I refused his single offer of a "taste.") I frequently checked to make sure that the tape recorder I'd borrowed from a business student down the hall from me was still working, I changed tapes until they ran out, I made detailed back-up notes with a ballpoint pen in a stenographic notebook. A couple of times, he played me sections of records that he wanted me to hear, and now and then he sang a couple of bars to make sure that I understood what he was telling me. He sat me in his only chair, and during the entire night stationed himself, dressed in his pork pie hat, a dark blue chalk-stripe suit, and white button-down shirt with a black knit tie, on the edge of his bed. This was a formal occasion. When I arrived at nine o'clock, he addressed me as "Mr. Leonard Feather" (the name of a well-known jazz critic), and when he opened his door at six-thirty the next morning, he called me "Miss Rosemary." By then, I knew that this was an allusion to Rosemary Clooney, whose singing I had learned that he liked, and that the nickname meant he liked me, too. It was not at all certain, however, that he remembered my actual name.

I had three sixty-minute tapes and a notebook filled with handwriting that gradually degenerated from my usual scrawl into loops and wiggles that resembled Arabic more than English. Over the next month, I spent whatever spare time I had transcribing the tapes and trying to decipher my own handwriting. I wasn't sure that what I had was an interview. My carefully prepared questions had been met either with evasions or blank, silent refusals to answer—he had simply started talking about something else. After about an hour, I realized that this was his interview, not mine, and let him roll.

After my notes had been typed up and the tapes transcribed, I put everything in a drawer and went back to work on my M.A. What I had was even more puzzling than I'd thought, and straightening it out would have taken more time than I could afford. So the rest of that academic year was a long grind of studying for the comprehensive exam and getting a thesis ready. Until I picked up an old *Time* magazine in the John Jay lounge and saw his name in the "Milestones" columns, I didn't even know that Hat had died.

Two months after I'd interviewed him, he had begun to hemorrhage on a flight back from France; an ambulance had taken him directly from the airport to a hospital. Five days after his release from the hospital, he had died in his bed at the Albert.

After I earned my degree, I was determined to wrestle something useable from my long night with Hat—I owed it to him. During the first weeks of that summer, I wrote out a version of what Hat had said to me and sent it to the only publication I thought would be interested in it. *Downbeat* accepted the interview, and it appeared there about six months later. Eventually, it acquired some fame as the last of his rare public statements. I still see lines from the interview quoted in the sort of pieces about Hat never printed during his life. Sometimes they are lines he really did say to me; sometimes they are stitched together from remarks he made at different times; sometimes, they are quotations I invented in order to be able to use other things he did say.

But one section of that interview has never been quoted, because it was never printed. I never figured out what to make of it. Certainly I could not believe all he had said. He had been putting me on, silently laughing at my credulity, for he could not possibly believe that what he was telling me was literal truth. I was a white boy with a tape recorder, it was Halloween, and Hat was having fun with me. He was *jiving* me.

Now I feel different about his story and about him, too. He was a great man, and I was an unworldly kid. He was drunk, and I was priggishly sober, but in every important way, he was functioning far above my level. Hat had lived forty-nine years as a black man in America, and I'd spent all of my twenty-one years in white suburbs. He was an immensely talented musician, a man who virtually thought in music, and I can't even hum in tune. That I expected to understand anything at all about him staggers me now. Back then, I didn't know anything about grief, and Hat wore grief about him daily, like a cloak. Now that I am the age he was then, I see that most of what is called information is interpretation, and interpretation is always partial.

Probably Hat was putting me on, jiving me, though not maliciously. He certainly was not telling me the literal truth, though I have never been able to learn what the literal truth of this case was. It's possible that even Hat never knew what was the literal truth behind the story he told me—possible, I mean, that he was still trying to work out what the truth was, nearly forty years after the fact.

2

He started telling me the story after we heard what I thought were gunshots from the street. I jumped from the chair and rushed to the windows, which looked out onto Eighth Avenue. "Kids," Hat said. In the hard yellow light of the street lamps, four or five teenage boys trotted up the Avenue. Three of them carried paper bags. "Kids shooting?" I asked. My amazement tells you how long ago this was.

"Fireworks," Hat said. "Every Halloween in New York, fool kids run around with bags full of fireworks, trying to blow their hands off."

Here and in what follows, I am not going to try to represent the way Hat actually spoke. I cannot represent the way his voice glided over certain words and turned others into mushy growls, though he expressed more than half of his meaning by sound; and I don't want to reproduce his constant, reflexive obscenity. Hat couldn't utter four words in a row without throwing in a "motherfucker." Mostly, I have replaced his obscenities with other words, and the reader can imagine what was really said. Also, if I tried to imitate his grammar, I'd sound racist and he would sound stupid. Hat left school in the fourth grade, and his language, though precise, was casual. To add to these difficulties, Hat employed a private language of his own, a code to ensure that he would be understood only by the people he wished to understand him. I have replaced most of his code words with their equivalents.

It must have been around one in the morning, which means that I had been in his room about four hours. Until Hat explained the "gunshots," I had forgotten that it was Halloween night, and I told him this as I turned away from the window.

"I never forget about Halloween," Hat said. "If I can, I stay home on Halloween. Don't want to be out on the street, that night."

He had already given me proof that he was superstitious, and as he spoke he glanced almost nervously around the room, as if looking for sinister presences.

"You'd feel in danger?" I asked.

He rolled gin around in his mouth and looked at me as he had in the alley behind the club, taking note of qualities I myself did not yet perceive. This did not feel at all judgmental. The nervousness I thought I had seen had disappeared, and his manner seemed marginally more concentrated than earlier in the evening. He swallowed the gin and for a couple of seconds looked at me without speaking.

"No," he finally said. "Not exactly. But I wouldn't feel safe, either."

I sat with my pen half an inch from the page of my notebook, uncertain whether or not to write this down.

"I'm from Mississippi, you know."

I nodded.

"Funny things happen down there. Back when I was a little kid, it was a whole different world. Know what I mean?"

"I can guess," I said.

He nodded. "Sometimes people disappeared. They'd be *gone*. All kinds of stuff used to happen, stuff you wouldn't even believe in now. I met a witchlady once who could put curses on you, make you go blind and crazy. Another time, I saw a mean, murdering son of a bitch named Eddie Grimes die and come back to life—he got shot to death at a dance we were playing, he was *dead*, and a woman went down and whispered to him, and Eddie Grimes stood right back up on his feet. The man who shot him took off double-quick and he must have kept on going, because we never saw him after that."

"Did you start playing again?" I asked, taking notes as fast as I could.

"We never stopped," Hat said. "You let the people deal with what's going on, but you gotta keep on playing."

"Did you live in the country?" I asked, thinking that all of this sounded like Dogpatch—witches and walking dead men.

He shook his head. "I was brought up in town, Woodland, Mississippi. On the river. Where we lived was called Darktown, you know, but most of Woodland was white, with nice houses and all. Lots of our people did the cooking and washing in the big houses on Miller's Hill, that kind of work. In fact, we lived in a pretty nice house, for Darktown—the band always did well, and my father had a couple of other jobs on top of that. He was a good piano player, mainly, but he could play any kind of instrument. And he was a big, strong guy, nice-looking, real light-complected, so he was called Red, which was what that meant in those days. People respected him."

Another long, rattling burst of explosions came from Eighth Avenue. I wanted to ask him again about leaving his father's band, but Hat once more gave his little room a quick inspection, swallowed another mouthful of gin, and went on talking.

"We even went out trick or treating on Halloween, you know, like the white kids. I guess our people didn't do that everywhere, but we did. Naturally, we stuck to our neighborhood, and probably we got a lot less than the kids from Miller's Hill, but they didn't have anything up there that tasted as good as the apples and candy we brought home in our bags. Around us, people made instead of bought, and that's the difference." He smiled at either the memory or the unexpected sentimentality he had just revealed—for a moment, he looked both lost in time and uneasy with himself for having said too much.

"Or maybe I just remember it that way, you know? Anyhow, we used to raise some hell, too. You were *supposed* to raise hell, on Halloween."

"You went out with your brothers?" I asked.

"No, no, they were—" He flipped his hand in the air, dismissing whatever it was that his brothers had been. "I was always apart, you dig? Me, I was always into my own little things. I was that way right from the beginning. I play like that—never play like anyone else, don't even play like myself. You gotta find new places for yourself, or else nothing's happening, isn't that right? Don't want to be a repeater pencil." He saluted this declaration with another swallow of gin. "Back in those days, I used to go out with a boy named Rodney Sparks—we called him Dee, short for Demon, 'cause' Dee Sparks would do anything that came into his head. That boy was the bravest little bastard I ever knew. He'd wrassle a mad dog. And the reason was, Dee was the preacher's boy. If you happen to be the preacher's boy, seems like you gotta prove every way you can that you're no Buster Brown, you know? So I hung with Dee, because I wasn't any Buster Brown, either. This is when we were eleven, around then—the time when you talk about girls, you know, but you still aren't too sure what that's about. You don't know what *anything's* about, to tell the truth. You along for the ride, you trying to pack in as much fun as possible. So Dee was my right hand, and when I went out on Halloween in Woodland, I went out with *him*."

He rolled his eyes toward the window and said, "Yeah." An expression I could not read at all took over his face. By the standards of ordinary people, Hat almost always looked detached, even impassive, tuned to some private wavelength, and this sense of detachment had intensified. I thought he was changing mental gears, dismissing his childhood, and opened my mouth to ask him about Grant Kilbert. But he raised his glass to his mouth again and rolled his eyes back to me, and the quality of his gaze told me to keep quiet.

"I didn't know it," he said, "but I was getting ready to stop being a little boy. To stop believing in little boy things and start seeing like a grown-up. I guess that's part of what I liked about Dee Sparks—he seemed like he was a lot more grown-up than I was, shows you what my head was like. The age we were, this would have been the last time we went out on Halloween to get apples and candy. From then on, we would have gone out mainly to raise hell. Scare the shit out of the little kids. But the way it turned out, it was the last time we ever went out on Halloween."

He finished off the gin in his glass and reached down to pick the bottle off the floor and pour another few inches into the tumbler. "Here I am, sitting in this room. There's my horn over there. Here's this bottle. You know what I'm saying?"

I didn't. I had no idea what he was saying. The hint of fatality clung to his earlier statement, and for a second I thought he was going to say that he was here but Dee Sparks was nowhere because Dee Sparks had died in Woodland, Mississippi, at the age of eleven on Halloween night. Hat was looking at me with a steady curiosity which compelled a response. "What happened?" I asked.

Now I know that he was saying *It has come down to just this, my room, my horn, my bottle.* My question was as good as any other response.

"If I was to tell you everything that happened, we'd have to stay in this room for a month." He smiled and straightened up on the bed. His ankles were crossed, and for the first time I noticed that his feet, shod in dark suede shoes with crepe soles, did not quite touch the floor. "And, you know, I never tell anybody everything, I always have to keep something back for myself. Things turned out all right. Only thing I mind is, I should have earned more money. Grant Kilbert, he earned a lot of money, and some of that was mine, you know."

"Were you friends?" I asked.

"I knew the man." He tilted his head and stared at the ceiling for so long that eventually I looked up at it, too. It was not a remarkable ceiling. A circular section near the center had been replastered not long before.

"No matter where you live, there are places you're not supposed to go," he said, still gazing up. "And sooner or later, you're gonna wind up there." He smiled at me again. "Where we lived, the place you weren't supposed to go was called The Backs. Out of town, stuck in the woods on one little path. In Darktown, we had all kinds from preachers on down. We had washerwomen and blacksmiths and carpenters, and we had some no-good thieving trash, too, like Eddie Grimes, that man who came back from being dead. In The Backs, they started with trash like Eddie Grimes, and went down from there. Sometimes, our people went out there to buy a jug, and sometimes they went there to get a woman, but they never talked about it. The Backs was *rough*. What they had was rough." He rolled his eyes at me and said, "That witch-lady I told you about, she lived in The Backs." He snickered. "Man, they were a mean bunch of people. They'd cut you, you looked at 'em bad. But one thing funny about the place, white and colored lived there just the same—it was *integrated*. Backs people were so evil, color didn't make no difference to them. They hated everybody anyhow, on principle." Hat pointed his glass at me, tilted his head, and narrowed his eyes. "At least, that was what everybody *said*. So this particular Halloween, Dee Sparks says to me after we finish with Darktown, we ought to head out to The Backs and see what the place is really like. Maybe we can have some fun.

"The idea of going out to The Backs kind of scared me, but being scared was part of the fun—Halloween, right? And if anyplace in Woodland was perfect for all that Halloween shit, you know, someplace where you might really see a ghost or a goblin, The Backs was better than the graveyard." Hat shook his head, holding the glass out at a right angle to his body. A silvery amusement momentarily transformed him, and it struck me that his native elegance, the product of his character and bearing much more than of the handsome suit and the suede shoes, had in effect been paid for by the surviving of a thousand unimaginable difficulties, each painful to a varying degree. Then I realized that what I meant by elegance was really dignity, that for the first time I had recognized actual dignity in another human being, and that dignity was nothing like the self-congratulatory superiority people usually mistook for it.

"We were just little babies, and we wanted some of those good old Halloween scares. Like those dumbbells out on the street, tossing firecrackers at each other." Hat wiped his free hand down over his face and made sure that I was prepared to write down everything he said. (The tapes had already been used up.) "When I'm done, tell me if we found it, okay?"

"Okay," I said.

3

"Dee showed up at my house just after dinner, dressed in an old sheet with two eyeholes cut in it and carrying a paper bag. His big old shoes stuck out underneath the sheet. I had the same costume, but it was the one my brother used the year before, and it dragged along the ground and my feet got caught in it. The eyeholes kept sliding away from my eyes. My mother gave me a bag and told me to behave myself and get home before eight. it didn't take but half an hour to cover all the likely houses in Darktown, but she knew I'd want to fool around with Dee for an hour or so afterwards.

"Then up and down the streets we go, knocking on the doors where they'd give us stuff and making a little mischief where we knew they wouldn't. Nothing real bad, just banging on the door and running like hell, throwing rocks on the roof, little stuff. A few places, we plain and simple stayed away from—the places where people like Eddie Grimes lived. I always thought that was funny. We knew enough to steer clear of those houses, but we were still crazy to get out to The Backs.

"Only way I can figure it is, The Backs was *forbidden*. Nobody had to tell us to stay away from Eddie Grimes' house at night. You wouldn't even go there in the daylight, 'cause Eddie Grimes would get you and that would be that.

"Anyhow, Dee kept us moving along real quick, and when folks asked us questions or said they wouldn't give us stuff unless we sang a song, he moaned like a ghost and shook his bag in their faces, so we could get away faster. He was so excited, I think he was almost shaking.

"Me, I was excited, too. Not like Dee—sort of sick-excited, the way people must feel the first time they use a parachute. Scared-excited.

"As soon as we got away from the last house, Dee crossed the street and started running down the side of the little general store we all used. I knew where he was going. Out behind the store was a field, and on the other side of the field was Meridian Road, which took you out into the woods and to the path up to The Backs. When he realized that I wasn't next to him, he turned around and yelled at me to hurry up. *No,* I said inside myself, *I ain't gonna jump outta of this here airplane, I'm not dumb enough to do that.* And then I pulled up my sheet and scrunched up my eye to look through the one hole close enough to see through, and I took off after him.

"It was beginning to get dark when Dee and I left my house, and now it was dark. The Backs was about a mile and a half away, or at least the path was. We didn't know how far along that path you had to go before you got there. Hell, we didn't even know what it was—I was still thinking the place was a collection of little houses, like a sort of shadow-Woodland. And then, while we were crossing the field, I stepped on my costume and fell down flat on my face. Enough of this stuff, I said, and yanked the damned thing off. Dee started cussing me out, I wasn't doing this stuff the right way, we had to keep our costumes on in case anybody saw us, did I forget that this is Halloween, on Halloween a costume *protected* you. So I told I him I'd put it back on when we got there. If I kept on falling down, it'd take us twice as long. That shut him up.

"As soon as I got that blasted sheet over my head, I discovered that I could see at least a little ways ahead of me. The moon was up, and a lot of stars were out. Under his sheet, Dee Sparks looked a little bit like a real ghost. It kind of glimmered. You couldn't really make out its edges, so the darn thing like *floated*. But I could see his legs and those big old shoes sticking out.

"We got out of the field and started up Meridian Road, and pretty soon the trees came up right to the ditches alongside the road, and I couldn't see too well any more. The road seemed like it went smack into the woods and disappeared. The trees looked taller and thicker than in the daytime, and now and then something right at the edge of the woods shone round and white, like an eye—reflecting the moonlight, I guess. Spooked me. I didn't think we'd ever be able to find the path up to The Backs, and that was fine with me. I thought we might go along the road another ten-fifteen minutes, and then turn around and go home. Dee was swooping around up in front of me, flapping his sheet and acting bughouse. *He* sure wasn't trying too hard to find that path.

"After we walked about a mile down Meridian Road, I saw headlights like yellow dots coming towards us fast—Dee didn't see anything at all, running around in circles the way he was. I shouted at him to get off the road, and he took off like a rabbit—disappeared into the woods before I did. I jumped the ditch and hunkered down behind a pine about ten feet off the road to see who was coming. There weren't many cars in Woodland in those days, and I knew every one of them. When the car came by, it was Dr. Garland's old red Cord— Dr. Garland was a white man, but he had two waiting rooms and took colored patients, so colored patients was mostly what he had. And the man was a heavy drinker, *heavy* drinker. He zipped by, goin' at least fifty, which was mighty fast for those days, probably as fast as that old Cord would go. For about a second, I saw Dr. Garland's face under his white hair, and his mouth was wide open, stretched like he was screaming. After he passed, I waited a long time before I came out of the woods. Turning around and going home would have been fine with me. Dr. Garland changed everything. Normally, he was kind of slow and quiet, you know, and I could still see that black screaming hole opened up in his face—he looked like he was being tortured, like he was in Hell. I sure as hell didn't want to see whatever *he* had seen.

"I could hear the Cord's engine after the tail lights disappeared. I turned around and saw that I was all alone on the road. Dee Sparks was nowhere in sight. A couple of times, real soft, I called out his name. Then I called his name a little louder. Away off in the woods, I heard Dee giggle. I said he could run around all night if he liked but I was going home, and then I saw that pale silver sheet moving through the trees, and I started back down Meridian Road. After about twenty paces, I looked back, and there he was, standing in the middle of the road in that silly sheet, watching me go. Come on, I said, let's get back. He paid me no mind. Wasn't that

Dr. Garland? Where was he going, as fast as that? What was happening? When I said the doctor was probably out on some emergency, Dee said the man was going *home*—he lived in Woodland, didn't he?

"Then I thought maybe Dr. Garland had been up in The Backs. And Dee thought the same thing, which made him want to go there all the more. Now he was determined. Maybe we'd see some dead guy. We stood there until I understood that he was going to go by himself if I didn't go with him. That meant that I *had* to go. Wild as he was, Dee'd get himself into some kind of mess for sure if I wasn't there to hold him down. So I said okay, I was coming along, and Dee started swooping along like before, saying crazy stuff. There was no way we were going to be able to find some little old path that went up into the woods. It was so dark, you couldn't see the separate trees, only giant black walls on both sides of the road.

"We went so far along Meridian Road I was sure we must have passed it. Dee was running around in circles about ten feet ahead of me. I told him that we missed the path, and now it was time to get back home. He laughed at me and ran across to the right side of the road and disappeared into the darkness.

"I told him to get back, damn it, and he laughed some more and said I should come to *him*. Why? I said, and he said, Because this here is the path, dummy. I didn't believe him—came right up to where he disappeared. All I could see was a black wall that could have been trees or just plain night. Moron, Dee said, look down. And I did. Sure enough, one of those white things like an eye shone up from where the ditch should have been. I bent down and touched cold little stones, and the shining dot of white went off like a light—a pebble that caught the moonlight just right. Bending down like that, I could see the hump of grass growing up between the tire tracks that led out onto Meridian Road. He'd found the path, all right.

"At night, Dee Sparks could see one hell of a lot better than me. He spotted the break in the ditch from across the road. He was already walking up the path in those big old shoes, turning around every other step to look back at me, make sure I was coming along behind him. When I started following him, Dee told me to get my sheet back on, and I pulled the thing over my head even though I'd rather have sucked the water out of a hollow stump. But I knew he was right—on Halloween, especially in a place like where we were, you were safer in a costume.

"From then on in, we were in No Man's Land. Neither one of us had any idea how far we had to go to get to The Backs, or what it would look like

once we got there. Once I set foot on that wagon-track I knew for sure The
Backs wasn't anything like the way I thought. It was a lot more primitive
than a bunch of houses in the woods. Maybe they didn't even have houses!
Maybe they lived in caves!

"Naturally, after I got that blamed costume over my head, I couldn't see
for a while. Dee kept hissing at me to hurry up, and I kept cussing him out.
Finally I bunched up a couple handfuls of the sheet right under my chin
and held it against my neck, and that way I could see pretty well and walk
without tripping all over myself. All I had to do was follow Dee, and that
was easy. He was only a couple of inches in front of me, and even through
one eyehole, I could see that silvery sheet moving along.

"Things moved in the woods, and once in a while an owl hooted. To tell
you the truth, I never did like being out in the woods at night. Even back
then, give me a nice warm bar-room instead, and I'd be happy. Only animal
I ever liked was a cat, because a cat is soft to the touch, and it'll fall asleep
on your lap. But this was even worse than usual, because of Halloween,
and even before we got to The Backs, I wasn't sure if what I heard moving
around in the woods was just a possum or a fox or something a lot worse,
something with funny eyes and long teeth that liked the taste of little
boys. Maybe Eddie Grimes was out there, looking for whatever kind of
treat Eddie Grimes liked on Halloween night. Once I thought of that, I got
so close to Deep Sparks I could smell him right through his sheet.

"You know what Dee Sparks smelled like? Like sweat, and a little bit
like the soap the preacher made him use on his hands and face before
dinner, but really like a fire in a junction box. A sharp, kind of bitter smell.
That's how excited he was.

"After a while we were going uphill, and then we got to the top of the rise,
and a breeze pressed my sheet against my legs. We started going downhill,
and over Dee's electrical fire, I could smell wood smoke. And something
else I couldn't name. Dee stopped moving so sudden, I bumped into him.
I asked him what he could see. Nothing but the woods, he said, but we're
getting there. People are up ahead somewhere. And they got a still. We got
to be real quiet from here on out, he told me, as if he had to, and to let him
know I understood I pulled him off the path into the woods.

"Well, I thought, at least I know what Dr. Garland was after.

"Dee and I went snaking through the trees—me holding that blamed
sheet under my chin so I could see out of one eye, at least, and walk without
falling down. I was glad for that big fat pad of pine needles on the ground.

An elephant could have walked over that stuff as quiet as a beetle. We went along a little further, and it got so I could smell all kinds of stuff—burned sugar, crushed juniper berries, tobacco juice, grease. And after Dee and I moved a little bit along, I heard voices, and that was enough for me. Those voices sounded angry.

"I yanked at Dee's sheet and squatted down—I wasn't going any farther without taking a good look. He slipped down beside me. I pushed the wad of material under my chin up over my face, grabbed another handful, and yanked that up, too, to look out under the bottom of the sheet. Once I could actually *see* where we were, I almost passed out. Twenty feet away through the trees, a kerosene lantern lit up the grease-paper window cut into the back of a little wooden shack, and a big raggedly guy carrying another kerosene lantern came stepping out of a door we couldn't see and stumbled toward a shed. On the other side of the building I could see the yellow square of a window in another shack, and past that, another one, a sliver of yellow shining out through the trees. Dee was crouched next to me, and when I turned to look at him, I could see another chink of yellow light from some way off in the woods over that way. Whether he knew it not, he'd just about walked us straight into the middle of The Backs.

"He whispered for me to cover my face. I shook my head. Both of us watched the big guy stagger toward the shed. Somewhere in front of us, a woman screeched, and I almost dumped a load in my pants. Dee stuck his hand out from under his sheet and held it out, as if I needed *him* to tell me to be quiet. The woman screeched again, and the big guy sort of swayed back and forth. The light from the lantern swung around in big circles. I saw that the woods were full of little paths that ran between the shacks. The light hit the shack, and it wasn't even wood, but tar paper. The woman laughed or maybe sobbed. Whoever was inside the shack shouted, and the raggedy guy wobbled toward the shed again. He was so drunk he couldn't even walk straight. When he got to the shed, he set down the lantern and bent to get in.

"Dee put his mouth up to my ear and whispered, *Cover up—you don't want these people, to see who you are. Rip the eyeholes, if you can't see good enough.*

"I didn't want anyone in The Backs to see my face. I let the costume drop down over me again, and stuck my fingers in the nearest eyehole and pulled. Every living thing for about a mile around must have heard that cloth ripping. The big guy came out of the shed like someone pulled him out on a string, yanked the lantern up off the ground, and held it In our direction. Then we could see his face, and it was Eddie Grimes. You wouldn't want to run into Eddie Grimes anywhere, but The Backs was the last place you'd want to come across him. I was afraid he was going to start looking for us, but that woman started making stuck pig noises, and the man in the shack yelled something, and Grimes ducked back into the shed and came out with a jug. He lumbered back toward the shack and disappeared around the front of it. Dee and I could hear him arguing with the man inside.

"I jerked my thumb toward Meridian Road, but Dee shook his head. I whispered, *Didn't you already see Eddie Grimes, and isn't that enough for you?* He shook his head again. His eyes were gleaming behind that sheet. So what do you want, I asked, and he said, *I want to see that girl. We don't even know where she is,* I whispered, and Dee said, *All we got to do is follow her sound.*

"Dee and I sat and listened for a while. Every now and then, she let out a sort of whoop, and then she'd sort of cry, and after that she might say a word or two that sounded almost ordinary before she got going again on crying or laughing, the two all mixed up together. Sometimes we could hear other noises coming from the shacks, and none of them sounded happy. People were grumbling and arguing or just plain talking to themselves, but at least they sounded normal. That lady, she sounded like *Halloween*—like something that came up out of a grave.

"Probably you're thinking what I was hearing was sex—that I was too young to know how much noise ladies make when they're having fun. Well, maybe I was only eleven, but I grew up in Darktown, not Miller's Hill, and our walls were none too thick. What was going on with this lady didn't have anything to do with fun. The strange thing is, Dee didn't know that—he thought just what you were thinking. He wanted to see this lady getting humped. Maybe he even thought he could sneak in and get some for himself, I don't know. The main thing is, he thought he was listening to some wild sex, and he wanted to get close enough to see it. Well, I thought, his daddy was a preacher, and maybe preachers didn't do it once they got kids. And Dee didn't have an older brother like mine, who sneaked girls into the house whenever he thought he wouldn't get caught.

"He started sliding sideways through the woods, and I had to follow him. I'd seen enough of The Backs to last me the rest of my life, but I couldn't run off and leave Dee behind. And at least he was going at it the right way, circling around the shacks sideways, instead of trying to sneak straight through them. I started off after him. At least I could see a little better ever since I ripped at my eyehole, but I still had to hold my blasted costume bunched up under my chin, and if I moved my head or my hand the wrong way, the hole moved away from my eye and I couldn't see anything at all.

"So naturally, the first thing that happened was that I lost sight of Dee Sparks. My foot came down in a hole and I stumbled ahead for a few steps, completely blind, and then I hit a tree. I just came to a halt, sure that Eddie Grimes and a few other murderers were about to jump on me. For a couple of seconds I stood as still as a wooden Indian, too scared to move. When I didn't hear anything, I hauled at my costume until I could see out of it. No murderers were coming toward me from the shack beside the still. Eddie Grimes was saying *You don't understand* over and over, like he was so drunk that one phrase got stuck in his head, and he couldn't say or hear anything else. That woman yipped, like an animal noise, not a human one—like a fox barking. I sidled up next to the tree I'd run into and looked around for Dee. All I could see was dark trees and that one yellow window I'd seen before. To hell with Dee Sparks, I said to myself, and pulled the costume off over my head. I could see better, but there wasn't any glimmer of white over that way. He'd gone so far ahead of me I couldn't even see him.

"So I had to catch up with him, didn't I? I knew where he was going—the woman's noises were coming from the shack way up there in the woods—and I knew he was going to sneak around the outside of the shacks. In a couple of seconds, after he noticed I wasn't there, he was going to stop and wait for me. Makes sense, doesn't it? All I had to do was keep going toward that shack off to the side until I ran into him. I shoved my costume inside my shirt, and then I did something else—set my bag of candy down next to the tree. I'd clean forgotten about it ever since I saw Eddie Grimes' face, and if I had to run, I'd go faster without holding onto a lot of apples and chunks of taffy.

"About a minute later, I came out into the open between two big old chinaberry trees. There was a patch of grass between me and the next stand of trees. The woman made a gargling sound that ended in one of those fox-yips, and I looked up in that direction and saw that the clearing extended in a straight line up and down, like a path. Stars shone out of the patch of darkness between the two parts of the woods. And when I started to walk across it, I felt a grassy hump between two beaten tracks.

The path into The Backs off Meridian Road curved around somewhere up ahead and wound back down through the shacks before it came to a dead end. It had to come to a dead end, because it sure didn't join back up with Meridian Road.

"And this was how I'd managed to lose sight of Dee Sparks. Instead of avoiding the path and working his way north through the woods, he'd just taken the easiest way toward the woman's shack. Hell, I'd had to pull him off the path in the first place! By the time I got out of my sheet, he was probably way up there, out in the open for anyone to see and too excited to notice that he was all by himself. What I had to do was what I'd been trying to do all along, save his ass from anybody who might see him.

"As soon as I started going as soft as I could up the path, I saw that saving Dee Sparks' ass might be a tougher job than I thought—maybe I couldn't even save my own. When I first took off my costume, I'd seen lights from three or four shacks. I thought that's what The Backs was—three or four shacks. But after I started up the path, I saw a low square shape standing between two trees at the edge of the woods and realized that it was another shack. Whoever was inside had extinguished his kerosene lamp, or maybe wasn't home. About twenty-thirty feet on, there was another shack, all dark, and the only reason I noticed that one was, I heard voices coming from it, a man and a woman, both of them sounding drunk and slowed-down. Deeper in the woods past that one, another grease-paper window gleamed through the trees like a firefly. There were shacks all over the woods. As soon as I realized that Dee and I might not be the only people walking through the Backs on Halloween night, I bent down low to the ground and damn near slowed to a standstill. The only thing Dee had going for him, I thought, was good night vision—at least he might spot someone before they spotted him.

"A noise came from one of those shacks, and I stopped cold, with my heart pounding away like a bass drum. Then a big voice yelled out, *Who's that?*, and I just lay down in the track and tried to disappear. *Who's there?* Here I was calling Dee a fool, and I was making more noise than he did. I heard that man walk outside his door, and my heart pretty near exploded. Then the woman moaned up ahead, and the man who'd heard me swore to himself and went back inside. I just lay there in the dirt for a while. The woman moaned again, and this time it sounded scarier than ever, because it had a kind of a chuckle in it. She was crazy. Or she was a witch, and if she was having sex, it was with the Devil. That was enough to make me start crawling along, and I kept on crawling until I was long past the shack where the man had heard me. Finally I got up on my feet again, thinking that if I didn't see Dee Sparks real soon, I was going to sneak back to Meridian Road by myself. If Dee Sparks wanted to see a witch in bed with the Devil, he could do it without me.

"And then I thought I was a fool not to ditch Dee, because hadn't he ditched me? After all this time, he must have noticed that I wasn't with him any more. Did he come back and look for me? The hell he did.

"And right then I would have gone back home, but for two things. The first was that I heard that woman make another sound—a sound that was hardly human, but wasn't made by any animal. It wasn't even loud. And it sure as hell wasn't any witch in bed with the Devil. It made me want to throw up. That woman was being *hurt*. She wasn't just getting beat up—I knew what that sounded like—she was being hurt bad enough to drive her crazy, bad enough to kill her. Because you couldn't live through being hurt bad enough to make that sound. I was in The Backs, sure enough, and the place was even worse than it was supposed to be. Someone was killing a woman, everybody could hear it, and all that happened was that Eddie Grimes fetched another jug back from the still. I froze. When I could move, I pulled my ghost costume out from inside my shirt, because Dee was right, and for certain I didn't want anybody seeing my face out there on *this* night. And then the second thing happened. While I was pulling the sheet over my head, I saw something pale lying in the grass a couple of feet back toward the woods I'd come out of, and when I looked at it, it turned into Dee Sparks' Halloween bag.

"I went up to the bag and touched it to make sure about what it was. I'd found Dee's bag, all right. And it was empty. Flat. He had stuffed the content into his pockets and left the bag behind. What that meant was, I couldn't turn around and leave him—because he hadn't left me after all. He waited for me until he couldn't stand it any more, and then he emptied his bag and left it behind as a sign. He was counting on me to see in the dark as well as he could. But I wouldn't have seen it at all if that woman hadn't stopped me cold.

"The top of the bag was pointing north, so Dee was still heading toward the woman's shack. I looked up that way, and all I could see was a solid wall of darkness underneath a lighter darkness filled with stars. For about a second, I realized, I had felt pure relief. Dee had ditched me, so I could ditch him and go home. Now I was stuck with Dee all over again.

"About twenty feet ahead, another surprise jumped up at me out of darkness. Something that looked like a little tiny shack began to take shape, and I got down on my hands and knees to crawl toward the path when I saw a long silver gleam along the top of the thing. That meant it had to be metal—tar paper might have a lot of uses, but it never yet reflected starlight. Once I realized that the thing in front of me was metal, I remembered its shape and realized it was a car. You wouldn't think you'd come across a car in a down-and-out rathole like The Backs, would you? People like that, they don't even own two shirts, so how do they come by cars? Then I remembered Dr. Garland driving away speeding down Meridian Road, and I thought *You don't have to live in The Backs to drive there.* Someone could turn up onto the path, drive around the loop, pull his car off onto the grass, and no one would ever see it or know that he was there.

"And this made me feel funny. The car probably belonged to someone I knew. Our band played dances and parties all over the county and everywhere in Woodland, and I'd probably seen every single person in town, and they'd seen me, too, and knew me by name. I walked closer to the car to see if I recognized it, but it was just an old black Model T. There must have been twenty cars just like it in Woodland. Whites and coloreds, the few coloreds that owned cars, both had them. And when I got right up beside the Model T, I saw what Dee had left for me on the hood—an apple.

"About twenty feet further along, there was an apple on top of a big old stone. He was putting those apples where I couldn't help but see them. The third one was on top of a post at the edge of the woods, and it was so pale it looked almost white. Next to the post one of those paths running all through The Backs led back into the woods. If it hadn't been for that apple, I would have gone right past it.

"At least I didn't have to worry so much about being making noise once I got back into the woods. Must have been six inches of pine needles and fallen leaves underfoot, and I walked so quiet I could have been floating—I've worn crepe soles ever since then, and for the same reason. You walk *soft*. But I was still plenty scared—back in the woods there was a lot less light, and I'd have to step on an apple to see it. All I wanted was to find Dee and persuade him to leave with me.

"For a while, all I did was keep moving between the trees and try to make sure I wasn't coming up on a shack. Every now and then, a faint, slurry voice came from somewhere off in the woods, but I didn't let it spook me. Then, way up ahead, I saw Dee Sparks. The path didn't go in a straight line, it kind of angled back and forth, so I didn't have a good clear look at him, but I got a flash of that silvery-looking sheet way off through the trees. If I sped up I could get to him before he did anything stupid. I pulled my costume up a little further toward my neck and started to jog.

"The path started dipping *downhill*. I couldn't figure it out. Dee was in a straight line ahead of me, and as soon as I followed the path downhill a little bit, I lost sight of him. After a couple more steps, I stopped. The path got a lot steeper. If I kept running, I'd go ass over teakettle. The woman made another terrible sound, and it seemed to come from everywhere at once. Like everything around me had been *hurt*. I damn near came unglued. Seemed like everything was *dying*. That Halloween stuff about horrible creatures wasn't any story, man, it was the way things really were—you couldn't know anything, you couldn't trust anything, and you were surrounded by *death*. I almost fell down and cried like a baby boy. I was lost. I didn't think I'd ever get back home.

"Then the worst thing of all happened.

"I heard her die. It was just a little noise, more like a sigh than anything, but that sigh came from everywhere and went straight into my ear. A soft sound can be loud, too, you know, be the loudest thing you ever heard. That sigh about lifted me up off the ground, about blew my head apart.

"I stumbled down the path, trying to wipe my eyes with my costume, and all of a sudden I heard men's voices from off to my left. Someone was saying a word I couldn't understand over and over, and someone else was telling him to shut up. Then, behind me, I heard running—heavy running, a man. I took off, and right away my feet got tangled up in the sheet and I was rolling downhill, hitting my head on rocks and bouncing off trees and smashing into stuff I didn't have any idea what it was. *Biff bop bang slam smash clang crash ding dong.* I hit something big and solid and wound up half-covered in water. Took me a long time to get upright, twisted up in that sheet the way I was. My ears buzzed and I saw stars—yellow and blue and red ones, not real ones. When I tried to sit up, the blasted sheet pulled me back down, so I got a faceful of cold water. I scrambled around like a fox in a trap, and when I finally got so I was sitting up, I saw a slash of real sky out the corner of one eye, and I got my hands free and ripped that hole in the sheet wide enough for my whole head to fit through it.

"I was sitting in a little stream next to a fallen tree. The tree was what had stopped me. My whole body hurt like the dickens. I had no idea where

I was. Wasn't even sure I could stand up. Got my hands on top of the fallen tree and pushed myself up with my legs—blasted sheet ripped in half, and my knees almost bent back the wrong way, but I got up on my feet. And there was Dee Sparks, coming toward me through the woods on the other side of the stream.

"He looked like he didn't feel any better than I did, like he couldn't move in a straight line. His silvery sheet was smearing through the trees. *Dee got hurt, too,* I thought—he looked as if he was in some total panic. The next time I saw the white smear between the trees it was twisting about ten feet off the ground. *No,* I said to myself and closed my eyes. Whatever that thing was, it wasn't Dee. An unbearable feeling, an absolute despair, flowed out from it. I fought against this despair with every weapon I had. I didn't want to know that feeling—I was eleven years old. If that feeling reached me when I was eleven years old, my entire life would be changed, I'd be in a different universe altogether.

"But it did reach me, did it? I could say *no* all I liked, but I couldn't change what had happened. I opened my eyes and the white smear was gone.

That was almost worse—I wanted it to be Dee after all, doing something crazy and reckless, climbing trees, running around like a wild man, trying to give me a big whopping scare. But it wasn't Dee Sparks, and it meant the worst things I'd ever imagine were true. Everything was dying. You couldn't know anything. you couldn't trust anything, we were all lost in the midst of the death that surrounded us.

"Most people will tell you growing up means you stop believing in Halloween things—I'm telling you the reverse. You start to grow up when you understand that the stuff that scares you is part of the air you breathe.

"I stared at the spot where I'd seen that twist of whiteness, I guess trying to go back in time to before I saw Dr. Garland fleeing down Meridian Road. My face looked like his, I thought—because now I knew that you really *could* see a ghost. The heavy footsteps I'd heard before suddenly cut through the buzzing in my head, and after I turned around and saw who was coming at me down the hill, I thought it was probably my own ghost I'd seen.

"Eddie Grimes looked as big as an oak tree, and he had a long knife in one hand. His feet slipped out from under him, and he skidded the last few yards down to the creek, but I didn't even try to run away. Drunk as he was, I'd never get away from him. All I did was back up alongside the fallen tree and watch him slide downhill toward the water. I was so scared I couldn't even talk. Eddie Grimes' shirt was flapping open, and big long scars ran all across his chest and belly. He'd been raised from the dead at least a couple of times since I'd seen him get killed at the dance. He jumped back up on his feet and started coming for me. I opened my mouth, but nothing came out.

"Eddie Grimes took another step toward me, and then he stopped and looked straight at my face. He lowered the knife. A sour stink of sweat and alcohol came off him. All he could do was stare at me. Eddie Grimes knew my face all right, he knew my name, he knew my whole family—even at night, he couldn't mistake me for anyone else. I finally saw that Eddie was actually afraid, like he was the one who'd seen a ghost. The two of us just stood there in the shallow water for a couple more seconds, and then Eddie Grimes pointed his knife at the other side of the creek.

"That was all I needed, baby. My legs unfroze, and I forgot all my aches and pains. Eddie watched me roll over the fallen tree and lowered his knife. I splashed through the water and started moving up the hill, grabbing at weeds and branches to pull me along. My feet were frozen, and my clothes were soaked and muddy, and I was trembling all over. About half way up the hill, I looked back over my shoulder, but Eddie Grimes was gone. It was like he'd never been there at all, like he was nothing but the product of a couple of good raps to the noggin.

"Finally, I pulled myself shaking up over the top of the rise, and what did I see about ten feet away through a lot of skinny birch trees but a kid in a sheet facing away from me into the woods, and hopping from foot to foot in a pair of big clumsy shoes? And what was in front of him but a path I could make out from even ten feet away? Obviously, this was where I was supposed to turn up, only in the dark and all I must have missed an apple stuck onto a branch or some blasted thing, and I took that little side trip downhill on my head and wound up throwing a spook into Eddie Grimes.

"As soon as I saw him, I realized I hated Dee Sparks. I wouldn't have tossed him a rope if he was drowning. Without even thinking about it, I bent down and picked up a stone and flung it at him. The stone bounced off a tree, so I bent down and got another one. Dee turned around to find out what made the noise, and the second stone hit him right in the chest, even though it was his head I was aiming at.

"He pulled his sheet up over his face like an Arab and stared at me with his mouth wide open. Then he looked back over his shoulder at the path, as if the real me might come along at any second. I felt like pegging another rock at his stupid face, but instead I marched up to him. He was shaking his head from side to side. *Jim Dawg*, he whispered, *what happened to you?* By way of answer, I hit him a good hard knock on the breastbone. *What's the matter?* he wanted to know. *After you left me, I say, I fell down a hill and ran into Eddie Grimes.*

"That gave him something to think about, all right. Was Grimes coming after me, he wanted to know? Did he see which way I went? Did Grimes see who I was? He was pulling me into the woods while he asked me these dumb-ass questions, and I shoved him away. His sheet flopped back down over his front, and he looked like a little boy. He couldn't figure out why I was mad at him. From his point of view, he'd been pretty clever, and if I got lost, it was my fault. But I wasn't mad at him because I got lost. I wasn't even mad at him because I'd run into Eddie Grimes. It was everything else. Maybe it wasn't even him I was mad at.

"*I want to get home without getting killed,* I whispered. *Eddie ain't gonna let me go twice.* Then I pretended he wasn't there any more and tried to figure out how to get back to Meridian Road. It seemed to me that I was still going north when I took that tumble downhill, so when I climbed up the hill on the other side of the creek I was still going north. The wagon-track that Dee and I took into The Backs had to be off to my right. I turned away from Dee and started moving through the woods. I didn't care if he followed me or not. He had nothing to do with me any more, he was on his own. When I heard him coming along after me, I was sorry. I wanted to get away from Dee Sparks. I wanted to get away from everybody.

"I didn't want to be around anybody who was supposed to be my friend. I'd rather have had Eddie Grimes following me than Dee Sparks.

"Then I stopped moving, because through the trees I could see one of those grease-paper windows glowing up ahead of me. That yellow light looked evil as the Devil's eye—everything in The Backs was evil, poisoned, even the trees, even the air. The terrible expression on Dr. Garland's face and the white smudge in the air seemed like the same thing—they were what I didn't want to know.

"Dee shoved me from behind, and if I hadn't felt so sick inside I would have turned around and punched him. Instead, I looked over my shoulder and saw him nodding toward where the side of the shack would be. He wanted to get closer! For a second, he seemed as crazy as everything else out there, and then I got it: I was all turned around, and instead of heading back to the main path, I'd been taking us toward the woman's shack. That was why Dee was following me.

"I shook my head. No, I wasn't going to sneak up to that place. Whatever was inside there was something I didn't have to know about. It had too much power—it turned Eddie Grimes around, and that was enough for me. Dee knew I wasn't fooling. He went around me and started creeping toward the shack.

"And damndest thing, I watched him slipping through the trees for a second, and started following him. If he could go up there, so could I. If I didn't exactly look at whatever was in there myself, I could watch Dee look at it. That would tell me most of what I had to know. And anyways, probably Dee wouldn't see anything anyhow, unless the front door was hanging open, and that didn't seem too likely to me. He wouldn't see anything, and I wouldn't either, and we could both go home.

"The door of the shack opened up, and a man walked outside. Dee and I freeze, and I mean *freeze*. We're about twenty feet away, on the side of this shack, and if the man looked sideways, he'd see our sheets. There were a lot of trees between us and him, and I couldn't get a very good look at him, but one thing about him made the whole situation a lot more serious. This man was white, and he was wearing good clothes—I couldn't see his face, but I could see his rolled up sleeves, and his suit jacket slung over one arm, and some kind of wrapped-up bundle he was holding in his hands. All this took about a second. The white man started carrying his bundle straight through the woods, and in another two seconds he was out of sight.

"Dee was a little closer than I was, and I think his sight line was a little clearer than mine. On top of that, he saw better at night than I did. Dee didn't get around like me, but he might have recognized the man we'd seen, and that would be pure trouble. Some rich white man, killing a girl out in The Backs? And us two boys close enough to see him? Do you know what would have happened to us? There wouldn't be enough left of either one of us to make a decent smudge.

"Dee turned around to face me, and I could see his eyes behind his costume, but I couldn't tell what he was thinking. He just stood there, looking at me. In a little bit, just when I was about to explode, we heard a car starting up off to our left. I whispered at Dee if he saw who that was. *Nobody*, Dee said. Now, what the hell did that mean? Nobody? You could say Santa Claus, you could say J. Edgar *Hoover*, it'd be a better answer than Nobody. The Model T's headlights shone through the trees when the car swung around the top of the path and started going toward Meridian Road. *Nobody I ever saw before*, Dee said. When the headlights cut through the trees, both of us ducked out of sight. Actually, we were so far from the path, we had nothing to worry about. I could barely see the car when it went past, and I couldn't see the driver at all.

"We stood up. Over Dee's shoulder I could see the side of the shack where the white man had been. Lamplight flickered on the ground in front of the open door. The last thing in the world I wanted to do was to go inside that place—I didn't even want to walk around to the front and look in the door. Dee stepped back from me and jerked his head toward the shack. I knew it was going to be just like before. I'd say no, he'd say yes, and then I'd follow him wherever he thought he had to go. I felt the same way I did when I saw that white smear in the woods—hopeless, lost in the midst of death. *You go, if you have to,* I whispered to him, *it's what you wanted to do all along.* He didn't move, and I saw that he wasn't too sure about what he wanted any more.

"Everything was different now, because the white man made it different. Once a white man walked out that door, it was like raising the stakes in a poker game. But Dee had been working toward that one shack ever since we got into The Backs, and he was still curious as a cat about it. He turned away from me and started moving sideways in a straight line, so he'd be able to peek inside the door from a safe distance.

"After he got about half way to the front, he looked back and waved me on, like this was still some great adventure he wanted me to share. He was afraid to be on his own, that was all. When he realized I was going to stay put, he bent down and moved real slow past the side. He still couldn't see more than a sliver of the inside of the shack, and he moved ahead another little ways. By then, I figured, he should have been able to see about half of the inside of the shack. He hunkered down inside his sheet, staring in the direction of the open door. And there he stayed.

"I took it for about half a minute, and then I couldn't any more. I was sick enough to die and angry enough to explode, both at the same time. How long could Dee Sparks look at a dead whore? Wouldn't a couple of seconds be enough? Dee was acting like he was watching a goddamn Hopalong Cassidy movie. An owl screeched, and some man in another shack said *Now that's over*, and someone else shushed him. If Dee heard, he paid it no mind. I started along toward him, and I don't think he noticed me, either. He didn't look up until I was past the front of the shack, and had already seen the door hanging open, and the lamplight spilling over the plank floor and onto the grass outside.

"I took another step, and Dee's head snapped around. He tried to stop me by holding out his hand. All that did was make me mad. Who was Dee Sparks to tell me what I couldn't see? All he did was leave me alone in the woods with a trail of apples, and he didn't even do that right. When I kept on coming, Dee started waving both hands at me, looking back and forth between me and the inside of the shack. Like something was happening in there that I couldn't be allowed to see. I didn't stop, and Dee got up on his feet and skittered toward me.

"*We gotta get out of here*, he whispered. He was close enough so I could smell that electrical stink. I stepped to his side, and he grabbed my arm. I yanked my arm out of his grip and went forward a little ways and looked through the door of the shack.

"A bed was shoved up against the far wall, and a woman lay naked on the bed. There was blood all over her legs, and blood all over the sheets, and big puddles of blood on the floor. A woman in a raggedy robe, hair stuck out all over her head, squatted beside the bed, holding the other woman's hand. She was a colored woman—a Backs woman—but the other one, the one on the bed, was white. Probably she was pretty, when she was alive. All I could see was white skin and blood, and I near fainted.

"This wasn't some white-trash woman who lived out in The Backs— she was brought there, and the man who brought her had killed her. More trouble was coming down than I could imagine, trouble enough to kill lots of our people. And if Dee and I said a word about the white man we'd seen, the trouble would come right straight down on us.

"I must have made some kind of noise, because the woman next to the bed turned halfways around and looked at me. There wasn't any doubt about it—she saw me. All she saw of Dee was a dirty white sheet, but she saw my face, and she knew who I was. I knew her, too, and she wasn't any Backs woman. She lived down the street from us. Her name was Mary Randolph, and she was the one who came up to Eddie Grimes after he got shot to death and brought him back to life. Mary Randolph followed my dad's band, and when we played roadhouses or colored dance halls, she'd be likely to turn up. A couple of times she told me I played good drums—I was a drummer back then, you know, switched to saxophone when I turned twelve. Mary

Randolph just looked at me, her hair stuck out straight all over her head like she was already inside a whirlwind of trouble. No expression on her face except that look you get when your mind is going a mile a minute and your body can't move at all. She didn't even look surprised. She almost looked like she *wasn't* surprised, like she was expecting to see me. As bad as I'd felt that night, this was the worst of all. I liked to have died. I'd have disappeared down an anthill, if I could. I didn't know what I had done—just be there, I guess—but I'd never be able to undo it.

"I pulled at Dee's sheet, and he tore off down the side of the shack like he'd been waiting for a signal. Mary Randolph stared into my eyes, and it felt like I had to pull myself away—I couldn't just turn my head, I had to *disconnect*. And when I did, I could still feel her staring at me. Somehow I made myself go down past the side of the shack, but I could still see Mary Randolph inside there, looking out at the place where I'd been.

"If Dee said anything at all when I caught up with him, I'd have knocked his teeth down his throat, but he just moved fast and quiet through the trees, seeing the best way to go, and I followed after. I felt like I'd been kicked by a horse. When we got on the path, we didn't bother trying to sneak down through the woods on the other side, we fit out and ran as hard as we could—like wild dogs were after us. And after we got onto Meridian Road, we ran toward town until we couldn't run any more.

"Dee clamped his hand over his side and staggered forward a little bit. Then he stopped and ripped off his costume and lay down by the side of the road, breathing hard. I was leaning forward with hands on my knees, as winded as he was. When I could breathe again, I started walking down the road. Dee picked himself up and got next to me and walked along, looking at my face and then looking away, and then looking back at my face again.

"*So?* I said.

"*I know that lady*, Dee said.

"Hell, that was no news. Of course he knew Mary Randolph—she was his neighbour, too. I didn't bother to answer, I just grunted at him. Then I reminded him that Mary hadn't seen his face, only mine.

"*Not* Mary, he said. *The other one.*

"He knew the dead white woman's name? That made everything worse. A lady like that shouldn't be in Dee Sparks' world, especially if she's going to wind up dead in The Backs. I wondered who was going to get lynched, and how many.

"Then Dee said that I knew her, too. I stopped walking and looked him straight in the face.

"*Miss Abbey Montgomery,* he said. *She brings clothes and food down to our church, Thanksgiving and Christmas.*

"He was right—I wasn't sure if I'd ever heard her name, but I'd seen her once or twice, bringing baskets of ham and chicken and boxes of clothes to Dee's father's church. She was about twenty years old, I guess, so pretty she made you smile just to look at. From a rich family in a big house right at the top of Miller's Hill. Some man didn't think a girl like that should have any associations with colored people, I guess, and decided to express his opinion about as strong as possible. Which meant that we were going to take the blame for what happened to her, and the next time we saw white sheets, they wouldn't be Halloween costumes.

"*He sure took a long time to kill her,* I said.

"And Dee said, *She ain't dead.*

"So I asked him, What the hell did he mean by that? I saw the girl. I saw the blood. Did he think she was going to get up and walk around? Or maybe Mary Randolph was going to tell her that magic word and bring her back to life?

"*You can think that if you want to,* Dee said. *But Abbey Montgomery ain't dead.*

"I almost told him I'd seen her ghost, but he didn't deserve to hear about it. The fool couldn't even see what was right in front of his eyes. I couldn't expect him to understand what happened to me when I saw that miserable . . . that *thing.* He was rushing on ahead of me anyhow, like I'd suddenly embarrassed him or something. That was fine with me. I felt the exact same way. I said, *I guess you know neither one of us can ever talk about this,* and he said, *I guess you know it, too,* and that was the last thing we said to each other that night. All the way down Meridian Road Dee Sparks kept his eyes straight ahead and his mouth shut. When we got to the field, he turned toward me like he had something to say, and I waited for it, but he faced forward again and ran away. just ran. I watched him disappear past the general store, and then I walked home by myself.

"My mom gave me hell for getting my clothes all wet and dirty, and my brothers laughed at me and wanted to know who beat me up and stole my candy. As soon as I could, I went to bed, pulled the covers up over my head, and closed my eyes. A little while later, my mom came in and asked if I was all right. Did I get into a fight with that Dee Sparks? Dee Sparks was born to hang, that was what she thought, and I ought to have a better class of friends. *I'm tired of playing those drums, Momma*, I said, *I want to play the saxophone instead*. She looked at me surprised, but said she'd talk about with Daddy, and that it might work out.

"For the next couple days, I waited for the bomb to go off. On the Friday, I went to school, but couldn't concentrate for beans. Dee Sparks and I didn't even nod at each other in the hallways—just walked by like the other guy was invisible. On the weekend I said I felt sick and stayed in bed, wondering when that whirlwind of trouble would come down. I wondered if Eddie Grimes would talk about seeing me—once they found the body, they'd get around to Eddie Grimes real quick.

"But nothing happened that weekend, and nothing happened all the next week. I thought Mary Randolph must have hid the white girl in a grave out in The Backs. But how long could a girl from one of those rich families go missing without investigations and search parties? And, on top of that, what was Mary Randolph doing there in the first place? She liked to have a good time, but she wasn't one of those wild girls with a razor under her skirt—she went to church every Sunday, was good to people, nice to kids. Maybe she went out to comfort that poor girl, but how did she know she'd be there in the first place? Misses Abbey Montgomerys from the hill didn't share their plans with Mary Randolphs from Darktown. I couldn't forget the way she looked at me, but I couldn't understand it, either. The more I thought about that look, the more it was like Mary Randolph was saying something to me, but what? *Are you ready for this? Do you understand this? Do you know how careful you must be?*

"My father said I could start learning the C-melody sax, and when I was ready to play it in public, my little brother wanted to take over the drums. Seems he always wanted to play drums, and in fact, he's been a drummer ever since, a good one. So I worked out how to play my little sax, I went to school and came straight home after, and everything went on like normal, except Dee Sparks and I weren't friends any more. If the police were searching for a missing rich girl, I didn't hear anything about it.

"Then one Saturday I was walking down our street to go the general store, and Mary Randolph came through her front door just as I got to her house. When she saw me, she stopped moving real sudden, with one hand still on the side of the door. I was so surprised to see her that I was in a kind of slow-motion, and I must have stared at her. She gave me a look like an X-ray, a look that searched around down inside me. I don't know what she saw, but her face relaxed, and she took her hand off the door and let it close behind her, and she wasn't looking inside me any more. *Miss Randolph*, I said, and she told me she was looking forward to hearing our band play at a Beergarden dance in a couple of weeks. I told her I was going to be playing the saxophone at that dance, and she said something about that, and all the time it was like we were having two conversations, the top one about me and the band, and the one underneath about her and the murdered white girl in The Backs. It made me so nervous, my words got all mixed up. Finally she said *You make sure you say hello to your daddy from me, now*, and I got away.

"After I passed her house, Mary Randolph started walking down the street behind me. I could feel her watching me, and I started to sweat. Mary Randolph was a total mystery to me. She was a nice lady, but probably she buried that girl's body. I didn't know but that she was going to come and kill me, one day. And then I remembered her kneeling down beside Eddie Grimes at the roadhouse. She had been *dancing* with Eddie Grimes, who was in jail more often than he was out. I wondered if you could be a respectable lady and still know Eddie Grimes well enough to dance with him. And how did she bring him back to life? Or was that what happened at all? Hearing that lady walk along behind me made me so uptight, I crossed to the other side of the street.

"A couple days after that, when I was beginning to think that the trouble was never going to happen after all, it came down. We heard police cars coming down the street right when we were finishing dinner. I thought they were coming for me, and I almost lost my chicken and rice. The sirens went right past our house, and then more sirens came toward us from other directions—the old klaxons they had in those days. It sounded like every cop in the state was rushing into Darktown. This was bad, bad news. Someone was going to wind up dead, that was certain. No way all those police were going to come into our part of town, make all that commotion, and leave without killing at least one man. That's the truth. You just had to pray that the man they killed wasn't you or anyone in your family. My daddy turned off the lamps, and we went to the window to watch the cars go by. Two of them were state police. When it was safe, Daddy went outside to see where all the trouble was headed. After he came back in, he said it looked like the police were going toward Eddie Grimes' place. We wanted to go out and look, but they wouldn't let us, so we went to the back windows that faced toward Grimes' house. Couldn't see anything but a lot of cars and police standing all over the road back there. Sounded like they were knocking down Grimes' house with sledge hammers. Then a whole bunch of cops took off running, and all I could see was the cars spread out across the road. About ten minutes later, we heard lots of gunfire coming from a couple of streets further back. It like to have lasted forever. Like hearing the Battle of the Bulge. My momma started to cry, and so did my little brother. The shooting stopped. The police shouted to each other, and then they came back and got in their cars and went away.

"On the radio the next morning, they said that a known criminal, a Negro man named Edward Grimes, had been killed while trying to escape arrest for the murder of a white woman. The body of Eleanore Monday, missing for three days, had been found in a shallow grave by Woodland police searching near an illegal distillery in the region called The Backs. Miss Monday, the daughter of grocer Albert Monday, had been in poor mental and physical health, and Grimes had apparently taken advantage of her weakness to either abduct or lure her to The Backs, where she had been savagely murdered. That's what it said on the radio—I still remember the words. *In poor mental and physical health. Savagely murdered.*

"When the paper finally came, there on the front page was a picture of Eleanore Monday, a girl with dark hair and a big nose. She didn't look anything like the dead woman in the shack. She hadn't even disappeared on the right day. Eddie Grimes was never going to be able to explain things, because the police had finally cornered him in the old jute warehouse just off Meridian Road next to the general store. I don't suppose they even bothered trying to arrest him—they weren't interested in *arresting* him. He killed a white girl. They wanted revenge, and they got it.

"After I looked at the paper, I got out of the house and ran between the houses to get a took at the jute warehouse. Turned out a lot of folks had the same idea. A big crowd strung out in a long line in front of the warehouse, and cars were parked all along Meridian Road. Right up in front of the warehouse door was a police car, and a big cop stood in the middle of the big doorway, watching people file by. They were walking past the doorway one by one, acting like they were at some kind of exhibit. Nobody was talking. It was a sight I never saw before in that town, whites and colored all lined up together. On the other side of the warehouse, two groups of men stood alongside the road, one colored and one white, talking so quietly you couldn't hear a word.

"Now I was never one who liked standing in lines, so I figured I'd just dart up there, peek in, and save myself some time. I came around the end of the line and ambled toward the two bunches of men, like I'd already had my look and was just hanging around to enjoy the scene. After I got a little past the warehouse door, I sort of drifted up alongside it. I looked down the row of people, and there was Dee Sparks, just a few yards away from being able to see in. Dee was leaning forward, and when he saw me he almost jumped out of his skin. He looked away as fast as he could. His eyes turned as dead as stones. The cop at the door yelled at me to go to the end of the line. He never would have noticed me at all if Dee hadn't jumped like someone just shot off a firecracker behind him.

"About half way down the line, Mary Randolph was standing behind some of the ladies from the neighborhood. She looked terrible. Her hair stuck out in raggedy clumps, and her skin was ashy, like she hadn't slept in a long time. I sped up a little, hoping she wouldn't notice me, but after I took one more step, Mary Randolph looked down and her eyes hooked into mine. I swear, what was in her eyes almost knocked me down. I couldn't even tell what it was, unless it was pure hate. Hate and pain. With her eyes hooked into mine like that, I couldn't look away. It was like I was seeing that miserable, terrible white smear twisting up between the trees on that night in The Backs. Mary let me go, and I almost fell down all over again.

I got to the end of the line and started moving along regular and slow with everybody else. Mary Randolph stayed in my mind and blanked out everything else. When I got up to the door, I barely took in what was inside the warehouse—a wall full of bulletholes and bloodstains all over the place, big slick ones and little drizzly ones. All I could think of was the shack and Mary Randolph sitting next to the dead girl, and I was back there all over again.

"Mary Randolph didn't show up at the Beergarden dance, so she didn't hear me play saxophone in public for the first time. I didn't expect her, either, not after the way she looked out at the warehouse. There'd been a lot of news about Eddie Grimes, who they made out to be less civilized than a gorilla, a crazy man who'd murder anyone as long as he could kill all the white women first. The paper had a picture of what they called Grimes' 'lair,' with busted furniture all over the place and holes in the walls, but they never explained that it was the police tore it up and made it look that way.

"The other thing people got suddenly all hot about was The Backs. Seems the place was even worse than everybody thought. Seems white girls besides Eleanore Monday had been taken out there—according to some, there was even white girls living out there, along with a lot of bad coloreds. The place was a nest of vice, Sodom and Gomorrah. Two days before the town council was supposed to discuss the problem, a gang of white men went out there with guns and clubs and torches and burned every shack in The Backs clear down to the ground. While they were there, they didn't see a single soul, white, colored, male, female, damned or saved. Everybody who lived in The Backs had skedaddled. And the funny thing was, long as The Backs had existed right outside of Woodland, no one in Woodland could recollect the name of anyone who had ever lived there. They couldn't even recall the name of anyone who had ever gone there, except for Eddie Grimes. In fact, after the place got burned down, it appeared that it must have been a sin just to say its name, because no one ever mentioned it. You'd think men so fine and moral as to burn down The Backs would be willing to take the credit, but none ever did.

"You could think they must have wanted to get rid of some things out there. Or wanted real bad to forget about things out there. One thing I thought, Dr. Garland and the man I saw leaving that shack had been out there with torches.

"But maybe I didn't know anything at all. Two weeks later, a couple things happened that shook me good.

"The first one happened three nights before Thanksgiving. I was hurrying home, a little bit late. Nobody else on the street, everybody inside either sitting down to dinner or getting ready for it. When I got to Mary Randolph's house, some kind of noise coming from inside stopped me. What I thought was, it sounded exactly like somebody trying to scream while someone else was holding a hand over their mouth. Well, that was plain foolish, wasn't it? How did I know what that would sound like? I moved along a step or two, and then I heard it again. Could be anything, I told myself. Mary Randolph didn't like me too much, anyway. She wouldn't be partial to my knocking on her door. Best thing I could do was get out. Which was what I did. Just went home to supper and forgot about it.

"Until the next day, anyhow, when a friend of Mary's walked in her front door and found her lying dead with her throat cut and a knife in her hand. A cut of fatback, we heard, had boiled away to cinders on her stove. I didn't tell anybody about what I heard the night before. Too scared. I couldn't do anything but wait to see what the police did.

"To the police, it was all real clear. Mary killed herself, plain and simple.

"When our minister went across town to ask why a lady who intended to commit suicide had bothered to start cooking her supper, the chief told him that a female bent on killing herself probably didn't care *what* happened to the food on her stove. Then I suppose Mary Randolph nearly managed to cut her own head off, said the minister. A female in despair possesses a godawful strength, said the chief. And asked, wouldn't she have screamed if she'd been attacked? And added, couldn't it be that maybe this female here had secrets in her life connected to the late savage murderer named Eddie Grimes? We might all be better off if these secrets get buried with your Mary Randolph, said the chief. I'm sure you understand me, Reverend. And yes, the Reverend did understand, he surely did. So Mary Randolph got laid away in the cemetery, and nobody ever said her name again. She was put away out of mind, like The Backs.

"The second thing that shook me up and proved to me that I didn't know anything, that I was no better than a blind dog, happened on Thanksgiving day. My daddy played piano in church, and on special days, we played our instruments along with the gospel songs. I got to church early with the rest of my family, and we practiced with the choir. Afterwards, I went to fooling around outside until the people came, and saw a big car come up into the church parking lot. Must have been the biggest, fanciest car I'd ever seen. Miller's Hill was written all over that vehicle. I couldn't have told you why, but the sight of it made my heart stop. The front door opened, and out stepped a colored man in a fancy gray uniform with a smart cap. He didn't so much as dirty his eyes by looking at me, or at the church, or at anything around him. He stepped around the front of the car and opened the rear door on my side. A young woman was in the passenger seat, and when she got out of the car, the sun fell on her blond hair and the little fur jacket she was wearing. I couldn't see more than the top of her head, her shoulders under the jacket, and her legs. Then she straightened up, and her eyes lighted right on me. She smiled, but I couldn't smile back. I couldn't even begin to move.

"It was Abbey Montgomery, delivering baskets of food to our church, the way she did every Thanksgiving and Christmas. She looked older and thinner than the last time I'd seen her alive—older and thinner, but more than that, like there was no fun at all in her life anymore. She walked to the trunk of the car, and the driver opened it up, leaned in, and brought out a great big basket of food. He took into the church by the back way and came back for another one. Abbey Montgomery just stood still and watched him carry the baskets. She looked—she looked like she was just going through the motions, like going through the motions was all she was ever going to do from now on, and she knew it. Once she smiled at the driver, but the smile was so sad that the driver didn't even try to smile back. When he was done, he closed the trunk and let her into the passenger seat, got behind the wheel, and drove away.

"I was thinking, *Dee Sparks was right, she was alive all the time.* Then I thought, *No, Mary Randolph brought her back, too, like she did Eddie Grimes. But it didn't work right, and only part of her came back.*

"And that's the whole thing, except that Abbey Montgomery didn't deliver food to our church, that Christmas—she was traveling out of the country, with her aunt. And she didn't bring food the next Thanksgiving, either, just sent her driver with the baskets. By that time, we didn't expect her, because we'd already heard that, soon as she got back to town, Abbey Montgomery stopped leaving her house. That girl shut herself up and never came out. I heard from somebody who probably didn't know any more than I did that she eventually got so she wouldn't even leave her room. Five years later, she passed away. Twenty-six years old, and they said she looked to be at least fifty."

4

Hat fell silent, and I sat with my pen ready over the notebook, waiting, for more. When I realized that he had finished, I asked, "What did she die of?"

"Nobody ever told me."

"And nobody ever found who had killed Mary Randolph."

The limpid, colorless eyes momentarily rested on me. "Was she killed?"

"Did you ever become friends with Dee Sparks again? Did you at least talk about it with him?"

"Surely did not. Nothing to talk about."

This was a remarkable statement, considering that for an hour he had done nothing but talk about what had happened to the two of them, but I let it go. Hat was still looking at me with his unreadable eyes. His face had become particularly bland, almost immobile. It was not possible to imagine this man as an active eleven-year-old boy. "Now you heard me out, answer my question," he said.

I couldn't remember the question.

"Did we find what we were looking for?"

Scares—that was what they had been looking for. "I think you found a lot more than that," I said.

He nodded slowly. "That's right. It was more."

Then I asked him some question about his family's band, he lubricated himself with another swallow of gin, and the interview returned to more typical matters. But the experience of listening to him had changed. After I had heard the long, unresolved tale of his Halloween night, everything Hat said seemed to have two separate meanings, the daylight meaning created by sequences of ordinary English words, and another, nighttime meaning, far less determined and knowable. He was like a man discoursing with eerie rationality in the midst of a surreal dream—like a man carrying on an ordinary conversation with one foot placed on solid ground and the other suspended above a bottomless abyss. I focused on the rationality, on the foot placed in the context I understood; the rest was unsettling to the point of being frightening. By six-thirty, when he kindly called me "Miss Rosemary" and opened his door, I felt as if I'd spent several weeks, if not whole months, in his room.

PART THREE
1

Although I did get my M.A. at Columbia, I didn't have enough money to stay on for a Ph.D., so I never became a college professor. I never became a jazz critic, either, or anything else very interesting. For a couple of years after Columbia, I taught English in a high school, until I quit to take the job I have now, which involves a lot of traveling and pays a little bit better than teaching. Maybe even quite a bit better, but that's not saying much, especially when you consider my expenses. I own a nice little house in the Chicago suburbs, my marriage held up against everything life did to it, and my twenty-two year old son, a young man who never once in his life for the purpose of pleasure read a novel, looked at a painting, visited a museum, or listened to anything but the most readily available music, recently announced to his mother and myself that he has decided to become an artist, actual type of art to be determined later, but probably to include aspects of photography, video tape, and the creation of "installations." I take this as proof that he was raised in a manner that left his self-esteem intact.

I no longer provide my life with a perpetual sound track (though my son, who has moved back in with us, does), in part because my income does not permit the purchase of a great many compact discs. (A friend presented me with a CD player on my forty-fifth birthday.) And these days, I'm as interested in classical music as in jazz. Of course, I never go to jazz clubs when I am home. Are there still people, apart from New Yorkers, who patronize jazz nightclubs in their own hometowns? The concept seems faintly retrograde, even somehow illicit. But when I am out on the road, living in airplanes and hotel rooms, I often check the jazz listings in the local papers to see if I can find some way to fill my evenings. Many of the legends of my youth are still out there, in most cases playing at least as well as before. Some months ago, while I was San Francisco, I came across John Hawes' name in this fashion. He was working in a club so close to my hotel that I could walk to it.

His appearance in any club at all was surprising. Hawes had ceased performing jazz in public years before. He had earned a great deal of fame (and undoubtedly, a great deal of money) writing film scores, and in the past decade, he had begun to appear in swallow-tail coat and white tie as a conductor of the standard classical repertoire. I believe he had a permanent post in some city like Seattle, or perhaps Salt Lake City. If he was spending a week playing jazz with a trio in San Francisco, it must have been for the sheer pleasure of it.

I turned up just before the beginning of the first set, and got a table toward the back of the club. Most of the tables were filled—Hawes' celebrity had guaranteed him a good house. Only a few minutes after the announced time of the first set, Hawes emerged through a door at the front of the club and moved toward the piano, followed by his bassist and drummer. He looked like a more successful version of the younger man I had seen in New York, and the only indications of the extra years were his silvergray hair, still abundant, and a little paunch. His playing, too, seemed essentially unchanged, but I could not hear it in the way I once had. He was still a good pianist—no doubt about that—but he seemed to be skating over the surface of the songs he played, using his wonderful technique and good time merely to decorate their melodies. It was the sort of playing that becomes less impressive the more attention you give it—if you were listening with half an ear, it probably sounded like Art Tatum. I wondered if John Hawes had always had this superficial streak in him, or if he had lost a certain necessary passion during his years away from jazz. Certainly he had not sounded superficial when I had heard him with Hat.

Hawes, too, might have been thinking about his old employer, because in the first set he played "Love Walked In," "Too Marvelous For Words," and "Up Jumped Hat." In the last of these, inner gears seemed to mesh, the rhythm simultaneously relaxed and intensified, and the music turned into real, not imitation, jazz. Hawes looked pleased with himself when he stood up from the piano bench, and half a dozen fans moved to greet him as he stepped off the bandstand. Most of them were carrying old records they wished him to sign.

A few minutes later, I saw Hawes standing by himself at the end of the bar, drinking what appeared to be club soda, in proximity to his musicians but not actually speaking with them. Wondering if his allusions to Hat had been deliberate, I left my table and walked toward the bar. Hawes watched me approach out of the side of his eye, neither encouraging nor discouraging me. When I introduced myself, he smiled nicely and shook my hand and waited for whatever I wanted to say to him.

At first, I made some inane comment about the difference between playing in clubs and conducting in concert halls, and he replied with the non-committal and equally banal agreement that yes, the two experiences were very different.

Then I told him that I had seen him play with Hat all those years ago in New York, and he turned to me with genuine pleasure in his face. "Did you? At that little club on St Mark's Place? That sure was fun. I guess I must have been thinking about it, because I played some of those songs we used to do."

"That was why I came over," I said. "I guess that was one of the best musical experiences I ever had."

"You and me both." Hawes smiled to himself. "Sometimes, I just couldn't believe what he was doing."

"It showed," I said.

"Well." His eyes slid away from mine. "Great character. Completely otherworldly."

"I saw some of that," I said. "I did that interview with him that turns up now and then, the one in *Downbeat*."

"Oh!" Hawes gave me his first genuinely interested look so far. "Well, that was him, all right."

"Most of it was, anyhow."

"You cheated?" Now he was looking even more interested.

"I had to make it understandable."

"Oh, sure. You couldn't put in all those ding-dings and bells and Bob Crosbys." These had been elements of Hat's private code. Hawes laughed at the memory. "When he wanted to play a blues in G, he'd lean over and say, 'Gs, please.'"

"Did you get to know him at all well, personally?" I asked, thinking that the answer must be that he had not—I didn't think that anyone had ever really known Hat very well.

"Pretty well," Hawes said. "A couple of times, around '54 and '55, he invited me home with him, to his parents' house, I mean. We got to be friends on a Jazz at the Phil tour, and twice when we were in the South, he asked me if I wanted to eat some good home cooking."

"You went to his hometown?"

He nodded. "His parents put me up. They were interesting people. Hat's father, Red, was about the lightest black man I ever saw, and he could have passed for white anywhere, but I don't suppose the thought ever occurred to him."

"Was the family band still going?"

"No, to tell you the truth, I don't think they were getting much work up toward the end of the forties. At the end, they were using a tenor player and a drummer from the high school band. And the church work got more and more demanding for Hat's father."

"His father was a deacon, or something like that?"

He raised his eyebrows. "No, Red was the Baptist minister. The Reverend. He ran that church. I think he even started it."

"Hat told me his father played piano in church, but . . ."

"The Reverend would have made a hell of a blues piano player, if he'd ever left his day job."

"There must have been another Baptist church in the neighborhood," I said, thinking this the only explanation for the presence of two Baptist ministers. But why had Hat not mentioned that his own father, like Dee Sparks's, had been a clergyman?

"Are you kidding? There was barely enough money in that place to keep one of them going." He looked at his watch, nodded at me, and began to move closer to his sidemen.

"Could I ask you one more question?"

"I suppose so," he said, almost impatiently.

"Did Hat strike you as superstitious?"

Hawes grinned. "Oh, he was superstitious, all right. He told me he never worked on Halloween—he didn't even want to go out of his room on Halloween. That's why he left the big band, you know. They were starting a tour on Halloween, and Hat refused to do it. He just quit." He leaned toward me. "I'll tell you another funny thing. I always had the feeling that Hat was terrified of his father—I thought he invited me to Hatchville with him so I could be some kind of buffer between him and his father. Never made any sense to me. Red was a big strong old guy, and I'm pretty sure a long time ago he used to mess around with the ladies, Reverend or not, but I couldn't ever figure out why Hat should be afraid of him. But whenever Red came into the room, Hat shut up. Funny, isn't it?"

I must have looked very perplexed. "Hatchville?"

"Where they lived. Hatchville, Mississippi—not too far from Biloxi."

"But he told me—"

"Hat never gave too many straight answers," Hawes said. "And he didn't let the facts get in the way of a good story. When you come to think of it, why should he? He was Hat."

After the next set, I walked back uphill to my hotel, wondering again about the long story Hat had told me. Had there been any truth in it at all?

2

Three weeks later I found myself released from a meeting at our Midwestern headquarters in downtown Chicago earlier than I had expected, and instead of going to a bar with the other wandering corporate ghosts like myself, made up a story about having to get home for dinner with visiting relatives. I didn't want to admit to my fellow employees, committed like all male business people to aggressive endeavors such as racquetball, drinking, and the pursuit of women, that I intended to visit the library. Short of a trip to Mississippi, a good periodical room offered the most likely means of finding out once and for all how much truth had been in what Hat had told me.

I hadn't forgotten everything I had learned at Columbia—I still knew how to look things up.

In the main library, a boy set me up with a monitor and spools of microfilm representing the complete contents of the daily newspapers from Biloxi and Hatchville, Mississippi, for Hat's tenth and eleventh years. That made three papers, two for Biloxi and one for Hatchville, but all I had to examine were the issues dating from the end of October through the middle of November—I was looking for references to Eddie Grimes, Eleanore Monday, Mary Randolph, Abbey Montgomery, Hat's family, The Backs, and anyone named Sparks.

The Hatchville *Blade*, a gossipy daily printed on peach-colored paper, offered plenty of references to each of these names and places, and the papers from Biloxi contained nearly as many—Biloxi could not conceal the delight, disguised as horror, aroused in its collective soul by the unimaginable events taking place in the smaller, supposedly respectable town ten miles west. Biloxi was riveted, Biloxi was superior, Biloxi was virtually intoxicated with dread and outrage. In Hatchville, the press maintained a persistent optimistic dignity: when wickedness had appeared, justice official and unofficial had dealt with it. Hatchville was shocked but proud (or at least pretended to be proud), and Biloxi all but preened. The *Blade* printed detailed news stories, but the Biloxi papers suggested implications not allowed by Hatchville's version of events. I needed Hatchville to confirm or question Hat's story, but Biloxi gave me at least the beginning of a way to understand it.

A black ex-convict named Edward Grimes had in some fashion persuaded or coerced Eleanore Monday, a retarded young white woman, to accompany him to an area variously described as "a longstanding local disgrace" (the *Blade*) and "a haunt of deepest vice" (Biloxi) and after "the perpetration of the most offensive and brutal deeds upon her person" (the *Blade*) or "acts which the judicious commentator must decline to imagine, much less describe" (Biloxi) murdered her, presumably to ensure her silence, and then buried the body near the "squalid dwelling" where he made and sold illegal liquor. State and local police departments acting in concert had located the body, identified Grimes as the fiend, and, after a search of his house, had tracked him to a warehouse where the murderer was killed in a gun battle. The *Blade* covered half its front page with a photograph of a gaping double door and a bloodstained wall. All Mississippi, both Hatchville and Biloxi declared, now could breathe more easily.

The *Blade* gave the death of Mary Randolph a single paragraph on its back page, the Biloxi papers nothing.

In Hatchville, the raid on The Backs was described as an heroic assault on a dangerous criminal encampment which had somehow come to flourish in a little-noticed section of the countryside. At great risk to themselves, anonymous citizens of Hatchville had descended like the army of the righteous and driven forth the hidden sinners from their dens. Troublemakers, beware! The Biloxi papers, while seeming to endorse the action in Hatchville, actually took another tone altogether. Can it be, they asked, that the Hatchville police had never before noticed the existence of a Sodom and Gomorrah so close to the town line? Did it take the savage murder of a helpless woman to bring it to their attention? Of course Biloxi celebrated the destruction of The Backs—such vileness must be eradicated—but it wondered what else had been destroyed along with the stills and the mean buildings where loose women had plied their trade. Men ever are men, and those who have succumbed to temptation may wish to remove from the face of the earth any evidence of their lapses. Had not the police of Hatchville ever heard the rumor, vague and doubtless baseless, that operations of an illegal nature had been performed in the selfsame Backs? That in an atmosphere of drugs, intoxication, and gambling, the races had mingled there, and that "fast" young women had risked life and honor in search of illicit thrills? Hatchville may have rid itself of a few buildings, but Biloxi was willing to suggest that the problems of its smaller neighbor might not have disappeared with them.

As this campaign of innuendo went on in Biloxi, the *Blade* blandly reported the ongoing events of any smaller American city. Miss Abigail Montgomery sailed with her aunt, Miss Lucinda Bright, from New Orleans to France for an eight-week tour of the continent. The Reverend Jasper Sparks of the Miller's Hill Presbyterian Church delivered a sermon on the subject "Christian Forgiveness." (Just after Thanksgiving, the Reverend Sparks's son, Rodney, was sent off with the blessings and congratulations of all Hatchville to a private academy in Charleston, South Carolina.) There were bake sales, church socials, and costume parties. A saxophone virtuoso named Albert Woodland demonstrated his astonishing wizardy at a well-attended recital presented in Temperance Hall.

Well, I knew the name of at least one person who had attended the recital. If Hat had chosen to disguise the name of his hometown, he had done so by substituting for it a name that represented another sort of home.

But, although I had more ideas about this than before, I still did not know exactly what Hat had seen or done on Halloween night in The Backs. It seemed possible that he had gone there with a white boy of his age, a preacher's son like himself, and had the wits scared out of him by whatever had happened to Abbey Montgomery—and after that night, Abbey herself had been sent out of town, as had Dee Sparks. I couldn't think that a man had murdered the young woman, leaving Mary Randolph to bring her back to life. Surely whatever had happened to Abbey Montgomery had brought Dr. Garland out to The Backs, and what he had witnessed or done there had sent him away screaming. And this event—what had befallen a rich young white woman in the shadiest, most criminal section of a Mississippi county—had led to the slaying of Eddie Grimes and the murder of Mary Randolph. Because they knew what had happened, they had to die.

I understood all this, and Hat had understood it, too. Yet he had introduced needless puzzles, as if embedded in the midst of this unresolved story were something he either wished to conceal or not to know. And concealed it would remain; if Hat did not know it, I never would. He had deliberately obscured even basic but meaningless facts: first Mary Randolph was a witch-woman from The Backs, then she was a respectable church-goer who lived down the street from his family. Whatever had really happened in The Backs on Halloween night was lost for good.

On the *Blade*'s entertainment page for a Saturday in the middle of November I had come across a photograph of Hat's family's band, and when I had reached this hopeless point in my thinking, I spooled back across the pages to look at it again. Hat, his two brothers, his sister, and his parents stood in a straight line, tallest to smallest, in front of what must have been the family car. Hat held a C-melody saxophone, his brothers a trumpet and drumsticks, his sister a clarinet. As the piano player, the Reverend carried nothing at all—nothing except for what came through even a grainy, sixty-year old photograph as a powerful sense of self. Hat's father had been a tall, impressive man, and in the photograph he looked as white as I did. But what was impressive was not the lightness of his skin, or even his striking handsomeness: what impressed was the sense of authority implicit in his posture, his straightforward gaze, even the dictatorial set of his chin. In retrospect, I was not surprised by what John Hawes had told me, for this man could easily be frightening. You would not wish to oppose him, you would not elect to get in his way. Beside him, Hat's mother seemed vague and distracted, as if her husband had robbed her of all certainty. Then I noticed the car, and for the first time realized why it had been included in the photograph. It was a sign of their prosperity, the respectable status they had achieved—the car was as much an advertisement as the photograph. It was, I thought, an old Model T Ford, but I didn't waste any time speculating that it might have been the Model T Hat had seen in The Backs.

And that would be that—the hint of an absurd supposition—except for something I read a few days ago in a book called *Cool Breeze: The Life of Grant Kilbert*.

There are few biographies of any jazz musicians apart from Louis Armstrong and Duke Ellington (though one does now exist of Hat, the title of which was drawn from my interview with him), and I was surprised to see *Cool Breeze* at the B. Dalton in our local mall. Biographies have not yet been written of Art Blakey, Clifford Brown, Ben Webster, Art Tatum, and many others of more musical and historical importance than Kilbert. Yet I should not have been surprised. Kilbert was one of those musicians who attract and maintain a large personal following, and twenty years after his death, almost all of his records have been released on CD, many of them in multi-disc boxed sets. He had been a great, great player, the closest to Hat of all his disciples. Because Kilbert had been one of my early heroes, I bought the book (for thirty-five dollars!) and brought it home.

Like the lives of many jazz musicians, I suppose of artists in general, Kilbert's had been an odd mixture of public fame and private misery. He had committed burglaries, even armed robberies, to feed his persistent heroin addiction; he had spent years in jail; his two marriages had ended in outright hatred; he had managed to betray most of his friends. That this weak, narcissistic louse had found it in himself to create music of real tenderness and beauty was one of art's enigmas, but not actually a surprise. I'd heard and read enough stories about Grant Kilbert to know what kind of man he'd been.

But what I had not known was that Kilbert, to all appearances an American of conventional northern European, perhaps Scandinavian or Anglo-Saxon, stock, had occasionally claimed to be black. (This claim had always been dismissed, apparently, as another indication of Kilbert's mental aberrancy.) At other times, being Kilbert, he had denied ever making this claim.

Neither had I known that the received versions of his birth and upbringing were in question. Unlike Hat, Kilbert had been interviewed dozens of times both in *Downbeat* and in mass market weekly news magazines, invariably to offer the same story of having been born in Hattiesburg, Mississippi, to an unmusical, working-class family (a plumber's family), of knowing virtually from infancy that he was born to make music, of begging for and finally being given a saxophone, of early mastery and the dazzled admiration of his teachers, then of dropping out of school at sixteen and joining the Woody Herman band. After that, almost immediate fame.

Most of this, the Grant Kilbert myth, was undisputed. He had been raised in Hattiesburg by a plumber named Kilbert, he had been a prodigy and high-school dropout, he'd become famous with Woody Herman before he was twenty. Yet he told a few friends, not necessarily those to whom he said he was black, that he'd been adopted by the Kilberts, and that once or twice, in great anger, either the plumber or his wife had told him that he had been born into poverty and disgrace and that he'd better by God be grateful for the opportunities he'd been given. The source of this story was John Hawes, who'd met Kilbert on another long JATP tour, the last he made before leaving the road for film scoring.

"Grant didn't have a lot of friends on that tour," Hawes told the biographer. "Even though he was such a great player, you never knew what he was going to say, and if he was in a bad mood, he was liable to put down some of the older players. He was always respectful around Hat, his whole style was based on Hat's, but Hat could go days without saying anything, and by those days he certainly wasn't making any new friends. Still, he'd let Grant sit next to him on the bus, and nod his head while Grant talked to him, so he must have felt some affection for him. Anyhow, eventually I was about the only guy on the tour that was willing to have a conversation with Grant, and we'd sit up in the bar late at night after the concerts. The way he played, I could forgive him a lot of failings. One of those nights, he said that he'd been adopted, and that not knowing who his real parents were was driving him crazy. He didn't even have a birth certificate. From a hint his mother once gave him, he thought one of his birth parents was black, but when he asked them directly, they always denied it. These were white Mississippians, after all, and if they had wanted a baby so bad that they taken in a child who looked completely white but maybe had a drop or two of black blood in his veins, they weren't going to admit it, even to themselves."

In the midst of so much supposition, here is a fact. Grant Kilbert was exactly eleven years younger than Hat. The jazz encyclopedias give his birth date as November first, which instead of his actual birthday may have been the day he was delivered to the couple in Hattiesburg.

I wonder if Hat saw more than he admitted to me of the man leaving the shack where Abbey Montgomery lay on bloody sheets; I wonder if he had reason to fear his father. I don't know if what I am thinking is correct—I'll never know that—but now, finally, I think I know why Hat never wanted to go out of his room on Halloween nights. The story he told me never left him, but it must have been most fully present on those nights. I think he heard the screams, saw the bleeding girl, and saw Mary Randolph staring at him with displaced pain and rage. I think that in some small closed corner deep within himself, he knew who had been the real object of these feelings, and therefore had to lock himself inside his hotel room and gulp gin until he obliterated the horror of his own thoughts.

THREE DOORS
Norman Partridge

Norman Partridge's tale involves a prosthetic hand its owner believes will magically open three doors; anyone waiting on the other sides of those doors will be his to command.

Going door-to-door and begging is not the only custom involving doors and Halloween. In some cultures doors and are left open on Halloween for visiting family spirits to easily enter and depart. The parshell—a cross made of straw or corn husks hung inside over the doorway each Halloween as protection against evil and sickness for the year—was an Irish custom. Many other magical protections involve doors: Celts sought to appease fairies by leaving milk and food on doorsteps. In Britain, rowan branches or osier twigs were placed above a door to keep witches out. Horseshoes offer similar protection. Doors and gateways were frequently attacked in various ways in the days of serious pranking.

When Halloween rolled around that year, Johnny Meyers painted his right hand black.

Of course, that right hand didn't really belong to Johnny. It was made of rubber, and he'd only had it three months. Brought it back from the war with him. Doesn't matter which war. They're all the same.

Now, Johnny didn't paint his hand black because he wanted a costume. Sure, it was Halloween, but he didn't care about that. It was more like he wanted that hand to do some things for him—things he couldn't manage if it were pink and clean and ordinary.

So Johnny got out some black enamel he'd used to paint model cars when he was a kid. He loosened up a stiff brush in a jar of thinner, and he painted the hand from its fake fingertips to its socketed rubber wrist. Then he sat and watched a monster movie while the paint dried. Trick or treaters knocked on the front door that Johnny never answered, and

Frankenstein and the Wolf Man went at it on the TV. But Johnny Meyers paid no attention. He sat there as still as could be, cradling that rubber hand in his lap.

An hour ticked by. The drying paint stretched like a new skin over Johnny's prosthetic hand, pulling those rubber fingers tight, curling them into a fist sealed up by a rubber thumb.

That was all right with Johnny.

Tonight he needed a fist.

Because a fist was built for knocking.

Now, maybe that's a little hard to believe. Not the part about a fist being built for knocking, but the part about a rubber hand curling into a fist because of a little black paint. But, hey . . . it doesn't really matter if you believe it or not. That's the way it happened. You can go ahead and fill in the blanks yourself if you need to. Figure someone cast a bucket of mojo over that fake hand while Johnny was in the hospital. Figure that a dying patient sweated some magic into that hand before he kicked off, and the folks in the PT unit decided to save the government a few bucks and pass on that five-fingered hunk of rubber to Johnny. Hell, you can figure the damn hand came from some haunted curio shop over on the far side of *The Twilight Zone* if you want to.

Doesn't matter to me how you explain it.

See, I'm not here to draw you a diagram.

I'm just here to tell you a story.

So when Johnny got up out of his chair, he knew exactly what that mojo hand could do for him. He'd been thinking about it all week long—listening to dry leaves churn out there in the black October night . . . eyeing those fat pumpkins waiting for knives on all those neatly swept porches over in town . . . watching spookshows on his little excuse for a TV when sleep wouldn't come.

What Johnny was thinking about was the power that painted hand would hold tonight, on Halloween, when witches and broomsticks and all that other crap that goes bump in the night holds sway. And what Johnny's brain told him was this: his mojo hand would give him three magic knocks on three ordinary doors. And it didn't matter who waited behind those doors—every one of them would open for Johnny Meyers, and whoever waited on the other side would be his to command.

▼▼▼▼▼

And I know what you're thinking now. Sure—I've heard of "The Monkey's Paw." Who the hell hasn't? A bucket of sour mojo, three wishes going bad, a dead guy knocking on his momma's door . . . all that. But that was W. W. Jacobs' story. This one's mine, and I'll play it my way. It's about a rubber hand that's painted black, and a guy named Johnny, and three doors he'll be knocking on before midnight rolls around.

So Johnny moved on—the screen door banged shut behind him, heavy footfalls thudded across the porch, dry leaves crackled beneath his boots as he crossed the yard to the gravel driveway.

Johnny's pickup waited by the mailbox. It wasn't much to look at. More rust than steel—a little bit like Johnny himself.

A yank courtesy of Johnny's real hand, and the door ratcheted open like an old man's jaw.

Johnny climbed behind the wheel, started the engine, and notched that sucker into gear.

Lucky for Johnny, the truck was an automatic. Would have been hell shifting with a rubber hand if he'd had a manual transmission. But Johnny's truck was easy—the only thing he'd really had to do as far as conversion was tighten down a clamp that attached a little knob to the steering wheel. After that, all he had to do was grab hold of that knob with his good hand, and he could make his turns one-handed.

Johnny headed up a two-lane road. Country—not many lights out there unless you knew where to look for them. The truck's radio didn't work, and neither did the heater. The cab was cold enough to make a rattler sleep through the whole damn winter without feeling a thing. Johnny himself didn't feel it much. He was a big guy. Lots of meat on him—minus that right hand, of course.

It was a familiar road, and it brought familiar memories. There were lots of things Johnny remembered about the way things were before the war. Lots of things he'd forgotten, too . . . but, hey, a couple of grenades send you twenty feet in the air and take a couple pounds of skin and bone off you in the bargain, you'd figure it would shake a few parts loose in your brainpan, too.

That's the way it was with Johnny. Of the stuff he remembered, most of it was good. Like drives with Elena on nights like this. Banging around country roads in the old pickup, just the two of them. Driving down to the river where the water seemed to run cold and clear any time of year.

Finding the moon down there waiting above the trees like some kind of searchlight, and finding the shadows that could hide them from it.

Laughter in the dark. Just the two of them. That was the way Johnny liked remembering it. Those nights by the river, and other nights before he'd gone away. That was what he had. See, Johnny hadn't seen Elena since he'd come home. Mostly, it was because of her parents. They had their reasons. In fact, her dad had Johnny over for a beer when he first got home. Sat him down at the table. No one else in the house—not Elena, not her mom. The old man wasn't what you'd call talkative but there were words, the kind that barely peak above a whisper. He explained things to Johnny, told him why he couldn't see Elena anymore. But the words didn't matter to Johnny. For him, those words were curled fists, banging away on a closed door inside . . . one that was locked and bolted and wouldn't open for any-goddamn-one.

But Johnny didn't want to think about that. He rolled down the window, searching for those other memories. The good ones. The side mirror caught the moonlight, but he didn't try to hide from it at all. No. This night was different. He'd do his hiding later, when Elena was with him.

He drove on. The cold air combed through his hair, and he caught the smell of a dirt road still damp with the first rain of the season mixed up with the scent of the wild apple orchard that stretched from the county road to the banks of the cold, clear river below.

The night was crisp and tart with the smell of ripening apples. Johnny didn't like it much. Somehow it made him think of Elena's father, and the things he'd said after Johnny came home. So Johnny rolled up the window and went searching for more pleasant scents that lingered in his memory.

Like roses.

Elena loved roses.

Johnny brought them for her all the time.

By any other name, they were just as sweet.

That was Johnny's first stop. A little florist shop downtown.

The truck door creaked open and Johnny stepped out. It was almost midnight now. Pretty deserted on the streets. He walked across the parking lot, black rubber hand swinging at his side, heart pounding so hard he couldn't hear his own footsteps. Giddy as a little kid. Because the whole deal was getting too close now, playing out in Johnny's head like quick-cut scenes in those late night creepshows he'd been watching all week. But these scenes weren't creepshows at all. Uh-uh. No way.

These scenes were sweet. Johnny saw his beater of a pickup truck, that rusty bed heaped with more roses than anyone could imagine. The perfume washed over him, almost smothered him as he drove up the little dirt road that led to Elena's place, and he imagined her expression when she caught sight of him with all those roses—

At the florist shop door, his reflection waited on the glass.

He raised his hand, put black rubber knuckle to its twin.

And he waited some more.

Turned out, he waited a long damn time.

The door didn't open. Johnny just stood there, staring at his magic hand, wondering what had gone wrong. And then it came to him. What had he been thinking? The florist shop had been closed since five o'clock that afternoon. There wasn't anyone inside. So it didn't matter that Johnny had himself a black fist that could work wonders. If there wasn't anyone behind the door to hear his knock, that five-fingered hunk of painted rubber was useless. Even a mojo hand couldn't command an empty building.

It took him awhile to get a hold of that idea. But once he got hold of it, he decided it didn't much matter. He'd lived in the real world for a long long time, and there were other tools at his disposal besides the mojo hand.

He went back to the truck and got two of them.

One was a .38, which he slipped behind him, under his belt, barrel along his spine.

The other was a cinder block.

Now, a lot of people in town didn't want anything to do with Johnny when he came marching home from the war. Ray Barnes was one of those.

Sheriff Ray Barnes, to be correct. Small-town cop going nowhere fast. Guy like that, of course he's going to have a hard-on for a war hero with a drawer full of medals. But Barnes wasn't prejudiced. He didn't much like *anyone*, and that made Halloween his favorite night of the year. People did stupid things, and Barnes made sure he was around when they did them. That's why the trunk of his cruiser was heavy with several cases of confiscated beer, courtesy of the town's teenage population. Up front, the sheriff had a bag of candy he'd snatched from some little window-soaper over at the church, even had the sawed-off runt's monster mask. Later tonight, Barnes figured he'd spook the little sweetheart over at dispatch with that mask. Make her jump right out of her skin.

But right now Barnes was chewing on one of the window-soaper's Hershey's bars and cruising the streets. That's the kind of guy he was. And that's why he got damn excited when a burglar alarm call directed him to a parking lot over on West Seventh. Because there was the war hero himself, Johnny Meyers, coming through the busted plate-glass door of the florist shop with an armful of roses, just as sweet as sweet could be.

Barnes grew a smile that was about half a yard wide. Everyone in town knew that Meyers was crackers, but the sheriff was the only one who was waiting to grind the soldier boy under his heel. Barnes hit the brakes. Ditched that Hershey's bar. Had his hand on his sidearm before he even released his seat belt, which was a bitch to undo, but he did it.

His free hand found the door.

He was just about to open it when black rubber knuckles rapped the glass.

Hard. None of that *gently rapping, rapping at my chamber door* Eddie Poe stuff. This rap was loud enough to make Barnes' spine snap purely vertical. Then his head swiveled like a ventriloquist dummy's, and he saw Meyers standing right there at his side window, and the synapses in his miserable excuse for a brain fired off one serious barrage.

Barnes opened that car door double-quick.

Meyers didn't budge.

He held out an open hand. The one that wasn't rubber.

"Trick or treat, Sheriff," was all he said.

Goddamned if he knew why, but Barnes just couldn't help himself.

He put down his pistol.

He picked up a Snickers bar, and he placed it in Johnny Meyers' hand.

Johnny ate that Snickers as Barnes drove across town. He wasn't sure why he took the cop with him, but he did. The guy really was Johnny's to command. Barnes was as docile as a puppy. And with the burglar alarm going off back there, and Johnny's truck sitting smack dab in the middle of the parking lot—well, Johnny figured it wouldn't hurt to have the sheriff at his disposal should any other law come sniffing around.

Johnny thought things over as they drove. At least his mojo hand really worked. That was the good news, and Barnes proved it. But the bad news was that Johnny wasn't sure how many times he'd used his hand. He'd knocked on Barnes' squad car door, and that one surely counted. But he didn't know about the florist shop. He'd knocked there, too—only no one had answered. He had no way of knowing if that knock counted or not.

So maybe he'd used one knock, and maybe he'd used two. He'd planned to use that second knock over at the jewelry store, where he wanted to pick out a diamond ring for Elena. But that was going to have to wait. For one thing, he'd already set off one burglar alarm in town. For another, if there was only one knock left in that magic hand he had to save it for Elena's door . . . and for the man who answered it.

Familiar road now. Familiar moonlight, too. And through the cracked window, the familiar scent of the river and that dirt road still wet with rain that cut through farmland. And then that other smell—that crisp, tart apple smell that reminded Johnny of Elena's father.

It sliced straight through him like a knife. Johnny rolled up the window. Now all he could smell were the roses—the bouquet of white ones he'd managed to grab at the florist shop before Barnes showed up. He tried to settle in on it, but he had a hard time.

Johnny couldn't finish the Snickers bar. He tossed it back in the bag Barnes had stolen from a kid. Then he noticed something else in there. A monster mask, some kind of rattlesnake man with great big fangs. Johnny pulled it out and looked it over. Ran his hand over those scales. Rattlers were cold-blooded; they'd sleep through a night like this. They'd sleep through a whole damn winter. Johnny wished he could be that way, but he was sweating something fierce.

Barnes turned onto the little dirt road that led to Elena's house, and Johnny's heart started thundering. He was thinking about Elena's father, thinking how things would play out once the old man answered that door.

Barnes pulled to a stop.

Johnny swallowed hard.

He crumpled up that monster mask, shoved it into his coat pocket like a snakeskin charm.

He grabbed the white roses in his good hand.

He got out of the car and walked to the door.

He knocked.

It took a while before the door opened, but it did. And there stood Elena's father, his eyes tired, his heart heavy. Johnny told him what he wanted. But somehow, Johnny's words didn't seem to matter to the old man any more than Johnny's mojo hand mattered. Because Elena's father didn't have any more left in his heart or his house than he did in his words, and though he spoke them under the sway of Johnny's magic hand, they were words that did not rise above a whisper, and they were the same words that had knocked hard on Johnny's heart when he'd come home from the war three months before.

Johnny had denied those words entrance then, but he couldn't deny them now. Not as the three of them drove to the cemetery across the road from the apple orchard gone wild. The crisp, tart scent sawed at Johnny as he got out of the cruiser, and he remembered the things Elena's father had told him that day three months ago, and he recalled the details of a death that had come quietly while he was half a world away.

And now he remembered about the cemetery. And the smell of apples. And the scent of roses, too, for there were roses on Elena's grave. White roses . . . just like the ones he'd stolen from the florist shop. And suddenly Johnny felt like he was coming apart, felt like a busted puppet ready to topple among the tombstones.

He reached into his coat pocket. He squeezed that rattlesnake face in his good hand. Then he took the mask out of his pocket and put it on. He knew what he had to do.

Of course, a one-handed man couldn't use a shovel. Johnny didn't have time for that, anyway. So he started up the backhoe the gravediggers used and he set to work, digging like a combat knife in a tin of rations. Elena's father watched without a word. Ray Barnes watched too, chewing on a Snickers bar while he sat on a tombstone. And while Johnny worked the backhoe's gears, his stump of a wrist sweated inside the sleeve of his magic prosthetic hand, and his tears lined the inner skin of that rattlesnake mask.

But none of it mattered anymore. Not the mojo hand, not the white roses chewed under the teeth of the backhoe's bucket. Not what Johnny remembered, and not what he'd forgotten. That's what he thought as he emptied out that hole, and that's what he thought as he climbed down onto the lid of Elena's coffin with a dozen crushed roses and a rubber hand that had started off the evening swollen with the promise of three magic knocks.

One or none—how many magic knocks were left in that hand didn't matter at all. Johnny knew that deep inside, even as he held that rubber hand poised above the metal casket, even as he cried inside that rattlesnake mask.

Even as he brought his fist down on that lid.

▼ ▼ ▼ ▼ ▼

And here's your kicker, folks—Johnny was right.

Because it doesn't really matter what happened next, any more than it matters why Johnny's hand was charged up with those three magic knocks in the first place. That's not what this story's about, because knocking on his dead love's coffin wasn't the worst thing that ever happened to Johnny Meyers. Not by a longshot.

The worst thing that ever happened to Johnny was ending up down in that hole at all.

The worst thing that happened was falling that deep, and that hard.

So . . . that's where Johnny is.

That's how he got there.

And that's where we'll leave him . . . tonight.

AUNTIE ELSPETH'S HALLOWEEN STORY, OR THE GOURD, THE BAD, AND THE UGLY

Esther M. Friesner

A carved pumpkin lit from within—the jack o' lantern—is probably the single most identifiable symbol of Halloween. (Look at our cover!) But the now-ubiquitous jack o' lantern is really a fairly recently acquired holiday icon. As you may recall from the introduction, the term "jack o' lantern" was first associated with marsh gas, transmuted through folklore into association with the Devil, and then twisted into many variations. Around the beginning of the twentieth century he evolved into a jolly decoration. Jack o' lanterns have a dual nature these days. They are still cheery neighborhood beacons of a happy Halloween, but they are also creepy incarnations of frightful evil.

Esther Friesner's subversively hilarious Auntie Elspeth combines both in her tale of Jo-Jo . . .

Hello, children, what brings you here to see your kindly old Auntie Elspeth? Parents fed up with you again? Well, never you mind. Auntie Elspeth knows what it's like to be unwanted, especially by the very same people who claim to love and cherish you, but who'll shove you into a so-called senior citizens' community—spelled "hellhole"—so fast that your wheelchair leaves skidmarks on the linoleum.

Now, now, don't whimper, and for heaven's sake don't look at me with those great big sad puppydog eyes. You don't want to know what I did to the last real puppydog who tried that crap on me. Face the facts, kiddies: Mommy and Daddy want you the hell out of their hair for awhile, probably because they want to play Hide the Hamster—no, you do not need to know what that means—but they also want an ooey-gooey feelgood excuse for doing it. That's why they parked you here with me. Probably said something like, "Oh my, won't dear old Auntie Elspeth love having some quality time with the children?"

No, Tommy, the word you are looking for to describe what Mommy and Daddy said is not "fibbing." The word you want is "bullshit." See if you can remember to say that when Mommy and Daddy come to pick you up, you and the rest of this clutch of young harpies-in-training. You see, dearie? Being with Auntie Elspeth is *educational*. That's another word Mommy and Daddy use a whole lot, I'll bet, especially when they want to justify plunking you brats down for a four-hour stint in front of the television.

As long as we're stuck with each other for— When did your parents say they were coming back? What? That long?! Why, those stinking, lousy, rotten sons-of—! Just because I'm old, do they think I've got nothing better to do with my time than hang out with the spawn of their loins? Bah.

Oh, to hell with it. Open the top drawer of that nightstand over there, kids; it's full of candy. Help yourself to as much as you want. Maybe if I send you back to them tanked up on sugar they'll think twice before farming you out to me again.

Hm? What's that, Cindy? You don't want any candy? What the hell's the matter with you?

Ohhhh. Not hungry, just bored. And bor-*ing* too, for the record. You want a story? Well, here's one: Once upon a time there was a nice old woman who was minding her own business when her nephew and his bimbo wife dumped their three kids on her doorstep and as soon as the old lady got the chance she sold the little buggers to a traveling circus where they had to spend the rest of their days biting the heads off chickens. The. End.

Happy?

Damn it, shut your yap and quit your bawling before one of the guards sticks his thick head in here. I'm not supposed to have all that candy, you know. Lousy screws will confiscate it if they find it. Look, I tell you what: How about if kindly old Auntie Elspeth tells you a *different* story? Once upon a time there were three little trichinosis-infected pigs who—

What?

You don't want that story either? Picky little snot, ain'tcha. Well then, what kind of story *does* Her Royal Heinieness desire?

A Halloween tale? Child there just might be some hope for you, after all. October is getting on. Halloween will be at our throats before you know it, and it just so happens to be your kindly old Auntie Elspeth's favorite holiday.

I heard that, Billy. If you're going to be malicious, at least have the stones to do it out loud so a person can hear you. Halloween is not my favorite holiday because I'm an old witch, I don't care what your Mommy said, Your Mommy also said she was a virgin when she married your Daddy, but between you and me and the Seventh Fleet—

Cindy, dear, it's not polite to interrupt. However, since you *did* ask, a virgin is a mythological creature, okay? Sort of like a dragon or a unicorn or a compassionate conservative or—

Look, grow up, learn to read, look up the words you don't know in the dictionary, and shut the hell up for two seconds. I don't have time to answer a lot of stupid questions.

Daddy told you there's no such thing as a stupid question? Daddy was wrong.

Do you want a Halloween story or not?

Now this is called "How the Vampire Prince Plunged His Fangs into the Heaving White Bosom of the Helpless Maiden and Devoured Her Stifl-Beating Heart." Once upon a time—

Now what?

Yes, Tommy, I know that Cindy is only four years old. Yes, I know that your Mommy and Daddy don't want any of you mini-weasels exposed to undue levels of violence. Speaking of which, where did a peewee pissant like you come up with such a mouthful of buzzwords?

Ah. Educational television. I should have known. All right, in that case I suppose I could tidy up the vampire story a bit and—

No vampires allowed? None at all? Not even a little one? He doesn't have to devour the maiden's still-beating heart, if you're going to be a big bunch of wussies about it. He can just devour it after he's sated his hellish thirst on the helpless maiden's blood and her heart stops beating, all right?

Okay, fine. Be that way. Sissies.

Ahem: The merciless sun of the Egyptian desert beat down upon the City of the Dead, but within the tomb of the Pharaoh's daughter it was cold; cold as the bellies of the deadly native vipers whose bite means a lingering, agonizing death; cold as the blade of a fanatical assassin as it slits the throat of the foreign devil rash enough to defy the ancient curses sealing the princess' final resting place; cold as the steely nerves of Sir Henry Battabout-Montescue as he strode into the burial chamber and laid

impious hands upon the lid of the princess' sarcophagus. But before he
could defile the royal virgin's eternal sleep, an unholy roar came from
behind him. He turned in time to see the figure of a mummy—a hideous,
deformed, desiccated corpse, rank with the putridity of centuries, trailing
the dusty wrappings of its entombment-come lurching toward him. Hands
like the talons of the sacred vulture closed around his windpipe and his
last breath was overwhelmed by the fetor of the creature's—

Good Lord, *now* what's wrong, Cindy? Stop making noises like a
dachshund with the hiccups and speak up! Billy, Tommy, try to make
yourselves useful for a change and get that rabbity little sister of yours to
stop crying.

What do you mean, I scared her? How could a simple little story about
one insignificant, bloodthirsty, vengeance-obsessed mummy bother anyone?
It's even got a *moral*, for pity's sake: If you touch stuff you're told not to
touch, you die a hideous, unnatural death. That's an *excellent* moral, in my
humble opinion. Eminently practical. And the story's full of all kinds of
fascinating facts about ancient Egypt. It's *educational*!

Gawd.

You know, in my day when we asked for a Halloween story we wanted
to be scared spitless. And we all dressed up like ghosts and ghouls and
goblins because we wanted to scare all the other kids so bad they'd walk
home with their shoes squishing. At least tell me that hasn't changed.

Oh. So Cindy's going to be a fairy princess and Billy's going to be a
teddy bear. Pass me that plastic basin from under the nightstand, Tommy;
Auntie Elspeth's feeling a mite poorly and I don't want to pitch my porridge
all over my clean shoes.

And what are you going to be this Halloween? A tofu burger?

Ahhhh, a *ghost*! Good boy. At least that's a step in the right—

The ghost of Anton van Loewen*who*?

Jesus, take me now. Do you little fluff-bunnies have blood in your veins
or maple syrup?

Look, grab another fistful of taffy, stop your gobs, and Auntie Elspeth
is going to tell you a Halloween story if it kills me. (Which it will, if there's
a just and merciful God who doesn't want to see me suffer away the rest
of this afternoon.) Don't worry, it won't be about vampires or mummies
or zombies or anything nifty like that. It's going to be just the way your
parents want you to be: Sweet and safe and sanitized for their protection.
All that Auntie Elspeth's going to ask of you darling moppets is that you

sit down, pay attention, and let your imaginations take you down the lovely garden path that leads to the Enchanted Pumpkin Patch, because *this*, children, is the story of Jo-Jo the Jolly Jack o' Lantern:

Once upon a time there was a little pumpkin named Jo-Jo. He grew up round and plump and happy with all of his little pumpkin friends in old Farmer Nosferatu's pumpkin patch. Oh, such jolly times they all had! The sun warmed them and the rain watered them and every time a traveling salesman came a-calling at the farmhouse, old Farmer Nosferatu would invite him inside, out of sight, and very soon afterwards he'd make a special trip down to the pumpkin patch to give the happy little pumpkins a great big dose of bone meal fertilizer. *Dear* old Farmer Nosferatu!

It was a good life, but it wasn't enough for JO-JO. You see, Jo-Jo was a pumpkin with a dream. More than anything else, Jo-Jo wanted to grow up to be big enough and round enough and just the perfect shade of orange to be made into a jack o' lantern in time for Halloween.

Now Jo-Jo didn't really know all there was to know about being a jack o' lantern, because he had still been only a seed the last time October 31 rolled around. Everything he'd ever heard about Halloween came from wise old Mr. Hooty Owl who lived in the lightning-blasted tree over by the north fence near the graveyard. Night after night, wise old Mr. Hooty Owl would scare himself up a fine fuzzy field mouse dinner, then sit on the pumpkin patch fence while he gobbled down every juicy morsel. And in between munchy, crunchy bites he'd tell all of the little pumpkins stories about Halloween.

"It's just the most wonderful holiday that ever was," he'd say. "It's the time of year when magic happens—real, honest-to-goodness magic! But if it weren't for you pumpkins, Halloween wouldn't be half so grand nor magical, no indeedy. You see, when the air starts to snap like a bone-crushing bear trap and the leaves on the tree bleed red and purple and gold, and the night starts to come in darker and sooner, crowded with lorn, lost souls, why that's when Halloween comes dancing down the lane. And that's when folks start looking for pumpkins to make into jack o' lanterns to light up the nights and keep away whatever's wandering in the dark."

What's that, Billy? What *is* wandering in the dark that the jack o' lanterns have to keep away? Gracious, I can't tell you that. Your parents wouldn't approve. So I guess you'll just have to sit up at night all by yourself, staring out into the darkness, and *imagine* what might be waiting out there waiting and watching and biding its time until it knows you're sound asleep and can't see it coming. Mercy sakes, whatever *might* it be? Will it have fangs or scales or claws or all three or something even worse than that? Will it be hungry? Will it know how to climb up walls and through windows, even when they're locked down tight, or will it just ring the doorbell, hmm? I won't tell—that would spoil the surprise—but you go right ahead and imagine it.

Won't that be fun?

You know, none of the little pumpkins who lived in Jo-Jo's patch ever interrupted wise old Mr. Hooty Owl when *he* was telling a story. They knew that if they did, wise old Mr. Hooty Owl would ring for the nurse and pretend he wanted to take a nap and all the blabby little pumpkins would have to sit in the sunroom where the only channel you can get on the television is CNN. And because they were smart little pumpkins and really didn't enjoy the smell of bleach and wee-wee they didn't butt in on wise old Mr. Hooty Owl's story any more.

"Oh, it's marvelous to be a jack o' lantern," wise old Mr. Hooty Owl would say. "One minute you're a pumpkin like a hundred others, the next you're all aglow with light, just like a star. Then people put you in their windows or out on their front steps or balanced on the porch railing so that all the world can see just how bright and beautiful you are. They're pleased as punch to have you—almost think of you like a member of the family, they do—and when the little children see you, their eyes get that wide, and their mouths become just as round as can be, and they can't help but cry out over what a fine jack o' lantern you are. Yes, sir—" And he bit off the dead mouse's head and chewed it contentedly while he finished his speech. "—Halloween's a magical time to be a pumpkin."

Of course that was when a big chunk of mouse skull went down the wrong way and choked the life out of wise old Mr. Hooty Owl because wise old Mr. Hooty Owl wasn't quite wise enough and didn't know any better than to talk with his mouth full.

Jo-Jo couldn't wait for Halloween to come. All through the summer he did his best to soak up the sun and the rain until his round little body swelled up like a tick and he went from a teensy-weensy green thing the size of a tennis ball to a great big orange thing the size of a full-grown pumpkin.

Okay, so I never said my name was Auntie Metaphor. Sue me.

Pretty soon it got on for being close to Halloween and old Farmer Nosferatu came out to harvest his pumpkin patch. He was very pleased with what he saw, but not half so pleased as Jo-Jo. That clever little pumpkin knew from the way Farmer Nosferatu smiled down at him that he was a fine, ripe pumpkin and would be chosen to become a for-real-and-for-true jack o' lantern. Jo-Jo was so proud and so happy that he didn't even mind the searing pain he endured when Farmer Nosferatu took out his ever-so-sharp sickle and slashed through the stem holding Jo-Jo to the pumpkin vine.

Actually I'm lying. He *did* mind it. In fact, *minding* it doesn't even begin to cover little Jo-Jo's feelings. He hated it. It *hurt* to be cut off the vine. It hurt so bad that I can't tell you. You just imagine how *you*'d feel if you were holding hands with your Mommy and someone came along who wanted to snatch you away, only you were holding onto Mommy's hand so tight that they couldn't make you let go and so they had to take a great big ax and chopped right through your—

But I don't need to tell you everything, do I? You're such bright children. You can imagine that for yourselves.

Poor little Jo-Jo passed out entirely from the pain and when he woke up again, his stem throbbing, he discovered that he was sitting in a market. I'll spare you the tedious details and all the philosophical crap about what Jo-Jo learned from observing the interactions of human society. (See, Tommy? You're not the only show-off who watches educational television.) Jo-Jo wasn't paying a whole lot of attention to the people in the market anyhow. He was concentrating on his future, and what a merry future it would be once he became a jack o' lantern. It helped to take his mind off the pain.

How happy Jo-Jo was on the day that a dear little boy name Jeremy Jinx came into the market with his mommy and picked three pumpkins! There was no doubt what Jeremy Jinx and his mommy were going to do with those pumpkins, no sirree, because Jo-Jo heard Jeremy Jinx ask his mommy right out loud, "Can we have this pumpkin to make into a jack o' lantern for Halloween? And this one? And this one? Oh, and this one, too? And that one over there? And the big one? Can we, can we, can we, huh, please, please, please?" And he heard Jeremy Jinx's mommy reply, "We shall pick out one pumpkin for you, and one for me, and one for your darling daddy. And then you can put a sock in it because I've got a three-martini headache so have some mercy and shut up."

Jeremy Jinx looked at all the pumpkins on display. Jo-Jo watched him. If he'd had a heart it would have been in his mouth, if he'd had a mouth. *Pick me!* he thought fiercely. *I want to be a jack o' lantern more than anything else in the whole, wide world. I want to be your jack o' lantern! Oh, please, please, please pick me!*

Lo and behold, Jo-Jo's fervent wish was granted, for little Jeremy Jinx looked straight at him, and put his dear, chubby little arms around him, and lifted him right off the display and said, "I want this one, Mommy. He's my very special friend, and he told me that more than anything else in the whole, wide world, he wants to be *my* jack o' lantern, and I love him."

"Great, now the kid's talking to vegetables," his mommy muttered. She picked out two other pumpkins and dumped them in her shopping cart. "As soon as we get home, I'm calling your therapist."

Pretty soon Jo-Jo was safe and warm in his new home. He sat on the kitchen table with the other two pumpkins that Jeremy Jinx and his mommy had chosen. He looked around, but he really wasn't paying attention to his surroundings. He was still thinking about becoming a jack o' lantern. In fact, Jo-Jo never thought about anything much except becoming a jack o' lantern. Come to think of it, Jo-Jo had a very unhealthy psychological obsession with becoming a jack o' lantern, so it's no wonder that when he finally learned the truth about jack o' lanterns—

But I'm getting ahead of myself.

On second thought, no, I'm not. Because you see, the very next morning, just as soon as Jeremy Jinx got on the school bus, when the air was fresh with frost and the sun was peeking in through the fluffy white curtains at the kitchen window, Jeremy Jinx's mommy spread a double layer of old newspaper over the kitchen table, set the first pumpkin right in the middle of it, took the biggest, sharpest knife in the whole kitchen, and plunged it straight through the soft and yielding skin right near the stem, ker-CHUNK!!!

Poor Jo-Jo! He was so shocked by this apparent act of wanton cruelty that he couldn't bring himself to look away. So he was still watching while Jeremy Jinx's mother sawed her knife all the way around the stem and pulled out the plug of dripping orange meat and then jabbed a big metal spoon deep into the helpless pumpkin's body. Jo-Jo saw how coolly the she-beast ladled out glob after sticky glob of seeds and dumped them into the garbage can, casually destroying generations of pumpkins yet unborn, but there was only so much a young vegetable could take. The horror was overwhelming and Jo-Jo fainted.

He awoke to a pain that made old Farmer Nosferatu's assault on his stem seem like a walk in the park. Mercifully, he passed out again before it completely registered on him that the source of his agony was because it was his turn under the knife and the spoon.

When Jo-Jo next became aware of the world around him, he felt strangely light-headed, or perhaps I ought to say light-shelled. Kids, can you say "dramatic irony"?

Well, I'll bet you could say it if you'd stop goggling at me like a bunch of strangled frogs. Oh, never mind.

Anyhow, Jo-Jo felt different, very, very different from the innocent little pumpkin he used to be.

"What has happened to me?" he asked. Then he did a double take. Had those words actually come out of his *mouth*?

But pumpkins don't have mouths.

Jack o' lanterns do.

Jo-Jo was still coming to grips with an altered reality when he glanced to his left. There was something shiny there, something that looked like a small silver box. Jo-Jo had no way of knowing that this was a toaster. All he knew was that when he turned, he could see himself in the brightly polished surface.

Oh, what a sight he was! For Jeremy Jinx's mommy had taken all of the impotent rage she always kept bottled up inside her—a ferocious, long-smoldering rage which came from years of living under the regime of a repressive, patriarchal society—and had used it. And how had she used it? Why on carving the Halloween pumpkins, of course! She had given each of them the scowliest eyes and the pointiest noses and the biggest, widest, most sinister grins you can imagine.

And what is a big, wide, sinister grin unless it's full of big, sharp, nastily pointed teeth?

"Wow," said Jo-Jo, giving his reflection the once-over. "Cool."

"It won't be cool for long, squashboy," came an unfamiliar voice. Jo-Jo turned-very slowly and in a wobbly manner-to confront the other two pumpkins that Jeremy Jinx's mother had also carved into jack o' lanterns. The one that had called out to Jo-Jo looked a lot like him, only not quite so scary, but the other one—

The other one was hollow and smashed and dead.

Jo-Jo gasped at the shattered, oozing shell. "What—what happened to her?" he demanded.

If a pumpkin could shrug, that's exactly what the other jack o' lantern would have done. "Mulch happens. The knife slipped. So the seed-scooping monster lost her temper and knocked the poor kid smack off the table by . . . 'accident.'"

"How awful!" Jo-Jo cried. Fat, slimy tears dripped from his freshly gouged-out eyeholes.

"Save your tears for yourself," the other pumpkin told him. "As soon as the seed-scooper comes back with the candies, it's all over for us."

Jo-Jo didn't understand.

"Geez, sprout, didn't anyone ever tell you?" the other pumpkin said. "Don't you know what it means to be a jack o' lantern?"

So Jo-Jo told the other pumpkin all about the pumpkin patch back home, and old Farmer Nosferatu, and wise old Mister Hooty Owl's stories. And when he was done, the other pumpkin was laughing fit to burst himself into a pile of puréed pie filling.

"Funny, you don't *look* green," he said when he finally got control of himself. "And you *believed* those stories? Sprout, those are the sort of thing 'most everyone tells you when you're young because being young means being dumb as a rock and it's fun to see just how many lies you'll swallow before you wise up!"

"Then it wasn't true?" Jo-Jo said, and he sounded so sorrowful and pathetic it would've made a high school guidance counselor cry real tears. "Not a single word?"

"Bless your blossoms, there's *some* truth to what you were told," the other pumpkin said. "All the best lies come wrapped up in half-truths so they're easier to believe. Halloween is a magical time of year for us poor pumpkins. How else do you think you got the power to move yourself around like that, even a little, and to talk like we're doing right now? But the magic doesn't last and neither do we. Oh, they'll use us to light up their Halloween night, all right! But how do you think they make us glow? Not by magic, nuh-uh. By fire."

Jo-Jo gasped. Fire was something he understood. It was something all vegetables understood without ever needing to be taught, a primal fear bred so deeply into every leaf and stem, fruit and flower, that it came to them as natural as soaking up sunlight and rain. Fire cooked. Fire killed.

"That's right, sprout, I said fire," the other pumpkin went on. "Something called a candle. They lift off the top of your shell, stick that thing upright inside you, and then they set it aflame. And as soon as the first little spark of it catches hold and the fire blazes up in your shell, the magic's over. You're dead. Beautiful and bright, but dead."

"Nooooooo!" Jo-Jo wailed. And he rocked back and forth on the kitchen table, because the magic of Halloween had given him the power to move himself around like that, in a most un-vegetable-like manner. More tears streamed from his eyeholes and he wiped them away frantically.

Then he realized something. *What* was he using to wipe away his tears?

"Where in heck did these come from?" he asked, holding up a pair of prehensile leaves. They trembled before his eyeholes, having burgeoned from the ends of a pair of sturdy pumpkin vines that had somehow erupted from the sides of his shell.

The other pumpkin chuckled. "Beats me, sprout. More of that 'magic of Halloween' crap in action, I guess. They say that if you want something bad enough, tonight of all nights, you get it. Anything short of wanting to save your own life, that is. Candle or no candle, we've only got until dawn."

"But I never wished for *these*," Jo-Jo protested, waving his vines about wildly.

"Hey, some things you want without knowing you want them," the other pumpkin said. "Some things, the magic knows you want them before you know it yourself."

Jo-Jo grew thoughtful. He continued to study his miraculous leaves and vines, flexing them testing them, reaching out with them, using them to pluck at the corners of the sodden newspapers still covering the kitchen tabletop. The leaves were very dexterous, just like human hands, only somehow Jo-Jo knew that the vines he'd grown instead of arms were much stronger than human arms.

"I guess the magic does know best," he said at last. "There is one thing I want to do before I go, and I won't so much mind dying after I've done it." As the other pumpkin watched, Jo-Jo began to shake and shiver, then all of sudden he sprouted two more vines, right out from under himself. Using his leaves, he laid hold of the table and let himself drop over the side just as his rapidly growing leg-vines reached their full size.

"Hey, sprout, what do you think you're—?" the other pumpkin began to ask. Just then the kitchen door swung open and Jeremy Jinx's mommy came in with a couple of fat, white candles in her hands.

The other pumpkin saw Jo-Jo's vines snake back up onto the table top, lay hold of the carving knife and the scooping spoon, and drop from sight again just before he heard Jeremy Jinx's mommy begin to scream.

The end.

What's that, Tommy? What do you mean, it can't be the end? Sure it can! Who's telling this story, huh? I'm only doing what your Mommy and Daddy want, shielding you, sheltering you from all the icky-sticky details. Why should I have to tell you what happened next, what Jo-Jo did with that carving knife and that scooping spoon and those candies? Can't you guess what little Jeremy Jinx found sitting on the front porch steps, waiting for him when he came home from school that day? It was a surprise, I can at least tell you that. A gaping, grinning surprise with a candle burning oh, ever so brightly inside!

Surely you don't need me to tell you what it was, do you? I didn't think so. Or to tell you what it was that little Jeremy Jinx found smeared all over the sharp, pointed, nastily carved teeth of the jolly jack o' lantern that sat on the other side of the front porch steps? A child's imagination is such a precious gift, dearie me, yes. Use it, yard-apes.

But what's that tapping at the door? Could it possibly be Jo-Jo the Jolly Jack o' Lantern, come to call? No, it's just your Mommy and Daddy, here to take you home again, thank God. Give Auntie Elspeth a kiss and— Oh, fine, no kiss, just try to stop screaming, okay?

Bye-bye, darlings. Happy Halloween.

STRUWWELPETER

Glen Hirshberg

Der Struwwelpeter (1845) by Heinrich Hoffmann is a book of ten cautionary tales in verse meant to teach children that misbehavior had consequences. Despite a subtitle of "Merry Stories and Funny Pictures," Herr Hoffman's consequences were dire indeed: play with matches and you will burn to death, suck your thumb and a sadistic tailor will cut it off, refuse to eat your soup and you'll dies of starvation in less than a week . . . "Struwwelpeter" is one of the milder story-poems. "Shock-haired" Peter doesn't comb his hair, clean his face, he never cuts his filthy nails, so people loathe him. Glen Hirshberg's Peter is disliked too, and the author chooses a haunted house and Halloween—its spookiness, its supernatural possibilities—to tell masterfully us his story. You'll find, however, that Halloween has little to do with the real horror of "Struwwelpeter."

"The dead are not altogether powerless."
—Chief Seattle

This was before we knew about Peter, or at least before we understood what we knew, and my mother says it's impossible to know a thing like that anyway. She's wrong, though, and she doesn't need me to tell her she is, either.

Back then, we still gathered, afterschool afternoons, at the Andersz' house, because it was close to the locks. If it wasn't raining, we'd drop our books and grab Ho Hos out of the tin Mr. Andersz always left on the table for us and head immediately toward the water. Gulls spun in the sunlight overhead, their cries urgent, taunting, telling us, *you're missing it, you're missing it.* We'd sprint between the rows of low stone duplexes, the sad little gardens with their flowers battered by the rain until the petals looked bent and forgotten like discarded training wheels, the splintery, sagging blue walls of the Black Anchor restaurant where Mr. Paars used to hunker alone and murmuring over his plates of reeking lutefisk when he wasn't stalking 15th Street, knocking pigeons and homeless people out of the way with his dog-head cane. Finally, we'd burst into the park, pouring down the avenue of fir trees like a mudslide and scattering people, bugs, and birds before us until we hit the water.

For hours, we'd prowl the green hillsides, watching the sailors yell at the invading seals from the top of the locks while the seals ignored them, skimming for fish and sometimes rolling on their backs and flipping their fins. We watched the rich-people sailboats with their masts rusting, the big gray fishing boats from Alaska and Japan and Russia with the fishermen bored on deck, smoking, throwing butts at the seals and leaning on the rails while the gulls shrieked overhead. As long as the rain held off, we stayed and threw stones to see how high up the opposing bank we could get them, and Peter would wait for ships to drift in front of us and then throw low over their bows. The sailors would scream curses in other languages or sometimes ours, and Peter would throw bigger stones at the boat-hulls. When they hit with a thunk, we'd flop on our backs on the wet grass and flip our feet in the air like the seals. It was the rudest gesture we knew.

Of course, most days it was raining, and we stayed in the Andersz' basement until Mr. Andersz and the Serbians came home. Down there, in the damp—Mr. Andersz claimed his was one of three basements in all of Ballard—you could hear the wetness rising in the grass outside like lock-water. The first thing Peter did when we got downstairs was flick on the gas fireplace (not for heat, it didn't throw any), and we'd toss in stuff: pencils, a tinfoil ball, a plastic cup, and once a broken old 45 which formed blisters on its surface and then spit black goo into the air like a fleeing octopus dumping ink before it slid into a notch in the logs to melt. Once, Peter went upstairs and came back with one of Mr. Andersz' red spiral photo albums and tossed it into the flames, and when one of the Mack sisters asked him what was in it, he told her, "No idea. Didn't look."

The burning never lasted long, five minutes, maybe. Then we'd eat Ho Hos and play the Atari Mr. Andersz had bought Peter years before at a yard sale, and it wasn't like you think, not always. Mostly, Peter flopped in his orange beanbag chair with his long legs stretched in front of him and his too-long black bangs splayed across his forehead like the talons of some horrible, giant bird gripping him to lift him away. He let me and the Mack sisters take turns on the machine, and Kenny London and Steve

Rourke, too, back in the days when they would come. I was the best at the basic games, Asteroids and Pong, but Jenny Mack could stay on Dig Dug forever and not get grabbed by the floating grabby-things in the ground. Even when we asked Peter to take his turn, he wouldn't. He'd say, "Go ahead," or, "Too tired," or, "Fuck off," and once I even turned around in the middle of losing to Jenny and found him watching us, sort of, the rainy window and us, not the TV screen at all. He reminded me a little of my grandfather before he died, all folded up in his chair and not wanting to go anywhere and kind of happy to have us there. Always, Peter seemed happy to have us there.

When Mr. Andersz got home, he'd fish a Ho Ho out of the tin for himself if we'd left him one—we tried to, most days—and then come downstairs, and when he peered out of the stairwell, his black wool hat still stuck to his head like melted wax, he already looked different than when we saw him at school. At school, even with his hands covered in yellow chalk and his transparencies full of fractions and decimals scattered all over his desk and the pears he carried with him and never seemed to eat, he was just Mr. Andersz, fifth-grade math teacher, funny accent, funny to get angry. At school, it never occurred to any of us to feel sorry for him.

"Well, hello, all of you," he'd say, as if talking to a litter of puppies he'd found, and we'd pause our game and hold our breaths and wait for Peter. Sometimes—most times—Peter would say, "Hey" back, or even, "Hey Dad." Then we'd all chime in like a clock tolling the hour, "Hey Mr. Andersz," "Thanks for the Ho Hos," "You're hat's all wet again," and he'd smile and nod and go upstairs.

There were the other days, too. A few, that's all. On most of those, Peter just didn't answer, wouldn't look at his father. It was only the one time that he said, "Hello, Dipshit-Dad," and Jenny froze at the Atari and one of the floating grabby things swallowed her digger, and the rest of us stared, but not at Peter, and not at Mr. Andersz, either. Anywhere but there.

For a few seconds, Mr. Andersz seemed to be deciding, and rain-rivers wriggled down the walls and windows like transparent snakes, and we held our breath. But all he said, in the end, was, "We'll talk later, Struwwelpeter," which was only a little different from what he usually said when Peter got this way. Usually, he said, "Oh. It's you, then. Hello, Struwwelpeter." I never liked the way he said that, as though he was greeting someone else entirely, not his son. Eventually, Jenny or her sister Kelly would say, "Hi, Mr. Andersz," and he'd glance around as though he'd forgotten we were there, and then he'd go upstairs and invite the Serbians in, and we wouldn't see him again until we left.

The Serbians made Steve Rourke nervous, which is almost funny, in retrospect. They were big and dark, both of them, two brothers who looked at their hands whenever they saw children. One was a car mechanic, the other worked at the locks, and they sat all afternoon, most afternoons, in Mr. Andersz' study, sipping tea and speaking Serbian in low whispers. The words made their whispers harsh, full of Z's and ground-up S's, as though they'd swallowed glass.

"They could be planning things in there," Steve used to say. "My dad says both those guys were badass soldiers." Mostly, as far as I could tell, they looked at Mr. Andersz's giant library of photo albums and listened to records. Judy Collins, Joan Baez. Almost funny, like I said.

Of course, by this last Halloween—my last night at the Andersz house—both Serbians were dead, run down by a drunken driver while walking across Fremont Bridge, and Kenny London had moved away, and Steve Rourke didn't come anymore. He said his parents wouldn't let him, and I bet they wouldn't, but that isn't why he stopped coming. I knew it, and I think Peter knew it, too, and that worried me a little, in ways I couldn't explain.

I almost didn't get to go, either. I was out the door, blinking in the surprising sunlight and the wind rolling off the Sound through the streets, when my mother yelled, "ANDREW!" and stopped me. I turned to find her in the open screen door of our duplex, arms folded over the long, gray coat she wore inside and out from October to May, sunlight or no, brown-gray curls bunched on top of her scalp as though trying to crawl over her head out of the wind. She seemed to be wiggling in mid-air like a salmon trying to hold itself still against a current. Rarely did she take what she called her *frustrations* out on me, but she'd been crabby all day, and now she looked furious, despite the fact that I'd stayed in my room, out of her way, from the second I got home from school because I knew she didn't really want me out tonight. Not with Peter. Not after last year.

"That's a costume?" She gestured with her chin at my jeans, my everyday black sweater, too-small brown mac she'd promised to replace this year.

I shrugged.

"You're not going trick or treating?"

The truth was, no one went trick or treating much in our section of Ballard, not like in Bellingham where we'd lived when we lived with my dad. Too wet and dismal, most days, and there were too many drunks lurking around places like the Black Anchor and sometimes stumbling down the duplexes, shouting curses at the dripping trees.

"Trick or treating's for babies," I said.

"Hmm, I wonder which of your friends taught you that," my mother said, and then a look flashed across her face, different than the one she usually got at times like this. She still looked sad, but not about me. She looked sad for me.

I took a step toward her, and her image wavered in my glasses. "I won't sleep there. I'll be home by eleven," I said.

"You'll be home by ten, or you won't be going anywhere again anytime soon. Got it? How old do you think you are, anyway?"

"Twelve," I said, with as much conviction as I could muster, and my mother flashed the sad look again.

"If Peter tells you to jump off a bridge. . ."

"Push him off."

My mother nodded. "If I didn't feel so bad for *him* . . . " she said, and I thought she meant Peter, and then I wasn't sure. But she didn't say anything else, and after a few seconds, I couldn't stand there anymore, not with the wind crawling down the neck of my jacket and my mother still looking like that. I left her in the doorway.

Even in bright sunlight, mine was a dreary neighborhood. The gusts of wind herded paper scraps and street-grit down the overflowing gutters and yanked the last leaves off the trees like a gleeful gang on a vandalism rampage. I saw a few parents—new to the area, obviously—hunched into rain-slickers, leading little kids from house to house. The kids wore drug-store clown costumes, Darth Vader masks, sailor caps. They all looked edgy, miserable. At most of the houses, no one answered the doorbell.

Outside the Andersz' place, I stopped for just a minute, watching the leaves leaping from their branches and tumbling down the wind, trying to figure out what was different, what felt wrong. Then I had it: the Mountain was out. The endless fall rain had rolled in early that year, and it had been weeks, maybe months, since I'd last seen Mount Rainier. Seeing it now gave me the same unsettled sensation as always. "It's because you're looking south, not west," people always say, as if that explains how the mountain gets to that spot on the horizon, on the wrong side of the city, not where it actually is but out to sea, seemingly bobbing on the waves, not the land.

How many times, I wondered abruptly, had some adult in my life asked why I liked Peter? I wasn't cruel, and despite my size, I wasn't easily cowed, and I did okay in school—not as well as Peter, but okay—and I had "a gentleness, most days," as Mrs. Corbett (WhoreButt, to Peter) had written on my report card last year. "If he learns to exercise judgment—and perhaps gives some thought to his choice of companions—he could go far."

I wanted to go far from Ballard, anyway, and the locks, and the smell of lutefisk, and the rain. I liked doorbell ditching, but I didn't get much charge out of throwing stones through windows. And if people were home when we did it, came out and shook their fists or worse, just stood there, looking at us the way you would a wind or an earthquake, nothing you could slow or stop, I'd freeze, feeling bad, until Peter screamed at me or yanked me so hard that I had no choice but to follow.

I could say I liked how smart Peter was, and I did. He could sit dead still for twenty-seven minutes of a thirty-minute comprehension test, then scan the reading and answer every question right before the teacher, furious, hovering over him and watching the clock, could snatch the paper away without the rest of us screaming foul. He could recite the periodic table of elements backwards, complete with atomic weights. He could build skyscrapers five feet high out of chalk and rubber cement jars and toothpicks and crayons that always stayed standing until anyone who wasn't him tried to touch them.

I could say I liked the way he treated everyone the same, which he did, in a way. He'd been the first in my grade—the only one, for a year or so—to hang out with the Mack sisters, who were still, at that point, the only African-Americans in our school. But he wasn't all that nice to the Macks, really. Just no nastier than he was to the rest of us.

No. I liked Peter for exactly the reason my mother and my teachers feared I did: because he was fearless, because he was cruel—although mostly to people who deserved it, when it wasn't Halloween—and most of all, because he really did seem capable of anything. So many of the people I knew seemed capable of nothing, for whatever reason. Capable of nothing.

Out on the whitecap-riddled Sound, the sun sank, and the Mountain turned red. It was like looking inside it, seeing it living. Shivering slightly in the wind, I hopped the Andersz' three stone steps and rang the bell.

"Just come in, Fuck!" I heard Peter yell from the basement, and I started to open the door, and Mr. Andersz opened it for me. He had his gray cardigan straight on his waist for once and his black hat was gone and his black-gray hair was wet and combed on his forehead, and I had the horrible, hilarious idea that he was going on a date.

"Andrew, come in," he said, sounding funny, too formal, the way he did at school. He didn't step back right away, either, and when he did, he put his hand against the mirror on the hallway wall, as though the house was rocking underneath him.

"Hey, Mr. Andersz," I said, wiping my feet on the shredded green mat that said something in Serbian. Downstairs, I could hear the burbling of the Dig Dug game, and I knew the Mack sisters had arrived. I flung my coat over Peter's green slicker on the coat rack, took a couple steps toward the basement door, turned around, and stopped.

Mr. Andersz had not moved, hadn't even taken his hand off the mirror, and now he was staring at it as though it was a spider frozen there.

"Are you all right, Mr. Andersz?" I asked, and he didn't respond. Then he made a sound, a sort of hiss, like a radiator when you switch it off.

"How many?" he muttered. I could barely hear him. "How many chances? As a teacher, you know there won't be many. You get two, maybe three moments in an entire year . . . Something's happened, there's been a fight or someone's sick or the soccer team won or something, and you're looking at a student . . . " His voice trailed off, leaving me with the way he said 'student.' He pronounced it "stu-DENT." It was one of the things we all made fun of, not mean fun, just fun. "You're looking at them," he said, "and suddenly, there they are. And it's them, and it's thrilling, terrifying, because you know you might have a chance . . . an opportunity. You can say something."

On the mirror, Mr. Andersz' hand twitched, and I noticed the sweat beading under the hair on his forehead. It reminded me of my dad, and I wondered if Mr. Andersz was drunk. Then I wondered if my dad was drunk, wherever he was. Downstairs, Jenny Mack yelled, "Get *off!*" in her fighting voice, happy-loud, and Kelly Mack said, "Good, come on, this is *boring.*"

"And as parent . . . " Mr. Andersz muttered. "How many? And what happens . . . the moment comes. . . but you're missing your wife. Just right then, just for a while. Or your friends. Maybe you're tired. It's just that day. It's rainy, you have meals to make, you're tired . . . There'll be another moment. Surely. You have years. Right? You have years . . . "

So fast and so silent was Peter's arrival in the basement doorway that I mistook him for a shadow from outside, didn't even realize he was there until he pushed me in the chest. "What's your deal?" he said.

I started to gesture at Mr. Andersz, thought better of it, shrugged. Footsteps clattered on the basement stairs, and then the Macks were in the room. Kelly had her tightly braided hair stuffed under a black, backward baseball cap. Her bare arms were covered in paste-on snake tattoos, and her face was dusted in white powder. Jenny wore a red sweater, black jeans. Her hair hung straight and shiny and dark, hovering just off her head and neck like a bird's crest, and I understood, for the first time, that she was pretty. Her eyes were bright green, wet and watchful.

"What are you supposed to be?" I said to Kelly, because suddenly I was uncomfortable looking at Jenny.

Kelly flung her arm out to point and did a quick, ridiculous shoulder-wriggle. It was nothing like her typical movements; I'd seen her dance. "Vanilla Ice," she said, and spun around.

"Let's go," Peter said, stepping past me and his father and tossing my mac on the floor so he could get to his slicker.

"You want candy, Andy?" Jenny teased, her voice sing-songy.

"Ho Ho?" I asked. I was talking, I suppose, to Mr. Andersz, who was still staring at his hand on the mirror. I didn't want him to be in the way. It made me nervous for him.

The word "Ho Ho" seemed to rouse him, though. He shoved himself free of the wall, shook his head as if awakening, and said, "Just a minute," very quietly.

Peter opened the front door, letting in the wind, and Mr. Andersz pushed it closed, not hard. But he leaned against it, and the Mack sisters stopped with their coats half on. Peter just stood beside him, his black hair sharp and pointy on his forehead like the tips of a spiked fence. But he looked more curious than angry.

Mr. Andersz lifted a hand to his eyes, squeezed them shut, opened them. Then he said, "Turn out your pockets."

Still, Peter's face registered nothing. He didn't respond to his father or glance at us. Neither Kelly nor I moved, either. Beside me, Jenny took a long, slow breath, as though she was clipping a wire on a bomb, and then she said, "Here, Mr. A," and she pulled the pockets of her gray coat inside out, revealing two sticks of Dentyne, two cigarettes, a ring of keys with a Seahawks whistle dangling amongst them, and a ticket-stub. I couldn't see what the ticket was from.

"Thank you, Jenny," Mr. Andersz said, but he didn't take the cigarettes, hardly even looked at her. He watched his son.

Very slowly, after a long time, Peter smiled. "Look at you," he said. "Being daddy." He pulled out the liner of his coat pockets. There was nothing in them at all.

"Pants," said Mr. Andersz.

"What do you think you're looking for, Big Bad Daddy?" Peter asked. "What do you think you're going to find?"

"Pants," Mr. Andersz said.

"And what will you do, do you think, if you find it?" But he turned out his pants pockets. There was nothing in those, either, not even keys or money.

For the first time since Peter had come upstairs, Mr. Andersz looked at the rest of us, and I shuddered. His face looked the same way my mother's had when I left the house: a little scared, but mostly sad. Permanently, stupidly sad.

"I want to tell you something," he said. If he spoke like this in the classroom, I thought, no one would wedge unbent paperclips in his chalkboard erasers anymore. "I won't have it. There will be no windows broken. There will be no little children terrorized—"

"That wasn't our fault," said Jenny, and she was right, in a way. We hadn't known anyone was hiding in those bushes when we toilet-papered them, and Peter had meant to light his cigarette, not the roll of toilet paper.

"Nothing lit on fire. No one bullied or hurt. I won't have it, because it's beneath you, do you understand? You're the smartest children I know." Abruptly, Mr. Andersz' hands flashed out and grabbed his son's shoulders. "Do you hear me? You're the smartest child I've ever seen."

For a second, they just stood there, Mr. Andersz clutching Peter's shoulders as though trying to steer a runaway truck, Peter completely blank.

Then, very slowly, Peter smiled. "Thanks, Dad," he said.

"Please," Mr. Andersz said, and Peter opened his mouth, and we all cringed.

But what he said was, "Okay," and he slipped past his father and out the door. I looked at the Mack sisters. Together, we watched Mr. Andersz in the doorway with his head tilted forward on his neck and his hands tight at his sides, like a diver at the Olympics getting ready for a back flip. He never moved, though, and eventually, we followed Peter out. I was last, and I thought I felt Mr. Andersz' hand on my back as I went by, but I wasn't sure, and when I glanced around, he was still just standing there, and the door swung shut.

I'd been inside the Andersz' house fifteen minutes, maybe less, but the wind had whipped the late afternoon light over the horizon, and the Mountain had faded from red to gray-black, motionless now on the surface of the water like an oil tanker, one of those massive, passing ships on which no people were visible, ever. I never liked my neighborhood, but I hated it after sundown, the city gone, the Sound indistinguishable from the black, starless sky, no one walking. It was like we were someone's toy set that had been closed up in its box and snapped shut for the night.

"Where are we going?" Kelly Mack said, her voice sharp, fed up. She'd been sick of us, lately. Sick of Peter.

"Yeah," I said, rousing myself. I didn't want to soap car-windows or throw rocks at street signs or put on rubber masks and scare trick or treaters, exactly, but those were the things we did. And we had no supplies.

Peter closed his eyes, leaned his head back, took a deep breath of the rushing air and held it. He looked almost peaceful. I couldn't remember seeing him that way. It was startling. Then he stuck one trembling arm out in front of him, pointed at me, and his eyes sprung open.

"*Do you know . . .* " he said, his voice deep, accented, a perfect imitation, "*what that bell does?*"

I clapped my hands. "*That bell. . .*" I said, in the closest I could get to the same voice, and the Mack sisters stared at us, baffled, which made me grin even harder, "*raises the dead.*"

"What are you babbling about?" said Kelly to Peter, but Jenny was looking at me, seawater-eyes curious and strange.

"You know Mr. Paars?" I asked her.

But of course she didn't. The Macks had moved here less than a year and a half ago, and I hadn't seen Mr. Paars, I realized, in considerably longer. Not since the night of the bell, in fact. I looked at Peter. His grin was as wide as mine felt. He nodded at me. We'd been friends a long time, I realized. Almost half my life.

Of course, I didn't say that. "A long time ago," I told the Macks, feeling like a longshoreman, a lighthouse keeper, someone with stories who lived by the sea, "there was this man. An old, white haired-man. He ate lutefisk— it's fish, it smells awful, I don't really know what it is—and stalked around the neighborhood, scaring everybody."

"He had this cane," Peter said, and I waited for him to go on, join me in the telling, but he didn't.

"All black," I said. "Kind of scaly. Ribbed, or something. It didn't look like a cane. And it had this silver dog's head on it, with fangs. A doberman—"

"Anyway . . . " said Kelly Mack, though Jenny seemed to be enjoying listening.

"He used to bop people with it. Kids. Homeless people. Whoever got in his way. He stomped around 15th Street terrorizing everyone. Two years ago, on the first Halloween we were allowed out alone, right about this time of night, Peter and I spotted him coming out of the hardware store. It's not there anymore, it's that empty space next to the place where the movie theatre used to be. Anyway, we saw him there, and we followed him home."

Peter waved us out of his yard toward the locks. Again, I waited, but when he glanced at me, the grin was gone. His face was normal, neutral, maybe, and he didn't say anything.

"He lives down there," I said, gesturing to the south toward the Sound. "Way past all the other houses. Past the end of the street. Practically in the water."

Despite what Peter had said, we didn't head that way. Not then. We wandered toward the Locks, into the park. The avenue between the pine trees was empty except for a scatter of solitary bums on benches, wrapping themselves in shredded jackets and newspapers as the night nailed itself down and the dark billowed around us in the gusts of wind like the sides of a tent. In the roiling trees, black birds perched on the branches, silent as gargoyles.

"There aren't any other houses that close to Mr. Paars'," I said. "The street turns to dirt, and it's always wet because it's down by the water. There are these long, empty lots full of weeds, and a couple sheds, I don't know what's in them or who owns them. Anyway, right where the pavement ends, Peter and I dropped back and just kind of hung out near the last house until Mr. Paars made it to his yard. God, Peter, you remember his yard?"

Instead of answering, Peter lead us between the low stone buildings to the canal, where we watched the water swallow the last streaks of daylight like some monstrous whale gulping plankton. The only boats in the slips were two sailboats, sails furled, rocking as the waves slapped against them. The only person I saw on either stood at the stern of the boat closest to us, head hooded in a green oil-slicker, face aimed out to sea.

"Think I could hit him from here?" said Peter, and I flinched, looked at his fists expecting to see stones, but he was just asking. "Tell them the rest," he said.

I glanced at the Macks and was startled to see them holding hands, leaning against the rail over the canal, though they were watching us, not the water. "Come on, already," Kelly said, but Jenny just raised her eyebrows at me. Behind her, seagulls dipped and tumbled on the wind like shreds of cloud that had been ripped loose.

"We waited, I don't know, a while. It was cold. Remember how cold it was? We were wearing winter coats and mittens. It wasn't windy like this, but it was freezing. At least that made the dirt less muddy when we finally went down there. We passed the sheds and the trees, and there was no one, I mean no one, around. Too cold for any trick or treating anywhere around here, even if anyone was going to. And there wasn't anywhere to go on that street, regardless.

"Anyway. It's weird. Everything's all flat down there, and then right as you get near the Paars place, this little forest springs up, all these thick firs. We couldn't really see anything."

"Except that it was light," Peter murmured.

"Yeah. Bright light. Mr. Paars had his yard floodlit, for intruders, we figured. We thought he was probably paranoid. So we snuck off the road when we got close and went into the trees. In there, it was wet. Muddy, too. My mom was so mad when I got home. Pine needles sticking to me everywhere. She said I looked like I'd been tarred and feathered. We hid in this little grove, looked into the lawn, and we saw the bell."

Now Peter turned around, his hands flung wide to either side. "Biggest fucking bell you've ever seen in your life," he said.

"What are you talking about?" said Kelly.

"It was in this . . . pavilion," I started, not sure how to describe it. "Gazebo, I guess. All white and round, like a carousel, except the only thing inside was this giant white bell, like a church bell, hanging from the ceiling on a chain. And all the lights in the yard were aimed at it."

"Weird," said Jenny, leaning against her sister.

"Yeah. And that house. It's real dark, and real old. Black wood or something, all sort of falling apart. Two stories, kind of big. It looked like four or five of the sheds we passed sort of stacked on top of each other and squashed together. But the lawn was beautiful. Green, mowed perfectly, like a baseball stadium."

"Kind of," Peter whispered. He turned from the canal and wandered away again, back between buildings down the tree-lined lane.

A shiver swept up the skin on my back as I realized, finally, why we were going back to the Paars' house. I'd forgotten, until that moment, how scared we'd been. How scared Peter had been. Probably, Peter had been thinking about this for two years.

"It was all so strange," I said to the Macks, all of us watching the bums in their rattling paper blankets and the birds clinging by their talons to the branches and eyeing us as we passed. "All that outside light, the house falling apart and no lights on in there, no car in the driveway, that huge bell. So we just looked for a long time. Then Peter said—I remember this, exactly—'*He just leaves something shaped like that hanging there. And he expects us not to ring it.*'

"Then, finally, we realized what was in the grass."

By now, we were out of the park, back among the duplexes, and the wind had turned colder, though it wasn't freezing, exactly. In a way, it felt good, fresh, like a hard slap in the face.

"I want a shrimp-and-chips," Kelly said, gesturing over her shoulder toward 15th Street, where the little fry-stand still stayed open next to the Dairy Queen, although the Dairy Queen had been abandoned.

"I want to go see this Paars house," said Jenny. "Stop your whining." She sounded cheerful, fierce, the way she did when she played Dig Dug or threw her hand in the air at school. She was smart, too, not Peter-smart, but as smart as me, at least. And I think she'd seen the trace of fear in Peter, barely there but visible in his skin like a fossil, something long dead and never before seen, and it fascinated her. That's what I was thinking when she reached out casually and grabbed my hand. Then I stopped thinking at all. "Tell me about the grass," she said.

"It was like a circle," I said, my fingers still, my palm flat against hers. Even when she squeezed, I held still. I didn't know what to do, and I didn't want Peter to turn around. If Kelly had noticed, she didn't say anything. "Cut right in the grass. A pattern. A circle, with this upside down triangle inside it, and—"

"How do you know it was upside down?" Jenny asked.

"What?"

"How do you know you were even looking at it the right way?"

"Shut up," said Peter, quick and hard, not turning around, leading us onto the street that dropped down to the Sound, to the Paars house. Then he did turn around, and he saw our hands. But he didn't say anything. When he was facing forward again, Jenny squeezed once more, and I gave a feeble squeeze back.

We walked half a block in silence, but that just made me more nervous. I could feel Jenny's thumb sliding along the outside of mine, and it made me tingly, terrified. I said, "Upside down. Right-side up. Whatever. It was a symbol, a weird one. It looked like an eye."

"Old dude must have had a hell of a lawn-mower," Kelly muttered, glanced at Peter's back, and stopped talking, just in time, I thought. Mr. Andersz was right. She was smart, too.

"It kind of made you not want to put your foot in the grass," I continued. "I don't know why. It just looked wrong. Like it really could see you. I can't explain."

"Didn't make *me* want not to put my foot in the grass," Peter said.

I felt Jenny look at me. Her mouth was six inches or so from my hair, my ear. It was too much. My hand twitched and I let go. Blushing, I glanced at her. She looked surprised, and she drifted away toward her sister.

"That's true," I said, wishing I could call Jenny back. "Peter stepped right out."

On our left, the last of the duplexes slid away, and we came to the end of the pavement. In front of us, the dirt road rolled down the hill, red-brown and wet and bumpy, like some stretched, cut-out tongue on the ground. I remembered the way Peter's duck-boots had seemed to float on the surface of Mr. Paars' floodlit green lawn, as though he was walking on water.

"Hey," I said, though Peter had already stepped onto the dirt and was strolling, fast and purposeful, down the hill. "Peter," I called after him, though I followed, of course. The Macks were beside but no longer near me. "When's the last time you saw him? Mr. Paars?"

He turned around, and he was smiling, now, the smile that scared me. "Same time you did, Bubba," he said. "Two years ago tonight."

I blinked, stood still, and the wind lashed me like the end of a twisted-up towel. "How do you know when I last saw him?"

Peter shrugged. "Am I wrong?"

I didn't answer. I watched Peter's face, the dark swirling around and over it, shaping it, like rushing water over stone.

"He hasn't been anywhere. Not on 15th Street. Not at the Black Anchor. Nowhere. I've been watching."

"Maybe he doesn't live there anymore," Jenny said carefully. She was watching Peter, too.

"There's a car," Peter said. "A Lincoln. Long and black. Practically a limo."

"I've seen that car," I said. "I've seen it drive by my house, right at dinner time."

"It goes down there," said Peter, gesturing toward the trees, the water, the Paars house. "Like I said, I've been watching."

And of course, he had been, I thought. If his father had let him, he'd probably have camped right here, or in the gazebo under the bell. In fact, it seemed impossible to me, given everything I knew about Peter, that he'd let two years go by.

"Exactly what happened to you two down there?" Kelly asked.

"Tell them now," said Peter. "There isn't going to be any talking once we get down there. Not until we're all finished." Dropping into a crouch, he picked at the cold, wet dirt with his fingers, watched the ferries drifting out of downtown toward Bainbridge Island, Vashon. You couldn't really make out the boats from there, just the clusters of lights on the water like clouds of lost, doomed fireflies.

"Even the grass was weird," I said, remembering the weight of my sopping pants against my legs. "It was so wet. I mean, everywhere was wet, as usual, but this was like wading in a pond. You put your foot down and the whole lawn rippled. It made the eye look like it was winking. At first we were kind of hunched over, sort of hiding, which was ridiculous in all that light. I didn't want to walk in the circle, but Peter just strolled right through it. He called me a baby because I went the long way around."

"I called you a baby because you were being one," Peter said, but not meanly, really.

"We kept expecting lights to fly on in the house. Or dogs to come out. It just seemed like there would be dogs. But there weren't. We got up to the gazebo, which was the only place in the whole yard with shadows, because it was surrounded by all these trees. *Weird* trees. They were kind of stunted. Not pines, either, they're like birch trees, I guess. But short. And their bark is black."

"Felt weird, too," Peter muttered, straightening up, wiping his hands down his coat. "That bark just crumbles when you rub it in your hands, like one of those soft block-erasers, you know what I mean?"

"We must have stood there ten minutes. More. It was so quiet. You could hear the Sound, a little, although there aren't any waves there or anything. You could hear the pine trees dripping, or maybe it was the lawn. But there weren't any birds. And there wasn't anything moving in that house. Finally, Peter started toward the bell. He took exactly one step into the gazebo, and one of those dwarf-trees walked right off its roots into his path, and both of us started screaming."

"What?" said Jenny.

"I didn't scream," said Peter. "And he hit me."

"He didn't hit you," I said.

"Yes he did."

"Could you shut up and let Andrew finish?" said Kelly, and Peter lunged, grabbing her slicker in his fists and shoving her hard and then yanking her forward so that her head snapped backward and then snapped into place again.

It had happened so fast that neither Jenny or I had moved, but Jenny hurtled forward now, raking her nails down Peter's face, and he said, "*Ow!*" and fell back, and she threw her arms around Kelly's shoulders. For a few seconds, they stood like that, and then Kelly put her own arms up and eased Jenny away. To my astonishment, I saw that she was laughing.

"I don't think I'd do that again, if I were you," she said to Peter, her laughter quick and hard, as though she was spitting teeth.

Peter put a hand to his cheek, gazing at the blood that came away on his fingers. "Ow," he said again.

"Let's go home," Jenny said to her sister.

No one answered right away. Then Peter said, "Don't." After a few seconds, when no one reacted, he said, "You've got to see the house." He was going to say more, I think, but what else was there to say? I felt bad without knowing why. He was like a planet we visited, cold and rocky and probably lifeless, and we kept coming because it was all so strange, so different than what we knew. He looked at me, and what I was thinking must have flashed in my face, because he blinked in surprise, turned away, and started down the road without looking back. We all followed. Planet, dark star, whatever he was, he created orbits.

"So the tree hit Peter," Jenny Mack said quietly when we were halfway down the hill, almost to the sheds.

"It wasn't a tree. It just seemed like a tree. I don't know how we didn't see him there. He had to have been watching us the whole time. Maybe he knew we'd followed him. He just stepped out of the shadows and kind of whacked Peter across the chest with his cane. That black dog-head cane. He did kind of look like a tree. His skin was all gnarly, kind of dark. If you rubbed him between your fingers, he'd probably have crumbled, too. And his hair was so white.

"And his voice. It was like a bullfrog, maybe even deeper. He spoke real slow. He said, '*Boy. Do you know what that bell does?*' And then he did the most amazing thing of all. The scariest thing. He looked at both of us, real slow. Then he dropped his cane. Just dropped it to his side. And he smiled, like he was daring us to go ahead. '*That bell raises the dead. Right up out of the ground.*'"

"Look at these," Kelly Mack murmured as we walked between the sheds.

"Raises the dead," I said.

"Yeah, I heard you. These are amazing."

And they were. I'd forgotten. The most startling thing, really, was that they were still standing. They'd all sunk into the swampy grass on at least one side, and none of them had roofs, not whole roofs, anyway, and the window-slots gaped, and the wind made a rattle as it rolled through them like a wave over seashells, over empty things that hadn't been empty always. They were too small to have been boat sheds, I thought, had to have been for tools and things. But tools to do what?

In a matter of steps, the sheds were behind us, between us and the homes we knew, the streets we walked. We reached the ring of pines around the Paars house, and it was different, worse. I didn't realize how, but Peter did.

"No lights," he said.

For a while, we just stood in the blackness while saltwater and pine-resin smells glided over us like a mist. There wasn't any moon, but the water beyond the house reflected what light there was, so we could see the long, black Lincoln in the dirt driveway, the house and the gazebo beyond it. After a minute or so, we could make out the bell, too, hanging like some bloated, white bat from the gazebo ceiling.

"It *is* creepy," Jenny said.

"Ya think?" I said, but I didn't mean to, it was just what I imagined Peter would have said if he were saying anything. "Peter, I think Mr. Paars is gone. Moved, or something."

"Good," he said. "Then he won't mind." He stepped out onto the lawn and said, "Fuck."

"What?" My shoulders hunched, but Peter just shook his head.

"Grass. It's a lot longer. And it's wet as hell."

"What happened after '*That bell raises the dead?*'" Jenny asked.

I didn't answer right away. I wasn't sure what Peter wanted me to say.

But he just squinted at the house, didn't even seem to be listening. I almost took Jenny's hand. I wanted to. "We ran."

"Both of you? Hey, Kell . . . "

But Kelly was already out on the grass next to Peter, smirking as her feet sank. Peter glanced at her cautiously. Actually uncertain, for once. "You would have, too," he said.

"I might have," said Kelly.

Then we were all on the grass, holding still, listening. The wind rushed through the trees as though filling a vacuum. I thought I could hear the Sound, not waves, just the dead, heavy wet. But there were no gulls, no bugs.

Once more, Peter strolled straight for that embedded circle in the grass, still visible despite the depth of the lawn, like a manta-ray half-buried in seaweed. When Peter's feet crossed the corners of the upside-down triangle—the tear-ducts of the eye—I winced, then felt silly. For all I knew, it was a corporate logo; it looked about that menacing. I started forward, too. The Macks came with me. I walked in the circle, though I skirted the edge of the triangle. Step on a crack and all. I didn't look behind to see what the Macks did, I was too busy watching Peter as his pace picked up. He was practically running, straight for the gazebo, and then he stopped.

"Hey," he said.

I'd seen it, too, and I felt my knees lock as my nervousness intensified. In the lone upstairs window, there'd been a flicker. Maybe. Just one, for a single second, and then it was gone again. "I saw it," I called, but Peter wasn't listening to me. He was moving straight toward the front door. And anyway, I realized, he hadn't been looking upstairs.

"What the hell's he doing?" Kelly said as she strolled past me, but she didn't stop for an answer. Jenny did, though.

"Andrew, what's going on?" she said, and I looked at her eyes, green and shadowy as the grass, but that just made me edgier, still.

I shook my head. For a moment, Jenny stood beside me. Finally, she shrugged and followed her sister. None of them looked back, which probably meant that there *hadn't* been rustling behind us just now, back in the pines. When I whipped my head around, I saw nothing but trees and twitching shadows.

"Here, puss-puss-puss," Peter called softly. If the grass had been less wet and I'd been less unsettled, I'd have flopped on my back and flipped my feet in the air at him, the seal's send-off. Instead, I came forward.

The house, like the sheds, seemed to have sunk sideways into the ground. With its filthy windows and rotting planks, it looked like the abandoned hull of a beached ship. Around it, the leafless branches of the dwarf-trees danced like the limbs of paper skeletons.

"Now, class," said Peter, still very quietly. "What's wrong with this picture?"

"I assume you mean other than giant bells, weird eyeballs in the grass, empty sheds, and these whammy-ass trees," Kelly said, but Peter ignored her.

"He means the front door," said Jenny, and of course she was right.

I don't even know how Peter noticed. It was under an overhang, so that the only light that reached it reflected off the ground. But there was no doubt. The door was open. Six inches, tops. The scratched brass of the knob glinted dully, like an eye.

"Okay," I said. "So the door didn't catch when he went in, and he didn't notice."

"When who went in?" said Peter, mocking. "Thought you said he moved."

The wind kicked up, and the door glided back another few inches, then sucked itself shut with a click.

"Guess that settles that," I said, knowing it didn't even before the curtains came streaming out the single front window, gray and gauzy as cigarette smoke as they floated on the breeze. They hung there a few seconds, then glided to rest against the side of the house when the wind expired.

"Guess it does," said Peter softly, and he marched straight up the steps, pushed open the door, and disappeared into the Paars house.

None of the rest of us moved or spoke. Around us, tree-branches tapped against each other and the side of the house. For the second time I sensed someone behind me and spun around. Night-dew sparkled in the lawn like broken glass, and one of the shadows of the towering pines seemed to shiver back as though the trees had inhaled it. Otherwise, there was nothing. I thought about Mr. Paars, that dog-head cane with its silver fangs.

"What's he trying to prove?" Kelly asked, a silly question where Peter was concerned, really. It wasn't about proving. We all knew that.

Jenny said, "He's been in there a long time," and Peter stuck his head out the window, the curtain floating away from him.

"Come see this," he said, and ducked back inside.

Hesitating, I knew, was pointless. We all knew it. We went up the stairs together, and the door drifted open before we even touched it. "Wow," said Kelly, staring straight ahead, and Jenny took my hand again, and then we were all inside. "Wow," Kelly said again.

Except for a long, wooden table folded and propped against the staircase like a lifeboat, all the furniture we could see had been draped in white sheets. The sheets rose and rearranged themselves in the breeze, which was constant and everywhere, because all the windows had been flung wide open. Leaves chased each other across the dirt-crusted hardwood floor, and scraps of paper flapped in mid-air like giant moths before settling on the staircase or the backs of chairs or blowing out the windows.

Peter appeared in a doorway across the foyer from us, his black hair bright against the deeper blackness of the rooms behind him. "Don't miss the den," he said. "I'm going to go look at the kitchen." Then he was gone again.

Kelly had started away, now, too, wandering into the living room to our right, running her fingers over the tops of a covered couch as she passed it. One of the paintings on the wall, I noticed, had been covered rather than removed, and I wondered what it was. Kelly drew up the cover, peered beneath it, then dropped it and stepped deeper into the house. I started to follow, but Jenny pulled me the other way, and we went left into what must have been Mr. Paars' den.

"Whoa," Jenny said, and her fingers slid between mine and tightened.

In the dead center of the room, amidst discarded file folders that lay where they'd been tossed and empty envelopes with plastic address-windows that flapped and chattered when the wind filled them, sat an enormous, oak, roll-top desk. The top was gone, broken away, and it lay against the room's lone window like the cracked shell of a dinosaur egg. On the surface of the desk, in black, felt frames, a set of six photographs had been arranged in a semi-circle.

"It's like the top of a tombstone," Jenny murmured. "You know what I mean? Like a . . . what do you call it?"

"Family vault," I said. "Mausoleum."

"One of those."

Somehow, the fact that two of the frames turned out to be empty made the array even more unsettling. The other four held individual pictures of what had to be brothers and one sister—they all had flying white hair, razor-blue eyes—standing, each in turn, on the top step of the gazebo outside, with the great bell looming behind them, bright white and all out of proportion, like the Mountain on a too-clear day.

"Andrew," Jenny said, her voice nearly a whisper, and in spite of the faces in the photographs and the room we were in, I felt it all over me. "Why Struwwelpeter?"

"What?" I said, mostly just to make her speak again.

"Struwwelpeter. Why does Mr. Andersz call him that?"

"Oh. It's from some kids' book. My mom actually had it when she was little. She said it was about some boy who got in trouble because he wouldn't cut his hair or cut his nails."

Jenny narrowed her eyes. "What does that have to do with anything?"

"I don't know. Except my mom said the pictures in the book were really scary. She said Struwwelpeter looked like Freddy Krueger with a 'fro."

Jenny burst out laughing, but she stopped fast. Neither of us, I think, liked the way laughter sounded in that room, in that house, with those black-bordered faces staring at us. "*Struwwelpeter*," she said, rolling the name carefully on her tongue, like a little kid daring to lick a frozen flagpole.

"It's what my mom called me when I was little," said Peter from the doorway, and Jenny's fingers clenched hard and then fell free of mine. Peter didn't move toward us. He just stood there while we watched, paralyzed. After a few, long seconds, he added, "When I kicked the shit out of barbers, because I hated having my haircut. Then when I was just being bad. She'd say that instead of screaming at me. It made me cry." From across the foyer, in the living room, maybe, we heard a single, soft bump, as though something had fallen over.

With a shrug, Peter stepped past us back into the foyer. We followed, not touching, now, not even looking at each other. I felt guilty, amazed, strange. When we passed the windows the curtains billowed up and brushed across us.

"Hey, Kelly," Peter whispered loudly into the living room. He whispered it again, then abruptly turned our way and said, "You think he's dead?"

"Looks like it." I glanced down the hallway toward the kitchen, then into the shadows in the living room, which seemed to have shifted, somehow, the sheet some way different as it lay across the couch. I couldn't place the feeling; it was like watching an actor playing a corpse, knowing he was alive, trying to catch him breathing.

"But the car's here," Peter said. "The Lincoln. Hey, *Kelly!*" His shout made me wince, and Jenny cringed back toward the front door, but she shouted, too.

"Kell? *Kell?*"

"Oh, what is *that?*" I murmured, my whole spine twitching like a severed electrical wire, and when Jenny and Peter looked at me, I pointed upstairs.

"Wh—" Jenny started, and then it happened again, and both of them saw it. From under the half-closed door at the top of the staircase—the only door we could see from where we were—came a sudden slash of light which disappeared instantly, like a snake's tongue flashing in and out.

We stood there at least a minute, maybe more. Even Peter looked uncertain; not scared, quite, but something had happened to his face. I couldn't place it right then. It made me nervous, though. And it made me like him more than I had in a long, long time.

Then, without warning, Peter was halfway up the stairs, his feet stomping dust out of each step as he slammed them down, saying, "Fucking hilarious, Kelly. Here I come. Ready or not." He stopped halfway up and turned to glare at us. Mostly at me. "Come on."

"Let's go," I said to Jenny, reached out on my own for the first time and touched her elbow, but to my surprise she jerked it away from me. "Jenny, she's up there."

"I don't think so," she whispered.

"Come *on*," Peter hissed.

"Andrew, something's wrong. Stay here."

I looked into her face. Smart, steely Jenny Mack, first girl ever to look at me like that, first girl I'd ever wanted to. And right then, for the only time in my life, I felt—within *me*—the horrible thrill of Peter's power, and realized I knew the secret of it. It wasn't bravery and it wasn't smarts, although he had both those things in spades. It was simply the willingness to trade. At any given moment, Peter Andersz would trade anyone for anything, or at least could convince people that he would. Knowing you could do that, I thought, would be like holding a grenade, tossing it back and forth in the terrified face of the world.

I looked at Jenny's eyes, filling with tears, and I wanted to kiss her, though I couldn't even imagine how to initiate something like that. What I said, in my best Peter-voice, was, "I'm going upstairs. Coming or staying?"

I can't explain. I didn't mean anything. It felt like playacting, no more real than holding her hand had been. We were just throwing on costumes, dancing around each other, scaring each other. Trick or treat.

"KELLY?" Jenny called past me, blinking, crying openly, now, and I started to reach for her again, and she shoved me, hard, toward the stairs.

"Hurry up," said Peter, with none of the triumph I might have expected in his voice.

I went up, and we clumped side by side to the top of the stairs. When we reached the landing, I looked back at Jenny. She was propped in the front door, one hand on the doorknob and the other wiping at her eyes as she jerked her head from side to side, looking for her sister.

At our feet, light licked under the door again. Peter held up a hand, and we stood together and listened. We heard wind, low and hungry, and now I was sure I could hear the Sound lapping against the edge of the continent, crawling over the lip of it.

"OnetwothreeBOO!" Peter screamed and flung open the door, which banged against a wall inside and bounced back. Peter kicked it open again, and we lunged through into what must have been a bedroom once and was now just a room, a blank space, with nothing in it at all.

Even before the light swept over us again, from *outside*, from the window, I realized what it was. "Lighthouse," I said, breathless. "Greenpoint Light."

Peter grinned. "Oh, yeah. Halloween."

Every year, the suburbs north of us set Greenpoint Light running again on Halloween, just for fun. One year, they'd even rented ferries and decked them out with seaweed and parents in pirate costumes and floated them just offshore, ghost-ships for the kiddies. We'd seen them skirting our suburb on their way up the coast.

"Do you think—" I started, and Peter grabbed me hard by the elbow. "Ow," I said.

"Listen," snapped Peter.

I heard the house groan as it shifted. I heard paper flapping somewhere downstairs, the front door tapping against its frame or the inside wall as it swung on the wind.

"*Listen*," Peter whispered, and this time I heard it. Very low. Very faint, like a finger rubbed along the lip of a glass, but unmistakable once you realized what it was. Outside, in the yard, someone had just lifted the tongue of the bell and tapped it, oh so gently, against the side.

I stared at Peter, and he stared back. Then he leapt to the window, peering down. I thought he was going to punch the glass loose from the way his shoulders jerked.

"Well?" I said.

"All I can see is the roof." He shoved the window even farther open than it already was. "*Clever girls!*" he screamed, and waited. For laughter, maybe, a full-on bong of the bell, something. Abruptly, he turned to me, and the light rolled across him, waist-high, and when it receded, he looked different, damp with it. "Clever girls."

I whirled, stepped into the hall, looked down. The front door was open, and Jenny was gone. "Peter?" I whispered, and I heard him swear as he emerged onto the landing beside me. "You think they're outside?"

Peter didn't answer right away. He had his hands jammed in his pockets, his eyes cast down at the floor. He shuffled in place. "The thing is, Andrew," he said, "there's nothing to do."

"What are you talking about?"

"There's nothing to do."

"Find the girls?"

He shrugged.

"Ring the bell?"

"They rang it."

"You're the one who brought us out here. What were you expecting?"

He glanced back at the bedroom's bare walls, the rectangular, dustless space in the floor where, until very recently, a bed or rug must have been, the empty light fixture overhead. Struwwelpeter. My friend. "Opposition," he said, and shuffled off down the hall.

"Where are you going?" I called after him.

He turned, and the look on his face stunned me, it had been years since I'd seen it. The last time was in second grade, right after he punched Robert Case, who was twice his size, in the face and ground one of Robert's eyeglass-lenses into his eye. The last time anyone who knew him had dared to fight him. He looked . . . sorry.

"Coming?" he said.

I almost followed him. But I felt bad about leaving Jenny. And I wanted to see her and Kelly out on the lawn, pointing through the window at us and laughing. And I didn't want to be in that house anymore. And it was exhausting being with Peter, trying to read him, dancing clear of him.

"I'll be outside," I said.

He shrugged and disappeared through the last unopened door at the end of the hall. I listened for a few seconds, heard nothing, turned, and started downstairs. "Hey, Jenny?" I called, but got no answer. I was three steps from the bottom before I realized what was wrong.

In the middle of the foyer floor, amidst a swirl of leaves and paper, Kelly Mack's black baseball cap lay upside down like an empty tortoise shell. "Um," I said to no one, to myself, took one more uncertain step down, and the front door swung back on its hinges.

I just stared, at first. I couldn't even breathe, let alone scream, it was like I had an apple-core lodged in my throat. I just stared into the white spray-paint on the front door, the triangle-within-a-circle. A wet, wide-open eye. My legs wobbled, and I grabbed for the banister, slipped down to the bottom step, held myself still. I should scream, I thought. I should get Peter down here, and both of us should run. I didn't even see the hand until it clamped hard around my mouth.

For a second, I couldn't do anything at all, and that was way too long, because before I could lunge away or bite down, a second hand snaked around my waist, and I was yanked off my feet into the blackness to my left and slammed against the living room wall.

I wasn't sure when I'd closed my eyes, but now I couldn't make them open. My head rang, and my skin felt tingly, tickly, as though it was dissolving into the atoms that made it up, all of them racing in a billion different directions, and soon there'd be nothing left of me, just a scatter of energy and a spot on Mr. Paars' dusty, decaying floor.

"Did I hurt you?" whispered a voice I knew, close to my ears. It still took me a long time to open my eyes. "Just nod or shake your head."

Slowly, forcing my eyes open, I nodded.

"Good. Now sssh," said Mr. Andersz, and released me.

Behind him, both Mack sisters stood grinning.

"You like the cap in the middle of the floor?" Kelly said. "The cap was a good touch, no?"

"Sssh," Mr. Andersz said. "Please. I beg you."

"You should see you," Jenny whispered, sliding up close. "You look so damn scared."

"What's—"

"He followed us to see if we were doing anything horrible. He saw us come in here, and he had this idea to get back at Peter."

I gaped at Jenny, and then at Mr. Andersz, who was peering very carefully around the corner, up the stairs.

"Not to get back," he said, so serious. It was the same voice he'd used in his own front hallway earlier that evening. He'd never looked more like his son than he did right then. "To reach out. Reach him. Someone's got to do something. He's a good boy. He could be. Now, please. Don't spoil this."

Everything about Mr. Andersz at that moment astounded me. But watching him revealed nothing further. He stood at the edge of the living room, shoulders hunched, hair tucked tight under his dock-worker's cap, waiting. Slowly, my gaze swung back to Jenny, who continued to grin in my direction, but not at me, certainly not with me. And I knew I'd lost her.

"This was about Peter," I said. "You all could have just stuck your heads out and waved me down."

"Yep," said Jenny, and watched Mr. Andersz, not me.

Upstairs, a door creaked, and Peter's voice rang out. "Hey, Andrew."

To Jenny's surprise and Mr. Andersz' horror, I almost answered. I stepped forward, opened my mouth. I'm sure Jenny thought I was getting back at her, turning the tables again, but mostly, I didn't like what Mr. Andersz was doing. I think I sensed the danger in it. I might have been the only one.

But I was twelve. And Peter certainly deserved it. And Mr. Andersz was my teacher, and my friend's father. I closed my mouth, sank back into the shadows, and did not move again until it was over.

"Andrew, I *know you can hear me!*" Peter shouted, stepping onto the landing. He came, clomp clomp clomp, toward the stairs. "*Ann-drew!*" Then, abruptly, we heard him laugh. Down he came, his shoes clattering over the steps. I thought he might charge past us, but he stopped right where I had.

Beside the couch, under the draped painting, Kelly Mack pointed at her own hatless head and mouthed, "Oh, yeah."

But it was the eye on the door, I thought, not the cap. Only the eye would have stopped him, because like me—and faster than me—Peter would have realized that neither Mack sister, smart as they were, would have thought of it. Even if they'd had spray paint. *Mr. Andersz had brought spray paint?* Clearly, he'd been planning this—or something like this—for quite some time. If he was the one who'd done it, that is.

"What the fuck," Peter muttered. He came down a step. Another. His feet touched flat floor, and still Mr. Andersz held his post.

Then, very quietly, Mr. Andersz said, "Boo."

It was as if he'd punched an ejector-seat button. Peter flew through the front door, hands flung up to ward off the eye as he sailed past it. He was fifteen feet from the house, still flying, when he realized what he'd heard. We all saw it hit him. He jerked in mid-air like a hooked marlin reaching the end of a harpoon rope.

For a few seconds, he just stood in the wet grass with his back to us, quivering. Kelly had sauntered past Mr. Andersz onto the front porch, laughing. Mr. Andersz, I noticed, was smiling, too, weakly. Even Jenny was laughing quietly beside me.

But I was watching Peter's back, his whole body vibrating like an imploded building after the charge has gone off, right at the moment of collapse. "No," I said.

When Peter finally turned around, though, his face was his regular face, inscrutable, a little pale. The spikes in his hair looked almost silly in the shadows, and also made him look younger. A naughty little boy. Calvin with no Hobbes.

"So he *is* dead," Peter said.

Mr. Andersz stepped outside. Kelly was slapping her leg, but no one paid her any attention.

"Son," said Mr. Andersz, and he stretched one hand out, as though to call Peter to him. "I'm sorry. It was . . . I thought you might laugh."

"He's dead, right?"

The smile was gone from Mr. Andersz' face now, and from Jenny's, I noted when I glanced her way. "Kelly, shut up," I heard her say to her sister, and Kelly stopped giggling.

"Did you know he used to teach at the school?" Mr. Andersz asked, startling me.

"Mr. Paars?"

"Sixth grade science. Biology, especially. Years ago. Kids didn't like him. Yes, Peter, he died a week or so ago. He'd been very sick. We got a notice about it at school."

"Then he won't mind," said Peter, too quietly, "if I go ahead and ring that bell. Right?"

Mr. Andersz didn't know about the bell, I realized. He didn't understand. I watched him look at his son, watched the weight he always seemed to be carrying settle back around his shoulders, lock into place like a yoke. He bent forward a little.

"My son," he said. Uselessly.

So I shoved past him. I didn't mean to push him, I just needed him out of the way, and anyway, he gave no resistance, bent back like a plant.

"Peter, don't do it," I said.

The eyes, black and mesmerizing, swung down on me. "Oh. Andrew. Forgot you were here."

It was, of course, the cruelest thing he could have said, the source of his power over me and the reason I was with him (other than the fact that I liked him, I mean). It was the thing I feared most, in general, no matter where I was.

"*That bell. . .*" I said, thinking of the dog's-head cane, that deep and frozen voice, but thinking more, somehow, about my friend, rocketing away from us now at incomprehensible speed. Because that's what he seemed to be doing, to me.

"Wouldn't it be great?" said Peter. And then, unexpectedly, he grinned. He would never forget I was there, I realized. Couldn't. I was all he had.

He turned and walked straight across the grass. The Mack sisters and Mr. Andersz followed, all of them seeming to float in the long, wet green like seabirds skimming the surface of the ocean. I did not go with them. I had the feel of Jenny's fingers in mine, and the sounds of flapping paper and whirling leaves in my ears, and Peter's last, surprising smile floating in front of my eyes, and it was enough, too much, an astonishing Halloween.

"This thing's freezing," I heard Peter say, while his father and the Macks fanned out around him, facing the house and me. He was facing away, toward the trees. "Feel this." He held the tongue of the bell toward Kelly Mack, but she'd gone silent, now, watching him, and she shook her head.

"Ready or not," he said. Then he reared back and rammed the bell-tongue home.

Instinctively, I flung my hands up to my ears, but the effect was disappointing, particularly to Peter. It sounded like a dinner bell, high, a little tinny, something that might call kids or a dog out of the water or the woods at bedtime. Peter slammed the tongue against the side of the bell one more time, dropped it, and the peal floated away over the Sound, dissipating into the salt air.

For a few breaths, barely any time at all, we all stood where we were. Then Jenny Mack said, "Oh." I saw her hand snake out, grab her sister's, and her sister looked up, right at me, I thought. The two Macks stared at each other. Then they were gone, hurtling across the yard, straight across that wide-open white eye, flying toward the forest.

Peter whirled, looked at me, and his mouth opened, a little. I couldn't hear him, but I saw him murmur, "Wow," and a new smile exploded, one I couldn't even fathom, and he was gone, too, sprinting for the trees, passing the Macks as they all vanished into the shadows.

"Uh," said Mr. Andersz, backing, backing, and his expression confused me most of all. He was almost laughing. "I'm so sorry," he said. "We didn't realize . . . " He turned and chased after his son. And still, somehow, I thought they'd all been looking at me, until I heard the single, sharp thud from the porch behind me. Wood hitting wood. Cane-into-wood.

I didn't turn around. Not then. What for? I knew what was behind me. Even so, I couldn't get my legs to move, quite, not until I heard a second thud, closer this time, as though the thing on the porch had stepped fully out of the house, making its slow, steady way toward me. Stumbling, I kicked myself forward, put a hand down in the wet grass and the mud closed over it like a mouth. When I jerked it free, it made a disappointed, sucking sound, and I heard a sort of sigh behind me, another thud, and I ran, all the way to the woods.

Hours later, we were still huddled together in the Andersz' kitchen, wolfing down Ho Hos and hot chocolate. Jenny and Kelly and Peter kept laughing, erupting into cloudbursts of excited conversation, laughing some more. Mr. Andersz laughed, too, as he boiled more water and spooned marshmallows into our mugs and told us.

The man the bell had called forth, he said, was Mr. Paars' brother. He'd been coming for years, taking care of Mr. Paars after he got too sick to look after himself, because he refused to move into a rest-home or even his brother's home.

"The Lincoln," Peter said, and Mr. Andersz nodded.

"God, poor man. He must have been inside when you all got there. He must have thought you were coming to rob the place, or vandalize it, and he went out back."

"We must have scared the living shit out of him," Peter said happily.

"Almost as much as we did you," said Kelly, and everyone was shouting, pointing, laughing again.

"Mr. Paars had been dead for days when they found him," Mr. Andersz told us. "The brother had to go away, and he left a nurse in charge, but the nurse got sick, I guess, or Mr. Paars wouldn't let her in or something.

Anyway, it was pretty awful when the brother came back. That's why the windows were all open. It'll take weeks, I bet, to air that place out."

I sat, and I sipped my cocoa, and I watched my friends chatter and eat and laugh and wave their arms around, and it dawned on me, slowly, that none of them had seen. None of them had heard. Not really. I almost said something five different times, but I never quite did, I think because of the way we all were, just for that hour, that last, magical night: triumphant, and windswept, and defiant, and together. Like real friends. Almost.

That was the last time, of course. The next summer, the Macks moved to Vancouver, although they'd slowly slipped away from Peter and me anyway by then. Mr. Andersz lost his job—there was an incident, apparently, he just stopped teaching and sat down on the floor in the front of his classroom and swallowed an entire box of chalk, stick by stick—and wound up working in the little caged-in accounting office at the used car lot in the wasteland down by the Ballard Bridge. And slowly, over a long period of time, it became more exciting, even for me, to talk about Peter than it was to be with him.

Soon, I think, my mother is going to get sick of staring at the images repeating over and over on our TV screen, the live reports from the rubble of my school and the yearbook photo of Peter and the video of him being stuffed into a police car and the names streaming across the bottom of the screen like a tornado warning, except too late. For the fifteenth time, at least, I see Steve Rourke's name go by. I should have told him, I thought, should have warned him. But he should have known. I wonder why my name isn't up there, why Peter didn't come after me. The answer, though, is obvious. He forgot I was there. Or he wants me to think he did.

It doesn't matter. Any minute, my mother's going to get up and go to bed, and she's going to tell me I should, too, and that we'll leave here, get away and never come back.

"Yes," I'll say. "Soon."

"All those children," she'll say. Again. "Sweet Jesus, I can't believe it. Andrew." She'll drop her head on my shoulder and throw her arms around me and cry.

But by then, I won't be thinking about the streaming names, the people I knew who are people no longer, or what Peter might have been thinking tonight. I'll be thinking, just as I am now, about Peter in the grass outside the Paars house, at the moment he realized what we'd done to him. The way he stood there, vibrating. We didn't make him what he was. Not the

Macks, not his dad, not me—none of us. But it's like he said: God puts something shaped like that in the world, and then He expects us not to ring it.

And now there's only one thing left to do. As soon as my mom finally lets go, stops sobbing, and stumbles off to sleep, I'm going to sneak outside, and I'm going to go straight down the hill to the Paars house. I haven't been there since that night. I have no idea if the sheds or the house or the bell even exists, anymore.

But if they do, and if that eye in the grass or any of its power is still there . . . well, then. I'll give a little ring. And then we'll know, once and for all, whether I really did see *two* old men, with matching canes, on the porch of the Paars house when I glanced back right as I fled into the woods. Whether I really did hear rustling from all those sideways sheds as I flew past, as though, in each, something was sliding out of the ground. I wonder if the bell works only on the Paars family, or if it affects any recently deceased in the vicinity. Maybe the dead really can be called back for a while, like kids from recess.

And if they do come back—and if they're angry, and they go looking for Peter, and they find him—well. Let the poor, brilliant, fucked-up bastard get what he deserves.

HALLOWE'EN IN A SUBURB

H.P. Lovecraft

H.P. Lovecraft is best known for his weird fiction, but he wrote quite a bit of poetry as well. Although this one could be termed "cosmic horror," he did not confine himself only fantastic or horrific themes.

One thing about this poem bothered me, however. In the last verse HPL refers to lemurs. He used the word in his story "The Horror at Red Hook" too. Why, in the name of Yog-Sothoth, would prosimians native to Madagascar be barking in the suburbs, even if the hounds of Time have done their rending?

I believe Lovecraft meant the Latin lemurēs, a particularly nasty type of Roman ghost. Most appropriate—but the three syllables would not have fit rhythmically, so he used the two-syllable lemurs. Lovecraft may have been known lemurs as an Anglicized version of the word or from Goethe's Faust. Goethe's Lemuren were sometimes translated into English as Lemurs. For Goethe they were creatures of a "half-patched nature" (Geflickte Halbnature) with enough ligaments, tendons, and bones (Bändern, Sehnen, und Gebein) to dig graves for Mephistopheles.

The steeples are white in the wild moonlight,
    And the trees have a silver glare;
Past the chimneys high see the vampires fly,
    And the harpies of upper air,
    That flutter and laugh and stare.

For the village dead to the moon outspread
    Never shone in the sunset's gleam,
But grew out of the deep that the dead years keep
    Where the rivers of madness stream
    Down the gulfs to a pit of dream.

A chill wind blows through the rows of sheaves
    In the meadows that shimmer pale,
And comes to twine where the headstones shine
    And the ghouls of the churchyard wail
    For harvests that fly and fail.

Not a breath of the strange grey gods of change
    That tore from the past its own
Can quicken this hour, when a spectral power
    Spreads sleep o'er the cosmic throne,
    And looses the vast unknown.

So here again stretch the vale and plain
    That moons long-forgotten saw,
And the dead leap gay in the pallid ray,
    Sprung out of the tomb's black maw
    To shake all the world with awe.

And all that the morn shall greet forlorn,
    The ugliness and the pest
Of rows where thick rise the stones and brick,
    Shall some day be with the rest,
    And brood with the shades unblest.

Then wild in the dark let the lemurs bark,
    And the leprous spires ascend;
For new and old alike in the fold
    Of horror and death are penned,
    For the hounds of Time to rend.

ON THE REEF
Caitlín R. Kiernan

Halloween's ancient beginnings are obscured by time, so it should come as no surprise that there would be a connection between this powerful time of year and the worship of the Elder Gods. Some fret about Satanic connections to Halloween; if you really want to worry, consider the so-called fictional mythos created by H.P. Lovecraft and ceremonies such as the one portrayed here by Caitlín Kiernan. Rites so potent the waking minds of men and women are suddenly, briefly, obscured by thoughts too wicked to ever share and, if asleep and dreaming, their dreams are turned to hurricane squalls and drownings and impossible beasts stranded on sands the color of a ripe cranberry bog.

Man is least himself when he talks in his own person.
Give him a mask, and he will tell you the truth.
—Oscar Wilde (1891)

There are rites that do not die. There are ceremonies and sacraments that thrive even after the most vicious oppressions. Indeed, some may grow stronger under such duress, stronger and more determined, so that even though devotees are scattered and holy ground defiled, the rituals will find a way. The people will find a way back, down long decades and even centuries, to stand where strange beings were summoned—call them gods or demons or numina; call them what you will, as all words only signify and may not ever define or constrain the nature of these entities. Temples are burned and rebuilt. Sacred groves are felled, but new trees take root and flourish.

And so it is with this ragged granite skerry a mile and a half out from the ruins of a Massachusetts harbor town that drew its final, hitching breaths in the winter of 1928. Cartographers rarely take note of it, and when they do, it's only to mark the location for this or that volume of local hauntings or guides for legend trippers. Even the teenagers from Rowley and Ipswich have largely left it alone, and the crumbling concrete walls are almost entirely free of the spray-painted graffiti that nowadays marks their comings and goings.

Beyond the lower falls of the Castle Neck (which the Wampanoag tribes named Manuxet), where the river takes an abrupt southeastern turn before emptying into the Essex Bay, lies the shattered waste that once was Innsmouth. More than half buried now by the tall advancing dunes sprawls this tumbledown wreck of planks weathered gray as oysters, a disarray of cobblestone streets and brick sidewalks, the stubs of chimneys, and rows of warehouses and docks rusted away to almost nothing. But the North Shore wasteland doesn't end at the shore, for the bay is filled with sunken trawlers and purse seiners, a graveyard of lobster pots and steel hulls, jute rope and oaken staves, where sea robins and flounder and spiny blue crabs have had the final word.

However, the subject at hand is not the fall of Innsmouth town, nor what little remains of its avenues and storefronts. The subject at hand is the dogged persistence of ritual, and its tendency to triumph over adversity and prejudice. The difficulty of forever erasing belief from the mind of man. We may glimpse the ruins, as a point of reference, but are soon enough drawn back around to the black granite reef, its rough spine exposed only at low tide. Now, it's one hour after sundown on a Halloween night, and a fat Harvest Moon as fiery orange as molten iron has just cleared the horizon. You'd think the sea would steam from the light of such a moon, but the water's too cold and far too deep.

On this night, there's a peculiar procession of headlights along the lonely Argilla Road, a solemn motorcade passing all but unnoticed between forests and fallow fields, nameless streams and wide swaths of salt marsh and estuary mudflat. *This* night, because this night is one of two every year when the faithful are drawn back to worship at their desecrated cathedral. The black reef may have no arcade, gallery, or clerestory, no flying buttresses or papal altar, but it *is* a cathedral, nonetheless. Function, not form, makes of it a cathedral. The cars file down to the ghost town, the town which is filled only with ghosts. They park where the ground is firm, and the drivers and passengers make their way by moonlight, over abandoned railroad tracks and fallen telegraph poles, skirting the pitfalls of old wells and barbed-wire tangles. They walk silently down to this long stretch of beach, south of Plum Island and west of the mouth of the Annisquam River and Cape Ann.

Some have come from as far away as San Francisco and Seattle, while others are locals, haling from Boston and Providence and Manhattan. Few are dwellers in landlocked cities.

Each man and each woman wears identical sturdy cloaks lined sewn from cotton velveteen and lined with silk, cloth black as raven feathers. Most have pulled the hoods up over their heads, hiding their eyes and half hiding their faces from view. On the left breast of each cape is an embroidered symbol, which bears some faint resemblance to the *ikhthus*, secret sign of early Christian sects, and before that, denoting worshipers at the shrines of Aphrodite, Isis, Atargatis, Ephesus, Pelagia, and Delphine. Here, it carries other connotations.

There are thirteen boats waiting for them, a tiny flotilla of slab-sided Gloucester dories that, hours earlier, were rowed from Halibut Point, six miles to the east. The launching of the boats is a ceremony in its own right, presided over by a priest and priestess who are never permitted to venture to the reef out beyond the ruins of Innsmouth.

As the boats are filled, there's more conversation than during the walk down to the beach; greetings are exchanged between friends and more casual acquaintances who've not spoken to one another since the last gathering, on the thirtieth of April. News of deaths and births is passed from one pilgrim to another. Affections are traded like childhood Valentines. These pleasantries are permitted, but only briefly, only until the dories are less than a mile out from the reef, and then all fall silent in unison and all eyes watch the low red moon or the dark waves lapping at the boats. Their ears are filled now with the wind, wild and cold off the Atlantic and with the rhythmic slap of the oars.

There is a single oil lantern hung upon a hook mounted on the prow of each dory, but no other light is tolerated during the crossing from the beach to the reef. It would be an insult to the moon and to the darkness the moon pushes aside. In the boats, the pilgrims remove their shoes.

By the time the boats have gained the rickety pier—water-logged and slicked with algae, its pilings and boards riddled by the boring of shipworms and scabbed with barnacles—there is an almost tangible air of anticipation among these men and women. It hangs about them like a thick and obscuring cowl, heavy as the smell of salt in the air. There's an attendant waiting on the pier to help each pilgrim up the slippery ladder.

He was blinded years ago, his eyes put out, that he would never glimpse the faces of those he serves; it was a mutilation he suffered gladly. It was a small enough price to pay, he told the surgeon.

Those who have come from so far, and from not so far, are led from the boats and the rotting pier out onto the reef. Each must be mindful of his or her footing. The rocks are slippery, and those who fall into the sea will be counted as offerings. No one is ever pulled out, if they should fall. Over many thousands of years, since the glaciers retreated and the seas rose to flood the land, this raw spit of granite has been shaped by the waves. In the latter years of the eighteenth century, and the early decades of the nineteenth—before the epidemic of 1846 decimated the port—the reef was known as Cachalot Ledge, and also Jonah's Folly, and even now it bears a strong resembles to the vertebrae and vaulted ribs of an enormous sperm whale, flayed of skin and muscle and blubber. But after the plague, and the riots that followed, as outsiders began to steer clear of Innsmouth and its harbor, and as the heyday of New England whaling drew to a close, the rocks were rechristened Devil Reef. There were odd tales whispered by the crews of passing ships, of nightmarish figures they claimed to have seen clambering out of the sea and onto those rocks, and this new name stuck and stuck fast.

Late in the winter of 1928, the submarine USS 0-10 was deployed to these waters, from the Boston Navy Yard. The one hundred and seventy-three foot vessel's tubes were armed with a complement of twenty-nine torpedoes, all of which were discharged into an unexpectedly deep trench discovered just east of Devil Reef. The torpedoes detonated almost a mile down, devastating a target that has never been publicly disclosed. But the pilgrims know what it was, and that attack is to them no less a blasphemy than the destruction of synagogues and cathedrals during the firestorms of the two World Wars, no less a crime than the razing of Taoist temples by Chinese communists, or the devastation of the Aztec Templo Mayor by Spaniard conquistadores after the fall of Tenochtitlan in 1521. And they remember the benthic mansions of Y'ha-nthlei and the grand altars and the beings murdered and survivors left dispossessed by those torpedoes. They remember the gods of that race, and the promises, and the rites, and so they come this night. They come to honor the Mother and the Father, and all those who died and who have survived, and all those who have yet to make the passage, but yet may. The old blood is not gone from the world.

Two are chosen from among the others. A box carved from jet is presented, and two lots are drawn. On each lot is graven the true name of one of the supplicants, the names bestowed in dreamquests by Father Dagon and Mother Hydra. One male and one female, or two female, or two male. But always the number is two. Always only a single pair to enact the most holy rite of the Order. There is no greater honor than to be chosen, and all here desire it. But, too, there is trepidation, for one may not become an avatar of gods without the annihilation of self, to one degree or another. And becoming the avatars of the Mother and the Father means utter and complete annihilation. Not physical death. Something far more destructive to both body and mind than mere death. The jet box is held high and shaken once, and then the lots are drawn, and the names are called out loudly to the pilgrims and the night and the waters and the glaring, lidless eye of the moon.

"The dyad has been determined," declares the old man who drew the lots, and then he steps aside, making way for the two women who have been named. One of them hesitates a moment, but only a moment, and only for the most fleeting of moments. They have names, in the lives they have left behind, lives and families and careers and histories, but tonight all this will be stripped away, sloughed off, just as they now remove their heavy black cloaks to reveal naked, vulnerable bodies. They stand facing one another, and a priestess steps forward. She anoints their forehead, shoulders, bellies, and vaginas with a stinking paste made of ground angelica and mandrake root, the eyes and bowels of various fish, the aragonite cuttlebones of Sepiidae, foxglove, amber, frankincense, dried kelp and bladderwrack, the blood of a calf, and powdered molybdena. Then the women join hands, and each receives a wafer of dried human flesh, which the priestess carefully places beneath their tongues. Neither speaks. Even the priestess does not speak.

Words will come soon enough.

And now it is the turn of the Keeper of the Masks, and he steps forward. The relics he has been charged with protecting are swaddled each in yellow silk. He unwraps them, and now all the pilgrims may look upon the artifacts, shaped from an alloy of gold and far more precious metals, some still imperfectly known (or entirely unknown) to geologists and chemists, and some which have fallen to this world from the gulfs of space. To an infidel, the masks might seem hideous, monstrous things. They would miss the divinity of these divine objects, too distracted by forms they have been taught are grotesque and too be loathed, too unnerved by the almost inexplicable angles into which the alloy was shaped long, long ago, geometries that might seem "wrong" to intellects bound by conventional mathematics. Sometime in the early 1800s, these hallowed relics were brought to Innsmouth by the hand of Captain Obed Marsh himself, delivered from the Windward Islands of French Polynesia and ferried home aboard the barque *Sumatra Queen*.

The Keeper of Masks makes the final choice, selecting the face of Father Dagon for one of the two women, and the face of Mother Hydra for the other. The women are permitted to look upon the other's mortal countenance one last time. And then the Keeper hides their faces, fitting the golden masks and tying them tightly in place with cords woven from the tendons of blood sacrifices, hemp, and sisal. When it is certain that the masks are secure, only then does the Keeper step back into the his place among the others. And the two women kneel bare-kneed on stone worn sharp enough to slice leather.

"Iä!" cries the priestess, and then the Keeper of the Masks, and, finally, the man who drew the lots. Immediately, the pilgrims all reply, "Iä! Iä! Rh'típd! Cthulhu fhtagn!" And then the man who drew the lots, in a somber voice that barely is more than an awed whisper, adds "Ph'nglui mglw'nafh Cthulhu R'lyeh wgah'nagl fhtagn. Rh'típd qho'tlhai mal." His words are lost on the wind, which greedily snatches away each syllable and strews them to the stars and sinks them to that immemorial city far below the waves, its spires broken and crystalline roofs splintered by naval munitions more than eighty years before this night.

"You are become the Mother and the Father," he says. "You are become the living incarnation of the eternal servants of R'lyeh. You are no more what you were. Those former lives are undone. You are become the face of the deep and the eyes of the heavens. You are on this night forever more wed."

The two kneeling women say nothing at all. But the wind has all at once ceased to blow, and around the reef the water has grown still and smooth as glass. The moon remains the same, though, and leers down upon the scene like a jackal waiting for its turn at someone else's kill, or Herod Antipas lusting after dancing Salomé. But no one among the pilgrims looks away from the kneeling women. No one ever looks away, for to avert their eyes from the sacrament would be unspeakable offense. They watch, as the moon watches, with great anticipation, and some with envy, that their names were not chosen from the bag of lots.

To the west—over the wooded hills beyond Essex Bay and the vast estuarine flats at the mouth of the Manuxet River—there are brilliant flashes of lighting, despite the cloudless sky. And, at this moment, as far away as Manchester-by-the-Sea, Wenham and Topsfield, Georgetown and Byfield, hounds have begun to bay. Cats only watch the sky in wonder and contemplation. The waking minds of men and women are suddenly, briefly, obscured by thoughts too wicked to ever share. If any are asleep and dreaming, their dreams turn to hurricane squalls and drownings and impossible beasts stranded on sands the color of a ripe cranberry bog. In this instant, the land and the ocean stand in perfect and immemorial opposition, and the kneeling women who wear the golden masks are counted as apostates, deserting the continent, defecting to brine and abyssal silt. The women are tilting the scales, however minutely, and on this night the sea will claim a victory, and the shore may do no more to protest their desertion than sulk and drive the tides much farther out than usual.

No one on the reef turns away. And they don't make a sound. There's nothing left for the pilgrims but to bear silent witness to the transition of the anointed. And that change is not quick, nor is it in any way merciful; neither woman is spared the least bit of agony. But they don't give voice to their pain, if only because their mouths have been so altered that they will nevermore be capable of speech or any other utterance audible to human ears. The masks have begun to glow with an almost imperceptible phosphorescence, and will shortly drop away, shed skins to be retrieved later by the Keeper.

Wearing now the mercurial forms of Mother Hydra and Father Dagon, the lovers embrace. Their bodies coil tightly together until there's almost no telling the one from the other, and the writhing knot of sinew and organs and rasping teeth glistens wetly in the bright moonlight. The two are all but fused into a single organism, reaffirming a marriage first made among the cyanobacterial mats of warm paleoarchaen lagoons, three and a half billion years before the coming of man. There is such violence that this coupling looks hardly any different from a battle, and terrible gaping wounds are torn open, only to seal themselves shut again. The chosen strain and bend themselves towards inevitable climax, and the strata of the reef shudders repeatedly beneath the feet of the pilgrims. Several have to squat or kneel to avoid sliding from the rocks to be devoured by the insincere calm of the sea. In the days to come, none of them will mutter a word about what they've seen and heard and smelled in the hour of this holy copulation. This is a secret they guard with their lives and with their sanity.

No longer sane, the lovers twist, unwind, and part. The Father has already bestowed his gift, and now it is the Mother's turn. A bulging membrane bursts, a protuberance no larger than the first of a child, and she weeps blood and ichor and a single black pearl. It is *not* a pearl, but by way of the roughest sort of analogy or approximation. One may as well call it a pearl as not. The true name for the Mother's gift is forbidden. It drops from her and lies quivering in a sticky puddle, to be claimed as the masks will be claimed. And then they drag themselves off the steep eastern lip of the reef, slithering from view and sinking into the ocean as the waves and wind return. They will spend the long night spiraling down and down, descending into that same trench the *O-10* torpedoed eighty-two Januaries ago. And by the time the sun rises, and Devil Reef is once more submerged, they will have found the many-columned vestiges of the city of Y'ha-nthlei, where they will be watched over by beings that are neither fish nor men nor any amphibious species cataloged by science.

By then, the cars parked above the ghost town will have gone away, carrying the pilgrims back to the drab, unremarkable lives they will live until the end of April and the next gathering. And they will all dream their dreams, and await the night they may wear the golden masks.

THE STICKS

Charlee Jacob

Charlee Jacob's story is set in the Deep South—one so deep it seems located closer to some strange dark world than to the rest of the North American continent. And, on this one night of the year when other worlds and uncanny beings converge on our usual reality, The Sticks is not a place you'd care to be. In The Sticks, a swamp-surrounded backwater town, Halloween is not a celebration. The children don't don costumes, go to parties, or trick or treat. They stay home—alone behind locked doors—put on pajamas, robes, and slippers, say their prayers in case they don't get the chance later, and prepare for a long, terrifying vigil which will take them past midnight . . . they hope.

~

Shshsh, he thought. *Shshhhhhhhhhhhhhhh.*

His face mimed the sound even if he didn't make it out loud. His lips pursed just so, his teeth couldn't chatter.

The sun was setting as twelve-year-old Greenboy turned on the porch light. His six year-old sister, Early, toured the house with a book of matches, lighting candles in every room—even in the bathrooms and down the hall. It was the same thing all through their neighborhood: kids getting ready for Halloween. They put on pajamas, robes, and slippers, saying prayers in case they didn't get the chance later, preparing for a long vigil which would take them—hopefully—past midnight.

Was this how children celebrated in other towns? They knew it wasn't. Hell, these kids watched television—an occupation they shared with the rest of America. They knew that in other parts of the country youngsters donned costumes, took up bags, and entered the darkness crying TRICK OR TREAT! for a deliciously good time. They went door to door, begging candy, making empty threats good naturedly, bringing home sacks of miniature candy bars and peanut butter taffies, popcorn balls and skull-shaped gum. Doing this as red and gold leaves drifted off tree branches and as frost nipped at eager faces.

It wasn't how things were done in this little backwater town. Not in The Sticks, what some city founder more than a hundred years ago had named the place. It wasn't much better than saying you were from The Boons or Podunk or Bugtussle. This was deep south, so south if you went any farther you ended up out of the swamps and in salt water swimming for the equator, black gators sending messages for the sharks to head you off at the pass.

The Sticks was a place positively sodden with history. In 1812 men toting empty muskets lured invading British Redcoats into tangles of cottonmouth snakes. In 1831 slaves led rebellions, put down by mosquitoes and fever. Sherman's Union galloped through in 1864 with torches to turn everything to ash. History was all about mortality. The kind written down in books came from the living, but the sort the land imprinted came from the dead.

Each year on October 29 everyone woke up to the occasion of white-mouthed water moccasins wriggling through the streets. These deadly S's had crawled a couple of miles from the belly of the swamp, writhing and knotting, going from one end of The Sticks to the other. There was no school that day. Nobody went to work either. They stayed in their houses, shut up tight—even if steaming hot with late Indian summer, sticky as a vat of rotten peaches. Night would come for the 29th and they'd hear those snakes slide past their doors, gliding over windows, across rooftops. Sometimes a few managed to locate a passage down a chimney. Folks scrambled with pokers, machetes and guns to kill them soon as they landed—spitting, hissing, snapping—in the hearth.

By October 30 the snakes were always vanished yet mosquitoes descended in thick swarms, a fog loud as a buzzsaw full of them. Nobody went out then either. Rarely the town might get lucky and the air would be cool. But usually the heat was intolerable, no way around keeping a blaze in the fireplace, in case tendrils of that fog infiltrated the chimney. They sat with even the keyholes stuffed, wondering why they endured this like the plagues sent to Egypt, sweating out the end of the 30th. Simply the idea of those skeeters outside made their flesh itch until they had to scratch, scratching until they bled, leaving furrows on flesh like ancient ritual tattoos stained a pagan red.

One might've thought it fair that these people would leave. Surely they'd move to the next town, go to Atlanta or New Orleans or even Biloxi.

Evacuating to somewhere which had kept up with the times. But people will remain in their homes on the slopes of active volcanoes, won't they? They'll live on a flood plain. They'll persevere on coastline regularly blown to pieces by hurricanes. It might be because they're stubborn, believing humanity is justification enough, refusing dictation by nature. Or it may be they can't—or won't—recognize a curse as old as a stain carried by original settlers, hair still reeking with the smoke of those their ancestors or they themselves had persecuted and burned or hanged. Sins of the fathers . . . and mothers.

Just for the sake of stating a "for instance": say that back in the old country a group practicing Samhain rites for the Old Religion was attacked in the woods. Suppose Majesty had attended this functional soiree, fragrant incense curling up through tree branches, stars bright as jagged flint, wine catching and holding an image of the moon. Then a posse of torch-bearing Christians descended to wipe them out for no particular reason. To the gods, a couple hundred years is nothing to wait. A thousand years may be a reasonable amount of time to fester. Further exposition might not be necessary.

But it all boiled down to the people in The Sticks waking up on October 31 to find the mosquitoes gone. Autumn had taken a sudden turn. It wasn't one of bronze and scarlet hues, or a gentle drifting of leaves to golding grass. The leaves and grass had turned black as if burned to ash. Heavy smoke tainted the air in clouds wafting about like the swarms of mosquitoes had the day before. There were smears of charcoal in runes upon the whitewashed walls of houses, sifting from the impaling points on picket fences, creating leering jack o' lantern faces in bold negative on windows. Still people stayed home, kids studying for when they returned to school, playing at tossing bones and dice or using the bones as skeletal erector sets to build little faerie castles and tiny old Roman forts. Their elders worked on costumes for the evening's festivities, scissors snapping like cottonmouth jaws, threaded needles sharp as the mosquito's bite.

Parents dressed up: faces painted green or gray, eyes and mouths outlined in lipstick. Hair teased to stand up in tufts as if rolling over in graves might've been responsible for tousling it—or slicked down and dripping joke-shop bottled slime to portray decomposed bodies risen from the swamp. Impromptu gowns with elaborate trains and winding cerement clothes dragged in tatters, fabric across the floor going *Shshshhhhhhhhhh.* Greenboy and Early heard the crowd down the street, crunching on gravel driveways, shaking bags full of teeth and bells. No hush now. The crowd called out, walking up and down for hours, frisky with theatrical noise, going from one front porch to the next, or turning around, going back the way they'd come. They didn't knock, not yet. They just tramped door to door.

"Where you think they're goin' to end up?" Early asked her brother, mindful of keeping her voice down, hard for someone her age. She stared at how the candlelight flickered in the windows and how it reflected in the glass.

He shrugged, then replied softly. "Don't do no good to try and guess."

He bit his lip, glancing at the large barrel his father had set near the door. He heard movement in there and it made him feel queasy. He wanted to rub his stomach but he didn't want Early to see how it made him sick. His sister didn't look at it at all but turned her head as she made a wide path around it. She put her palm up to shield her eyes so she didn't have to take note of it.

The crowd had just visited next door. Greenboy was sure he sensed John-Moseby, his best friend, sitting in an oversized and overstuffed chair by the door, nervously cracking his knuckles. He'd have been eating from a big bowl of chocolate pudding, so dark it didn't shine even in direct light, thick as something found between the stones in a dead man's gut. Some of it would've dribbled onto John-Moseby's chin, leaving him with a spattering of freckles like black water droplets from the River Styx. He'd be tensed, tempted to bolt should that feared knock come at the door. But where would John-Moseby run to if it did? He couldn't go out the back for the crowd always surrounded a house after they chose it. And he couldn't flee up the stairs for they'd simply come in after him. Naturally, at least one had the key.

Well, it didn't matter at this house. For three days ago Greenboy watched his father remove the back door. Now it was solid wall in the kitchen, icy smooth plaster.

"They're comin' up our walk," Early whispered, feathery white-blond hair framing her face until—with her large eyes—she resembled a backwoods owl. "Is it time, Greenboy? How long's it been?"

When you speak in a hush and you're only six years old, the *s*'s lisp until you seem to be underlining your speech with *Shshsh*.

She peered at a table where a clock, set into the belly of a porcelain bobcat, ticked. She hadn't yet learned to tell time. It had been dark outside for a spell, maybe for fewer hours than she thought. It always seemed to be longer than it really was, didn't it? The devil must've invented waiting.

Greenboy's eyes darted to the clock, too. "It's almost eight-thirty. But don't mean nothin'. Ain't no set hour or minute. Just has to be by midnight."

Feet moved outside, across black earth, shuffling up the sidewalk, snapping slick ebon twigs and crackling scoops of corrupted leaves. He couldn't help it—he went to the window as homemade noisemakers rang and clattered. Some faces he glimpsed beyond were nightmarish, others silly. But the way candles inside the darkened room reflected on the glass, every adult out there was on fire.

Because her brother looked, Early couldn't resist the impulse. She climbed up on a stool. "Don't you think they look dead, Greenboy?"

"They're s'pose to," he replied, hearing his own muffled S's.

"I see Momma and Daddy," she said almost inaudibly. "They're walkin' beside Mr. and Mrs. Rodell."

Early shivered and climbed back down, sharing a look with her brother. The Rodells lived on the other side of them from the one John-Moseby's family was. Last Halloween they lost one of their twin girls. Now the surviving twin waited next door: thinking what, feeling what?

Greenboy wondered if she shared the fear or pain. Twins were said to be mysteriously linked. He'd see Emily Rodell at school. She never seemed to blink. Her eyes bulged wide every second, as anybody's would from glimpsing something horrible. And her mouth always hung open as if she couldn't breathe. There'd be a trickle of silvery drool on her chin. (Had a water moccasin kissed her?) Her grades weren't very good anymore. She couldn't concentrate.

But the weirdest thing was she always smelled a bit rancid now. Like a dead squirrel struck by a car on a late Indian summer morning might smell on the way home from school in the afternoon.

"They're goin' away," Greenboy announced under his breath, letting out a gasp he'd only intended to be a sigh.

The crowd indeed stalked back down the walkway, teeth and bells in little plastic sandwich bags providing a jarring, primitive marimba. They traveled across the lawn, downright bypassing the Rodell's. Had that family given enough? Could anybody ever give enough?

Greenboy heard the water pipes groan. The toilets—one down the hall off the kitchen and the other upstairs—both flushed simultaneously, then gurgled as if all the liquid was being drawn down under the building. There must be bubbles in the swamp. He almost felt those, too, rising in fetid microcosms, necrotic rainbow circles in the moonlight. Daddy told them that every time the house pipes made this sound, it was because the swamp connection was uneasy. It caused a drop in pressure. Roots grown into the works or moss choking a valve someplace connected with the bog's throat.

A few years ago, when Greenboy was only five and before Early had yet to be born, one of those popular riverboats full of gambling tourists sank during a storm. The people submerged, screams softened into droning drowned. The county couldn't dredge even one for burial. Then suddenly at night, months later, those bloated bodies came up together. They'd drifted under the water, moving miles from the river's deepest center to the swamp, though nobody guessed how. One or two might've managed it, relocated by another storm or dragged by gators, but all? There were so many end on end that Daddy said you could've walked from one side of the swamp to the other, crossing a bridge. The water pressure dropped low—like voices in a church—and no one was able to make coffee or bathe or even flush their toilets for a week. And the stench! All over The Sticks the odor of carrion was pervasive.

"I'm sleepy," Early said after the crowd moved off toward the end of the block. She rubbed her eyes. "Can't I go to bed?"

"No," her brother muttered, tired himself. He glanced at the clock. Nine-thirty. Where had the whole last hour gone? Maybe the adults went away, clear to the other side of The Sticks by now. "You can lie down on the sofa but you have to stay downstairs."

And you must be so quiet. Respectful. Careful as a baby chick at a red-tailed hawk convention. Early curled on her side on the couch, knees up to her chest, fists under her cheek. Greenboy took his jacket off the back of a chair. He passed the barrel, a soft shuffling coming from within. He shuddered and wanted to throw the coat over it so he wouldn't see it. But instead he used the jacket over to blanket his sister. He hoped he wasn't going to have to wake her up later.

"How can you just sleep like nothin's goin' on?" He marveled mutely, able to close his eyes and shrug it away. Of course she could do that. She'd never seen anything. She knew the rules and was a good girl. She accepted the admonition to be quiet as a mouse, same as she did during the annual Christmas mass or Easter pageant, baby Jesus being revered in a simulated manger and then, enigmatically, admired as the older version died in contortions upon a replicated cross. She watched as adults did incomprehensible things because grown-ups did stuff that never made sense. Kids always pestering their parents with why this and why that got whippings, and she didn't like being punished.

But it took more than being told what to do and then doing it to understand.

The autumn Greenboy was five, he'd stared out the window as a child across the street was sucked beneath the crowd like under the wheels of a train. That house had candles in all its windows, too—not bright like Christmas, only glowing like Halloween, glass panes ruddy with it as if smeared with cherry ice. And one minute there were teeth and bells, shrieks added to them. Then those candles went out.

The Sticks once had a cemetery, same as most towns. But the swamp overtook it, black water creeping up a little each night. Finally one morning every grave was a sump hole. So the mayor and council hired local boys to move it to the other side of town. But without the bog making sink holes through the neighborhoods and downtown—in other words without visually creeping through the center to reach the end—the swamp simply appeared in that new location, too. Had it slid underneath them? Poisoned, motionless muck threaded the underground until it became soft with decay. Not more than a month later that new graveyard went to quicksand and gators, stinking bayou and snakes. They tried twice again to relocate so that cemeteries were eventually attempted north, south, east, and west. It always ended the same way, eventually encircling The Sticks with swamp. They'd needed to build bridges to get across.

Now the town's official policy mandated funerals at water's edge, Spanish moss rustling like a mortuary's velvet curtains as they gave their dead to the swamp. Same as burials at sea.

When the family held the funeral for Granddad two years ago, Greenboy stood on the bank. It had been a horrible feeling, ground sucking at his feet, hungry and too-soft. Water seeped into his good shoes. Full of tiny things, water actually wriggled, spreading around his ankles and between his toes as if it had places to go and bones to build sewers in.

Greenboy figured the reason he recalled the thing about the cemetery at that moment, as he remembered what he'd seen when he was five, was because as that hapless child went down across the street, it seemed there were suddenly lots more folks outside. The black earth gurgled and they came up out of the ground. They rose like bubbles of gas and gator jaws stretching wide. They multiplied in the dark—so dark he couldn't be sure of what he'd seen—flat as the shawls of moss, shadows starting out black, then turning red as they took on a substance of bloody imagination, next going briefly yellow-white as the candle flames, finally winking out just as suddenly as the candles themselves had reverted to ash.

He'd cracked the window open that night years ago, just a sliver, trying to make out what these shapes were. The whiff he caught from the wind was foul. It reminded him of his grandmom's leg which had developed gangrene because of her diabetes. The doctors had cut the black limb off, saying they did it to keep it from rotting away the rest of her.

How had the grown-ups known then to stop their parade at the house across the street? There must've been a signal but he'd never heard anything beyond the teeth-and-bell castanets, the adults' calling, his own *shshsh* to himself as a reminder not to cry. Maybe the ground had turned muddy, the swamp coming up. Or the air began to stink like corpses shot out of a big cannon (what he smelled). Had balls of swamp gas led the way like a troop of cotton-mouthed faeries pointing the direction to who'd been chosen this year? Perhaps gators had come in and could talk, lizard voices sibilant with *Shshshow's over here, ya'll. Shshshame and shshshin-bone shshshivaree. This year's shshshrine . . .*

The next morning he'd seen the mother from that house, hysterical on the lawn. The paint on her face from the night before streaked from sweat, frozen to her skin because the wind had come in cold. Happened even in the deep, deep south sometimes. She ran around the yard, dropping to her knees, digging up bloody little bones which lay just beneath the surface of the ground, hugging them to her chest, kissing them as she wept.

And his own momma told his daddy, "Jake, promise me . . ."

And then last year, when the Rodell's lost their twin girl . . . Momma sat at the breakfast table the morning after, face scrubbed raw and her nails cut so short the quicks were bruised. She stared into a cup of coffee like its blackness came straight from the swamp. She was unable to look at Greenboy or Early. She said to Daddy, "I can't do it. Not if it comes down to either of ours."

And this year, this fall, the day before October 29 came around and the plagues of their own personal Egypt descended, she said it again. Not softly, not in any kind of a whisper, but loud so that Daddy put a hand over her mouth. He feared the neighbors would hear. It might carry to the swamp which encircled The Sticks. There was a flicker in her eyes, of candles and madness. She pried his fingers away and begged Daddy to promise. He sat down, using the end of a paring knife to clean under his own nails. They weren't dirty but he went after them as if there something nasty under them. He scraped and scraped until they bled. Eventually he nodded.

Greenboy now heard the brattle of teeth and bells. Footsteps came up the street: some in shoes, some in boots, others barefoot. It had become so still that Greenboy himself must've fallen asleep, remembering those things. But sounds woke him. Early, too. She yawned and sat up, his jacket falling away from her.

He glanced at the clock. Eleven-forty-five. Had it happened yet? Where?

No, it hadn't happened. If it had, the adults would be quiet. They would've stuck those sandwich baggies with the teeth and the bells into their pockets. They'd be somber, the *shshsh*'s having gotten them. They'd creep down the street toward their homes. A few would murmur prayers for forgiveness, even as they wondered who the hell they were supposed to be asking forgiveness of.

It was nearly midnight and the crowd moved back this way.

Early jumped up and climbed back onto the stool, looking out the window. Greenboy shook his head, thinking how, for a second, she was like a little kid searching for Santa Claus. He went to stand beside her. Of course, he was twelve years tall as a cattail and didn't need to stand on anything to see out the window.

"I still think they look dead," she told him out loud.

"Hush, Early," he reminded her.

She slapped her hand over her mouth. Her breath made a little whistle. Then she turned to him, both hands going to perch at the windowsill, her mouth twisted. He felt her trembling next to him. This time her voice was the barest sniffle. "Greenboy? ARE they dead right now?"

No, he wanted to answer. But it would soon be true. Even if only for a few minutes, it would be true: most of what was out there would be dead.

They came up the walk. The candles had been going for hours and were waxy puddles, wicks burning, floating in individual swamps. The group parted and began to go around the house, circling it just like the swamp did The Sticks.

He pictured those cartoon gators. *Shshshow's over here, ya'll.*

Heavy boots clomped onto the porch. There was a knock at the door.

"Early, get upstairs. Now!" Greenboy commanded as softly as he could, lifting her down from the stool and setting her on the floor.

"But, Greenboy . . . "

"You saw what's in that barrel? Now git!" He'd barely aspirated the words through his clenched teeth.

She took off. He grunted and heaved to push the barrel over, hoping the top would come away by itself. It didn't, sealed tight with six strong metal tabs that went one direction to press the wooden top and moved another to swing free. The shuffling inside had grown louder but was still hard to hear over the racket the grown-ups created outside. Greenboy moaned, kicking at the lid and jumping back. Still it didn't come loose. He'd have to take the lid off himself. He crept up, fingers twitching, arm not wanting to stick the hand out to pry at those tabs. His flesh sidewindered.

There was another knock at the door.

"Don't wait," Daddy had told him after he'd taken out that kitchen door and covered up the entrance. "Do it fast, then cut out. Don't hesitate and don't come back down lookin' to see what's goin' on, no matter what you hear."

And then, October 29, Daddy opened up the chimney for a little while. He set the big barrel underneath it, sitting there with a pistol prepared to shoot anything that missed going inside.

Greenboy held his breath and reached out, flicking open the first metal tab. The click made him start. He undid the next one, wishing that would be enough except it wasn't. He moved the third tab, sensing vibration in the barrel as it juddered through the steel tongue. With the fourth tab, he felt that vibration stiffening the fine hairs on his arm. With the fifth tab the lid bulged, pressed from within, the contents aching to swell out.

He was too afraid to undo the final tab. He stepped back, watching the lid's edges tap. White forks licked from the seams. The top would explode out when he undid that last lock, wouldn't it? And he'd be caught too close to ground zero. But he had to do it for he heard another turning in the keyhole. Yet the door didn't open. He heard somebody (Daddy?) say, "Wrong key."

The noise of teeth and bells clashing together, people howling, and something similar to the sound bacon made when it sizzled into ruin echoed in his head until the boy couldn't think straight. Shadows pressed against the window, nearly spent candles folding them across the furniture and walls, resembling gators capering on hind legs.

. . . This here's this year's shshshrine!

A clatter, a jangle. Noises of a struggle as the crowd realized stall tactics when they saw them. Somebody had grabbed the keys away and tried one in the door.

Greenboy leaned forward like a runner poised for the gun to signal the beginning of a race, body straining to the starting line, legs stretched with the torso balanced upon the good graces of the fingers. He reached for that final tab, shocked to find the metal in it hot as a stove burner. He thought at first the hiss he heard was from the barrel's insides as they reached with magic intent through the solid lid to bite him. But it was only the skin of his fingertips blistering on that last lock. He flicked it and jerked away. He scampered backward toward the stairs, stumbling upon the bottom step.

The lid just plopped toward the carpet like a fallen drawbridge. Then it bounced to roll like a bicycle tire across the floor. The snakes coiled out at last, jaws widened to expose glistening fangs in cottony mouths.

Whoever had taken the keys finally found the right one as Greenboy turned to run up the stairs. He didn't pause to look behind him. But he noted the strong septic smell: of clogged sewers and flooded graves, of necrotic snakebite wounds and the not-completely cremated in their cold ashes.

People poured in through the doorway, unaware the cottonmouths were mad as hell and ready to strike. They pressed behind those who stumbled in first and fell, bitten. There was a bottleneck over the knots of water moccasins as some realized the danger and tried to rush back out—only to be trampled.

Upstairs, Greenboy locked the bedroom door. There was a sound under his sister's bed. Early had skittered down to hide there, the bedskirt stirring. He didn't blame her. But ever the witness, he watched from a window.

It had become apparent to those on the lawn and over the sidewalk that something was wrong. People screamed and no child had been delivered out. But the moss-flat shadows still oozed from the ground, bumping together like bodies rising bloated in the swamp. Shapes were of mud and fuzzy sump, with features dripping or smiles rigid as a gator's jaws. Shapes were spindly and gnarled as the trees bereft of their foliage.

Somebody scratched on the other side of the bedroom door, pleading to be let in. Their voice grew rough, loud as a shotgun, then faded to a faintly desperate purling. He heard a couple others as they managed to crawl up the stairway only to collapse at the top, one falling back down the steps, thrumming the banister.

Greenboy wanted to cry. Terror gathered thickly in his throat. His body twitched, trying to shake the sobs out. Yet he held them in, pressing burned fingertips hard against his chest as if they were the tab locks on the top of the barrel. He pursed his lips and managed only *Shshshhhhhhhh!* Something was out there he still had to be respectful to. Not just the silence of those trying to hide, trying not to be noticed and sniffed out, but the sign of obedience to the incomprehensible.

Some adults began running away. Others folded down under the moss or sank, shrieks effervescing. Greenboy lifted the candle still burning at that window and brought it near to his face, so close it might have singed his eyelashes. The light made it harder to see outside. It blinded him to the dark, flashing onto his retinas until all he saw was flame.

The minutes ticked by. Soon it was after midnight. The squeals and wailing stopped, nothing on the lawn but ash. The wind had risen, carrying a norther. Soon it would be cold thereabouts. Happened sometimes even in the Deep South.

Greenboy wondered if his parents were among those to escape. He was certain Daddy deliberately fumbled with the keys, able to keep a presence of mind about that barrel of deadly cottonmouths. Maybe he'd slipped off the porch, taking Momma to the far edge of the crowd. They'd been part of the group the boy had seen running off.

He let himself think happy thoughts about the morning to be. Momma and Daddy would return. They'd slide the body away from the bedroom door. They'd shoot whatever snakes still slithered through the house. They'd pack up the kids and move away.

It occurred to him that the candles down the block hadn't gone out. They still winked in windows or burned like steady eyes. But he was exhausted. Greenboy blew out the candle and closed the curtains. He turned to go to bed. Water swirled up in the carpet around his feet, sucking at them . . . hungry. And there was a stench welling up, so putrid it suffocated him, choking like bile in his throat.

The skirt around the bottom of the bed rustled. In another moment a long black snout came smiling out at him.

RIDING BITCH

K.W. Jeter

Jeter's narrator's problems involve more than Halloween—a lot more—but he does have a point about the holiday changing from a child-oriented celebration to an occasion for adults to get "all tarted up" or prove you can be a "beer-soaked trashbag." Nowadays, the kiddies may still have their day, but the holiday has also become a carnival that allows grown-ups to assume different identities and exceed the bounds of usual propriety. Costumes and disguises, the presence of tolerant co-conspirators, the indulgence—even encouragement—of the community in the festivities are now, for better or worse, a part of our ever-evolving conception of the season. Of course death is always part of the concept . . .

A lot was still going to happen.

He would stand at the bar, he knew, locked in the embrace of his old girlfriend.

"Probably wasn't your smartest move." Ernie the bartender would run his damp rag along the wood, polished smooth by the elbows of generations of losers. "Sounds like fun at the beginning, but it always ends in tears. Trust me, I know."

He wouldn't care whether Ernie knew or not. The beer wouldn't do anything to numb the pain. Not the pain of having a dead girl, whom once he'd loved, draped across his shoulders. Her left arm would circle under his left arm. When she'd been alive, whenever she'd conked out after too many Jägers and everything else, she'd always wrapped herself around him just like that, from the back. Up on tiptoes in her partying boots, just blurrily awake enough to clasp her hands over his heart.

He would knock back the rest of the beer in front of him, remembering how he'd carried her, plenty of nights, when there'd still been partying left in him. He'd shot racks of pool like this, leaning over the cue with her negligible weight curled on top of his spine like a drowsy cat, her face dropping close beside his, exhaling alcohol as took his shot, skimming past the eightball . . .

Her breath wouldn't smell of anything other than the formaldehyde or whatever it was that Edwin had pumped her full of, back at the funeral parlor. And it wouldn't really be her breath, anyway, her not having any in that condition. He would gaze at the flickering Oly Gold neon in the bar's bunker-like window, and swish another pull of beer around in his mouth, as though it could Listerine away the faint smell in his nostrils. The dead didn't sweat, he would discover, but just exuded—if you got that close to them—an odor half the stuff hospital floors were mopped with, half Barbie-doll plastic.

"Those look like they chafe."

Ernie the bartender would catch him tagging at the handcuffs, right where the sharp edge of metal would be digging through his T-shirt and into the skin over his ribs.

"Yeah," he'd say, "they do a bit." *Should've thought of that before you let 'em strap her on.* "I wasn't thinking too clearly then."

"Hm?" Ernie wouldn't look over at him, but would go on peering into the beer mug he'd just wiped with the bar towel.

"I blame it on Hallowe'en," he would explain.

"Hallowe'en, huh?" Ernie would glance at the Hamms clock over the bar's entrance. "That was over three hours ago." Ernie would lick a thumb and use it to smear out a grease spot inside the mug. "Over and done with, pal."

"Couldn't prove it around here." The bar would be all orange-'n'-blacked out, with the crap that the beer distributors unloaded every year, cheap cardboard stand-up's of long-legged witches with squeezed cleavage, grinning drunk pumpkins Scotch-taped to the wall over by the men's room, bar coasters with black cats arched like croquet wickets, Day-Glo spiderwebs, dancing articulated skeletons with hollow eyes that would've lit up if the batteries hadn't already run flat by the 30th, everything with logos and trademarks and brand names.

"Why do you let them put all that up, Ernie?"

"All what up?" The bartender would start on another mug, scraping away a half-moon of lipstick with his thumbnail. "What're you talking about?"

He'd give up then. There'd be no point. What difference would it make? He'd shift the dead girl a little higher on his shoulder, balancing her against the tidal pull of the beers he would put away. The combination of low-percentage alcohol with whatever the EMTs would huff him up with, when they scraped him off the road and into their van, would wobble his knees. Hanging onto the edge of the bar, instead of trying to walk, might be the only good idea he'd have that night.

And not all the ideas, the weird ones, would be his. There would still be that whole trip the other guys in the bar would come up with, about the reason Superman flies in circles.

But everything else—that would still be Hallowe'en's fault. Or what Hallowe'en had become. That was what he had told the motorheads, back when the night had started.

No—Cold lips would nuzzle his ear. *You've got it all wrong.*

He'd close his eyes and listen to her whisper.

It's what you became. What we became. That's what did it.

"Yeah . . ." He'd whisper to himself, and to her as well, so no-one else could hear. "You're right."

"I blame it all on Hallowe'en."

"That so?" The motorhead with the buzz cut didn't even look up from the skinny little sportbike's exhaust. "What's Hallowe'en got to do with your sorry-ass life?"

He hadn't wanted to tell someone else exactly what. He hadn't wanted to tell himself, to step through the precise calculus of regret, even though he already knew the final sum.

"It's not me, specifically," he lied. "It's what it did to everything else. It's frickin' Satanic."

That remark drew a worried glance from Buzz Cut. "Uhh . . . you're not one of those hyper-Christian types, are you?" He fitted a metric wrench onto a frame bolt. "This isn't going to be some big rant, is it? If it is, I gotta go get another beer."

"Don't worry." Something he'd thought about for a long time, and he still couldn't say what it was. Like humping some humungous antique chest of drawers out through a doorway too small for it, and getting it stuck halfway. He could wrestle it around into some different position, with the knobs wedged against the left side of the doorjamb rather than the right, but it would still be stuck there. "It's just . . ."

"Just what?"

He tried. "You remember how it was when you were a kid?"

"Vaguely." Buzz Cut shrugged. "Been a while."

"Regardless. But when we were kids, Hallowe'en was, you know, for kids. And the kids got dressed up, like little ghosts and witches and stuff. The adults didn't get all tarted up. They stayed home and handed out the candy."

"True. So?"

"So you've got three hundred and sixty-four other days, including Christmas, to act like a cheap bimbo, or to prove that you're a beer-soaked trashbag. Why screw around with Hallowe'en?"

"Dude, you have got to stop thinking about stuff like this." Buzz Cut went back to wrenching on the bike. "It's messing up your head."

He couldn't stop thinking about it, if pictures counted as thought. Didn't even have to close his eyes to see the raggedy pilgrimage, the snaking lines of pirates and bedsheeted ghosts and fairy princesses, and the kids you felt sorry for because they those cheap store-bought costumes instead of ones their mothers made for them. All of them trooping with their brown paper grocery bags or dragging old pillowcases, already heavy with sugar loot, from the sidewalk up to the doorbell and back out to the sidewalk and the next house, so many of them right after each other, that it didn't even make sense to close the door, just keep handing out the candy from the big Tupperware bowl on the folding TV tray. And if you were some older kid—too old to do that stuff anymore, practically a sneering teenager already—standing behind your dad and looking past him, out through the front door and across the chill, velvety-black night streets of suburbia, looking with a strange-crazy clench in your stomach, like you were first realizing how big and fast Time was picking you up and rolling and tumbling you like an ocean wave, head over heels away from the shore of some world from which you were now forever banished—looking out as though your front porch were now miles up in the starry-icy air and you could see all the little kids of Earth winding from door to door, coast to coast, pole to pole, stations of a spinning cross . . .

No wonder these guys think I'm messed up. He had managed to freak himself, without even trying. *Like falling down a hole.* He tilted his head back, downing the rest of the beer, as though he could wash away that world on its bitter tide.

"So how's the nitrous set-up working for you?"

Blinking, he pulled himself back up into the garage. Around him, the bare, unpainted walls clicked into place, the two-by-four shelves slid across them as though on invisible tracks, the cans of thirty-weight and brake fluid lining up where they had been before.

He looked over toward the garage door and saw the other motorhead, the redhaired one, already sauntered in from the house, picking through the butt-ends of a Burger King french fires bag in one hand.

"The nitrous?" It took him a couple seconds to remember which world that was a part of. At the back of his skull, a line of little ghosts marched away. An even littler door closed, shutting off a lost October moon. "Yeah, the nitrous . . ." He shrugged. "Fine. I guess."

"You guess," said Buzz Cut. "Jesus Christ, you pussy. We didn't put it on there so you could *guess* whether it works or not. We put it on so you'd use it. Least once in a while."

"Hey, it's okay." They'd both ragged him about it before. "It's enough to know I got it. Right there under my thumb."

Which was true. Even back when he and the motorheads had been installing the nitrous oxide kit on the 'Busa, he hadn't been thinking about ever using it. The whole time that the motorheads had been mounting the pressurized gas canister on the right flank of the bike—"Serious can of whup-ass," Buzz Cut had called it—and routing the feeder line to the engine, all 1298 cubic centimeters of it, they'd been chortling about how much fun would ensue.

"There's that dude with the silver Maserati Quattroporte, you see all the time over around Flamingo and Decatur. Thinks he's bad 'cause his machine can keep up with a liter bike."

"Hell." A big sneer creased Red's face. "I've smoked the sonuvabitch plenty of times."

"Not by much. That thing can haul ass when it's in tune and he's not too loaded to run it through the gears." Buzz Cut had tapped an ominous finger on the little nitrous can, *tink tink tink* like a bomb. "But when this shit kicks in, Mister Hotshot Cager ain't gonna see anything except boosser taillight fading in the distance." He had looked away from the bike and smiled evilly. "Won't that be a gas? For real?"

He had supposed so, out loud, just to shut the two of them up. Neither motorhead, Buzz Cut or Red, had a clue about potentialities. How something could be real—realer than real—if it just hung there in a cloud of *still could happen*. Right now, the only way that he even knew the rig worked was that the motorheads had put the 'Busa on the Piper T&M dynamometer at the back of their garage and cranked it. Stock, they'd gotten a baseline pull of 155 point nine horsepower. Tweaking the nitrous set-up with a number 43 jet, they'd wound up at 216 and a half, with more to go. "Now that's *serious* kick," Buzz Cut had judged with satisfaction.

It didn't matter to him, though. He sat in his usual perch on the greasy workbench, where he always sat when he came by the motorhead house, adding empty beer cans to the litter of tools and shop catalogues, and thought about the way their heads worked.

They didn't work the way his did. That was the problem, he knew. Nobody's did. *Or maybe mine doesn't work at all.* He had to admit that was a possibility. There'd been a time when it had—he could remember it. When it hadn't gone wheeling around in diminishing circles, like a bike whose rider had been scraped off in the last corner of the track. Gassing on about Hallowe'en and nitrous oxide buttons that never got punched and somehow that made it all even realer than the little ghost kids had been—

Inside his jacket, his cellphone purred. He could have burst into tears, from sheer relief. He dug the phone out and flipped it open.

Edwin calling, from the funeral parlor. He didn't have to answer, to know; he recognized the number that came up on the postage-stamp screen. And he didn't have to answer, to know what Edwin was calling about. Edwin only ever called about one thing. Which was fine by him, since he needed the job and the money.

"I'll see you guys later." He pocketed the phone and slid down from the workbench. "Much later."

"Yeah, maybe." Buzz Cut had finished with his customer's bike, standing back from it and wiping his hands on a shop rag. "Maybe next Hallowe'en."

"So what is the big deal?" Behind Edwin, the grandfather clocks lining the hallway ticked like ratcheting crickets. "You take it *from* here, you take it *to* there. You drop it off. And you get paid." Edwin's manicured hand drew out an eelskin wallet; a finger with a trimmed, glistening nail flicked through the bills inside. "So why are you making it so hard on yourself?"

The tall clocks—taller than him, way taller than Edwin—were part of the funeral parlor decor. They had been Edwin's father's clocks, back when the old guy had run the place, and Edwin's grandfather's, who had started it all. Edwin had inherited the family business, right down to the caskets in the display room. You could hear the clocks all over the place, in the flower-choked foyer and past the softly murmuring, endlessly repeating organ music in the viewing rooms. Maybe they reminded the customers in the folding chairs of eternity, or the countdown to when they'd be lying in a similar velvet-lined box. So they had better talk to the funeral director on the way out and make arrangements.

"I don't know . . ." He looked down the hallway. Past Edwin's office was the prep room, where the public didn't go, where it was all stainless steel and fluorescent bright inside, and smelled chemical-funny. Edwin had taken him in there one time, when it had been empty, and shown him around. Including the canvas-strapped electrical hoist mounted on the ceiling, that Edwin's father had installed when his back had gone out from flipping over too much cold dead weight. "This is kinda different . . ."

"What's different?" Edwin's face was all puffy and shiny, as though he hadn't actually swallowed anything he drank—the glass with the melting ice cubes was still in his hand—and now the alcohol was leaking out through his skin. "It's the same as before."

"Well . . . no, actually." It puzzled him, that he had to explain this. "Before, there was like a van. Your van. And all I had to do was help you load it up, and then drive it over there."

"The van's in the shop."

That didn't surprise him. Everything about the funeral parlor was falling apart, gradually, including Edwin. Things stopped working, or something else happened to them, and then they were supposedly getting fixed but that never happened, either. Which was the main reason that all the funeral business now went over to the newer place over on the west side of town. With a nice big sweep of manicured lawn and a circular driveway for the mourners' cars, and an overhang jutting out from the glass-walled low building, so the casket could get loaded in the hearse without the flowers getting beaten up on a rainy day. All Edwin got was the occasional cremation, because the oven his father had installed was right there on the premises, in a windowless extension behind the prep room.

Or used to get—Edwin had managed to screw that up as well. To keep the money from dwindling away quite so fast, what he'd gotten after his dad died, he'd taken on a contract from the local animal shelter, to take care of the gassed dogs and cats, the ones too ugly or old or mean to get adopted out in ninety days. An easy gig, and reliable—the world never seemed to run out of stiff, dead little corpses—but Edwin hadn't been picky enough about raking out the ashes and the crumbly charred bits from the cooling racks. Edwin had still gotten some human-type jobs, family leftovers from his father and grandfather running the place, and some old widow had opened up the canister that nothing but her husband's remains was supposed to be in, and had found the top half of a blackened kitten skull looking back all hollow-eyed at her. Things like that were bad for business, word-of-mouth-wise. Even the animal shelter had unplugged itself from Edwin, and then the state had revoked the cremation license, and now the oven also wasn't working, or Edwin hadn't paid the gas bill or something like that. Edwin had told him what the deal was, but he hadn't really paid attention.

"I don't get it." He pointed down the ticking hallway, toward the prep room. "Why do they keep dropping jobs off here, anyway?"

"Hey." Edwin was sensitive about some things. "This is still an ongoing business, you know. Mortenson's gets booked up sometimes. They're not *that* big." That was the name of the other place, the nicer one. "So I can take in jobs, get 'em ready, then send 'em over there. Split the fees. Works for them, works for us. This is how you get paid, right?"

Barely, he thought. Hard to figure that the other funeral parlor did a fifty-fifty with Edwin, since they would do all the flowers and the setting up of the casket in the viewing room, the hearse and the graveside services, all of that. The actual getting the body into the ground. What would they pay Edwin for providing a slab-tabled waiting room? Not much. So no wonder that the most he got from Edwin, for driving the van back and forth, was a ten-dollar bill or a couple of fives. Only this time, there was no van.

"Actually," he mused aloud, "you should pay me more for this one. If I were to do it at all. Since I'd be providing the wheels."

"How do you figure that?" Impatience lit Edwin's pudgy face even brighter and shinier. "Gas is cheaper for a motorcycle than a van. Even a hopped-up monster like yours."

If he hadn't finished off the six-pack, back at the motorheads' place, he might have been able to come up with an argument. *It's my gas*, he thought. *I paid for it*. But Edwin had already steered him down the hallway, past the clocks, and right outside the prep room door.

"Just do it, okay?" Edwin pushed the door open and reached in to fumble for the light switch. "We'll work out the details later."

Edwin had another sideline to get by with, dealing cigarettes dipped in formaldehyde, the being something he had gallon jugs of. The customers at the funeral parlor's back door were all would-be hoody teenagers, slouching and mumbling. Their preferred brands seemed to be Marlboros and those cheesy American Spirits from the Seven-Eleven. Edwin fired one up, puffed, then handed it to him. "Just to calm you down."

It had the opposite effect, as usual. The chemical smoke clenched his jaw vise-tight, the edges of the contracting world burnt red. He exhaled and followed Edwin inside the prep room.

"This better not be a bag job." He handed the dip back to Edwin. "Like that one that got hit by the train. That sucked."

"All in one piece." Edwin pulled the sheet off. "Looks like she's sleeping."

He looked down at what lay on the table, then shook his head. "You sonuvabitch." His fist was ready to pop Edwin. "This is not right."

"For Christ's sake. Now what's the matter?"

"What's the matter? Are you kidding?" The table's cold stainless-steel edge was right at his hip as he gestured. "I dated her."

"How long?"

He thought about it. "Four years. Practically."

Edwin took another hit, then snuffed the dip between his thumb and forefinger. "Not exactly being married, is it?"

"We lived together. A little while, at least."

"Like I said. Come on, let's not make a big production about this. Let's get her over to Mortenson's, let's get paid, let's get you paid. Done deal."

He turned back toward the table. At least she was dressed; that much was a comfort. She had on her usual faded jeans, with a rip across the right knee, and a sweatshirt he remembered buying her, back when they'd been an item. The sweatshirt said UNLV across her breasts. For some reason, she'd had a thing about college basketball, even though they'd never gone to a game. There was a cardboard box full of other Rebels junk, sweats and T-shirts and caps, that she'd left when she moved out of his apartment. Plenty of times, he'd come home drunk and lonely and horny, and he'd pull the box out of the closet, kneel down and bury his face in its fleecy contents, lifting out the tangled sweatshirts and inhaling the faded, mingled scent of her sweat and Nordstrom's cosmetics counter perfumes, more stuff that he'd bought, usually around Christmastime. He still kept in his wallet the list she'd written out for him, the stuff she wore. Which meant that now, every time he opened it up to pay for a drink, he'd catch a glimpse of the little folded scrap of paper tucked in there, and his equally frayed heart would step hesitantly through its next couple of beats, until the wallet was safely tucked in his back pocket again and he was recovered enough to continue drinking. Which helped. Most of the time.

He didn't have to ask how she'd wound up here. She'd had bad habits, mainly the drinking also, back when they'd been hooked up. But he'd heard they had gotten worse after the split-up. He had mixed feelings about that. On one hand, there was a certain satisfaction in knowing that she was as screwed up about him as he was about her. On the other, a certain pang that came with the thought of her heart wheezing to a stop under the load of some cheap street crap.

Which was apparently what had happened. He could tell. Whatever prep work Edwin had done, it wasn't enough to hide the blue flush under her jawline. He'd had buddies go that way, and they'd all had that delicate Easter egg color beneath the skin.

"So you're gonna do it, right? Don't be a schmuck. Think about her. For once. If you don't take her over to Mortenson's, I'll have to dump her in a wheelbarrow and take her over there myself."

"Yeah, like that's gonna happen." He knew it wouldn't; Edwin got winded just heading upstairs to get another drink. "This is gonna be double."

"Fine. You got me in a jam. Just do it, okay?"

It struck him that maybe this was some elaborate joke on Edwin's part. What would the punchline be? Her sitting up on the table, opening her eyes and flashing her old wicked smile at him?

I wish. That was something else that wasn't going to happen.

"Exactly how do you propose I'm gonna get this done?" He knew from previous jobs that she wouldn't be stiff anymore. She didn't even smell stiff. "Maybe I could sling her over the back of the bike and bungee her down. Or maybe across the front fender, like those guys who go out deerhunting with their pickup trucks." He nodded. "Yeah, just strap her right on there. Who'll notice?" The dip load in his brain talked for him. "Maybe we could make a set of antlers for her out of some coat-hangers."

"Look," said Edwin, "you don't have to get all pissy about this. I'm the one doing you a favor, remember? I thought of you because you're always going on about how you need the money."

Which was true. He nodded again, deflated. "All right. So what exactly did you have in mind?"

Edwin had already thought it through. He pulled the handcuffs out of his jacket pocket and held them up. "These'll do the trick. We just sit her on the bike behind you, throw her arms around your chest, clip these on her wrists and you're all set. Anybody sees you, just another couple cruising along. Young love."

"No way. She never liked to ride bitch." He'd found that out after he'd already pulled the stock seat off the 'Busa and put on a Corbin pillion for her. "She always wanted her own scoot. Remember, I was gonna buy her that Sportster? The powder blue one."

"Yeah, yeah, yeah." Edwin gave him a wearied look. "It's not as if she's in a position to complain about it, is she?"

The guy had a point there.

Took a lot of wrestling—for which Edwin was no frickin' use—but he finally got on the road. With her.

He rolled on the throttle, in the dark, kicking it up from fifth to sixth gear as the single lane straightened out. The chill of her bloodless hands, icy as the links of the handcuffs, seeped through his leather jacket and into his heart.

He stayed off Boulder Highway and the bigger, brighter main streets, even though it meant racking up extra miles. There was a helmet law in this state, though he'd never heard of the cops enforcing it. Or anything else for that matter—you'd have to shoot the mayor to get pulled over in this town.

Still, just his luck, the one time some black-'n'-white woke up, to get nailed with a corpse on back of the 'Busa. Cruel bastards to do it, though. He could see, without looking back over his shoulder, how her hair would be streaming in the wind, a tangling flag the color of night. With her pale cheek against his neck, she'd look as though she were dreaming of pure velocity, the destination that rushed just as fast to meet you, always right at the headlight's limit.

And if he closed his own eyes, as if he were sharing the same furious pillow of air with her . . .

Not a good idea. He didn't even see the patch of gravel, dropped on the asphalt by some construction truck. His eyes snapped open when the rear wheel started to skid out from beneath him. He yanked the 'Busa straight from the curve he'd banked into. The bike felt awkward and top-heavy with her weight perched a couple inches higher than his own. He steered into the skid, wrestling the bike back under control, his knee clearing the guardrail as he trod down on the the rear brake.

That all took about one second. But that was enough to have shifted his cold passenger around on the seat behind him. The handcuffs rode up under his armpit, her face with its closed, sleeping eyes no longer close to his ear but now pushed into the opposite sleeve of his jacket, down below his shoulder. One of the boots that Edwin had worked back onto her ivory, blue-nailed feet had popped loose from the rear peg. Her denim-clad leg trailed behind the bike, the boot's stacked heel skittering on the road. The body slewed around even more as he squeezed the front brake tight. By the time he brought the 'Busa to a halt, she was almost perpendicular on the seat behind him, her hair dangerously close to snagging in the wheel's hub.

"God damn." Edwin and his stupid ideas—this whole job was becoming more of an annoyance than it was worth. He levered the kickstand down and leaned the bike's weight onto it. Her hair swept a circle in the roadside debris. He was annoyed at her as well. If she had still been alive, he would have figured she was doing it on purpose. Drunk and screwing around again. Her weight toppled him over as he swung his own leg off the bike.

Now she was underneath him. As though she had brought him down in a wrestling hold—back when they had lived together, he had taught her a couple of moves he remembered from the junior varsity squad. Above him, the stars of the desert sky spun, wobbled, then held in place. If he rolled his eyes back, he could just see her face, somewhere by his ribs. If she had opened her eyes, she could've seen the stars, too.

His thin gloves scuffed in the sharp-edged rocks as he rolled onto his hands and knees, pulling her up on top of himself. That much effort winded him. It wasn't that she was so heavy, but every part of her seemed to have cooked up its own escape plan, as though none of her wanted to get dumped off at another funeral parlor. Her legs sprawled on his other side, the boots twisting at the ankles.

The handcuffs had been an even dumber idea. Edwin probably got some thrill out of the notion. It would've worked better if they had dug up a roll of duct tape and strapped her tight to his body. This way, she had just enough of a hold on him to be a nuisance. In that, not much had changed from when she had been alive. He rooted around in his jacket pocket for the key; couldn't find it. It must've popped out, somewhere on the ground.

He tried standing up, and couldn't make it. He toppled forward and grabbed the bike to keep his balance. The near-vertical angle rolled her weight forward, the handcuffs sliding onto his shoulderblade, her head lolling in front of him. The bike gave way, the kickstand scything through the loose dirt. The hot engine burned through his trouser knee as he fell.

The three of them—corpse, motorcycle and its rider—hit the side of the road hard. He could smell gasoline leaking from the tank's filler cap. The links of the handcuffs gouged the middle of his spine. She was sandwiched between him and the toppled bike, her face upturned toward him, as though waiting for a kiss, one denimed leg wedged into his groin.

He pushed himself away from the bike, dragging her up with him. The handcuffs slithered down to the small of his back as he managed to stand upright at last. That brought her face down to his belt level.

Well, that's sweet. He stroked her tangled, dusty hair back from her brow. Just like old times. Memory tripped through his head, strong enough to screw him up worse.

"Come on," he spoke aloud. "Nice and all, but we gotta get going."

He reached down, grabbed her above the elbows and lifted. She only came up a few inches before he realized he was pulling up his trousers as well, the frayed denim cuffs sliding above the tops of his own boots.

"What the—" He looked down. His eyes had adjusted enough to the slivered moonlight, that he could see her hair had snagged in the trousers' zip.

It must've happened while he and the corpse had been wrestling on top of the fallen motorcycle. Every stupid, annoying thing was happening tonight. That brought back memories as well.

Her cold face was caught so close to him, he couldn't even slide his hands down between her cheek and the front of the trousers. Not without undoing his buckle first; the loose ends of his belt flapped down beside her shoulders. He sucked in his gut and managed—barely—to pinch the zipper's metal tag. "Damn," he muttered. "Come on, you bastard." Half-inch by reluctant half-inch, he worked the zipper open, his knuckles chilled against her brow. Loosened, the trousers slid partway down his hips.

The world lit up. Headlight beams raked across him, a car rounding the road's curve. He shielded his eyes from the probing glare. His shadow, and hers, spilled back across the empty landscape.

He could see the silhouettes of the people inside. The driver, his wife beside him, a couple of little kids in the backseat, their faces pugnosing against the side windows as they got a better look. He glanced down and saw how perfectly the white, shifting light caught her profile. Or at least the part of it that wasn't shadowed by his open fly.

Then the headlight beams swung away from him and down the length of road farther on. The car was right next to him; he could have let go of her arm and rubbed his hand across the car's flank as it sped past. Close enough that the people in the car didn't need the headlights to see what was going on, or think they saw. There was enough moonlight to glisten on the handcuffs' links as the driver looked up to his rear-view mirror, the wife and kids gaping through the rear window.

My life's complete now. He had been there when some tourist yokels from Idaho or some other numb-nut locale had caught a glimpse of another world, where other stuff happened. Like the tightly rolled-up windows of their rental car had been the inch-thick glass of some darkened aquarium, that you could push your nose up hard against and witness sharks copulating with jellyfish, all blurry and wet. It would give them something to talk about when they got back to Boise, especially the bit about the poor ravaged girl being handcuffed around the guy's waist.

Two streaks of red pulsed down the asphalt. The car had hit its brakes. Worse; he turned, looked over his shoulder and saw another red light come on, above the car. It flashed and wavered, with blue-white strobes on either side. They weren't tourists from out of state; he saw that now. He watched as a Metro patrol car threw a U-turn, one front wheel crunching across the gravel, then bouncing the suspension as it climbed back onto the road.

"Shit." The headlights pinned him again. He looked down and saw, as if for the first time, how luminous pale her skin was. *They could tell*, he thought in dismay. One thing to be spotted getting skulled on the side of the road, even with the handcuffs involved—that was probably happening all over this town at any given moment, not worth the police's attention. But with a corpse—was that a felony or just a misdemeanor? It didn't matter, what with him still being on parole for things he couldn't even remember when he was straight.

He lifted harder this time, his hands clamped to her rib cage, hard enough to snap free a lock of her hair and leave it tangled in his zipper. Her arms still encircled him; that actually made it easier to sling her against one hip, his other hand tugging his trousers back in place. The difficult part was getting the bike upright again, but somehow he managed, even as the patrol car's siren wailed closer. Red flashes bounced off the tank and the inside of the windscreen, as he lugged her onto the seat behind him, the cuffs slipping across the front of his jacket once more.

The 'Busa coughed to life. As he kicked it down to first and let off the clutch, the cop car slewed a yard in front of him, spattering road grit against the front fender. He yanked the bike hard to the right, bootsole scraping the asphalt, then wrenched it straight again, pouring on the throttle. Something loose—maybe her boot?—clipped the patrol car's taillight as he jammed past.

He was already into fourth, redlining the tach, by the time he heard the siren coming up behind him. Fifth, and the yowl faded for a moment, then just as loud again as the driver cop stood on the accelerator pedal. Hitting the nitrous button wouldn't do him any good. The road was too straight; if they had been up in the mountains with some tight twisties to slalom through, he could've left the cops way behind. Out here in the flat desert, though, they could just keep hammering on top of him, long after the nitrous canister was exhausted, until he either gave up or sliced a curve's guardrail too close. The first would leave him on the ground, but alive at least, with a tactical boot on his throat and a two-handed forty-four pointed between his eyes. The second would probably leave two corpses on the ground, one freshly bleeding from the impact.

Just as he hit sixth, the 'Busa screaming into triple digits, the siren and the flashing red light jumped in front of him. *How'd that happen?* He didn't have time to wonder. A shining white wall reared before him. The 'Busa's headlight painted a big red X in the middle of it. That was all he saw as the brakes grabbed hold, too late to keep the bike from hitting broadside, even as it fell.

"You with us, pal? How many fingers?"

He wasn't sure. "Two?"

"Close enough."

He tried to turn over on his side, but couldn't. She was still hooked up to him, arms encircling him on the cot where they lay.

The paramedic van was like the inside of his head. Eye-achingly lit up, smelling of chemicals, and filled with mysterious objects that he didn't recognize.

"You hit us a good one." One of the EMTs had a knotted ponytail. He pointed to a spot near the van's floor. "You can see the dent from in here."

"I can pay for it." He pushed himself up on his elbow. "Not right now, but—"

"Forget that." The other EMT, looking back from the driver's seat, had tattoos and smoke-reddened eyes. The whole van reeked of party atmosphere. "This is not good."

"Yeah, yeah, I know." He tugged at the handcuffs but they stayed locked. "Look, just don't hand me over to the cops—"

"Cops? What cops?" The EMTs glanced at each other, above him. "We didn't see any cops."

A small comfort, that he was just screwed up and not pursued. *I must've made 'em up.* Another good reason for not riding in that kind of condition—all that beer and the hit off the dip that Edwin had given him.

"I'll just be on my way." The van's interior swam and tilted as he sat up, dragging her with him. "You don't have to report this—"

"Report it? Are you kidding? This is a frickin' fatality situation."

"What?" Then he realized what the tattooed one was talking about. "Uhh . . . actually, she was this way before."

They weren't listening to him. "I'm not calling it in," said Ponytail. "*You* call it in."

"Screw that. I'm not filling in all that paperwork again. I did the last one we had. Remember? The coronary?"

"Guys—"

"Well, we can't just let him walk."

"Why not?"

They both looked at him, then at each other, then back to him. Ponytail slowly nodded. "Maybe . . ."

He put his weight on his left foot. The resulting bolt through his spine nearly took the top of his skull off. He collapsed backward, propped up by the dead girl.

"You're not going anywhere in that condition, pal."

He looked down at himself and saw how ripped-up his trousers were. The whole long seam along the left leg had been torn open, the skin beneath bruised and chewed red by a skid over asphalt. God knew what condition the bike was in.

"I don't care." He gripped the edge of the cot with sweating hands, trying to keep from passing out. "I gotta get out of here. I got a delivery to make."

"Her?" Ponytail nodded toward the shackled weight, with the long dark hair and dreaming face.

"Give him something," said the driver. "Just get him on the road. Long as I don't have to fill out any paperwork, it's cool."

"Right—" Ponytail nodded as he fumbled around with the equipment shelved on either side. He spun a valve on a chrome canister, the tethered plastic mask to his own face. He inhaled deeply, then held it out. "Here, try this."

The van expanded and dissolved with the first hit. The blood throb in his battered leg faded, along with any other sensation of having a body.

All he could feel was her pulseless hug around his chest. He pushed the mask away. The paramedic van slowly coalesced, now formed of sheets of vaguely transparent gelatin, warping beneath him and yielding to a poke of his finger.

"Off you go, pal." Ponytail maneuvered him toward the van's open doors, like a parade balloon. "You have a good night. Try and stay out of trouble, okay?"

He found himself standing in the middle of an empty road, his wavering legs straddling a long scrape mark gouged out of the pavement. At its end, the 'Busa leaned on its kickstand. The EMTs must have picked it up after he T-boned their van. He wanted to thank them, but they were already gone.

He pulled his passenger along with himself, over toward the bike. She seemed weightless as well, the handcuffs the only thing keeping her from floating away, into the glittering night sky. The toes of her boots seemed to barely trail across the earth's surface.

"That was nice of them." He laid his hands on the tank. He could smell gasoline, but the bike didn't seem in too bad of a shape. The left fairing was a total write-off; that must have been the side he laid it down on. The pegs and bits of engine on that flank were scraped gleaming and raw. It could probably be ridden, if he could figure a way of holding on to it without getting blow away by the wind, like roadside scrap paper.

Whatever the EMTs had given him, he was still way slammed by it. The chemical tides in his bloodstream would have to roll out a bit—or a lot—before he'd be able to climb on the 'Busa again. *Sleep it off*, he told himself. Maybe he could just curl up at the side of the road, wrap her tighter around himself, spooning like old times . . .

Better not. A soft voice whispered at his ear. *I can't keep you warm anymore. Not like this.*

That was when he knew exactly how screwed up he was. And not by whatever was still percolating in his brain. That you could get over. The past, you never did.

He looked around and spotted, if not refuge, at least a waiting room. One that both of them were familiar with. How had he wound up in this part of town?

It didn't matter. He gripped her arms and brought her up higher on his back, her cheek close beside his, and stumbled toward the bar's sputtering neon.

▼▼▼▼▼▼

"The problem's not Hallowe'en," said Ernie. "It's you."

Don't listen to this guy.

He didn't know if the bartender could hear what she said. Maybe the dead spoke only in private whispers. Like lovers. He knocked back the latest beer that had been placed in front of him. "Why is it me?"

Like I said. Her voice again. *This one was always full of crap.*

"You really want to know why?"

He shrugged. "Do I have a choice?"

"You don't even want one." Ernie wiped his sodden towel across the bar. "Here's the deal. You're blaming the world for what happened to you. That's all backwards."

Right now, the world consisted of this bar and its tacky, orange-'n'-black decorations, courtesy of the beer distributors. He looked around at the dangling pasteboard junk, then back to Ernie. "I didn't do this." He pointed to the grinning, long-legged witches. "You can't blame me."

Yes, he can. You just wait.

The bar had emptied. He was the only one left inside, after Ernie the bartender had switched off the outside neon. While he had nursed one of the string of beers, Ernie had started stacking the chairs up on the tables. Then he had come back behind the bar to finish sorting out the world's problems.

"Just hear me out," said Ernie. "I mean, it's cool that you came here with your iced old lady cuffed to you. That shows some effort on your part."

"Hey. We broke up, remember?"

Did we?

He ignored her whisper. "Long time ago," he told the bartender.

Not long enough.

"Whatever." Ernie seemed not to have heard anything she said. "But that doesn't suffice. You gotta look inside yourself. It's not what Hallowe'en did to you. It's what you did to Hallowe'en."

He wished Ernie hadn't said that. Not because the bartender was wrong. But because he knew—standing at the edge of a vast, lightless abyss inside himself, looking down into it—he knew that the bartender might be right. About too much.

"You can't expect things to stay the same," said Ernie, "and you just get to change all you want. Like there's no connection between the two." Ernie uncapped another beer and set it on the bar. "But there is."

"He knows that," said another voice. "But he's got it backward. Like usual with him."

He turned and saw, a little farther down the bar, Buzz Cut taking a pull at a half-empty bottle. The other motorhead, the one with the red hair, sat on the next stool over, drinking and nodding slowly in agreement.

"You should've heard him before," continued Buzz Cut. "With his whole Hallowe'en rap. Boo hoo hoo. It's all so frickin' sad."

He had thought the bar had all cleared out. Where'd these guys come from?

"Sad, all right." Red set his own bottle down. "Just listening to him."

"He's got this whole thing, you see." Buzz Cut tried to explain it to Ernie the bartender. "About how Hallowe'en has changed. It's like really important to him. The poor sad bastard."

"Yeah, right. I've heard it." Ernie pointed around at the decorations. "He goes off about all this stuff, too."

"Wait a minute." It ticked him off, the way they were talking about him. In the third person, like he wasn't even there. When he wasn't even sure that they were there, or were just drug vapors. "Just because you guys—"

Set me as a seal upon your heart.

The whole bar went silent. As though they all could hear her now.

For a moment, she wasn't draped across his back, her pale hands cuffed in front of his chest. She sat right next to him, leaning forward, those hands wrapped around her own beer. She turned and looked at him, beautiful and unsmiling, her dark hair a veil.

As a seal upon your arm, she whispered. *For love is strong as death, passion fierce as the grave.* She took a sip, then continued. *Its flashes are flashes of fire, a raging flame . . .*

"Okay, now I'm totally spooked." He gripped the edge of the bar, forcing it to become real and solid. "Give me a break."

She leaned over and kissed him. *If all the wealth of our house were offered for love*, she said, *it would be utterly scorned.* When he opened his eyes, she wasn't sitting there anymore. Her hands pressed against his heart once more, her cold arms wrapped around him.

Still full of surprises, even dead; he had to give her that. Though not totally a surprise; she'd come up with stuff like that when they'd been together the first time. Pentecostalist childhood, for both of them. He recognized it: Song of Solomon, chapter eight, verses six and seven. There were some hot bits in that Bible book, favorites of hers. Though he couldn't recall her spouting that one before.

"You gotta go back." Ernie's voice penetrated his meditations. "That's what she's trying to tell you."

Maybe they had heard her. He didn't know what that might mean. "Go back where? I already been all over town."

"Not where. When. You gotta go back to when you went wrong. The two of you. And then do it right."

"He'll never make it." Another voice came from the end of the bar. He looked and saw Edwin down there, stubbing out a cigarette butt in a drained highball glass. "He's too screwed up."

"Up yours." The motorheads came to his defense. Buzz Cut nodded along with Red. "He can do it. We gave him all he needs. In this world, at least."

"I'm not following this . . ."

"Pay attention." Ernie leaned over the bar, bringing his face close to his and the dead girl's, as if they were in a football huddle. "I heard you out before. I know where you're coming from. Believe me, I've heard it from other guys like you. You think the world changed out from under you, and that's why things are all wrong." Ernie tapped him on the brow. "But it's the other way around. *You* changed. You gave up the old faith. You thought you could mess around all you wanted, and the world would still be the way it was, the way it's supposed to be, when you got done. It doesn't work that way."

"Listen to the man." Somebody shouted that from one of the tables in the corner of the bar. He glanced over his shoulder and saw the EMTs sitting there, empty bottles soldiered in front of them. And outside the bar—he could sense the Metro patrol car and the tourist family from Idaho, slowly circling around. Except that he had made them up. So they at least were gone.

"Is this one of those *Twilight Zone* bits?" He felt even creepier than before. "You know, like where the guy is dead, only he thinks he's still alive?"

"You should be so lucky," said Ernie. "Don't change the subject. Don't try to get yourself off the hook. You want the world to be the way it should be? Then you need to go back and be the way you should've been. You and her." Ernie reached out and stroked her dark hair, tenderly. "You should've been different. All this screwing around, and being trashy and wild—yeah, that's fun and I'm happy to help you do it, but it doesn't get the job done."

"What job?"

"Come on. You and her, you were supposed to be the people handing out the candy. To the kids. On Hallowe'en. You were supposed to have a house, with a front door, and the bowlful of candy beside it. That's what you were supposed to do. That was your job. Instead, you screwed around.

All of you." Ernie gestured toward the bar's walls. "You think all this crap isn't here for a reason? It's because of you. People like you. Not doing your job. That's how it got here."

"Yeah, well, that's real great. Telling me where—or when—I need to go, and all. Only problem is, there's no way of getting there. It's gone."

"Strictly a technical problem." Buzz Cut shrugged. "Just need to know how. That's why you have friends like us."

"What's the matter?" Edwin had the kind of sneer that revealed a line of yellow teeth. "Didn't you read Superman comics when you were a kid? You weren't one of those Marvel faggots, were you?"

"What's Superman got to do with it?"

"Don't you remember?" Buzz Cut regarded him with pity. "Jeez, what a wasted childhood you must've had. No wonder you turned out this way."

"When Superman needed to go back," said Ernie, "remember how he did it?"

"Uh, that was a comic book."

"Regardless. Remember how?"

"He went real fast." A page full of bright yellows and reds and blues surfaced in his memory. "In a circle. Spinning, like."

"Going in a circle doesn't cut it. If you think about this." Buzz Cut might have been explaining the difference between Keihin carbs and direct fuel injection. "It's the going fast that does the trick. Obviously. Go fast enough, you can get anywhere. Or when. The spinning around in a circle, that was just so Superman would still be where he started out. Right? Otherwise, he would've gone back, but he would've been out around Neptune. Or Alpha Centauri or some other rat-ass place like that."

"Going fast, huh?"

"That's why people like to do it. Go fast, I mean. Even when they have no place to get to. Even when they're just going around in circles. They know what they're doing. They're trying to get back. And you know what?" Buzz Cut leaned toward him, imparting a secret, but loud enough that everyone in the bar could hear. "Sometimes they do."

Some of it made sense, some of it didn't. "Don't you have to go as fast as Superman? To make it work. Super fast?"

"Hell, no. That was just because Superman had to go back to ancient Egypt, or go fight dinosaurs or something. *You* don't have that far to go."

Red chimed in. "You just have to get back to where you went wrong. And start over. The two of you. That's just not that far back."

It's not. Her whisper. *Let's go for it.*

"And no circles?"

"I told you already. Head down, full tuck and accelerate." Buzz Cut got nods of agreement from the others along the bar. "Strictly straight line."

"Kinda hard to tuck down behind the windscreen, with . . ." He tilted his head toward hers. "You know . . ."

"Do the best you can," said Buzz Cut. "Do it right, you won't even be outside the city limits. When you make it there."

He knew what they were all going on about. "You mean the nitrous."

"Well, of course. We put it on there for a reason. Now you know."

Go for it.

They all watched him. Their gaze weighed heavier on him than she ever had.

They were right. Buzz Cut and the others, Ernie the bartender, even Edwin. They were right.

"I'm not paying you, though." Edwin had pointed that out. "This is some other deal you got going."

Once he got himself and her on the 'Busa again, and started it up, he realized how right they were. He didn't make it to the city limits. Out in empty desert again, sawtooth mountain silhouettes against the night sky—but if he had looked over his shoulder, he would still have been able to see the city's clustered neon, a single blue-white beam bending its trajectory above him.

He didn't need to look back. Her face was right next to his, her eyes closed, dreaming into the wind.

Straight shot, up into sixth gear, the road a knife's edge in front of them, throttle rolled to the max. Nothing left but the red button on the handlebars, his leathered thumb already resting upon it.

Now's the time.

Her whisper a kiss at his ear; he turned his cheek closer against the brush of her cold lips. He could barely breathe, she held him so tight. If his heart beat any stronger, it would break the links of the little chain.

Come on . . .

Or maybe the handcuffs had snapped apart already—he couldn't feel them—and it was her own locked grip binding her to him. The way it had before, her eyes closed, velocity and dreamless. His hand at the center of a small world, trembling with both their pulses, every small motion a new possibility.

The button rose to meet his thumb. He pushed as hard as she did.

Then he knew why he had waited so long.

First to go was the 'Busa's fairing, where it had cracked in the spill before. As the nitrous oxide poured into the engine and ignited, the stars blurred horizontal. A wall of air hit him, almost peeling him off the bike. In the rush that enveloped him, he could see but not hear the crack along the left side widen bigger than his gloved fist. It spidered into a jigsaw cobweb for only an instant, then shattered, the razor fragments swirling around him, then gone in the bike's streaming wake.

Pinned, the tach and speedometer were useless now. He couldn't even see them, unable to bring his sight down from the black horizon racing toward him.

Do it, she whispered somewhere. *Harder.*

The wind tore his jacket into tatters, stripped it from his chest. Her hands held tight, cupping his heart.

The front wheel came up from the road, spun free in hurtling air. The distant mountains tilted as he rolled in her embrace, face full against hers. He let go of the handlebars and pulled her tighter to himself, her knees crushing his hips. Beneath them, the motorcycle broke apart, into fire as meteors do, a match flame struck against the earth's atmosphere. Fiery bits of metal skittered along the road, white heat dying to red sparks.

"We're not going back." He turned and kissed her. "We're here already."

Lies and stories. There'd never been any going back. That'd all been crap they'd told him, that he'd told himself, to get to this point.

The old faith would have to do without them. If the children out at night looked up at the incendiary wound bleeding across the dark, they could take it as a sign.

Just before they struck the earth, she opened her eyes and looked into his. The road would strip their flesh away, their entwined bones charring to ash.

"Fierce." She smiled. "As the grave."

MEMORIES OF EL DÍA DE LOS MUERTOS

Nancy Kilpatrick

Nancy Kilpatrick sets her haunting story on the Latin American holiday el Día de los Muertos. It's not exactly Halloween, but it occurs about the same time of year and, like Halloween, its origins can be traced back to pre-Christian culture. The Catholic Church adapted an Aztec festival for the Queen of the Dead, the goddess Mictecacihuatl, with All Saints and All Souls Days. Like Guy Fawkes Day/Night in England, the nearness of the dates brings some crossover with Halloween, but the connection to death and the dead give the Days of the Dead an even closer affinity. Various observances of the Mexican Days of the Dead are, more and more, combining with U.S. customs in many areas.

You call me death bringer, as though ancient words can wound me. When I was mortal, as you are still, that name filled me with loathing. Now, because I live forever, because I have seen your grandparents rot and will watch *los Gusanos* devour your children, your words fade like the ghosts of memories.

This eve of the Day of the Dead—my day, although you do not yet realize there are many ways to be dead—I watch you enter the cemetery just after sunset. The crude wooden crosses as well as those of fine marble are draped with fragrant bougainvillea and gardenia and you add your marigolds—the flowers of the dead—to the stones you stop beside. I see your wife spread a colorful blanket over the graves of your ancestors and open jars and boxes for the long night of sharing. A night when the dead will consume the spirit of the food you offer. Food you expect to devour.

Your son and two daughters pulse with life. Life I no longer possess. They skip along the dusty paths eating sugar skulls and clutching papier-mâché skeletons until the sky blackens and the few fires scattered throughout the graveyard become the only light under a moonless sky. The children fall silent and huddle near you, fearful, expectant. You tell them a story. Of how the dead, on this Day, return to converse with the living. To fulfil promises and offer guidance. To bring good fortune. As you strum your guitar and sing a song, your eyes are sad and fearful. Years have passed since you have visited the dead. Few still come here to spend the night.

By the flickering embers you stare at the worn oval photograph of your mother and imagine her returning. You want this yet fear it. To speak with her again, to feel her bless you and the ones you love . . .

Your son and daughters have fallen asleep. Your wife is drowsy. She leans back and closes her eyes, her long black hair and the crucifix she wears falling away from her throat. You are alone.

Outside the cemetery walls the mariachi band has stopped playing. A cool wind caresses you, blowing hair up the back of your head, exposing your neck. You shiver. I laugh, and you turn abruptly at the sound. Familiar. Alien. Darkness presses in on you and the dead beneath you struggle to call a warning, but their voices were silenced long ago by the worms. You look again to the picture of your mother, then to the sky, and cross yourself, sensing she can no longer help you.

Something flies through the night air, beyond the illumination of the fire. A bat, you hope. Wings flap and you listen as though to a voice. The tequila bottle is less than half full; you take another swallow and I can see you are wondering how you will endure this night.

Once, long ago, when your ancestors and I walked in daylight together, I sat where you sit now. Honoring the dead. Singing sad and joyous songs to them. Telling their tales of grief and bitterness and of how they loved. Of how they lived, and died. Memories stir in me like petals rustled by a breeze.

At last you see me, a shadow among shadows. The guitar slips from your hands. I have come for you. Your eyes are red-rimmed with the knowledge. You plead. Your wife, you say, and your children. There are things you have not yet done. You beg me to spare you until morning, imagining I do not know my powers will wane with the sun. I laugh as tears spill down your weathered face. I am incapable of pity. When I reach out to stroke your cheek, to feel the warmth pushing against your flesh, salty wetness coats my dead fingers. Astonished, I remember.

On a Day of the Dead such as this, when I sat where you sit now, my loved ones beside me, music floating on the cool breezes drifting down from the mountains, I, too, wept. My vulnerable tears betrayed me then, as yours betray you now. My tears did not save me.

What warms your body will soon warm mine. I nod at the boy child, the youngest. A substitute. You decline, as I knew you must. I do not see this as heroism or bravery, simply what you would do.

You turn to the picture of your mother. She will intercede, you think. You pray to her. To anyone. A small iguana springs onto the tombstone next to the melting candle you have placed there. He pauses to stare at you; he is a sign, you believe, good or ill, how can you be certain? I step into the firelight. Neither the dead nor the living can help you now.

"Why?" you ask me. This question I have heard many times over the years. Many times. It is a question for which there is no answer. Your life does not mean to me what it means to you. I feel no love or sympathy, no pity; I no longer understand remorse. All I can tell you is that I long for your hot blood to swirl through my cold body. Your eyes are the only reflection I am capable of seeing and in them I find myself as I once was but am no longer. This image cannot sway me. What I need I must have.

You suddenly understand a horror that all your life you have avoided. You find this incomprehensible: dead exist to whom you mean nothing. And yet even you must know that blood is all that matters on this day when *los Muertos* are honored.

Across the graveyard another calls his ghosts and I listen, intrigued by the bitter-sweet song. The night is long; there are many here with offerings. Many. To one such as myself, all are equal.

Before I turn away, I glimpse disbelief in your eyes. Gratitude. You cross yourself and fall on your knees before your mother. Before me.

I drift between the worn stones toward new warmth. You are a memory already fading. A memory that will die. A memory of the dead.

HALLOWEEN STREET
Steve Rasnic Tem

Steve Rasnic Tem has written a fair number of Halloween tales. The two included here—actually thirteen since the second is a dozen linked vignettes set a single night—involve Halloween Street. It's one of those mysterious locales that may exist the entire year, but becomes significant on this one special night . . . the night when even those born "out of place" find their places.

Halloween Street. No one could remember who had first given it that name. It had no other. There was no street sign, had never been a street sign.

Halloween Street bordered the creek, and there was only one way to get there—over a rickety bridge of rotting wood. Gray timbers had worn partway through the vague red stain. The city had declared it safe only for foot or bike traffic.

The street had only eight houses, and no one could remember more than three of those being occupied at any one time. Renters never lasted long.

It was a perfect place to take other kids—the smaller ones, or the ones a little more nervous than yourself—on Halloween night. Just to give them a little scare. Just to get them to wet their pants.

Most of the time all the houses stayed empty. An old lady had supposedly lived in one of the houses for years, but no one knew anything more about her, except that they thought she'd died there several years before. Elderly twin brothers had once owned the two center houses, each with twin high-peaked gables on the second story like skeptical eyebrows, narrow front doors, and small windows that froze over every winter. The brothers had lived there only six months, fighting loudly with each other the entire time.

The houses at the ends of the street were in the worst shape, missing most of their roof shingles and sloughing off paint chips the way a tree sheds leaves. Both houses leaned toward the center of the block, as if two great hands had attempted to squeeze the block from either side. Another three houses had suffered outside fire damage. The blackened boards looked like permanent, arbitrary shadows.

But it was the eighth house that bothered the kids the most. There was nothing wrong with it.

It was the kind of house any of them would have liked to live in. Painted bright white like a dairy so that it glowed even at night, with wide friendly windows and a bright blue roof.

And flowers that grew naturally and a lawn seemingly immune to weeds.

Who took care of it? It just didn't make any sense. Even when the kids guided newcomers over to Halloween Street they stayed away from the white house.

The little girl's name was Laura, and she lived across the creek from Halloween Street. From her bedroom window she could see all the houses. She could see who went there and she could see everything they did. She didn't stop to analyze, or pass judgments. She merely witnessed, and now and then spoke an almost inaudible "Hi" to her window and to those visiting on the other side. An occasional "Hi" to the houses of Halloween Street.

Laura should have been pretty. She had wispy blond hair so pale it appeared white in most light, worn long down her back. She had small lips and hands that were like gauges to her health: soft and pink when she was feeling good, pale and dry when she was doing poorly.

But Laura was not pretty. There was nothing really wrong about her face: it was just vague. A cruel aunt with a drinking problem used to say that "it lacked character." Her mother once took her to a lady who cut silhouette portraits out of crisp black paper at a shopping mall. Her mother paid the lady five dollars to do one of Laura. The lady had finally given up in exasperation, exclaiming, "The child has no profile!"

Laura overheard her mother and father talking about it one time. "I see things in her face," her mother had said.

"What do you mean?" Her father always sounded impatient with her mother.

"I don't *know* what I mean! I see things in her face and I can never remember exactly what I saw! Shadows and . . . white, something so white I feel like she's going to disappear into it. Like clouds . . . or a snowbank."

Her father had laughed in astonishment. "You're crazy!"

"You know what I mean!" her mother shouted back. "You don't even look at her directly anymore because you *know* what I mean! It's not exactly sadness in her face, not exactly. Just something born with her, something out of place. She was born out of place. My God! She's eleven years old! She's been like this since she was a baby!"

"She's a pretty little girl." Laura could tell her father didn't really mean that.

"What about her eyes? Tell me about her eyes, Dick!"

"What *about* her eyes? She has nice eyes . . . "

"*Describe* them for me, then! Can you *describe* them? What color are they? What shape?"

Her father didn't say anything. Soon after the argument he'd stomped out of the house. Laura knew he couldn't describe her eyes. Nobody could.

Laura didn't make judgments when other people talked about her. She just listened. And watched with eyes no one could describe. Eyes no one could remember.

No, it wasn't that she was sad, Laura thought. It wasn't that her parents were mean to her or that she had a terrible life. Her parents weren't ever mean to her and although she didn't know exactly what kind of life she had, she knew it wasn't terrible.

She didn't enjoy things like other kids did. She didn't enjoy playing or watching television or talking to the other kids. She didn't *enjoy*, really. She had quiet thoughts, instead. She had quiet thoughts when she pretended to be asleep but was really listening to all her parents' conversations, all their arguments. She had quiet thoughts when she watched people. She had quiet thoughts when people could not describe her eyes. She had quiet thoughts while gazing at Halloween Street, the glowing white house, and all the things that happened there.

She had quiet thoughts pretending that she hadn't been born out of place, that she hadn't been born anyplace at all.

Laura could have been popular, living so close to Halloween Street, seeing it out of her bedroom window. No other kid lived so close or had such a good view. But of course she wasn't popular. She didn't share Halloween Street. She sat at her desk at school all day and didn't talk about Halloween Street at all.

▼▼▼▼▼▼

That last Halloween Laura got dressed to go out. That made her mother happy—Laura had never gone trick or treating before. Her mother had always encouraged her to go, had made or bought her costumes, taken her to parties at church or school, parties the other kids dressed up for: ghosts and vampires and princesses, giggling and running around with their masks like grotesquely swollen heads. But Laura wouldn't wear a costume. She'd sit solemn-faced, unmoving, until her mother finally gave up and took her home. And she'd never go trick or treating, never wear a costume.

After she'd told her mother that she wanted to go out that night her mother had driven her around town desperately trying to find a costume for her. Laura sat impassively on the passenger side, dutifully got out at each store her mother took her to, and each time shook her head when asked if she liked each of the few remaining costumes.

"I don't know where else we can try, Laura," her mother said, sorting through a pile of mismatched costume pieces at a drugstore in a mall. "It'll be dark in a couple of hours, and so far you haven't liked a *thing* I've shown you."

Laura reached into the pile and pulled out a cheap face mask. The face was that of a middle-aged woman, or a young man, cheeks and lips rouged a bright red, eye shadow dark as a bruise, eyebrows a heavy and coarse dark line.

"But, honey. Isn't that a little . . . " Laura shoved the mask into her mother's hand. "Well, all right." She picked up a bundle of bright blue cloth from the table. "How about this pretty robe to go with it?" Laura didn't look at the robe. She just nodded and headed for the door, her face already a mask itself.

Laura left the house that night after most of the other trick or treaters had come and gone. Her interest in Halloween actually seemed less than ever this year; she stayed in her bedroom as goblins and witches and all manner of stunted, warped creatures came to the front door singly and in groups, giggling and dancing and playing tricks on each other. She could see a few of them over on Halloween Street, not going up to any of the houses but rather running up and down the short street close to the houses in I-dare-you races. But not near as many as in years past.

Now and then her mother would come up and open her door. "Honey, don't you want to leave yet? I swear everybody'll be all out of the goodies if you don't go soon." And each time Laura shook her head, still staring out the window, still watching Halloween Street.

Finally, after most of the other kids had returned to their homes, Laura came down the stairs wearing her best dress and the cheap mask her mother had bought for her.

Her father and mother were in the living room, her mother having retrieved the blue robe from the hall closet.

"She's wearing her best dress, Ann. Besides, it's damned late for her to be going out now."

Her mother eyed her nervously. "I could drive you, honey." Laura shook her head.

"Well okay, just let me cover your nice dress with the robe. Don't want to get it dirty."

"She's just a *kid*, for chrissake! We can't let her decide!" Her father had dropped his newspaper on the floor. He turned his back on Laura so she wouldn't see his face, wouldn't know how angry he was with both of them. But Laura *knew*. "And that *mask*! Looks like a *whore's* face! Hell, how can she even see? Can't even see her eyes under that." But Laura could see his. All red and sad-looking.

"She's doing something normal for a change," her mother whispered harshly. "Can't you see that? That's more important."

Without a word Laura walked over and pulled the robe out of her mother's arms. After some hesitation, after Laura's father had stomped out of the room, her mother helped her get it on. It was much too large, but her mother gasped "How beautiful!" in exaggerated fashion. Laura walked toward the door. Her mother ran to the door and opened it ahead of her. "Have a good time!" she said in a mock cheery voice. Laura could see the near-panic in the eyes above the distorted grin, and she left without saying goodbye.

A few houses down the sidewalk she pulled the robe off and threw it behind a hedge. She walked on, her head held stiff and erect, the mask's rouge shining bright red in the streetlights, her best dress a soft cream color in the dimness, stirred lightly by the breeze. She walked on to Halloween Street.

She stopped on the bridge and looked down into the creek. A young man's face, a middle-aged woman's face gazed back at her out of dark water and yellow reflections. The mouth seemed to be bleeding.

She walked on to Halloween Street. She was the only one there. The only one to see.

She walked on in her best dress and her shiny mask with eyes no one could see.

The houses on Halloween Street looked the way they always did, empty and dark. Except for the one that glowed the color of clouds, or snow.

The houses on Halloween Street looked their own way, sounded their own way, moved their own way. Lost in their own quiet thoughts. Born out of place.

You could not see their eyes.

Laura went up to the white house with the neatly trimmed yard and the flowers that grew without care. Its color like blowing snow. Its color like heaven. She went inside.

The old woman gazed out her window as goblins and spooks, pirates and ballerinas crossed the bridge to enter Halloween Street. She bit her lip to make it redder. She rubbed at her ancient, blind eyes, rubbing the dark eyeshadow up into the coarse line of brow. She was not beautiful, but she was not hideous either. Not yet. In any case no one ever remembered her face.

Her fine, snow-white hair was beautiful, and long down her back.

She had the most wonderful house on the street, the only one with flowers, the only one that glowed. It was her home, the place where she belonged. All the children, all the children who dared, came to her house every Halloween for treats.

"Come along," she said to the window, staring out at Halloween Street. "Come along," she said, as the treat bags rustled and shifted around her. "You don't remember, do you?" as the first of the giggling goblins knocked at her door. "You've quite forgotten," as the door began to shake from eager goblin fists, eager goblin laughs. "Now scratch your swollen little head, scratch your head. You forgot that first and last, Halloween is for the dead."

TRICKS & TREATS:
ONE NIGHT ON
HALLOWEEN STREET

Steve Rasnic Tem

Halloween is a night when anything can happen. We sometimes forget that. The holiday is what anthropologists call an "inversion ritual": proper order and the usual ways of things are reversed. When we ritualize something, it retains its power, but it also becomes socially acceptable; normative. So, we have certain expectations of Halloween and feel there's no real harm, no actual consequence to intentionally inviting the world to be turned upside down and inside out. Tem reminds us our only expectation on Halloween should be to expect the unexpected.

TRICKS

It was supposed to be the last time they'd all go trick or treating together, but it didn't seem right that the gang go out now that Tommy was dead.

Every year all the gang had gone trick or treating together: Allison and Robbie, Maryanne and John, Sandra and Willona and Felix and Randall. And Tommy. They'd been doing it since fourth grade. Now they were teenagers, and they figured this was the last time. The last chance to do it up right.

Not that they'd ever done anything particularly malicious on Halloween. A few soaped windows. A few mailboxes full of cow shit. Not much more than that.

But Tommy had said this particular Halloween needed to be special. "For chrissakes, it's the last *time!*"

But then Tommy had died in that big pile up on the interstate. They'd all gone to the funeral. They'd seen the casket lowered into the ground, the earth dark as chocolate. It wasn't like in the movies. This movie, Tommy's movie, would last forever. Sandra kept saying that word, "forever," like it was the first time she'd ever heard it.

The dead liked playing tricks. She figured that out quick. Dying was a great trick. It was great because people just couldn't believe it. You'd play the trick right in front of their eyes and they still just couldn't believe it.

He'd only been dead a week when Sandra wondered if Tommy's life itself had been a trick. She couldn't remember his face anymore. Even when she looked at pictures of him something felt wrong. Tommy had this trick: he was never going to change, and because he didn't change she couldn't remember what he looked like.

Sandra and Willona had both had crushes on Tommy. And now he was going to be their boyfriend forever. He used to take them both to the horror shows, even the ones they were too young for. He knew places he could get them in. Sandra thought about those shows a lot—she figured Willona did, too. Tommy loved the horror shows. Now he was the star of his own horror show that played in their heads every night. He'd always be with them, because they just couldn't stop thinking about him.

Sometimes it felt so great just to be alive, now that somebody you knew was dead. Sandra thought that must be the ugliest feeling in the world, but it was real. That was what Halloween was all about, wasn't it? Remembering the dead and celebrating hard because you weren't one of them.

Tommy had liked Halloween the best of all of them—he'd been the one who'd organized all their parties, the one who'd come up with the tricks they would play. So this last night as they went door to door they thought of him when they called out "Trick or treat!" They thought of him while they munched on the candy on their way to the next house, like they were eating his memory a piece at a time.

Halloween Street was always the last place to go. It was traditional. You could play the best tricks on Halloween Street, too, since none of the neighbors ever came out to bother you. You could just do whatever you pleased.

Sandra led the way to the first house on the street: a tall thing missing most of its roof and leaning toward the rest of the block like it was drunk. She knocked on the door and knocked on the door until finally they gave up and started to go away. But as they turned away the door opened and oranges came rolling out for all of them. They put them into their sacks and walked on down the street.

At the next house, a wide place with fire damage on the outside walls, Willona did the knocking. An old man with no teeth gave each of them a peanut butter log and then they left and walked on down the street.

The middle two houses looked even emptier than the others, twins that seemed to be looking at each other all the time with small window eyes. Maryanne and John knocked at both houses and at each house one of the old twin brothers who lived there gave them a box of raisins.

By the time they all got to the end of the street the sacks were getting heavy, unbelievably heavy and Sandra insisted that they sit down to rest. The gang sat in a circle and reached into their sacks for the goodies.

When Sandra looked into her sack her orange had turned into Tommy's head, bleeding from a gash that crossed the crown of his head.

When Willona reached into her sack for the peanut butter log she found a slippery finger instead, Tommy's ring wedged on it so tightly she couldn't get it off no matter how hard she tried.

What John and Maryanne found in their sacks when they went looking for the raisins was a mass of black insects, each one carrying a small pale bit of Tommy's broken flesh.

But the gang never said a word to each other about what they had found, nor did they show any alarm on their faces. They went on munching and smacking their lips, giggling to themselves because it was so good to be alive on this the final Halloween of their childhoods.

And thinking about how this was Tommy's last trick on them—and what a grand trick it was!—and how this was their last trick on Tommy.

THE INVISIBLE BOY

J.P. was acting stupid again. Susan was sorry she'd brought him along, as usual, but she never had any choice anyway. J.P. always went where he wanted to go, and unfortunately the places he wanted to go always seemed to be the places she wanted to go.

She tried to walk as far away from him as possible so that maybe people wouldn't know that he was her brother. But people always knew anyway. Like she had a big sign: J.P.'s SISTER, painted on her forehead.

He looked so stupid in his regular street clothes on Halloween night. That yellow shirt and those brown corduroy pants he always wore. Always. He never took them off, and she didn't think he ever washed them. It made her mad that Mom let him get away with stuff like that.

J.P. was so ignorant. *I'll be the invisible boy,* he said, and laughed that stupid horse laugh of his. *I'll wear my same old clothes but I'll be the invisible boy so that no one can see me!*

"J.P., you're so ignorant!" she'd said but he'd just laughed at her. That stupid laugh. Here she'd worked forever on her fairy princess costume—it had wings and everything—and her brother thought he could be the invisible boy just by saying he was the invisible boy.

You can't see me! he'd said.

"J.P., that's dumb! Of course I can see you! You're wearing that stupid yellow shirt and those stupid brown pants and no way are you an invisible boy!"

He'd looked worried then. *Don't tell anybody you can see me, then . . . don't tell or you'll ruin everything!*

It made her mad when he asked her that because he knew she could never tell him no. He always took advantage of her. It made her feel stupid, too.

"Okay, okay . . . let's just go."

So they started across the street just as a car was coming across the bridge onto Halloween Street when J.P. turned to her and started making faces just like he always did. And Susan started screaming just like she always did.

And the car passed through J.P., the headlights trapped inside him for a second like he was burning smoke, just like it always did.

J.P., the Invisible Boy, turned around and looked at her and laughed that stupid horse laugh of his before jumping backwards onto the sidewalk and then walking backwards like that all the way up Halloween Street.

J.P. was so ignorant.

PAINTED FACES

She always thought that the costumes which were just painted faces were the best.

You could make almost any kind of face with the paint. You could tear the skin in red or bruise it in blue. You could dirty it with brown or you could make it shine with the heat of the sun. If anybody said you were ugly you could make yourself beautiful.

And if anybody said you were beautiful you could make yourself ugly, too.

On Halloween Street the painted faces were always the best. Somebody would always paint themselves up to look like your mother or to look like your father, your brother or your sister. Faces you knew so well but which you were afraid you really didn't know at all.

Because faces were painted and you could always wash them off. Because faces were painted and you could always change them.

Every once in awhile she would reach up to her mom or her dad's face and rub and rub as hard as she could.

And sometimes, after a long time of rubbing and crying about the rubbing, the paint would come off.

SACK LUNCH

He was just a little boy but he carried the biggest treat sack any of the kids had ever seen. It grew out of his hands like a big dark hole and it reached to the ground and even dragged behind him for several feet.

Some of the big boys thought it was silly—he looked crazy dragging that big sack around, almost tripping over it every second and stepping on it all the time. But what if he got more candy because he was such a little boy carrying such a great big sack? Adults were funny that way—they might think it was cute.

So they stopped him, and they took the big sack away from him, and just for a moment they considered dropping it and running away because the sack was so light, and felt so strange in their hands—like an oily cloud as it rose and drifted and hummed as the October wind wrapped it around them.

But they just had to look inside.

Later, when the little boy picked the big sack up out of the street it felt just a little heavier, and there were harsh whispers inside.

But they didn't last for long.

SWEET & SOUR

The boy loved the taste of sweet and sour. Sweet, then sour. Sour, then sweet. Ice cream, then pickles. Lemons, then peaches.

"That's the way of things," his daddy used to tell him. "You wouldn't know the good without the bad to compare it to." His daddy used to say that over and over to him, like some kind of preacher with his sermon. But his daddy just had no idea. Why was one thing good and the other thing bad? Sweet and sour. It was just another flavor, another kind of taste.

Grapefruit and strawberries. Kisses and slaps. Silk and razor blades. Living and dying.

The boy was too old to be out trick or treating. He knew that but he liked the candy too much. He had a sweet tooth. He had a sour tooth.

That night on Halloween Street he was having the best time. Hardly anyone seemed to be home in those houses but he didn't care. There were lots of little kids running up and down that street with their silly store-bought costumes and their grocery sacks full of treats.

He helped one little kid pick up all his spilled candy. He took another kid's mask off and threw it in the creek. He cut a little girl's arm with the penknife he carried and tried to comfort her when she cried. He pulled her arm up to his lips and teeth and tasted her frightened skin: he couldn't figure out if it tasted sweet or if it tasted sour, and finally decided it was both.

He ate as much of his favorite candy as he could steal, until he was almost sick with it. Almost, but not quite. Sweet and sour. Sour and sweet.

Rhubarb and honey. Sugar and alum.

He liked being the biggest one out on Halloween Street, using just his sweetest smile and his most twisted snarl for a costume. But that didn't mean he wanted to be an adult. Adults didn't know a thing, for all they acted like they knew everything. They didn't know that clover stems were sweet, or that dandelion stems were as sour as can be. They never tasted them like kids did.

Adults had the power, but they were just a few trick or treats away from dying. Sweet and sour. Sour and sweet. The boy didn't want to die, although sometimes he didn't much like living. Limes and strawberries. Hugs and teeth.

He ran up onto each house on Halloween Street, knocking on doors and ringing bells. Sometimes the curtains moved, but no one came to the door. Sometimes someone came to the door, but you couldn't see their face.

A little goblin came around the corner, an ugly mask on the beautiful little body. The boy smiled and frowned, took out his knife and went to give the goblin a little kiss.

The goblin reached up its arms to hug the big boy, but the goblin's little fingers were too sharp, and the big boy's skin too thin.

The boy smiled and frowned, and turned upside down.

He lay there until morning came up and his eyelids went down, smelling the fruit trees and tasting his own blood.

Was it Delicious? Or was it Granny Smith? The boy couldn't decide.

BUTCHER PAPER

Jean had spent weeks arranging the outing. The terminal kids got out all too rarely, although most of them were still ambulatory. Just bureaucratic hospital regs that made no sense. Anxieties over law suits. But she'd gotten to the right people and worn them down. And they put her in charge.

The kids were given any materials they wanted so that they might construct their own costumes. The first few days they'd just stared at the materials—picking up glue and markers and glitter and putting them right back down again, touching the giant roll of butcher's paper again and again as if it were silk

—as if these were alien artifacts that they were handling, objects which might have been contaminated with some rare disease.

She wasn't prepared for what the kids finally came up with.

Each kid had wrapped his or her body in the stiff brown butcher's paper. Wide rolls of tape were used to fasten the pieces together securely. When they were all done they looked like a walking line of packages. Packages of meat.

And that was the way they went out on Halloween Street. And that was the way they went out.

CLOWNS

The only ones that really scared her were the clowns. Clown masks always smiled, but that made it even harder to guess at the faces underneath.

Sometimes you could tell from the eyes inside the holes: they'd be red or dark above the impossible ugly smile. But sometimes you couldn't see the eyes.

Sometimes all you could see were the spaces where the eyes were missing. Sometimes all you could see was the space where the mouth was missing.

She thought it must be terrible pretending to smile all the time. She thought it must be terrible to be a smile.

But the clowns filled the streets during Halloween every year, more and more of them every year, and the most hideous of all the clowns seemed to be on Halloween Street this year. She saw clowns with large scars across their faces and big ball noses chewed by something worse than a rat. She saw clowns with vampire teeth sticking out from their messy red lips and clowns with mouths and ears sewn shut by bright blue shoelaces. There were mad clowns and suicidal clowns, crazed and sick and dead clowns. And half of them didn't carry treat sacks. And half of those were much too large to be children in disguise.

Laugh, child! said a voice behind her. She turned and there was the fattest clown she had ever seen, with rolls of brightly painted fat spilling out of his baggy white pants.

Be happy! said another voice, and suddenly there was the thinnest clown she had ever seen, his shirt torn away to show the white flesh like tissue covering the narrow rib cage.

Smile . . . said a crawling clown with a head like a snake. *Sing a merry tune* . . . said a leaping clown with red axes for hands.

And she felt so scared she did begin to laugh, laughing so hard until she peed her pants and then laughing some more. Laughing so hard that when a clown no more than six inches tall and with an orange rat's tail hanging out of the back of his pants handed her a tube of black grease paint she took it, and drew her own smile around her shrieking lips.

So that ever after that she could smile, no matter how she felt inside.

MASKS OF ME

Ronald went to the door and was surprised to see a little boy standing there wearing a mask that looked just like Ronald's own face.

"Where'd you get that mask of me?" Ronald asked, but the little boy just turned and ran away. Ronald went out on the front porch and yelled as loudly as he could, "WHERE'D YOU GET THAT MASK OF ME?" But the little boy just kept on running, and never looked back.

Ronald jumped off the porch and ran after the little boy. Behind him, he could hear his mother and father calling after him in panic, but Ronald kept running, just knowing that he *had* to catch that little boy and find out about the mask of his own face.

"I WON'T HURT YOU! I JUST WANT TO KNOW ABOUT THAT MASK OF ME!" he called, but the little boy just kept getting further and further away, like he had leopard legs or something. Leopard legs and Ronald's own face.

He chased that little boy with the mask of himself up Fredericks Lane and down Lincoln Avenue. He spun into Jangle Road so fast he almost fell down. The wind was blowing hard and the trees were moving like they were getting ready to dance and the whole thing made Ronald feel like he was flying, soaring after that little boy wearing his mask of Ronald.

"... where'd you get that mask of me ..." Ronald tried to say but the wind caught his words and blew them away so hard he could hardly hear them himself.

"... where'd you ... where'd you ..." the wind spat back at him.

Then finally the little boy turned onto Halloween Street and Ronald felt pretty good about that because he knew Halloween Street was a dead end. But he wasn't ready for all the kids trick or treating there, hundreds of them of all sizes, and all of them wearing these masks with Ronald's own face.

"Where'd you get those masks of me?" Ronald cried out in confusion.

"Where'd you get that mask of me?" they all chorused back in panic and fatigue.

"... where'd you ... where'd you ..." the wind gently crooned.

And then there was nothing else to say. All the children with Ronald's face sat down on Halloween Street and said nothing. Ronald wondered if maybe they were all waiting for the real Ronald to stand up, for the real Ronald to make it perfectly clear exactly who was who.

So the real Ronald stood up and tried to take his face off, just to show all the others that it wasn't a mask. And all the other real Ronalds stood up and tried to take their faces off, to finally put an end to the crowded masquerade.

And all of Ronald's faces did come off. And there were the Willies and the Anns and the Bobbies and the Janes. And there was no one named Ronald there at all.

And no one could remember ever knowing any kid with such a strange name.

PLAY PARTY

Ellen left the party early because she didn't belong.

Freddie left the party early because he didn't belong.

Willa left the party early because she didn't belong.

Johnny left the party early because he didn't belong.

They wandered their separate ways toward Halloween Street, empty and waiting sacks clutched desperately in their hands.

Behind them faded the community sounds, the get-together songs of cornhusking, apple paring, rock and roll dancing, bobbing for apples and stealing a kiss.

Come, all ye young people that's wending your way,
And sow your wild oats in your youthful day . . .
But there would always be a place where the loners could go.
So choose your partner and be marching along . . .
Halloween Street was always open to the Ellens, the Willas, the Freddies and Johnnys.
For daylight is past, the night's coming on . . .
Where the doors to the empty houses would open only to their special knocks.
And close them up safe. And close them up tight.

JACK

Marsha cut her thumb real bad last year carving pumpkins, so this year her dad said she couldn't carve pumpkins at all. He said she was too careless. She didn't understand how he could remember things that far back—sometimes she had trouble just remembering what happened last week—but he did. And she had made him mad the last couple of days and sometimes that made him remember more. She had let the soup boil over on the stove and she had borrowed her mother's ring and lost it and she had let the baby crawl away when she was supposed to be watching him. Sometimes it was hard for her to remember things especially when she was excited about something like Halloween. But Dad didn't seem to understand that at all. That's why she'd taken the knife out of the kitchen and hid it in her treat sack. There was a big pumpkin patch behind Halloween Street and she'd find herself one there to carve.

All up and down Halloween Street the jack o' lanterns were wonderful this year. She didn't know any of the people who lived on this street, and she didn't know anyone else who did either, and that made her wonder all the more what kind of people would carve such great pumpkins.

On the pumpkins there were faces with great moustaches and faces with huge noses. Enormous, deep-set eyes and mouths that stretched ear-to-ear. Some of the pumpkins had other vegetables attached—carrots and onions and potatoes and turnips—to make features that stood out on the pumpkin's head. There were pumpkin cats and pumpkin dogs, bats, walruses, spiders, and fish.

There was every kind of face on those pumpkins a person could imagine: faces Marsha had seen lots of times and faces Marsha had never seen once in her entire life.

But there wasn't a single pumpkin that matched anyone in her head she might have called a "Jack." As far as Marsha was concerned there wasn't a "Jack o' lantern" in the bunch. So she'd just have to make herself one.

She slipped down a well-worn pathway that ran between two dilapidated houses, crept along a waist-high fence whose paint had peeled and furred to the point where it gave her the creeps just to touch it, until finally she stepped out into the pumpkin patch: yards and yards of green foliage studded with the big orange pumpkins.

She couldn't see the ends of the patch—it stretched out as far as she could see on this side of the river. But for all the pumpkins to choose from, finding the right one for "Jack" was easy.

It was a squat, warped-looking thing just beginning to rot. But she could already see Jack's face in the bulgy softness of its sides. She cleared off the dirt from its surface, pulled out the knife, and stuck it in as deep as she could make it go. The patch sighed and shook as she wiggled the knife back and forth. It felt icky, like she was carving up a baby or something. Finally Jack's face started coming out of all that softness: a wide mouth with teeth as big as knife blades, a nose like a hog's nose, or maybe some other animal that liked to stick its face down in the mud, and two deep deep little eye holes, like the eyeballs had sunk way down so that you couldn't look at them, so that you could never know exactly what old Jack was feeling. That was the other thing—somehow Marsha just knew that Jack's face was old, as old a face as Marsha had ever seen. So old it was like Jack could have nothing in common with Marsha, or even care.

So that after she'd made Jack, Marsha decided she really didn't like him very much. The fact was, she hated him. So she dropped him on his big ugly face and ran out of there. She ran out of the patch and back down the path that led between the dark houses and out into the shadowy lane that was Halloween Street itself. Then she remembered she had forgotten the kitchen knife.

It wasn't an ordinary knife—it was part of a set her parents got for their wedding and it had a different sort of handle and once her dad found it gone then he would know who had taken it.

Marsha went back up the pathway slowly, but when she reached the pumpkin patch she saw that a man was standing there, right in the middle of the Halloween Street pumpkin patch, just staring at her.

He wore a big black coat and a big black hat and his hands had been swallowed up by big orange gloves.

And Marsha could see that he was standing right where she had dropped Jack. So her parents' kitchen knife had to be some place near his feet.

"Excuse me, sir?" she said and the man took a step toward he. "Did you see . . . " And the man took another step. " . . . a knife?" And the man stepped closer still.

When the man took several more fast steps Marsha turned and ran. She ran back down the path and she ran out in the street but when she turned her head the man was right there.

So she ran to the end of the street and beat on a door there but she could hear the man coming up the steps and so she ran to the edge of the porch and jumped off and ran to the next empty house with a pumpkin on the porch and then the next and then the next but nobody ever answered even though all the jack o' lanterns were lit and she could hear the man behind her with every terrified step.

Finally she was stuck in one corner of a dark yard and there was no place to turn and the man was coming right up to her he was so tall she couldn't see the top of him and he had one orange hand held up high.

"Your knife, I've got your knife, little girl," the man said in a friendly voice and she felt all better again.

Until he took off his hat with that big orange glove of his and his head was that pumpkin she carved, that big old ugly Jack with the knife blade teeth and her parents' kitchen knife was stuck in all the way to the handle right beside his nose but he didn't seem to mind.

Owls

All night long the owls gathered in the trees up and down Halloween Street.

All night long they rustled their feathers and stared with their eyes of glass.

All night long they wept while the children played.

For owls know that some days the sacks are empty. For owls know a sack can't be filled with wishes.

And owls know the children eventually go home, lock their doors, and never come out again.

The children hooted and screeched their way from house to house, the tears of the owls glistening on their shoes.

TREATS

Almost midnight, when the last of the children should have been home, but were not, their bags too full of treats to carry, and Halloween Street full of the sounds of rustling costumes and laughter, candles were seen to light up all over the lane and both sides of the creek.

The children, if they hadn't been so excited by the bizarre and exciting shapes of each other, by the heady scent of colored sugars in their bags, might have been a little frightened by this, but for the moment it seemed like a great deal of fun. The world was full of treats for them, and each new event offered them more. They all laughed out loud.

Some of them cheered.

But then the individual flames began to drift away from their individual candletops, rising swiftly to join one another in the sky above, where they paused as if sad and reluctant before floating up into the dark night.

As quickly as that. As quickly as a hungry child emptying his bag of its bright and shiny, but ultimately unsatisfying, treats.

Only one child cried, but all the others recognized what he felt. For a brief moment they thought of the ends of things, of how alone they were in this dark and treatless night.

One by one the children drifted away to home and their separate dreams, even the youngest among them trying to pretend he was younger still, a baby, some unknowing sprite who might last this night forever.

MEMORIES

Peter Crowther

It has become a tradition to disguise oneself for Halloween. There are several theories about the origins of dressing up for the holiday. Some think it was first an attempt to impersonate the spirits in order to placate or confuse them; others posit obscuring identity may once have been seen as a way to trick ghosts, to keep them from recognizing you. Others see it simply as a way to protect those guilty of pranks—or worse. But what if . . . something . . . appeared and stole your identity, obliterated every trace of your existence: all memories and evidence there ever was a "you"? How would we even know such a threat existed? Perhaps Peter Crowther knows something we've . . . forgotten . . .

"Ezzie?"

"Bea, that you?"

"Yes, it's me."

"Why you whispering?"

"Where you been? I been calling you on and off for a couple hours now."

"I had to take the store keys into Mil. She's going in early in the morning. Jack took her bunch of keys by mistake." Then, "Why *are* you whispering, Bea?"

"Go to the window."

"What?"

"Go to your window and look over."

"Bea, I'm right in the mid-"

"Please, Ezzie. If you can't do this one thing for me then I just don't—"

"Okay, okay . . . but this had better be good."

The line went quiet for a minute or so and Beatrice Duke heard a laughtrack Doppler first into earshot and then out again as Elizabeth

Rafaelson walked from her kitchen, through the living area and into the hallway.

"Okay," she said. "I'm at the window."

"See anything?"

Elizabeth couldn't hide the chuckle—and maybe just a hint of frustration—from her voice. "Bea, you're gonna have to be just a little bit more specific. I see *lots* of—"

"Outside my place—can you see anyone? Outside my house?"

Ezzie flicked off the hall light, leaned on the windowsill and put her forehead against the glass. "Uh-uh," she said softly. Then, "Hey, now you've got *me* whispering!"

"Someone's out there, Ezzie."

"Yeah, there's lots of folks out there, Bea . . . kids mostly, and moms and dads herding them around door to door—it's Hallowe'en, for chrissakes. Every kid in the nighborhood is out there, armed with a cloak, some stick-in vampire dentures and a plastic punkin tub to store their plunder."

The line was silent for a few seconds and Ezzie moved back from the glass. Had she seen something out there? Just for a second, there had been the faintest hint of movement, over there behind the bushes that lined the pathway around the back of Bea's house. She was sure of it. She leaned forward again and, shielding her eyes as she squinted into the gloom between her house and the house across the street, she hit her head on the glass. On cue, the TV set behind her chose that very moment to burst into a wave of laughter. When Bea spoke again, it startled Ezzie.

"It's not kids, Ezzie."

"So if it's not kids, who is it?"

Silence. Then, "I dunno, but he does stuff . . . and then, I think he makes you forget. And he did something to little Billy Westlow."

It must be getting unseasonably cold, Ezzie thought and she wrapped her free arm around her tummy. Here it was only fall and already it felt like it was the depths of January. "This some kind of Hallowe'en prank, Bea because if it is then I tell you thi—"

As though reading her friend's mind, Bea said, "I called the police."

Somewhere outside, a siren wailed and Ezzie wondered if it was a police car or an ambulance.

"They came over? On Hallowe'en? Boy, you musta touched the hem of God's robe, girl. And the guy's stayed around with the cops tramping through the bushes?"

"He wasn't on my place. Not then."

"So . . . why'd you call the police?"

"Ezzie, do you remember Bill Westlow?"

"*Bill* Westlow? Bea, who's *Bill* Westlow? Don's brother? I didn't even know he had a—"

Bea let out a deep sigh that just stayed a breath short of all-out breaking down and crying. "He's Don and Margie's *boy*," she said. "Their *son*, Ezzie. Leastways, he *was*."

Ezzie turned away from the window. It sounded for a second there as though Bea's voice had drifted away off someplace. "Bea, you okay?"

No answer.

"Bea, Don and Margie don't have any kids. You know that."

"Ezzie, he was a *boy* . . . just a *kid*. And that . . . that thing—"

"Thing? What are you talking about, Bea?"

"It looks like . . . it looks like he's a man but I don't think—" She paused and lowered her voice to a whisper. "I don't think it is."

"You mean he's a woman?"

"No!"

Ezzie's hand came up to her neck involuntarily. "You mean to tell me he's one of them trans-vest-ite fellas?"

"For God's sake, Ezzie," Bea snarled.

"Hey, honey, will you just slow—"

Bea finally broke down in tears.

"Bea, you want me to come over? I got a cake in the oven but—"

"No!" Bea snapped. "Stay in your house."

There was that chill feeling again and Ezzie shivered. "Bea, please . . . come on now: you're scaring me."

"Ezzie, he's still out there."

"Who? *Who's* out there?"

Silence. Then, her voice even softer, Bea said, "I told you. The man. At least—" She lowered her voice even more. "—at least I *think* he's a man. And I think there are more of them out there."

Ezzie turned around again and squinted at the house across the street. "I'm looking at your house right now, Bea and there's—"

Wait a minute? What was that?

"Ezzie?"

"It's okay. I'm still here. I thought I saw something."

"What? What did you see?"

"Nothing, honey. I didn't see nothing at all. Just thought I did, is all."

"So what did you *think* you saw?"

Ezzie shook her head to the darkness that surrounded her in the hallway. "A shape," she said at last.

"A shape? Good God almighty, Ezz—"

"Hold on there. It was just a shadow, that's all. You got me all messed up here."

"Shadows only happen when something throws them."

"Not this one. It was just the clouds over the moon . . . something like that. Wasn't nothing more than that. Just clouds across the moon."

Ezzie tried to picture the two of them, standing in their respective hallways looking out of their homes at each other's home, not able to see the other person, talking about—

"What did he do to . . . to this boy?"

"Bill Westlow," Bea hissed, "little Billy Westlow. Never did anything to anyone. Good as gold he was." The line went quiet. "He should have had his mom with him, it being Hallowe'en and all."

Ezzie waited until the line went quiet again before saying, "So what did he do to him? The man?"

"I. Don't. Know." The words were clipped and deliberate. "He just kind of wrapped himself all around him. In a cloak."

"Get outta here! A cloak? Like Dracula? Boy, that's taking the Hallowe'en thing a little too—"

"You didn't *see* it, Ezzie. He wrapped the cloak around him out there on the grass, right at the side of the street, and he fell down on top of him so they were just like a big pile of cloth, the two of them together so you couldn't see any skin. Then the man stands up and . . . and Billy wasn't there. And—" She stopped dead.

"And what?"

"His mouth, Ezzie."

"What about his mouth?"

Ezzie had never appreciated how someone could shout while whispering . . . until right now, that was.

"It was big, Ez . . . so very big."

Elizabeth Rafaelson gave a shudder that travelled all the way down her body. It went like an avalanche, from the neck locket that her mom had passed on to her when Sydney Rafaelson (who could figure giving a man's name to a beautiful baby girl) found that the lump in her left breast was going to take her out, and all the way down to the cloud-patterned house-slippers that Ezzie had bought for $9.95 from T.J. Maxx, over to the Resthaven Mall outside of Forest Plains.

"Big?" was all Ezzie could think of to say to that, but she said it so low it was almost a mime. The answering silence made Ezzie think that maybe her friend hadn't heard her but then Bea went and said something so the gap must just have been Bea nodding. Ezzie had seen her doing it many times when she was listening to someone on the telephone, like the other party could see her doing it from miles away.

Bea said, "He ate him."

"He *ate* him?"

She was nodding again; Ezzie knew it.

"You telling me the guy with the big mouth just up and ate this kid? This Willie Westlow?"

"Billy," Bea said, her voice calm now. "It's Billy Westlow. Don and Margie's boy. You know that, Ez . . . please tell me you know that."

Ezzie wasn't going to say anything of the sort. Maybe Bea was having some kind of breakdown. Naybe she—Ezzie—should call the police herself. But then, hadn't Bea called them? Ezzie said, "So you called the police."

"So I called the police. First off I called you but you weren't there. So then I called the police. And . . . Ezzie?"

"Yeah? I'm still here."

"He saw me."

"Who saw you? The man? Saw you how?"

"I was on the phone, door wide open, watching him stand up while I waited for my call to connect."

Ezzie waited and then said, "What did he do? When he saw you?"

Ezzie could hear a hollow sound down the wire: it sounded like the wind but when she turned to the window there was no movement in the trees or the bushes. Then Bea said, "He just . . . disappeared."

Two small-sized bedsheets came into view walking along the sidewalk holding hands with a much taller Frankenstein's monster—Ezzie would recognise the creature's lumbering gait anywhere. It was Pete Winters and his twin sons, Benjamin and Jake.

"Disappeared?" Ezzie asked. It was like she was doing this whole thing for a script. None of it made any more sense than it did on TV shows when some poor shmuck was trying to come to terms with the downright absurd.

"Like . . . '*poof!*'" Bea said, wonder in her voice.

"Maybe you backed away, blinked or something."

Ezzie sensed her friend shaking her head. "Uh-uh. He just up and vanished. Like he was never there. But you know what?"

Ezzie was not sure she wanted to know anything more at all, but she grunted interest and waited.

"It was like he was surprised."

"Surpised?"

Nod nod. "Like he wasn't expecting me to be able to see him."

"Why would he be not expecting you to see him?"

"I dunno. But that's the way I felt." There was a brief silence and then Bea said, "I was just checking outside . . . make sure he hadn't come back."

"Come back? So he went away? When he saw you'd seen him?"

"Ezzie, he vanished."

"He vanished?" Ezzie repeated, suddenly feeling like one of the characters in an old Bob Newhart routine: *And then he lit it, Walt?* Ezzie half-expected some canned laughter but there was nothing.

"He . . . he waved to me, and then he disappeared."

Ezzie watched the bedsheets with a kind of detached feeling. One of them dropped something—a coin, maybe or one of the tiny chocolate lanterns or pumpkins that she'd seen in the store—and he stooped awkwardly to retrieve it while Frankenstein's monster stood by patiently, holding onto the other bedsheet. "Who came out?" she asked Bea at last—it was the only thing she could think of saying that might move the conversation on a little.

"Huh?"

"Who answered your call-out?"

"Ed Lacy."

"Did he come out?"

"Uh-uh. Too busy. I think he thought I'd been at the bottle."

"He say that?"

"He didn't need to. I know when I'm been patronized, girl."

Ezzie nodded. "How's his wife doing? I haven't seen her down at the store in ages."

"I think she's doing okay. He never mentioned Marnie."

The bedsheets had crossed the street and were now heading up Old Man Wilmetts's front walk to where a shining pumpkinhead sat on a porch table, candlelights glittering from behind its knife-slashed eyes.

I guess he wouldn't, Ezzie was tempted to say but she didn't, deciding it was better to leave the sheriff's wife's drinking problems well alone. The bedsheets had stopped on the sidewalk, heads tipped forward as they went through their spoils.

"Ezzie?"

"Yeah?"

"What if . . . what if there were things that could blank out your memories?"

"Like drugs?"

"Yeah, like drugs . . . but maybe these things are *people.* Or people-*sized,* anyways."

"Girl, you just are not making any sense here. And I got this cak—"

"And they feed off of people. And when they eat the people—these things—they can blanket everyone's memories so's it's like they never even existed."

Ezzie didn't know what to say. She moved the telephone into her other hand and waited.

"I can feel it happening with me, Ezzie. With—" She stopped. "Shit!"

"What is it?"

"His name. I forgot his name?"

"Whose name?"

"The boy. The second son I told you about."

"Westlow? You said Westlow. Don and Margie. A second son."

"That's it . . . Westlow." She paused. "What was his name? His first name?"

"Will—no, you said Bill. His name was Bill. Bill Westlow."

"But you never heard of him, right?"

Ezzie watched the bedsheets comparing swag. "No, I never heard of him. I never heard of him because he never existed, Bea."

"He did, Ezzie. But that . . . that thing out there, the thing that ate him up, it moved every trace of him from my memory."

Ezzie thought of that for a moment. Then she rationalized. "But what about the Westlows' house? And all the folks who had—who *have*—photographs of this Billy Westlow? What about them? And the school prizes, the morning register, the office of births, deaths and marriages? What about all the records there?"

Ezzie knew Bea was nodding.

"Yes, I thought of that. And that's what makes it worse."

Bea lowered her voice a few more notches.

"What if," she whispered, "what if somehow—and I have no idea how, so bear with me, now—what if this thing, or things if there's more than one of them . . . what if they're able somehow to wipe it all clean. Just like that—" Bea clicked her fingers.

"Doesn't make any sense," Ezzie said. "And anyways, it's not possible."

"What if—" Bea stuttered to find the words. "What if one time, a ways back, you had a sister-"

"I *do* have a sister, you know tha—"

"No, Ezzie, hear me out now. What if you had yourself a *second* sister—let's call her Maisie."

"*Maisie*? Why on God's green earth are my folks about to call—"

"And one day, who knows when, these things caught your sister. And they ate her. And then . . . then they blanked out all trace of her."

Ezzie looked across at the chest of drawers right there in the hallway, saw the framed photograph of her and Doreen, standing outside a beach-stand selling lobster rolls, each of them holding one of those rolls in their little fat hands and laughing fit to burst.

"Ezzie?"

"I'm here."

"You thinking about that? What I said?"

"I'm thinking about it." And she was. She squinted her eyes almost closed and imagined the Doreen half of the photograph suddenly getting itself all blanked out.And the books that Doreen had bought her, all of them either just disappearing or having the scribbled notes from the endpapers wiped clean. And no end of other stuff.

"And then," Bea said, "what if every now and again, someone catches them at it."

Outside, the bedsheets had returned to their work and, as Ezzie watched them, they reached old man Wilmetts's door, pulled the bell and waited. Ezzie fancied she could hear it chime, way deep in the house and all the way across the street. She was about to say something to Bea when a dark blot exploded from the dwarf rose bushes ringing the porch railings and enveloped one of the twins, knocking him to the ground.

"Oh, Jesus!" Ezzie exclaimed.

Frankenstein's monster and the other bedsheet looked around from the door at the tussle taking place on the walkway right at the very moment that Old Man Wilmetts opened the door and put on a mock scared face. The bedsheet turned back to face the door and, while Frankenstein's monster took a step back to let his son take center stage, the boy beneath proffered the hand holding his swag-collector.

"What is it?" Bea hissed down the telephone line.

On Old Man Wilmetts's walkway, the blot swirled like a dark mass of material and wrapped itself around the stricken bedsheet-clad form . . . and, the strangest thing happened then. Well, two things, if truth be told. The first thing was that the blot straightened itself up and became human again—

Human *again*? Ezzie thought. Then what had it been in the short timeframe when it was crumpled over the—?

—and that was the second thing right there. Just as the thought came into Elizabeth Rafaelson's head it was replaced with a blankness. Like an eraser taking out an annoying pencil slash on an otherwise pristine book cover. And the thing was that she could feel it happening and could even *see* it happening . . . could see it in her mind's eye, happening at a calm and measure pace but happening nevertheless. It was like someone was reaching into her head and removing certain items—she watched it happen and then, just as suddenly as it had started, it finished. The hand withdrew.

"Ezzie, you still there?"

"Still here."

Across the street, the bedsheet accepted something into his swag-bag while Frankenstein's monster tousled the sheet's head with one hand and shook old man Wilmetts with the other.

"Jeez," Bea said, the relief obvious in her voice. "I thought you'd gone off or something."

"Nope, still here. Thought I saw something but wasn't nothing. Just Ben Winters and his dad getting treats from old man Wilmetts."

She sensed her friend nodding and, just for a moment, wanted to correct herself—there was some distant nagging voice that made her want to call Ben by another name . . . Jack? Or Jeff? Now it was Ezzie's turn to shake her head.

Ezzie watched the old man close the door while the bedsheet and Frankenstein reached the sidewalk and turned right. The moon way up above and the pool of light from the streetlight made the two walking figures into a very poignant tableau, but some part of Ezzie felt there was something even more poignant about them. She glanced back at the grassy sward leading up to old man Wilmetts's porch and, just for a second, she thought she saw the outline of a dog—maybe even a fox. Jackie Gooding down at the general store had said there were a lot of them this year, getting ballsier in coming up into civilization. But whatever it was disappeared as fast as she noticed it . . . kind of unfurling itself (she couldn't think of any other way to put it) and then blowing like a black plastic bag across the next yard and up against Bea's porch.

A piece of plastic? Ezzie wondered.

A slab of gen-you-whine cape once belonging to a true Transylvanian count, perhaps? But she didn't think so.

Bea, Ezzie thought, reluctant to commit her unfounded and unreasonable fears to actual sounds, get out! Take off! Take a hike! Take a powder! Make like an egg and beat it, girl! That wasn't no piece of plastic just as it wasn't no five-and-dime Taiwan-made vampire cloak. It was an honest-to-God slice of October midnight hell-bent on dark mischief.

"Bea," Ezzie snapped, "you got to listen to me."

Jake, that was the other name she had been trying to think of. But Jake? Jake who?

She watched the air around her friend's house contract and expand like heat haze over the summertime blacktop, crinkling reality all around. Now the shape took form-

"Bea, are you listening to me?"

"That you, Ez?"

Is that me? Ezzie thought. What the hell kind of a question was that to ask a girl when you'd been on the telephone with her best part of a quarter-hour . . . and when she'd placed the damn call herself, for chrissakes.

—and now it reared up on what passed for legs and moved on towards Bea's door . . . reaching up a long arm now, the hand clenched into a fist and—

"Bea?" Ezzie wanted to explain to her lifelong friend that she needed to leave her home and hi-tail it to safety . . . walk or even run right out there into the night, no topcoat and maybe not even a sweater, phone hanging from the cradle, swinging in the now-empty house—but she didn't want to panic here. And, deep down, Ezzie wasn't sure at all if Bea would heed her words.

Then Bea said, "Oh for goodness' sake."

Ezzie could hear a rhythmic thumping from somewhere back in Bea's house and she looked back across the street and saw the Midnight Man (or whoever he was), his hand raised, repeatedly bringing it down on the door. And was it a trick of the light or did his whole head look like it was hinged around the mouth area?

"Someone at the damn door, Ez," Bea said, her voice a mixture of exasperation and relief: after all, it was Hallowe'en and here was someone knocking at her door to trick or treat her . . . and everyone surely knew the bogeyman didn't go around knocking on doors, no sir.

"*Bea*," Ezzie shouted again, shifting position so she could better see Bea's front door. "Don't answer the door."

"Hold on there," Bea shouted, her face away from the telephone.

"Bea!"

"Damn kids," Bea said, chuckling.

"It's not kids, Bea—"

No, it's the bogeyman hisownself come calling on you this All Hallows Eve and he's a mind to introduce you to all kinds of nastiness

"—it's . . . it's someone else."

The banging came again and Bea shouted, "Oh, hold your horses now all you little ghosts, ghouls, and goblins." Then, "Hold the line, Ez . . . I got a little treating to do here."

"Don't open the door, Bea!"

"'Don't open it'? Why, why ever not, Ez?"

Ezzie turned from the window and heard Bea's thick bolt hammering back, heard it even over her own cries. Then she heard the big key turning in the mortise lock that Virgil Duke ("God rest his philandering soul," Bea always said, followed by a mock spit) had taken almost an entire weekend to install.

"Bea!" Ezzie now screamed.

She heard a new sound on the telephone. It was the sound of the outside flooding into Bea's house. *Hello?* she heard Bea say, heard her say it again and then once more, as Ezzie's friend stepped out into Hallowe'en and looked around her yard.

Ezzie turned to the window and watched Bea, wiping back a streak of frizzled hair from her forehead and hugging her apron tight around her against the wind. "Oh, Bea," Ezzie whispered—no point in shouting now—"please be careful."

But as far as she could see, there was nobody out there to be careful about.

Bea retreated into her house and, without turning her attention away from the window, Ezzie heard the lock being turned once more and the bolt being thrust home.

Outside, the clouds had slid off of the moon and its light shone down onto the street. It had been raining, she now saw, slick puddles reflecting house-sides and street lamps and the occasional small vampire or hunch-back lumbering along the sidewalks, one hand held by tall helpers while the other clasped a trophy jar of nickels and dimes, candies and chocolate bars.

Then, just as she heard crackling on the telephone, Ezzie saw the shapes moving down the grass from around back of Bea's house, heading for the road, warping space around them, blistering reality the way the paint on the doors went when Ezzie's long-left husband, Wayne took a blowtorch to the them when he was re-painting the house.

"Hello?" Bea's voice said in Ezzie's ear.

"Bea, I see them."

There was a distinct hesitation. Then Bea said *hello* again . . . this time even more uncertain.

"Bea, it's me. They're moving away from your house." Why the hell was she whispering? There was no way these things could hear her. Was there? As they shifted in and out of vision, there seemed to be a real determination to them. They reached the sidewalk—she counted four, five . . . seven of them, maybe even more. And yes, there was something about their heads, flapping open around the middle of their dark and featureless heads and then flapping closed again.

"I'm sorry, but if this is some kind of a Hallow—"

"Bea, it's *me*. Ezzie."

"Ezzie?"

Ezzie stepped back carefully from the window as the black shapes stepped off the opposite sidewalk and onto the road, fanning out to either side as they slid and crept, like shadows on a wall bathed in the sudden light from a passing car's headlights . . . heading now across the road towards Ezzie's house. She reached out and turned the key in the lock and then crouched down, her back against the door.

"Bea, listen carefully to me."

"How do you know my name? Who are—"

"Bea! Shut up and listen. Your name is Beatrice Duke and we've—"

"I know who *I* am. Who are *you*?"

"My name is Elizabeth Rafaelson. We've been frie—"

"I don't *know* anyone called Eliz—"

"Bea, shut the fuck *up*. We've been friends for almost fifty years now. I live across—"

"I'm hanging up now, whoever you are."

"Bea! Bea! Don't hang up. I'm telling you . . . please don't hang up. I live just across the street from you—go to your window and-"

"I'm hanging up."

"Bea, can't you just do that one thing for me? Go to your window and look across at me—I'll wave to you and—"

"There's nothing across the street from me."

"What?"

"I said there's nothing across the street from me. Just spare ground."

"What?"

"I'm going. Goodbye."

"Bea!"

The line was dead.

And then, the telephone was no longer in Ezzie's hand—her hand was just there in front of her, clawed, the fingers wrapped around empty space.

Ezzie lifted her head and watched the overhead light pop out of existence along with the ceiling and the upstairs rooms and even the roof. Now there were just stars above her.

Suddenly, she felt the full might of the October chill and everywhere went dark. Still crouched down, Ezzie turned and stared across the street. There was grass beneath her . . . damp grass, she realised. Her skirt was getting wet. Just next to her, a tall beech stood majestically, bare branches spread out above her head.

Across the street, Bea Duke stood at her window, her hand pressed against the glass as she surveyed the spare land where Ezzie had once lived.

And then the shapes moved forward as one, their darkness filling everything. And those mouths—Bea had been right. So big.

As one of them came down towards her, right where her front door had been, Ezzie started to say, "Poor Billy Westlow." But she didn't quite finish the last word.

ULALUME: A BALLAD

Edgar Allan Poe

As far as I know, Edgar Allan Poe never specifically used the word Halloween *or any variation of it in his writing. But these lines seem to indicate the date: "For we knew not the month was October,/And we marked not the night of the year—/(Ah, night of all nights in the year!)" This is, of course, open to interpretation—the narrator may merely be referring to the anniversary of the burial of his lost love—but I think Poe meant All Hallows Eve. After all, it is the one night of the year when one might easily stroll ghoul-haunted woodlands, chat with ancient goddesses, and be tempted by a demon to visit a tomb?*

I've kept the poem's often omitted "secret" final stanza as originally published. Poe is known to have performed the poem complete with the verse at least once and included it in a consequent transcription. He must have felt it had meaning.

"Ulalume" was written with dramatic recitation in mind. Poe is known to have pronounced the title/name as you-la-lume. *He probably derived it from the Latin* ululare *(to wail, lament, howl, shriek) and* lumen *(light). Try reading it aloud.*

)

The skies they were ashen and sober;
   The leaves they were crispèd and sere,
   The leaves they were withering and sere;
It was night in the lonesome October
   Of my most immemorial year:
It was hard by the dim lake of Auber,
   In the misty mid region of Weir—
It was down by the dank tarn of Auber,
   In the ghoul-haunted woodland of Weir.

Here once, through and alley Titanic,
    Of cypress, I roamed with my Soul—
    Of cypress, with Psyche, my Soul.
These were days when my heart was volcanic
    As the scoriac rivers that roll—
    As the lavas that restlessly roll
Their sulphurous currents down Yaanek
    In the ultimate climes of the pole—
That groan as they roll down Mount Yaanek
    In the realms of the boreal pole.

Our talk had been serious and sober,
    But our thoughts they were palsied and sere—
    Our memories were treacherous and sere—
For we knew not the month was October,
    And we marked not the night of the year—
    (Ah, night of all nights in the year!)
We noted not the dim lake of Auber—
    (Though once we had journeyed down here)—
Remembered not the dank tarn of Auber,
    Nor the ghoul-haunted woodland of Weir.

And now, as the night was senescent
    And star-dials pointed to morn—
    As the star-dials hinted of morn—
At the end of our path a liquescent
    And nebulous lustre was born,
Out of which a miraculous crescent
    Arose with a duplicate horn—
Astarte's bediamonded crescent
    Distinct with its duplicate horn.

And I said—"She is warmer than Dian;
    She rolls through an ether of sighs—
    She revels in a region of sighs:
She has seen that the tears are not dry on
    These cheeks, where the worm never dies,
And has come past the stars of the Lion

To point us the path to the skies—
　　To the Lethean peace of the skies—
Come up, in despite of the Lion,
　　To shine on us with her bright eyes—
Come up through the lair of the Lion,
　　With love in her luminous eyes."

But Psyche, uplifting her finger,
　　Said: "Sadly this star I mistrust—
　　Her pallor I strangely mistrust:
Oh, hasten! oh, let us not linger!
　　Oh, fly!—let us fly!—for we must."
In terror she spoke, letting sink her
　　Wings until they trailed in the dust—
In agony sobbed, letting sink her
　　Plumes till they trailed in the dust—
　　Till they sorrowfully trailed in the dust.

I replied—"This is nothing but dreaming:
　　Let us on by this tremulous light!
　　Let us bathe in this crystalline light!
Its Sybilic splendour is beaming
　　With Hope and in Beauty tonight!—
　　See!—it flickers up the sky through the night!
Ah, we safely may trust to its gleaming,
　　And be sure it will lead us aright—
We safely may trust to a gleaming,
　　That cannot but guide us aright,
　　Since it flickers up to Heaven through the night."

Thus I pacified Psyche and kissed her,
　　And tempted her out of her gloom—
　　And conquered her scruples and gloom;
And we passed to the end of the vista,
　　But were stopped by the door of a tomb;
　　By the door of a legended tomb;
And I said: "What is written, sweet sister,
　　On the door of this legended tomb?"

She replied: "Ulalume—Ulalume—
'Tis the vault of thy lost Ulalume!"

Then my heart it grew ashen and sober
   As the leaves that were crisped and sere—
   As the leaves that were withering and sere;
And I cried: "It was surely October
   On *this* very night of last year
   That I journeyed—I journeyed down here!—
   That I brought a dread burden down here—
   On this night of all nights in the year,
Ah, what demon hath tempted me here?
   Well I know, now, this dim lake of Auber—
   This misty mid region of Weir—
Well I know, now, this dank tarn of Auber,—
   This ghoul-haunted woodland of Weir."

Said we, then—the two, then—"Ah, can it
   Have been that the woodlandish ghouls—
   The pitiful, the merciful ghouls—
To bar up our way and to ban it
   From the secret that lies in these wolds—
   From the thing that lies hidden in these wolds—
Had drawn up the spectre of a planet
   From the limbo of lunary souls—
This sinfully scintillant planet
   From the Hell of the planetary souls?"

MASK GAME

John Shirley

John Shirley captures a truly modern American family—functioning in its dysfunctionality—struggling to keep Halloween a "family" tradition, but ultimately being forced to strip off the guises they have employed to obscure the truth. We don't know the origination of associating masks with Halloween, but it probably lies in practices of mumming and pranking. And, like Halloween, masks are mysterious and magical in and of themselves. Masks have transformative power. In many cultures wearing a mask allowed a human to become or gain the power of that which the mask portrayed, or make contact with the spirit world. In Jungian terms, a mask functions as a mediator between archetypal powers of the collective unconscious and individual ego, connecting present to past and mundane to the supernatural. When wearing a mask, you are allowed to be something other than yourself, but it's not a permanent transformation—you become yourself again once you take it off. And, as in this story, masks tend to reveal rather than conceal

"Neva has a new Halloween game she wants us to play at the party," said Donny.

Juno looked across the room at her younger brother. "Say what, scrubster?"

Donny was barely thirteen. He surprised everyone in the family room by chiming in about the Halloween party, because he didn't seem to be paying attention to them at all; he was staring so fixedly into the video game he seemed in another room, another world: his fingers clicking the controller, his hands jabbed it in the air, his shoulders wrenched this way and that—as if these contortions could help his Killflyer safely pass the ice spikes hurtled by the enraged Living Mountains.

Juno, Donny's older sister, sat with the others at the breakfast table on the tile floor beyond the stained carpet of the game-dominated family room. On wicker chairs around the kitchen table were Donny's wearily obese mom, Juno and her best friend Linda, and Linda's always-smiling dad, Mr. Carpenter. According to Linda, Mr. Carpenter was "a heavily medicated soccer Dad."

Juno looked at her brother, saw him flying, in his mind and on-screen, into the box of the videogame—

One of those sickening feelings of unwanted scale came into Juno's mind again: she seemed to see Donny in the box of the TV screen, and the box was like a little puppet theatre in which he zipped around in a toy spaceship, shooting things; and that box was inside the box of the family room, next to the box of the kitchen, both in the box of the split-level house, which was in a grid of such house-boxes, in the Southerton suburb of Sacramento, in the middle of California, on the coast of North America—in her mind, she could see it all from space, the planet a ball in space: the boxes stuck to the big ball, the big ball itself hanging, in her imagination, in some vast transparent box that astronomers had failed to discover because they weren't supposed to, because . . .

Stop.

Dizzy, Juno pulled her mind back, and focused on the kitchen table; the crumbs of breakfast, the bowl of chips, the homely, comfortingly ordinary faces of her family and her friend Linda.

Donny was muttering something again about masks for the Halloween party. Focus on that.

"So you're, like, in on this Halloween party committee all of a sudden, scrubster?" Juno asked, fishing in the bowl for a taco chip that hadn't gotten limp by sitting out all night. "Ugh. Mom these chips are, like, blue food."

"Then throw them in the trash and put out some fresh, Juno," Mom said, distractedly looking at Donny.

Mr. Carpenter nodded his head in silent agreement at that. He was smiling but something in his expression said, *Spoiled kids.*

Donny was still staring into the screen, jerking his body around in a burlesque of his Killflyer's trajectory. He made it past the beetling visages of the Living Mountains, muttering, "Aw riiiiight," and flew on into the Jurassic Swamplands, where he began to systematically strafe the Village of the Swamp People.

"You have to kill people in some village, in that game?" Mom asked, frowning. "They look like, you know, innocent bystanders . . . "

Juno thought: *Like you'd do anything about it even if he had to torture them to death for points.*

"You get more points," Donny said, "if the people in the village have weapons. But yeah you kill everybody, if you want enough points to get the Annihilator. You can't really win unless you get the Annihilator . . . Yeah, uh Neva, anyway, said—shit . . . flew too low . . . "

"Neva said 'shit'?" Juno asked, pretending innocence. Linda giggled.

"You two watch your language," Mom said. Grunting, she heaved herself up, out of her chair: a big woman, she'd lost enough weight so that she didn't have to use a cane anymore, but she still breathed through her mouth when she moved. She looked at her watch—a tiny silver strip of watch on a big pink slab of arm—and decided it was close enough to lunchtime; she got her Slimfast from the fridge and drank it down hungrily.

"Neva said that uh, she . . . shit! Every time I come to this swamp part, their stupid trained dino-gator's vomiting those acid bombs. He always— whoa, got 'em! . . . Neva said she had a game she wanted to play with the kids at the party and she . . . she had prepared for it, for, like, months, and made special masks for everyone. Everyone's got their own mask. Kinda weird but that's what she said . . . . Dang little kid keeps escaping into the woods. Now I've gotta use my nuker on the woods to kill him . . . "

"She made the masks by hand?" Mr. Carpenter asked. He snapped his fingers in admiration. "*Gee*, that's great, I'd love to see them." He was a chiropractor who'd retired after losing a lawsuit with a patient. Something about spinal adjustments causing strokes. Mr. Carpenter's receding blond hair was going gray, but he still had a little ponytail, tied in the back. His head seemed slightly too long and narrow for his wide shoulders.

"She worked on it for *months*?" Juno asked. "The girl's, like, obsessed!"

"Rully," Linda said. "That's like so . . . " Her voice trailed off.

Linda was stocky like her dad, with that same long chin. Not as pretty as Juno; not as brave about expressing herself.

"Oh I think spending that long perfecting a craft to get it right, that's marvelous," said Linda's dad, as both Juno and Linda had known he would. "The masks must be *great*."

"That's right," Mom said. "I don't know how we all lost touch with craftsmanship and caring about doing things right. I'm not saying I'm much better. I guess, when we were younger we were having too much fun to think about getting some skills that mattered. Me, I mean—not you, Frank."

Mr. Carpenter nodded pleasantly.

Juno thought: *Mom's always saying things are screwed up, and then saying she's no better. But she starts out judging everything anyway—then she judges herself.*

Breathing through her mouth, Mom labored around the kitchen, dumping out the old chips, putting new chips in the big earthenware bowl. "Mo-om," said Juno, as soon as she was sure her mom had already done it. "I would've got those. I was going to."

Donny went on, barely audible: "Yuh, Neva said . . . said she wanted us to wear these special masks . . . and . . . she—" He broke off, for a long moment, staring at the screen, as it loaded another level. "—wants to show us how to play the game tonight . . . Oh, sweet: Next level is Kill-frenzy . . . Yeah she's coming tonight to . . . to . . . "

"Uh, *riiiiiight*, Donny" Juno said. She and Linda exchanged looks. It was like Donny was a Mynah bird, just repeating something.

Mom made one of her frustrated noises, a kind of a low growl, and went to the videogame—and surprised Juno by shutting it off. Donny looked at her in outraged shock. "I hadn't *saved* yet!"

"Tough," Mom said, "I'm sick of you doing all that video-killing and not participating in . . . in . . . family stuff."

"What—stuff like Halloween? Where we can, like, pretend to be Jason or Freddie and carry toy knives with fake blood on 'em and stuff? *That's* not violence? Shit, Mom, I was just about to—"

"Watch your language, buddy-boy! Now tell me what your cousin Neva was going to do with these masks? We're *trying* to plan the evening. We want to do something together as a family this year."

"Neva?" Donny brushed some lank brown hair out of his eyes and blinked at her. "Neva was going to do what?"

"You were just saying you'd talked to Neva?"

"Like, a month ago . . . well, not 'talked,' you know, she messaged me online . . . You could've warned me before you switched off the game so I coulda saved. Now I have to replay that level."

"That's, like, such a tragedy, losing your saved videogame," Juno said, dripping sarcasm. "It's tragic if you're a retard, I mean." She stared. "*God,* Donny you haven't even got any *pants* on—running around in a shirt and underwear . . . "

"That's just disrespectful," Linda said. "I have to say. None of my business but . . . I mean . . . Ex*cuse* me? It's like he's all . . . "

"Why're you looking at my ass, *Linda?*" Donny jeered, unfolding his long, bare legs to get up. He stalked angrily out, going down to his room; to his computer. He liked to walk out on things, on people, to make a point. The picture of Eminem on the back of his T-shirt glared a reproach at them, as if "getting Donny's back," all the way down the stairs. Slim Shady's printed-on face receded into the shadows of the downstairs hall.

"Donny's being such a butt-head," Juno said. "Like, he'll just not tell us now about Neva because he's mad."

"Boys are confused, at his age, pretty easily," said Mr. Carpenter, always the conciliator. "He'll be fine."

Juno wondered what Mr. Carpenter would say, instead, if he hadn't been taking his Paxil.

From Donny's room they heard the muted chiming of Instant Messages, one after another, as his Buddy List told his friends he was once more in their shared digital world.

Wearing only a bra and panties and feeling a little sick from the cooking smells of instant dinners coming up through the grate in the floor, Juno was standing in her bedroom-closet door with Linda, trying to decide what to put on. She was supposed to wear some artsy-craftsy mask that her weird cousin Neva had made, tonight—made for them without even asking them all first—and since she didn't know what mask she would have she didn't know what costume to put together to go with the mask.

"Some, like, tights—black tights and a leotard, that'd go with any mask. You look cute in tights anyway," Linda was saying. Linda took a fashion design course and was good with design software. She was into pictures, into color and texture, like her mom had been.

"I'm putting on weight, I can't wear tights," Juno said.

"You are so not putting on weight."

Juno whispered: "I'm scared I'll end up like . . . " She glanced at the door.

"You have more your dad's metabolism, from what your doctor said that time," Linda said, abstractedly, riffling the outfits hanging in the closet. "How about this?"

Then the doorbell rang, and the tightness started in her stomach: it was her dad.

"*Ju*-noooo!" her mom called, from downstairs. "Your dad's here!"

Dad was bringing her half-brother, six-year-old Little Mick, over for the party—probably Dad was going to some office Halloween thing with his wife. He worked for UniNet, where they were supposed to be "just like a family" and their CEO was heavy into having "family holidays" and it was so weird how that was like her mom lately, too. Mom was on a "family togetherness" kick. Like that would make up for Dad being married to some skinny lawyer bitch.

"Yeah, I'll put on my Danskins for now, I guess," Juno said. She took the tights off the shelf inside the closet, next to the hanging clothes, and drew them on, then shrugged and wriggled into a matching scoop-necked leotard; black Danskins. If Russell came over, it'd be worthwhile to wear clinging things.

She contemplated herself in the mirror, smoothing out wrinkles in the stretchy fabric; Linda pulled up on the elastic for her, from behind. "Yow, easy, I might want to have babies some day."

Linda giggled and the two looked critically at Juno: a tortoise-shell barrette flipped her long, wavy brown hair just a little to one side; her pert, angular face; the deep-set green eyes she got from her dad. Her glossy-black fingernails were already painted for Halloween, no reason to change that. But the almost painted-on Danskins—you could see her nipples—oh, so what, Mom probably wouldn't object. Mostly her objections were just noise anyway.

"*Don*-neeee! *Ju*-noooo!"

Juno exchanged a sigh with Linda and they went downstairs.

Mick was orbiting his dad, trailing one hand on his dad's legs as he circled him, making a *rrrrr* sound. Dad, still wearing his tieless suit, was tall, gangly, with glinting green eyes, a wide, easily-smiling mouth and lots of flashing white teeth.

Mick stopped dead still, his small round face beaming up at Donny when he came slouching into the front hall. "Donny!" Mick shrilled. "Can we play *Killforces*?"

"Yuh, sure—split screen, dude. Hi Dad."

"Hi Donny," Dad said. "So, are thirteen-year-old guys allowed to have any fun on Halloween?"

"Yuh sure, whatever. We're, like, having a party or something." Donny trailed Mick into the family room.

"You give Mick a chance to win!" Dad yelled after them, smiling. He pretended to gawk up at Juno as she descended the stairs. "Who's this terribly skinny vision in black?"

"Oh right like I'm so skinny." She made herself go to him for The Hug.

It was hard to be mad at him after six years, especially with him trying so hard when he came over. But it was hard to hug him too. She *wanted* to hug him—*and* she wanted to push him away; and the tug-of-war made that tight, ill feeling inside her when he came to visit.

He let her go. "So what's up tonight? Hi Linda!" He waved at Linda, who sat on a step halfway down.

"Hi Mr. Weiss."

"Um—we're not doing much," Juno said, relieved to be able to step back; to hug herself, instead. "Neva . . . cousin Neva . . . is coming over . . . bringing some masks . . . "

"Cousin Neva?" He frowned, looking puzzled—and shrugged. "I can't keep up. Time marches on. And so must I." He kissed her cheek. She let him. He grinned down at her—holding her shoulders cupped in his big hands for a moment, looking into her face.

Did he have to have that it's-all-good expression, when he didn't live with them? Like it was so good to be not married to her mom.

He squeezed her shoulders gently, once, and turned to go—then turned back long enough to check: "Oh—I think your mom has Mick's costume. He insists on wearing the same one from last year for trick or treating. Should still fit, one more time. Donny and Linda's dad are taking him . . . ?"

"Yep, that's the plan."

"That's a done deal, then. Okay kids—Happy Halloween." He blew Juno a kiss, waved to Linda and then he was gone, closing the door softly, swiftly, behind him.

It was after dark and they were in the living room, doing busywork to avoid the discomfort of having to wait for anything like a real party to start. Aunt Laura had set out punch and cookies and put on music: *Classics from the Crypt.* Mom, perched on the sofa, had Linda and Juno putting up the Halloween decorations she'd bought at The Big Halloween Store, a discount place that rented a space at the mall for one month out of the year. Juno grimaced at the decorations: cut-outs of clichéd witches, trite ghosts, hackneyed werewolves, stereotyped Frankenstein monsters: bright chirpy images printed on cereal-box cardboard.

Russell, the jerk, didn't come over. He would have some good excuse, he always did, and he'd been careful not to promise. They weren't really going steady, after all. One blowjob didn't make him her boyfriend.

Don't try to date somebody that popular, Linda had warned her, and she'd been right, as much as Juno hated to admit it.

Her friend Marcy couldn't come. She was volunteering to help run some dance at her Catholic school. They were really lame, the dances at that school—they played, like, Justin Bieber; would never play Lady Gaga—but it was a place to meet the boys from St Anthony's. Dandridge couldn't come, he was doing some DJ thing somewhere. Atesha and Ahmed had made excuses so lame that Juno couldn't even remember what they were. They knew what Mrs. Wiess's Halloween parties were like.

So it was just Linda and Mr. Carpenter—Linda's dad—after he got back with Donny and Little Mick and Mom and Juno and Mom's sister Laura. Aunt Laura was a nervously active, medium-sized woman with her rusty hair up in a bun and pants that were way too tight for her big derriere. Later, Granddad Morris, Mom's father, was supposed to come over. Thrill. Granddad was deadly dull when he wasn't bitching. Some Halloween party.

"What I hate," said Juno, looking around, "is how they make the 'monsters' in Halloween decorations all happy and jolly and grinning and . . . like they're trying to make you feel they couldn't really hurt you. Don't want to scare the kids on Halloween . . . "

"Or piss off the fundamentalists—the fascist scrubs—" said Linda, whose mother, Lupe, had been rather a political activist with the Catholic Workers before she'd died of an embolism when they were in fifth grade. "If you make Halloween stuff scary they think it's . . . it's . . . you know . . . "

Juno pushed a tack through a ghost's eye. "Like . . . demonic?"

The doorbell rang. Juno got the door, and there was Neva, and things were instantly more interesting. Neva had her jet-black hair in long, rank-looking dreadlocks; she had some kind of white coloring on her lips, not lipstick, more like white paint, so that they were dead white, and the same on her eyelids; her nose was doubly pierced by little emerald and ruby studs, her ears quadrupley hooped. Her heart-shaped face was pretty but abjectly solemn; her black eyes were like polished onyx. When she blinked, the flashing shift from bone-white to onyx was sometimes startling.

But her smile put Juno at ease. "Cousin *Juno!*" Neva said, reaching out to press Juno's hand; and Juno saw the shiny silver stud piercing Neva's tongue, in the dead center of that laughing, open-mouthed smile. "I haven't seen you since you were so little . . . and now you're bigger than me!"

It was true—Neva was probably in her twenties, but she was a small woman, a well-turned but pixyish shape, no more than five-foot-one. She wore a flat-white, sleeveless sash-belted shift like something a servant girl would wear in a movie about ancient Rome. The cloth was sewn, here and there, with runes. She had a silver armlet of a snake biting its own tail, and a really old, worn-out pair of sandals on her small feet.

Neva hesitated in the doorway as Juno frankly stared at her, forgetting her peevishness about the mask game, beginning to appreciate Neva's style. "Whoa, nice toenails," Juno said. Neva's toenails were alternately black and white. "Black and white and—"

"—and black and white and black and white!" Neva laughed. Her voice was both soft and husky, and her laugh was infectious so that Juno found herself laughing too. "And you've got all black fingernails, Juno! If you do a handstand next to me, just right, some piano player may stroke his fingers on the ends of us. I know just which octave I am too."

What a weird-ass little thing to say, Juno thought.

"Well do come *in*, for heaven's sake, Neva!" Mom called, from the sofa, where she was watching Linda put up black and orange crepe paper. "Juno you're making her stand out there!"

"Sorry." Juno closed the door behind Neva—who stood on the carpet, looking around, smiling like the Mona Lisa at their decorations. "Very . . . nice." She put down a large satiny black bag—the kind of material that was black and gold both, depending on how it shifted around in the light. The bag was full, its contents covered with a coarse white cloth. Neva gazed benignly at Mom. "Good to see you, Judith!"

Mom looked at Neva with slightly narrowed eyes, her head tilted. "Um . . . You too, Neva."

"Are those the masks you made?" Juno asked, looking at the bag. She was embarrassed, suddenly, by the party, and her family—Neva was so cool, so confident, and she found she wanted to know her better.

What did Neva *do* for a living? Juno couldn't remember. She remembered something about Neva, doing . . . what? Going off to school somewhere? Studying art in Europe or something? She must have: she was so effortlessly exotic.

"Yes, those are the masks," said Neva. "Oh! That music—*Night on Bald Mountain*. I like that."

"It's *Classics from the Crypt*," Aunt Laura said. She was stringing unnecessary crepe paper.

"Is that what it is? I'll bet it's much quieter in a crypt than that," said Neva.

Linda and Juno laughed. Aunt Laura turned and blinked at Neva in confusion, then managed a chuckle.

"Have some punch!" Mom said. "You can have the grown-up punch with the white wine in it . . . Laura would you get her some punch?"

Neva dutifully went to stand by the transparent plastic punchbowl, to wait for her drink. The bowls were on a folding table covered with black construction paper, set up against the wall. With exquisite care, Laura ladled out a waxed paper cup of wine and Hawaiian Punch from the "grown-up bowl." Juno got herself some punch from the other bowl—a mix of canned juices with floating orange slices.

"Mmm, thanks." She sipped at the cup, her eyes darting from one person to the next, and around the room. "Delightful. Lovely."

Mr. Carpenter had taken Donny and Little Mick out trick or treating. Mick was Batman. Donny had decided to design his own Halloween makeup—he'd ended up with scribbles on his face and what looked like unreadable graffiti.

The doorbell rang. Laura let Granddad Morris in. He stumped in on his aluminum cane that sprouted into four legs near the bottom; Granddad scowling, nodding, shuffling. "Thank you, Laura. Kids, how ya doing, there. Judith. Where's Little Mick?"

"Trick or treating, Dad. I've got your water heating . . . " Laura took his arm, and slowly escorted him into the kitchen for the instant de-caf coffee and Oreos he always had when he arrived.

The trick or treaters began to arrive. Neva stood near the punch, watched Juno and Linda take turns answering the door, offering the bowl of miniature Snickers and Mars bars and Baby Ruths to kids wearing store-bought masks of Freddie and Zero the Zombie; to more kids in green monster makeup their parents had put on them by hand. Now and then groups of black kids, most of them looking like they were at least fifteen, came to the door and mumbled, "Trickertreat"; they usually didn't bother with masks. Linda gave them candy.

Mom seemed to be watching Neva—Mom's gaze wandered from Neva's dreadlocks to her piercings, to the eyes that seemed so familiar and so unfamiliar . . .

. . . And watching Neva, Mom ruminatively ate mini-Mars bars from a sack, one after another, forgetting her diet, accumulating a pile of discarded candy bar wrappers.

Neva drifted over to the lamp table, beside Mom, where the wrappers were piling up and ran her fingers through the crinkly pile. "Like a heap of autumn leaves . . . "

"You can sit on the couch, you know, or a chair, hon," Mom said

"I need to stand for a while. But thank you."

She needs to stand? Juno thought.

Still gazing at Neva, Mom put a mini-Mars bar down half-eaten, and sat up a little straighter in sudden animation. "I remember . . . Gosh—you've grown so much, Neva . . . "

"Oh I wish I'd grow some more! I'm so damnedly short. But you get used to it. It gives you a more realistic sense of scale." She looked at Juno.

Mom cocked her head at this, considering it, frowning. Juno looked at Neva for a moment, some half-memory of what might've been a dream stirring in her . . . and then she turned away and emptied another family-size bag of Halloween candy into the trick-or-treat bowl.

Aunt Laura came in long enough to change the music to *Disco Inferno*; she did a few dance steps in place—it was disco music but she was doing an Irish folk dance, with her arms straight at her side. She'd taken lessons. She did all her dancing that way—she said Michael Flatley proved you could Irish-dance to anything.

Neva stared at Laura a moment, then drifted up beside Juno to watch as a disparate batch of masked kids came to the door at once—two Wolverines and one Mystique from the *X-Men* movies, one fourteen-year-old boy with *The Crow* makeup, one Fairy Princess with sparkles on her cheeks—not long out of diapers—holding her dad's hand, one *Scary Movie* mask.

"Some masks speak so deeply, Juno," Neva murmured. "—but some drip onto our faces from the glass screens . . . and some only mock us from dreams we forgot we had."

Juno looked at her, thinking: *What was that? Something from some lame community college drama class?* "When are you going to show us the masks you brought, Neva?"

"Soon as the trick or treating dies out," Neva said, going to stand by the punch table again. She'd stayed there most of the evening, but hadn't drunk anything else.

At the open door, Juno nodded toward a group of kids coming up the walk. "This bunch'll be one of the last . . . they stop around ten."

Neva was gazing out the open door, at the beacon of the moon in the black sky. As if drawn, she walked across the room to Juno, at the door, her gaze seamlessly on the moon. "It's not quite full, tonight. It's waxing. Growing."

"Yeah. The moon's really pretty tonight. It's so bright."

"It's *awesome*," Linda said, coming to join them. "It's all . . . " Her voice trailed off, as usual; they gazed together into the night sky, each with the moon in her mind's eye.

Then another group of kids came, yelling "trick or treat" in a listless, off-hand kind of way, accidentally knocking over potted plants as they came up the walk and not stopping to right them.

The doorbell stopped ringing about ten-thirty and, soon after, Neva closed the front door and said, "Almost time for the Mask Game."

Granddad Morris was in the Barcalounger. Donny, his makeup smeared— looking scowling and put-upon—was seated on the floor between Granddad and Aunt Laura; she sat stiffly on a kitchen chair she'd brought into the living room. Donny was industriously eating Halloween candy from a plastic orange trick-or-treat bag he'd brought back with him. Juno and Linda sat on the two arms of the overstuffed chair across from the sofa, under the painting of a troubadour singing to a Spanish girl on a balcony. Little Mick was playing *Destructo* on his PlayStation Portable, half curled up on the big chair. He had lost his beloved Batman mask somewhere, occasioning a minor crisis; but he'd forgotten about it when Donny pressed the PSP on him to quiet him down.

Mr. Carpenter was leaning on the back of a turned-around kitchen chair, rocking its front legs off the floor, humming to himself while gazing vaguely at the plaster light-bulb-lit jack o' lantern in the front window. Mom had wanted to carve real jack o' lanterns this year, but the kids had all made excuses, and the uncut pumpkins were still sitting on the back porch.

"Could we put on music?" Donny was saying. "And for once could we listen to something I like, something that's good for Halloween? There's that song 'Kim'—"

Juno groaned, "Not Eminem, please God."

"Juno come on, it's Hallo-*ween* stuff—it's a scary story about this guy who kills this girl and tells his daughter it's all just a game but he's getting the kid to help dump her in the lake . . . It's just like a horror movie."

"It's his sick fantasy about murdering his wife—*that's* not Halloween—"

"Actually," Neva said, mildly, as she took the cloth covering off the masks in the sack. "I agree with Donny, I have heard that song and it is a Halloween story, very much so. A good one too. But music right now would be distracting . . . we have storytelling of our own to do with the help of the masks . . . ." With a mask gazing empty-eyed from her hand, she straightened up and announced with just the right air of mystery: "For now commences our Halloween Mask Game!"

And she went counter-clockwise, starting with Grandad, passing out masks, one to each.

The masks were like glazed papier-mâché—but it wasn't paper, exactly. It was more like crushed straw, Juno thought, looking at the back: Some kind of fibrous plant. The front was beautifully painted, and shaped; they were human faces—familiar faces—not monsters. The workmanship was indeed of a quality beyond merely professional. It was "the art of the hands."

"Can I have that one . . . ?" Juno asked, pointing at a mask of an old woman.

"No, I'm sorry, that one is mine," Neva said sweetly, huskily. "Each has his own mask. Try yours on—it should fit quite well to your features."

Juno took her own mask: it was a mask of her mom's face, not a mocking caricature, just Mom younger than now, more slender. Juno hesitated, not quite wanting to put it on.

With a deeply-etched scowl, Granddad was staring at his own mask—which stared sightlessly back from his trembling, blue-veined hands. He grunted, and shook his head. The mask was a parody of his own face—much younger. "Me in Vietnam," he said. "About that time . . . I was thirty-two. How'd she know how to . . . ?"

Mom gazed at her own mask. "Why that's my mother, rest her soul. They really are beautifully made. Neva's done her research. I . . . it gives me such a funny feeling . . . You know, I should have done another art course. People give up so easily, when they try to take classes, and . . . I guess I did too. I wish I'd done some more art classes . . . like Lupe—but she was so good at them . . . "

At the mention of Lupe, Mr. Carpenter glanced at Mom, then looked quickly back at the mask in his hands.

"Oh yes," Aunt Laura said, "Lupe was very talented. You know, I'd have to be talented at something to really want to learn it—an art, I mean. I . . . I wanted to do more dancing but I didn't think I had . . . " She broke off, seeming embarrassed, as if she'd exposed herself.

"Mine's not like the others," Mick said, tossing his PSP aside to take his mask. "It doesn't have a face and it's made of something else."

"It *is* made of something different! You're a sharp boy!" said Neva, all charming encouragement as she pulled his Batman shirt off over his head, so that he was bare-chested. "It doesn't have much of a face yet, but just wait. We need at least one real honest monster on Halloween." She put the mask gently on his face and began to . . .

What is she *doing*? Juno wondered.

The mask had started out without any character to it; just a generic face. She was shaping the mask, under her fingers, as she spoke. "The other masks are made of something similar to paper, and they're fixed in one shape by a glaze. This one is of a kind of special, stiff cloth that's very easy to mold . . . "

The mask took shape, suggesting a werewolf. Not any particular werewolf; not Lon Chaney Jr, nor the Wolfen. Not Eddie Munster. But it was more or less, thought Juno, what Little Mick would look like if he turned into some kind of wolfboy.

"There—you're a werewolf!" Neva said, clapping her hands, just once. "You go on now, and be a werewolf boy! Explore that! Go see in the bathroom mirror what it looks like!"

"Ow-WOOO!" Mick howled, to nervous laughter. His eyes sparkled at the attention; at everyone looking at him and laughing. Then he ran down the hall to the bathroom to look in the mirror.

The laughter died down as everyone looked at their masks.

"After you've had a good look at them, put the mask on," Neva said.

Everyone obediently put their masks on, except Granddad Morris. There was no string, no rubber band on the back of the mask—the top of the mask curved back into a kind of cap that held the mask on the head and against the face. It clung to Juno's face with such unnatural steadiness, she took it off and put it back on a couple of times, just to reassure herself that she *could* take it off.

Weird ideas get into your head at Halloween, she thought.

Every mask fit perfectly, so far as Juno could see. How had Neva done that, without measuring everyone? Juno found she was afraid to ask.

"Whoa-hey—like a glove!" Aunt Laura said, giggling faintly. Laura's own mask was an image of herself as a teenager about Juno's age.

"No, it's some kind of mean joke," Granddad said, staring at his mask. Even as he said, "I won't put it on."—he put it on.

"You just did put it on, Granddad," Donny said.

"I won't put it on," Granddad said again, his voice muffled from behind his mask.

Juno started to laugh—then realized there was no humor in Granddad Morris's voice. He wasn't kidding.

She was starting to get scared . . . Which was good, wasn't it? Weren't you supposed to feel scared on Halloween, at least some of the time? But then this wasn't that kind of scared. It'd never occurred to her before that there was a good scared—and a bad scared.

Linda's mask was of her mother, Lupe, a pretty woman, half-Latino.

Linda's dad, Mr. Carpenter asked, jovially, "How d'I look?"

"Like yourself, but younger," Mom said.

"What I want is the other way around—to be younger, but myself, Judith," he said, chuckling.

Donny's mask looked like his dad—but younger. "We're . . . we're all each other," he said, "or . . . the same but younger or . . . "

"Not you, you're not someone here," said Juno. "And Mom is her mom—and you're Dad." For some reason, the remark seemed to hang in the air, as if it wasn't through releasing all its meaning.

"But who are you, Neva?" Aunt Laura asked, as Neva put on her own mask.

"I'm a grandmother crone," said Neva. "Any grandmother crone. One of this family's ancestors, perhaps—or another. It doesn't matter." Her mask was of a very old woman's face, but not a scary-witch face—more like a matriarch, smiling softly but also determined, firm in her convictions. Looking at Neva in her mask, it was difficult to remember her original face.

Neva was switching off the lights, one by one, lastly the ones in the living room, making darkness fall across the room like a "wipe" in an old fashioned movie. No one objected—this was a Halloween party.

"Maybe we should have candles," Aunt Laura said tentatively. "I could get some. I think there's some in the garage . . . " Her masked face, in the shadows, seemed a frightened child—though the mask's expression hadn't seemed frightened before she'd put it on.

"We don't need candles, we have the moon herself," Neva said, and she pulled the bottom of the front window shade to make it snap up. Suddenly moonlight flooded into the room. It brought only a little clarity, but it changed the character of the room. And Neva turned to them and intoned, with more simple declaration of conviction than drama: "The waxing moon—a moon pregnant with Harvest." Even in this faint light the edge of the mask Neva wore could be seen—yet the features moved like a natural face as she spoke. It made Juno shudder. "Tonight," Neva went on, "there are solar flares, so the moon is even brighter than normal, reflecting the petulant fury of the sun. Lunar flares! We forget that moonlight is reflected sunlight—sunlight that has been stolen by the moon, and re-directed. This very light you see here—" She lifted her hand so that it was bathed in moonlight. "This light on my hand first struck the surface of the moon, before it struck my hand—it struck the filmy coating of moondust hundreds of thousands of miles out there, it struck the cratered hills of the moon—and it bounced off that moonscape, and came here, to us, to all of us in this room. But it still has in it something of the dead dust of those bleak, shadow-etched craters . . . and something else—a power we can use . . . "

"Gosh she's good at that, isn't she?" Mr. Carpenter chuckled. But there was a quaver, the faintest quaver, of uncertainty in his voice.

"I knew it," Juno whispered to Linda, "she's been taking drama or something."

Linda suppressed a snigger. But Juno was far from certain that Neva was dramatizing. Even when she said something poetic, she seemed so unaffected about it all, as if she were speaking of the weather, or the stock market.

"Now, each of you knows who your mask is," Neva said, turning to them, silhouetted against the tarnished silver of the moonlit window. "To play the game, you need only listen to the mask. It will tell you what your part is, and how to play the role. Now stand you up, all of you . . . you too, Donny . . . Yes, and you too Clarence . . . " Clarence was Granddad Morris's first name. "Good. Now we stand here, facing one another . . . and we each take a step back, and as we do we step back from the people we pretended we were before—we step into the reality of the masks . . . into the people who *are* these masks, the masks who are these people . . . . "

Playing along—or perhaps caught up in some kind of eternity-touched ritual of solemnity they couldn't articulate–they each took a step back, out of the pool of moonlight . . .

Each masked face receded into the shadows, as they stepped back, so that only the faintest moonlit sketches of the masks remained, hanging unsupported, like bodiless specters, in the dim reaches of the room . . .

Little Mick kept going back to the mirror. The bathroom was lit only by a nightlight in the wall outlet next to the mirror. It was sort of dark but he could see the wolfboy's reflection well enough.

He'd stand on the toilet lid and gaze into the dark glass. And every time he looked at the face reflected there—at the mask that was like an angry dog, to him who'd never seen a wolf . . .

Every time . . .

. . . the face seemed a little more powerful, more independent. But he never felt scared of it—it was not like the face was some monster.

In fact this time, when he looked at the face, it seemed more like him—like Mick Weiss . . .

After each mirror-look he would get down on the floor, and go prowling about the bathroom, growling, swaying his head from side to side; sometimes chuckling in wonder at the good feeling the growling and skulking gave him. He snarled at some plastic family-size bottles of bubble bath and hair conditioner on the edge of the tub—and struck out at them with his clawed, furred hands, knocking them into the tub, where the hollow ring of their bouncing sounded like frightened yelps.

Mick went to the mirror one more time—and then the mask was finished, somehow. It hadn't been finished till that moment.

He climbed down and began to prowl down the hall . . . and into the kitchen, then out the back door, into the cool night air.

"What . . . do we do now?" came Aunt Laura's voice, a little angry, from the darkness.

"Listen . . . " came Neva's voice urgently. " . . . just try not to think about anything, even if only for a second or two, and listen, and you'll hear what you should say . . . what the mask you're wearing wants to say."

Then they heard Grandad Morris speak, and saw him step out of the shadows, into the moonlight, without his cane. He was still an old, bent figure, but he was moving easily now, and his voice seemed a little younger—though you could hear the age in it too. It was as if he were doing an uncanny mimicry of himself as a younger man.

"Judith, get your heinie in here!" he snarled.

Juno watched in fascination as her Mom stepped into the moonlight. A big shape but with that young, more slender woman's face: the mask of Judith's mother, Juno's deceased grandmother.

But Mom wasn't in character yet. "Dad . . . ? Gosh you're so . . . Are you all right? I'm not sure about this game . . . "

"*Listen* to your mask, Judith," Neva prompted. "Even if it doesn't speak in words, it will guide you. Give it a chance and the miraculous may come!" Neva spoke again—but not out loud. Her voice seemed to come from within each of them, in that moment, speaking without words. It seemed to say that something precious would be lost if they didn't play the game. So persuasive was Neva's own voice, in that moment, that all of them listened intently to the silence that preceded the murmur of their masks, and the drama began to unfold . . .

"Yes, Daddy?" Judith's voice, younger—and then Juno realized it had come from *her*. Judith's voice coming from Juno!

She found herself stepping into the light—as her mother stepped back into the shadows. She'd spoken in her mother's voice, saying what her mask wanted her to say.

"You going to marry this fella, Judith?" Granddad Morris asked.

Juno—the mask of Judith—answered, hesitantly: "I expect so . . . But Daddy, I—"

"You're not sure? You're not sure you're pregnant? You're not sure he knocked you up?"

Juno falling into it now . . . hearing the words in her mind, even as she spoke them—almost like a memory, though it was one she couldn't have. "Daddy . . . " She found she was crying. "Daddy I didn't want to . . . "

Yes, Juno decided—there was such a thing as a good scared—and a really *bad* scared.

She wanted to shout for Neva to stop this. But she couldn't. Like the others, she was carried inexorably along—she was watching it all from some distant part of herself . . .

Then Aunt Laura, the teen-aged Laura, stepped up; the mask spoke: "Daddy—stop it. She couldn't help it. He was too much for her. He sent her poetry every day. She had to."

"Had to!" He laughed sadly, contemptuously. "Laura—well hell, now I see you're in danger of becoming exactly what your sister is. You're right in her goddamn shadow! I will not spawn a family of whores!"

"Clarence!" It was Juno's mom—in her mother's mask. Her mother's voice. "I won't have you speaking to the girl like that. "

"She has to learn what life is—it's time, goddammit!" His voice shook with emotion. "This world is without pity, without mercy! I saw it! I saw them butcher innocent women and children, in 'Nam, butchered like sheep! That's the kind of world this is—there is no pity in it. Women who lay themselves down to be used will be destroyed! People will see them as whores!"

"Clarence—this is a foul way to talk around Laura . . . "

"Talk? I won't talk to her! I'll *show* her!" Still raging, he stepped over to Aunt Laura and slapped her, hard, across the face. The mask she wore didn't budge from its place. Laura staggered and covered her eyes, then went slumping to her knees, as he shouted, "That's how the world treats whores—better get used to it!"

Strange, Juno thought, *how the moonlight seemed to spotlight one person, then the other, as the drama unfolded . . .*

Juno—as her mom—pulled him away from Laura. "Stop it! You're hurting her for what I did!"

"Really, Clarence!" His wife's outrage was palpable—but ineffectual. Juno's mom as Grandma, Clarence's wife.

"You will marry that slick son of a bitch or you'll get twice what she got and more! And I'll see to it he marries you, you may depend on it!"

Aunt Laura was sobbing . . . or the Laura mask was sobbing . . .

Juno, as Judith, protested: "Daddy—I don't think he really loves me. It was like he was . . . he was practicing on me. I don't want to marry him. If I marry him now . . . "

"You should have thought of that before you opened your dirty little legs!" He backed away, shaking, into the shadows, the mask fading from sight. " . . . your dirty . . . little legs . . . "

The moonlight seemed to dim on Juno and Laura and Mom—and to increase near Neva, as she emerged from the shadows. "As time passes," intoned the old woman of Neva's mask, with simple conviction, "it pulls things this way and that—they move in one direction and then they're pulled in another; they resist and yet they submit, and in the struggle comes their shape; and so a tree becomes gnarled, a vine becomes tangled, a face becomes imprinted with selfishness, or kindness. And time pulls, and tugs against us, and we're shaped by the struggle with time and the world . . . "

The moonlight shifted, like shafts of light underwater as clouds boil and the surface roils, and Juno seemed to see another room, in her mind's eye; another place: She saw Donny approaching her, wearing his father's face, speaking in a voice that was his own, but with an adult resonance—a voice that went with the mask he was wearing. His mask didn't move its lips, yet it seemed to take on shadings, emphasis in light and shadow that underscored the words of the drama; as all the masks did.

" . . . but, a chiropractor, Judith?" said the mask of Dad to Juno.

To Juno who wore, who *was*, the mask of her mom. Juno as Judith.

"He made me feel like something again . . . he called me every day—"

"You weren't something already?" The voice of a man, only a little too high, through the mask of that man, coming from the body of a boy.

There was no way Donny could make this stuff up on his own, thought Juno in some distant part of herself.

"You were a wife, a mother. You've got Juno, and Donny now . . . "

"He said . . . I wanted to learn something, to be something . . . I could be a homeopathist maybe . . . "

"What the hell is that?"

"It's this new thing—it's not new, it's ancient but it's sort of new to us—"

"Forget it, I don't care, for God's sake. Good Lord above, couldn't he have paid for a motel room?"

Juno . . . Judith . . . was weeping. "I'm so sorry . . . sorry about you finding us like that . . . We got carried away."

"And you wanted to be 'something'-like Lupe with her gallery shows? What good did it do her—he cheated on her anyway."

"She's so caught up in her career . . . She hasn't got much time for him . . . "

"Oh yeah, I feel *so* fucking sorry for him. I feel sorry for our kids—that's who I feel sorry for."

"Look, I've told him I won't see him again . . . "

"Then you won't have either one of us," he said, relishing it.

"What?"

"You heard me. I've already packed. I'm gone. There's a lady who's interning for my attorney . . . you should see the way she smiles at me. If I were free . . . "

"You've walked out on me before . . . "

"And came back. That'll be the difference this time. This time I won't come back."

"But you enjoy it so much—walking out on people. You even walked out on your kids when they forgot Father's Day. When I reminded them, they wanted to take you out to dinner—but you used the excuse to play golf . . . "

"You think I enjoy this? I won't enjoy being separated from my kids—or paying you child support, for Chris'sakes . . . And the alimony . . . Oh no. But I'll enjoy not having to wonder what I'll find in my bed when I come home . . . "

He turned and walked out of the moonlight . . . Donny being Dad walking out . . .

Judith . . . Juno . . . tried to follow—and a door slammed in her face, though there was no door in that wall.

Then Mom—as her own mom, Juno's grandmother—stepped out of the shadows, and said, "Judith? Go after him. This isn't right."

"I deserve it, Mother," said Juno—said Juno as her mom. "I deserve it."

"This is hurting me, Judith. I don't want to go out this way . . . "

"What are you talking about?"

"I'm not sure—I'm getting a second opinion. You'd better take me to Kaiser to get the results . . . Oh Judith I don't want to die with you kids breaking up like this . . . "

"And that's my fault too, I guess? I don't know . . . I don't know . . . "

Little Mick had pulled off his clothing, his shoes, and, taking a feral joy in the cool October air on his skin, he crouched ankle deep in the Gundersons' koi pond, snarling, swiping at the blotchy black and gold carp.

The moonlight seemed to infuse the fish with a glowing energy. Swipe, splash, he had one. He could hear—and almost taste—the blood pumping through its frightened heart. But it slithered and flopped back into the pond before he could tear into it.

He went all statue-still, to make the fish think he'd gone. The rippling water slowly quieted, and his face came into reflective focus in the pond at his feet—the triumphantly bestial, powerful face that showed who he was now.

He lifted his head as he heard a muted yowl from the back porch. He moved slowly, carefully, on hind legs and all fours by turns, crept away from the pond and across the back yard toward the back porch. The cat made a growl of warning—which only drew him more quickly toward it . . .

He could see the ghostly white outline of the cat against the glass back door—a white cat. His other self, his unmasked self, knew its name, and sometimes played with it.

He couldn't remember its name, and he didn't care about playing. Mick He was hungry, achingly hungry.

He could smell the warm life of the fat white cat from here.

He set himself . . .

▼▼▼▼▼▼

The moonlight had tripped away and returned, time had passed, and now Frank Carpenter was emerging from the shadows, wearing his mask, putting his hand on Juno's arm. Only it was Juno's mom he was touching, in their drama—Judith Weiss: Juno's mask.

"If Lupe won't let you go . . . we can't really fight that . . . " said Juno, through the mask of her mom.

"She's Catholic. She tries to be so modern, with her progressive Catholic Worker crowd—but she's still Catholic," Frank said. "She won't agree to a divorce. I just want to know–if she were out of the picture, if she were gone—"

"You mean she's fallen in love with someone, Frank? She wants to marry someone else?"

"If she were gone in any sense. If Lupe were gone in any sense—you'd marry me, Judith?"

"I'd do anything for you, Frank. You're all I have."

"That sounds like it's me by default, Judith. That's why you'd do anything for me? Because you couldn't be without . . . someone?"

"No, no—I mean—you're everything to me. Of course I'd marry you if she . . . if she left or whatever."

The room darkened; the darkness lingered; there was muffled sobbing. Juno almost came back to control of herself. But then some unseeable hand dialed up the reflected glamour of the moon, and a lunatic spotlight caught Linda in the mask of her mother, Lupe—and her dad, Frank Carpenter, in the mask of his younger self. Only the mask seemed to have aged a little. It was Frank Carpenter six or seven years ago. He was approaching Linda, who was curled up on the sofa, wearing the mask of her mother Lupe. "Frank?" asked Linda as Lupe, sleepily. "Is that you?"

"Lupe . . . Did you think it over? You said you'd think it over . . . "

She stretched, yawning, though her mouth couldn't be seen under the mask. "I prayed over it, anyhow. I spoke to Father Devsky. I just can't in good conscious say yes to a divorce. And what's come between us, I mean, really? Infidelity, Frank. If you're screwing someone else, how can you say you're working on your marriage? No, I can't do it. I can't live with a divorce. Look, I couldn't sleep last night and I finally managed to take a nap . . . Let's talk later."

"I'll let you sleep," came Mr. Carpenter's voice, from behind the mask.

As Juno breathlessly watched, from that dim place faraway behind her own mask, Mr. Carpenter seemed to struggle within himself—or with the mask. He reached up toward the mask, as if about to take it off. His hands froze. His shoulders trembled. Then his reach changed direction: he reached for the pillow behind Linda's head, pulled it out from under her head as she—as Lupe—shouted in protest, just once, before he pressed the pillow over her face, holding her down; she flailed; her feet kicked.

"I'll let you sleep," Mr. Carpenter said again hoarsely.

Juno tried to drag leaden limbs across the room to stop him . . . She managed a few steps . . .

But then Little Mick burst the drama apart. He ran into the living room, naked and streaming blood . . .

Vomiting blood as he came, then wailing . . .

The electric lights came back on. The room flooded with artificial light.

The smeared mask fell away from Mick, falling into fibrous streamers, so that they could see the gobbets of red-sticky white fur rimming his mouth like a hideous parody of a beard; fur gore-pasted to his own baby teeth; blood-soaked fur vomiting up to splatter the very center of the caramel-colored carpet.

Mr. Carpenter stood up straight—free now, to pull his mask away—and he threw it aside.

Linda sat up, unhurt, pulling her own mask away—

Mom lumbered toward Mick but she hadn't taken her mask off yet and he screamed and floundered back, falling, scrambling across the floor to get away from her; from the disorienting mock of Judith's face. She flung the mask aside and went ponderously to her knees beside him, scooped him up though he were her own child.

"Oh Mick—what happened . . . ?"

"What happened to all of us?" Donny asked wonderingly, tossing his mask aside.

Juno was looking for Neva . . .

The front door was open. Neva was gone; her bag was gone too.

Juno went to the porch and shouted for her. She walked out to the sidewalk, and looked up and down the street, and saw no one but a car full of laughing, drunken teenagers weaving down the cross street, on their way to being in a newspaper article.

Juno was lying on her back in the bottom bunk, looking through the window at the gibbous moon; the moon shattering and reforming, breaking and becoming whole between the brown, shedding leaves as the big tree in the back yard surged in the night wind. Juno was hoping that alien sense of connectedness to cosmic scale would come back, if she looked at the moon—usually it scared her, but now it made her feel like she didn't have to be part of this family . . .

Linda was sleeping in the top bunk that Mick slept in when he was visiting his half-siblings. Linda wouldn't stay at Mr. Carpenter's house anymore; wouldn't stay in a room with him, her own dad. Knowing he was a murderer.

Mick had gone back to his mom and dad, the next morning—washed and numb and quiet.

An insomniac old man had seen a small, masked boy running naked through the yards, Halloween night; the naked boy had snarled at some little girl, and chased her, and rooted through her dropped candy bag, finding nothing he wanted; then he'd leaped a fence and splashed through a goldfish pond; and he'd trapped and killed a cat with his hands and with the sharp edge of a garden stone. The old man hadn't known the boy. Only Juno's family knew who the boy was.

Juno thought about the others. Granddad Morris had been hospitalized with a stroke the very next day, at five a.m. He was lingering in critical care. He was not expected to live long. Juno was only a little ashamed when she realized she was glad he was dying. The way he'd treated her mom . . .

Laura claimed she was moving to Ireland, been selling her furniture and things. She'd always wanted to live in Ireland, though she was not in the least Irish.

Juno sat up, thinking about checking the doors again. She wanted to make sure they were locked.

Mom had had the locks changed, because of Frank Carpenter. He had threatened her, when she'd gone to the police and said she wanted to testify. She signed a paper saying that Frank Carpenter had told her that he'd killed his wife, Lupe; that she'd been afraid to speak out till now.

He'd been arrested. Linda's dad, arrested. He'd put up the bond and now—as far as they knew—he was alone in his own house, though Linda thought he might jump bail.

Now, Linda's voice floated out of the darkness. "Juno . . . ?"

"I thought you were asleep."

"Sort of, for a while. But sometimes when I start . . . .you know . . . "

"Drifting off?"

"Yeah, I–feel the . . . the thing . . . "

"The mask?"

"Yeah. I can feel it on my face."

"We burned the masks," Juno said, though she knew what Linda meant.

"It's just a feeling—it's sort of a dream. And then I feel I'm my mom . . . and my dad is . . . "

Juno didn't finish that one for her. She could hear Linda's soft weeping. After a while, Juno said, "Linda . . . chill. You can always stay with us."

"I can't stay here all that long . . . I don't want to. Your mom *knew*."

"She didn't tell him to kill Lupe. She never, like, said to do it. She told me everything—she said she didn't know he was going to do that shit."

"But she didn't turn him in when he told her."

"She was afraid they'd take her kids away, because she was half way mixed up in it . . . I mean, seriously, why do you think Mom got so fat? She didn't used to be like that. She was so neurotic about the whole thing, she was just freaked—but she couldn't talk about it. It was like she had to hide it under . . . just *more body*, or something. And—your dad just kept saying, 'I did it for you, I did it for you' and she couldn't tell him to go away, he was so—he was, like, all dependent on her somehow. But she stopped, you know, going over to . . . "

"Don't say it. I don't want to think about my . . . about him and your mom . . . "

"I know. Especially now."

They were quiet for a few moments. The wind rattled the window; the moonlight falling on the floor shifted nervously.

"Juno? Did you guys ever find Neva?"

"No. Linda—there's something I haven't told you. Mom didn't want me to talk about this . . . Linda . . . " It was hard to say because it was hard to accept. It sounded like a lie. But it was true. "Linda . . . *we don't have a cousin Neva*. We never did. When we heard her name, we were all . . . it was like we sort of remembered her . . . we pictured her at the family things, you know, Thanksgiving or something . . . we, like, saw her in our memories? But it was all like . . . something was suggesting it to us. Linda—we never heard of Neva before Halloween. Linda? Are you listening?"

Silence.

"Linda?"

"She's asleep, Juno. She won't wake till morning, now."

Oh no.

The voice had come from the window. Neva was sitting on the dresser, her head haloed by the tossing gold of the moon, her legs primly crossed. Dressed exactly as she had been on Halloween.

"It wasn't a costume . . . " Juno murmured.

"No. Juno, it wasn't. I've come here to—"

Juno rounded on her. *"What did you do to Mick?"*

"Don't shout, Juno, you'll wake your mother. I only gave Mick the experience he wanted—and I showed him something special. He has seen the Beast that all men live with, the bestial god they share their bodies with, the one they must contend with if they are to climb the hidden staircase. But few choose to climb it. Mick, now, will climb it—because he has seen, he has known the Beast, and he cannot forget it. You were afraid he was going to become some kind of . . . what? One of those who murders for pleasure?"

"You made him a psychokiller . . . or . . . the beginning of one."

"I have seen what will become of him, or more accurately what he will choose to become. He has seen his dark self, and this will give him awareness. He will one day climb the staircase. He will be a leader, and lead people away from the thing he met that night. "

"Neva . . . Are you . . . ?"

"Yes. I'm really here. You and I are here together. You called me, after all."

"I did not."

"You did. You called me, Juno. You have that power—you have that natural 'connectedness' to the cosmic, to the real source of Life. You're like me . . . and it was you who really made the mask game possible. You knew somehow what Frank had done to Lupe. And to your mother. You felt it. You knew about the sickness in your family, and the masks behind the masks behind the masks . . . "

"Go away. Get away from my house."

"Juno—You knew, and *you called me.* Now I'm calling you, Juno. You try to be one of these haunters of malls, these ghosts in chat rooms. But you don't belong there. You're more substantial than that. If you choose . . . it's all a matter of choice . . . Linda will be all right. Your mom will take care of her. Linda will let her atone. All you have to do is listen to what the night has to say. Just listen . . . to the silence between breath, between heartbeats . . . just listen, and know . . . And ask yourself—'What do I really want?'"

In the morning, Mom found Linda, deeply asleep, and smiling, dreaming sweetly.

But as for Juno . . .

They never did find Juno. She didn't even leave a note.

A year passes, like a twisting root, shaped by impulse and resistance; by time and struggle.

It is Halloween, in Portland, Oregon, just after sunset. The smallest trick or treaters are already going from door to door, holding their mothers' hands.

Mr. Stroud is the only one carving the pumpkin on the porch with a kitchen knife. He couldn't get the kids interested. He is listening to the radio he'd set up in the window, the classic rock station's Jimi Hendrix marathon, Jimi playing "Voodoo Child." And Stroud was watching the sidewalk; expecting visitors. He saw the two young women walking up toward him from half a block away. Yes, they are turning in at the walk to the front door, coming up between the juniper hedges.

One of them—the darker one, maybe, in a sort of Roman costume— that must be cousin Neva, from the letter Angela had gotten. Maybe she was one of his half-sister Doreen's kids. She looked vaguely familiar. Sort of.

I'm a voodoo child, voodoo child . . .

And that other one must be Neva's friend, Juno. The two of them were supposed to teach the family a new Halloween game.

Well. What the hell. It would be good to do something different, this year.

BY THE BOOK
Nancy Holder

It's the Debs of the world who make the mundane type of Halloween magic. They cut out invitations; sew costumes; stick sequins on masks and devise clever makeup designs; buy the treats, make caramel apples, and bake the cupcakes; organize the parties; fetch bales of hay, pumpkins, and dried cornstalks in the minivan for seasonal decor; know how to provide spooky special effects with a green light bulb, dry ice, and a Crock-Pot . . . and are generally underappreciated, overworked, and often desperate for a bit of help. Nancy Holder's harried mom, Deb, gets some help—and not just with the holiday season—from an entirely unexpected source.

"What you need," Ellen told Deb, "is a little something for yourself. And I've got just the thing."

Picture-perfect, Ellen reached into her embroidered tote bag, which was decorated with Halloween pumpkins and candy corn. Deb, slouchy and unprepared for visitors, had her arms filled with a tower of black construction paper topped with a black cat invitation template, and she desperately kept Ellen blockaded in the entryway of the house. The place was a disaster; Kevin had stayed home from work with the flu and there were piles of tissues everywhere. Andy's pajamas were wadded up in the middle of floor, and the kitchen was covered with ants because Sarah hadn't put away her Sugar Pops before informing Deb that Deb just didn't understand, that Sarah hated her, and she might as well be dead.

Ellen had just given Deb the paper and the pattern to transform the paper into invitations for the Boy Scouts Halloween party. Both their sons were Cubs. It was going to be a big 'do, and suddenly Deb had sixty–three black cats to cut out. Today. And speaking of cats, the cat box reeked. Deb hadn't noticed it before, but now as she stalled Ellen, who clearly thought coffee and something fragrant and homemade should come forth during the handoff, her eyes were almost watering. Cleaning the cat box Sarah's job. So were last night's dishes, but Deb just wouldn't understand why they'd gone undone.

"Okay, well, thank you," Deb said, as Ellen topped the tower with a thick paperback book. Deb stared down cross-eyed at it. It was a romance novel. Silver embossed letters read *No Time for Love.* Below the title, a woman with waist-length curly blond hair, dressed in a silver gown with a plunging neckline, clung to a man with a sharp profile wearing a pirate shirt exposing bulging pecs. He had miles of dark curly brown hair. Their lips were open, their eyes were closed . . .

. . . and Deb couldn't even remember the last time she'd thought about romance, much less had any. Her ponytail was held back with a rubber band; she wasn't wearing any makeup; and she had on a ratty old sweater, a pair of too-tight jeans, and one blue sock and one green sock.

"It saved my life," Ellen said, tapping the book with one of her perfectly manicured fingernails, and there was something in her voice, an odd sort of catch, that made Deb blink. "You really should read it."

"Okay, thanks," Deb replied. "I'll get the invitations done by tomorrow."

Ellen sneezed. Maybe it was the cat box. Mortified, Deb closed her eyes and willed her to leave.

"Be good to yourself." Ellen's charm bracelet—witches, pumpkins, and black cats—jingled as patted the book. Then she reached back into her tote and pulled out a key ring. The heart shape said *World's #1 Mom.* She had five kids. Deb had two.

At last she was gone, and Deb shut the door—and her cell went off. Balancing the tower of paper and the book, she fished in her jeans for the phone. Everything tumbled to the floor, the paper flapping like bats. And it was then—and only then—that she discovered that the cat had left a gift on the floor, perhaps in retaliation for the filthy litter box: a round little—

She closed her eyes in shame as the purring motor of Ellen's car hummed down the street. The phone trilled again and she managed to connect.

"Mom, I don't have my gym shoes!" Sarah shrieked. "I thought I put them in my locker but they're not here! I'll get a nonsuit! No field trip!"

"Oh, no," Deb said. Sarah's PE class was going to a performing arts center tomorrow. Sarah was a dancer and an actress; she hardly ever wore her gym uniform, hence no need for shoes.

"*Mom!*" Sarah wailed.

"I'll find them. I'll bring them," Deb promised.

They were underneath Kevin's briefcase in the hall. And on the way to Sarah's school, she ran out of gas.

"You should have made sure you had your shoes," Kevin said to Sarah that evening, as he blew his nose again and dropped the tissue onto another stack beside the couch. Sixty pounds overweight, in need of a shave, wearing his favorite sweats and a ragged bathrobe, he was draped with a fuzzy dark blue throw covered with cat hair, and he had been there all day, watching TV. Deb had told Andy to pick up his LEGOs, but the TV had him hypnotized.

"I *did* make sure," Sarah huffed. She rolled her heavily made-up eyes. She was thin and wiry, a dancer. Her black hair was long and dramatic, a drama student. "Andy must have hidden them."

"Why—?" Kevin began, but something on the TV caught his eye. He picked up the remote.

"God!" Sarah bellowed. Then she stormed out of the room. Deb heard her door slam. Andy didn't move. He hadn't heard a word.

Kevin blew his nose and put the tissue on the coffee table. "Sorry again about the gas," he said. "I thought *you* had gassed up."

"I want a baby brother," Andy announced.

"I think something's burning in the oven." Kevin picked up the remote and continued to surf.

It was after one in the morning. Kevin was asleep on the couch, so Deb would have the bedroom to herself. Which was nice, because Kevin snored. The doctor said if Kevin lost a few pounds, the snoring might go away.

From the chuckles and clacking emanating from Sarah's room, Deb guessed she was on her laptop, chatting with her friends. Sarah's punishment for not doing the dishes last night was to do tonight's as well, but she hadn't emerged from her room all evening, not even to eat. Sarah also still hadn't cleaned the cat box. Better to leave her alone and let her get over her sulk, Deb decided. So Deb did her chores, loading the dishwasher with great care so as not to wake Kevin.

Then she picked up the construction paper and the black cat pattern from the breakfast bar, where she'd left them, and absently grabbed Ellen's romance novel as well. Wearily, she shuffled into the master bedroom, flicked on the lights, and shut the door.

Scissors, she thought, as she laid everything on the bed. Sighing, she turned to go back into the kitchen. The silver letters of the book cover gleamed, catching her eye. *No Time for Love.* That guy was so handsome, in an outrageous sort of way. Huge chest, arm muscles bulging all over the place . . .

It saved my life.

As she rummaged through the kitchen drawers for the scissors, Kevin snuffled from the couch and she tried to look more quietly. They weren't anywhere; she was about to knock on Sarah's door when she noticed that the sliver of light beneath it was gone. Sarah had gone to bed. She tiptoed into Andy's room, her stockinged foot coming down hard on a LEGO block. She winced and bit her lip as she spied the prize on top of a pile of paper, markers, and glue sticks: some bright blue kiddie scissors about three inches long.

She plucked them up and limped back out of the room, down the hall, and into the master bedroom again. She picked up the black cat template and three piece of black paper, and looked down at her scissors. This was ridiculous; she *had* good scissors. If whoever had taken them would have just put them back . . .

No Time for Love.

She sat down on the bed and moved the scissors around the tail of the cat pattern, then along the arched back toward the head. It was hard to cut through three layers with the funky scissors. Her thumb was already hurting. Then she accidentally ripped the tail.

Frustrated, she unthreaded her fingers and flexed them, cricking her neck left and right. This was crazy. She could do it tomorrow. After the carpool and paying the bills and seeing what she could do about the ants.

She put the whole mess on the nightstand. The book was left behind on her mattress. Feeling a little sheepish—she'd never read a romance novel in her life—she opened it to page one.

He stood on the beach, his rough muslin shirt dangling open, the cold air washing his broad chest, his muscular thighs girded with chain mail.

She blinked. Did the man on the cover have on chain mail? She checked. No, no chain mail. Leather trousers. Snug, too. Wow. *very* snug.

Aidan's long, brown, curly hair waved in the wind as he thought of his woman in the arms of the sheikh . . .

"His woman gets a pirate *and* a sheikh?" she murmured.

*He balled his fists and swore that nothing would come between them,
not even his honor . . . or hers . . .*

"Wow." Flushing, she felt a little thrill at the base of her spine. This was
pretty hot stuff. She kept reading.

She was his, and his world would end if he could not have her . . . .

Then she thought she heard something, some kind of rushing noise.
Was it the TV in the living room? They kept the heater down low for a
reason, and that reason was called *money*.

She looked up from the book, dropped it, and would have screamed if
the man looming over her hadn't covered her mouth with his large hand
and gazed into her eyes with fiery passion. It was Aidan, from the cover,
with his pirate shirt and his broad, masculine chest and his legs girded in
chain mail.

"Mmmwh," she managed behind his hand. She had to be asleep. She
was having a dream.

Gently he pushed her back against the pillows, moving one clanking
leg onto the bed. Her eyes widened. The sound she was hearing was the
ocean, and she smelled salt and . . . whoa . . . *him* . . .

"*Nothing shall come between us. Nothing*," he whispered in a deep,
masculine voice. With his other hand, he caressed her cheek. His fingertips
were calloused. His eyes burned with lust.

I am definitely asleep, she thought, as her heart pounded and she tingled
all over. *But I sure don't feel like it.*

"*I, Aidan, am here*," he declared, with a smoldering look as he trailed
his fingertips over her mouth. "*And all I want . . . is you.*"

In the morning, Deb jerked awake to the blaring alarm as the black
construction paper cascaded, once again, to the floor. She rolled over the
other way, and found Ellen's book under her hip. She smiled. Nice dream.
Then she laughed. Who was she kidding? It had been a great dream. The
best dream of her life, in fact.

But the morning was here way too early and she had carpool. She slung
her legs over the bed.

"Mom, there are ants *everywhere*!" Andy shouted.

"You little freak!" Sarah screamed. "You freak, you freak! *Mom!*"

▼▼▼▼▼

"Thank you so much for doing this," Ellen said, taking the invitations as Deb blocked her view of the house once more. Ellen was wearing *another* Halloween-themed ensemble—a black sweater with silver moons over matching black trousers, and silver moons dangling from her ears. She even had a crescent-moon watch with a black leather band. "I hope you didn't go to a lot of trouble."

"Oh, no, it was fine," Deb lied. Her fingers were killing her. She had never found the good scissors. Andy had dribbled ketchup all over Sarah's costume for her dance performance and Deb had spent the majority of the day first trying to clean it, then figuring out how to replace the ruined sections. Andy swore it was an accident. He'd been trying to kill the ants that had also invaded the bathroom. With ketchup. Kevin had done nothing but snuffle and cough on the couch.

"Did you start the book?" Ellen asked. Her smile was sly.

"Um, yes, it's great," Deb replied vaguely, trying to translate that smile, blazing with embarrassment over her hot, hot dream. As she looked down, she discovered a spot of ketchup on her black sweatshirt. Then she nearly choked as she noticed the time on Ellen's half-moon watch. "Our cat has a vet appointment," she announced.

"Oh. My husband takes care of our dog." Ellen smiled very sweetly. "If I could trouble you to make some cupcakes for the party?" Inwardly, Deb groaned. But she smiled and said, "Of course."

"Thank you *so* much. Well, I'll get out of your hair." She glanced at Deb's hair, and Deb blanched. She'd been meaning to get a cut . . . .

"You are perfect just the way you are," Aidan murmured into her frizzy shag six hours later. Kevin was still on the couch, thank goodness. *"I adore you."*

"You're really here," Deb whispered, touching his broad chest with her fingertips. She'd been on page seventeen, third paragraph down, when suddenly, he'd appeared, as he had the night before. Except tonight . . .

. . . no chain mail.

"Mom!" Sarah bellowed. "Mom, I need a towel!"

She sighed. He caught her hand and brought it to his lips.

"I am really here. And all I want is . . . you. Kiss me, my beauty."

"Mom!" Sarah cried. "There is cat hair all over the floor and my wet feet will get all gross! *Mom!*"

"Shut up!" Andy shouted. Pounding rattled the hallway wall. "Me and Dad are watching the game!"

"*Stay here, with me,*" Aidan begged her, grabbing her hand. "*Stay here.*"

"Sarah needs a towel," she told him.

"*But I need you.*" He eased her back against her pillow. "*I need you as no other needs you.*"

"Here!" Andy yelled. "Catch!"

"Ouch! *Mom!*"

"Stay." He kissed her.

And she stayed.

"Thanks," Deb said absently to Kevin, whom she had convinced to stay on the couch by claiming that she had caught his cold. He'd been there for four nights now. He seemed perfectly content, eating potato chips, drinking beer, channel surfing. As thunder rumbled overhead and rain poured down the sliding-glass door, she glided way, the hem of her light blue chenille bathrobe catching on one of the heaps of tissues, sending a cascade to the floor. In the hall, she stepped on a LEGO, and then on a wet washcloth.

"We're out of Sugar Pops," Sarah informed her from the doorway of her room. "We're out of *everything*. And I don't have any more clean jeans."

"I'm so sorry, sweetie," she said, gliding on.

"What is *wrong* with you?" Sarah demanded, then huffed and slammed her door as Deb glided past. "I don't know," Sarah muttered behind the closed door. "I swear my mom has gone psycho."

Deb went into her bedroom . . . or rather, where he bedroom used to be. Now it was their secret tropical cove of passion. Aidan's pirate ship, *The Treasure*, bobbed in the distance, and Aidan himself lay bare-chested in the filigree bed he had carried from his quarters aboard ship and settled firmly in the fine, warm sand. A canopy of shimmering Indian silk was strung from one gently curving palm tree to the other, and he was lying on his side, his broad chest glistening with a sheen of manly perspiration, his long brown hair hanging low. A parchment map was spread on the bed; he was drinking from a sterling silver goblet. At his tanned elbow, an empty silver platter studded with jewels gleamed in the sun.

"*My love,*" he said, eyes drinking in the sight of her. "*I've been waiting for an eternity for you.*"

"Sorry, sorry," she murmured. "My family . . . " She shrugged and held out her hands.

"*I am your family now*," he said, reaching for her wrists and drawing her toward him. "*Come to me, my beauty*."

Her stomach growled. She had made tomato soup and grilled cheese sandwiches for dinner, burned the last of the bread—her own sandwich—while reading chapter seventeen. Thirty-six pages of love scene.

She could hardly wait.

She sat down beside him on the bed. His eyes blazed with pleasure. Her stomach growled again and she said, "What were you eating? Is there more?"

"*Iced shrimp and papaya*," he told her. "*Of course there's more*."

He leaned over the side of the bed and brought up another platter laden with delicate pink shrimp and golden slivers of papaya. And chocolates.

"You're a lifesaver," she murmured, as he began to feed her.

"Yes, I really do still have a cold," she told Kevin, blowing her nose as if to make a point. It had been a week. She looked down at the pile of tissues beside the couch and wondered why on earth he didn't throw them away himself. He was back at work, which got the daytime TV off, thank God.

The hallway was littered with dirty clothes and there was a paper towel roll outside the bathroom. The kids had been making do since the toilet paper ran out. Kevin kept apologizing for forgetting to get some at the store on his way home from the strip of fast food restaurants he had begun to frequent. Sarah wasn't talking to Deb; she had forgotten to do the carpool and everyone had been late for school. *Twice*. She felt a twinge. Slight, but present.

She heard someone crying in Sarah's room.

"I don't know what's wrong with her, Andy," Sarah said. "Maybe she's got a fever and she's delirious."

"But I *have* to bring the cupcakes to the Scout party. It's my responsibility!" Andy ground out.

"Maybe Dad can buy you some," Sarah ventured.

Deb stepped around the hallway clutter and went into the bedroom. And there he was, lying in bed, sipping rum and eating a banana. Sun-streaked highlights gleamed in his hair. When he saw her, he beamed with joy and held out the cup to her.

"*Where have you been, my beauty?*" he demanded hotly. "*The hours have dragged like years.*"

She climbed onto the bed. "I don't suppose you know how to make cupcakes."

He slid his arms around her. "*No, but I know how to make you happy.*"

Sighing, she picked up the goblet and swallowed down the rum. He kissed her. Again. And again. He ran his fingers through her hair and marveled aloud at how exquisitely, achingly beautiful she was. He wept with joy that they had found each other at last.

"What about the cupcakes? I have to make cupcakes. I'm supposed to take them to Ellen's after drop-off tomorrow."

He eased her onto her back and gazed with limpid desire into her eyes.

"*Forget them,*" he urged her in his deep, barrel-chested voice. "*There's nothing but you . . . and me. Nothing in the world but our passion.*"

He was almost right about that. But Andy's tears echoed in her mind as she slumbered beside Aidan. She tossed and turned. Then at four a.m., she got up and started making the batter. She'd bought all the makings the first day she'd read Aidan into her life. While digging for the extra package of butter in the freezer, she discovered a treasure trove of microwave meals and frozen vegetables. Kevin and the kids didn't have to eat so much fast food. They'd had food in the house all along. But no one had looked for it. No one else seemed to be able to cook. And why was that?

In the next room on the couch, Kevin snored on.

Yawning, exhausted, Deb made chocolate cupcakes with orange frosting, each one topped with a gumdrop spider and legs of black licorice. Four dozen. Her eyes were bloodshot and lined with sandpaper by the time she finished, just as the sun came up. And as she awakened her son with the wonderful news, he just stared at her in horror.

"Four dozen? You were supposed to make *six* dozen," he said.

She realized with dawning horror that he was right. She'd miscounted. She'd been too distracted—too tired, and too eager to get back in bed with Aidan.

"Ellen, hi, I'm sorry," she said, calling Ellen on her cell phone. "I hit a snag," she said. "I'll bring the cupcakes over a little later today."

"Oh," Ellen said, sounding surprised. "All right."

Andy didn't talk to her the entire way to school. He sat in the back, sulking beside Sarah, who was also sulking, because she was gaining weight and her face was breaking out from all the fast food.

"Sarah, if you don't like all the stuff Daddy's been buying, why haven't you zapped any of the meals in the freezer?" Deb asked her daughter.

"*Me?*" Sarah asked, stunned. "*You're* the mom."

Deb jerked as if she'd been pelted with a water balloon. She blinked, stunned, at what a curt, spoiled, thoughtless child her daughter was. And her son, glowering at her because she was two dozen cupcakes short of a Halloween party.

I'm the mom, Deb thought, as she dropped her kids off at their schools. It became a litany with the swish-swoosh of the windshield wipers as the sleet crackled down on her windshield. *The mom, the mom, the mom.*

She did feel guilty, but more than that, she was angry. She went home to her filthy house, half-covered with ants, and the cupboards and trashcans overflowing with fast-food containers and tissues; and the nest Kevin had made on the couch, and the remote on the floor. She looked at it all and she blasted into the bedroom, where she found Aidan lying in bed, the light in his eyes leaping to life as she stomped toward him.

"*At last,*" he said. "*How I have been pining for you, my beauty.*"

She stared at him. "Do you love me?"

His chest swelled. His eyes welled with tears. "*Oh, yes. I love you, with all my heart, and my soul. You are my life. Without you, I'm . . . I'm nothing.*"

"Then why didn't you help me with the cupcakes last night?" she demanded. "Because I'm the *mom?*"

"*You are my one true love.*" He looked puzzled. "*Come to me, be with me . . .*"

"I can't," she said miserably. "It's all getting worse. It's going to be overwhelming if I don't get back to work." She broke down sobbing. "Because I'm *the mom.*"

"*No, you are my beloved. My darling. My life.*" He enveloped her in a loving embrace and kissed her tears away. "*Don't cry, my heart, my wonder, my sweetling.*"

"Can't you help me?" she asked him. "If you love me?"

"*Help you . . . yes, I will help you, yes, my darling,*" he said. "*We'll weigh anchor in an hour and be gone from here forever.*" He pulled the rubber band from her hair and clutched her face, kissing her long and hard. "*My beauty.*"

"Make it two hours," she pleaded.

"*For you . . . an eternity,*" he whispered moistly into her ear. "*Soon, we will leave all this behind.*"

She left the bedroom, but she didn't make the extra two dozen cupcakes. Trembling, she loaded what she had into the car and drove straight to Ellen's house. She'd never been there before, but as her arms shook around the Tupperware containers loaded in her arms, she noted the impeccable lawn, the little Japanese footbridge, and the stone lanterns on either side of the entrance. WELCOME FROM THE DEWITT FAMILY, said a little sign on the door with two big cherry blossoms and five little ones.

Balancing the containers, she rang the doorbell and tried to catch her breath. She thought she was going to faint. As dots of yellow swam before Deb's eyes, Ellen opened the door. Every hair in place, she was dressed in her black moon sweater, jeans, and black Uggs. She was taking off a pair of rubber gloves.

"Oh, good," she said. "Come on in. I was just cleaning up."

Deb stumbled across the foyer into a homey living room filled with antiques. Pushed against the wall beneath a painting of an old forest, there were five large plastic bins, each one labeled with a name: SEAN, MARCIE, HAILEY, DOUG, STEPHANIE. The names of her children.

Deb and Ellen went down a hall where various certificates were framed—soccer, softball, good citizenship, honor roll—and a large white board labeled CHORES. The children's names were written there, too, with a series of checkmarks beside each one. To the right that were at least half a dozen calendars, hung up side by side, each with a different theme— puppies, baseball, France, sunsets, motorcycles. The squares for October were all filled in, with different handwriting for each calendar.

Ellen caught her looking. "Each of my children has their own calendar," she said. She laughed. "Of course I have one for my husband, and one for me. And I keep it all on a spreadsheet."

Deb stared at Ellen as if she were speaking a foreign language. She swayed behind Ellen as she led her into her kitchen. It was blue and white, and it was immaculate, from the white grout between the white tile squares on the counter, to the white tile floor and the white appliances. Tidy refrigerator art. A pumpkin candle sat in the kitchen bay window, overlooking a perfectly manicured yard. There was one orange coffee cup decorated with a black cat in the dish drainer. Ellen laid the rubber gloves on a stand that hung over the sink, wiped her hands on a brown dishtowel with a smiling jack o' lantern on it, and reached for the containers.

"I'm sorry, I'm so sorry, there are only four dozen," Deb said in a rush, "but I had to talk to you. What did you do? Did you come back, or ... or ... ?" She trailed off as Ellen cocked her head quizzically and set the containers beside each other, burping open the nearest one.

"What *adorable* cupcakes. Did you run out of supplies? I always keep some mixes on hand. I get them when they're on sale."

Deb stared at her. "Ellen, what did you do about *Aidan*?"

"Aidan?" Ellen said, opening her cupboard. She pulled out a box of chocolate cake mix. "Who—"

"*You* know," Deb said. "The man . . . in the book."

"Oh." She laughed. "You see, I have it all blocked out. " She smiled at Ellen. "On my calendar." As Deb blinked, she walked back to the row of calendars and pointed to the one closest to them, themed with sunsets. She tapped her finger on Wednesday's square. "See? Nine to ten p.m. tonight. Mom's Reading Time. I'm halfway through a great new one about a highlander." She leaned toward Deb. "Scorching. I'll give it to you after I'm finished."

"Reading time," Deb said, trying to make sense. "Scorching."

Ellen. "My husband teases me about my romance novels but I'd go crazy if I didn't have some 'me' time, you know?"

"Me," Deb said.

"No one better interrupt my reading time," Ellen declared. "It's my life saver."

Deb flopped backwards against the wall. Ellen peered at her. "Are you all right?"

"Dinner," she blurted desperately, scanning the chore list. "Do they make dinner? Do you have . . . what about the store? If you run out of toilet paper . . . ."

"Let me get you a glass of water." She left Deb, who had slid halfway down the wall, and went back into the kitchen. She got Deb some water and brought it back to her. "It's Doug's turn to make dinner. Of course all of them have chores. And if they don't do them, well, they might say I'm too hard on them but it's all about consistency, you know?" She wrinkled her nose. "And boundaries."

"Oh, my God, I'm going crazy," Deb said, gulping down the water. "Completely crazy."

"Is there someone I can call?" Ellen ventured, taking the empty glass. "Do you need something, some medication or—"

"I need to go," Deb announced. She pushed herself away from the wall.

"You can keep the book," Ellen assured her. "I just recycle them when I'm finished."

Deb lurched to the door. "Okay. Okay, thank you."

"Are you sure you can drive? If there's anything I can do? I'll make the last two dozen cupcakes. Don't worry about that."

Ellen hovered at the door of her perfect home as Deb staggered out to her car. Her messy, stinky car that was almost out of gas again.

I'm the mom I'm the mom I'm the mom.

I am the mom, she thought. *Me.*

She did a lot of thinking on the way home. Once there, she threw open the door to the master bedroom. Aidan had on his shirt, and the bed was gone.

"At last. I have been waiting," he said.

She crooked her finger. "We're not going anywhere."

Six months later, and the dark days were over. It was spring.

The calendars were up. The bins were in the hall. Andy was putting away the groceries, including the items Sarah had requested for her dinner preparation. As was indicated on her calendar—ballerinas—it was her turn.

"Hey, are you ready?" Kevin asked Sarah, as he strode into the room in his new track shorts and a freshly laundered T-shirt. It had been Andy's turn to fold and put away. He was clean-shaven, and he had lost forty pounds. Deb had promised Ellen she would have the bright green Camporee invitations finished by this evening at seven.

"Yes. Hold on," she told him.

While Kevin jogged in place, she went to the master bedroom and rapped lightly on the door. It was their code, giving Aidan permission to exist.

She opened the door and there he was, lying beneath the canopy of Indian silk, naked from the waist up. His eyes beamed with joy at the sight of her.

"My beauty, my joy," he whispered. *"How I need—"*

She glanced down at the paltry pile of invitations beside his elbow. The scissors in his hand caught the light. "You should get the sheikh to help you," she told him.

He sighed unhappily. *"But my beloved, I need—"*

"*I* need those invitations. Pronto." She blew him a kiss as he huffed and picked up the scissors.

Smiling, she shut the door, and retraced her steps back down the hall. Stopping at Sarah's door, she gave it a soft rap.

"How's it going?" she asked.

"Mom," Sarah said, "do I *have* to make dinner *and* the dishes?"

"Yes," Deb replied. "You forgot to clean the cat box. That's the punishment."

"It's not fair!"

"I know." Deb smiled to herself.

"But then why do I have to do it?"

Deb couldn't wait to say it. She loved saying it.

"Because I'm the mom."

And Deb set sail for her walk.

HORNETS

Al Sarrantonio

"Hornets," along with some of Al Sarrantonio's other seasonal fare, is set in the fictional upstate New York town of Orangefield, the pumpkin capital of New England. As any Orangefieldian could probably tell you, pumpkins are native to the New World. When planted in late May in northern fields (as late as early July in extremely southern locations), they are perfect for pre-Halloween harvest and many seasonal uses—including the fairly recent invention of pumpkin chunking. (A "sport" in which competitors contrive a device to hurl the orange vegetable as far as possible.)

Orangefield, however, has a connection to Halloween far weirder than growing gourd-like squashes (or chunking them). Detective [Bill] Grant, who appears in this story, must annually deal with both human and supernatural strangeness.

Too warm for late October.

Staring out through the open door of his house, Peter Kerlan loosened the top two buttons of his flannel shirt, then finished the job, leaving the shirt open to reveal a gray athletic T-shirt underneath. Across the street the Meyer kids were re-arranging their newly purchased pumpkins on their front stoop—first the bigger of the three on the top step, then the middle step, then the lower. They were jacketless, and the youngest was dressed in shorts. Their lawn was covered, as was Kerlan's, with brilliantly colored leaves: yellow, orange, a dry brown. The neighborhood trees were mostly shorn, showing the skeleton fingers of their branches; the sky was a sharp deep blue. Everything said Halloween was coming—except for the temperature.

Jeez, it's almost hot!

Behind him, out through the sliding screen door that led to the back yard, Peter could hear Ginny moving around, making an attempt at early Sunday gardening.

Maybe it's cold after all.

He opened the front screen door, retrieved the morning newspaper he had come for, and turned back into the house, unfolding the paper as he went.

In the kitchen, he sat down at the breakfast table and studied the front page.

The usual assortment of local mayhem—a robbery, vandalism at the junior high school, a teacher at that same school suspended for drug use.

In the back, Ginny cursed angrily; there was the sound of something being knocked against something else.

"Peter!" she called out.

He pretended not to hear her for a moment, then answered, "I'm eating breakfast!" and began to study the paper much more closely then it deserved.

On the second page, more local mayhem, along with the weather—sunny and unseasonably warm for at least the next three days—as well as a capsule listing of the rest of the news, which he scanned with near boredom.

Something caught his eye, and he gave an involuntary shiver as he turned to the page indicated next to the summary and found the headline: Hornets Attack Preschoolers

Another shiver caught him as he noted the picture embedded in the story—a man clothed in mosquito netting and a pith helmet holding up the remains of a huge papery nest; one side of the structure was caved in and within he could make out the clumped remains of dead insects—

Again he gave an involuntary shiver, but went on to the story:

(Orangefield, Special to the Herald, Oct. 24) Scores of preschoolers were treated today for stings after a small group of the children inadvertently stirred up a hornets nest which had been constructed in a hollow log. The nest, which contained hundreds of angry hornets, was disturbed when a kick ball rolled into it. When one of the children went to retrieve the ball, the insects, according to witnesses, "attacked and kept attacking."

Twenty-eight children in all were treated for stings, and the Klingerman Pre-School was closed for the rest of the day.

The nest was removed by local bee keeper and exterminator Floyd Willims, who said this kind of attack is very common. "The nests are

mature this time of year, and can hold up to five hundred drones, along with the Queen. Actually, new drones are maturing all the time, and can do so until well into fall. With the warm weather this year, their season is extended, probably well into November. The first real cold snap will kill them off."

Willims continued, "Everyone thinks that yellow jackets are bees, but they're not. They're hornets, and can get pretty mean when the nest is threatened. At the end of the season, next year's Queens will leave the nest, and winter in a safe spot, before laying eggs and starting the whole process over again with a new nest."

As of last night, none of the hornet stings had proved dangerous, and Klingerman Pre-School will reopen tomorrow.

Peter finished the story, looked at the picture again—the bee keeper holding the dead nest up with a triumphant grin on his face—and gave a third involuntary shiver.

Ugh.

At that moment Ginny appeared at the back sliding door, staring in through the screen. He looked up at her angry face.

"I can't get that damned shed door open!" she announced. "Can you help me *please*?"

"After I finish my breakfast—"

Huffing a breath, she turned and stormed off.

"Aren't you going to eat with me?" he called after her, hoping she wouldn't turn around.

She stopped and came back. "Not when you talk to me with that tone in your voice."

"What tone?" he protested, already knowing that today's version of "the fight" was coming.

She turned and gave him a stare—her huge dark eyes as flat as stones. She was as beautiful as she had ever been, with her close-cropped blond hair and anything but boyish looks. "Are we going to start again?"

"Only if you want to," he said.

"I never want to. But I don't know how more of this I can take."

"How much more of *what*?"

She stalked off, leaving the door open. After a moment, Peter threw down the paper and followed her, closing the sliding screen door behind him and dismounting the steps of the small deck. She was in front of the garden shed, a narrow, four foot deep, one story-high structure attached to the house to the right of his basement office window.

"Well, I'm here," he said, not at all surprised that she momentarily ignored him.

Jeez, it is *hot!* he thought, looking up at a sun that looked summer-bright, and then surveying the back yard. The colored leaves fallen from the tall oaks that bordered the backyard looked incongruous, theatrical. There was an uncarved pumpkin on the deck of the house behind theirs; it looked out of place in the heat.

Peter turned to stare at Ginny's little garden, to the right of the shed, which displayed late annuals; they were a riot of summer color which normally would have been gone by this time of year, killed by the first frost which had yet to come.

"I've been weeding by hand," she explained, "but I'd like to get some of the tools out and get ready for next spring. I've been having trouble with the shed door again."

He stepped around her, pulled at the structure's wooden door, which gave an angry creak but didn't move.

"Heat's got the wood expanded; I'll have a look at it when I get a chance." He gave it a firmer pull, satisfied that it wouldn't move.

"Isn't there anything you can do about it *now*?"

"No." He knew he sounded nasty, but didn't care.

She reddened with anger, then brought herself under control. "Peter, I'm going to try again. We've been through this fifty times. You're punishing me, and there isn't any reason. I *know* it's been rocky between us lately. But I don't want it to be like that! Can't you just meet me halfway on this?"

"Halfway to hell?"

She was quiet for a moment. "I love you," she said, "but I just can't live like this."

"Like what?" he answered, angry and frustrated.

"No matter what I do you find something wrong with it—all you do is criticize!"

"I . . . don't," he said, knowing as it came out that it wasn't true.

She took a tentative step forward, reached out a hand still covered in garden loam. She let the hand fall to her side.

"Look, Peter," she said slowly, eyes downward. "I know things haven't been going well for you with your writing, believe me I do. But you can't take it out on me. It's just not fair."

Male pride fought with truth. He took a deep breath, looking at her, as beautiful as the day he met her—he was driving her away and didn't know how to stop.

"I . . . know I've been difficult—" he began.

She laughed. "*Difficult?* You've been a monster. You've frozen me out of every corner of your life. We used to *talk*, Peter; we used to try to work things out together. You've gone through these periods before and we've always gotten through them *together*. Now . . . " She let the last word hang.

He was powerless to tell her how he felt, the incomprehensible frustration and impotence he felt. "It's like I'm dry inside. Hollow . . . "

"Peter," she said, and then she did put a dirt-gloved hand on his arm. "Peter, talk to me."

He opened his mouth then, wanting it to be like had been when they first met, when he had poured his heart out to her, telling her about the things he had inside that he wanted to get out, the great things he wanted to write about, his ambition, his longings—she had been the only woman he ever met who would listen to it, really *listen* to it. He had a sixth sense that if he did the wrong thing now it would mean the end, that he had driven her as far away as he dared, and that if he pushed her a half step farther she would not return.

He said, "Why bother?"

Again she reddened with anger, and secretly he was enjoying it.

"I'm going out for the day. We'll talk about this later."

"Whatever you say." He gave her a thin smile.

She turned away angrily, and after a moment he heard the screen door slide shut loudly, the front door slam, and the muted roar of her car as she left.

Why did you do that? he asked himself.

And a moment later he answered: *Because I wanted to.*

The screen was still blank.

At his desk in his basement office, Kerlan sat staring at the white clean sheet of the word processing program. It was like staring at a clean sheet of paper. *Maybe that's why they settled on that color, so that writer's block would be consistent in the computer age.*

He cringed at the words: *writer's block.*

After a moment he looked up over the top of the monitor at the casement window over his desk. Outside the sky was high and pallid blue and the window itself was open, letting the unnatural warmth in. It felt more like late August.

While he watched, a hornet bumped up against the window screen, followed by another. After tapping at the unbroken screen in a few spots, trying to find entry, they moved off with a thin angry buzz.

Not gonna get in here, boys.

Again the thrill of a shiver went up his spine as he remembered the story from the morning paper.

Too bad I can't turn that *into a piece for* Parade *magazine . . .*

The phone rang.

He grabbed at it, as much in relief from the prospect of work as in annoyance.

"Pete, that you?" a falsely hearty voice said.

"Yeah, Bill, it's me."

His agent Bill Revell's voice became guarded. "I hesitate to bother you on a Sunday, but . . . "

"I'm not finished with it, Bill."

A slow long breath on the other end of the line. "They need the story by Tuesday, Pete. Halloween's a week from today and they have to coordinate artwork with it and—"

"I know all that, Bill," he said, with annoyance. "It's just going slow is all."

"All that research stuff you found—did it do you any good?"

"Fascinating stuff. But it hasn't helped me yet. I just can't seem to get a handle on this one."

"Jeez—" Revell started to sound frustrated, but held it in check. "Come on, Pete. You're one of the most popular children's horror authors on the planet. Your stories have sold in the millions in every language on Earth. You can do this stuff in your sleep. Bogey man, a nice little scare, kids save the day, end of story. Tuesday. Two days. Can you do it?"

"Sure I can do it. In their hands Tuesday."

"You sure, bud?" Revell sounded doubtful.

"No problem."

There was a hesitation. "You . . . sure you're all right, Pete?"

"Why do you ask?"

"You sound . . . weird. A little strange." A pause. "You been drinking?"

"Hell, no."

"Everything okay between you and Ginny?"

Maybe I should ask you that, you bastard.

He said, with sarcasm, "Sure, Bill. Just fine."

"Oh." After a long moment, Revell added, "Anything I can do?"

"Fifteen percent worth of advice?"

"No need to get nasty, Pete. I'm just trying to help."

Before Kerlan could stop himself it came out: "You've already helped plenty, Bill."

The longest pause yet. "I told you, Pete, there was never anything between Ginny and me."

"You know how much I believe you, Bill? Fifteen percent."

"Perhaps we shouldn't work together any longer, if that's the way you feel."

"You really want that, Bill?"

"Actually no, I don't. But if you can't get over this idea that Ginny and I had an affair, I think we'd better think about it."

Something far in the back of his mind, in the place that still was rational and mature, told him to stop.

He took a long breath. "Let's just forget it," he said, reasonably.

There was a long breath on the other end of the line. "I'd like that, Pete. Get back to where things were."

Continuing in a reasonable tone, Kerlan said: "I'll have that piece in by Tuesday."

"Tuesday it is, bud. Maybe we can meet up early next week for a Halloween drink?"

"Sure, Bill. Whatever you say."

"Talk to you soon."

"Right."

There was a click and the phone went dead.

He held it in his hand for a moment, staring at it. *Did she have an affair with him or not?* The truth was, he didn't know. He was smart enough to know that the root of his problem with Ginny was deeper than that—deeper in himself. She was perfectly correct when she told him that all of his problems were rooted in his own frustration with his writing. He knew that was true. But didn't everything else flow out of that? He'd always been a grouch—but had his moods grown so dark in the last months that he was actually driving her away from him?

Wasn't it reasonable to supposed that if he was driving her away, she would be driven into the arms of someone else? Someone like Bill Revell, who was handsome, and younger than he was, and made plenty of money?

Did it matter that he had absolutely no evidence of an affair between the two of them, except for that fact that he realized he was such rotten company that she *had* to fall into someone else's arms?

That and the fact that he'd seen Revell put the moves on Ginny once?

God, Kerlan, you're an asshole.

He still loved Ginny, still loved her with all his heart—but had no idea how to tell her that.

The phone receiver still clutched in one hand, he lowered it slowly to its cradle and reached for the half empty fifth of Scotch, which had been open since noon. He poured two fingers of the honey-colored liquid into the tumbler to the left of the keyboard.

I do think I'll have that drink with you now, Bill, he thought, staring at the white sheet of the computer screen in front of him.

Four more fingers of Scotch and two hours later, he was no closer to filling the white blank space with words, but was at least enmeshed in the research in front of him.

Why the hell can't I get this down on paper?

It *was* fascinating stuff, the legends of Halloween and how they eventually became the relatively benign children's holiday of the present age. It was not always so. Halloween's roots were deep in pagan ritual, specifically the Celtic festival of Samhain, the Lord of Death. Samhain had the power to return the souls of the dead to their earthly homes for one evening— the evening which eventually became known in the Christian era as All Hallows Eve.

Why can't I turn this into a nice, not-too-scary children's story for the Sunday supplements?

He'd tried it a thousand ways—with pets, with witches, with scary monsters—but always it came out too frightening, too strong for children. Always it came out with Samhain as something not benign at all—but rather a hugely frightening entity to be feared more than life itself.

How the hell do you turn the Lord of Death into a warm, fuzzy character?

How the hell do you keep making a living, and straighten your life out, you dumb, useless bastard?

After another two fingers of Scotch, and another two hours, he gave up, went upstairs, and fell asleep on the couch in the living room, dreaming of endless white pages filled with nothing.

▼▼▼▼▼▼

He heard Ginny come in, heard her hesitate as she beheld his prone body on the couch, heard her mutter, "Wonderful," and waited until she stalked off to the bedroom and slammed the door before trying to rouse himself. Blearily opening his eyes, he saw the orange sun setting through the living room window. It looked like a fat pumpkin.

Maybe there's something I can use there, he thought blearily. *A fat old pumpkin named Pete . . . .*

He closed his eyes and drifted back to sleep.

A noise roused him. He knew it was much later, because it was dark through the window now. A dull white streetlight lamp glared at him where the sun had been.

He stared at the grandfather clock in the adjacent dining room, and saw that it was nearly eleven o'clock.

He heard noise off in the hallway leading to the front door.

He hoisted himself into a sitting position on the couch. Head in his hands, he saw the empty Scotch bottle on the floor on its side between his legs.

"Wonderful indeed," he said, remembering Ginny's use of the word hours before, as the first poundings of an evening hangover began in his temples.

He stood, and discovered he was still mildly drunk.

And there, piled in the hallway leading to the front door, was much of what Ginny owned, neatly stacked and suitcased.

Holy shit.

He suddenly discovered he wanted another drink. He found his way to the liquor cabinet, and was rooting around for an unopened bottle of Scotch when Ginny returned.

In a cold, even tone, she said, "Don't you think you've had enough to drink for one day?"

"Just one more, to clear my head," he said. "I get the feeling I'm going to need it."

She was beside him, her hand on his arm as he removed the discovered fifth of Dewers. To his surprise, her grip was gentle.

"Please don't," she said, and moved her hand down to take the Scotch from him.

Sudden resentment and anger boiled up in him. He pulled the bottle away, keeping it in his own hand. He turned away from her and twisted the cap off, looking unsteadily back into the living room for the glass tumbler he had used.

Ginny, amazingly, kept the gentle tone, but it had hardened slightly into urgency: "Please don't, Peter—"

"Just one!" he said, swiveling back to take a fresh tumbler from top of the liquor cabinet, where they stood, cut crystal sparkling like winking eyes.

He poured and drank.

"I really can't take this any longer," Ginny said quietly, and the continued mild tone of what she said made him focus on him.

"Take what? Me?"

"Yes."

He grunted a laugh. "So you're going to—leave?"

"I think I have to."

"You gonna run to your lover? Jump into Bill Revell's arms?" Even as he said it, even with his drunkenness, he knew it was a mistake.

Silence descended on the room like a cold hand. "I told you, Peter—"

He poured another drink, downed it. "You told me! You told me!" He waved the tumbler at her. "What if I don't believe you?"

With iron control she motioned toward the dining room table. "Sit down, Peter."

He moved the neck of the Scotch bottle to the tumbler, but her hands were firmer this time, yanking the bottle and glass out of his grip.

"*Sit down.*"

He did so, fumbling at the chair until she pulled it out for him. He sat, and watched her sit on the opposite side of the table. Startled, he saw that there were tears in her eyes.

"I'm going to say this for the last time, Peter," she began, and suddenly he was focused on her as if he'd been struck suddenly sober. He knew by everything—by her posture, her voice, the tears in her eyes—that this was the pivotal moment they had been moving toward for the past weeks.

"I'm listening," he said, the fight out of him before it had even begun.

She studied his face for a moment. "Good. Then please listen closely, because this is the best I can do to explain what's happened to us." She took a deep breath. "First of all, I never had an affair with Bill Revell, and never would. He's your agent, and, quite frankly, I don't like him. He's smart but he's ruthless, and the only reason he's with you is that you're making him money. We both know he would drop you in a second if you stopped producing."

Kerlan thought of his conversation that afternoon with Revell. "You're right about—" he began, but Ginny cut him off.

"Let me finish. I was merely being polite to him at that party in September. He tried to kiss me and I didn't let him. End of story."

"I saw—"

"You saw him *try*. I turned my cheek and let him peck me there. That's what you saw. After you turned away I told him as nicely as I could that if he ever tried to kiss me again I'd knee him in the balls."

Kerlan felt an odd urge to laugh—this sounded so much like the old Ginny, the one he had fallen in love with. But instead he just stared at her.

"You said that? You never told me—"

"You never let me tell you. For the last month you've been treating me like a leper. Ever since you started that Halloween magazine assignment Revell got you."

He found that his head had cleared to a miraculous extent. It was as if the importance of the moment had surged through him, canceling out the liquor.

"You know I've been having trouble with it—"

Ginny laughed. "Having trouble? Like I said this morning, you've been nothing but a monster since you began researching it."

"The money's too good—"

"To hell with the money—and to hell with Bill Revell! Just tell him you can't do it!"

"I've never had trouble with anything before—"

She leapt on his words as if she had been waiting for them. "Isn't that what this is all about, Pete? Isn't this all about you not being able to pull the trigger when you want to? It's always come easy, hasn't it? You've always been able to write when you wanted or needed to—and now for the first time you've got . . . writer's block—"

"Don't say that!" he nearly screeched. She had touched the nerve, and even she seemed to know she had gone too far.

"All right then," she said, backing off. "Let's just say you're having trouble with this one. Isn't that the root of all our problems lately?"

After a moment, when he found there was nothing else he could say, he said, "Yes."

She seemed to give a huge sigh of relief. In the gentlest voice he had ever heard her use, she said, "Peter, do you think we can stop fighting?"

His eyes were drawn to the pile of her belongings waiting in the hallway. He found that the last thing in the world he wanted was for her to leave. To hell with his work—to hell with everything. He wanted her to stay.

"I . . . love you, Ginny. I'm . . . sorry for everything I've done."

Then suddenly she was around the table and holding him, and they both were crying.

"Oh, Peter, it's all right, everything's going to be all right."

"Yes, Ginny, I promise . . . "

"And you'll tell Revell you can't do that piece?"

He stiffened, and she pulled away from him.

"You'll tell him that?" she repeated.

The old anger tried to boil up in him—all the feelings of inadequacy, of helplessness, of everything that was mixed in with it, of him hitting middle age, getting older, afraid of losing his talent, afraid of losing *her*—

With a huge effort, he brought himself under control and said, "If it doesn't work in the next day or so, I'll toss it."

"You mean it?" Her huge beautiful eyes were searching his own, studying him, begging him—

Again he had to control himself, and knew she sensed it. She was waiting for him—

"Yes."

She hugged him tighter. "I can't tell you how happy I am. I didn't want to leave. I was going to go to my sister's, and you know I can't stand her—"

"Neither can I," Kerlan said dryly, and Ginny laughed.

"I love you more than anything in the world, Peter," she said, kissing him. "Don't ever doubt that."

She kissed him again, and Peter said, "I love you, too. More than you'll ever know."

She pulled away from him, smiling, and said, "I'll put everything away in the morning. It's Monday, and I want to get the rest of my gardening done early, before I go to work. I'll put my stuff away after I get home tomorrow night, all right?"

"All right," he answered, smiling back at her.

"You coming to bed?"

He almost said yes, sensing from the look in her eyes that she might want more than sleep, but instead he said, "I'm going to spend a little time in my office."

Her face darkened slightly. "You're not going to—"

"If it doesn't work immediately, I'm giving it up. Let's call this a last stand."

He could tell she was thinking of arguing, but instead she nodded. "All right, Peter. Give it one more try."

"I'll be up later."

She stopped, looked back at him. "I'll wait up for you, if I can keep my eyes open."

"See you later."

She went down the hall to the bedroom. Kerlan, grunting with the continuance of a well deserved hangover, made his way downstairs.

At three in the morning, he was finally ready to give up. The piece, no matter how he came at it, was just much too dark. The more he delved into the character of Samhain, the more frightening the Celtic Lord of Death became. There were hints of human sacrifice as tribute for good crops and prosperity. There were various dark tales of horrible deaths and evil perpetuated in his name. There was just no way to lighten him up. Peter tried making him into a character with a black cloak and pumpkin for a head—but when he read over what little he had written, the Lord of the Dead was just too scary for children. It just seemed that nomatter what he tried to make the Samhain character do, he always ended up surrounded by death.

The *real* stuff.

And if little kids didn't like one thing, it was the real stuff.

He stared at a sketch he'd made of Samhain to help him, with the folds of his bright pumpkin head set back into the dark shadows of his cowl, a horrid sickle grin on his cut-out face, a spark of terrifying fire deep in the ebony eye sockets, stark white bone hands reaching from beneath the folds of the cloak, and shivered.

"Hell," he muttered to the picture, at the end of his rope, realizing that it just wasn't going to work, "*I'd* even pay tribute to you, Sam, if you'd help me finish this damn story."

Suddenly, as if a switch had been thrown, it came to him.

Sam.

That was it!

Call him Sam.

Almost before he knew it, he was tearing through the story, and, in what seemed like no time at all, it lay all but finished in front of him.

He came out of what felt like a trance, but what must actually be, he realized, a mixture of waning work-adrenaline, the remains of a Scotch hangover, and just plain tiredness. Through the window above his desk, the sun had already circled the globe and come up over the back of the house. Brighter than it had been the evening before, when it had hovered in the living room window, it now resembled a happy pumpkin.

By the clock, he saw that it was eight in the morning.

I worked five hours straight. Amazing.

Three tiny shadows passed by the window in front of the sun, hovering briefly before the screen, and he saw that they were yellow jackets. Briefly, he remembered the newspaper story from the day before. A shiver started, but was suppressed by tiredness.

He stretched, suddenly remembering Ginny.

I hope she just drifted off to sleep, and didn't wait for me.

He rose, stretched as if his frame had been locked into a sitting position for a year, rubbing his eyes while yawning, and left the office, tramping upstairs.

He thought of making coffee, but knew he would never stay awake while it brewed.

In the front hallway, he walked around Ginny's pile of belongings, noting with curiosity that the front door was open.

Upstairs, Ginny was not in the bedroom.

She was nowhere in the house.

On the pile of her belongings, perched like a bird, was a note: *Peter, I'm sorry, but I have to leave . . . .*

"And there's a possibility the note may have been written the previous night, before your reconciliation?"

"Yes."

"Thing I don't get is, Mr. Kerlan: why'd she leave without her things?"

Detective Grant had been nice enough in the beginning, even solicitous; but now, standing with the man in the front hallway of the house, Peter sensed a change in the atmosphere, an aggressiveness that hadn't been present before. At first all the questions had been about Ginny, where she might have gone, why she would have left, but now, Grant couldn't seem to take his eyes off the pile of belongings in the hallway. Peter could tell it stuck like a wad of gum to the roof of the man's mouth.

"I told you, detective, we had a fight Sunday. A big one. I was sleeping on the couch when she came home, and when I woke up all of her stuff was in the hallway—"

"She packed while you were asleep—"

"Yes. And when I woke up we started the fight all over again. By the end of it we had squared things away, I thought. Ginny went up to bed and I went down to my office to work—"

"This was late, almost midnight—?"

"Yes."

"And you worked through the entire night—" Grant said, referring to his notes. "And when you went upstairs—"

He looked up at Kerlan from his pad, and for the first time Peter sensed a faint belligerence from the man.

"When I went upstairs she was gone."

The detective snapped his fingers. "Just like that?"

"Yes."

"Left her belongings, her car, just took off after you had supposedly settled everything?" He gave a twist in emphasis to the word "supposedly," making it sound almost sinister.

"That's exactly right."

"And you called us after you spent yesterday looking everywhere she might have gone, including her sister; an—" he consulted his notes "—uncle in Chicago, her best friend from college, and even your own mother." He glanced sideways from his notebook at Kerlan. "*Your* mother?"

"My mother and Ginny are very close. I could see her going there, yes. Ginny's own parents are dead."

Grant nodded briefly, went back to his notes. "You called all the local motels and hotels . . . that about the whole story?"

"Yes."

Grant straightened his heavy frame, turning his notebook to a new page. "Well, maybe not exactly, Mr. Kerlan. I'd like to fill in a few blanks, if you don't mind."

"Anything you want."

"All right, then. Let's see . . . " Grant was running his eyes down a notebook page, flipped back to the previous page and did the same. His eyes, which were bright blue in a rough, stubbled face, making them startling, pinned Peter suddenly.

"Let's start with you being asleep on the couch on Sunday. You were taking a *nap*?" Again the emphasis on a word, this time "nap," which made Grant sound incredulous.

"I'd had a few drinks, and was sleeping that off."

"Ah." This seemed to satisfy Grant and he went on searching his notes. Kerlan had the feeling that the detective already had a list of laser sharp questions in a neat list in his head, and was only scanning the notebook for effect.

"You had *two* fights with your wife that day?"

"One at breakfast time and then another that night."

"You fought a lot?"

"Recently, yes."

"Marital . . . trouble?" Grant let this hand in the air, waving his pencil in a little circle to make the question more than it was.

"I've been having trouble with my work. It carried over."

"Any other obvious difficulties? Money? Sex life? You having an affair, maybe?"

Kerlan blinked, surprised at the question. "No. Nothing like that."

"Nothing like that." Grant nodded to himself, making a note on his current page. "You drink a lot, Mr. Kerlan?"

Again, he was taken aback. "No. Occasionally I have a few."

"Have a few . . . .You ever hit your wife? Slap her around?"

Now Peter became angry. "No."

Grant nodded, made a note.

"You can't think of anywhere else she might have gone, anyone else she might have gone to see?"

"No."

The detective eyed the pile of goods stacked in the hallway for perhaps the twentieth time. "Any idea why she left her stuff behind, Mr. Kerlan?"

"That's the part I don't get."

"Me too. If you were running away, would you leave all your things behind after spending the time and trouble to stack it all up in the hallways by the front door?"

"No, I wouldn't."

Suddenly the detective straightened again, turning it into a stretch. He flipped the notebook closed and pocketed his pen in the side pocket of his jacket. His tie was loosened, Peter noticed.

Without warning, Grant smiled, making Peter blink.

"Thanks, Mr. Kerlan. I've got everything I need for now. We'll check over everything you did, and widen the motel and hotel search a little into the next county. It's kind of early yet to be too worried. I'll be in touch." He suddenly winked, and held out his hand. "If she shows up give me a call, will you?"

Peter went to shake the hand but then saw that there was a business card in it, which he took automatically.

"I will, detective."

"Do that." Grant turned on his heels and was out the front door and into his sedan almost before Peter could answer. Peter saw him light a cigarette as he climbed into the car.

He watched the detective pull out of the driveway over a mat of yet-to-be-raked leaves. In the last two days the trees had denuded themselves completely, leaving a riot of reds and yellows on his lawn. Peter idly noticed that the Meyers' had cleared and bagged their own front yard, the neatly clipped grass of which showed yellow green. Their three pumpkins had settled into a neat row—smallest at the top, fattest of the three at the bottom. In their picture window were Halloween cut-outs: a jointed white skeleton with a toothy grin, a black-clad witch riding a broomstick angled up toward a sickle reddish moon.

Halloween was only five days away.

And it was still too damned hot.

He turned away from the front door, confronted by the mute pile of Ginny's belongings.

For a moment, tears welled up in his eyes.

Ginny, where are you?

I thought we had fixed it? I thought we were okay?

The boxes, the suitcases, the bags of clothing, remained mute.

He first felt not a sting, but the vague, insistent, faint, tiny itch of an insect on his leg.

He swiveled in his armchair, bending his left leg and at the same time brushing at the itch; something small, dark and solid dropped from his leg and melded with the carpet beside his desk. It wriggled there for a moment, righting itself in a tiny lifting of small wings, and he bent to examine it, suppressing a sudden shudder.

It was a hornet, not much past pupae stage, its tiger stripes muted into almost orange and black.

He remembered the story in the newspaper; the children stung by a legion of hornets from a nest they had disturbed—

"How in hell—" he said, lifting his carpeted slipper almost without thinking to grind the insect into the carpet before it could advance or, possibly, take flight.

Suppressing another shudder, he drew his foot away, dragging it across the carpet to rid the slipper's bottom of the creature's remains. A diminishing line of bug guts, looking dry and powdery and papery, trailed the low cut gray rug till they came to a point and disappeared.

Have to clean that later, he thought, turning back to his work.

The basement office's single screened window was open above his desk, and for a moment he idly heard a buzz and looked up.

There, outside, was a fat bumblebee, just bumping the screen before lumbering airily off.

Before turning back to his work he let his eyes roam over the screen, looking for torn corners or holes; there were none.

Didn't get in that way.

He turned back to his work, which was still going well; after sending the Halloween story to *Parade* magazine on Monday he'd discovered he had more to say on the subject of Samhain—or, as he called his own cute little version, Sam.

Almost immediately the phone rang, and he clutched his pencil, almost throwing it down angrily, before dropping it on the desk and, with a sigh, picking up the receiver.

"Yes?"

It was Ravell on the other end of the line, asking after him.

"I'd be doing a lot better," Peter said, trying to keep the testiness out of his voice, "if I didn't have people like you bothering me."

Ravell said with false concern, "I'm just worried about you, Pete."

Are you?

"Thanks for the concern."

"You heard anything more from the police?"

"No. They don't have anything new."

Unless Ginny's with you after all, you bastard.

"Well, let me know if you need anything," Revell said. "I—"

Peter cut him off. "I really have to get back to work."

"Nothing wrong with that Take your mind off what you're going through. Actually, that's the reason I called—"

Of course it is, you bastard. He recalled what Ginny had said: "He would drop you in a second if you stopped producing . . . "

"I've got to go. I'll call you soon."

Like hell I will.

He half-slammed the phone down, stared at the wall next to his desk.

Something was crawling up it, above the wooden filing cabinet that held his printer, muted orange and black stripes—

"What the fu—"

He reached out a palm, hit it flat; the hornet, still whole, tumbled from the wall behind the metal filing cabinet and was lost to view.

He was on his feet, pushing his swivel chair back and pressing his head against the wall to try to locate the insect behind the cabinet; unable to, he stalked from the office in anger and went to his messy workbench at the other end of the basement, pushing objects aside—a power screwdriver, coffee tin of miscellaneous nails—until he located a flashlight. He turned back toward the office, flipping the flashlight switch, which produced a click but no light beam.

"Shit!"

He reversed stride, rummaged through the wreckage on top of the workbench, then pulled drawers open until he found an opened four pack of D cells; he unscrewed the flashlight's top, turned it over impatiently, dropping one of the two batteries within from his waiting palm to the floor where it rolled beneath the bench.

"Shit! Shit!" He kicked the bench once, pulled back his slipper to kick it again before breathing deeply and turning his attention to the new batteries, which he shoved viciously into the flashlight's tubular body before screwing the head back on and flipping it on once more.

Light shone this time, blinked out until his smacked the tool against his palm, hard.

The beam stayed on.

He strode back to the office and played the beam on the wall above he filing cabinet. Getting closer, he was about to shine it behind the cabinet when he saw an immature hornet crawling over the printer's paper tray, and another on the wall beside it.

He cursed, put the flashlight down on the desk, looked for something to hit the insects with, and found a recent trade journal, which he rolled up, smacking the two hornets with it.

One dropped away to the rug; the other lay squashed against the printer's paper roll.

Wary now, he looked in increments behind the printer, saw another insect making its way up the wall behind, and what looked like two others below it, showing movement.

Shivering, he drew back, moved away from the desk and toward the office's door, his eyes glancing at the rug, the walls, the ceiling.

He closed the door behind him, dropped the rolled up magazine and climbed the steps to the house's first floor two at a time.

He made his way to the front door, pushing his way past piles of Ginny's clothes, Ginny's books, her CDs.

He yanked open the front door, pushed open the screen, descended the porch's four steps and walked quickly to the western rear corner of the house, which fronted his basement office and the bedroom above it.

The cable television and phone line entry, as well as the house's gas main, were clustered near the side corner. He examined them, seeing no entry for an insect where the wires and gas line led into the house's siding; everything was sealed and caulked.

He moved closer; a hornet flew past him, then another, and he spotted the entry, below the siding level. He watched a moment, saw a hornet fly to a spot near the corner of the house, where foundation met siding, land and crawl underneath the siding.

Edging closer, he crouched nearly to the ground, turning his head to examine beneath the siding.

There was a gap there in the wooden sill plate on which the house rested above the concrete foundation; it looked like the two boards which met at the corner had either not been properly butted, or that the butting board had shrunk, leaving an opening into an area between the house's first floor and basement.

"Jesus," he said, as a hornet crawled out from the space, flying past him with a rush as another crawled into the opening.

They had obviously built a nest back there.

"*Damn.*"

Filled with fury and resolve, he got to his feet, returned to the house and kicked his slippers off in the living room, looking for his deck shoes; they were no where to be seen and his searched down the hallway, almost reaching the back bedroom before finding the shoes nestled one against the other just outside the bedroom door.

He slipped them on, checked the pockets of his shorts for his car keys and then moved back outside, slamming the house door behind him.

I'll take care of you, you bastards.

He got into his Honda, nearly leaving rubber as he backed out of the driveway, and was back in twenty minutes with two cans of Hornet and Wasp Killer. Barely reading the instructions, he pulled the safety tab from the top of one can, shoved the thin, hard plastic straw that came with it into the can's top nozzle and shook the can as he marched back to the outside corner of the house.

Want to eat this? Enjoy it!

He stopped before the spot, watched a hornet alight and then crawl into the hidden opening, watched another crawl out and fly off. He crouched, thrusting the can's nozzle forward and awkwardly trying to fit it under and into the opening.

The hard plastic straw missed, sliding away as a hornet, angered, crawled out, followed by another.

Flinching, he pressed the nozzle, watching the acrid spray cover the two insects; they froze and dropped to the ground.

And now the rest of you bastards.

Still spraying, he crouched lower, his eye level below that of the foundation, and found the opening.

He angled the nozzle's straw in and tightened his grip on the can's trigger.

A single hornet fought its way out, dropped immediately to the ground. Another, coming from the outside, circled the opening, caught a wiff of escaping spray and also dropped.

He emptied the can, pushed himself back as three returning hornets began to circle the hole widely; one of the insects ventured into the hole, immediately retreated and then dropped to the ground. There was a long stain of spilled pesticide spray down the foundation under the hole, which began to dry as he watched.

A cloud of hornets circled the sprayed opening, darting toward it, landing tentatively on the lowest level of siding over the opening, took off again.

He shook the can, let a final spray cover them; all but one dropped to the ground as the remaining one flew off.

That'll take care of you.

Breathing deeply, the adrenalin rush that had sustained him for the past hour receding, he went into the house, scooping up the second can of insect spray where he had deposited it on the front stoop, in time to hear the telephone begin to ring.

It was Bill Revell again.

"Pete, I'm sorry to bother you again but you didn't let me finish before. *Parade* was so wild about that Halloween piece you did that I showed it to Doubleday and they flipped. They'd like you to do more, and turn it into a book. We're talking high five figures, maybe low six for this one—"

"I'll think about it."

"Jeez, what's to think about? Just say yes and I'll take care of the rest. They're talking about publishing next Halloween, cash register dumpster display, a real push. These characters of yours could become perennials—you could turn one out every Halloween, have the kids waiting in line—"

"I said I'd *think about it*—"

"I know you're worried about Ginny, bud, but this one could set you up with a guaranteed every year for the next five years at least. Can I at least negotiate a three-book deal?"

He said nothing, and Revell went on: "The characters are great, Pete! A real Halloween character! Named Sam no less! And I *love* Holly Ween! I've got feelers out already to television, and I think we can expect a *big* bite on that—half hour like *It's the Great Pumpkin, Charlie Brown*. We're talking ancillary—lunch boxes, tees, the whole nine—"

"*Do whatever the hell you want!*" Kerlan shouted, and slammed down the phone.

He gripped the receiver tightly as he suddenly began to cry.

If she wasn't with Revell, she was with someone else.

And he'd driven her away.

She's gone and I know it.

Gone for good.

He let the second can of bug spray slip to the floor as he covered his face with his hands and wept, and kept weeping.

After trying to watch television, and trying to eat, he went to bed early and as a consequence rose early the next morning.

With a tepid cup of instant coffee in his hand, he made his way down to he basement office.

Even before reaching it, the faint, acrid smell of bug spray tickled his nostrils.

"Christ," he said, wincing as he walked into the room; it was even worse than the faint, musty odor the basement room sometimes held in the summer months, when the foundation walls behind the sheetrock-covered studs picked up humidity from the ground. The smell had been particularly noticeable this year.

He stood up on his swivel chair, cursing sharply as it tried to turn sideways with his weight, then leaned out over his desk to open the room's single casement window.

"*Shit.*" he said, recoiling; in the casement box were the bodies of five small hornets, all but one seemingly dead; the live one moved feebly, its small wings opening once, then again. Behind the casement, somewhere behind the room's wall, he heard a faint buzzing sound.

He climbed down from the chair, nearly ran to the workbench area, and returned with the basement's wet/dry vacuum.

He plugged the vacuum into the wall socket between his desk and the printer stand, turned it on, and angled the hose nozzle up into the casement, sucking up all of the hornets.

His eye caught movement by the printer, and he saw another small insect body crawling up the wall over the machine.

I thought I wiped you bastards out yesterday!

He covered the hornet with the sucking nozzle, then looked wildly around the walls, then at the floor.

"Shit!"

There was a cluster of dead bodies fanned out in the corner just to the left of the printer stand, where a heat register ran across the wall at floor level; two live hornets were just crawling out of the bottom of the register itself.

"Shit! Shit!" he said, fighting an uncontrollable chill, thrusting the vacuum head around the area and plugging it into the corner under the register as far as it would go.

He heard the tap of insect bodies rushing up the vacuum's soft plastic accordion hose and into the wet-vac's drum.

Another crawled out onto the rug from behind the printer stand, and he speared it, then put the nozzle back into the corner. He kept it there, feeling another tiny body sucked up into the machine, and then another.

He gave up all thoughts of work, and fled the office; at the doorway he saw a feebly moving hornet on the rug by the sill, and mashed it with his foot, closing the door behind him.

"Sounds weird enough, Mr. Kerlan, but they all sound weird to me. One time—"

"Can you come today?" Peter said into the phone, cutting the bee keeper off before he went into yet another anecdote. "This infestation is in the place I work, and I need it taken care of."

"Sure," the other said, slowly. "I suppose I can be there this afternoon. We'll take care of you."

"I hope so," Kerlan said, slamming down the phone.

He stole a glance into his office, opening the door a crack. By now all sorts of nightmares preyed on his mind: the room filled with flying insects; a swarm waiting for him, covering him as he opened the door—

All inside seemed quite; the casement window threw a rectangular shaft of light against the far wall's built-in bookcase.

He opened the door wider, listening for buzzing.

Maybe I wiped them out after all.

His relief was short-lived; as he stepped toward his desk his foot covered three squirming hornet bodies, and he saw a few more scattered here and there, some unmoving, others moving as if drunk; there were three or four on the walls, also, and more, perhaps a dozen, covering the casement's window itself, silhouetted dots against the light.

He reached for the wet/dry vac, recoiled as a hornet brushed his hand as it fell from the hose; others were crawling over the instrument's drum, one hiding coyly by one of the rolling wheels.

Once again he fled, and closed the door.

"What you've got here is a classic case of wall infestation," the bee keeper, whose name was Floyd Willims, said. He worked part time as the local exterminator, but he *looked* like a bee keeper, was tall and thin-haired and preoccupied when he stepped from his dirty white van; and now even more so, dressed almost comically in a pith helmet whose brim was ringed with mosquito netting; from the back of his van he pulled a thick pair of rubber gloves from a soiled box. He held up the gloves for inspection. "Triple thickness," he said, almost proudly; "stingers can't get through." After retrieving a powder filled canister and what appeared to be a pump hose from the van, he turned back to Kerlan and said, "Proceed!"

Kerlan had already showed him the corner of the house where the hornets had gained access; they returned to that spot now and the bee keeper knelt, put the thin end of the hose which led into the canister in the opening, and began to puff powder into it.

"This'll kill 'em dead," he said. "Whichever ones return will carry the powder into the nest and spread it to the others."

As if on cue, as the bee keeper removed the hose from the opening a hornet alighted and crawled into it.

"Now let's have a look at the nest," the bee keeper said, heading for the house with Kerlan.

They had already studied the office on the bee keeper's arrival, and the bee keeper had helped Kerlan move furniture so that the upper corner of the wall, behind which the bee keeper said they would find the nest, was exposed; luckily, there would be access through a nearby panel, behind which the house's electrical box was located. To either side of the box was packed insulation, which the bee keeper began to remove.

The smell of insect spray became stronger in the room.

The bee keeper lay the strips of insulation on the floor; Kerlan was repulsed to see hornets crawling feebly over the pink spun glass fibers of its back.

The bee keeper held up a strip, examined the five hornets on it carefully.

"You zapped them pretty good with that off-the-shelf stuff you sprayed into the nest yesterday," he said. "If you'd gotten them at dusk, when they were all in the nest, you might have killed them all. What we're looking at are the dregs, I think."

"How did they get in here to begin with? How many openings does the nest have?"

Willims had shown him a picture of a typical paper hornet's nest; a nearly round structure with a single opening, usually at the bottom.

"They either made another exit, or left an opening near the top," he said. "This isn't quite a typical nest. They were drawn to the light in your office." He pointed to the baseboard, the corner of the floor where the heat register butted the wall. "There's an opening down there, I'm sure. Doesn't take much, just a quarter inch." He squinted through his mosquito netting at the molding along the rug where the printer stand had been before they moved it. "There may be others. Like I said, a quarter inch is all they need."

An involuntary chill washed over Kerlan as a hornet crawled onto the bee keeper's glove and onto his shirt sleeve. The bee keeper regarded it for a moment and then flicked it to the floor. "Like I said, you must have hit them good. If they were healthy they'd be all over us, because of the light." He turned to Kerlan as if having a sudden thought. "Sure you don't want to leave?"

"I'll stay, if you think it's safe."

The bee keeper laughed. "Safe enough. If they pour out of the walls when I remove the rest of this insulation, I'll yell and you can run."

Kerlan's eyes enlarged in alarm but the bee keeper added, "Not likely to happen.

At that moment the bee keeper pulled the last strip of insulation out with a grunt.

Nothing happened; the bee keeper angled his head, aiming a flashlight up into the exposed cavity, and called back, "Yeah, you hit 'em pretty good."

Kerlan leaned over, trying to see; pulled back and a fist-shaped clutch of dead hornets fell from the space between the open cavity and the bee keeper's body.

The bee keeper angled his arm up into the cavity.

"I'll . . . get it out if I can—"

He pulled a huge chunk of dark papery gray material out of the cavity, let it drop to the floor.

"Nest," he said in explanation. It was followed by a bigger chunk, mottled and round on the inside; within it's crushed interior were dead hornets and a few feebly live ones.

"Ugh," Kerlan said.

"Pretty big nest," the bee keeper said, continuing to pull sections of the structure out. Mixed with the leavings now were the familiar honeycombed sections that Kerlan knew contained the pupae. Most but not all were empty. "About the size of a soccer ball. They built it right up in the corner beneath the floor above. As they built the nest it forced the insulation back. Amazing critters."

He continued his work, and Kerlan shivered.

An hour later the office was more or less back to normal, and Kerlan was writing the bee keeper a check.

"You'll want to caulk that hole they used in a couple of weeks," Willims said. That powder I sprayed around it will take care of any stragglers."

"Why not plug it now?"

"Well, you could, but there could still be a few females outside the nest; they'd just start another one."

Kerlan had forgotten that each nest held a queen.

"Didn't we kill off this nest's queen?"

"You can be pretty much certain of that. But even so, any female can become a queen. They'll just start another nest." He grinned. "Summer's not quite over, you know. I'll be getting calls like yours 'till mid-November, if the heat holds out."

"Christ."

The bee keeper folded the check and turned toward his dirty white van. Kerlan had a sudden thought.

"You're sure my nest is dead?"

The bee keeper shrugged. "Pretty sure. You may see a few strays wander out of your baseboard gaps looking for light, but believe me, that nest is dead. Only other problem you could have is if two females got in there originally and the second one started another nest somewhere else inside the wall, farther down." Seeing Kerlan's eyes widen he laughed. "Not likely that happened, though. Plug the gaps in the baseboard if you can; you can use a wad of scrunched up cellophane tape. Call me if you have any more problems."

Kerlan nodded as the van drove off.

A single yellow jacket brushed by his face as he entered the house.

The next morning he entered his office to work. The evening before, he had moved along the edge of the baseboard where he could get at it, pushing cellophane tape into anything that looked like an opening. By the baseboard he had found a huge hole surrounding the heat pipe that let into the register; around it were tens of dead yellow jackets and a very alive spider as big as a thumb nail, feeding on them. There was a sour smell emanating from the vent: a mixture of fading bug spray and the strong damp smell from the cavity behind. After recoiling he cleaned the area out with the wet/dry vac and then plugged it with insulating material. The smell receded.

He vacuumed the rug thoroughly, sucking up dead hornet bodies, and then replaced his furniture and turned on his computer.

There came a tapping at the casement window above him and he started, looking up; it was just a fat bumblebee, probably the same from the other day, which ambled sluggishly off.

He let out a deep breath and turned to the screen.

He typed out the words *Sam Hain and the Halloween That Almost Wasn't* and suddenly, for the next hours, he was lost in the characters as words poured out of him in a torrent. Nothing like this had happened to him in the last twenty years. Page after page scrolled down the screen, and he knew they were all good. He finished one story and the ideas for two others came into his head unbidden. He typed so fast his fingers began to ache—something he hadn't felt since the days of electric typewriters, when the constant kickback of the keys would rattle his knuckles and literally make his fingers sore. It was a marvelous feeling. And still he wrote on, completing outlines for two more stories before finally letting himself fall back into his swivel chair, breathing hard. It was as if he had run a marathon, and he couldn't believe the mass of material now stored on his hard drive.

Without thinking, he sent it all as an attached file to Bill Revell, with a curt note: "Like I said, do whatever the hell you want."

He knew that would keep the bastard busy for a while, and off his back.

Even now, he felt another itch at the back of his brain, which would turn into more work tomorrow. He knew it. It had been so long since this had happened to him, this creative torrent, that he'd forgotten what it was like.

Oh, Ginny, if only you were here now! The problem's gone! I can write again!

It was the only sour note in what had been a marvelous day. He looked up at his casement window and saw that night had fallen, and that a waxing moon was rising. It looked huge and orange-tinged, and even that gave him a new idea for a story: *Sam and Holly and the Halloween Moon.*

Quickly he wrote it down in outline, and when he looked up again the moon was high and the clock said it was midnight.

He stumbled upstairs, past Ginny's things, and walked down the hall to bed, where he dreamed of black and orange things, and a cute character named Sam Hain, a squat fellow that looked like a comical skeleton with a wide happy grin and a spring in his step, who danced through a children's Halloween world with his blonde-curled friend Holly. It was a world of orange and yellow and red, of perpetually falling leaves that danced and dervished, and trick-or-treat bags that were always open and bottomless, and Jack o' lanterns that never sputtered or grew burned black inside or soft rotten, and winds that were blustery and just cold, and clouds that made the fat full moon wink, and a night that was always All Hallows Eve, with hoots in the air, and scary costumes that weren't really scary at all—

—and in the dream Sam Hain changed, even as the night changed, as he grew from a fat happy children's character into a monstrous terrifying thing, black and tall and cold as space, his bone hands bone white and hard as smooth stones, his eyes deeper than black empty wells, his grin not happy but ravenous, his breath ancient and colder than space, and sour with death as he bent to whisper into Kerlan's ear something soft and horrible, and which made him scream even as it filled him with joy—

Two days, it said. *You'll see her in two days.*

He awoke, covered in sweat, with the moon higher than his window and the night suddenly chilly, and for a moment he thought he saw something that looked like Ginny lying on the bed next to him, something which turned to writhing tiny balls of dust and then vanished.

He sat up in bed breathing heavily, drenched in cold sweat, eyes wide with fear, and then he lay down again, and the room grew warm, and he slept again, dreamless.

The day next he sat in front of his screen again oblivious, until a sound, a tiny insistent buzzing, made him look up.

He already had outlines for two more Sam Hain stories, and was in the middle of a third. Groggily, he glanced up at his window and saw a hornet buzz by outside the screen.

He went back to work, but the tiny insistent buzzing remained. It was like an itch at the back of his mind.

If anything, the weather had grown even hotter. The radio, which he had listened to briefly while making coffee, mentioned a record-breaker of 82 degrees for this date, October 30th. The leaves on the front lawn were wilting, turning dry and crackly like they normally did in deep winter. The Meyer kids, he barely noticed, were now all in shorts and short sleeve shirts.

As he worked, the faint buzz remained, but he tuned it out, and kept tapping at the keys.

Sometime in early afternoon, after ignoring two phone calls, he hit a lull and reached blindly for the phone when it rang again.

"Yes?" he said curtly.

There was a slight pause, and then a voice said: "Mr. Kerlan? This is Detective Grant."

For a moment that meant nothing to him, but then he focused on the name.

"Are you there, Mr. Kerlan?" the detective asked.

"Yes, I'm here."

"I was wondering if you've heard from your wife."

He remembered the dream from the night before. "Have *you* heard from her?" he said with hope.

Again a pause. "No, I haven't. Frankly, I don't see why I would. I'm just checking in to see if by any chance she made contact with you, or anyone else you know."

"I haven't heard from her."

"That's too bad." Another pause, which Kerlan waited patiently through.

"Mr. Kerlan, do you mind if I ask you a few more questions?"

Peter's attention now was on everything Grant said. His hands left the keyboard reluctantly. "Sure, go ahead."

"Thank you. I was . . . wondering if perhaps your wife had gone to . . . someone other than a family member?"

"Like who?"

"Someone . . . perhaps she was . . . " Grant laughed with slight embarrassment. "I don't know quite how to say this, except to just say it."

Peter waited.

"Mr. Kerlan, was your wife having an affair?"

He instantly thought of Revell.

"Who told you that?"

"Well . . . I shouldn't say this, but one of her relatives told me that there had been some . . . friction between your wife and yourself lately over the question of her, perhaps, seeing someone else . . . "

A kind of relief flooded through him; he'd though perhaps the detective had dug up facts when, in fact, he had obviously been talking to Ginny's big mouthed sister, who would have known about their problems.

"Did Ginny's sister Anna tell you that?"

Grant said, "Well . . . "

"If she did, there's nothing to it. I had a fit of jealousy but there was nothing behind it."

"That's what your agent said when I talked to him, but you never know with these things. People try to . . . keep things quiet sometimes . . . "

"Revell."

"Yes, William Revell. So as far as you know your wife wasn't having an affair with Mr. Revell?"

"Absolutely not."

"But you *did* think he was, for a time."

"For a brief time, yes. I was wrong."

"Jealousy, you said . . . " Grant replied, and Peter could picture the man consulting his cursed note pad, flipping pages . . .

"Is there anything else, detective? I'm busy—"

"Just a few more questions. Unless you'd like me to drop by later . . . "

Peter sighed. "That's all right. I'll answer whatever you want now."

"Thank you for taking the time, Mr. Kerlan. Now . . . "

Peter could *hear* the rustling of notebook pages. He waited.

Grant finally said, "Ah. What I wanted to know was, if it possible, I mean, could it be possible, that your wife is not missing, but has been murdered?"

Peter's vision went black for a moment. "What?"

"What I mean is," Grant said, in the same casual tone, "do you think it's possible?"

"Murdered? By whom?"

"That's the question, isn't it? But what we've got here, Mr. Kerlan, is a woman who threatened to run away, who may have had an affair, and, when she did finally leave, did not go anywhere logical, to family or friend, or even to the man with whom she may have been having an affair—"

"I *told* you, there was no affair. You talked with Revell, didn't you say?"

"Oh, yes, he was very helpful. Told me just what you're telling me now. But what I'm thinking is that, if there was the *perception* of an affair, even for a time . . . "

"Detective Grant, I may be dense but I'm not *that* dense. Are you telling me you think I killed my wife?"

"Not at all!" Grant gave a falsely hearty laugh. "Did I say that?"

"Not in so many words. But the way you're talking . . . "

Another pause. "Let me put it this way, Mr. Kerlan. Usually when we have this kind of situation, a missing person the way we have here, a few logical possibilities usually present themselves. The most logical in this case is that your wife left, and went to someone close to her. That hasn't happened. Another logical possibility is that she took off on a whim, and went to a faraway place, on an airplane, perhaps, or a train or bus. Since she didn't take her car, this is the way we think. We've checked on this end as far as we could, and that doesn't seem to have happened. And if it had, usually after two or three days she would have contacted you, or one of the other people close to her, to talk or just to let someone know she was all right. This is the kind of logic we use. After those two scenarios are excluded, there's another that often presents itself. That is, of course, that she never left at all. That she was . . . "

"Murdered. By me."

"Or someone else, Mr. Kerlan. Is there anyone else we should be looking at?"

"Could it have been a random thing, a serial killer—"

He had the feeling Grant almost laughed, but instead the detective said, "That's not a logical scenario at the moment, Mr. Kerlan. Like I said, is there anyone else . . . ?"

"No. Nobody I can think of."

"Then if you were me, and thinking logically . . . "

"You think I killed her. You think I went into a jealous rage, and murdered her, and hid her body, chopped it up with an ax, put it in a blender . . . "

Grant wasn't laughing on the other end of the line, and Kerlan suddenly realized the man might take him literally.

"I write horror fiction for a living, detective."

"Yes, I know." The voice was a bit harder-edged.

"I didn't chop her up and put her in a blender."

Silence.

"Should we be talking further about this, Mr. Kerlan? With perhaps a lawyer present?"

"I didn't kill my wife, detective."

Almost all of the civility was gone from Grant's voice. "Didn't you, Mr. Kerlan?"

"I didn't."

"Can you blame me for thinking such . . . well, horrible thoughts?"

"I can't, but you're wrong. If Ginny is dead I didn't kill her."

"Do you think she's dead, Mr. Kerlan? After what I've said?"

His voice caught. "I don't know. I hope to God she isn't."

"I'll be in touch, Mr. Kerlan," Grant said, and there was an ominous note to his voice.

The line went dead.

Tomorrow, Peter thought, the previous night's dream coming into his head. *He said I'd see her tomorrow.*

He worked the rest of the day and into evening in a fog. Two more complete Sam Hain outlines rolled across his monitor, along with sketches for three more already begged for his attention. And all the while he heard the faintest of buzzings, going so far as to stop his feverish work at one point and search his office. But No matter where he searched the buzzing was faint and out of reach, and finally he went back to pounding the keys until exhaustion made him stop, with yet another moon, even fatter, rising across the window over his desk.

Without eating, he fell into bed and dreamed again of the black shrouded specter, the bleach-bones fingers gripping his shoulder, the whispering voice, dry as August in his ear: *Tomorrow* . . . .

He awoke to Halloween.

Even after all that had happened, the day was somehow different than all other days. He noted a slight cooling in the air, and saw with surprise that the sky was the deep sapphire blue of a true autumn day. The radio promised dropping temperatures all day, into the forties by dusk. Perfect Halloween weather.

Across the street the Meyer kids were busy, along with every other kid on the block. The streets and lawns were full of children, mounting decorations, stringing pumpkin shaped lights, transforming the neighborhood into the festival of orange and black it always became. Pumpkins seemed to have sprung up everywhere—not only on stoops and porches but in windows, perched on flower boxes, back decks, and, at one house, lined along the entire front of the house, an orange army guarding the lawn and fallen leaves. At the house next to the Meyers, a huge spiders web of pale rope was being erected, pinned from the highest bare tree limb and stretching to the house's gutter, anchored in three places on the ground to make it stretch like a sail; two boys were hauling a huge and ugly black plastic spider from the garage to mount in its lair.

A steaming mug of coffee in his hand, Peter watched the frantic progress that would continue all day and culminate in a wonderland of Halloween by the time the moon replaced the sun.

He felt the first tendrils of cold weather coming, and shivered for many reasons, turning to go down to his office and work.

When he entered he heard insistent buzzing, and the chill down his spine broadened.

It's got to be in my mind.

He sat down before his monitor and began to work.

Another Sam Hain outline. And another. Sam and Holly on Mars. Sam and Holly Meet the Undergrounders. Sam and Holly and the Halloween Comet.

The buzzing wouldn't go away.

Morning melted into afternoon. Through the open casement window he heard shouts and laughter, and, finally, felt a cold breeze which deepened to the point where he had to close the window. For the first time since the previous winter, the house was chilly. Somewhere upstairs he heard the heat tick on.

Have to close those windows later.

At the casement window, leaves rattled against the screen, and something else bumped it and stayed.

A hornet.

He stared at it, as another joined it, crawling, half flying, almost hopping, from the left of the window to cling to the screen.

What the—

The hornets, looking sluggish, crawled off, one of them making an attempt at flying before falling back with the aid of the wind to cling to the screen before dropping from sight.

He remembered what the bee keeper had said: that they would be active until the first cold spell, which would slow them down and then kill them off.

Another hornet appeared, and another.

With effort, he turned his mind back to the screen and continued to work, pausing to bundle what he had done for the day and send it as an attachment to Revell. He was rewarded with an almost instantaneous return email which effused: "Keep 'em comin', son! They love everything I've showed them so far! You'll be doing these wonderful things for the next ten years—THE KIDS WILL EAT THEM UP!"

He erased the message and went back to work.

In the back of his mind, like a growing hope, was the promise of the dream, that today he would see Ginny.

Please, he thought, *please let her come back.*

But the buzzing sound increased, becoming insistent, almost angry now. He paused once, thinking to do anything necessary to make it stop—rip the walls out, burn down the house, but the computer screen drew his eyes back:

Sam and Holly and the Texas Tornado.

Sam and Holly Meet the Leprechauns.

Sam and Holly and the Hornets of Doom.

He stopped, breathing hard, and stared at the screen.

That's it, he thought. *Enough.*

He pushed himself away from the desk, turned in his swivel chair and got unsteadily to his feet.

The buzzing sound was getting louder.

"*Stop!*" he shouted, putting his hands to his ears.

He pushed himself from the office, stumbled to the basement stairs, somehow dragged himself up to the main floor.

The house was dark, and cold, and suffused only by orange light from outside.

For a moment he was disoriented. Then he remembered it was Halloween.

He staggered to a window, closed it, and looked out.

A wonderland of orange met his eyes.

The lights in the neighborhood had been lit—strings of them in trees and across gutters and around door frames, orange and white. And all the pumpkins had been carved and lit with flickering light—the world was filled with sickle grins, some with crooked teeth, all with round or triangle noses and evil triangle eyes. As he closed another window he could smell pumpkins, their scooped insides sweet-cold and wet, the smell of whispered cinnamon, allspice.

For a moment he was lost in the smell and lights, and tears ran down his face and he was cold and helpless—

Ginny, come back to me!

The doorbell rang, a jarring, booming sound, and he stood rooted for a moment before stumbling over Ginny's things in the hallway to get to the door.

Maybe it was her!

God, please!

He yanked the door open, throwing on the porch light as he did so, and blinked at two miniature pirates who held open pillow sacks out to him.

"Trick or treat!"

He stood staring at them for a moment, and then the smaller, bolder one thrust his sack out again and demanded, "Trick or treat, mister!"

"Just . . . a moment," he blurted, turning to stumble into the kitchen where he rummaged in an overhead cabinet where he knew they kept the candy they had bought on sale weeks before. He saw flour and unopened cans—and then, behind them, his fingers found the bags and he pulled them out.

Two were filled with candy bars melted from the recent heat—a third contained miniature boxes of jawbreakers. He tore that bag open, took two handfuls of candy and went back to the front door.

The smaller pirate was scowling; his buccaneer friend already turning away.

"We thought you was gonna welsh," the little one said.

Peter pushed open the door, thrust a multitude of tiny boxes into the pirate's bag. He followed it with his other handful.

"For your friend," he said.

"Thanks, Mister!" the kid shouted, turning away to consult with his compatriot. Peter looked out to see the street filled with children in groups, cars and vans moving slowly up one side of the street and down the other, ferrying other costumed congregations.

He went back to retrieve whatever candy they had, and spent the next hour stationed at the door, pushing candy into the open mouths of trick-or-treat bags.

He noticed one car parked in front of his house that didn't move with the others.

A curl of cigarette smoke rose from the open window on the driver's side, and he noticed the man sitting there looking his way now and then.

It looked like Grant, but he couldn't be sure.

The night grew colder, more blustery; leaves began to dance around the few remaining children, until the groups trickled to a few older uncostumed kids, out for fun with shaving cream cans or rolls of toilet paper.

Then, abruptly, it was quiet. The vans, engorged with little riders, drove off, leaving only the single car in front of Kerlan's house, and the curl of smoke.

Some of the lights went out; pumpkin flames were snuffed by the wind, leaving the block quieter, more eerie.

He closed the front door; locked it; closed the remaining windows, found a sweater in his bedroom and went back down to his office.

It was cold inside—and was filled with the sound of buzzing.

When he stepped into the room, his foot crushed something alive and wriggling on the carpet.

A hornet.

Others were moving over the rug, crawling slowly up the walls from behind the couch; one made a feeble try at flying up toward the light but fell back, exhausted, to land on the coffee table which held manuscripts in front of the sofa.

"What in God's name—!"

He ran to his desk, jabbed at the phone, rifled through the stacks of papers on his desk, looking for the phone number of Willims, the bee keeper.

A hornet was crawling tiredly across the front edge of the desk, and he swatted it angrily to the floor.

There was more yellow jackets, scores of them, moving toward the desk from the far end of the office, more climbing up the walls—

He found the number, punched keys, waiting impatiently.

Be there, dammit!

A sleepy voice answered the phone, yawned "Hello?"

Peter identified himself, and almost shouted into the receiver: "They're back, dammit! All over the place! What the hell is going on?"

The bee keeper yawned again. "Fell asleep in front of the TV," he explained. "Watching *Frankenstein Meets the Wolfman*. Good flick." He laughed. "Don't get many trick or treaters. Kids are afraid of bees." Another, more drawn-out yawn. "You say they came back? Impossible. We killed that nest dead."

"*Then what the hell is happening?*"

A pause. "Only thing I can think of is that there was a second nest, like a mentioned to you. Real unusual, but it does happen. Two females, probably from the same brood originally, established nests near each other. This ain't the original nest we're talking about, but a whole new one. Wow. Haven't seen this in a long time."

"Can you get rid of it?"

"Sure. What's probably happening now is the cold is killing off the drones. You must have missed a spot in the baseboard, and they're being driven from the nest to the light and heat in your office. Why don't you look for the opening in the baseboard while I get over there—plug that up with tape and that'll take care of your office. Then we'll find the new nest and knock 'em out in no time. They're on the way out anyway." He laughed shortly, giving a half-yawn. "Wow. Two nests. That's somethin' . . . "

"Just get over here!"

Peter slammed down the phone and stalked to the sofa. He moved the coffee table in front of it, then angled the couch out, away from the wall.

A mass of sluggish hornets were clustered on the rug in front of a gap in the baseboard.

More in anger than in fright, he grabbed a wad of papers from the coffee table, rolled them into a makeshift tube and cleared the front of the opening of hornets. They moved willingly. He ran back to his desk, retrieved a length of cellophane tape, and, with a practiced motion, wadded it as he went back to the baseboard.

Already another hornet, followed by yet another sluggish insect, was crawling through the space.

Peter thrust the wadded cellophane at the opening, pushing the two new intruders backwards as the hole was plugged.

The sound of buzzing was very loud behind the wall.

And now, being this close to the wall, he noticed another sound.

A rustling movement, a thin sound as if someone was scratching weakly against the other side of the wall.

And then a pained, tepid whisper:

"Peter . . . ."

"What—"

He stood up, brushing a few slow-crawling hornets from the wall and put his ear flush against it.

It came again, the thinnest of rustling breaths heard behind a thick chorus of buzzing: *"Peter, help me . . . "*

"Ginny!" he shouted.

"Yes . . . ."

"My God—"

"Peter . . . ."

He drew back from the wall, balling his fists as if he would smash through it—then he turned, throwing open the office door and dashing through and up the stairs. He ran for the back sliding door, nearly tripping over Ginny's things in the hallway, his mind feverish.

"My God, Ginny . . . "

He pushed himself out into now-cold night, a full October chill hitting his face as he shouted, "Ginny!"

The backyard was lit by the sharp circle of the moon, by a few orange and white lights still lit in houses behind his visible through denuded oaks. A pumpkin on a back deck railing, now carved, was still lit, the candle within it flickering wildly in the chill breeze, making the features wild.

"Ginny, where are you!"

He heard a rustle to his right, against the house, in darkness.

He stumbled down the back deck steps.

"Ginny!"

"Here, Peter, help me . . . "

Breathing heavily, he found himself standing before the garden shed, its bulk looming in front of him. The sound of buzzing was furious, caught in the cold wind.

"Peter . . . "

He screamed, an inarticulate sound, and pulled at the shed's door, which wouldn't budge.

My God, she must have been caught inside the shed. The door must have closed on her and trapped her inside!

His mind filled with roiling thoughts. He pulled and clawed and banged at the door, trying to open it.

"Help me please, Peter . . . "

"Jesus!" The door wouldn't move. He looked wildly around for a tool, something to pry it open with—and then spied the short handle of a spade lying close by on the grass.

He picked it up, noting faint scratches on the spade's face—this must have been how Ginny had gotten the door open originally . . .

"Peter . . . "

"I'm coming!"

Mad with purpose, he pried the spade into the thin opening between wooden door and jamb, began to work it back.

There was a creaking sound, but the door held firm.

"Dammit!"

"Peter, please . . . "

He hammered on the handle of the spade, driving it deeper into the opening. He angled it sideways and suddenly the wooden handle broke away, leaving him with the metal arm which had been imbedded in it, attached to the blade. He pushed at the blade, getting faint purchase but shouting with the effort.

"Dammit!" The handle slipped, slicing into his hand, but he ignored the pain, the quick line of blood, and kept pushing and banging.

The door gave a bit, but still wouldn't open.

Buzzing filled his ears, an angry sound now—he realized that when he opened the door the hornets might rush out at him but he didn't care. He drove the thought from his mind.

"Peter . . . "

The voice was growing fainter.

He shouted, and became aware that lights were going on around him—still he beat at the handle.

The door gave way another fraction; it was almost open—

"Jesus! Open, dammit!"

With a supreme effort, which caused the broken metal handle of the spade to push painfully into his open wound, the door opened with a huge groaning creak and flew back on its hinges.

"Ginny!"

"Peter . . . "

There was darkness within, a seething fog of flying things—and then something stumbled out into his arms, something white and alive, a human skeleton with a skin made of hornets. Writhing alive orange and black insects covered her skull, her arms, her fingers gripped him tightly as he stumbled backwards screaming in its embrace. The thing walked with him, holding him tightly, hornets making Ginny's face, boiling alive in the empty eye sockets to make eyes, and hair, and lips on the skeletal mouth.

The mouth moved, the opening jawbone hissing with the movement of hornets. The writhing face showed something that was almost tenderness.

"Kiss me, Peter. Kiss me . . . "

He screamed, pushing at the thing which would not let him go, aware suddenly that there were others nearby. He turned his head to see detective Grant and the bee keeper Willims standing side-by-side, rooted with horror to the spot they stood in, flashlights trained on him.

"Kiss me, Peter. Samhain let me come back. The Lord of the Dead let me come back but only for tonight. Only for Halloween. I never stopped loving you . . . "

And now Peter felt the first stings as the hornets began to peel away from Ginny's skeleton, covering his own face, attacking him—

"Help me!" he screamed.

Ginny melted away in his arms, the bones collapsing to a clacking pile as Peter fell to the ground, covered in angry hornets. Through his burning eyes he saw the bee keeper standing over him, wide-eyed, waving his arms, his flashlight beam bouncing, shouting something which Peter could no longer hear through his swollen ears, his screaming mouth filled with soft angry hornets, his throat, his body covered inside his clothing.

He gave a horrid final choking scream, and was silent.

"And that's the way you'd like the record to read?" District Attorney Morton said. He was shaking his head as he said it—but then again, he had been shaking his head since the informal inquest had begun two hours ago.

Detective Grant spoke up. "This will be sealed, right?"

Morton laughed shortly, a not humorous sound. "You bet your ass it will be. We're lucky nobody from the press got wind of this." He looked sideways at the bee keeper. "We're not going to have any trouble from you, are we, Mr. Willims?"

The bee keeper nearly gulped. "Are you kidding? If Detective Grant hadn't been standing next to me, do you think the bunch of you would have believed me? I'd be in a looney bungalow right now."

Morton nodded. "Yes, you would be. But since the two of you saw it—"

The bee keeper gulped again, and Grant nodded curtly.

"At least I don't think he killed his wife," Grant said. "It looks to me like she got herself stuck in that gardening shed, and the hornets got to her." He looked at Willims, and suddenly everyone was looking at the bee keeper.

"You want me to tell you this all could happen? Sure, I'll tell you—but I still don't believe it. Could hornets strip a human body clean in a few days? Well, maybe. Usually hornets won't eat human flesh, but if the opportunity presents itself, I guess they might. They probably stung her to death after she got trapped in the shed. And then the body was in there with them . . . so, sure, I guess it could happen."

"And what about the supposed . . . " Morton consulted the papers before him. " . . . mobility of the skeleton . . . ?" He let the question hang, and Grant finally spoke up.

"The damn thing looked like it stumbled out of the shed. But it could have been a trick of the light. If the skeletal remains had been propped against the door when Kerlan opened it, which would have been consistent with his wife's trying to get out of the shed until she was overcome by the hornets, then, sure, it could have tumbled out into his arms."

He looked over at the bee keeper, who looked at his shoes. "Yeah, I guess that's what I saw too."

Morton addressed the bee keeper: "And the bees covering Mrs. Kerlan like skin—that could have been a 'trick of the light' too?"

"Well . . . "

Willims looked up from his shoes to see Grant glaring at him.

"Sure, I guess so. And I guess the words we heard her say could have been in our minds—"

For a moment he looked defiant, before collapsing. "All right. It was all in our heads."

"Fine," Morton said. He had gained a satisfied look. He turned to the medical examiner. "Jim, you're okay with the cause of death in both cases as being extreme toxic reaction to hornet stings?"

The M.E. nodded once. "Yep."

"And there was nothing the two of you could have done to save him?" he asked Grant and Willims.

The bee keeper said, "By the time we got to him he'd already been stung hundreds of times. I was able to get some of them off, but it was too late. The weirdest thing is that they wouldn't respond to light, which threw me. When I shined my flashlight on them they should have flocked to it."

"But they could have been so angry at that point that they would have ignored the light, correct?" Morton said sharply.

"I guess so. But I still say they should have attacked the light, and left Mr. Kerlan alone."

"But you're fine with the way we wrote it up in this report?" Morton said, daring the bee keeper to contradict him.

"Yes, I suppose so."

"Good. Anything else?" Morton patted his knees, making as if to rise, daring anyone in the room not to let him end the proceedings.

There was a glum silence. Once again the bee keeper was staring at his own shoes.

"I want to re-emphasize, Mr. Willims, that you aren't to speak to anyone of what went on in here today. We're all sworn to secrecy. This record *will* be sealed. Whatever was said in this room remains in this room. I don't want to see anything in the newspapers about humans made out of yellow jackets or . . . " here he consulted his notes again, " . . . Samhain, the Lord of the Dead. You understand?"

Without lifting his gaze, Willims answered, "Sure."

Letting a hard edge climb into his tone, Morton said, "If any of this finds its way into the press, or anywhere else outside this room, I'll know who to call on, won't I, Mr. Willims?"

The bee keeper nodded. His gaze shifted momentarily to Grant, but the detective's face was blank; he had obviously decided the best course of action for himself.

"Just so you understand," Morton continued. "There are licenses and such in your profession, and I would hate for you to have trouble in that area."

The bee keeper nodded.

Morton's tone switched suddenly from hard to hearty. "All right, then— that's it!" He stood and stretched, glancing at the M.E. "Jim—lunch?"

"Yep," the M.E. said.

On the way out of the room, the District Attorney put his arm briefly around the bee keeper's shoulder and said, "Just forget about it, Willims. Chalk it up to professional strangeness."

Willims looked up at the D.A., and for a moment his face was haunted.

"The thing I can't get over," he said, "is the stuff she was saying about the Lord of the Dead, how she'd been brought back only for Halloween—"

Morton's scowl turned to an angry frown. "I warned you in there, Willims—"

"I heard you," the bee keeper said resignedly. "Believe me, I heard you."

Morton removed his arm from the other man's shoulder, giving him a slight shove forward. "Just don't forget what I said."

They were in the marbled hallway of the court building, leading toward the revolving doors to the outside world. Morton watched Willims go through them, slouching with unhappiness.

I'll have to watch that one, he thought.

The M.E. came up behind him and tapped him on the shoulder.

"Meet you at the restaurant," he said laconically. "I've got to dip into my office upstairs for a minute."

"Fine."

The M.E. peeled off into another hallway, his footsteps echoing away on the polished stone floor.

After a moment, the D.A. composed himself into his public face of smiling bluster, and drove through the revolving doors.

Outside it was cold and bright, early November chill making the recent October heat wave a memory.

The D.A. shivered, wishing he had remembered his topcoat. But the restaurant was only a block away.

He began to descend the wide stone steps of the courthouse, which led to the street, when something small and striped orange and black, an insect, brushed by his ear and settled lightly there.

He heard the faintest of whispers before he swatted it away—as if someone were talking to him from a far distance. Later he would wonder if he had heard at all what it said:

"Next Halloween . . . "

PRANKS

Nina Kiriki Hoffman

Although preceded by a number of "begging" customs—including guising in Scotland and souling in England—trick or treating, as we know it and by that name, did not become part of Halloween tradition until the 1930s. The activity seems to have started in the western states of the U.S. and then moved eastward. During World War II, sugar rationing (and its effect on candy production) stymied its spread until after the war, but by the early 1950s the custom had gone nationwide.

Nina Hoffman introduces us to a true trickster who really doesn't care much about the candy.

The energy for good or ill was always stronger around Halloween, and this year he decided to accept it into his spirit and form himself a body, instead of jumping from one to another of the people already running around dressed as people they weren't. He chose to become someone small, a child; that made a good use of the energy he could gain without too much trouble. He would spend it all before the night was over, causing mischief, but first he would look and listen.

He made himself small and dark and then drew fire from air to dress himself in clothes like flames. He made the flames settle into solid, streamers of spider silk, quieting their heat, light, and appetite. When he had drawn enough fire to cover himself except for head and hands, he ran down out of the forest on the hilltop and into the neighborhood, where children in costumes dashed from one lighted front door to another, while adults in normal dress waited on the sidewalk, watching.

The flame child joined a group of children who had separated from their grown-up. He slipped among them as they climbed the steps to a front door. The pirate girl he stood beside noticed him; she lifted her eye patch to look, but she didn't say anything. The boy dressed as a dog on his other side was too busy knocking on the door to pay attention. The others, a ghost, a zombie, a witch, pressed forward, sacks held open.

A woman answered the door. She also was dressed as a witch, only an ugly witch, with stick-on warts and ragged gray hair, more cobweb than homegrown. All her clothes were dark green or black, and she cackled at them. "Trick!" she screeched before the children could yell the usual question.

Dog-boy stumbled backward, confused. The other children looked at each other. Jack, the name the flame child had decided to call himself, moved up a step and gestured toward the witch. He set her tall pointed hat on fire. "Trick," he said.

She shrieked and snatched the hat off her head, dropped it, and stomped the fire out. "What was that?" she yelled. "Do you want me to call the police?"

"No," said the pirate girl. "You told us to trick you. We did. Happy Halloween!" She grabbed Jack's arm and ran down the front path toward the street. The other children followed.

"That was the coolest," said the pirate girl. "How'd you do it?"

"I used up my little finger." Jack waved his left hand, showing that it only had three fingers and a thumb left.

"Ewww!" said three of the children.

"What happened?" asked the grownup waiting in the street for them.

"She told us to trick her!" said the dog. "She didn't give us any candy," yelled the zombie. "She was trying to scare us," said the witch, "but then her hat burned."

"Really?" asked the grownup, a tall slender woman with long dark hair, wrapped in a big dark coat with a collar lined in brown fake fur.

"She said she'd call the police on us," said the pirate girl.

"That doesn't sound good," said the grownup. "Let's get out of here." She switched on a flashlight and led the flight down the street.

They ran until they turned the block, passing a number of groups of other kids, some of whom cackled at them or shrieked things.

When they slowed, the pirate girl said, "What's your name?"

"Jack," said Jack. "What's yours?"

"Nell. The dog is Ben, and the witch is Amber. The ghost and the zombie are friends of Ben's. I don't know them."

"Do you not like them?"

"That thing you did with your finger," said the witch, Amber, joining them. "Was that a magic trick?"

"I guess," said Jack.

"Did you set the fire by magic?" asked Nell.

"It was all part of the same trick," said Jack.

"Can you do it again?" asked the ghost.

"I don't like to repeat myself," said Jack.

"Wait a sec," said the grownup. "You set the fire? Who are you, anyway?"

"This is my friend Jack," said Pirate Nell. "I asked him to join us."

"Jack," said the grownup. "I'm Ben's big sister Sandra. I'm supposed to be in charge here. I'd prefer to know who is in the party. Did I hear right? You set the witch's hat on fire?"

"Yes," said Jack.

"I'm not sure that was a good idea."

"I'm not about good ideas. I'm about doing things that make me laugh," said Jack. He thought back. He hadn't laughed about this one yet, though it had struck him as funny. The look on her face—

He laughed, enjoying the trick in hindsight. In a moment, the rest of them were laughing too, though the zombie looked confused. Maybe he didn't get the joke. Even the grownup laughed.

"Let's do another," said Jack. He led them up a path to a front porch and rang the doorbell. The other kids were close behind. As the occupant of the house opened the door, all the children screamed, "Trick or treat!"

The bald man laughed and held out a bowl of candy. "Help yourselves," he said.

Jack lifted a hand, but Nell took his arm. "You don't trick them if they offer you a treat," she whispered.

"But I want to," he said. While the other children selected candy from the bowl, Jack spent a finger and a thumb convincing the man's hair to come back, wildly. Dark brown hair waved up out of the man's scalp.

"What?" he said. He set the bowl of candy on a nearby table and reached up as hair grew out of his scalp and flowed down around his shoulders. Jack spent another finger to inspire the man's beard and mustache to grow out, too. "Hey!" The man didn't seem so much angry as astonished. "What the hell?"

All the kids had gotten candy except Jack. "Run away," Nell said, and they pelted across the man's lawn back to Sandra.

"Now what?" Sandra asked.

"He was nice and gave us candy, but Jack played a trick on him anyway," said Ben.

"Did you?" Sandra asked. "I guess we better run again." They ran around another corner.

"It was a good one!" Jack said when they stopped running. He laughed, and again the rest of them laughed too. They couldn't help themselves.

"How'd you do that?" Ben asked when they had laughed themselves silly.

"Used up some more fingers." Jack held up his hand. He had only an index finger left.

Sandra gripped his hand. "Oh my god oh my god oh my god, we better get you to a hospital," she said.

"No," said Jack, and he spent his index finger and palm turning Sandra into a child, younger than the rest of them, swallowed by her grown-up's clothes.

"What?" she cried, her voice much higher than it had been.

Jack laughed. They all did. Nell stopped first, and said, "Jack? I don't know if I like you anymore."

This troubled Jack, because he liked Nell. He spent his other hand making her like him no matter what he did, but some hard part of her fought that. It made it even more fun. He liked that she was hard to convince.

Sandra strode up to him, elbows out, hands on her hips, her clothing bagging around her and almost tripping her. She was a head shorter than he was. "Hey."

Nell gripped his shoulder. "Be nice."

"You need a costume," Jack said, to be nice. He spent a forearm spinning Sandra's clothes into a tight-fitting black cat costume, complete with whiskers growing from below her nose. Even her eyes changed, yellow with slit pupils.

"Rowr," she said. "Why does everything look different?" She studied her forearms (black), flexed her now-black fingers and watched claws emerge from her fingertips. "Hey."

"Let's get candy," said the ghost, and before Nell or Sandra could object, the rest of them ran up a front walk to another front door, this one decorated with a glow-in-the-dark skeleton. The zombie pressed the doorbell.

"Well, aren't you the cutest little monsters I ever did see," said the large smiling woman who opened the door. "I have just the thing for you to polish your fangs with after you eat all that candy." She gave them each a toothbrush.

"Trick." Amber nudged Jack.

He spent a toe giving the woman long, pointy teeth so large she couldn't close her lips over them. She lifted a hand to her mouth, her eyes wide, and Ben ran, the others following. They laughed so hard they couldn't breathe. "I bet she bites through the floss," said the ghost.

Sandra tugged on Jack's streamers. "How long do these tricks last?"

"Always."

She narrowed her yellow eyes. "I'll wake up tomorrow as a dwarf cat?"

"The costume will come off."

"But her teeth—?"

"I might be lying," Jack said. He didn't think he was.

"I'd like it if you turned Sandra back into herself," said Nell.

"Maybe later." Should he spend some more body parts to make Nell stop telling him what to do?

"Candy!" Ben yelled, and they approached another house.

"Trick," Amber whispered to Jack before anyone rang the bell. She had laughed the hardest of them all. Jack wondered if he liked her more than he did Nell.

A woman wearing a short black dress and black-and-white striped stockings opened the door. Her hair was big and green. She smiled while the children yelled, "Trick or treat!" and offered them candy bars. As Jack leaned over the bowl, she snagged his shoulder and said, "Trade you treats for a trick!" Her hand was sticky; he couldn't shake it off. "How silly you are to walk around like that, such a tempting little powerball," said the witch. "I know what to do with you!"

"You can't have him," said Nell, who liked Jack no matter what. "He's mine."

"Finders keepers," said the witch. She wadded Jack up as though he were a bundle of rags and stuffed him into a silver bag she wore at her waist.

Nell lunged forward and bit the witch's hand, snatched the bag from her belt, and ran.

"A curse on you!" cried the witch, but Nell ran so fast the curse was lost before it reached her. She ran so fast she left all the other children behind. She stopped in the forest on the hill, and then she opened the bag and pulled out what was left of Jack.

He uncrumpled into the form of a boy missing parts, and lay on the ground looking up at her. He was glad to be rescued, though he was sure the witch would have made more mischief with him.

"Can you take back the things you did?" Nell asked.

"No, only do different things," said Jack. He felt tired now, less inspired.

"Never mind, then," Nell said. She sat on the fallen leaves and looked down at the neighborhood. Jack pulled himself together and decided to spend the rest of himself on Nell. He seeped into her skin and made her into someone who would play tricks on others and laugh.

Nell, itchy, irritated, different, rose to her feet and headed downhill. Her fingers tingled with trickery.

PUMPKIN NIGHT

Gary McMahon

Gary McMahon provides us with a gruesome little tale involving a creature with a pumpkin for a head. Most likely, this isn't the first story you've ever read featuring a squash-noggin (and it won't be the last you'll find in this anthology).

Literature's most famous pumpkinhead, however, may not be exactly as you've seen depicted or recall. In Washington Irving's "The Legend of Sleepy Hollow" (1820), Ichabod Cranes sees "a horseman of large dimensions . . . mounted on a black horse of powerful frame," and later sees "the goblin rising in his stirrups, and in the very act of hurling his head at him." The next morning "the tracks of horses' hoofs deeply dented in the road, and evidently at furious speed, were traced to the bridge, beyond which, on the bank of a broad part of the brook, where the water ran deep and black, was found the hat of the unfortunate Ichabod, and close beside it a shattered pumpkin." Despite the usual illustrations and depictions, Irving did not mention if the pumpkin had a faced carved into it.

"Men fear death as children fear to go in the dark; and as that natural
fear in children is increased with tales, so is the other."
—Sir Francis Bacon, "Of Death," *Essays* (1625)

The pumpkin, faceless and eyeless, yet nonetheless intimidating, glared up at Baxter as he sat down opposite with the knife.

He had cleared a space on the kitchen table earlier in the day, putting away the old photographs, train tickets, and receipts from restaurants they had dined at over the years. Katy had kept these items in a large cigar box under their bed, and he had always mocked her for the unlikely sentimentality of the act. But now that she was dead, he silently thanked her for having such forethought.

He fingered the creased, leathery surface of the big pumpkin, imagining how it might look when he was done. Every Halloween Katy had insisted upon the ritual, something begun in her family when she was a little girl. A carved pumpkin, the task undertaken by the man of the house; the seeds and pithy insides scooped out into a bowl and used for soup the next day. Katy had always loved Halloween, but not in a pathetic Goth-girl kind of way. She always said that it was the only time of the year she felt part of something, and rather than ghosts and goblins she felt the presence of human wrongdoing near at hand.

He placed the knife on the table, felt empty tears welling behind his eyes.

Rain spat at the windows, thunder rumbled overhead. The weather had taken a turn for the worse only yesterday, as if gearing up for a night of spooks. Outside, someone screamed. Laughter. The sound of light footsteps running past his garden gate but not stopping, never stopping here.

The festivities had already started. If he was not careful, Baxter would miss all the fun.

The first cut was the deepest, shearing off the top of the pumpkin to reveal the substantial material at its core. He sliced around the inner perimeter, levering loose the bulk of the meat. With great care and dedication, he managed to transfer it to the glass bowl. Juices spilled onto the tablecloth, and Baxter was careful not to think about fresh blood dripping onto creased school uniforms.

Fifteen minutes later he had the hollowed-out pumpkin before him, waiting for a face. He recalled her features perfectly, his memory having never failed to retain the finer details of her scrunched-up nose, the freckles across her forehead, the way her mouth tilted to one side when she smiled. Such a pretty face, one that fooled everyone; and hiding behind it were such *unconventional* desires.

Hesitantly, he began to cut.

The eyeholes came first, allowing her to see as he carried out the rest of the work. Then there was the mouth, a long, graceful gouge at the base of the skull. She smiled. He blinked, taken by surprise. In his dreams, it had never been so easy.

Hands working like those of an Italian master, he finished the sculpture. The rain intensified, threatening to break the glass of the large kitchen window. More children capered by in the night, their catcalls and yells of "Trick or treat!" like music to his ears.

The pumpkin did not speak. It was simply a vegetable with wounds for a face. But it smiled, and it waited, a noble and intimidating presence inhabiting it.

"I love you," said Baxter, standing and leaning towards the pumpkin. He caressed it with steady hands, his fingers finding the furrows and crinkles that felt nothing like Katy's smooth, smooth face. But it would do, this copy, this effigy. It would serve a purpose far greater than himself.

Picking up the pumpkin, he carried it to the door. Undid the locks. Opened it to let in the night. Voices carried on the busy air, promising a night of carnival, and the sky lowered to meet him as he walked outside and placed Katy's pumpkin on the porch handrail, the low flat roof protecting it from the rain.

He returned inside for the candle. When he placed it inside the carved head, his hands at last began to shake. Lighting the wick was difficult, but he persevered. He had no choice. Her hold on him, even now, was too strong to deny. For years he had covered-up her crimes, until he had fallen in line with her and joined in the games she played with the lost children, the ones who nobody ever missed.

Before long, he loved it as much as she did, and his old way of life had become nothing but a rumor of normality.

The candle flame flickered, teased by the wind, but the rain could not reach it. Baxter watched in awe as it flared, licking out of the eyeholes to lightly singe the side of the face. The pumpkin smiled again, and then its mouth twisted into a parody of laughter.

Still, there were no sounds, but he was almost glad of that. To hear Katy's voice emerging from the pumpkin might be too much. Reality had warped enough for now; anything more might push him over the edge into the waiting abyss.

The pumpkin swivelled on its base to stare at him, the combination of lambent candlelight and darkness lending it an obscene expression, as if it were filled with hatred. Or lust.

Baxter turned away and went inside. He left the door unlocked and sat back down at the kitchen table, resting his head in his hands.

Shortly, he turned on the radio. The DJ was playing spooky tunes to celebrate the occasion. "Werewolves of London," "Bela Lugosi's Dead," "Red Right Hand" . . . songs about monsters and madmen. Baxter listened for awhile, then turned off the music, went to the sink, and filled the kettle. He thought about Katy as he waited for the water to boil. The way her last days had been like some ridiculous horror film, with her bedridden and coughing up blood—her thin face transforming into a monstrous image of Death.

She had not allowed him to send for a doctor, or even call for an ambulance at the last. She was far too afraid of what they might find in the cellar, under the shallow layer of dirt. Evidence of the things they had done together, the games they had played, must never be allowed into the public domain. Schoolteacher and school caretaker, lovers, comrades in darkness, prisoners of their own desires. Their deeds, she always told him, must remain secret.

He sipped his tea and thought of better days, bloody nights, the slashed and screaming faces of the children she had loved—the ones nobody else cared for, so were easy to lure here, out of the way, to the house on the street where nobody went. Not until Halloween, when all the streets of Scarbridge, and all the towns beyond, were filled with the delicious screaming of children.

There was a sound from out on the porch, a wild thrumming, as if Katy's pumpkin was vibrating, energy building inside, the blood lust rising, rising, ready to burst in a display of savagery like nothing he had ever seen before. The pumpkin was absorbing the power of this special night, drinking in the desires of small children, the thrill of proud parents, the very idea of spectres abroad in the darkness.

It was time.

He went upstairs and into the bedroom, where she lay on the bed, waiting for him to come and fetch her. He picked her up off the old, worn quilt and carried her downstairs, being careful not to damage her further as he negotiated the narrow staircase.

When he sat her down in the chair, she tipped to one side, unsupported. The polythene rustled, but it remained in place.

Baxter went and got the pumpkin, making sure that the flame did not go out. But it never would, he knew that now. The flame would burn forever, drawing into its hungry form whatever darkness stalked the night. It was like a magnet, that flame, pulling towards itself all of human evil. It might be Halloween, but there were no such things as monsters. Just people, and the things they did to each other.

He placed the pumpkin in the sink. Then, rolling up his sleeves, he set to work on her body. He had tied the polythene bag tightly around the stump of her neck, sealing off the wound. The head had gone into the ice-filled bath, along with . . . *the other things*, the things he could not yet bring himself to think about.

The smell hit him as soon as he removed the bag, a heavy meaty odor that was not at all unpleasant. Just different from what he was used to.

Discarding the carrier bag, he reclaimed the pumpkin from the sink, oh-so careful not to drop it on the concrete floor. He reached out and placed it on the stub of Katy's neck, pressing down so that the tiny nubbin of spine that still peeked above the sheared cartilage of her throat entered the body of the vegetable. Grabbing it firmly on either side, a hand on each cheek, he twisted and pressed, pressed and twisted, until the pumpkin sat neatly between Katy's shoulders, locked tightly in place by the jutting few inches of bone.

The flame burned yellow, blazing eyes that tracked his movements as he stood back to inspect his work.

Something shifted, the sound carrying across the silent room—an arm moving, a shoulder shrugging, a hand flexing. Then Katy tilted her new head from side to side, as if adjusting to the fit.

Baxter walked around the table and stood beside her, just as he always had, hands by his sides, eyes wide and aching. He watched as she shook off the webs of her long sleep and slowly began to stand.

Baxter stood his ground when she leaned forward to embrace him, fumbling her loose arms around his shoulders, that great carved head looming large in his vision, blotting out the rest of the room. She smelled sickly-sweet; her breath was tainted. Her long, thin fingers raked at his shoulder blades, seeking purchase, looking for the familiar gaps in his armor, the chinks and crevices she had so painstakingly crafted during the years they had spent together.

When at last she pulled away, taking a short shuffling step back towards the chair, her mouth was agape. The candle burned within, lighting up the orange-dark interior of her new head. She vomited an orangery-pulp onto his chest, staining him. The pumpkin seeds followed—hundreds of them, rotten and oversized and surging from between her knife-cut lips to spatter on the floor in a long shiver of putrescence. And finally, there was blood. So much blood.

When the stagnant cascade came to an end, he took her by the arm and led her to the door, guiding her outside and onto the wooden-decked porch, where he sat her in the ratty wicker chair she loved so much. He left her there, staring out into the silvery veil of the rain, breathing in the shadows and the things that hid within them. Was that a chuckle he heard, squeezing from her still-wet mouth?

Maybe, for a moment, but then it was drowned out by the sound of trick or treaters sprinting past in the drizzly lane.

He left the door ajar, so that he might keep an eye on her. Then, still shaking slightly, he opened the refrigerator door. On the middle shelf, sitting in a shallow bowl, were the other pumpkins, the smaller ones, each the size of a tennis ball. He took one in each hand, unconsciously weighing them, and headed for the hall, climbing the stairs at an even pace, his hands becoming steady once more.

In the small room at the back of the house, on a chipboard cabinet beneath the shuttered window, there sat a large plastic dish. Standing over it, eyes cast downward and unable to lift his gaze to look inside, Baxter heard the faint rustle of polythene. He straightened and listened, his eyes glazed with tears not of sorrow but of loss, of grief, and so much more than he could even begin to fathom.

Katy had died in childbirth. Now that she was back, the twins would want to join their mother, and the games they would play together promised to be spectacular.

THE UNIVERSAL SOLDIER
Charles de Lint

There are innumerable Halloween tales, but Charles de Lint explains there's a story in everything and everybody. Lots of stories. There's the one that's inside you and then all the other ones that get born when your story bangs up against somebody else's story. Belinda and Jane—rather special folk themselves—collect these stories. One Hallows Eve, the one day when the dead can walk around wearing skin and bones like the living, they encounter the ghost of a soldier come to meet his true love as promised . . .

"They're gemmin," the janitor told me when I asked. "Little mobile histories of a place. Kind of like fairies, if you think of them as the spirits of some particular area or space. They soak up stories and memories, and then one day they're all full up and off they go."

"Where do they go?" I said.

"I don't know. I just know they go and they don't come back. Not the same ones, anyway."

—from "Sweet Forget-Me-Not" by Ahmad Nasrallah

"Excuse me," the soldier said. "If it's not too much trouble, could you tell me the best way for me to take get to the Lakefront Pier?"

The two girls looked at one another and began to giggle.

"Did you ever—"

"Not me."

They spoke at the same time, stopped to let the other continue, then started to giggle again when neither did.

The dark-haired soldier waited patiently for them to finish before repeating his question.

"We're not supposed to talk to strangers," Belinda said.

Jane nodded in agreement. "That's what Charlotte says, and she should know. She's older than us."

"By three days."

"Which still makes her older."

"But we do, anyway."

"Speak to strangers, that is."

"But only if they have kind eyes."

"Which you have, by the way."

Belinda nodded. "Kind, but haunted."

Belinda was the blonde, taller and far more buxom than the petite Jane, with her boyish figure and short dark hair. Jane wore a top hat, a pair of tight faded blue jeans, and a black jacket that was cropped on the front and sides, but had tuxedo tails at the back. Belinda was in a vintage pink tulle dress with a lace bodice and a full skirt that cascaded to her knees in a froth of white and pink with accents of fine black netting. They were both barefoot and could have been going to a prom, except today being Halloween, he assumed they were either on their way to an early costume party, or they simply liked dressing up.

It was hard to tell their age because of their artfully applied make-up. The soldier put them at somewhere between fifteen and twenty. He had five sisters and knew that girlish giddiness wasn't attributable to any particular age.

"Perhaps if I introduced myself first," he tried. "Then you might discover that we're not so much strangers as simply old friends meeting for the first time. My name's Parker Paul. I know that's confusing, having a first name for a surname and vice versa, but I assure you, the choice was entirely out of my hands."

"Why do you talk so funny?" Belinda asked.

Parker raised his eyebrows. "Do you mean my accent?"

"That, too. It's just—"

"You talk like someone in a movie," Jane finished for her.

Belinda nodded. "Yes, you're very wordy."

"That comes from two years in an English boarding school, I'm afraid."

"Of what?" Belinda asked.

"I'm sorry?"

Jane cocked her head. "Why?"

Parker smiled. He was used to this, too. Two of his sisters were considerably younger than him and delighted in pretending to take everything he said literally and then pestering him with questions. Time spent with them had obviously been a training ground for just this sort of situation.

He looked from one girl to the other, his dark brown eyes solemn.

"I suppose it all depends," he said, "on the color of the spoon."

The girls clapped their hands.

"Oh, very good," Jane told him. "You really must be a long-lost friend."

"Oh, yes," Belinda agreed. "Moon-wise and spinning very still."

"And since you're an old friend . . . "

" . . . we won't tell you how to get to the Pier . . . "

" . . . we'll take you there, our very own selves."

With that they slipped up on either side of him and hooked their arms in his.

"It's this way, Mr. Paul," Belinda said.

They led him off down the sidewalk, deftly steering him through the crowd so that while it seemed as though they were forever about to run into this oncoming pedestrian or that one, they always managed to find some way to walk three abreast without bumping into anyone.

"Are you of the Stanton Street Pauls?" Jane asked.

He looked in her direction and nodded.

"You know they don't live there anymore, don't you?" Belinda added.

She had her head cocked prettily, the question repeated in the arch of her eyebrows.

"No, I hadn't heard," he said. "It's been so long since I've been back and everything has changed."

"How long have you been away?"

"It feels like a very long time. I've been . . . overseas."

Belinda nodded. "Is that where it happened?"

"Where what happened?"

"Where you died," Jane said.

Parker stopped and disengaged their arms from his. He looked from one guileless face to the other.

"What a thing to say," he told them.

"I suppose it was rude," Jane said, "just coming out with it like that."

"Though that doesn't make it any less true," Belinda added. "Does it?"

"I . . . "

"You can't pretend you don't know," Jane said.

Belinda nodded. "Because if you didn't, how would your ghost know to be waiting for the moon to rise at the very place of its death, on today, the one day when the dead can walk around wearing skin and bones like the living?"

Parker studied her for a long moment, but all he said was, "You seem to know a lot about ghosts."

"Not really. Mostly they just drift around, all . . . "

She looked for the word.

"Ghostly," Jane said.

Belinda nodded. "Exactly. We can hardly see them and they certainly aren't able to have an actual conversation—at least not usually—never mind hold your hand or give you a kiss."

"I'm not giving you a kiss," Parker said.

"I know," Belinda said. "Because you already have a sweetheart. Or you did, before you died. And you hope to see her on the Pier."

"How do you know that?"

"We might not know a lot about ghosts," Jane told him, "but we do know about love."

"Is that so."

"Oh, don't go all huffy," Jane said. "We're bringing you to the Pier, aren't we? Or at least we were until you stopped in the middle of the sidewalk and became an immovable object." She gave him a little poke with a finger. "See? You can't be budged."

Belinda gave him a poke as well.

"He's like a lamppost," she said. "Rooted to the pavement."

"Stop that," Parker said as she went to poke him again.

Jane looked at her wrist, though she wasn't wearing a watch.

"Time's a-wasting," she told the soldier. "If you want to make your rendezvous, we should keep walking."

"Unless you have money for a bus?" Belinda asked, her voice hopeful.

"I don't have any money."

Jane nodded. "Neither do we. We keep telling Charlotte that we should have money, but she doesn't seem to think it's necessary."

"Because she doesn't have to walk all the way to the Pier," Belinda said.

"That's twice you've mentioned someone named Charlotte," the soldier said.

"Is it? I wasn't keeping count."

She looked at Belinda who shook her head.

"I wasn't either," Belinda said.

"It's a good thing someone was," Jane told the soldier.

Parker sighed. "I only meant that as a preamble to asking you who she was."

"Not dead, that's for sure," Belinda said.

"Who she *is* then."

"Ah." Jane took his arm again. "She's like our sister."

She slipped her arm in his and started to walk once more and the soldier let her lead him off. Belinda fell in step beside him and took his other arm.

"But she's not really your sister," Parker said.

"That depends," Jane said. "Let's say you have handful of seeds that all come from the same plant. When some of them sprout, are they siblings?"

"I can't even pretend to understand what that means," Parker told her.

"Well," Belinda said, "you know how, for a ghost to be born, someone has to die first? It's like that, except totally different."

"Totally," Jane agreed. "But otherwise, just like that."

Parker decided that to press for clarification would only make him more confused, but he still found himself asking, "And that would make Charlotte?"

"Definitely the oldest," Belinda said.

"Of the three of you."

"Five, actually," Jane said. "You can't forget Gina and Kathy."

Belinda nodded. "Well, you could, but it wouldn't be very polite."

"So there are five of you."

"Yes," Jane agreed. "There are five of us in our little pod."

Belinda shook her head. "Pod doesn't sound right. Maybe we should say flock."

"But we're not birds. How about gang?"

"Tribe."

"Clan."

"Posse."

"Which do you like best?" Belinda asked the soldier.

"I don't feel qualified to offer an opinion," he said.

"Oh, pooh. Everybody has opinions."

"I meant an informed opinion," he told her. Then for lack of anything better to say, he added, "I have five sisters."

"Sisters!" Jane said. "That's perfect. Sisters. As in 'sisters in crime,' or 'sisters of the heart.' I like it."

"It *is* perfect," Belinda agreed. "You're a clever soldier."

"Do you miss *your* sisters?" Jane asked the soldier.

Parker nodded. "I think of them often."

"Then how could you just leave them behind to go off and fight in some silly old war?"

"Not to mention your true love," Belinda added.

"It was my duty," he told them. "When I serve and protect my country, I serve and protect them as well."

"So you volunteered?"

He nodded. "My father didn't want me to go. He told me that soldiering was for poor people who didn't have any other options for their future, not for bright young men with the whole of the world waiting for them. But I disagreed. If our country was going to war, it was the duty of all of us to defend our freedoms and rights. We argued. A lot. But I signed up anyway."

"And then you died," Jane said.

Parker's brow furrowed. "It was a car bombing . . . this time . . . "

"What do you mean this time?" Belinda asked.

The soldier brought them all to a stop once more. He again disengaged his arms from theirs and rubbed his brow. He looked up into the sky but his gaze was turned inwards.

"I . . . I seem to remember dying more than once . . . " he told them.

"You sound like us," Jane told him. "We sort of die all the time, but then we come back. Or some part of us comes back—enough so that it might as well be us."

"Except it's not," Belinda said.

Jane nodded. "No, not at all. But it all feels familiar because we know what to do and where to go and what stories to collect."

"I don't understand," the soldier said.

"Well, you know how everybody—"

"Every*thing*," Belinda interrupted.

"Everything," Jane agreed. "There's a story in everything and everybody. Lots of stories. There's the one that's inside them and then all the other ones that get born when they bang up against somebody else's story."

The solider gave a slow nod.

"Well, we're the ones who collect those stories," Belinda said.

Parker wasn't quite sure what they were telling him.

"What do you do with them?" he finally asked.

"They fill us up and then we go away and other girls come along to collect more stories."

"Go where?"

Belinda gave a breezy wave with her hand. "Oh, you know. Away. Back into the bigger story of the world."

"You mean you die?"

Jane giggled. "Oh, no no no. How can we die when we were never born?"

"Are you telling me you're not human?"

Jane looked at Belinda. "Says the ghost of a dead soldier."

"But I *was* human."

"Oh, like ever having been human's such a big deal."

The soldier shook his head. "What are you?"

The girls shrugged. "What are you?"

"Apparently, the ghost of a dead soldier. One who's died more than once. I . . . if I let myself think about it too much, I can't count all the battlefields . . . the times I've died . . . "

"It sounds like reincarnation," Jane said.

"I don't believe in reincarnation."

Belinda laughed. "If something exists, it doesn't matter if you believe in something or not. It still *is*."

"Is that what happens to you?"

"We're not sure," Jane said.

Belinda nodded. "And besides that, it's not important."

"Our stories aren't important."

"Just the ones we collect."

"I would think," the soldier said, "that every story is as important as another. Otherwise it means that hierarchies and caste systems and however else we divide ourselves are real."

Belinda cocked her head. "That's probably right." She turned to Jane. "After all, we're carrying around our own stories, too. We just don't have to collect them."

"Because we live them," Jane said.

Belinda nodded. "Which means they'll come with us whether we want them to or not."

"But they're not as interesting to us," Jane told the soldier. "We'd much rather hear other people's stories. And we especially want to hear your stories."

"Why would that be?" Parker asked.

"Because normally ghosts don't talk. Normally we can't even see them."

"And when we do," Belinda added, "they're all drifty and focused on what they can't have."

"Or what to set right."

"I don't feel either impulse," Parker said.

"Oh no? Then why are you going to meet your true love on the Pier?"

"Because I said I would."

"When did you make that promise?" Belinda asked.

"I . . . I don't remember."

"Well, I think it's terribly romantic," Jane said.

Belinda nodded. "And a bit sad."

"Bittersweet," Jane said.

"Bittersweet," Belinda agreed. "Exactly."

"You don't know that," the solider said. "What makes you think she won't come?"

"Well, if you're one of the Stanton Street Pauls," Jane said, "it has to turn out sad because they moved away ages ago. That means your going away and dying and all happened ages ago, too. So even if your true love is still alive, she'd be really old."

Parker smiled. "Old? As in her mid-thirties?"

"No, *really* old. Like in her fifties or something."

"She might be too old and decrepit to come," Belinda said. "No offense."

"None taken," Parker told her. "But she will come."

"How can you be so sure?"

"Because I promised her and she promised me."

The two girls exchanged a worried look, then Jane sighed.

"Well, come on then," she said, taking his arm once more. "We shouldn't keep her waiting, should we?"

The soldier let them lead him off again, one girl on either arm. He tried not to gawk at their surroundings as they walked, but it was hard to stop. Everything had changed—drastically. The buildings were impossibly tall, all metal and glass. There was so much traffic, the vehicles all so sleek. And the crowds of people, hurrying, chattering into their cell phones, dressed in an array of styles that bewildered the eye . . .

Except . . . except . . .

It was all familiar as well.

They were walking down the sidewalk of this busy street with traffic rushing by, the tall buildings on either side. But at the same time they were walking through an older version of the city. Many older versions that flitted in and out of his awareness. One moment a modern bus was pulled up at a stop. The next it was an old streetcar. Then there were only horse-drawn buggies slowly passing by, the horse hooves clopping on cobblestones. Then it was a dirt road. Then a field and they were following a narrow game trail.

Then, just as abruptly, the modern city was back.

"Which one are you now?" Jane asked.

He looked at where she walked on his right, arm linked with his.

"What do you mean?"

"You keep changing," she said. "Your hair goes from short to long and then back again."

"And your skin changes color."

"And your uniform changes, too."

"Sometimes you're hardly wearing anything—"

"—and then you're smartly dressed again," Jane said.

"How do you do it?" Belinda asked.

"I don't know," the soldier said. "I'm just me. Parker Paul."

Except that didn't seem to be the right name. Parker had died in the trenches in France during the Second World War. While he . . . he'd died in the desert. He'd been part of a combat patrol, west of the city, when their attacker detonated explosives directly under their vehicle . . .

No, he'd died in a jungle, cut down by a sniper . . .

He'd died in a forest of pines and cedars, struck by an arrow that had come whistling from between the trees, the bowman unseen . . .

He'd died at sea, when a broadside struck down their mast and he'd come tumbling down from the crow's nest . . .

He'd died in a gray uniform, fighting his brother who wore the blue . . .

He'd died under the clubs of another tribe's warriors . . .

He'd died . . . he'd died . . . he'd died . . .

But he was still Parker. Or at least Parker was still a part of him.

He brought them all to a halt again.

"It's not so far now," Jane assured him.

Belinda nodded. "We really do know where we're going."

"It's not that," he told them. "It's . . . there's something wrong with me. I'm too many people, all at the same time."

"Maybe you're the unknown soldier," Jane said. "There was probably one in every war."

"More than one," Belinda added.

Jane nodded. "Sadly, that's true."

Parker shook his head. "No. If I concentrate, I know who every one of these people inside me are."

"Then maybe you're the well-known soldier," Belinda said, then added, "Sorry. I didn't mean to make that sound like a joke."

"She didn't," Jane said.

The soldier nodded. "I know."

They began to walk again. In the far distance, they could finally catch glimpses of the lake, a shimmer of water between the canyon of buildings on either side of the street.

"How did you know I was a ghost?" the soldier asked after they'd gone a few more blocks.

"We just *did*," Jane told him.

Belinda nodded. "It's what we know."

"Who's human and who's not."

"Do you meet a lot of people who aren't human?" Parker asked.

"You'd be surprised."

"Though maybe not," Jane said. "Do ghosts get surprised?"

"That's right," Belinda said. "You don't hear of ghosts hanging a-round because they're surprised. They're usually sad or angry or lost or something."

"You surprise me," the soldier said. "Every time you open your mouths."

They walked in silence for a few moments, the girls opening and closing their mouths with great exaggeration.

"How many times were you surprised?" Jane asked after a half block of that.

"You're very strange girls," he told them.

Belinda grinned. "Says the ghost."

"If you think we're strange," Jane said, "you should meet Gina. She collects bobby pins."

"But only ones she finds on the street," Belinda said.

"And then she arranges them in patterns on the tar of a roof that overhangs the alley where we were born-ish."

"She says 'born-ish'," Belinda explained, "because that's the easiest way to describe how one day we were just there."

"When the day before we weren't."

"I still think you're stranger," Parker said.

"Is that a good thing or a bad thing?" Jane asked.

"It's neither," Belinda said before the soldier could reply. "It just is."

"You mean like there's no box to fit us in?"

"There could never be a box to fit you in," Parker said.

"I don't know," Jane told him. "I've seen some big boxes."

"I meant metaphorically."

"I knew that," Jane said, then stuck out her tongue at him.

Belinda suddenly stopped, bringing them all to a halt. She reached up and straightened the soldier's tie.

"We're almost there now," she said, "and you need to look your best."

Parker looked up and saw that they were only a couple of blocks from the street that ran parallel to the lake. The two girls industriously brushed dust—real and imagined—from his jacket while he stood and stared. He didn't recognize any of the stores on this street, but he knew the shapes of the older buildings. And he knew the old hotel he could see down by the shore front. The Pier would be to its right, hidden from sight at the moment by the buildings on the other side of the street.

"Are you nervous?" Jane asked.

He shook his head.

"Of course he's not nervous," Belinda said. "He's a soldier. They're brave and never get nervous."

"That's not true," he told them. "I'm always nervous in battle. Sometimes I get so scared I don't know if I'll be able to hold my rifle."

"But you do."

He nodded. "You have to. The men you're with are depending on you. At that moment, the reason you're there, the reason you're fighting, doesn't mean much at all. You just want to get the mission done and survive, protecting as many of your companions as you can."

"Hence the brave part," Belinda said.

"I suppose."

Parker felt uncomfortable. There was nothing glamorous about war. Time spent on the front lines was an even mixture of boredom, fear and the horror of combat. You didn't remember to appreciate the boredom until the night was filled with mortar shells and bullets.

He wasn't sure how to convey that to his two young companions. Wasn't sure he even wanted them to carry the burden of the knowledge.

"You're not our first soldier," Jane said. "That's how we know you must be brave."

Belinda nodded. "You're not even our first ghost."

"Except the others never talked to us."

"Why not?" he asked.

"I guess we didn't meet them on Halloween."

"I need to go," he said.

Jane gave his sleeve a last brush with her fingers.

"Of course you do," she said.

"Do you mind if we follow?" Belinda asked.

"We won't come too close."

"And we won't interrupt or eavesdrop or anything."

"We're very good at not being seen."

"Or at least, people don't see us unless they need to."

"What does that mean?" the soldier asked.

Belinda shrugged. "I don't know. It's just that if a person's open enough, and seeing us can make a difference, then they often do."

"And for some reason," Jane added, "it makes them feel better."

"Well, I know that feeling," he told them.

"So can we tag along?" Belinda asked.

"We'll be ever so . . . " Jane looked at Belinda. "What's the word I'm looking for?"

"Inconspicuous."

Jane nodded. "Exactly. We'll be so totally inconspicuous that not even a super secret agent spy-type satellite could hope to conspicuous."

Parker laughed. "Of course you can come. I'd like you to meet Angeline."

"That's a pretty name," Belinda said, linking her arm with his again.

Jane did the same on the opposite side and they continued down the last couple of blocks until they finally reached Lakeside Drive and there was only the wide street and lakefront hotels between themselves and the lake. Wolf Island was half-hidden in mists, but they could clearly see the Pier and the ferry that was just leaving port on the far side of the long wooden and concrete structure. The wind blowing in from the lake held a faint echoing scent of fish and weeds.

"At least that hasn't changed," Parker said.

"Do you mean the Pier?"

He nodded. "The Pier. The restaurant at its far end. The ferries. The island. It's all the way I remember it—or at least, more so than the walk we just took to get here."

They crossed Lakeside and walked in the shadow of the hotels until they reached the parking lot in front of the Pier.

"But they didn't charge to park your car back then," the soldier said as they walked by the booth where a man sat waiting for customers to be either entering or leaving his lot.

"Everything costs money now," Jane told him.

"It would have back then, too," Parker said. "If they'd only come up with the idea and thought they could get away with it."

"Do you see her?" Belinda asked.

They stepped from the sidewalk onto the Pier and Parker shaded his eyes to look down towards the restaurant. A radiant smile woke on his face.

"I'm guessing you do," Jane said.

She and Belinda disengaged their arms from his and let him go on ahead. They watched him approach an old woman in her sixties whose own face lit up as he reached her. They embraced.

"I knew it was going to be sad," Jane said.

Belinda nodded. "She's so old and . . . " She peered more closely. "Oh, my."

"Yes, she's a ghost, too," a voice said from behind them.

The two girls turned to look at the man standing behind them. He was tall and handsome and also dressed in a soldier's uniform, although his was more contemporary than Parker Paul's and his skin was a dark brown where Parker's was pale.

"Do we know you?" Jane asked.

"Only a piece of me," the soldier said.

Belinda looked back down the Pier to where Parker and Angeline walked towards the restaurant at the far end.

"The piece that was Parker Paul?" she asked.

The new soldier nodded.

"You're not a ghost," Jane said.

He nodded again.

"But you're not human either. Who are you?"

"Most recently, I was Tim Sanders," he said. "But I'm Parker Paul, too.

I'm Nadiv Levy, Dasya Rao, Akio Yamamoto, Asgrim son of Bodvar, Zerind Nagy, Bobby Whitecloud, Emilio Sanchez, Tai Phan, Jason Smith . . . "

He changed as he spoke, becoming each man, showing a wide variety of races and uniforms. Occasionally, there wasn't even a uniform. Just a loincloth. Or a vest and leggings made of animal skins.

He let his voice trail off.

"You're all the soldiers Parker thought he was," Belinda said.

"I am."

"But if he's a part of you," Jane said, "how come he's walking down the Pier with his true love? How's that even possible?"

The soldier shrugged. "His duty's long done and love is stronger. So I let him go."

"So he does get a happy, romantic ending," Belinda said.

"He does."

"Except she's old and he's not."

"You don't see her through his eyes."

"But you do."

"Easily."

"Because he's still a part of you," Jane said.

The soldier nodded. "And so long as there are wars, I'll be other soldiers with other names. We fight and die and then we're born to fight again. It's been like this since the first time one tribe of early men fought with another and will go on for as long as men wage war against each other."

"And you're okay with that?"

The soldier gave her a sad smile. "It's not something I would chose. It's just the way of my world."

"So you never get a happy ending," Belinda said.

He shook his head.

"We're more alike than you think," he told them. "We both carry the stories of the world. The difference is, mine are born on the battlefield."

"And now your story's part of ours," Jane said.

"I hope it's not too dreary."

"Well, it's sad," Belinda said, "but that's the thing with stories. You don't get to choose what kind you find."

"And maybe, if they were all happy," Jane said, "a person wouldn't appreciate how good they had it when their story was good."

Belinda sighed. "That's a dumb reason to have a sad story."

"I know. It's just a theory."

"I don't know why there are sad stories," the soldier said, "or why there have to be wars. You'd think that eventually people would realize that we're all the same under our skin. That the enemy that we hurt is no different from our own brother or son."

"You'd think," Jane said.

"But I'm happy to have met you," the soldier told them. "Now I have the cheerful memory of the pair of you to sustain me the next time I'm viewing an enemy through the site of my rifle."

"I suppose," Belinda said, not particularly comforted by the idea.

Except why did he have to go to these wars in the first place? Couldn't he just refuse? And if he did, then who would fight the war? No one. So it seemed very much up to him.

She wondered what the polite way to tell him this was, but before she could say anything more, he faded away with a ghostly "farewell." She looked back down the Pier and saw that Parker and Angeline were gone as well.

"This," she told her companion, "has been a particularly weird day."

"It has," Jane agreed. "And we never did get to meet Angeline."

Belinda nodded. "But I suppose that doesn't matter, because at least Parker did."

Jane smiled. "He did, didn't he?"

"I liked him," Belinda said with a touch of wistfulness in her voice.

"What wasn't to like?"

"Well, he was dead, for one thing."

"That wasn't his fault."

"And he already had a true love."

"Maybe you'll find one, too."

Belinda's features brightened. "That's true. I should go look for one right now."

Jane took her hand.

"I'll help you," she said.

Hand in hand, they turned their backs on the Pier and the lake and walked back into the city, where the thousands and thousands of stories they hadn't met awaited them.

And maybe a true love, too.

NIGHT OUT

Tina Rath

As Muriel says in this story, everyone needs an evening out sometimes. One of Muriel's special nights happens to be Halloween. To say much more at this point would spoil Tina Rath's brief tale, but I'll add a note at the end . . .

Mrs. Padgett gave a final glance round the kitchen, mentally ticking off her list of tasks: Cat's tray? Filled with clean litter. Cat's bowl? Filled with fresh food. He wouldn't eat anything, of course, but she had to be on the safe side. Casserole? In the oven, keeping warm. Fruit salad? In the fridge, keeping cool. And some plain yogurt to go with it, not cream. She had read, somewhere, that cream was bad for you, though her own mother, still very much alive, and a force to be reckoned with, had eaten a bowl of porridge with cream (and white sugar) every day of her life. Or so she said. Perhaps there was some ingredient in porridge that cancelled out the evil effects of cream . . .

Mrs. Padgett brought her mind back firmly from scientific speculation, and checked the bread bin. A whole fresh loaf. Good. But could that be all? Doubt paralyzed her for a moment. How could she be sure that she had thought of everything? But then she gave herself the mental bracer that had proved so effective in the past.

"Buck up, Muriel," she told her middle-aged self silently, just as she had once told her much younger self, about to walk down the aisle in her white dress to become the bride of an almost unrecognizably younger Mr. Padgett. And just look what that had led to!

And now all she had to do was to give her family their last-minute instructions, check her handbag (compact? door key? purse?) and walk out the front door.

Everyone has an evening out alone sometimes.

She said "Buck up, Muriel," again, aloud this time, and went into the sitting room.

Mr. Padgett was watching the news. Timothy, her youngest (he had been quite a surprise, almost an embarrassment at first, although it was quite funny now to remember how shy she had been at those ante-natal classes with girls young enough, some of them, to be her own daughters), was doing his homework. Neither of them looked up when she came in. Her middle child, Sara, soon to walk down the aisle on her own account, was out doing some necessary shopping, but she would be back in time for dinner. Mrs. Padgett waited until the weather forecast came on.

Then she said, "I'm off now. You know about the casserole, don't you? Don't burn yourself when you get it out of the oven, you'll find the oven gloves hanging right next to the stove . . ." They always hung right next to the stove, but last time Mr. Padgett had searched through all the kitchen drawers and found a lace tablecloth to muffle his hands, ruining it, and very nearly his fingers, in the process. She suppressed that memory firmly.

"There are some jacket potatoes as well, and I don't expect Sara will want one . . . "

No, she certainly would not. She intended to wear a wedding dress that was a mere slip of white satin (Mrs. Padgett's mother had said she'd worn a bigger nightie than that on her wedding night, never mind what she'd worn to church) and it would contour itself to every mouthful of potato. It seemed so unfair. Timothy, who was never likely to wish to appear in public in a white satin slip, seemed to eat twice his own weight in starch every day, and never put on an ounce.

Remembering Timothy's appetite she said, "There's heaps of bread as well. Don't leave anything for me, you know we get a lovely meal. Oh, and if any children should knock . . . "

Mr. Padgett, withdrawing his gaze from the television screen for the first time since she had come into the room, stared blankly at her and she hastened to explain, "It's Hallowe'en, dear. They may come round asking for sweets. Trick or treat, you know. Well, there are some bags of sweets and things all ready on the hall table."

Mr. Padgett thought about this for a moment, and came to a suitably managerial decision. "I'll leave all that to young Sara," he said firmly.

"Yes, dear," said Mrs. Padgett. "Now, you will be all right, won't you?"

"We'll be fine," said Mr. Padgett, who had never cooked a meal in his life. "We're used to fending for ourselves, aren't we, Tim? You go off and enjoy yourself. You don't often get out on your own."

Four times a year, Mrs. Padgett thought, with uncharacteristic sharpness. I must manage it about four times a year. And I'm not surprised when I have to plan everything like a military campaign. Three times as much work beforehand and heaven only knows what my kitchen will look like when I get back. For a moment she wondered if it was all worth it. She was tired, and no wonder, and she had a slight, but nagging, headache.

Perhaps it would be better just to go upstairs and lie down.

Timothy looked up at last. "Are you going out, Mum?" he asked.

Mrs. Padgett was saved from anything she might have said by her husband saying: "She's having a night out with the girls. Aren't you, Mu? At least that's what she tells us. I bet we'd be surprised at what she really gets up to."

Mrs. Padgett smiled nervously. "Are you sure there's nothing you need, before I go?"

She hovered, fighting with those awful guilt feelings, waiting to see if her husband and son had any last requests, but Mr. Padgett had gone back to the television and Timothy to his book. If she was going, and it seemed as if she must be, there was no sense in being late.

She went up to her bedroom. Now—coat, gloves, handbag. A quick glance in the mirror to check her neat but timid bob and that pink lipstick she could never quite get used to. Her elder daughter, Melanie, living a life of married bliss in Pinner, who could drive, and went out alone in the evenings two or three times a month, had persuaded her to abandon her old-fashioned red lipstick, but she was still not sure about it. After all, if red lipstick was so completely out of fashion, why were they still making it? For a moment she hesitated in front of the mirror, thinking, not of her lipstick but of Melanie. No sign of ante-natal classes for her, and yet she seemed happy enough . . .

Perhaps she should phone her . . . No, not tonight.

"Buck up, Muriel!" she said, quite loudly and fiercely to her reflection. "You know you'll enjoy it once you get going."

She picked up her handbag and, calling a cheerful goodbye to her son and her husband she went out, closing the front door carefully behind her.

The garden was dark and smelt of wet leaves. If Mr. Padgett, or Timothy, had looked out of the window and seen her walking, not down the drive, but across the lawn to the tool shed they would have been surprised. They might even have been a little disturbed. But the sitting room windows were tightly curtained. Still, Mrs. Padgett moved quietly. She had oiled the hinges on the door earlier that day, and it opened with barely a whisper. The cat, who had been waiting in the shrubbery, hurled himself forward with a squeak of excitement but Mrs. Padgett hushed him firmly.

Very, very quietly she took the garden besom from its rack and carried it outside.

Decorously she sat herself astride the handle while the cat leaped up behind her. Guilt was forgotten in a flood of glorious excitement. She recited her spell and the broom rose smoothly into the air. She pointed its head in the direction of their meeting place and set off for the greatest witches' festival of the year.

The broom banked high over the house, skittish after its long confinement. Mrs. Padgett, feeling the wet wind rush through her hair, took a firm grip on her handbag and shrieked aloud her delight and anticipation.

Far below Mr. Padgett roused himself momentarily from his television programme, catching the echo of that eldritch cry. He turned to his son.

"Do you know, I could have sworn I heard someone shriek "Buck up, Muriel," he said.

But Timothy was reading.

The stereotypical Halloween witch is old and ugly, wears a black pointed hat, rides a broomstick, has a black cat, and is probably in league with the Devil. She usually has a cauldron nearby bubbling with . . . something. Lately, however, this portrayal of witches is being at least supplemented with an attractive younger, often sexy version—a new cliché. The character of Muriel falls somewhere between the two extremes: a mundane matron who secretly practices a (probably) benign form of witchcraft

ONE THIN DIME

Stewart Moore

Stewart Moore's "William Wildhawk" indulges in old memories and inquires about the past in "One Thin Dime." On Halloween we can transcend time. As supernatural as that may seem, consider your own Halloweens. Keeping traditions, adding new ones, passing them on to the next generation—this might be considered a way of extending yourself into the future. Each Halloween also connects to those of your past—you may dig out decorations that are decades old, think back on holidays past, perhaps revisit your childhood, rediscover seasonal memories—all for better or worse. Does visiting the past necessarily involve magic or just a willingness to make the journey?

It had to be a great house for candy. Anyone who decorated their house that much for Halloween must have great candy, and lots of it. Old-style carnival posters filled the yard, proclaiming the wonders of Doug the Dinosaur Boy, The Real Jack Pumpkinhead, The Mysterious Blackwidow, and Kate the Lion-Tailed Girl. Each poster was carefully framed, its yellowing paper sealed behind glass. Each one hung from a stake driven deep into the dew-damp grass. They stood, arrayed like a band of goblins, guarding the house. That house itself—so white and plain by daylight—was draped in shadows that dripped from the branched fingers of old oak trees. A simple, single-toothed jack o' lantern grinned its candlelit grin from the porch, and right at the top of the steps, a real, honest-to-goodness, enormous witch's cauldron smoked and steamed. There had to be great candy in there.

The problem was that there were no lights on in the house, no lights at all, and so the little pirate stood on the sidewalk, shifting from foot to foot, trying to decide whether to go up and knock. In the glass frame of every poster, his reflection danced nervously.

The little pirate's mother had warned him not to go up to any house that didn't have its lights on—and especially not to go up to this house. This house had been empty for years and years, but just last month someone had moved in. Grown-ups never talked about the new owner except in whispers. The little pirate watched the cauldron steam. He was sure he had heard his mother whisper the word, "Witch."

It didn't help that the moon was full, that the last dry leaves on the trees rattled like tiny bones in the cold wind, and that somewhere, in the darkness, an owl was hooting. These things didn't help at all.

Finally, the little pirate decided not to try it. As he turned to go to the next, friendly, well-lit house, a shadow moved among the deeper shadows of the porch, and a smooth, clear voice spoke: "And what are you tonight, my dear little monster?"

The trick or treater froze. It was a woman's voice, a young woman's voice: younger than his mother, older than his babysitter. The voice spoke quietly, but still he could hear it clearly over the soft bubbling of the cauldron: "Well?"

The trick or treater began his shuffling dance again. He looked down at his costume as if to be sure: at his oversized white shirt, his black pants, his buckled shoes; at the shiny plastic hook that hid his left hand. He felt the eye patch and the bandanna he wore on his head. Finally, uncertainly, he croaked an answer. " . . . I'm a pirate?"

The woman in the shadows laughed. It was a friendly laugh, not the sort of gurgling chuckle you might expect to hear from a darkened porch on Halloween night.

"That I can see," the voice said. "But which one? Are you that Blackbeard Edward Teach, who died with twenty-six bullets in his body and his beard full of other men's blood? Or perhaps you're Jean LaFitte, the voodoo master of New Orleans, who used his own, dead sailors to guard his treasures? Or even . . . no, you couldn't be . . . so bloody a man as Captain William Davey, a man so evil he named his ship 'The Devil'? They say that before he was caught and dangled, he made his crew swallow his gold and jump overboard, so that they could bring his treasure back to him in Hell, ten thousand doubloons clinking in their bellies. Are you such a man as that?"

The trick or treater's ideas concerning pirates came mostly from *Scooby-Doo*. The names the shadowy woman had rolled out to him spoke of blood, and he didn't like them. He tried, quickly, to think of a name for himself, a good piratical name, but now all the names he could think of sounded like they belonged to very, very bad men. At a loss, he looked down at his feet and mumbled, "I'm a pirate."

"And a fine one you are, too. But you weren't going to pass me by, were you?"

"You're light's a-pposed to be on." The little pirate felt that on this point, the Halloween rules, as they had been explained to him by his mother, were quite clear, and he felt confident enough to assume a reproachful tone.

"I know," said the voice, unfazed even by this clear admission of rule breaking. "It burned out. Don't you want a trick or treat?"

The little pirate's father was fond of this exact same trick question, and so he knew the proper follow-up: "Which one?"

The voice laughed again. "A treat. For you—most certainly a treat. All you have to do . . . " The voice paused for a very long time, as if waiting for an owl to hoot eerily in the silence—which, at last, one did. "All you have to do is reach into the pot."

The cauldron still bubbled and steamed, but did not choose this moment to do anything threatening, like spitting out a shower of particolored sparks, or allowing a greasy gray tentacle to slither briefly over its lip. Uncertain, but drawn on by the promise of treats, the little pirate began inching his way up the walkway. "What's your name?" he asked. With a name, he would at least be on firmer ground.

"Oh, no," the voice purred. "You're not supposed to tell names on Halloween. It's dangerous. You don't know what might be listening. Do you?"

The shadow that spoke from the shadows finally stirred, and stepped forward into the light. A young woman appeared, with long golden hair and tawny skin, wearing a red lion-tamer's jacket and a black top hat. She also had a long, golden-furred tail that swished idly back and forth behind her.

"But Long John Silver," she said, "where's your parrot?"

The little pirate looked at the poster nearest the house: Kate the Lion-Tailed Girl looked exactly like the coolly smiling woman standing over the cauldron.

"You're in the poster," he said.

"Yes . . . " Kate winked. "Well, don't you have something to say?"

The pirate only looked down at his hook.

"Trick . . . " Kate prompted.

" . . . or treat?"

"And which would you prefer?"

"Treat, please," said the pirate quickly.

"Of course!" Kate opened her arms in a wide gesture of welcome. "Go ahead. I've got very good candy. Reach in. I won't move a muscle."

The little pirate climbed the steps to the porch, much more slowly than many a real pirate had climbed the stairs to the gallows. He stopped on the last step, refusing actually to stand on the same porch as the lion-tailed girl. Her tail, he saw, was twitching much faster now. He tried to look into the cauldron, but all he could see was white smoke bubbling inside it.

"You said . . . good candy?"

"Very good, I said." Kate grinned.

The white cloud inside the cauldron spat out a tendril of mist, and the pirate shrank back. The candy he'd already collected rattled inside his plastic pumpkin: not very much so far. And the cauldron was very, very big. There was a lot of room for a lot of candy. Finally, he screwed his courage to the sticking-place and, squinting his eyes tightly, reached into the pot. His hand sank beneath the surface of a cold liquid. He'd expected heat, and snatched his hand back. It was covered in strawberry syrup, but it wasn't strawberry syrup. He knew what it was. He knew what it was, it was—

"Oh, how silly!" Kate laughed. "You said treat, didn't you?" Cat-quick, she reached into the cauldron herself, and her hand came out, not scarlet, but clutching a crinkling mass of candy bars. She held it out, patiently waiting for the little pirate to hold up his pumpkin. Trembling, he did. But before she dropped the treasure, she tilted her head and asked, "But are you sure you wouldn't like to see what the real trick is?"

He shook his head so violently his eye patch slid down to his cheek. Kate laughed and dropped the candy into his pumpkin. On the instant, the pirate ran off like a cannon shot for saner quarters. She called after him: "I hope you find your parrot!"

A little ways down the road, under a streetlight, an old, old man was watching, his hands buried deep in the pockets of a coat that might have fought at Verdun. As the boy ran off, the old man walked nearer, stopping at the same spot the little pirate had stood for so long before his fateful decision to go up the walkway. The old man tipped his hat. "You set to bothering the young ones there?" he asked.

"Can I help you?" Kate asked, stepping back slightly towards her shadows.

The old man took off his hat. His wisps of white hair shivered in the wind. He held his hat like a bowl. "Trick or treat?"

"Where's your costume?" Kate took a half-step back towards the light.

"Right on my face!" the old man said. "I'm a genuine Egyptian mummy, ten thousand years old and falling to pieces right before your eyes. You got any magic tanis root in that pot there?"

Kate regarded him sidelong, her arms crossed. "Reach in and see."

"Oh, no. Not after what I just saw. My heart couldn't take the strain, I'm afraid."

"That is a pity," Kate said, and tossed him a candy bar. He caught it in his hat and slipped it in his pocket.

"Much obliged, Miss Kate," he said, as he put his hat back on.

"That's trouble," she said. "How do you know my name?"

"Well, there's the convenience of putting it on that poster there."

"That poster," she said, "is older than you are."

"And besides that, you're about the only thing this town has talked about since you moved in last month. It's behavior like this—plus having a tail, I suppose—that's done it all, you know."

Kate half-smiled. "So it's Halloween night, and you know my name. That gives you quite an advantage. But who are you?"

The old man tipped his hat once more, and said, "Name's William Wildhawk."

Kate laughed, surprised, delighted. "No, it isn't!"

"Of course not. But it sounds like the sort of name a fellow ought to have when the woman he's talking to has a tail, doesn't it?"

"It does indeed," she said, and her tail arched upward with pleasure. "But what brings a man named William Wildhawk to my doorstep on such a night as this? Surely not free candy bars. With a name like that, you need dragons to slay."

The old man looked around, as if Kate might have a dragon waiting in the shadows on a leash. "No, not me," he said. "I doubt I have anything that would slay a dragon. Why, do you know where one might be found?"

"I used to," Kate said, a faraway look coming over her face. William glanced at the poster of Doug the Dinosaur Boy, a tyrannosaurus in a schoolboy's tie and short pants. Would he be the sort of thing that counted for a dragon in this mechanized day and age? he thought.

Kate shook her head. " . . . But I think he's most likely moved on by now." Far away, something howled. It was certainly a dog. It couldn't possibly be a wolf. It couldn't possibly be a lonely timberwolf keening over its empty belly. The wind cut through the thin places in the old man's coat. He shuddered, and wrapped his arms around himself.

Kate forced a smile. "You should think about getting yourself home soon, William. It's Halloween, and things will be coming out to play soon. This is a night for haunts and fairies."

William winked. "Goblins, too?"

"What!" gasped Kate, in tones of deepest mortification. "A goblin, me?"

"And where else would a tail like that come from?"

Kate huffed. Her tail flicked indignantly. "From my mother's side of the family. And you watch your mouth, or you'll be a toad come morning."

"Your mother had a tail, too?" William asked.

"She had a nicer tail than I, but she took better care of it. French shampoo, German vitamins, and plenty of exercise."

"And what about her mother?"

Kate looked down at William for a long time. Her tail was stiff and still. "My grandmother's tail was the world champion. She could serve tea with it. She even traveled around with a carnival for a while. That's where all the posters come from." She stepped down off the porch, standing on the first stair, her hands on her hips, her tail slowly arching. "You knew her, didn't you?"

William shook his head. "No. But I saw her once, just once, when her circus passed through. I must have been, oh, twelve. Around there. That was the last year before I was too old to let my friends know that I still liked circuses, and too young to know that they all felt the same way. In fact, that was the last circus I ever went to, till I had kids of my own and a good excuse. And I was just on my way home that night, licking the cotton candy off my fingers, when I saw the Lion-Tailed Girl herself in front of the old freakshow tent, working the crowd for their last dimes."

Kate jumped down onto the grass in the midst of her posters, landing on her feet without a sound. "Ladies and gentlemen!" she called out to an invisible crowd, and though she did not shout, still every word rang down the street and around the corner. Her voice circled around William's ears and would not be ignored. "Ladies and gentlemen! Every one of you knows the wonders that God made in the six days of Genesis. But have you seen what his hands made in those same six nights, in the dark, when no one was looking?"

She strode over to a poster filled entirely by a mass of swirling darkness, with two large eyes in the midst of it. "Have you seen our famous Blackwidow, the most horrifying perversion of nature in history? She's inside, just a dime away."

Kate's fingers slipped into a jacket pocket, and came back up with a thin dime flashing, rolling over her knuckles. "Have you seen the real refugee from Oz, our own Jack Pumpkinhead?" She pointed to a poster of a huge, smiling, orange, empty-eyed face. It must have been a mask, because it looked exactly like a tall, thin man with a pumpkin for a head.

"They're all inside, and it only takes a dime to see them, just the skinniest coin of all, slap it down and walk on in." Kate hopped back onto her porch and flung her front door open wide. Darkness gaped inside. "If you walk away now, you'll wake up in the night, in the dark, and wonder what it was you missed. But you can see it now. For one dime. Just one—thin—dime!"

Kate froze in a theatrical pose, both hands pointing into the darkness inside her house. William had watched it all with misty eyes. He shook his head.

"You are her spirit and image," he said. "You are that."

Kate relaxed and leaned against her porch railing. "So I'm told." She shrugged. Her tail drooped.

"You know," William said, "I always wondered what was that Black-widow's 'perversion of nature' that was so horrifying?"

"You mean you didn't go in?"

"No. I spent my last dime on one of the games. Throwing baseballs at milk bottles." He reached into one of his deep pockets and pulled an ancient flattened rag doll into the light: a lion, with a mangy mane and a wind-up key in its back. "I won this for knocking them over three times in a row. I named him Raleigh. He used to play a little song when you wound him up."

"What was the song?" Kate asked.

"I don't really remember anymore. It was . . . " He closed his eyes, and, after a moment, began to hum. He hummed a tune that was somehow melancholy and jaunty at the same time: the sort of tune you might want to hear after a long, bad night, in the blue, foggy light, just before the sun rose. Finally, he gave up. "But it wasn't really like that at all . . . Oh well. It's a funny thing about music, isn't it? You can still feel what it sounded like, years and years ago, even if you can't really remember how it went."

"And what happened to Raleigh?" Kate sat down on her top step, her chin in her hands, her tail curled around her side. "One day you wound him up too tight, and something deep down inside of him snapped?"

"No, no. Truth to tell, I just set him down one day and forgot all about him. I found him in a box, years later. And he just wouldn't play anymore.

I turned the key, and nothing happened. I kept him around, ever since, but . . . nothing, of course. I took him to a toy shop once, to see if I could get him fixed, but the man said he'd have to cut Raleigh open, and I couldn't do that."

"May I see him?" Kate asked. William slowly walked forward, through the midst of the faded carnival posters, and gently laid the little lion in her hands.

"You know," he said, "I thought, that night, I might give him to your grandmother. But she'd already gone inside the tent. I'm sure she could have gotten one of her own, of course, but . . . " He shrugged. "I was twelve."

Kate gently turned Raleigh over and over in her hands. "Those carnival games were all rigged," she said softly. "Grandmother told me. The balls were full of sawdust, and the bottles were nailed down."

"Maybe I really wanted that lion." William chuckled. "Maybe I just believed I could do it." He reached into yet another pocket and brought an ancient, yellow baseball up into the light. He tossed it from one hand to the other. "Maybe I switched the balls. This one has lug nuts in the middle."

"What don't you have in that coat?" Kate asked.

"The devil's three golden hairs and a cure for cancer. I've got just about everything else, though."

Kate smiled and held Raleigh out for William to take back. William shook his head.

"No," he said. "He's most of why I came by. He's always been your grandmother's, really, at least to my mind. So that pretty much makes him yours."

"Thank you," Kate said, and she hugged the little lion tightly.

"Not at all," said William. He touched the brim of his hat, and turned away.

"Blackwidow's act," she said, and he stopped. "It was pretty simple. She could swallow a four-inch-long tarantula and bring it up again, alive."

William shuddered. "That's it?"

"Well, she could do some other things, too, but they were too much for the show. And you don't want to know, even if you think you do."

"Ah well. I suppose that's what I get for spending my dime on milk bottles instead of the show." He walked back down the walkway, but stopped on the curb. He half-turned back. "So your grandmother's name was Kate, too, then?"

Kate's tail twitched. "And my mother's. It's a popular name in the family."

William tipped his hat one last time. "You have a good rest of your Halloween, Miss Kate."

As quick as a big cat pouncing, Kate jumped down from the porch and ran up to William. She pressed her dime into his palm, and whispered, "One more ticket to see the show." She smiled. "Save it this time."

"Thank you much," said William, closing his hand tightly around the little coin.

"Good night to you, William Wildhawk," said Kate over her shoulder as she walked back to her house, her tail swishing.

"Goodbye," said William Wildhawk. Kate ran lightly up the stairs and inside, shutting the door behind her.

For a long time, the old, old man did not walk down the road. He stood beneath the streetlight, looking at the dime flashing in his hand: purple-white, when it reflected the halogen lamp above his head; blue, when he tilted it to catch the moonlight. And then there was another light caught in the coin's face, a warm and golden light that he hadn't seen in years, the kind of light you could only get from old, old bulbs, like the ones over a carnival midway. He looked up, and saw that warm light flashing inside Kate's house. She passed by a window, and she waved to him, a flourish of fingers matched by a flourish of her tail, and then the curtains fell closed, and the lights went off.

As William turned away, he thought he could hear music playing from somewhere far away: a simple music-box tune, somehow both jaunty and sad, the sort of tune you might hear at the end of a long, cold night, as the sky grows blue, just before the sun rises.

He held the dime tightly, and shoved both hands deep into his pockets. "Just one thin dime," he chuckled, "to see the show." And he walked slowly towards home, humming the little tune to himself as he stepped into the shadows.

MAN-SIZE IN MARBLE

E. Nesbit

In her long career as an author Edith Nesbit published over a hundred books, but she is best remembered for her many children's books, most notably The Railway Children *(1906). Considered by many as the first "modern" children's writer, she often connected the "real world" with the magical. Her influence on children's literature and fantasy is considerable. Nesbit also wrote a number of supernatural stories. This one was first published (1893) in the late Victorian era when telling ghost stories at Halloween parties was part of the spooky fun. Few Victorian stories refer to the holiday directly, but this one does. It also uses two interesting terms which may be unfamiliar:* bier-balk *and* corpse-gate. *The first is a path in an English churchyard (or across a nearby field) along which a bier or coffin is carried. A corpse-gate—also known as a* lich-gate *or* lych-gate—*is a roof over a gate where the bier stands during the reading of the first portion of the funeral service before it is carried inside.*

Although every word of this story is as true as despair, I do not expect people to believe it. Nowadays a "rational explanation" is required before belief is possible. Let me then, at once, offer the "rational explanation" which finds most favour among those who have heard the tale of my life's tragedy. It is held that we were "under a delusion," Laura and I, on that 31st of October; and that this supposition places the whole matter on a satisfactory and believable basis. The reader can judge, when he, too, has heard my story, how far this is an "explanation," and in what sense it is "rational." There were three who took part in this: Laura and I and another man. The other man still lives, and can speak to the truth of the least credible part of my story.

I never in my life knew what it was to have as much money as I required to supply the most ordinary needs—good colors, books, and cab-fares—and when we were married we knew quite well that we should only be able to

live at all by "strict punctuality and attention to business." I used to paint
in those days, and Laura used to write, and we felt sure we could keep
the pot at least simmering. Living in town was out of the question, so we
went to look for a cottage in the country, which should be at once sanitary
and picturesque. So rarely do these two qualities meet in one cottage that
our search was for some time quite fruitless. We tried advertisements,
but most of the desirable rural residences which we did look at proved to
be lacking in both essentials, and when a cottage chanced to have drains
it always had stucco as well and was shaped like a tea-caddy. And if we
found a vine or rose-covered porch, corruption invariably lurked within.
Our minds got so befogged by the eloquence of house-agents and the rival
disadvantages of the fever-traps and outrages to beauty which we had
seen and scorned, that I very much doubt whether either of us, on our
wedding morning, knew the difference between a house and a haystack.
But when we got away from friends and house-agents, on our honeymoon,
our wits grew clear again, and we knew a pretty cottage when at last we
saw one. It was at Brenzett—a little village set on a hill over against the
southern marshes. We had gone there, from the seaside village where we
were staying, to see the church, and two fields from the church we found
this cottage. It stood quite by itself, about two miles from the village. It
was a long, low building, with rooms sticking out in unexpected places.
There was a bit of stone-work—ivy-covered and moss-grown, just two old
rooms, all that was left of a big house that had once stood there—and
round this stone-work the house had grown up. Stripped of its roses and
jasmine it would have been hideous. As it stood it was charming, and
after a brief examination we took it. It was absurdly cheap. The rest of
our honeymoon we spent in grubbing about in second-hand shops in the
county town, picking up bits of old oak and Chippendale chairs for our
furnishing. We wound up with a run up to town and a visit to Liberty's,
and soon the low oak-beamed lattice-windowed rooms began to be home.
There was a jolly old-fashioned garden, with grass paths, and no end of
hollyhocks and sunflowers, and big lilies. From the window you could see
the marsh-pastures, and beyond them the blue, thin line of the sea. We
were as happy as the summer was glorious, and settled down into work
sooner than we ourselves expected. I was never tired of sketching the view
and the wonderful cloud effects from the open lattice, and Laura would
sit at the table and write verses about them, in which I mostly played the
part of foreground.

We got a tall old peasant woman to do for us. Her face and figure were good, though her cooking was of the homeliest; but she understood all about gardening, and told us all the old names of the coppices and cornfields, and the stories of the smugglers and highwaymen, and, better still, of the "things that walked," and of the "sights" which met one in lonely glens of a starlight night. She was a great comfort to us, because Laura hated housekeeping as much as I loved folklore, and we soon came to leave all the domestic business to Mrs. Dorman, and to use her legends in little magazine stories which brought in the jingling guinea.

We had three months of married happiness, and did not have a single quarrel. One October evening I had been down to smoke a pipe with the doctor—our only neighbor—a pleasant young Irishman. Laura had stayed at home to finish a comic sketch of a village episode for the *Monthly Marplot*. I left her laughing over her own jokes, and came in to find her a crumpled heap of pale muslin weeping on the window seat.

"Good heavens, my darling, what's the matter?" I cried, taking her in my arms. She leaned her little dark head against my shoulder and went on crying. I had never seen her cry before—we had always been so happy, you see—and I felt sure some frightful misfortune had happened.

"What *is* the matter? Do speak."

"It's Mrs. Dorman," she sobbed.

"What has she done?" I inquired, immensely relieved.

"She says she must go before the end of the month, and she says her niece is ill; she's gone down to see her now, but I don't believe that's the reason, because her niece is always ill. I believe someone has been setting her against us. Her manner was so queer—"

"Never mind, Pussy," I said; "whatever you do, don't cry, or I shall have to cry too, to keep you in countenance, and then you'll never respect your man again!"

She dried her eyes obediently on my handkerchief, and even smiled faintly.

"But you see," she went on, "it is really serious, because these village people are so sheepy, and if one won't do a thing you may be quite sure none of the others will. And I shall have to cook the dinners, and wash up the hateful greasy plates; and you'll have to carry cans of water about, and clean the boots and knives—and we shall never have any time for work, or earn any money, or anything. We shall have to work all day, and only be able to rest when we are waiting for the kettle to boil!"

I represented to her that even if we had to perform these duties, the day would still present some margin for other toils and recreations. But she refused to see the matter in any but the grayest light. She was very unreasonable, my Laura, but I could not have loved her any more if she had been as reasonable as Whately.

"I'll speak to Mrs. Dorman when she comes back, and see if I can't come to terms with her," I said. "Perhaps she wants a rise in her screw. It will be all right. Let's walk up to the church."

The church was a large and lonely one, and we loved to go there, especially upon bright nights. The path skirted a wood, cut through it once, and ran along the crest of the hill through two meadows, and round the churchyard wall, over which the old yews loomed in black masses of shadow. This path, which was partly paved, was called the "bier-balk," for it had long been the way by which the corpses had been carried to burial. The churchyard was richly treed, and was shaded by great elms which stood just outside and stretched their majestic arms in benediction over the happy dead. A large, low porch let one into the building by a Norman doorway and a heavy oak door studded with iron. Inside, the arches rose into darkness, and between them the reticulated windows, which stood out white in the moonlight. In the chancel, the windows were of rich glass, which showed in faint light their noble coloring, and made the black oak of the choir pews hardly more solid than the shadows. But on each side of the altar lay a gray marble figure of a knight in full plate armor lying upon a low slab, with hands held up in everlasting prayer, and these figures, oddly enough, were always to be seen if there was any glimmer of light in the church. Their names were lost, but the peasants told of them that they had been fierce and wicked men, marauders by land and sea, who had been the scourge of their time, and had been guilty of deeds so foul that the house they had lived in—the big house, by the way, that had stood on the site of our cottage—had been stricken by lightning and the vengeance of Heaven. But for all that, the gold of their heirs had bought them a place in the church. Looking at the bad hard faces reproduced in the marble, this story was easily believed.

The church looked at its best and weirdest on that night, for the shadows of the yew trees fell through the windows upon the floor of the nave and touched the pillars with tattered shade. We sat down together without speaking, and watched the solemn beauty of the old church, with some of that awe which inspired its early builders. We walked to the chancel and looked at the sleeping warriors. Then we rested some time on the stone seat in the porch, looking out over the stretch of quiet moonlit meadows, feeling in every fibre of our being the peace of the night and of our happy love; and came away at last with a sense that even scrubbing and blackleading were but small troubles at their worst.

Mrs. Dorman had come back from the village, and I at once invited her to a tête-à-tête.

"Now, Mrs. Dorman," I said, when I had got her into my painting room, "what's all this about your not staying with us?"

"I should be glad to get away, sir, before the end of the month," she answered, with her usual placid dignity.

"Have you any fault to find, Mrs. Dorman?"

"None at all, sir; you and your lady have always been most kind, I'm sure—"

"Well, what is it? Are your wages not high enough?"

"No, sir, I gets quite enough."

"Then why not stay?"

"I'd rather not"—with some hesitation—"my niece is ill."

"But your niece has been ill ever since we came."

No answer. There was a long and awkward silence. I broke it.

"Can't you stay for another month?" I asked.

"No, sir. I'm bound to go by Thursday."

And this was Monday!

"Well, I must say, I think you might have let us know before. There's no time now to get any one else, and your mistress is not fit to do heavy housework. Can't you stay till next week?"

"I might be able to come back next week."

I was now convinced that all she wanted was a brief holiday, which we should have been willing enough to let her have, as soon as we could get a substitute.

"But why must you go this week?" I persisted. "Come, out with it."

Mrs. Dorman drew the little shawl, which she always wore, tightly across her bosom, as though she were cold. Then she said, with a sort of effort—

"They say, sir, as this was a big house in Catholic times, and there was a many deeds done here."

The nature of the "deeds" might be vaguely inferred from the inflection of Mrs. Dorman's voice—which was enough to make one's blood run cold. I was glad that Laura was not in the room. She was always nervous, as highly-strung natures are, and I felt that these tales about our house, told by this old peasant woman, with her impressive manner and contagious credulity, might have made our home less dear to my wife.

"Tell me all about it, Mrs. Dorman," I said; "you needn't mind about telling me. I'm not like the young people who make fun of such things."

Which was partly true.

"Well, sir"—she sank her voice—"you may have seen in the church, beside the altar, two shapes."

"You mean the effigies of the knights in armor," I said cheerfully.

"I mean them two bodies, drawed out man-size in marble," she returned, and I had to admit that her description was a thousand times more graphic than mine, to say nothing of a certain weird force and uncanniness about the phrase "drawed out man-size in marble."

"They do say, as on All Saints' Eve them two bodies sits up on their slabs, and gets off of them, and then walks down the aisle, *in their marble*"— (another good phrase, Mrs. Dorman)—"and as the church clock strikes eleven they walks out of the church door, and over the graves, and along the bier-balk, and if it's a wet night there's the marks of their feet in the morning."

"And where do they go?" I asked, rather fascinated.

"They comes back here to their home, sir, and if any one meets them—"

"Well, what then?" I asked.

But no—not another word could I get from her, save that her niece was ill and she must go. After what I had heard I scorned to discuss the niece, and tried to get from Mrs. Dorman more details of the legend. I could get nothing but warnings.

"Whatever you do, sir, lock the door early on All Saints Eve, and make the cross-sign over the doorstep and on the windows."

"But has any one ever seen these things?" I persisted.

"That's not for me to say. I know what I know, sir."

"Well, who was here last year?"

"No one, sir; the lady as owned the house only stayed here in summer, and she always went to London a full month afore the night. And I'm sorry to inconvenience you and your lady, but my niece is ill and I must go on Thursday."

I could have shaken her for her absurd reiteration of that obvious fiction, after she had told me her real reasons.

She was determined to go, nor could our united entreaties move her in the least.

I did not tell Laura the legend of the shapes that "walked in their marble," partly because a legend concerning our house might perhaps trouble my wife, and partly, I think, from some more occult reason. This was not quite the same to me as any other story, and I did not want to talk about it till the day was over. I had very soon ceased to think of the legend, however. I was painting a portrait of Laura, against the lattice window, and I could not think of much else. I had got a splendid background of yellow and gray sunset, and was working away with enthusiasm at her lace. On Thursday Mrs. Dorman went. She relented, at parting, so far as to say—

"Don't you put yourself about too much, ma'am, and if there's any little thing I can do next week, I'm sure I shan't mind."

From which I inferred that she wished to come back to us after Hallowe'en. Up to the last she adhered to the fiction of the niece with touching fidelity.

Thursday passed off pretty well. Laura showed marked ability in the matter of steak and potatoes, and I confess that my knives, and the plates, which I insisted upon washing, were better done than I had dared to expect.

Friday came. It is about what happened on that Friday that this is written. I wonder if I should have believed it, if any one had told it to me. I will write the story of it as quickly and plainly as I can. Everything that happened on that day is burnt into my brain. I shall not forget anything, nor leave anything out.

I got up early, I remember, and lighted the kitchen fire, and had just achieved a smoky success, when my little wife came running down, as sunny and sweet as the clear October morning itself. We prepared breakfast together, and found it very good fun. The housework was soon done, and when brushes and brooms and pails were quiet again, the house was still indeed. It is wonderful what a difference one makes in a house. We really missed Mrs. Dorman, quite apart from considerations concerning pots and pans. We spent the day in dusting our books and putting them straight, and dined gaily on cold steak and coffee. Laura was, if possible, brighter and gayer and sweeter than usual, and I began to think that a little domestic toil was really good for her. We had never been so merry since we were married, and the walk we had that afternoon was, I think, the happiest time of all my life. When we had watched the deep scarlet clouds slowly pale into leaden gray against a pale-green sky, and saw the white mists curl up along the hedgerows in the distant marsh, we came back to the house, silently, hand in hand.

"You are sad, my darling," I said, half-jestingly, as we sat down together in our little parlour. I expected a disclaimer, for my own silence had been the silence of complete happiness. To my surprise she said—

"Yes. I think I am sad, or rather I am uneasy. I don't think I'm very well. I have shivered three or four times since we came in, and it is not cold, is it?"

"No," I said, and hoped it was not a chill caught from the treacherous mists that roll up from the marshes in the dying light. No—she said, she did not think so. Then, after a silence, she spoke suddenly—

"Do you ever have presentiments of evil?"

"No," I said, smiling, "and I shouldn't believe in them if I had."

"I do," she went on; "the night my father died I knew it, though he was right away in the north of Scotland." I did not answer in words.

She sat looking at the fire for some time in silence, gently stroking my hand. At last she sprang up, came behind me, and, drawing my head back, kissed me.

"There, it's over now," she said. "What a baby I am! Come, light the candles, and we'll have some of these new Rubinstein duets."

And we spent a happy hour or two at the piano.

At about half-past ten I began to long for the good-night pipe, but Laura looked so white that I felt it would be brutal of me to fill our sitting-room with the fumes of strong cavendish.

"I'll take my pipe outside," I said.

"Let me come, too."

"No, sweetheart, not tonight; you're much too tired. I shan't be long. Get to bed, or I shall have an invalid to nurse to-morrow as well as the boots to clean."

I kissed her and was turning to go, when she flung her arms round my neck, and held me as if she would never let me go again. I stroked her hair.

"Come, Pussy, you're over-tired. The housework has been too much for you."

She loosened her clasp a little and drew a deep breath.

"No. We've been very happy to-day, Jack, haven't we? Don't stay out too long."

"I won't, my dearie."

I strolled out of the front door, leaving it unlatched. What a night it was! The jagged masses of heavy dark cloud were rolling at intervals from horizon to horizon, and thin white wreaths covered the stars. Through all the rush of the cloud river, the moon swam, breasting the waves and disappearing again in the darkness. When now and again her light reached the woodlands they seemed to be slowly and noiselessly waving in time to the swing of the clouds above them. There was a strange gray light over all the earth; the fields had that shadowy bloom over them which only comes from the marriage of dew and moonshine, or frost and starlight.

I walked up and down, drinking in the beauty of the quiet earth and the changing sky. The night was absolutely silent. Nothing seemed to be abroad. There was no scurrying of rabbits, or twitter of the half-asleep birds. And though the clouds went sailing across the sky, the wind that drove them never came low enough to rustle the dead leaves in the woodland paths. Across the meadows I could see the church tower standing out black and gray against the sky. I walked there thinking over our three months of happiness—and of my wife, her dear eyes, her loving ways. Oh, my little girl! my own little girl; what a vision came then of a long, glad life for you and me together!

I heard a bell-beat from the church. Eleven already ! I turned to go in, but the night held me. I could not go back into our little warm rooms yet. I would go up to the church. I felt vaguely that it would be good to carry my love and thankfulness to the sanctuary whither so many loads of sorrow and gladness had been borne by the men and women of the dead years.

I looked in at the low window as I went by. Laura was half lying on her chair in front of the fire. I could not see her face, only her little head showed dark against the pale blue wall. She was quite still. Asleep, no doubt. My heart reached out to her, as I went on. There must be a God, I thought, and a God who was good. How otherwise could anything so sweet and dear as she have ever been imagined?

I walked slowly along the edge of the wood. A sound broke the stillness of the night, it was a rustling in the wood. I stopped and listened. The sound stopped too. I went on, and now distinctly heard another step than mine answer mine like an echo. It was a poacher or a wood-stealer, most likely, for these were not unknown in our Arcadian neighbourhood. But whoever it was, he was a fool not to step more lightly. I turned into the wood, and now the footstep seemed to come from the path I had just left. It must be an echo, I thought. The wood looked perfect in the moonlight. The large dying ferns and the brushwood showed where through thinning foliage the pale light came down. The tree trunks stood up like Gothic columns all around me. They reminded me of the church, and I turned into the bier-balk, and passed through the corpse-gate between the graves to the low porch. I paused for a moment on the stone seat where Laura and I had watched the fading landscape. Then I noticed that the door of the church was open, and I blamed myself for having left it unlatched the other night. We were the only people who ever cared to come to the church except on Sundays, and I was vexed to think that through our carelessness the damp autumn airs had had a chance of getting in and injuring the old fabric. I went in. It will seem strange, perhaps, that I should have gone half-way up the aisle before I remembered—with a sudden chill, followed by as sudden a rush of self-contempt—that this was the very day and hour when, according to tradition, the "shapes drawn out man-size in marble" began to walk.

Having thus remembered the legend, and remembered it with a shiver, of which I was ashamed, I could not do otherwise than walk up towards the altar, just to look at the figures—as I said to myself; really what I wanted was to assure myself, first, that I did not believe the legend, and, secondly, that it was not true. I was rather glad that I had come. I thought now I could tell Mrs. Dorman how vain her fancies were, and how peacefully the marble figures slept on through the ghastly hour. With my hands in my pockets I passed up the aisle. In the gray dim light the eastern end of the church looked larger than usual, and the arches above the two tombs looked larger too. The moon came out and showed me the reason. I stopped short, my heart gave a leap that nearly choked me, and then sank sickeningly.

The "bodies drawn out man-size" *were gone*, and their marble slabs lay wide and bare in the vague moonlight that slanted through the east window.

Were they really gone? Or was I mad? Clenching my nerves, I stooped and passed my hand over the smooth slabs, and felt their flat unbroken surface. Had some one taken the things away? Was it some vile practical joke? I would make sure, anyway. In an instant I had made a torch of a newspaper, which happened to be in my pocket, and lighting it held it high above my head. Its yellow glare illumined the dark arches and those slabs. The figures *were gone*. And I was alone in the church; or was I alone?

And then a horror seized me, a horror indefinable and indescribable—an overwhelming certainty of supreme and accomplished calamity. I flung down the torch and tore along the aisle and out through the porch, biting my lips as I ran to keep myself from shrieking aloud. Oh, was I mad—or what was this that possessed me? I leaped the churchyard wall and took the straight cut across the fields, led by the light from our windows. Just as I got over the first stile, a dark figure seemed to spring out of the ground. Mad still with that certainty of misfortune, I made for the thing that stood in my path, shouting, "Get out of the way, can't you!"

But my push met with a more vigorous resistance than I had expected. My arms were caught just above the elbow and held as in a vice, and the raw-boned Irish doctor actually shook me.

"Would ye?" he cried, in his own unmistakable accents—"would ye, then?"

"Let me go, you fool," I gasped. "The marble figures have gone from the church; I tell you they've gone."

He broke into a ringing laugh. "I'll have to give ye a draught tomorrow, I see. Ye've bin smoking too much and listening to old wives' tales."

"I tell you, I've seen the bare slabs."

"Well, come back with me. I'm going up to old Palmer's—his daughter's ill; we'll look in at the church and let me see the bare slabs."

"You go, if you like," I said, a little less frantic for his laughter; "I'm going home to my wife."

"Rubbish, man," said he; "d'ye think I'll permit of that? Are ye to go saying all yer life that ye've seen solid marble endowed with vitality, and me to go all me life saying ye were a coward? No, sir—ye shan't do ut."

The night air—a human voice—and I think also the physical contact with this six feet of solid common sense, brought me back a little to my ordinary self, and the word "coward" was a mental shower-bath.

"Come on, then," I said sullenly; "perhaps you're right."

He still held my arm tightly. We got over the stile and back to the church. All was still as death. The place smelt very damp and earthy. We walked up the aisle. I am not ashamed to confess that I shut my eyes: I knew the figures would not be there. I heard Kelly strike a match.

"Here they are, ye see, right enough; ye've been dreaming or drinking, asking yer pardon for the imputation."

I opened my eyes. By Kelly's expiring vesta I saw two shapes lying "in their marble" on their slabs. I drew a deep breath, and caught his hand.

"I'm awfully indebted to you," I said. "It must have been some trick of light, or I have been working rather hard, perhaps that's it. Do you know, I was quite convinced they were gone."

"I'm aware of that," he answered rather grimly; "ye'll have to be careful of that brain of yours, my friend, I assure ye."

He was leaning over and looking at the right-hand figure, whose stony face was the most villainous and deadly in expression.

"By Jove," he said, "something has been afoot here—this hand is broken."

And so it was. I was certain that it had been perfect the last time Laura and I had been there.

"Perhaps some one has tried to remove them," said the young doctor.

"That won't account for my impression," I objected.

"Too much painting and tobacco will account for that, well enough."

"Come along," I said, "or my wife will be getting anxious. You'll come in and have a drop of whisky and drink confusion to ghosts and better sense to me."

"I ought to go up to Palmer's, but it's so late now I'd best leave it till the morning," he replied. "I was kept late at the Union, and I've had to see a lot of people since. All right, I'll come back with ye."

I think he fancied I needed him more than did Palmer's girl, so, discussing how such an illusion could have been possible, and deducing from this experience large generalities concerning ghostly apparitions, we walked up to our cottage. We saw, as we walked up the garden-path, that bright light streamed out of the front door, and presently saw that the parlour door was open too. Had she gone out?

"Come in," I said, and Dr. Kelly followed me into the parlour. It was all ablaze with candles, not only the wax ones, but at least a dozen guttering, glaring tallow dips, stuck in vases and ornaments in unlikely places. Light, I knew, was Laura's remedy for nervousness. Poor child! Why had I left her? Brute that I was.

We glanced round the room, and at first we did not see her. The window was open, and the draught set all the candles flaring one way. Her chair was empty and her handkerchief and book lay on the floor. I turned to the window. There, in the recess of the window, I saw her. Oh, my child, my love, had she gone to that window to watch for me? And what had come into the room behind her? To what had she turned with that look of frantic fear and horror? Oh, my little one, had she thought that it was I whose step she heard, and turned to meet—what?

She had fallen back across a table in the window, and her body lay half on it and half on the window-seat, and her head hung down over the table, the brown hair loosened and fallen to the carpet. Her lips were drawn back, and her eyes wide, wide open. They saw nothing now. What had they seen last?

The doctor moved towards her, but I pushed him aside and sprang to her; caught her in my arms and cried—

"It's all right, Laura! I've got you safe, wifie." She fell into my arms in a heap. I clasped her and kissed her, and called her by all her pet names, but I think I knew all the time that she was dead. Her hands were tightly clenched. In one of them she held something fast. When I was quite sure that she was dead, and that nothing mattered at all any more, I let him open her hand to see what she held.

It was a gray marble finger.

THE GREAT PUMPKIN ARRIVES AT LAST

Sarah Langan

It's the Great Pumpkin Charlie Brown is playing in the background of Sarah Langan's short and not-so-sweet story. The animated feature was first aired on October 17, 1966 and has been re-aired annually. Written by Charles Schultz, it was produced and animated by Bill Melendez with music by Vince Guaraldi. Based on characters from Schultz's Peanuts *cartoon-strip characters—The Great Pumpkin was first mentioned in* Peanuts *in 1959—the story revolves around Linus van Pelt's belief that The Great Pumpkin rises from the pumpkin patch on Halloween and delivers gifts to those who sincerely believe.*

Tom wasn't happy about this. Not even a smidge. But life, it makes its decisions for you, so what could he do?

He took a drag and held it. Count of three. Let it go. On television, Linus van Pelt was babbling about The Great Pumpkin. On the floor, Laura was down on her hands and knees, drawing a pentagram inside a circle with chalk. She pretended to be all kooky and shit, but he got the feeling she learned her craft from old episodes of "Charmed." The chalk was pink, by the way. And she'd bought the Parker Brothers Ouija board from Walmart. Which made her a capitalist, not a wiccan.

She looked up at him. Pretty brown eyes, short, pixie hair that framed her face. *I'm a serial killer for Halloween,* she'd said when she arrived an hour ago. *I don't need a costume. We look just like everybody else.* Then she giggled, because he'd been his donning his housemate's discarded red plastic pirate boots and an eye patch, like an asshole.

"What kind of cowboy wears an Ironman T-shirt?" she'd asked, her eyes watering with glee.

"The kind that will brand-your-ass!" That got a laugh, which was pretty great, which had led to a screw, which had been even better. Then they'd lay there, the middle of the day like a couple of slugs. He'd let his finger trace the smooth seams of her skin, and then she'd sat up fast, covering her nakedness with a dingy sheet.

"I can see him," she said. "He's got green eyes you like you."

Tom and Laura had nothing in common. She was three years older than him, with a degree in world religion under her belt, and a scholarship to Rome to study the Etruscan civilization scheduled for the spring. Basically, they were doomed, so he probably shouldn't have agreed to all her spirit nonsense in the first place. But her optimism was contagious, and he held some hopes that together, they might endure.

"You nervous?" she asked from the floor. Pink chalk scrape-scraping.

He took another drag. Counted to three. Thought about the Bud in the fridge. He was waiting until after the séance, because he'd heard drunk people can get possessed. Were there four left, or five? Because if Laura wanted one, he wouldn't have enough to last the night. Wait, had she asked him a question? "What?"

She wiped the sweat from her brown with the back of her arm. This apartment was overheated. "You're so high. That's not good. Why do you always get so high?"

He decided to answer the first question, because the second was too involved. "I'm not scared. This is bullshit. I'm only doing it for you," he said, even though, looking at that crazy-ass pink pentagram, his stomach slid down, abandoning its post, and was now living in his large intestine.

She finished drawing, and started lighting candles. Good thing his housemates were out for the night, because this was really weird. They were all sophomores, but he was a left-back junior. That's what happens when you don't show up for class. In the short term, it's awesome, but it was the long term he was worried about.

Out the window, a couple of kids dressed as Michael Myers and Freddie Kreuger rang his bell. He kind of wished he could rewind his day right now, and save a few bucks for candy corn instead of spending it all on sweet air. Like a Time Bandit, only taller and less ugly.

The bell rang again. *Zzzt! Zzzt!* Sounded like a bug killer. Laura looked at him. Shook her head slowly like: *you fuck up.* Then she laughed, so he laughed, too. "Tommy, Tommy, Tommy," she said, like that was all she needed to say. Her hands were pink with chalk—murder light.

The bell rang one more time before the kids turned back down the walk. They smashed the jack o' lantern he'd carved beneath the hedges, that had gotten soft in the middle, and rotted, so its face was black. Which was mean, but in character for Myers and Krueger, which in turn reminded him of his brother.

Hey Tommy, you really stink, Michael had once said to him, then started laughing, because he'd emptied his bedpan under Tommy's sheets. Hardy-har-har.

Tommy took another drag. Then pulled a Bud from the fridge. The fall leaves outside were bright red. The sunlight reflected off them now, and shone through his window, so the house looked it was on fire.

"We're almost ready," Laura said. She breathed the words instead of saying them, and the arms of her peasant blouse were wet with sweat, which made him wonder if she was scared, too.

The candles were the vanilla scented kind. Everything smelled like his mother's bathroom back in West Hempstead. All the entrances there still had wheelchair ramps, which probably explained why he never visited.

Hey Tommy? Wanna touch my leg? Michael used to say before the amputation, because he'd lost feeling by then, and unwittingly bumped it so often that it oozed.

Laura dusted the chalk from her hands by wiping them on her jeans. Then she smiled crookedly, like she was half-happy, half-terrified. "You don't think I'm crazy, do you?"

He'd picked her up about a month ago in front of Hofstra's anthropology building. She'd seemed like a real sweetheart, sitting on that bench, her lips moving as she silently read her book: *The Widening Gyre*. Round, rosy cheeks, legs crossed at the ankles. Old fashioned pea coat. No make-up. She'd been a teaching assistant in his freshman religion class, delivering impassioned speeches about man's boundless potential for redemption, and marking wrong answers with "Nice try!" Seeing her there, looking lonely but content, like somebody who knows the secret to life, but hasn't found anyone to share it with, he'd wanted to sweep her up and carry her away. Save her from the mean world that would surely break her, once she started living in it.

Hey, Tommy? Why ya crying? You never touched a dead cat before?

He'd watched Laura on that bench for a long while, and tried to remember a time when things in his life had been good. Maybe before his big brother got sick. Maybe when he was a toddler. Maybe never.

"Hey, Laura DeGraff from World Religions!" he'd said, then sat next to her.

She'd startled, like she'd been alone for so long that she was unaccustomed to other people. So for the first few minutes, he'd done the talking. At first, she was nervous, chewing her thin red lower lip. But then he got her to laugh, and he knew he had her: "Admit it," he said. "You used to be on the Mickey Mouse Club. You were the one with the lazy eye and the middle part, right?"

She'd looked at him, and then, with a grin, crossed her eyes and giggled. Damn if in that instant, she hadn't stolen his heart.

He'd learned early how to charm, and because of that he'd had friends his whole life, and got more breaks than he deserved. It was all about listening, and then mimicking: You like Yeats? I do, too! Never talk about yourself too much, or your audience gets bored. Instead, reinforce what they've already told you, because everyone likes to be reassured. If they're mean, make a joke at someone else's expense. If they're nice, talk about saving the whales and your decision to become a vegan. If you're good at it, you always think you're telling the truth, even when you're lying.

With a bat-shit crazy brother like Michael, he'd learned to smile a lot, and pretend things were better than they were. And maybe that had taken its own kind of toll, because he got high a lot, too, and when he woke up in the morning, he didn't look forward to much. But looking at Laura's earnest, open face that crisp day in September, he'd thought she might be different from anyone he'd ever known. Maybe his days as a slug were numbered, because she was about to make him a better man.

He took her out for a burger that night at B.K. Sweeney's. A workaholic holding a full load of graduate courses, it was probably the first time she'd been off campus since school started. After that, they went back to her dorm room, whose walls were painted black.

"Nice," he'd said.

"Not really," she'd told him, "But I get distracted by color. I see too much."

Given her shyness, she was easier than he'd expected. But maybe she was lonely. She didn't have pictures of friends anywhere, and except when a professor called, her cell phone never rang. Surprisingly, her bra had been frilly lace, and her bed had smelled like talcum powder. She was the eighteenth girl he'd slept with, which was high, but not ridiculous. He rated her somewhere at the bottom, but he figured she'd get better with time. After they were done, he picked up and replaced the knick-knacks on her dresser. A porcelain cat, a signed photo of Christian Bale, a voodoo doll wrapped in rosary beads.

"You're kind of a freak, huh," he'd said, more to the Bale photo than the voodoo doll, which he'd in fact found endearing.

"Actually, I'm a psychic," she'd answered. "I communicate with the dead."

Hey Tommy! You wanna find out what happens to a cat when you put it under water?

Tom had looked at her for a long time to see if he should laugh. But it turned out, she wasn't kidding. Then he'd done a full circle around the room, but all he'd seen was black.

"I noticed something from the second you sat down with me at the bench. It's been following you all night," she'd told him, then lit a candle in the dark, as if to scare it away.

Over the next few weeks, they spent a lot of time together. She slept at his place most nights, or else he stayed at the dorm. She dressed mostly in black, and his housemates called her the freaky bitch, until one day he decided enough was enough, and told them to stop. He liked her black room, and he liked her short hair, and he liked her sweet smile, like everything hurt her just a little bit, because her feelings ran so deep.

"What do you see in me?" she'd asked early on, her wet eyes reflecting the light of his joint.

He could have told her she was fun, or she had a nice laugh, or that she woke something inside him that he'd been missing for a long time. "You need to get out more, or your wouldn't ask that," he said instead.

The number of dead people she'd seen: five. Her grandmother, who stopped by on her way from heaven to say *see you later.* Some old guy who hung out near the swings at her day camp, though she could never figure out if he was dead or just weird. The rest had been less distinct: a black spot, an aura, a baloney sandwich. They were old and faded, or else, maybe not really ghosts, but stains of something that had once happened, and left a wound.

And that made sense. Tommy was full of wounds. Most of them, he'd forgotten about, because forgetting is a lot easier than you'd think. There was his first girlfriend Janine—they lost their virginities to each other when they were thirteen, and afterward, crying, she'd told him that if she'd known it was going to hurt that much, she'd rather have joined a convent. After that, he'd made virgins his thing, just to right the wrong. Then there was his best friend Steven—they'd been thick as thieves until Tommy's foot started bothering him, and he had to quit little league football. Overnight, Steven stopped saying hello in the halls, like they hadn't build pillow forts at each others' houses for the last five years. There was the bottle his mother broke when Michael got sick, and the way she'd crawled on the floor with a rag, bloodying her knees, because she'd wanted to clean it up fast so his father didn't smell the gin. There was his father, who got sick of the smell of alcohol and hospitals, so he left the whole damn family for the fresh young thing who typed his letters.

And then there was Michael, who'd pulled the metal rod from his back brace, and punched it through Tom's foot, then guilted him into keeping it there for two days while their parents were out of town, because at least he wasn't dying of a rare neurological ataxia. "It's only fair, Tommy," he'd said twelve years ago. "If I'm hurting, you should hurt, too." When the doctors finally took it out, he was left with a permanent limp that kept him from joining sports, or running, which was sort of why he took up pot. Hanging out behind the 7-Eleven after school had been a hell of a lot better than watching his mom get drunk.

Yeah. There were a lot of things he'd forgotten, but over that time with Laura, he told her everything. And, tears in her eyes, because her sympathy never ran dry, she listened, and he started to feel saved.

She'd brought up the idea of a séance as a lark, but soon presented it more often, and more fervently. She said the stain had gotten darker since they'd been together, and that it never left, not even to sleep. Even when they made love, it watched.

"I don't have a lot of real life experience with all this—just what I've read. But most people, when this happens to them, they feel it. They see it. They're haunted. Their lives aren't right because these spirits won't let them alone. Aren't you haunted?" she'd asked.

Hey Tommy? That your girlfriend, or monkey?

"No," he'd said.

Probably, he should have found another girl, because clearly Laura was from Mars. But he didn't believe in the power of Parker Brothers' Ouija Boards, and he didn't believe in spirits, either, so what was the harm?

On the television, Sally and Linus were sitting in the pumpkin patch. He'd always thought her hair was pretty stupid, but at least she wasn't mean, like Lucy. On the ground, Laura was chanting. It sounded Gregorian. She was sitting Indian style with her hands on her knees, palms-up.

"So what does this spirit look like?" he asked when she was done, even though they'd been through this before.

She sighed. "Dark. It has a human shape. Kind of twisted, like. I don't know, like its arms and legs are wrong." She told him she'd been born psychic the way some people are blonde. She'd always known things before she got told, and picked winning lotto numbers, and seen the things people hide. She'd never done a séance, but she'd read Halloween was the best night for it.

Hey Tommy? How'd football practice go today? You think you're gonna make the team?

"Michael was a shit. If it's him, I don't think we want to say hello," he told her.

On the television, the kids woke up on the Day of the Dead, and the Great Pumpkin never showed. Out the window, a couple of clowns rang the bell, and he felt so bad about that stupid candy corn that he was tempted to run out and throw pennies.

Laura's eyes got wet in sympathy. She really needed to get out more. "Don't you see?" she sniffled. The candles around her glowed, and the whole thing was starting to feel unpleasantly real. "He's like a weight that holds you down. Maybe he isn't even real—just something your mind has produced. But it doesn't matter. I . . . I can't stand him."

It broke his heart a little, that she said that. Because it felt like something he'd done wrong. "What if it tells us something terrible?" he asked. "What if it's Michael and he turns you against me?"

She shook her head. "Everything I need to know about you I saw the first day we met, when you folded my clothes for me, and got me that Coke, so I didn't have to get out of bed. You're such a good person inside. But he follows you, and it's too much for me. You see? I can't be around you all the time, because it's always there. It never lets us be."

See this, Tommy? Michael had asked, as his involuntary muscles had quit on him, and his body had shivered. *When I die, I'll haunt you. I'll give you my disease.*

Tom sighed. "So really, if I want to keep you, I've got no choice," he said.

"I don't want it to come off that way."

The day Michael stopped breathing, the fall leaves out the window they shared had watched in silence, painting the walls red. No one was home, so it had been Tommy and the body, alone. He'd put his hand over his brother's mouth, and felt for breath.

"Please," she said. "Let's just see what he wants."

He sighed, and joined her inside the circle. The hairs on the back of his neck stood at attention, and he crossed his arms as if to protect from something without, or maybe within. "Okay."

She did some more weird chanting. It was hard to look at her now, without being angry. Hard not to blame her, for putting him here.

She closed her eyes. He was supposed to as well, but he didn't. She licked her lips, which ten minutes ago, he'd thought was cute. Everything was blurry. He was high as Mackenzie Phillips.

"Is the spirit here?" she asked.

Nothing happened. It was still light out, and kids in costumes roamed the streets. He felt her fingers move the planchette to "yes." Not a ghost, her fingers. There was relief in that. Disappointment, too. His girlfriend was batshit.

"What is your name?" she asked, eyes still closed. Rocking a little. She moved the chip across the letters that spelled "Michael." He flinched, because impersonating somebody's dead brother is pretty low.

Then the money question. "What is it you want?"

One of the candles blew out, and she snapped open her eyes. Her fingers weren't on the planchette anymore. Instead they were on his thighs, holding fast.

"Murder," the board spelled. Tommy's stomach dropped. "Murder," it spelled again. He wet-heaved in his mouth, and spit to his side. Three times. "M-U-R-D-E-R."

Hey Tommy? What'd you do to that cat? And in Tommy's hands, Whiskers wet and still, because Michael had promised he'd float.

"The cat," Tommy mumbled, remembering now, as if for the first time. "I did it. Because he made me. Because I had to sleep in the same room as that monster every night for six years. Because I was angry, and it wouldn't stop rubbing my leg."

"Were you murdered?" Laura asked. The planchette kept moving. He couldn't look anymore. On the television, Linus was screaming about the Great Pumpkin's return, next year. Out the window, the sun was just starting to set.

He looked back down for a second, and saw it spell out: "Want a body."

Laura's face was pale. Tears streamed down either cheek. He kind of noticed, and kind of didn't. A little part of him turned off, and a different part turned on. "He wants your body. That's why he stays. He wants to take it over. Because . . . You killed him, didn't you?"

Tom wiped his face like he was trying to pull it off.

Swallow this, Tommy. That way you won't be able to breathe, either, he'd said toward the end, after crawling down to the basement, and peeling asbestos from the wall.

Tommy had been high even then, at fifteen. And still dumb enough to consider it, just to make his brother happy, or maybe just to shut him up. Instead, he'd picked up the white pillow. Light as air. Michael fought. Striking at first forcefully, and then weakly. By then he'd lost both legs. Afterward, Tommy climbed in bed, and slept next to his brother's corpse. If anyone guessed what he'd done when they found the body the next morning, they never said so.

He looked at Laura. "Now I've got to kill you."

She jumped up, but by then he had her arm. "What are you doing?" she cried.

I'll haunt you until the day you die. And I'll never let you have anything I can't have. Because we're brothers. Because I hate you.

"You'll tell. And I can't have that, you know? I really can't." He was crying as he said it.

"Tom. You love me. I know you do."

"Yeah," He said. "But I'm really good at forgetting."

He put his hands around her throat. It was satisfying to see the expressions change on her face from bewilderment, to betrayal, to comprehension, as she realized what dark thing over the last few weeks, she'd woken up. So yeah, maybe she was a psychic. And yeah, maybe she really had finally made him whole. He and Michael, together at last.

As he pressed, the candles went out. The sun tore through the house, like it was on fire, and he wondered, since Michael lingered, if she would, too. And then he thought about how nice it would be to have a collection of them, and how right it was that Laura was his first. He'd read his books, too. The first is always the one you love.

Before he carried out her body, and dropped it in the sump, he took off his red boots and eye patch, so that he would look like everyone else.

SUGAR SKULLS
Chelsea Quinn Yarbro

*Our second story connected to el Día de los Muertos highlights sugar skulls
(calaveras de azúcar), a candy that is an art form, a memorial to the dead, a
sweet treat, and—as in this story—a magical artifact. Colorfully decorated
with icing and foil, the skulls often bear the names of the beloved dead.
Although Day of the Dead customs differ by locale, in general the skulls are
placed along with marigolds, candles, incense, and other special foods on a
home altar, the ofrenda, or taken to graves to welcome the spirits. Smaller,
less ornate skulls are also given to the living: "eating death" is a reminder
that death is merely passing from this life to another.*

The day after tomorrow would be el Día de los Muertos, the Day of the Dead,
the Feast of All Souls. Today was the Eve of the Feast of All Saints, when
children in the big country to the north put on foolish clothing and went to
take food from their neighbors, or played tricks on them for refusing their
demands—it was one of the many strange customs that prevailed among
those people with their big houses and big cars and yellow-haired women.

Refugio shook her head as she followed her grandmother's instructions
and continued to mix the shining white sugar into the whipped egg whites
that would permit them to shape the mixture into the hard-set celebratory
skulls. Already most of the candies were made, ranging in size from that
of a cup to a few as large as a real skull, with scenes inside them when you
looked through the frosting-outlined eyes. Many had names of the loved
dead written on the skulls in her grandmother's square letters made of red
or black frosting. Refugio wanted to write some of the names herself, and
imbue them with her emotions as she did.

"Abuela Concepcion," she said, reaching for another bowl of whipped
egg white and starting to measure in the sugar. She had been helping her
grandmother since shortly after dawn, knowing that this was the only day

on which they could prepare these candies, and wanting to make as many of them as possible.

"Sí?" her grandmother answered, not taking her eyes from the small molds she was filling; these would be the smallest skulls, hardly larger than a thumb and given minimal decoration. They would be sold five for a peso, and consumed by the handful. So far there were three hundred of the finished skulls sitting out on trays in the dining room, their licorice dots for eyes and missing teeth making them seem unusually stark. By the next morning, there would be at least double that number waiting, like small versions of the stone carvings of racks of skulls that stood at the end of the main street, next to a wide avenue of old, old stones that led to a crumbling mound behind the cemetery, and the first tangle of trees, many perched on hillocks said to be haunted. These sugar skulls seemed pale echoes of the overgrown stone ones.

"Tell me, how much longer do we have to work before we eat? The mid-day bell sounded a while ago. Can't we stop for a moment?" She summoned up all her nerve to ask, for Abuela Concepcion took her skull-making very seriously and begrudged every single moment such mundane tasks demanded. "I'm hungry. I'm sorry, but I am."

Abuela Concepcion sighed. "It is almost time for it, you're right. But I will have to work through siesta to get all this done. There's a lot left to do. I must have the skulls ready before first Mass tomorrow, or sin by working on the Feast of All Saints. No. We make skulls today and sell them tomorrow. That is the only day people will buy." She put her hands on the table and leaned forward.

"I'll stay up through siesta if it will help. But I need to eat and have a little chocolate to drink, or I won't be able to help you the way I should." She turned her melting dark eyes on her grandmother. "Please, Abuela." She hoped her grandmother couldn't read her thoughts, or take notice of her dark intentions.

It took Concepcion Molero a little while to decide what to do. "All right, chica, but it will be nothing fancy. For all it's almost a feast-day."

Refugio laughed. "That doesn't bother me," she said with all the confidence of her eleven years. "I will honor the saints as best I can by helping you sell the skulls tomorrow. That should make it all right."

"Don't you want to join the celebration in the evening?" her grandmother asked. "There is going to be a fine gathering in the square."

"No particularly," she lied heroically; she loved the excitement of town festivities, for it was the only time she could feel herself expand beyond her limited world and embrace everything that lay beyond the town market of Santa Luz, which was what tempted her more than anything else she could imagine. "I know you need my help to finish."

Abuela Concepcion moved to the ancient stove on the far side of her kitchen. "Soup and tortillas with a little cheese and a cup of chocolate, then," she said, using a match to start the stove.

"This was easier when Mama was alive to help you, wasn't it? You miss her being here?" Refugio asked in a small voice as she went to wash her hands in the old zinc basin immediately below the pump. She worked the worn handle vigorously and made sure she used soap as well as water, as her mother had taught her.

When Abuela Concepcion answered her voice was muffled. "Yes. This is the hardest year, since it is the first we have had to make the skulls without her, and you miss her as much as I do. It is difficult for both of us."

"If Papa weren't in prison, he'd help," said Refugio, although she doubted it.

"If your Papa weren't in prison, he'd be off in the forest with his friends, pretending to be soldiers fighting the government, and we should have to leave this town," Abuela Concepcion said bitterly. She plunked the lid on her soup-pot with more force than usual.

"Well, I'll help you as much as I can," Refugio said, and meant it in more ways than her grandmother guessed.

"I know you will. And you're a good girl for it," said her grandmother, going to pump water into her kettle, then returning to the stove to set it heating. She had made tortillas the night before and there were still a few left for their lunch. She wrapped them in a damp cloth and put the in the warming oven in the pipe above the stove. The gas was working well today, and the soup warmed quickly, its fragrance filling the kitchen with a heady mix of herbs, onions, peppers, garlic, and goat. Concepcion went to find the wedges of cheese in the cooler, and brought them out, one pale as milk, the other a light golden shade and slightly firmer than the first; she cut a portion from each and reached for the grater. "Here, Refugio. You do this. I have to finish these skulls." She offered a shallow dish to her granddaughter. "Use them both."

"All right," said Refugio, and set her bowl of sugared egg whites aside and covered them with a swath of fine cotton. Grating cheese was a pleasant change, so long as she was careful not to scrape her knuckles on the sharpened holes in the grater. As soon as she was done she wiped her hands carefully and turned to Abuela Concepcion. "There."

"Very good. I'll make chocolate for you, but you have to get back to your mixing." She sighed as she looked at her tray of molds. "I have to get more of these. They always sell better than the rest."

"Because they are small," said Refugio, "and you sell them for so little."

"Because they are the cheapest of all I make." Abuela Concepcion shrugged, accepting the iron rule of poverty.

Refugio went back to stirring the skull-making mixture. "Will we need more eggs?"

"I hope not," said her grandmother, busy with making chocolate. "I don't think Jorje or Ysidro have any to spare, and Lupe charges too much."

"I could ask, if you like. They might let me have one or two more they can spare for us," said Refugio. She had begun to notice that she was able to persuade her neighbors to help her on the strength of her youth and misfortune. It was a beginning, she thought, a first step to her freedom. "Let me go ask."

"I don't want you trading on tragedy, chica. You should have more pride than that." Abuela Concepcion was sternly disapproving. Her busy hands kept at her work, independent of her speaking.

"Padre Cazdor says pride is a sin," Refugio reminded her with a hint of mischief in her smile. "A very bad sin."

"And so it is, when it flies in the face of God. But pride that is born of dignity is entirely different. You want the respect of your neighbors, not their pity," said Abuela Concepcion, stirring the chocolate in the small saucepan.

Refugio thought about this as she continued to stir the contents of her bowl. "What if I offered to work in exchange for the eggs? I could tend their chickens."

"I doubt they'd let you do that," said Abuela Concepcion, continuing to fill the molds. "Not their chickens; they'd worry you'd filch eggs or take one of the chicks or some such prank. If you'd be willing to milk their goats for two or three mornings, they might accept a trade." She looked aside, suddenly ashamed. "No. You should not have to get eggs for me that way."

"Well, we must have them, and you cannot spare any time. It makes sense that I should do it," said Refugio, feeling suddenly very grown up. "Everyone knows you make the best skulls in the town. If you have a few more to sell, you will make a little more money. And I will only be doing what Mamacita would do, if she were here."

"But I don't want you to bear this burden, chica, nor did your mother. It shouldn't be yours. There are so many things you can do—you're smart, you think about things. Your mother wanted you to have a chance to continue in school and to make something of yourself. Of all of us, you are the one with the ability to do it, your Mama told me. She knew you aren't like most of the children in Santa Luz; you're clever, not like most of the others. You ask questions no one, not even Padre Cazador can answer. Everyone knows you're smart, that you could go a long way in the world if you were taught properly. You could have a life very different than the one your Mama had. I pray it will be longer and much better than hers." Abuela Concepcion stopped her labor for a moment. "I promised your mother to give you that chance."

"The bruja has said she'll teach me her skills," said Refugio.

"No!" Abuela Concepcion held up her hand almost as if to strike Refugio. "You should have nothing to do with her—nothing!"

"But she'll teach me for nothing. She wants to teach me. She said so," Refugio felt her confidence slipping away. She knew her grandmother disliked the old witch-woman who lived near the ruins beyond the graveyard and was said to commune with ghosts there.

"You won't learn anything worthwhile from her, chica," Abuela Concepcion threatened. "She is a superstitious old fool."

"But everyone is afraid of her, aren't they?" Refugio asked.

"That means nothing! You must not let the foolishness of others—" She crossed herself. "That old woman preys on those who are not wise enough to realize that—I'll hear nothing more about her!"

Refugio knew it was useless to argue; they had been over this very question many times in the last six months. "But I want to study something, Abuelita. Yes, I like school. It is good to learn. But most girls my age leave school and learn to manage a household. There isn't much more I can study here in Santa Luz if I can't learn from Viuda Estrella."

"Yes, most girls end their schooling at your age. But you must not, and you must not become a student of Viuda Estrella, for that would be worse than sending you to be a housemaid in the city," said Abuela Concepcion. "Your mother would have done anything to see you be properly educated, with a degree and good employment before you. She said if you were not educated, smart as you are, it would be a great injustice. It could lead to trouble for you, as well. Padre Cazador says you are the brightest pupil the school has had in years. Not that you should boast of it, for it is a gift from God, not anything of your doing, but as God's gift, you must not disdain it. It would be a sign of ingratitude for what God has done if you were to turn away from learning, which Viuda Estrella would be the epitome of insult for your gifts. Padre Cazador says that you deserve a good education, not the superstition and sorcery Viuda Estrella professes."

"If he says so, then he should help me get one," Refugio exclaimed with more emphasis than she had intended.

"Refugio!" Abuela Concepcion admonished her. "This isn't a wealthy town. The parish cannot afford to give money to children who will not devote themselves to the Church. Everyone knows that." She finished with the skull molds and stepped back. "If you had a vocation, it would be otherwise, but you haven't one, have you?"

"No, Abuela. I couldn't be a nun, with those hours and hours of praying," said Refugio apologetically. "I can't live as they do, all my time set out, order in everything, and accusing myself of sins I can only imagine." She angled her head upward in defiance. "You can tell Padre Cazador if you think he has to know."

"I wouldn't do that," said Abuela Concepcion. "He wouldn't be surprised in any case."

Without warning Refugio grinned. "No. I ask too many questions in class—he's told me so. He says some of the questions aren't proper at all, but I can't help it."

Abuela Concepcion nodded. "I know. That is your nature. A pity you weren't a boy: more could be done for you. But it doesn't matter—you have to follow where your curiosity leads. Your mother made it clear to me how it is with you."

"Yes," said Refugio. "And what can I do?"

"Mayor Arrugaverde isn't likely to pay any attention to people like us—we have nothing he wants, and we none of his friends. He never has extended himself on our behalf in the past. He is not interested in the poor except when he needs someone to vote for him, and then it is only a sham fellowship he offers. The richest man I know is the mechanic, Justino Caida, and he has six children of his own to provide for." She went to rinse her hands and took down two white stoneware bowls. "Get the spoons, chica."

Refugio set her bowl aside and followed her grandmother to the pump.

She dried her hands on the hanging scrap of towel, then took two steps across the kitchen and opened the drawer in the worn cabinet, removing two soup spoons, a knife, and two frayed napkins. She went into the alcove that served as a dining room and put on the small round table the spoons and napkins flanking the bowls, and laid the knife on the smaller clay trivet. "I'll fetch the butter," she said, and went back into the kitchen to the cooler. Taking out the small tub of butter, she stood aside to permit Abuela Concepcion to carry the soup-pot to the table.

"The tortillas will be quite warm by now," said Abuela Concepcion as she set the pot down on the larger trivet. She returned to the kitchen to retrieve them.

When Abuela Concepcion returned, she and Refugio sat down and bowed their heads for the short prayer of thanks: *"God, Who gives this food, let it nourish my body as Your Word nourishes my soul. Amen."*

After echoing the *Amen*, Refugio waited for Abuela Concepcion to ladle out her soup. The steam rising from it was delicious, and Refugio licked her lips in anticipation; her long morning of working with food had made her hunger sharper, and she anticipated eating with appreciation. "This is wonderful, Abuela."

"It's good of you to say so, chica," said Abuela Concepcion, pleased that Refugio had such good manners, for they both knew the meal was very simple. "Take a tortilla."

Refugio did as she was told, cutting a few curls of butter from the tub and spreading them carefully on the golden cornmeal round. She rolled this up and took hold of it as if it were an edible cigar. "Jorje will have more goat for sale soon."

"And after this Dia de los Muertos, we'll have money enough to afford some," said Abuela Concepcion.

"It is all to the good," said Refugio, who knew she was expected to speak only of pleasant things at table.

Abuela Concepcion tasted her soup and let the spoon drop back in the bowl. "Too hot," she muttered, and opened the small bottle of mineral water that was her usual drink at lunch. "I will set up my booth first thing in the morning, while you attend Mass. Then you may keep the booth while I go to the second Mass."

"Of course, Abuela," said Refugio, and bit into the roll of her tortilla.

"You're not to bargain with anyone, or to promise what you cannot deliver. Tell them you cannot do it because I order it so," said Abuela

Concepcion. "Everyone in town knows me. They will believe I would tell you such things."

"Si, Abuela." Another bite of tortilla and Refugio dared to test her soup. It was very hot but not scalding.

"Be pleasant to everyone, especially the important families. They always buy skulls from me, and if they do, everyone else does, too." She took a tortilla and rolled it up without the luxury of butter; she dunked one end into her soup, then chewed thoughtfully on it for a short while. "I must find some way to get a patron for you, chica. You cannot go about the world nothing more than a peasant when you have it in you to be much more." She stared toward the small window where a wedge of brilliant light made the little alcove glow.

Refugio knew better than to interrupt her grandmother's thoughts. She continued to eat her meal, saving the chocolate for last. Finally, as she buttered a second tortilla, she looked toward the front door on the far side of the scrupulously clean main room. "The special skulls—who is coming for them?"

"Dominga Caida. She should be here after siesta, unless she sends one of her children—she's almost ready to deliver, and it isn't easy for her to get about just now." Abuela Concepcion frowned. "If only she would introduce me to her uncle in Cedro Cima, something might be arranged. He has money, and to spare."

"Why would she do that?" Refugio asked with an innocence she did not feel. "Doesn't she have children of her own to look out for?"

"She does, and two of them are already promised work on their great-uncle's land. He has orchards and a mine and he raises cattle, pigs, and goats." Her brow darkened as she continued to think. "His sons have been sent to university."

"That doesn't mean he'll send me," said Refugio, suddenly struck with a new plan. "We could do as they do in the north—dress up in demons' clothing and demand help or promise to blow up their houses. Viuda Estrella says that much can be done on this night." She grinned as she weighed the options this could give. "I could walk to Cedro Cima this afternoon and I could waylay Dominga Caida's uncle after sundown."

Abuela Concepcion looked outraged. "Refugio! Never even *think* such evil thoughts. That is an affront to our faith! You ought to go to the church and confess at once! To have such thoughts on the Eve of All Saints."

But Refugio was too enchanted by the idea to accept the reprimand. "He wouldn't know it was me. I'd talk in a big, deep voice, and I wouldn't let him see me very well. I'd tell him I came from Los Angeles and I expected him to do as men in Los Estados Unidos do, taking care of those who are intelligent and making them rich and powerful, just as was done for Carlos Istmo—he has three restaurants in Texas. The same could be done for me." Her grin widened. "I'd say he had to do this or else!"

"You mustn't. That is worse than going to the witch-woman—which I forbid you to do! Promise me you won't do anything so foolish. Promise me you won't even think about it again." Abuela Concepcion was truly worried, for she knew her granddaughter had great determination and a recklessness that could easily mean trouble for a girl.

Refugio could see she had gone too far. "I wouldn't do it, Abuelita, not really. But it is fun to wonder what might happen."

"No, it isn't. It's wrong and it could bring you into great trouble." Abuela Concepcion was still very much worried about Refugio. "What sort of satisfaction could you take in anything so . . . so criminal?"

"I said I wouldn't do it," Refugio reminded her, beginning to pout. "Do you doubt me, when I promise you?"

"I worry about you. I worry you'll let your disappointments drag you into trouble," said Abuela Concepcion.

"You have no reason to worry," said Refugio, relieved that this, at least, was the truth. "I will not do anything that will harm me."

"Very well; I will trust you," said Abuela Concepcion. "You and I will forget you have ever said such things. I know you are not an evil child. You will stay away from Viuda Estrella, and abandon such dreadful thoughts as you've told me today. I will take this as the power of the saints, who are very near now. So, in the presence of the saints, you swear that you will being no disgrace upon our family. Do this for me, and for the memory of your Mama." She tried to resume eating but found her own cooking now to lack savor, and she soon found an excuse to stop eating. "You have the rest of your meal. I have to get back to making skulls."

Knowing she was still in disfavor, Refugio only nodded and added some grated cheese to her soup. There were some things she had learned from Viuda Estrella already, and she could use them without her grandmother knowing. There had to be a way to go to Viuda Estrella without offending either the Padre or her grandmother. She made plans as she ate. When she had finished, she took her bowl and utensils to the sink, worked the pump, and washed them, then added the last of her grandmother's soup to the slop-bucket and cleaned her bowl and utensils as well. Only when she had dried the flatware and bowls and put them away did she speak again. "I'm sorry, Abuela."

"Be sure you are," said Abuela Concepcion as she worked on filling another tray of molds. "I don't want you to put yourself in danger."

"You can't blame me for wanting to do something to make things better for us," she said in a small voice.

"No. But if you do something wrong it will make things much worse," said Abuela Concepcion. "Isn't having your father in prison enough?"

This stung Refugio, and she blinked back sudden tears. "I won't go to prison, Abuela. I wouldn't do that."

"Well, pranks like the ones you proposed can get you there," said Abuela Concepcion. "Come on, chica. We have many more skulls to make." This was a peace offering, and Refugio accepted it as such.

"I will," she said with relief, and went to resume whipping sugar into egg-whites.

"I know you say these things to cheer me," Abuela Concepcion said a bit later. "But, chica, they are not easily understood by most people, who may think you are serious if you talk of these things where you can be overheard."

"I won't blather," Refugio promised, all the while trying to think of some means to gain the advantage she sought in a way that would not upset her grandmother.

"No, I don't suppose you will," said Abuela Concepcion, her face long and serious as she interrupted her labor on the skulls. "I will need more licorice."

"There is still a lot in the pantry," said Refugio. "Do you want me to fetch it?"

"No. I'll attend to it myself," said Abuela Concepcion, and set her immediate work aside to retrieve a handful of licorice strings for making eyes and lost teeth for the skulls.

"They say that if you have some hair from a rich man, and you write his name on a skull and then he eats it, his treasure will become yours," said Refugio as she watched her grandmother ornament the sugar skulls.

"That's nonsense. Only old people believe such things," scoffed Abuela Concepcion. "Old people and Viuda Estrella."

"You don't believe it," said Refugio.

"No, and for good reason," said Abuela Concepcion. "I don't want to hear any more nonsense out of you, chica. Not today, not tomorrow, not ever."

"Oh, very well," said Refugio, but her mind continued to play with all the various stories she had heard about ways to draw good fortune to you on these special feast days. There had to be something she could do to end the hard life she and her grandmother had been living. Perhaps, she thought, I will make a skull of my own, and make sure it has everything to bring me money so I can continue to study. That idea thrilled her, and she let her imagination wander while she prepared more sugared egg-whites. Suddenly she dared to speak. "Abuela, tell me—would you permit me to make a skull of my own? I'd do it when we've finished for the day, and I wouldn't make a very big one, not a little one, but the teacup size. I just thought it would be nice, for Mama. So I can remember all that she wanted for me." She felt a little uncomfortable with this little lie, but told herself it wasn't so far from the truth. Her mother wanted her to be educated, so making a skull to do a fortune spell wasn't exactly a lie.

Abuela Concepcion stopped her work and stood quite still for a short while, then said, "If that would please you, then keep out enough mix to make a skull. Not the very smallest, but not the largest, either."

"Thank you, Abuelita," said Refugio with her most winsome smile. It would be a fine thing to cast such a spell as the skull would contain.

"But you must continue to work now. There's still more to finish, and time is getting short." She sounded almost gruff, as if the reminder of her daughter had taken her by surprise and left her feeling bereft.

"I will," said Refugio, and resumed her labors with renewed energy as she thought of how she would prepare the skull for its magical purpose.

"Very good," said Abuela Concepcion, preparing more molds. "You are being a great help to me today, chica. I want you to know how much that pleases me."

"You're good to me, Abuela," said Refugio. Her grandmother blinked, and Refugio could see tears on her lashes. "Please don't be sad."

"I can't help it, Refugio. I don't want to see your life go to waste as so many others have done. Your father has been reckless, and some of it is in your nature as well. You should learn prudence, chica. It is one thing if children are foolish or have no capacity for study, but you are bright and you are happiest when you're reading, and that is a good thing. I should be able to do something for you. If your father hadn't got himself on the wrong side of the regional government, something might be done. But with him in jail and no money, and that awful Viuda Estrella hoping to bring you into her—" She blotted her tears with the hem of her apron.

"I'll think of something," said Refugio, making it a promise.

"I hope you will, for I haven't been able to," Abuela Concepcion admitted as if confessing to a great sin. She shoved Refugio away gently and then wiped her hands before going back to her work. "When you make your skull, ask God for help."

"I'll do what I can," said Refugio, and went back to the tasks her grandmother had imposed upon her.

By the time all the molds had been filled and the skulls were drying on the narrow racks, it was dark. Dominga Caida had come and gone, taking the special skulls away with her, and leaving behind full payment with an extra peso for having the skulls ready on time. Now, as dusk thickened, there were four lights in Abuela Concepcion's house, one in each room—bare, glaring bulbs set in the ceiling, lending their brightness to the encroaching night. Abuela Concepcion finished washing up all the bowls but one.

"Shall I make my skull now?" Refugio asked as she looked at the last small egg waiting on the table. At least she hadn't had to go out to try to get another.

"Yes, if you still want to," said Abuela Concepcion. She didn't want Refugio to know how tired she was or how much her feet hurt, so she declared, "I'm going to listen to the radio, to find out if there's any news."

"Oh, all right," said Refugio, paying less than half her attention to what her grandmother said. She was thinking about her skull, and what she would do with it. Working with great care, she took the second-largest mold and began to spread the egg-white-and-sugar mixture on it, pausing now and again to write down what she wanted from the spirits that hovered over Santa Luz. Whispering her invocation, she worked with great care, remembering how important it was to show respect for the spirits whose aid she sought. It would be very late when the skull was ready, but Viuda Estrella said that tonight of all nights she would be awake almost until dawn. Refugio was careful to follow the instructions the witch-woman had given her to the letter, for if she botched any part of it, the results could be calamitous. "This is for money so I can study," she said, pressing a tiny round of gold-colored foil from a candy-wrapper. "This is for protection." If Abuela Concepcion knew what Refugio was doing, she would forbid it and would destroy the skull. She looked about as if expecting to see her grandmother watching her from the doorway, but no, Refugio was alone. When she had finished filling the mold, she set it on the windowsill, facing the east, where the moon would shortly rise. Viuda Estrella had been most specific about that, and Refugio complied. "There," she said to the skull that had her own name on it. "Let the moon see you."

By the time Abuela Concepcion turned off the radio and made her way to bed, Refugio had already donned her good white-cotton dress with the lace edging, just as Viuda Estrella had told her to do. She had a flashlight and a sack for the skull she had made, and she loaded it carefully before letting herself out through the narrow door at the back of the pantry. Thinking of how much her life was about to change, she almost skipped with excitement. She kept the flashlight off until she was on the road outside of Santa Luz, for she didn't want anyone to see her as she made her way toward the ancient, tumbled stones and the house where Viuda Estrella was waiting to work her most potent conjuration on Refugio's sugar skull on this most magical of all nights. Her future would be so much better than Abuela Concepcion feared. Viuda Estrella would teach her all she needed to know to make her way in the world, to be a woman of importance. Then she would go to the school in Guanajuanto, and after that, she would venture out into the wider world, with the education her grandmother wanted for her and the strength of Viuda Estrella to give her power.

As she walked Refugio sang to the skull wrapped in her handkerchief, telling it of all she wanted, confident that the saints and her mother heard her. The beam of the flashlight was a cone of brightness in the dark, lighting her way. She felt deeply happy, and for the first time in her life, she believed she would be able to achieve all she wanted, for the skull and her industry, combined with the might of the saints that could be invoked on this night, would remove all obstacles before her. There was so much to look forward to, she thought, and took the path to Viuda Estrella's house.

ON A DARK OCTOBER
Joe R. Lansdale

According to Joe Lansdale, "On a Dark October" was originally written for
Twilight Zone magazine, but editor T.E.D. Klein felt it was too dark. And
even though David Silva published it in his magazine, The Horror Show, *he*
had similar reservations as well. Considering the graphic horror Lansdale
was known for at the time, the author was somewhat surprised by their
concern. Seems the problem was with the story's social commentary. Real
horrors make folks nervous. The history of Halloween in the twentieth and
twenty-first centuries is a reflection American culture—and the reflection is
often ugly. Lansdale serves up a story that evokes uncomfortable "reality,"
and adds a dollop of the supernatural to make sure you squirm.

The October night was dark and cool. The rain was thick. The moon
was hidden behind dark clouds that occasionally flashed with lightning,
and the sky rumbled as if it were a big belly that was hungry and needed
filling.

A white Chrysler New Yorker came down the street and pulled up next
to the curb. The driver killed the engine and the lights, turned to look at
the building that sat on the block, an ugly tin thing with a weak light bulb
shielded by a tin-hat shade over a fading sign that read BOB'S GARAGE. For
a moment the driver sat unmoving, then he reached over, picked up the
newspaper-wrapped package on the seat and put it in his lap. He opened it
slowly. Inside was a shiny, oily, black-handled, ball peen hammer.

He lifted the hammer, touched the head of it to his free palm. It left a
small smudge of grease there. He closed his hand, opened it, rubbed his
fingers together. It felt just like . . . but he didn't want to think of that. It
would all happen soon enough.

He put the hammer back in the papers, rewrapped it, wiped his fingers
on the outside of the package. He pulled a raincoat from the back seat and

put it across his lap. Then, with hands resting idly on the wheel, he sat silently.

A late model blue Ford pulled in front of him, left a space at the garage's drive, and parked. No one got out. The man in the Chrysler did not move.

Five minutes passed and another car, a late model Chevy, parked directly behind the Chrysler. Shortly thereafter three more cars arrived, all of them were late models. None of them blocked the drive. No one got out.

Another five minutes skulked by before a white van with MERTZ'S MEATS AND BUTCHER SHOP written on the side pulled around the Chrysler, then backed up the drive, almost to the garage door. A man wearing a hooded raincoat and carrying a package got out of the van, walked to the back and opened it.

The blue Ford's door opened, and a man dressed similarly, carrying a package under his arm, got out and went up the driveway. The two men nodded at one another. The man who had gotten out of the Ford unlocked the garage and slid the door back.

Car doors opened. Men dressed in raincoats, carrying packages, got out and walked to the back of the van. A couple of them had flashlights and they flashed them in the back of the vehicle, gave the others a good view of what was there—a burlap-wrapped, rope-bound bundle that wiggled and groaned.

The man who had been driving the van said, "Get it out."

Two of the men handed their packages to their comrades and climbed inside, picked up the squirming bundle, carried it into the garage. The others followed. The man from the Ford closed the door.

Except for the beams of the two flashlights, they stood close together in the darkness, like strands of flesh that had suddenly been pulled into a knot. The two with the bundle broke away from the others, and with their comrades directing their path with the beams of their flashlights, they carried the bundle to the grease rack and placed it between two wheel ramps. When that was finished, the two who had carried the bundle returned to join the others, to reform that tight knot of flesh.

Outside the rain was pounding the roof like tossed lug bolts. Lightning danced through the half-dozen small, barred windows. Wind shook the tin garage with a sound like a rattlesnake tail quivering for the strike, then passed on.

No one spoke for a while. They just looked at the bundle. The bundle thrashed about and the moaning from it was louder than ever.

"All right," the man from the van said.

They removed their clothes, hung them on pegs on the wall, pulled their raincoats on.

The man who had been driving the blue Ford—after looking carefully into the darkness—went to the grease rack. There was a paper bag on one of the ramps. Earlier in the day he had placed it there himself. He opened it and took out a handful of candles and a book of matches. Using a match to guide him, he placed the candles down the length of the ramps, lighting them as he went. When he was finished, the garage glowed with a soft amber light. Except for the rear of the building. It was dark there.

The man with the candles stopped suddenly, a match flame wavering between his fingertips. The hackles on the back of his neck stood up. He could hear movement from the dark part of the garage. He shook the match out quickly and joined the others. Together, the group unwrapped their packages and gripped the contents firmly in their hands—hammers, brake-over handles, crowbars, heavy wrenches. Then all of them stood looking toward the back of the garage, where something heavy and sluggish moved.

The sound of the garage clock—a huge thing with DRINK COCA-COLA emblazoned on its face—was like the ticking of a time bomb. It was one minute to midnight.

Beneath the clock, visible from time to time when the glow of the candles was whipped that way by the draft, was a calendar. It read OCTOBER and had a picture of a smiling boy wearing overalls, standing amidst a field of pumpkins. The 31st was circled in red.

Eyes drifted to the bundle between the ramps now. It had stopped squirming. The sound it was making was not quite a moan. The man from the van nodded at one of the men, the one who had driven the Chrysler. The Chrysler man went to the bundle and worked the ropes loose, folded back the burlap. A frightened black youth, bound by leather straps and gagged with a sock and a bandana, looked up at him wide-eyed. The man from the Chrysler avoided looking back. The youth started squirming, grunting, and thrashing. Blood beaded around his wrists where the leather was tied, boiled out from around the loop fastened to his neck; when he kicked, it boiled faster because the strand had been drawn around his neck, behind his back and tied off at his ankles.

There came a sound from the rear of the garage again, louder than before. It was followed by a sudden sigh that might have been the wind working its way between the rafters.

The van driver stepped forward, spoke loudly to the back of the garage. "We got something for you, hear me? Just like always we're doing our part. You do yours. I guess that's all I got to say. Things will be the same come next October. In your name, I reckon."

For a moment—just a moment—there was a glimmer of a shape when the candles caught a draft and wafted their bright heads in that direction. The man from the van stepped back quickly. "In your name," he repeated. He turned to the men. "Like always, now. Don't get the head until the very end. Make it last."

The faces of the men took on an expression of grimness, as if they were all playing a part in a theatric production and had been told to look that way. They hoisted their tools and moved toward the youth.

What they did took a long time.

When they finished, the thing that had been the young black man looked like a gigantic hunk of raw liver that had been chewed up and spat out. The raincoats of the men were covered in a spray of blood and brains. They were panting.

"Okay," said the man from the van.

They took off their raincoats, tossed them in a metal bin near the grease rack, wiped the blood from their hands, faces, ankles, and feet with shop rags, tossed those in the bin and put on their clothes.

The van driver yelled to the back of the garage. "All yours. Keep the years good, huh?"

They went out of there and the man from the Ford locked the garage door. Tomorrow he would come to work as always. There would be no corpse to worry about, and a quick dose of gasoline and a match would take care of the contents in the bin. Rain ran down his back and made him shiver.

Each of the men went out to their cars without speaking. Tonight they would all go home to their young, attractive wives and tomorrow they would all go to their prosperous businesses and they would not think of this night again. Until next October.

They drove away. Lightning flashed. The wind howled. The rain beat the garage like a cat-o'-nine-tails. And inside there were loud sucking sounds punctuated by grunts of joy.

THE VOW ON HALLOWEEN

Lyllian Huntley Harris

Halloween is full of mysteries and deception, but little did I know I'd uncover both when I chose this tale for inclusion. I found it in a 1985 anthology compiled by Peter Haining. He had attributed it to Irish author Dorothy Macardle, who is now best remembered for her novel Uneasy Freehold *(1941), published in the U.S. as* The Uninvited *(1942), and then filmed under that name in 1944.*

When the table of contents for Halloween *were announced online, Douglas A. Anderson emailed me and soundly refuted Macardle as the author. Anderson and Peter Beresford Ellis have researched Dorothy Macardle, and when they discovered this story republished under her name, they immediately knew it was not by the author. Macardle's few elegantly written short stories usually combined her interests in contemporary Irish politics and the supernatural. This story bears no resemblance to her style. Moreover, Anderson (and others) have noted that Haining is known to have cited incorrect sources in other cases.*

Anderson tracked the original publication of the story to Weird Tales*, Vol. 4, No. 2, May-June 1924, authored by Lyllian Huntley Harris. This was easily verified—but here the mystery arises. Who was Lyllian Huntley Harris and did she ever write anything else? All we know of her—other than this story—is that Lyllian Huntley Harris (1885-1939) was a Georgia native, the wife of a lawyer John Joseph Harris and that she is buried in Sandersville, Georgia.*

This short story of supernaturally blighted love is pure pulp and quaintly romantic. It may not be—in modern eyes—a great work of literature, but it is a type of story that was quite popular in its era. It also gives us a glimpse of a holiday party of the early 1920s.

It was Halloween, the time of revelry, when mysticism holds full sway and hearts are supposed to be united beneath the magic glow of dim lanterns. It was the time of apple bobbing, fortune telling, and masking in motley raiment, the whole glamoured over by the light of wishing candles.

Amid such scenes one never thinks of tragedy, but it treads apace, sometimes among the gay revelers, and many a domino or cowl covers that which would make the staunchest heart quake and is as different from the gay exterior as darkness is from light.

The lanterns glimmered, the varicolored lights shading and darkening with the winds that soughed through the beautiful old garden where the fête was held.

The pergolas, standing whitely aloof from surrounding density, made wonderful trysting places for the age-old stories of love to be whispered.

"You have made me very happy tonight, Audrey," a deep voice was whispering. "I think that all my life after will be a paean of gratitude for this moment of bliss. When you would vouchsafe no word of hope, not even one of pity, I felt hopeless, broken. Life seemed as senseless as a stupid rhyme! But now, dearest, life's cup is filled to overflowing!"

His lips met hers in a lingering caress.

For a moment the lanterns seemed to flicker and dim. A slight shudder ran over her slender frame. She freed herself gently.

"I cannot expect you to understand, Arthur," Audrey replied, "why you were kept waiting. The silence encompassed the whole of the earth and sky to me. It has been a frightful reality, which my tongue refused to explain until today, and my mental anguish has well nigh swayed my reason. A year ago tonight I experienced a terrible ordeal, more uncanny because it has seemed impossible for me to shake off the pall of it. It has changed the course of my life. For a year I have lived the life of a senseless thing, a piece of clay, merely breathing, eating, sleeping, but with no soul left me—"

Her voice trailed off into nothingness, and for a while both were silent. He was awed by her utterances. His arm tightened about her.

"Poor Audrey," he whispered, "you must have worried yourself needlessly. Is not illusion a sort of night to the mind which we people with dreams?"

"It was no illusion, Arthur, but grim reality. But last night a dream came to me which seemed to awaken my dead sensibilities, cut loose the spell under which I was living. In it I was commanded to tell you all."

Gently he caressed her.

"Tell me what you wish, dear, and nothing more. Remember, hope is better than memory. I am listening."

"I shall tell you all. You suffered, so nothing shall be withheld. My troubles began when my father had financial reverses. I gave music lessons to eke out a meager income. About this time, Rothschild Manny came into my life. He loved me at sight, as intensely as I loathed him. One glance from his slanting, shifty eyes was sufficient to set me cowering in my chair, and if his hand by chance touched mine, cold chills chased over my body. He was like some demon, waiting his chance to spring upon his prey.

"Imagine my dismay, when my parents immediately began insisting on my marriage with this monster! His fortune would retrieve ours and would regain the position we had lost by financial reverses. The horror of it! After one lengthy argument I felt my brain reel, and I fell upon my knees crying and imploring my father to spare me this ordeal. He was obdurate and insisted upon my consent. Finally he sent for Manny, placed my hand in his, and gave me to him formally. But not once did I encourage him, and he seemed to change into a veritable demon. His eyes would become crafty as he looked at me and his face assume an expression of sardonic intensity.

"One day, the day that is seared upon my memory, one year ago tonight, he sought me out. I was alone in the house, my father having gone to the lodge. Manny was trembling under some terrible emotion.

" 'Your welcome does not shine forth from your eyes, my dear,' he said as he seated himself and took my hand.

"With a gesture of horror I jerked it away. The motion seemed, to infuriate him, and deepened the intensity of his eyes.

" 'I came to take you driving,' he said, with a quick intake of his breath. 'The night is lovely and my new car is outside. It will be yours when you are mine.'

"There was a steely intensity in his gaze directed upon me.

" 'I don't care to go,' I said quietly.

" 'Pray reconsider. I may be able to persuade you to feel differently if you give me a chance.'

"Here I interrupted.

" 'I will do nothing of the sort,' I cried, 'I will go nowhere with you. I want nothing to do with you, and God willing, I will never be your wife!'

"My words infuriated him. He was under some powerful influence of evil. He seized my wrist and, jerking me out of my chair, shook me violently. My senses reeled, and I must have lost consciousness. All I remember was being held up by brute force, those horrible evil eyes boring malevolently into mine while he shouted in my ear:

" 'Remember, young lady, you will drive with me yet! Maybe not now, but some day! This is not a threat, it is a declaration, and neither stars, moon, nor even heaven itself, shall deliver you from it.'

"I was thrown violently upon the floor. Merciful oblivion came to me.

"For days I was ill—not knowing, not caring what happened, craving death to relieve me from the sinister influence and deliver me from the effect of that horrible vow on Halloween. When I recovered I learned that

Manny, driving his car that day madly, had lost control and had come to a horrible end. His evil influence seemed to hold me drugged in its power. I longed to die. But death does not come when one craves it. I lived, a piece of senseless clay, until you came to me; and when I looked into your eyes I felt that heaven had been kind in denying me my desire. My heart, my soul, went out to you, but I couldn't let you know. I could never become your wife with that terrible vow sounding in my ears, that terrible power controlling me.

"Then yesterday, in the dim watches of the night a dream came to me. A voice spoke and said: 'Love beyond price is yours. Take and cherish it, lest this priceless gift be withdrawn!'

"I awoke, happy, myself once more, grateful that life could come to me again."

She nestled close and his hand caressed her hair.

"My darling, how you have suffered. My whole life shall be spent in keeping you free of the mirage of this terrible experience—"

"Beg pardon," a suave voice interrupted, and a cowled figure drew near, "This is my dance, I believe. Is it not too warm to repair to the ballroom? I have my car here. A spin will refresh us both."

The cowled figure bowed low. Audrey glanced at her dance card, and arose with a little laugh.

"You will excuse me, Arthur, won't you? It seems that this august domino person has prior claim."

With a light hand on the newcomer's arm she was lost in the crowd. The music from the palm-shaded orchestra stirred forth, hummed, throbbed, and sobbed into a soft requiem.

Two days later, some belated wayfarers came upon a young woman, who seemed unable to move from her seat in an automobile. Upright beside her was a skeleton, whose sightless eye sockets even then bored into the soul from which the light of reason had fled forever more!

Manny had kept his threat.

And in an old moonlit garden, under the white pergola where he had lived his one moment of bliss, a figure fell, turned into sudden clay, as the smoking weapon in his hand could testify.

THE OCTOBER GAME

Ray Bradbury

Ray Bradbury's Halloween fiction is so notable (and influential) he's fondly known as "Mr. October. His novel The Halloween Tree (1972) *has been called "a poetic instruction manual for the understanding of Halloween and its background history and mythology." His early story "Homecoming" (1946) centers around a young outsider—born mortal in a family of supernatural beings—and his emotions as his preparations are made for an All Hallows Eve celebration. The story "Heavy-Set" deals with a man whose attachment to the childish aspects of Halloween leads us to understand a horrific situation. According to F. Paul Wilson, Bradbury is somewhat ambivalent about "The October Game" these days—still appreciative of his youthful technique, but now somewhat appalled by the subject matter. I think, however, you'll find it remains a stunning piece.*

He put the gun back into the bureau drawer and shut the drawer.

No, not that way. Louise wouldn't suffer that way. She would be dead and it would be over and she wouldn't suffer. It was very important that this thing have, above all duration. Duration through imagination. How to prolong the suffering? How, first of all, to bring it about? Well.

The man standing before the bedroom mirror carefully fitted his cuff links together. He paused long enough to hear the children run by swiftly on the street below, outside this warm two-story house, like so many gray mice the children, like so many leaves.

By the sound of the children you knew the calendar day. By their screams you knew what evening it was. You knew it was very late in the year. October. The last day of October, with white bone masks and cut pumpkins and the smell of dropped candle fat.

No. Things hadn't been right for some time. October didn't help any. If anything it made things worse. He adjusted his black bow tie. If this were spring, he nodded slowly, quietly, emotionlessly, at his image in the mirror, then there might be a chance. But tonight all the world was burning down into ruin. There was no green spring, none of the freshness, none of the promise.

There was a soft running in the hall. "That's Marion," he told himself. "My little one. All eight quiet years of her. Never a word. Just her luminous gray eyes and her wondering little mouth." His daughter had been in and out all evening, trying on various masks, asking him which was most terrifying, most horrible. They had both finally decided on the skeleton mask. It was "just awful!" It would

"scare the beans" from people!

Again he caught the long look of thought and deliberation he gave himself in the mirror. He had never liked October. Ever since he first lay in the autumn leaves before his grandmother's house many years ago and heard the wind and saw the empty trees. It has made him cry, without a reason. And a little of that sadness returned each year to him. It always went away with spring.

But, it was different tonight. There was a feeling of autumn coming to last a million years.

There would be no spring.

He had been crying quietly all evening. It did not show, not a vestige of it, on his face. It was all hidden somewhere and it wouldn't stop.

The rich syrupy smell of sweets filled the bustling house. Louise had laid out apples in new skins of toffee; there were vast bowls of punch fresh-mixed, stringed apples in each door, scooped, vented pumpkins peering triangularly from each cold window. There was a water tub in the center of the living room, waiting, with a sack of apples nearby, for dunking to begin. All that was needed was the catalyst, the inpouring of children, to start the apples bobbling, the stringed apples to penduluming in the crowded doors, the candy to vanish, the halls to echo with fright or delight, it was all the same.

Now, the house was silent with preparation. And just a little more than that.

Louise had managed to be in every other room save the room he was in today. It was her very fine way of intimating, Oh look Mich, see how busy I am! So busy that when you walk into a room *I'm* in there's always something I need to do in *another* room! Just see how I dash about!

For a while he had played a little game with her, a nasty childish game. When she was in the kitchen then he came to the kitchen saying, "I need a glass of water." After a moment, he standing, drinking water, she like a crystal witch over the caramel brew bubbling like a prehistoric mudpot on the stove, she said, "Oh, I must light the pumpkins!" and she rushed to the living room to make the pumpkins smile with light.

He came after, smiling, "I must get my pipe."

"Oh, the cider!" she had cried, running to the dining room.

"I'll check the cider," he had said. But when he tried following she ran to the bathroom and locked the door.

He stood outside the bathroom door, laughing strangely and sense-lessly, his pipe gone cold in his mouth, and then, tired of the game, but stubborn, he waited another five minutes. There was not a sound from the bath. And lest she enjoy in any way knowing that he waited outside, irri-tated, he suddenly jerked about and walked upstairs, whistling merrily.

At the top of the stairs he had waited. Finally he had heard the bathroom door unlatch and she had come out and life belowstairs had resumed, as life in a jungle must resume once a terror has passed on away and the antelope return to their spring.

Now, as he finished his bow tie and put his dark coat there was a mouse-rustle in the hall. Marion appeared in the door, all skeletonous in her disguise.

"How do I look, Papa?"

"Fine!"

From under the mask, blond hair showed. From the skull sockets small blue eyes smiled. He sighed. Marion and Louise, the two silent denouncers of his virility, his dark power. What alchemy had there been in Louise that took the dark of a dark man and bleached and bleached the dark brown eyes and black hair and washed and bleached the ingrown baby all during the period before birth until the child was born, Marion, blond, blue-eyed, ruddy-cheeked? Sometimes he suspected that Louise had conceived the child as an idea, completely asexual, an immaculate conception of contemptuous mind and cell. As a firm rebuke to him she had produced a child in her *own* image, and, to top it, she had somehow *fixed* the doctor so he shook his head and said, "Sorry, Mr. Wilder, your wife will never have another child. This is the last one."

"And I wanted a boy," Mich had said eight years ago.

He almost bent to take hold of Marion now, in her skull mask. He felt an inexplicable rush of pity for her, because she had never had a father's love, only the crushing, holding love of a loveless mother. But most of all he pitied himself, that somehow he had not made the most of a bad birth, enjoyed his daughter for herself, regardless of her not being dark and a son and like himself. Somewhere he had missed out. Other things being equal, he would have loved the child. But Louise hadn't wanted a child, anyway, in the first place. She had been frightened of the idea of birth. He had forced the child on her, and from that night, all through the year until the agony of the birth itself, Louise had lived in another part of the house. She had expected to die with the forced child. It had been very easy for Louise to hate this husband who so wanted a son that he gave his only wife over to the mortuary.

But—Louise had lived. And in triumph! Her eyes, the day he came to the hospital, were cold. I'm alive they said. And I have a *blond* daughter! Just look! And when he had put out a hand to touch, the mother had turned away to conspire with her new pink daughter-child—away from that dark forcing murderer. It had all been so beautifully ironic. His selfishness deserved it.

But now it was October again. There had been other Octobers and when he thought of the long winter he had been filled with horror year after year to think of the endless months mortared into the house by an insane fall of snow, trapped with a woman and child, neither of whom loved him, for months on end. During the eight years there had been respites. In spring and summer you got out, walked, picnicked; these were desperate solutions to the desperate problem of a hated man.

But, in winter, the hikes and picnics and escapes fell away with leaves. Life, like a tree, stood empty, the fruit picked, the sap run to earth. Yes, you invited people in, but people were hard to get in winter with blizzards and all. Once he had been clever enough to save for a Florida trip. They had gone south. He had walked in the open.

But now, the eighth winter coming, he knew things were finally at an end. He simply could not wear this one through. There was an acid walled off in him that slowly had eaten through tissue and bone over the years, and now, tonight, it would reach the wild explosive in him and all would be over!

There was a mad ringing of the bell below. In the hall, Louise went to see. Marion, without a word, ran down to greet the first arrivals. There were shouts and hilarity.

He walked to the top of the stairs.

Louise was below, taking wraps. She was tall and slender and blonde to the point of whiteness, laughing down upon the new children.

He hesitated. What was all this? The years? The boredom of living? Where had it gone wrong? Certainly not with the birth of the child alone. But it had been a symbol of all their tensions, he imagined. His jealousies and his business failures and all the rotten rest of it. Why didn't he just turn, pack a suitcase, and leave? No. Not without hurting Louise as much as she had hurt him. It was simple as that. Divorce wouldn't hurt her at all. It would simply be an end to numb indecision. If he thought divorce would give her pleasure in any way he would stay married the rest of his life to her, for damned spite. No he must hurt her. Figure some way, perhaps, to take Marion away from her, legally. Yes. That was it. That would hurt most of all. To take Marion away.

"Hello down there!" He descended the stairs beaming.

Louise didn't look up.

"Hi, Mr. Wilder!"

The children shouted, waved, as he came down.

By ten o'clock the doorbell had stopped ringing, the apples were bitten from stringed doors, the pink faces were wiped dry from the apple bobbling, napkins were smeared with caramel and punch, and he, the husband, with pleasant efficiency had taken over. He took the party right out of Louise's hands. He ran about talking to the twenty children and the twelve parents who had come and were happy with the special spiked cider he had fixed them. He supervised pin the tail on the donkey, spin the bottle, musical chairs, and all the rest, amid fits of shouting laughter. Then, in the triangular-eyed pumpkin shine, all house lights out, he cried, "Hush! Follow me!" tiptoeing toward the cellar.

The parents, on the outer periphery of the costumed riot, commented to each other, nodding at the clever husband, speaking to the lucky wife. How *well* he got on with children, they said.

The children, crowded after the husband, squealing.

"The cellar!" he cried. "The tomb of the witch!"

More squealing. He made a mock shiver. "Abandon hope all ye who enter here!"

The parents chuckled.

One by one the children slid down a slide which Mich had fixed up from lengths of table-section, into the dark cellar. He hissed and shouted ghastly utterances after them. A wonderful wailing filled dark pumpkin-lighted house. Everybody talked at once. Everybody but Marion. She had gone through all the party with a minimum of sound or talk; it was all inside her, all the excitement and joy. What a little troll, he thought. With a shut mouth and shiny eyes she had watched her own party, like so many serpentines thrown before her.

Now, the parents. With laughing reluctance they slid down the short incline, uproarious, while little Marion stood by, always wanting to see it all, to be last. Louise went down without help. He moved to aid her, but she was gone even before he bent.

The upper house was empty and silent in the candle-shine. Marion stood by the slide. 'Here we go,' he said, and picked her up.

They sat in a vast circle in the cellar. Warmth came from the distant bulk of the furnace. The chairs stood in a long line along each wall, twenty squealing children, twelve rustling relatives, alternatively spaced, with Louise down at the far end, Mich up at this end, near the stairs. He peered but saw nothing. They had all grouped to their chairs, catch-as-you-can in the blackness. The entire program from here on was to be enacted in the dark, he as Mr. Interlocutor. There was a child scampering, a smell of damp cement, and the sound of the wind out in the October stars.

"Now!" cried the husband in the dark cellar. "Quiet!"

Everybody settled.

The room was black black. Not a light, not a shine, not a glint of an eye.

A scraping of crockery, a metal rattle.

"The witch is dead," intoned the husband.

"Eeeeeeeeeeeeeeeeeeee," said the children.

"The witch is dead, she has been killed, and here is the knife she was killed with." He handed over the knife. It was passed from hand to hand, down and around the circle, with chuckles and little odd cries and comments from the adults.

"The witch is dead, and this is her head," whispered the husband, and handed an item to the nearest person.

"Oh, I know how this game is played," some child cried, happily, in the dark. "He gets some old chicken innards from the icebox and hands them around and says, 'These are her innards!' And he makes a clay head and passes it for her head, and passes a soup bone for her arm. And he takes a marble and says, 'This is her eye!' And he takes some corn and says, 'This is her teeth!' And he takes a sack of plum pudding and gives that and says, 'This is her stomach!' I know how this is played!"

"Hush, you'll spoil everything," some girl said.

"The witch came to harm, and this is her arm," said Mich.

"Eeeeeeeeeeee!"

The items were passed and passed, like hot potatoes, around the circle. Some children screamed, wouldn't touch them. Some ran from their chairs to stand in the center of the cellar until the grisly items had passed.

"Aw, it's only chicken insides," scoffed a boy. "Come back, Helen!"

Shot from hand to hand, with small scream after scream, the items went down, down, to be followed by another and another.

"The witch cut apart, and this is her heart," said the husband.

Six or seven items moving at once through the laughing, trembling dark.

Louise spoke up. "Marion, don't be afraid; it's only play."

Marion didn't say anything.

"Marion?" asked Louise. "Are you afraid?"

Marion didn't say anything.

"She's all right," said the husband. "She's not afraid."

On and on the passing, the screams, the hilarity.

The autumn wind sighed about the house. And he, the husband stood at the head of the dark cellar, intoning the words, handing out the items.

"Marion?" asked Louise again, from far across the cellar.

Everybody was talking.

"Marion?" called Louise.

Everybody quieted.

"Marion, answer me, are you afraid?"

Marion didn't answer.

The husband stood there, at the bottom of the cellar steps.

Louise called "Marion, are you there?"

No answer. The room was silent.

"Where's Marion?" called Louise.

"She was here," said a boy.

"Maybe she's upstairs."

"Marion!"

No answer. It was quiet.

Louise cried out, "Marion, Marion!"

"Turn on the lights," said one of the adults.

The items stopped passing. The children and adults sat with the witch's items in their hands.

"No." Louise gasped. There was a scraping of her chair, wildly, in the dark. "No. Don't turn on the lights, oh, God, God, God, don't turn them on, please, *don't* turn on the lights, *don't!*" Louise was shrieking now. The entire cellar froze with the scream.

Nobody moved.

Everyone sat in the dark cellar, suspended in the suddenly frozen task of this October game; the wind blew outside, banging the house, the smell of pumpkins and apples filled the room with the smell of the objects in their fingers while one boy cried, "I'll go upstairs and look!" and he ran upstairs hopefully and out around the house, four times around the house, calling, "Marion, Marion, Marion!" over and over and at last coming slowly down the stairs into the waiting breathing cellar and saying to the darkness, "I can't find her."

Then . . . some idiot turned on the lights.

THE NOVEMBER GAME

F. Paul Wilson

"The November Game" was written for a "tribute" anthology honoring Ray Bradbury that William F. Nolan edited some years back. It's a sequel to Ray Bradbury's classic "The October Game." This is the first time the two stories have ever been published together in one volume.

As F. Paul Wilson noted to me: "Part of me hopes you're reprinting 'The October Game' along with this, and part of me hopes you're not. Ray's story is a masterpiece of subtly growing menace, and one of the most perfectly focused short stories ever written, as effective today as it was when he wrote it. Put my story alongside it and it will look like such a pallid little thing in comparison.

"I first read it on a summer night in 1959 in Hitchcock's 13 More Stories They Wouldn't Let Me Do On TV, *and I consider that night one of the pivotal moments in my life. I was thirteen at the time. The last line ('Then . . . some idiot turned on the lights.') blew me away, utterly and completely. Left me gasping. Lowered the temperature of the night by twenty degrees, easy. And made me decide that I had to write horror fiction some day.*

"So . . . 'The November Game' picks up shortly after Ray's story ends. It's lurid where Ray was subtle, but that seemed the way to go. Over the years I've been unable to let go of the notion that poor Marion's killer has to get his. What goes around, comes around. And now . . . it's Daddy's turn."

I'm sure you'll find Wilson's story much more than a "pallid little thing."

Two human eyeballs nestle amid the white grapes on my dinner tray. I spot them even as the tray is being shoved under the bars of my cell.

"Dinner, creep," says the guard as he guides the tray forward with his shoe.

"The name is Mich, Hugo," I say evenly, refusing to react to the sight of those eyes.

"That translates into *creep* around here."

Hugo leaves. I listen to the squeaky wheels of the dinner cart echo away down the corridor. Then I look at the bowl of grapes again.

The eyes are still there, pale blue, little-girl blue, staring back at me so mournfully.

They think they can break me this way, make me pay for what I did. But after all those years of marriage to Louise, I don't break so easily.

When I'm sure Hugo's gone I inspect the rest of the food—beef patty, string beans, French fries, Jell-O. They all look okay—no surprises in among the fries like last night.

So I take the wooden spoon, the only utensil they'll let me have here, and go to the loose floor tile I found in the right rear corner. I pry it loose. A whiff of putrefaction wafts up from the empty space below. Dark down there, a dark that seems to go on forever. If I were a bit smaller I could fit through. I figure the last occupant of this cell must have been a little guy, must have tried to dig his way out. Probably got transferred to another cell before he finished his tunnel, because I've never heard of anyone breaking out of here.

But *I'm* going to be a little guy before long. And then I'll be out of here.

I upend the bowl of grapes and eyeballs over the hole first, then let the rest of the food follow. Somewhere below I hear it all plop onto the other things I've been dumping down there. I could flush the eyes and the rest down the stained white toilet squatting in the other corner, but they're probably listening for that. If they hear a flush during the dinner hour they'll guess what I'm doing and think they're winning the game. So I go them one better. As long as they don't know about the hole, I'll stay ahead in their rotten little game.

I replace the tile and return to my cot. I tap my wooden spoon on the Melmac plates and clatter them against the tray while I smack my lips and make appropriate eating noises. I only drink the milk and water. That's all I've allowed myself since they put me in here. And the diet's working. I'm losing weight. Pretty soon I'll be able to slip through the opening under that tile, and then they'll have to admit I've beaten them at their own rotten game.

Soon I hear the squeak of the wheels again. I arrange my tray and slip it out under the bars and into the corridor.

"An excellent dinner," I say as Hugo picks up the tray.

He says nothing.

"Especially the grapes," I tell him. "The grapes were delicious—*utterly* delicious."

"Up yours, creep," Hugo says as he squeaks away.

I miss my pipe.

They won't let me have it in here. No flame, no sharps, no shoelaces, even. As if I'd actually garrote myself with string.

Suicide watch, they call it. But I've come to realize they've got something else in mind by isolating me. They've declared psychological war on me.

They must think I'm stupid, telling me I'm in a solitary cell for my own protection, saying the other prisoners might want to hurt me because I'm considered a "short eyes."

But I'm not a child molester—that's what "short eyes" means in prison lingo. I never molested a child in my life, never even *thought* of doing such a thing. Especially not Marion, not little eight-year-old Marion.

I only killed her.

I made her part of the game. The October game. I handed out the parts of her dismembered body to the twenty children and twelve adults seated in a circle in my cellar and let them pass the pieces around in the Halloween darkness. I can still hear their laughter as their fingers touched what they thought were chicken innards and grapes and sausages. They thought it was a lark. They had a ball until some idiot turned on the lights.

But I never molested little Marion.

And I never meant her any harm, either. Not personally. Marion was an innocent bystander caught in the crossfire between her mother and father. Louise was to blame. Because it was Louise I wanted to hurt. Louise of the bleached-out eyes and hair, Louise the ice princess who gave birth to a bleached-out clone of herself and then made her body incapable of bearing any more children. So where was my son—my dark-eyed, dark-haired counterpoint to Marion?

Eight years of Louise's mocking looks, of using the child who appeared to be all of her and none of me as a symbol of my failures—in business, in marriage, in fatherhood, in life. When autumn came I knew it had to stop. I couldn't stand the thought of another winter sealed in that house with Louise and her miniature clone. I wanted to leave, but not without hurting Louise. Not without an eight-year payback.

And the way to hurt Louise most was to take Marion from her.

And I did. Forever. In a way she'll never forget.

We're even, Louise.

(suck . . . puff)

"And you think your wife is behind these horrific pranks?" Dr. Hurst says, leaning back in his chair and chewing on his pipe stem.

I envy that pipe. But I'm the supposedly suicidal prisoner and he's the prison shrink, so he gets to draw warm, aromatic smoke from the stem and I get pieces of Marion on my food tray.

"Of course she is. Louise was always a vindictive sort. Somehow she's gotten to the kitchen help and the guards and convinced them to do a *Gaslight* number on me. She hates me. She wants to push me over the edge."

(suck . . . puff)

"Let's think about this," he says. "Your wife certainly has reason to hate you, to want to hurt you, to want to get even with you. But this conspiracy you've cooked up is rather farfetched, don't you think? Focus on what you're saying: Your wife has arranged with members of the prison staff to place pieces of your dismembered daughter in the food they serve you. Would she do something like that with her daughter's remains?"

"Yes. She'd do anything to get back at me. She probably thinks it's poetic justice or some such nonsense."

(suck . . . puff)

"Mmmmm. Tell me again what, um, parts of Marion you've found in your food."

I think back, mentally cataloging the nastiness I've been subjected to.

"It started with the baked potatoes. They almost fooled me with the first one. They'd taken some of Marion's skin and molded it into an oblong hollow shape, then filled it with baked potato. I've got to hand it to them. It looked quite realistic. I almost ate it."

Across his desk from me, Dr. Hurst coughs.

(suck . . . puff)

"How did you feel about that?"

"Disgusted, of course. And angry too. I'm willing to pay for what I did. I've never denied doing it. But I don't think I should be subjected to mental torture. Since that first dinner it's been a continual stream of body parts. Potato after potato encased in Marion's skin, her fingers and toes amid the French fries, a thick slice of calf's liver that didn't come from any calf, babyback ribs that were never near a pig, loops of intestine supposed to pass at breakfast as link sausage, a chunk of Jell-O with one of her vertebrae inside. And just last night, her eyes in a bowl of grapes. The list goes on and on. I want it stopped."

(suck . . . puff)

"Yes . . . " he says after a pause. "Yes, of course you do. And I'll see to it that it is stopped. Immediately. I'll have the warden launch a full investigation of the kitchen staff."

"Thank you. It's good to know there's at least one person here I can count on."

(suck . . . puff)

"I'm sure it is. But tell me, Mich. What have you done with all these parts of Marion's body you've been getting in your food? Where have you put them?"

A chill comes over me. Have I been wrong to think I could trust Dr. Hurst? Has he been toying with me, leading me down the garden path to this bear-trap of a question? Or *is* it a trap? Isn't it a perfectly natural question? Wouldn't anyone want to know what I've been doing with little Marion's parts?

As much as I want to be open and honest with him, I can't tell him the truth. I can't let anyone know about the loose tile and the tunnel beneath it. As a prison official he'll be obligated to report it to the warden and then I'll be moved to another cell and lose my only hope of escape. I can't risk that. I'll have to lie.

I smile at him.

"Why, I've been eating them, of course."

(suck . . .)

Dr. Hurst's pipe has gone out.

I'm ready for the tunnel.

My cell's dark. The corridor has only a single bulb burning at the far end. It's got to be tonight.

Dr. Hurst lied. He said he'd stop the body parts on my trays but he didn't. More and more of them, a couple with every meal lately. But they all get dumped down the hole along with the rest of my food. Hard to believe a little eight-year old like Marion could have so many pieces to her body. So many I've lost track, but in a way that's good. I can't see that there can be much more of her left to torment me with.

But tomorrow's Thanksgiving and God knows what they'll place before me then.

It's got to be tonight.

At least the diet's working.

Amazing what starvation will do to you. I've been getting thinner every day. My fat's long gone, my muscles have withered and atrophied. I think I'm small enough now to slip through that opening.

Only one way to find out.

I go to the loose tile and fit my fingers around its edges. I pried it up with the spoon earlier and left it canted in its space. It comes up easily now. The putrid odor is worse than ever. I look down into the opening. It's dark in my cell but even darker in that hole.

A sense of *waiting* wafts up with the odor.

How odd. Why should the tunnel be waiting for me?

I shake off the gnawing apprehension—I've heard hunger can play tricks with your mind—and position myself for the moment of truth. I sit on the edge and slide my bony legs into the opening. They slip through easily. As I raise my buttocks off the floor to slide my hips through, I pause.

Was that a sound? From below?

I hold still, listening. For an instant there I could have sworn I heard the faintest rustle directly below my dangling feet. But throughout my frozen, breathless silence, I hear nothing.

Rats. The realization strikes me like a blow. Of course! I've been throwing food down there for weeks. I'd be surprised if there *weren't* a rat or two down there.

I don't like the idea but I'm not put off. Not for a minute. I'm wearing sturdy prison shoes and stiff, tough prison pants. And I'm bigger than they are.

Just like I was bigger than Marion . . .

I slip my hips through the opening, lower my waist through, but my chest and shoulders won't go, at least not both shoulders at once. And there's no way to slip an arm through ahead of me.

I can see only one solution. I'm not comfortable with it but there's no way around it: I'm going to have to go down headfirst.

I pull myself out and swivel around. I slip my left arm and shoulder through, then it's time for my head. I'm tempted to hold my breath but why bother? I'm going to have to get used to that stench. I squeeze my head through the opening.

The air is warm and moist and the odor presses against my face like a shroud freshly torn from a moldering corpse. I try to mouth-breathe but the odor worms its way into my nose anyway.

And then I hear that sound again, a rustle of movement directly below me—a wet rustle. The odor grows stronger, rising like a dark cloud, gagging me. Something has to be behind that movement of stinking air, propelling it. Something larger than a rat!

I try to back up out of the opening but I'm stuck. Wedged! The side of my head won't clear the edge. And the odor's stronger, oh god, it's sucking the breath right out of me. Something's near! I can't see it but I can hear it, sense it! And it wants me, it *hungers* for me! It's so close now, it's—

Something wet and indescribably foul slides across my cheek and lips. The taste makes me retch. If there were anything in my stomach it would be spewing in all directions now. But the retching spasms force my head back out of the hole. I tear my arm and shoulder free of the opening and roll away toward the bars, toward the corridor. Who would have thought the air of a prison cell could smell so sweet, or a single sixty-watt bulb a hundred feet away be so bright.

I begin to scream. Unashamed, unabashed, I lay on my belly, reach through the bars and claw the concrete floor as wails of abject terror rip from my throat. I let them go on in a continuous stream until somebody comes, and even then I keep it up. I plead, sob, *beg* them to let me out of this cell. Finally they do. And only when I feel the corridor floor against my knees and hear the barred door clang shut behind me, does the terror begin to leach away.

"Dr. Hurst!" I tell them. "Get Dr. Hurst!"

"He ain't here, creep."

I look up and see Hugo hovering over me with two other guards from the third shift. A circle of faces completely devoid of pity or compassion.

"Call him! Get him!"

"We ain't disturbin' him for the likes o' you. But we got his resident on the way. Now what's this all—?"

"In there!" I say, pointing to the rear of the cell. "In that hole in the back! Something's down there!"

Hugo jerks his head toward the cell. "See what he's yapping about."

A young blond guard steps into my cell and searches around with his flashlight.

"In the back!" I tell him. "The right rear corner!"

The guard returns, shaking his head. "No hole in there."

"It must have pulled the tile back into place! Please! Listen to me!"

"The kid killer's doing a crazy act," Hugo says with a snarl. "Trying to get off on a section eight."

"No-no!" I cry, pulling at his trousers as I look up at him. "Back there, under one of the tiles—"

Hugo looks away, down the corridor. "Hey, doc! Can you do something to shut this creep up?"

A man in a white coat appears, a syringe in his hand.

"Got just the thing here. Dr. Hurst left a standing order in the event he started acting up."

Despite my screams of protest, my desperate, violent struggles, they hold me down while the resident jabs a needle into my right buttock. There's burning pain, then the needle is withdrawn, and they loosen their grip.

I'm weak from lack of food, and spent from the night's exertions. The drug acts quickly, sapping what little strength remains in my limbs. I go with it. There's no more fight left in me.

The guards lift me off the floor and begin to carry me. I close my eyes. At least I won't have to spend the night in the cell. I'll be safe in the infirmary.

Abruptly I'm dropped onto a cot. My eyes snap open as I hear my cell door clang shut, hear the lock snap closed.

No! They've put me back in the cell!

I open my lips to scream but the inside of my mouth is dry and sticky. My howl emerges as a whimper. Footsteps echo away down the corridor and the overheads go out.

I'm alone.

For a while.

And then I hear the sound I knew would come. The tile moves. A gentle rattle at first, then a long slow sliding rasp of tile upon tile. The stinking miasma from below insinuates its way into my cell, permeating my air, making it its own.

Then a soft scraping sound, like a molting snake sliding between two rocks to divest itself of old skin. Followed by another sound, a hesitant, crippled shuffle, edging closer.

I try to get away, to roll off the cot, but I can't move. My body won't respond.

And then I see it. Or rather I see a faint outline, greater darkness against lesser darkness: slim, between four and five feet high. It leans over the bed and reaches out to me. Tiny fingers, cold, damp, ragged fingers, flutter over my face like blind spiders, searching. And then they pause, hovering over my mouth and nose. My God, I can't stand the odor. I want to retch but the drug in my system won't let me do even that.

And then the fingers move. Quickly. Two of them slip wetly into my nostrils, clogging them, sealing them like corks in the necks of wine bottles. The other little hand darts past my gasping lips, forces its way between my teeth, and crawls down my throat.

The unspeakable obscenity of the taste is swept away by the hunger for air. Air! I can't breathe! I need *air!* My body begins to buck as my muscles spasm and cry for oxygen.

It speaks then. In Marion's little voice.

Marion's voice . . . yet changed, dried up and stiff like a fallen leaf blown by autumn gusts from bright October into lifeless November.

"Daddy . . . "

TESSELLATIONS

Gary Braunbeck

Braunbeck's novella is about a family and the ties that bind them together, even in death. Life and death are with us at all times, but it is only on Halloween that the barrier between the two is so permeable.

The L. Frank Baum character mentioned in the story, Jack Pumpkinhead, first appeared in The Marvelous Land of Oz, *the immediate sequel to* The Wonderful Wizard of Oz, *in 1904. A boy, Tip, makes the pumpkin-headed scarecrow in hopes of frightening the witch Mombi. Mombi, however, brings Jack to life. Although he appears in many of the Oz books—frequently replacing his ever-rotting head with a fresh pumpkin—he is featured in the twenty-third (the ninth penned by Ruth Plumly Thompson):* Jack Pumpkinhead of Oz *(1929). There's no direct connection between Baum's Jack Pumpkinhead and Halloween, but similar figures have become firmly associated with the holiday. He may have inspired Tim Burton's Jack Skellington, the "Pumpkin King" protagonist of the film* The Nightmare Before Christmas *(1993).*

"The whole conviction of my life now rests upon the belief that
loneliness, far from being a rare and curious phenomenon,
is the central and inevitable fact of human existence."
—Thomas Wolfe, "God's Lonely Man."

1

Make certain that all the tools you'll need for cutting materials for your patchwork quilt are properly sharpened so as to ensure each edge-cut is as clean as possible.

There is a certain night when stories of the darkness and that which calls it home are commonplace, accompanied by a host of spirits who wait patiently for their chance to set foot upon soil where unknowing humankind shrugs off its fear with laughter and candy and the celebrating of an ancient ritual. The mouth of this night is the choice hour for the formless, nameless, restless dead as they drift in low-moaning winds, searching for something—an errant wish, an echo of joy or terror, a blind spot in someone's peripheral vision—anything they can use to give themselves shape and dimension, however briefly. Many of them take joy in frightening the living out of the husk of their hearts; others wait quietly by the sides of those alone, a companion whose only wish is to bring a sense of friendship and comfort; still others are content to drift along, taking great pleasure in simply watching the bustle of humankind. The light that is shadowless, colorless, softer than moonglow shimmering over a snow-laden field, this light against which even the deepest darkness would appear bright as a star in supernova, this light is the place they call home.

The Romans called this night the Feast of Pomona; the Druids named it All Souls Day; in Mexico it is known as *el Dia de los Muertos.*

Most call it Hallowe'en.

The children here have a favorite story they like to tell one another as they pass down dark streets in search of houses whose porch lights bid welcome; it is a story that has been around as long as even many of the adults can remember, all about Grave-Hag and the Monster who lives with her, guarding her house from curiosity-seekers and passers-by until Hallowe'en arrives; *then,* say the tellers, *and only then, do the two of them slip out of the house and into the night, skulking through shadows toward some hideous task . . . .*

And so it begins, this tale best told under a full autumn moon when the wind brings with it a chill that dances through the bones and the sounds from beyond the campfire grow ominously semi-human.

A sad and damaged little town.

In its center, an October-lonely cemetery.

A lone figure holding two red roses stands near a pair of graves—one still quite fresh, the other settled, comfortable, long at home—listening to the echoing laughter of children dressed as beasties and hobgoblins.

A trace of unease.

The smoky scent of dried leaves burning in a distant, unseen yard.

A pulsing of blood through the temples.

And the unseen presence of regrets both new and old about to become flesh.

▼▼▼▼▼▼

2

Sort your materials into separate stacks, double check to make certain all detailing accessories have also been gathered and properly assembled into groups that correlate with their respective patches.

Marian knew that coming here first might be a mistake but, wanting to put off facing her brother, she came anyway. If the morbid tone of the phone call from Aunt Boots was any indication of what waited for her at the house, she wanted to avoid going there for as long as possible. After the paralyzing wreckage of the last few days she needed a quiet place to be alone, to find her bearings, to begin recovering from the awful thing that had happened and steel herself for whatever else was coming.

A small group of ghosts moved in the distance, bags in one hand, flashlights in the other, each giddy with anticipation of the treasures waiting—the candied apples, the chocolate bars, the popcorn balls and licorice sticks. Marian found herself envying them. The one night of the year when everyone—young and old, adult and child—cast away their fear of the dark for the sake of enjoying some good old-fashioned scares, decorating their houses with multicolored corn strung across doorways, pumpkins, stacked sheaves of straw leaning against the porch railings, even monster-masked scarecrows waiting on the steps.

The ghosts chanted: "*Tonight is the night when dead leaves fly/Like witches on switches across the sky . . .*"

Her smile widened as she remembered the path that ran next to the north side of the gate at Cedar Hill Cemetery, providing the trick or treaters with a shortcut through the gravestones. On many Hallowe'ens past she'd taken the shortcut herself, climbing the tiny embankment and following the path through this place of the resting dead until it emerged near North Tenth. Every town has that one special street where all the ghouls, withes, goblins, and their like head toward on Beggar's Night, that special street where the people gave out the best goodies in town, and in the case of Cedar Hill, that street was North Tenth. At least, that's the way it had been when Marian was a child. She wondered if that were still the case.

On those Beggars' Nights, so long ago, as she and Alan skulked their way past the tombstones and crypts and eternal flames, she would listen for the rhythmic thudding of the dead trying to beat their way out of their coffins—*Let-us-OUT! Let us OUT!*—all the while gripping her brother's hand *very* tightly as he spooked her with stories of warlocks and demons and fog-shrouded moors where rotting hands suddenly shot up out of graves to snatch away innocent children and drag them down into the pits of darkness where some terrible, slobbering, hairy, starving, unspeakably grouchy *Thing* waited. God, what fun it had been!

As the first group of ghosts disappeared into a thick patch of trees, another, smaller group of creatures emerged next to the gate and moved stealthily along; there were devils in this batch, werewolves and misshapen monstrosities followed by a princess or two who looked over their shoulders at a fast-approaching vampire brigade, who chanted around their plastic fangs: *"Tonight is the night when pumpkins stare/Through sheaves and leaves everywhere . . . "*

Not wanting to pull herself away from the sights and her memories, wishing there was some way she could avoid having to deal with any of this, Marian sighed, felt a small shudder snake down her spine, and, with a smooth deliberation she'd spent most of her adult and professional life perfecting, turned to the business at hand.

"Well, you two," she whispered, "looks like you can meet the rest of the family now." Then she chuckled, albeit a bit morbidly, under her breath. There was as much truth as there was displaced irony in that statement.

In the early days of Cedar Hill when the Welsh, Scotch, and Irish immigrants worked alongside the Delaware and Hopewell Indians to establish safe shipping lanes through places such as Black Hand Gorge, the Narrows, and Buckeye Lake, a devastating epidemic of cholera swept through the county. People died so fast and in such great numbers that corpses had to be collected in express wagons every eight hours. People were dying faster than healthy men could be found to bury them. But the " . . . plague" (as it was referred to in the journals of the time) passed, the town began to rebuild its citizenship (many widows and widowers moving beyond the barriers of their "own clans and communities" to marry and procreate), and later, in 1803, Cedar Hill Cemetery was established by the town's remaining founders as a place to permanently inter those who had died during the epidemic. Even though bodies were scattered for nearly seventy-five miles in all directions, groups of volunteers were assembled whose duty it was to locate and identify as many of the dead as possible, bring them back to Cedar Hill, and ensure each was given a " . . . burial befitting one of a good Christian community." Since most of the bodies had been buried with some sort of marker, locating them wasn't too difficult, nor, surprisingly, was identifying them, despite the ravages of time and disease on the bodies; every " . . . Hill citizen of Anglo descent" had been buried with a small Bible whose inside cover bore the name of its possessor, as well as those of his or her immediate family. Once found and returned, the bodies were placed in the cemetery according to family or clan, and over the decades it remained that way, albeit by unspoken agreement; members of families directly descended from Cedar Hill's founding fathers were buried in or as near as possible to the plats where their ancestors slept. But such were the ways of nearly two hundred years ago that a majority of people in Cedar Hill (both the cemetery and the town) were now related by ancestral blood; some within three or less generations, others quite distantly.

The graves of Marian's parents were located in front of a small abandoned church on the cemetery grounds. The long-forgotten architect who'd designed the church had, like Marian's dad, been an admirer of Antonio Gaudi's *Sagrada Familia* Cathedral in Barcelona. She thought of Gaudi now because he'd been something of a hero to her father, a man who laid bricks, cut lumber, and balanced beams for a living. Her parents had married on Hallowe'en nearly forty years ago (hence that day being the Big Celebration Day in the Quinlan household), then honeymooned in Barcelona where her father was awestruck by Gaudi's masterpiece: She could still recall the wonder in his face whenever he spoke of the experience, shaking his head in amazement that the plans for the cathedral's construction were so vast, complex, and precise it would take hundreds of years to complete.

"I wish I had that kind of talent," he'd said. *"To be able to create something like that, something that you don't just build, but something your soul goes into, something that will go on being created hundreds of years after you're gone, so you'll never be forgotten."*

"You know," said Mom, *"in that pamphlet they were giving out, it said that Gaudi was partly inspired by a quilt his mother had made when he was a child. I always wanted to get back to that quilt I was working on."*

Dad laughed. "Well, then; you got your dream project and I got mine."

A soft rustling of leaves somewhere behind told Marian that yet another band of demons and wizards and ghoulies was making its way through, but she did not turn to look; her gaze was still fixed on the crumbling church before her. Dad had always been fascinated by the church's obvious, though less extravagant, Gaudi influence, disregarding that the structure was merely the echo of another man's genius; from the blue marble inlay to the ominous gargoyles to the reproduction of the Virgin Mary over the rotting and sealed oak doors, the building seemed to apologize for what it wasn't rather than boast of its own virtues. Over the years sections of the front and side walls had collapsed, revealing parts of the interior. From where Marian stood she see exposed portions of both the belfry and the organ loft. Her dad once put in a bid to renovate this church, seeing it as his one and only chance to leave behind something to equal the glory of the *Sagrada Familia*—a wild and improbable dream, to be sure, but one that he'd nurtured for over half his life. It helped him to pass the long nights when his back pain kept him awake and the bills outweighed the bank balance—both conditions being part and parcel of an independent contractor's chosen occupation. The city later decided that renovating the church wasn't as important as building a new shopping mall and so dropped the project. Still, her father had kept the family gravesites near the structure; if he couldn't rest near his greatest triumph, he would rest near the symbol of what might have been.

Marian stared at the decaying church and sighed. Even in death her parents had to settle for second best. Their tombstones were side by side, with a third spot reserved—at his own request—for Alan.

There was no space for Marian; they'd always known she'd be the one to break away completely, to build a new life far away from this sad and tired little town that liked to call itself a city.

She hoped that her dad knew how hard she'd tried (*but not all* that *hard*, said something in the back of her mind) to get here in time.

Tried and failed.

As the beggars' retreating footsteps crunched through the dried leaves, Marian knelt down and placed one rose on each of her parents' graves, whispering a prayer taught to her by her mother at a time when the Mass was still spoken in Latin, the language of worship Mom had always preferred:

"*Intra tua vulnera aescode me,*" she said, hoping she was remembering it correctly.

She heard the approaching footsteps but paid them no mind.

"*Ne permittas me separari a te. Ab hoste maligno defende me. In hora mortis meae voca me; Et jub me venire ad te, Ut cum Sanctis tuis laudem—*"

She saw a shadow slowly rise up behind her to stretch over the graves.

Spindly, almost twig-like arms and hands; a slender, tubular trunk; and a large, rounded head with its stem jutting upward.

She smiled and felt a tear slip from her eye.

For a moment, kneeling there under the entwined shadows, she was six years old again, listening as Mom read to her from L. Frank Baum's *The Marvelous Land of Oz*, describing how Tip came to build Jack Pumpkinhead who would be his partner as they went in search of the Tin Woodsman and the Scarecrow. Jack Pumpkinhead, with his round eyes, three-cornered nose, and mouth like a crescent moon, living under the watchful gaze of Mombi the Sorceress. Jack had been Marian's imaginary friend through most of her childhood, always next to her during math tests at school, sitting by her bed at night after the Friday chiller movies to guard against the creatures she feared were waiting under the bed or crouching in the closet. Only she could see him then.

Just like now.

She was so pleased to have him with her again she almost couldn't finish the prayer.

"*In sa . . . sa . . .* "

"*In saecula saeculorum,*" said Jack Pumpkinhead behind her. "*Amen.*"

"Amen," echoed Marian.

Something brushed against her shoulder, then rested there.

A soft whisper, full of October melancholy: "Let's sing our special song."

She reached up and, not turning to look, touched the twig-fingers of Jack's hand. She knew his being here was just a bit of childhood whimsy she had never been able to discard (after all, a good actress was supposed to be able to *recall* feelings and experiences to enrich her performances), but, still, it amazed her how easily she was able to slip back into the Marian of childhood and find she still fit.

The shadow softly sang: "*Ol' Jack Pumpkinhead lived on a vine/Ol' Jack Pumpkinhead thought it was fine . . .* "

She thought there was something different about his voice, but not wanting to ruin this wonderful surprise by analyzing it to death, she answered in song, just as she always had: "*First he was small and green, then big and yellow/Ol' Jack Pumpkinhead is a very fine fellow.*"

She rose to her feet and turned to embrace him, dearest Jack who'd come back one last time to protect her from the grief and guilt she couldn't face.

His eyes glowed a sickly orange-red, casting diseased beams through the early evening mist. He was hunched and shuddering, a soul-sick animal.

"I thought you had forgotten about me," he said, and it was then that Marian knew what was different about his voice; it was no longer the light, happy tenor that she'd given him, it was the sound of an empty house when the door was opened, an empty bed in the middle of the night, or an empty crib that never knew an occupant; dead leaves skittering dryly across a cold autumn sidewalk; the low, mournful whistling of the wind as it passed through the branches of bare trees; it was a sound so completely, totally, irrevocably *alone* that hearing it just in a whisper's instant made her long for the warmth and safety of home and hearth: even if her company there was now superfluous, at least she wouldn't be alone as *that sound*.

A thin trickle of blood dripped from the corner of Jack's mouth.

She closed her eyes, wishing away this friend from her childhood, this dear friend who had been so horribly changed and misshapen—

—but why?

She felt the twigs that were his fingers grip her wrists. "I've really missed you, Marian. Please don't be afraid. It's so cold here, so lonely where everyone is sleeping and you have no friends."

She opened her eyes, knowing—praying—that his return to her was just a hallucination brought on from lack of sleep the past three days. Maybe she'd just seen one too many houses where the children had constructed horrible Hallowe'en effigies from straw and old clothes, then set them on the front porch to scare the monsters away.

One of Jack's twig-fingers broke through her flesh. She felt the warmth of her blood as it seeped out, staining her blouse's white sleeve.

Jack was wearing one of Dad's old shirts, the one Marian had bought him for Christmas last year.

"Jack Pumpkinhead is still a fine fellow," he whispered to in that voice. "The quilt's almost finished. And we put a light in the window for you."

The wind grew stronger. One of the bells in the church steeple swung back, then forth, ringing twice.

"Please come home now," said Jack. "You're needed."

Her blood was soaking into the bark of his hand.

Her legs began to buckle as Jack leaned forward to cover her lips with his crescent mouth in a welcome-home kiss.

Something moved in the distance; another group of tiny spirits broke through the bushes on their way to claim sugary treasures, singing: "*A goblin lives in OUR house, in OUR house, in OUR house, a goblin lives in OUR house, all the year round . . .*"

Marian broke away, slipped, and fell on top of her father's grave, half expecting his desiccated hands—

—*Let us OUT! Let us OUT!*—

—to break through the soil and grab her.

The church bell rang once more, a brassy chime, Mom's voice singing to her when she was young and sick with fever.

The children's laughter lingered as the bell fell silent.

Autumn-dried leaves blew past her, a few clinging to the hem of her dress.

Jack Pumpkinhead began to fade; color went first, draining away until Jack and everything surrounding him looked like part of an old sepia-toned photograph, disappearing very slowly, an image retained on the inside of the eyelid for an instant, then gone.

Rising unsteadily to her feet, Marian saw the second set of footprints that followed her own and stopped at the edge of the graves.

No. It wasn't him. It couldn't *have been. Someone must have been here before me and I just didn't notice the prints, that's all.*

As convincing an argument as it was, it still didn't stop her from half-sprinting out of the cemetery to her car. She needed to rest but couldn't until she saw her brother. Maybe seeing Alan after all this time would help to purge her of whatever had made her resurrect Jack.

She started the car, saw the ghostly effigies resting on the porches of nearby homes, and noticed the small gash on the side of her wrist.

Some of her blood dripped onto the steering wheel.

"*Goddammit,*" she whispered, bandaging the wound with her handkerchief. "Welcome home." Then, trying to force away the image of Jack's glowing eyes and the mournful echo of his voice, drove away toward the place she once called home.

3

Place two fabrics right sides together, making sure to rotary cut strips the width of the square template you are using; if the strips weren't compatible when you cut them, do so now, layering them, and making individual alterations as necessary in order to achieve conformity.

The house of her childhood stank of grief; even from outside, she could smell it. She slipped her key into the front door lock and held her breath, anxiously aware of the sound made by the October leaves as the wind scattered them across the pavement; the dry whisper of sorrow, the crackle of old guilts trying to step out of dank corners and pull her in with the stab of twig-fingers.

It wasn't your fault you missed the funeral, she told herself, hoping to believe it. *Alan will understand.*

She swallowed, released the breath she had been holding in since pulling up, felt her skin tingle with the bleak cold of descending night, and walked inside. Closing the door, she started slightly at the sound of the gas furnace snapping on, then removed her coat and tossed it into an empty chair.

Although it was barely seven-fifteen the interior of the house held layers of blackness that deepened with every step she took. She longed to be back in Los Angeles, but she had a responsibility to her brother.

Responsibility. It seemed like such a corrupt word right now. Alan had given over most of his youth to the responsibility of caring for the family; keeping the house clean, doing the laundry, the cooking, shopping for groceries, never moving out because that would've meant having to face the world without the security of a family—something Alan, for all his good intentions, could not live without. He had always been terrified of other people; it was amazing to Marian that he'd ever been married.

Next to the front door was a table that held three glass bowls filled with goodies for the trick or treaters; two were overflowing with candy, the third contained—

—she felt a shiver, shook it away—

—pumpkin seeds. Even now, with Dad less than a week in his grave, Alan still held fast to the family traditions; Dad always gave each beggar a handful of pumpkin seeds so they could plant them and grow their own jack o' lanterns for next year.

"Alan?" she called. When there was no answer, she walked into the living room. Ice formed on her spine as she saw what was draped over one of the recliners.

The stale aroma of a dead woman's perfume enveloped her as she leaned down toward her mother's old housecoat. It was arranged in such a way that Marian almost expected to see Mom descend from above, slip neatly into it, and ask that the television be turned on, she'd had a long day and was tired and wanted to see her shows, please.

Marian's faded and discolored First Communion dress was arranged on the couch so that it faced the television, Grandpa's old but well-kept three-piece (what he called his "church suit") was in the reading chair in the next room, a book on its lap, the light turned squarely on the open page.

"Alan? It's me."

No response.

She headed for the kitchen, stepping over innumerable pizza boxes and fast-food bags along the way. Her foot pressed down on something that was either growing brittle and stale or softening in decay; all she could be sure of was that it crunched under her foot and then squirted something thick and warm. She leaned against the wall and shook her foot until the muck fell away from the sole of her shoe, shimmering, landing in the center of long rug in the hallway. Leaning down, Marian saw that what she thought was light playing glissandos across its surface was actually a group of blowflies fighting for a prime location. She pulled in a deep breath, covering her mouth with her hand as she continued to the kitchen.

The table was cluttered with dishes holding the remnants of meals begun but never finished, now teeming with tiny crawling things she didn't want to look at. The sink was filled with various pots and pans, their exteriors badly scorched, some of the burnt black flecking away and mixing with the off-white, fungal-looking matter that floated on the surface of the still water, bloating the moldy bits of food that sucked in the water like sponges.

The Alan she remembered would never have allowed the house to disintegrate like this.

She thought she heard a muffled sound somewhere nearby, then something small and sticky squirmed up her calf. Marian let out a sharp cry of revulsion and batted it away, then returned to the living room and its collection of familiar outfits waiting for occupants.

"Alan? Come on, this isn't funny. Are you here?"

This was bad enough.

Upstairs was worse.

Grandma's favorite nightgown was spread upon the bed in the guest room, a Bible open next to the emptiness reaching from its right sleeve, a glass of orange soda sitting on the night stand next to the bed so she could have a drink if she was thirsty. That was always Grandma's nightly routine.

The bathroom was unspeakable; great smears of what must have been rust covered the inside of the bathtub, the toilet lid was up, the rim of the bowl nearly overflowing with waste, and the sink looked to have been recently vomited in. Underneath everything was a scent of copper. The cumulative stench made her gag, but she managed to open the medicine cabinet above the sink and remove what she needed to clean and dress the wound on her hand, which she did out in the hall.

But the worst thing, the most terrible thing, was in Alan's old bedroom.

On the bed lay his ex-wife Laura's black silk robe, the sash still around its waist, opened to expose the bright red bra and panties arranged in their proper positions—

—and the glistening, well-used, wet indentation of the mattress under the crotch of the panties, as if—

—*god, no*. Alan would never do something like . . . like that.

Brother, she thought.

My brother.

What's happened to you? Where are you now?

Marian shivered.

All through the house were the garments of the dead, the almost-forgotten, the moved-aways and just-lefts, awaiting someone to wear them, each carrying the scents of those who once did.

Back downstairs, Marian debated whether to continue searching the house or just grab her coat and cut her losses.

Something winked at her from the living room.

She turned toward it. It winked again, bright and fiery.

"Alan? Alan, please answer me if that's you."

"Over here." Though barely more than a whisper, his voice nonetheless startled her.

As her vision adjusted to the darkness, she saw her brother for the first time in what seemed an eternity; not a savior born under Bethlehem's star, not possessing the greatness that led other men to become leaders and poets and visionaries, not a man who wanted to change the world or even harbored the abilities to do so; just a son, a brother, a fine boy, a decent enough man who'd brought no shame to his family's good name, who'd studied for passing grades in school, who'd tried to build his own life with a fine woman by his side to love him, but then came the day she didn't love him anymore and so left, and with her his will to believe himself special in any way.

He was sitting very still, watching the cigarette between his index and middle finger burn down until the heat threatened to singe his flesh. He was wearing an old baseball cap, its brim turned toward the back of his head like a baseball catcher without the mask. He was a man she barely recognized—hair too gray for his thirty-three years, eyes that were dark and hopeless, blueblack crescents underneath, lines etched so deeply into his skin they looked like cracks in plaster; he looked as if he'd crumble into dust if shaken hard enough.

From outside came the cries of "*Trick or treat, smell my feet, give me something good to eat!*"

Alan turned his head toward the gray of evening that swept in from a wide part between the curtains over the only window in the room. "What? Did you expect to find me holed-up in the john weeping endlessly into a cracked mirror?" He took along drag from the cigarette.

Marian followed his gaze.

We put a light in the window for you.

There was, indeed, a light there; a big, beautiful jack o' lantern, facing outside, the candle within burning brightly, welcoming lost children home. Why hadn't she noticed that when she was on the front porch?

Because it wasn't there, came the answer.

"Are you here because you want to be," asked Alan, "or because Boots called you?"

"Because Boots called me." "Boots" was their nickname for Aunt Lucille, their dad's sister, for as far back as they could remember, though neither of them could have told you why she was called that.

Alan gave a short, empty laugh. "An honest one. I figured it was either Boots or Laura. God bless 'em both." He took another deep drag as he stared into the dim of fast-approaching night meandering in from the large window at the front of the house, bringing with it a grayness that did not so much cast shadows as rearrange them to suit the feelings of the thing that looked out from behind his eyes.

"I killed a man last night."

Marian heard the words but did not allow them to register. She took a deep breath and crossed toward her brother. "Alan, listen, I know you haven't been well, Laura told me, and I—"

"I really did it, you know. I really did. It helped. It helped a lot."

Marian knelt down, took away the cigarette and crushed it in the ashtray, then held Alan's hand between both of hers. "You look like hell. You need to get some sleep."

"Did you say hello to Jack? He's missed you quite a lot." Alan adjusted the baseball cap, then turned on a small table lamp, the light revealing Jack slumped on the couch, his legs spread wide and twisted, his arms akimbo, the glow of his inner-candle fire nearly extinguished. He looked no different from a dozen other homemade figures on a dozen other porches tonight.

Except that he was still wearing Dad's shirt.

Marian was too shocked to react right away.

Between Jack and her First Communion dress lay a thick, neatly-folded coverlet, its patchwork surface a mosaic of colors and shapes.

The Story Quilt, a family heirloom passed down from nearly a century-and-a-half ago, a perpetual work-in-progress; through various descendants to her great-grandmother to her grandmother to her own mother, the Story Quilt had always been a constant in Marian's life. Her mother had hoped Marian would continue working on it when the time came. Marian shivered at the thought; Mom had been working on it the day she'd suffered the stroke that would kill her within a few hours. Marian couldn't bring herself to touch the damn thing after that.

A click, a hiss and a hum; the distinctive noise of the television coming on, the picture coming into focus, the static fading out of the speaker as the sound of some country music program faded in.

She looked at her brother. He was not holding a remote control.

Because the set never had one.

"Seven-thirty," said Alan matter-of-factly. "Time for *Hee-Haw.*"

Marian balled her hands into fists, feeling her knuckles crack under the pressure. *Hee-Haw* had been her parents' favorite program.

"Come on, Alan. I'm going to take you back to my hotel room, get you cleaned up, then we're going to get something to eat, and then you're going to get some sleep. When you wake up we'll finalize details here, and you'll come with me to L.A. for a while."

"I can't leave. The family depends on me."

Only now did she notice that Alan was wearing Dad's favorite pajamas, the gray ones with the white and blue diamond pattern. A small bloodstain near the crotch had dried and stiffened.

Don't say anything, she thought. *Not yet.*

And don't think about that thing sitting on the couch behind you.

Alan smiled, a crooked smile that held some residue of the brother she remembered. "I'm sorry, Sis," he said, sitting down at the table. "I suppose I ought to explain things." He took hold of her shoulders. "Look at you, so nervous and frightened. Did I do that? I'd apologize for scaring you but, after all, it's Hallowe'en. Don't go anywhere, I've got something to show you.

It was going to be a surprise from Dad, but . . . ." He walked over to the television and pulled the cover off a new VCR perched atop the set. "Dad bought this not too long ago, after you got that national perfume commercial. He taped all of your commercials and those cop shows you did bit parts on. He was really looking forward to your sitcom pilot next month."

Marian was silent. For most of her adult life Dad had never said anything about her chosen profession, never given the smallest hint that he was proud of her accomplishments. She closed her eyes and tried to imagine her father sitting alone in this room, watching his daughter over and over as she sprayed herself with perfume or ran screaming from make-believe thugs. Would he have done all that if he hadn't been proud?

Why didn't you ever tell me? she wondered.

The doorbell rang, followed by a children's chorus: "Trick or treat!"

Alan raised a finger to his lips, signaling silence, then rolled up the sleeve of the pajama top, revealing the dark-stained bandage around his wrist.

The bell rang again, followed by insistent knocks. The children giggled.

"Just a minute," called Alan, walking over to the slumped figure of Jack Pumpkinhead, whose light was nearly gone. Alan grabbed Jack's stem and lifted the top off, then ripped the bandage from his arm.

"W-what're you doing?" said Marian.

"Jack needs a recharge. I can't deny him a drink when he needs one." Alan bit into his wrist and tore away a large, crusty scab, freeing his blood to drip into Jack's head.

The blood ignited Jack's inner flame, a brilliant flash of orange-red that sent a chill through Marian. She found herself staring at an exposed patch on the quilt, trying to remember when Mom had made it; she stared at it because as long as her gaze was elsewhere, she wouldn't have to acknowledge what was happening in the periphery, wouldn't have to admit that she wasn't imagining it, that Jack Pumpkinhead was rising off the couch, towering almost seven feet, reaching for his stem-cap.

So she stared at patch on the quilt, remembering . . .

High school was a breeze for Marian. Girl's Glee and Drama Club her sophomore year; Cheerleading Squad, Concert Choir, and Acting Ensemble her junior year, Pep Squad Captain, president of Dram Club, Swing Choir, and both the Homecoming Court and Prom Queen her senior year. If anyone's high school years could be called dream-perfect, they were Marian's. In those three years her sense of balance and security remained; every time she looked into the faces of her parents and brother, that expression of pride was there. A few times it bothered her that there seemed so little she could do to help her family, but those feelings quickly vanished when she told herself that she was doing everything she could to make them proud of her and that should be enough. She was only human.

A few weeks before graduation she was ecstatic to find she'd been granted a scholarship at one of the best Liberal Arts schools in the country, and—after a summer stint as a bank teller—she went on to study Theatre, the biggest love of her life. Mid-way through her second year she auditioned on a whim for a traveling company production of 'night, Mother and nearly fainted when the call came to her dorm room informing her that she'd been cast in the role of Jesse. It paid three hundred and twenty-five dollars a week, including the producers picking up all traveling and motel expenses.

It was a young actress's dream come true.

Through those first two years at college she rarely saw her family, except at Christmas. She wrote home once a week, faithfully, and never once had to ask them for any money to help her get by; she'd snatched up a teller position at the town's local bank and worked two days a week and on Saturday, which netted her enough money for groceries, books, and twice-monthly partying on the town; it was on one of these excursions that she read the notice for the traveling company's auditions. Theatre was her major, so she decided to go for it; after all, why go on studying to become an actress when there was a chance she could actually be one?

Her parents were very pleased with her good fortune but did not hide their dismay that she wouldn't be finishing college. Marian eased their fears by reminding them that she was a fine bank teller and could always find a job if things fell through. Mom and Dad had both smiled, but she sensed her confidence did little to ease their fears.

During the first leg of the tour she contented herself by having a brief affair with the stage manager and devouring her good reviews, which came as a relief to her. Marian had never been much for the Method school of acting but found herself, during the first weeks of rehearsal, wishing that she'd given Stanislavsky more credit and attention. The role of Jesse was a bitch to play, requiring her to show an emptiness and isolation she couldn't even imagine. Having never really experienced that measure of desperation she didn't know if she could pull it off.

Then her mother died of a stroke.

Marian was unable to cry at the funeral, though she very much wanted to. She was too busy studying her dad's ragged and lonely face, telling herself that *that* look was exactly what she needed for Jesse.

After the funeral she tried to talk with Alan, who only sat at the picnic table in Aunt Boots's back yard while the other guests snacked on after-burial munchies and offered polite sympathies. Eventually she wound up going off with Laura, then Alan's wife. Laura, though always beautiful, looked frazzled around the edges to her.

"What's wrong?" asked Marian.

"Your brother," she said. "I understand that when someone dies you have a natural proclivity to talk about them, but since your mother died he keeps . . . I don't know how to say it . . . *going on* about things." They sat in two folding lawn chairs at the far end of Boots's yard, picking at the two pieces of pound cake they'd taken from the snack table.

"He keeps talking about how bad he feels that your parents never had any time to do things they wanted to do."

"Why? It's not like that was his fault."

"Try telling *him* that!" said Laura. "At first I thought it was just the natural guilt someone feels when a parent dies, you know? 'I should have been around more.' That sort of thing."

"And now?"

"It's turning into a real problem. He can't stop thinking about it. He's had two states for the last week: he's either screaming at me like a lunatic or he's damn near catatonic."

Marian looked over at her brother, who was sitting very still, staring down into his drink, not looking up, not saying a word.

"Like now?" she asked Laura.

"Like now."

After the cautious kisses and awkward embraces she bid goodbye to her Dad, promising to write and call every week, and returned to Connecticut to resume rehearsals.

Though she did write, somehow the time to call became nonexistent during the hectic first weeks after the show hit the road, but Marian didn't worry over it; everyone had a copy of the schedule and knew where the show would be and when. If there was any problem Alan would call her. Or Laura would do it for him.

So she didn't worry. She also never really mourned her mother, though she loved her very much; from what Laura had said, Alan was mourning enough for the whole family.

She worried over her brother, but not too much. It seemed self-defeating.

The tour completed its first seven-month run well in the black; both Marian and Anna—the woman playing Thelma opposite her, a well-known soap-opera actress whose name on the marquee was the box-office draw—renegotiated their contracts for a second tour to commence six months down the line. During the break Marian appeared in an Equity dinner theatre production of Peter Schafer's *Black Comedy* in her first true ingénue role. The notices were excellent, and by the time the production closed Marian's reputation as an Actress To Watch was established.

Ten days of rehearsal was all it took for her and Anna to get their chemistry going again, and by the time the play began its second, sold-out tour, they were performing better than either of them ever had before.

Then came the night in Boston that Anna buckled over backstage one night after the curtain call, complaining of chest pains. She was taken to the hospital where she was diagnosed with angina. With only one performance left at the current stop, the producers decided Anna's understudy would go on the next night; after that, they wouldn't say.

Two hours later, after Marian and an admirer from the audience—a sinewy, rugged man named Joseph Comstock—had brought each other home (rather noisily) in her hotel bed, the phone rang and she answered it, sweaty, sore, and out of breath.

As she brought the receiver up to her face, she caught a glimpse of the small digital clock/calendar on the bedside table and noted, for some reason, that it was the same date as her mother's death nearly two years ago.

She listened as her aunt gave her the news.

Dad would now be keeping Mom company. Marian hung up and lay in Joseph's arms, thinking: *Father, my dear father. Where are you now?*

Joseph stayed for the rest of the night, comforting her, listening to her, but becoming more and more pensive as morning approached. As he was dressing to leave Marian realized—with much surprise—that she felt much better.

She wanted very much to see him again after that evening's performance, and he nodded his mute agreement. The funeral would be the day after tomorrow, so Marian planned to do one more performance then have her understudy take over for two nights while she went home. The fact that Joseph Comstock—this wonderful, understanding man—would come again tonight and see her through gave her some strength.

One of the most curious things about human behavior is how people will form a bond with those nearest them when bad news hits; the comforting words of an acquaintance suddenly become a declaration of love and caring never before imagined, the empathetic embrace of a friend becomes a life preserver thrown out before the third sinking, and the companionship of a stranger, a stranger who listens and who in their silence seem to give so much, this companionship often becomes the only thing one can count on until the storm has passed. Marian suddenly felt as if she'd been with Joseph Comstock all her life, and on that morning she felt secure.

Something in his face and behind his eyes told her that he knew her, and that she was being looked after.

He didn't show up for the performance that night, nor did he appear afterward. Marian returned to her hotel room alone. She watched television until nothing but snow stood before her gaze, and sometime around six a.m. fell into an uncomfortable sleep.

She was awakened a little after ten by her understudy knocking on the door. Marian rose, still groggy, threw on her bathrobe, and answered.

Her understudy told her how sorry she was about Marian's dad. Marian thanked her for her sympathy, wondering why her understudy hadn't simply called.

"Have you seen this morning's paper?" she asked Marian.

"I don't usually bother with local papers when we're there less than two weeks."

Saying nothing, her understudy handed Marian a copy of the morning edition, the lower half of the front page facing up. Marian took it, read the bold-faced words above the story, and felt her knees begin to buckle.

There was a picture of her sweet admirer next to an old photo of a house that had seen better days. A quick glance at the headline—MAN KILLS WIFE, CHILDREN, SELF—and the next thing she remembered was her understudy leading her back to the bed. Somewhere between dressing and talking to the police she threw up, but when she finally boarded the plane for home, Marian found that she didn't feel quite so bad anymore. A little shaky, yes, but not bad.

Not bad at all.

Until she found herself in the living room of her family's house, on her knees and staring at the quilt-patch that her mother had made from her graduation gown, depicting a lone shadow-figure standing on a stage beneath the brightly focused beam of a spotlight, staring at this patch so she wouldn't have to acknowledge the thing in her peripheral sight . . . .

4

Cut squares and nip off the corners, then chain pieces by picking up two squares at a time so they don't shift out of alignment. Alternate the fabric that is on top (this pair light on top, that pair dark). The chain can be as long as you want.

Jack's crescent mouth grew wider, a hideous phantasm of a smile. "Jack Pumpkinhead still works fine, honey," he said with *that voice*, then strode into the front room and filled his hands with candy and seeds before opening the front door.

Before Marian could move, Alan was behind her, one arm around her waist, the other across her collarbone, his hand covering her mouth. "Don't make a sound," he said. "I don't want to frighten the kids." Then: "I sent a telegram to your hotel in Boston the day your company arrived there. That was *five days* before Dad died, almost a week before Aunt Boots called to give you the news. So don't bother lying to me about how you didn't know in time, okay?"

Outside, the children were going *ooooh* and *aaaah* at the sight of Jack as he distributed the treats.

"Well, lookee what we got here," said Jack. "Is that a witch I see?"

Giggles and cackles.

"And what's this? Old Count Dracula come to sink his fangs?"

More giggles, excited whispering, the sound of wrapped candy softly plopping into paper bags as Jack lowered his voice and spoke to the children like a co-conspirator. "Come to the shortcut in the cemetery tonight and I'll have more surprises for you and your folks—make sure you bring 'em along. We're gonna have a bonfire and tell ghost stories. Remember to bring your pumpkins and your magic seeds." A soft, spattering sound— pumpkin seeds being sprinkled into each waiting bag.

The children all shrieked with joy, savoring the delight on this night when it was okay to be scared, then bustled off the porch toward more shivers and shakes.

"How did that man make such a neat costume, Daddy?" "I don't know

but it sure was spooky, wasn't it?" "Can we go to the bonfire later? Can we, huh?"

Jack Pumpkinhead closed the door, then turned to face Alan and Marian. His eyes, nose, and mouth glowed a deep, deep red now. A trickle of blood spilled over the jagged bottom of his mouth and spattered over the collar of Dad's shirt. He stood there, branch-arms crossed in front of him, long twig-fingers pressed against his shoulders; the sentinel.

. . . A goblin lives in OUR house, in OUR house, in OUR house . . .

Alan released Marian and she collapsed onto the couch, her heart hammering against her chest.

Alan adjusted his baseball cap once more, then knelt in front of her and took her hands in his. "There are some Eastern religions that believe a person's final thought before dying stays in the spot where that person dies, just sort of hanging in the air, waiting for someone to claim it. But the thing is, that final thought contains everything that ever went through that person's mind while they were alive, so whoever"—he looked at Jack and smiled—"or whatever claims that final thought has the power to bring that person back to life in some form."

Jack gave a nod of his head.

"For years I've been asking myself if I was my own man or just the sum of my family's parts," said Alan. "Now I know." He pointed at Jack.

"People die, Alan," said Marian. "Maybe some of them don't die pleasantly but they do die and there's nothing we can do about it except let them go." God, was this real?

Alan glared at her. "You're goddamned right some of them don't die pleasantly. Would you like to know about Dad's last night on this earth?"

"I don't see what that would accom—"

"The thing that's always pissed me off at you, Sis, is that you passionately avoid anything even remotely unpleasant—and I'm well aware of how you can let people go, thank you very much."

"That's not fair."

"Not fair?" He pulled away from her and began pacing the room. "Dad weighed ninety-one pounds when he bought it. He laid right there on the couch, in these pajamas, watching your tape over and over again, all the time hoping you'd show up to see him. He wanted to set things straight with you, wanted to let you know how much he loved you and how proud it made him that you were the first person in this family who didn't have to wash the stink of blue collar labor off your hands at the end of the day.

You were the one who was going to keep the family name alive long after the rest of us lived, died, and were buried in this fucking town!

"The man couldn't even get up to *pee* he was so eaten alive. I had to help him. I took a cup and opened the fly of his pajamas and took . . . took him out down there and put him in the cup and . . . and it hurt him *so much*, I saw the pain in his face as he tried to force the piss out of his bladder, he tried so hard, and when it finally came out"—he looked down at the stained pajama crotch—"it was more blood than piss. Then he *thanked* me, for chrissakes! Told me what a good boy I'd been and asked me to tell Mom to buy a real good pumpkin so he could carve it up nice and scary for *you*. How the hell could I remind him that Mom's been dead for four years?" He cast a pleading glance at Jack, who nodded, then gestured him *Continue*.

"So I went out and bought some pumpkins. He was bound and determined to build you a 'real' Jack Pumpkinhead for Hallowe'en. 'This'll show her how much I love her, how proud I am.' Christ! You'd've thought he was finally getting to build his own *Sagrada Familia*, his own little masterpiece, like Mom's unfinished quilt." He closed his eyes, took a deep breath to calm himself down, then started banging a fist against the side of his leg.

"He dragged out that old Oz collection that Mom used to read to you just so he'd make sure to get Jack's face exactly right. I lost count of how many times he cut himself while carving. He stopped worrying about it after a while and let himself bleed into the pumpkin, all over the seeds . . . "

Marian thought about the third bowl of treats: *Be sure to bring your magic seeds.*

" . . . but he couldn't finish," continued Alan, "the effort got to be too much. He made me promise I'd finish building Jack for you. Then he just . . . laid there. He was minutes away from dying and all he cared about was making you happy. He stared at the shadows and mumbled about Gaudi, coughed up a wad of something I don't even want to *think* about, and died. No wailing, no wringing of the hands, no sackcloth and ashes. Just sickness and pain and sadness, memories of mopping up the vomit in the middle of the floor because he couldn't get to the bathroom in time, or wiping his ass when he shit himself because he was too weak to get off the couch, or cleaning the blood from his face and nose after a violent coughing fit, all the time having to look in his eyes and see the regret and fear and loneliness in them—*that's* how his existence culminated; in a series of sputtering little agonies to signal the end of a decent man's life. And he never stopped hoping that you'd come see him."

Marian felt the heat brewing in her eyes, reached up to wipe away the first of the tears, and swallowed back the rest as best she could. She would not give in, would not feel bad, would not show weakness. "I'm sorry it was so hard on you, but people die and there's nothing—"

"—we can do about it except let go, yeah, yeah, yeah—you played that scene earlier, remember?"

The doorbell rang again: *Trick or treat, smell my feet* . . .

Jack opened the door. The children gasped in awe.

"Well, lookee here. Is that a mummy before me? And Spider-Man—I take it that the Green Goblin and Doc Oc are otherwise engaged?—how good of you to come!"

The giggles again, the whispers and *aaaah*s.

"So," said Alan, "what do you think?"

She was surprised at how steady her voice was. "I think that Aunt Boots told me you haven't been sleeping well, and you know what happens when a person doesn't get enough sleep? They start having waking dreams."

"That's my Marian, always the rational one. Okay, fine—if I'm having waking dreams, then explain Mr. Pumpkinhead over here."

"Come to the shortcut in the cemetery tonight," called Jack as he began closing the door, "and be sure to bring your pumpkins and your magic seeds."

She didn't have an answer. Alan was throwing too much at her too fast, she needed time to sort this out, she needed order and calm, needed .

"Alan, look, I . . . " She had to buy some time. She was letting herself be drawn into his world of grief and dementia. How romantic and seductive it seemed when one was this close. "I couldn't bring myself to come here any sooner. I couldn't just sit around here waiting for Dad to die. I can't stand anything like that, I never could. I need to be where everything is vibrant, healthy, *alive* . . . goddammit, I was too scared, I admit it, it's just that . . . I didn't know Dad wanted me here so much."

"Would it have made any difference?"

A beat, a breath. "No."

Jack poked his head around the corner. "Good girl."

Alan said, "Jack told me something about Mom. Did you know she always thought you didn't love her? She told Dad she thought you were embarrassed to have her for a mother because she was just an ignorant factory gal."

Marian felt something expand in her throat. "God, Alan, I *never* felt that way. I always thought she was a good—a *fine* woman. She almost never complained about things and always managed to come up with some extra money whenever we wanted something special. I don't think I ever saw her buy a thing for herself. How could she believe I thought so . . . *little* of her?"

"You never told her." His voice was empty.

Then Jack spoke. "The last time you kissed her, you were nineteen years old."

Alan took her hand. "Remember how we used to make fun of her getting tired so quickly? It never crossed our minds that she might be sick. That's why we were so shocked when she died."

Marian looked at Mom's favorite chair and remembered the way Dad had cried when he'd found her there, dead. "She never said anything."

"It wasn't her way," said Alan. "But we were her family. If we'd cared a little more, we would've known."

Marian hugged herself. She could feel the affliction and loss trapped within this house; the loneliness . . . *God*, the loneliness.

"It becomes easier, once you accept it," said Alan. "Love it. Embrace it as you would a child. Hold it against you. Let it suckle your breast like a baby would. Let it draw the life from you. Love the pain. Love the emptiness. Love the guilt and remorse, cherish the loneliness, love it all and it will make you strong. It's what makes us whole."

"No. I can't—I *won't* feel bad about not knowing. They could have said something to me, could have talked to me, asked me things. It's not my fault."

"I never said it was."

Marian rubbed her eyes, then held her hands against them for a moment. "Alan, please, I don't know what to . . . what to say or do . . . I don't understand how—"

"—how this started?"

Marian pulled her hands away from her face as Jack answered the call of more trick or treaters. "Yes."

"It started a long, long time ago, before either of us were ever born, I guess. But I suppose, for us—you and me—it started with Grandpa . . . "

It was three weeks after Alan's ninth birthday, about seven-thirty in the evening. Marian and her brother were settled in front of the television to watch the next hair-raising episode of *Batman*. The Green Hornet and his trusty aid Kato were making a special guest appearance tonight, so both were barely able to contain their excitement, stuffing popcorn into their mouths by the plentiful handful.

The opening credits were just starting when there came a knock at the front door; it was a timid, almost inaudible knock. Alan and Marian looked at each other.

"I'll bet it's that goony paper boy coming to collect," said Marian.

"He'll go away if we don't answer," said Alan. "That always works."

The knocking persisted just as they were being told it was another normal day in Gotham City as Commissioner Gordon and Chief O'Hara were—

—Knocking again. Louder this time.

"Alan? Marian?" called Mom, "will one of you answer the door? I'm in the bathroom."

When Alan looked at her and didn't move, Marian angrily slammed down her popcorn and stomped over to the front door, really ready to chew that paper boy out. How could anyone come around when *Batman* was on? You did *not* knock on their front door on *Batman* nights, and you *sure* didn't do it tonight of all nights, when the Green Hornet and Kato were going to be on! Whoever this was had better have a good reason, or Marian would . . . well . . . she'd sure do *something*, you could bet on that.

She had to fiddle with the deadbolt for a moment, and then with the stupid, stupid, *stupid* chain lock, but then it was off and dangling and the front door was wide open—

—and she was staring at Boris Karloff. She knew it wasn't *really* Boris Karloff, but the man who stood on their front porch looked enough like him to make her shiver for a moment, wondering if she hadn't woke up in the middle of a horror movie.

The man looked her up and down a couple of times, cleared his throat (it sounded like he really needed to hawk up a loogie), and spoke.

"Would you be Marian?"

"Yessir."

"Your mom at home?"

"Yessir."

"Would you mind gettin' her for me?" His voice was like rusty nails being pulled out of old and warped wood. It gave Marian the creeps.

She turned to call and saw her Mom standing in the doorway to the kitchen, an expression on her face that told Marian not only did Mom know who this man was, but that he was a Big Deal. You Stuck Around for Big Deals. Marian's mother wiped her hands on a small towel, but when she was done she didn't put the towel over the back of a chair or lay it on the table; she just let it drop to the floor.

Marian walked over and picked it up, but Mom took no notice. By this time Alan was standing by the door, looking at Mr. Karloff.

He wore an old floppy brown hat, straight-legged gray pants, dusty boots, a collarless green shirt with sleeves rolled up to the elbows. He was carrying a small suitcase. Mom said nothing for what seemed the longest time, and Marian found herself becoming afraid of this man, who looked at them through the reddest eyes she had ever seen, and even from where Marion was standing, the smell of tobacco and iodine was overpowering. His skin was all scratched and stained, like a piece of old leather left out in the sun too long. Marian looked at Alan, then to Mom, who was breathing very slowly, the strange expression on her face suddenly gone, replaced by nothing at all.

"Glad I found you at home," said Mr. Karloff.

"I worked day shift at the plant now," said Marian's mother.

"Days, huh? I'll bet that makes it nice for the kids here."

"I always have time for them," said her mother, which seemed to hurt Mr. Karloff in the doorway; his eyes started blinking rapidly and the hand which held the suitcase shook a little.

Marian was just plain scared now.

She looked more closely at Mr. K. and noticed that one of his eyes was half-closed, a deep cut on its lid, covered in iodine.

"I been in the V.A. hospital," he said. "I suppose you know that?"

"I heard about it," said her Mom, shaking.

From the living room Robin exclaim, "*Holy hornet's nest, Batman!*"

Piss off, Boy Wonder.

"You look good," said Mr. K. to Mom.

"You look like hell."

And that's when it happened.

Marian had never seen anything like it before. Mr. K. took a deep breath, turned as if he was going to leave, but then he seemed to spot something outside of the house that scared him. A lot. Enough to make him not want to go outside, and for the first time Marian realized that she wasn't alone in feeling this way; maybe everybody once in a while looked out their front doors or windows and saw something that scared them, things that maybe even weren't there most of the time but you saw them anyway. Maybe this old man could see something out there, maybe in a tree or behind a bush or a parked car or even in the shape of a cloud, but he saw it out there, he sure did, and he didn't want to walk out the door to face it, so he let his suitcase slip out of his hand and drop to the floor, turned back around, and without looking at Marian's mother started to speak.

His voice came out in low wheezes, fizzling in and out like whispers do. "I only got about twenty dollars to my name right now and I vas just wonderin' if . . . if you would mind terribly loaning me a couple of bucks. I ain't had me a thing to eat since about noon yesterday and I'm a bit hungry. I can't use this money for food 'cause it's got to go for a room of some kind. I wouldn't be bothering you otherwise honest. If it ain't too much trouble would you let me sleep on your sofa, just for tonight, until I can find me a room at the 'Y' or something? I haven't been feeling too good lately and don't got the energy to go stompin' around town tonight looking for a place. I'd much appreciate if you'd lend me a hand for the night. Whatta you say?"

His last few words were so soft Marian could barely understand what he was saying, so she looked up at her mother but Mom was staring down at her feet like she did when she wished things weren't happening, so Marian reached up and took her hand.

"Close the damn door and take your shoes off," said her mother, turning away and wiping something off her face. "I'm just getting ready to fix us some hamburgers." Marian wondered why Mom was telling Mr. K. that, because they'd just finished doing the supper dishes; they'd already *had* hamburgers.

Mr. K. was taking his boots off when Mom turned lack around.

"And I don't want hear any of this shit about you getting a room at the 'Y' or anything like that. If you help out you can stay here as long as you like. Just don't get in my way too much." She turned back into the kitchen, then called over her shoulder: "And I don't allow liquor in this house. Read me there?"

"I read you," said Mr. K. He looked at Alan and Marian, tried to smile, raised an eyebrow, and released a breath that sounded like he'd been holding it for years.

"So," he said, "you two are Alan and Marian, huh?"

"Yessir," they both replied.

"Don't you all be cablin' me 'sir,' that's too formal."

"What should we call you?" said Alan.

"I'd be your grandfather, boy. 'Grampa' will do just fine."

The next few weeks were a great time for Marian and her brother. Grampa taught them how to play Poker, how to make meatloaf and homemade bread, told them stories about how he fought in the war, helped with the dishes, and even did a lot of extra work on the house for Dad. Eventually Mom allowed Grampa to buy some beer, but only in a six-pack and only once a week. This seemed to make Grampa happy because he and Dad could drink while they were playing cards and smoking cigarettes. Marian really liked her Grampa, and so did Alan, but neither of them understood why Mom wouldn't talk to him more. When they finally asked her she just shrugged her shoulders and said, "It's of no concern to someone your age."

Grampa began getting some kind of checks in the mail shortly after he came to stay, but he never spent any of the money on himself—aside from a six-pack and a couple packs of cigarettes; he always gave a lot to mom, then spent the rest on Marian and her brother. Clothes, records, a new board game, whatever they wanted. And he always had such wonderful stories to tell them.

Toward the end of his first summer with them the card game became less frequent and he took to watching television. His favorite show was *Hee-Haw* and, even though she and Alan hated it, Marian would watch it with everyone else. Grampa seemed to enjoy having company while he sang along—always off-key—to the country music songs.

By fall all he did was go shopping once a week. He couldn't help Dad much with the house for some reason, and Mom wouldn't let him cook because she said he needed his rest.

Every once in a while Grandma came over to see how he was doing. Marian knew that her grandparents had not been married for a long time, but never asked anyone how come, or why Mom seemed to be made at Grampa about something, or why Grampa was doing all these things for them.

Winter rolled in and Mom rented Grampa a hospital bed from the drug store. Grampa seemed happy when it arrived because, he said, the sofa was starting to get to his back. When the checks came he insisted on paying the rental fee for the bed, but because of that he couldn't buy Marian and Alan anything. But they didn't mind that at all.

It was the first of December when things started going sour. Marian hadn't realized how sick Grampa was until then; he dropped several pounds in a short period of time and began spending more time in bed. He always kept apologizing to Marian and Alan because he didn't feel well.

One afternoon Marian and Alan came home after doing a little Christmas shopping, loaded down with presents from a small curiosity shop two blocks away. Both Mom and Dad were working extra shifts for the overtime, so the only person home was Grampa. They came through the door, set down the presents, and were just heading up stairs to get the wrapping paper and tape they'd stashed earlier when Marian heard Grampa call her name. He was in the bathroom, which was just off the kitchen, so Marian came back down and stood by the closed door.

"What is it?" she said.

"Could you . . . ?" His voice trailed off and a terrible sound came from him. The closest Marian had ever heard to that sound was from a small child down the block who once fell on the sidewalk in front of their house and scraped his knee badly; the child fell, rolled over, took in a sharp mouthful of air and held it until he was shaking from head to heel, his face turning red, his veins pounding in his head, but then he finally released the scream—

—but not before he let out one hideous little *squeak!* before the cries exploded.

That little squeak was the sound that followed Grampa's "Could you . . . ?"

"Grampa?" said Marian.

No answer.

She knocked on the door. "Grampa? Do you need some help with something?"

Squeak!

Marian pounded on the door with her fist. "Grampa! Grampa do you need—"

And from the other side of the door, so quietly she almost mistook it for the sound of her own breath leaving her throat and nose, Marian heard Grampa say one word: " . . . help."

She tried to yank open the door but Grampa had used the little eye-hook on the other side, and try as she did, pulling with all of her strength, Marian could not get the door to open, so she ran over and pulled open the cutlery drawer and took out Mom's biggest cutting knife and jammed it deep inside the crack beside the door and pulled it upward, then had to turn it around so that she was *pushing* it upward, instead, and somewhere she could hear Alan calling for her, asking *what's wrong Sis what is it* but she couldn't answer him, she needed to hold her breath and answering him would mean she'd have to let her breath out and if she did that she'd never get the door opened and if she never got the door opened then Grampa might die, so she closed her eyes and gritted her teeth and pushed up with knife as hard as she could, making sure to wiggle it from side to side as much as she could (a villain on *The Green Hornet* had done something like this once) and just when her arms were throbbing and her shoulders were screaming and she felt like she was going to pass out from being so dizzy, three things happened: she felt the hook wrench from the eye, heard the *thwack!* of the metal against the doorjamb, and released her breath it one massive puff; then she threw down the knife and threw open the bathroom door and saw that Grampa leaning against the sink, shaking, his face so red and sweaty Marian thought he might scream, but he never did, not once, not ever, because he was too busy gripping the sides of the sink, his wrinkly old arms looking like old sticks you used for kindling in the fireplace, and she realized that Grampa had been trying to sit down on the toilet when he got sick or felt the pain or whatever it was that happened to him, because the toilet seat was up and his pants were halfway down his legs but his underwear had gotten stuck and they had a big red stain spreading all over them and the more the blood spread the more Grampa shook and squeaked, and he pulled away one hand and said . . . " . . . these damned underpants, I can't never . . . ohgod . . . " and he tried to grab hold of them with one shuddering hand but he couldn't reach them, it hurt him too much, but then Alan was there, on his knees next to Grampa, grabbing the ruined shorts and pulling them down so they could get him on the toilet, and they did, she and Alan, Marian holding him around the waist while Alan took hold of his legs and they eased him down onto the toilet seat and all the time Marian just wanted to cry for how much Grampa was hurting, but Alan was being the big cry baby, whining over and over *Grampa I'm so sorry you're so sick I love you I don't want you to die*, but then Grampa was on the toilet and breathing okay, his face wasn't as red now, that was good, and Marian almost smiled when he looked up and winked at her.

"Got it that time, didn't we?" he said. He reached out with an unsteady hand and grasped Marian's arm.

"Thank you both very much," he said. "Now go." There was a hideous sound from below his waist as his ruined bowels exploded.

Marian grabbed Alan and went back out, closing the door behind them. They stood there for a moment listening for him in case he needed more help.

"You two can go about your Christmas wrappin' business," he said. "I'm almost eighty years old and I been in worse situations than this. I got me no intention of dying on a goddamned toilet seat. Now move along."

They were heading back upstairs for the paper and the tape when Alan squeezed her hand and said, "He's so sad."

"He's just sick," replied Marian. "He'll be better."

"I don't want him to feel sad. I love him."

Marian looked at her brother and shook her head. "I love him, too. But I don't think that's enough to make him not sad anymore."

Alan looked heartbroken. "Not even a little?"

Marian shrugged. "Maybe a little. But what good's *that*, what good is a little?"

A few days later Grampa insisted that he was well enough to go do his own Christmas shopping, and Marian's mother made no attempt to stop him. When he came back with all the presents his check allowed him to afford he told everyone that he'd bought himself—of all things—a 45 r.p.m. record of some Neil Diamond song.

"I never bought a record before, but they was playing' this in the store where I was shopping and it was kinda pretty (which he pronounced 'purdy') so I bought it." After dinner when Mom was doing the dishes he went into the front room and put the record on Mom's old table-top hi-fi, then sat in the reading chair and listened to it. Marian stood in the doorway and watched Grampa as he closed his eyes and leaned back in the chair and seemed to . . . *deflate* like a balloon, sort-of, just a little bit.

She didn't say anything because he looked tired, so she just stood there and listened to the record. It was a song called "Morningside" and it was about this old man who lived alone and had no friends and when he died no one cried, and then people went to collect his things and they found this table he'd been building for a long time, and it was a beautiful table, the most beautiful table any of them had ever seen, and when they were moving it, they turned it upside-down and saw that he'd written a message underneath it that said *for my children.*

It was the saddest and most awful depressing song Marian had ever heard; sadder even more than "Puff, the Magic Dragon."

When the record was over the arm lifted up and swung back and set itself back down, the needle easing into the grooves with a brief *clikkity-click* before the song started again.

Grampa opened his eyes and rolled his head over and saw Marian standing there.

"That's kinda pretty in a . . . in a way, ain't it?" he asked, gesturing for her to climb up on his knee.

"Yes, it is," she said. And that wasn't a lie; it *was* pretty, but it was sad, too, and Marian didn't understand how something could be so sweet and so depressing at the same time.

Later that night Grampa was lying in his bed in the middle room and asked Mom if he could have a while alone with Marian and Alan. Mom said sure and kissed him goodnight. It was the first time Marian could remember seeing her mother kiss Grampa.

After Mom went to bed Grampa told Alan to go get him a small a can of soda pop and some chips, he was going to tell them a special story. When they were all situated and sipping away, he began.

"I wasn't too good to your mother when she was a little girl," he said. "I was young and had all this Get Up and Go. I liked to drink me a mighty good time, I did . . . so I's never around much. That's probably why your Grandma and me never made it. I left her to take care of your mother all by herself. That was back during the Depression. Thing's weren't good for a woman with a kid and no husband then. County had to finally take your mother away and put her in a children's home for a few years . . . until your Grandma could get enough money to give her a proper upbringing.

"Anyway . . . that ain't got a lot to do with what I wanted to tell you, but I seen the way you two've been watching me and your mother, and I know you're not stupid kids so you were probably wondering. I just thought you ought to know." He reached down under the blankets and took out a bottle. It was like no other bottle Marian had ever seen. It was made out of stone, and stoppered with an old cork. She was about to ask what it was but then Grampa started talking again; and all the time, his finger kept stroking the bottle's stone surface. "I got myself shot overseas during the war and it did something to the bones in my leg and the doctors, they had to insert all these pins and build me a new kneecap and calf-bone—it was awful. Thing is, when this happened, I only had ten months of service left. I was disabled bad enough that I couldn't return to combat but not so bad that they'd give me an early discharge, so they sent me back home and assigned me guard duty at one of them camps they set up here in the states to hold all those Jap-Americans.

"I guarded the gate at the south end of the camp. It was a pretty big camp, kind of triangle-shaped, with watchtowers and searchlights and barbed wire, the whole shebang. There was this old Jap tailor being held there with his family and this guy, he started talking to me during my watch every night. This guy was working on a quilt, you see, and since a needle was considered a weapon he could only work on the thing while a guard watched him, and when he was done for the night he'd have to give the needle back. Well, I was the guy who pulled 'Needle Patrol.'

"The old guy told me that this thing he was working on was a 'memory quilt' that he was making from all the pieces of his family's history. I guess he'd been working on the thing section by section for most of his life. It'd been started by his great-great-great-great-grandfather. The tailor, he had part of the blanket his own mother had used to wrap him in when he was born, plus he had his son's first sleeping gown, the tea-dress his daughter had worn when she was four, a piece of a velvet slipper worn by his wife the night she gave birth to their son . . . .

"What he'd do, see, is he'd cut the material into a certain shape and then use stuff like paint or other pieces of cloth stuffed with cotton in order to make pictures or symbols on each of the patches. He'd start at one corner of the quilt with the first patch and tell me who it had belonged to, what they'd done for a living, where they'd lived, what they'd looked like, how many kids they'd had, the names of their kids and their kids' kids, describe the house they had lived in, the countryside where the house'd been . . . it was really something. Made me feel good, listening to this old guy's stories, 'cause the guy trusted me enough to tell me these things, you see? Even though he was a prisoner of war and I was his guard, he told me these things.

"It also made me feel kind of sad, 'cause I'd get to thinking about how most people don't even know their great-grandma's maiden name, let alone the story of her whole life. But this old Jap—'scuse me, I guess I really oughtn't use that word, should I? Don't show the proper respect for the man or his culture—but you gotta understand, back then, the Japs were the enemy, what with bombing Pear Harbor and all . . . .

"Where was I? Oh yeah—this old tailor, he knew the history of every last member of his family. He'd finish talking about the first patch, then he'd keep going, talking on about what all the paintings and symbols and shapes meant, and by the time he came round to the last completed patch in the quilt, he'd covered something like six hundred years of his family's history. 'Every patch have hundred-hundred stories.' That's what the old guy said.

"The idea was that the quilt represented all the memories of your life—not just your own, but them ones that was passed down to you from your ancestors, too. The deal was, at the end of your life, you were supposed to give the quilt to a younger member of your family and it'd be up to them to keeping adding to it; that way, the spirit never really died because there'd always be someone and something to remember that you'd existed, that your life'd meant something. This old tailor was really concerned about that. He said that a person died twice when others forget that they'd lived.

"'Bout six months after I started Needle Patrol the old tailor came down with a bad case of hepatitis and had to be isolated from everyone else. While this guy was in the infirmary the camp got orders to transfer a hundred or so prisoners, and the old guy's family was in the transfer group. I tried to stop it but nobody'd lift a finger to help—one sergeant even threatened to have me brought up on charges if I didn't let it drop. In the meantime, the tailor developed a whole damn slew of secondary infections and kept getting worse, feverish and hallucinating, trying to get out of bed and babbling in his sleep. He lingered for about a week, then he died. As much as I disliked Japs at that time, I damn near cried when I heard the news.

"The day after the tailor died I was typing up all the guards' weekly reports—you know, them hour-by-hour, night-by-night deals. Turned out that the three watchtower guards—and mind you, these towers was quite a distance from each other—but all three of them reported seeing this old tailor at the same time, at exactly 3:47 in the morning. And all three of them said he was carrying his quilt. I read that and got cold all over, so I called the infirmary to check on what time the tailor had died. He died at 3:47 in the morning, all right, but he died the night *after* the guards reported seeing him—up till then, he'd been in a coma for most of the week.

"I tried to track down his family but didn't have any luck. It wouldn't have mattered much, anyway, 'cause the quilt come up missing.

"After the war ended and I was discharged, I decided to take your Grandma to New York. See, we'd gotten married about two weeks before I shipped out and we never got the chance to have a real honeymoon. So we went there and saw a couple of Broadway shows and went shopping and had a pretty good time. On our last day there, though, we started wandering around Manhattan, stopping at all these little shops. We came across this one antique store that had all this 'Early Pioneer' stuff displayed in its window. Your Grandma stopped to take a look at this big ol' ottoman in the window and asked me if I thought there were people fool enough to pay six-hundred dollars for a footstool. I didn't answer her. I let go of her hand and went running into that store, climbed over some tables and such to get in the window, and I tore this dusty old blanket off the back of a rocking chair.

"It was the quilt that Japanese tailor'd been working on in the camp. They only wanted forty dollars for it so you bet your butt I slapped down the cash. We took it back to our hotel room and spread it out on the bed—oh, it was such a beautiful thing. All the colors and pictures, the craftsmanship . . . I got teary-eyed all over again. But the thing that really got me was that, down in the right-hand corner of the quilt, there was this one patch that had these figures stitched into them. Four figures. Three of them was positioned way up high above the fourth one, and they formed a triangle. The fourth figure was down below, walking kind of all stooped over and carrying what you'd think was a bunch of clothes. I took one look and knew what it was—it was a picture of that tailor's spirit carrying his quilt, walking around the camp for the last time, looking around for someone to pass his memories on to because he couldn't find his family."

By now he'd slipped the stone bottle back under the blankets. He lay on his side, looking at them, his bone-thin hands kneading the pillow. "That's sort of what I'm trying to do here, you understand? I know that if I was to die real soon I wouldn't have no finished tapestry to show . . . mine's got all these holes in them. I wanna have a whole one, a finished one. I don't much fancy wandering' around all-blessed Night because God don't like what I show Him. I want to fill in the holes I made." He smiled. "I love you two kids. I truly do. And I love your mom and your Grandma and your dad, too. They're all real fine people. I just want you all to . . . I just wanted to tell you about that."

"Grampa," said Alan, softly. "Whatever happened to that man's quilt?"

Grampa pointed to his top blanket. Marian and Alan looked at one another and shrugged, then Grampa started to pull down the blanket but didn't have the energy to finish, so they did it for him.

Underneath the top blanket lay the quilt. Even though they could see only very little of it, both Alan and Marian knew it was probably the most beautiful thing they'd ever see.

"I wanna . . . I wanna be buried with this," said Grampa. "I already told your dad that." He gestured for Marian to lean down close so her could kiss her good-night. "Hon, I need to be alone with your brother for a few minutes, okay?"

" . . . 'kay."

"Good girl. You run along to bed and I'll see you in the morning.

Marian decided to sleep downstairs that night in case he woke up and needed something, so she went into the living room and laid down on the sofa.

She watched as Grampa gave Alan the stone bottle and explained something to him. Her brother looked so serious as he listened, more like an adult than a nine-year-old. Then she lifted her head and overheard Grampa say, " . . . wait here with me until your dad gets home . . . " but then she was too tired to keep her head up.

She woke up around two-thirty in the morning. Lifting her head, she saw her Dad's workboots setting next to the door. She wondered if he'd had a good night at work. Maybe he could quit soon, like he wanted, and start his own building business. She hoped so. It bothered her that Dad was never home nights.

She heard Grampa tapping against the railing of his bed with something. She went to him.

"You got good ears, little girl. You'll go far." He tried to raise himself up but couldn't.

"I gotta pee," he said. Marian wanted to go wake Alan or Dad but Grampa wouldn't hear of it. He finally laid down and pointed to his drinking glass. "Why don't you empty that damn thing out and I'll . . . I'll use it." She did as he asked, carrying the glass into the kitchen and pouring its contents down the sink. When she came back in Grampa had his hands at his sides and was staring at the ceiling.

"Marian, I hate like hell to ask this, hon, but, well . . . I can't seem to move my hands. Would you mind, uh . . . ?" Marian already had him out and in the cup, so there was no need for him to finish.

"You're a good girl," he said. "You make your mom and dad real proud, you hear?"

"Yessir," she said. His eyes then lit up, but only for a few moments.

"How's about puttin' . . . puttin' my record on real low so's we don't wake the whole house? I'd kinda like to hear it."

Again Marian did as she was asked.

When she came back Grampa was desperately trying to empty his bladder but couldn't get anything to come out. She wiped his forehead, then put her hand on Grampa's abdomen, pushing down gently. After a few moments the pained expression on his face relaxed as the urine started to fill the cup. He soon finished and nodded his thanks. Marian took the cup into the bathroom to empty it.

It was full of blood.

She washed her hands afterward and then asked him if there was anything else he needed.

"Could you maybe fix it so my record would play over a few times?"

She did, then kissed him good-night again, and went back to the darkness of the living room, where she sat on the sofa and listened for a while before falling asleep again, hoping that Grampa would feel better on the morningside.

When she woke up there was Mom, holding Grampa's head in her lap, rocking back and forth, stroking his hair and crying. "Yes, that's it . . . go to sleep, shh, that's it, you rest now. You rest . . . ."

Alan came over and hugged Marian. They stayed like that until Mom looked up and saw them and told them to come over and say good-bye to Grampa. Marian was suddenly afraid of the thing that mom was holding in her arms. It wasn't Grampa. It didn't even look like a human being.

She pulled away from her brother and saw that some of Grampa's blood was still on her fingers.

It took her forever to get that hand clean.

5

Press seam allowances toward the darker fabric. Cut apart in pairs. The squares are in their proper color placement and ready for sewing. Place the first pairs right sides together and sew into four patches.

Alan pressed the top of his baseball cap to make sure it was still in place, then reached into one of his pants pockets and removed the stone bottle. "When Dad came home that night Grampa had both of us cut our thumbs and put some of our blood into this bottle, along with his. Then he gave it to Dad to keep until it would be time to pass it on to me." He shrugged. "Guess it was some kind of Irish thing, some legend that our great-great-grandfather brought with him when he came to the States."

"What are you supposed to do with it?"

Alan shook his head. "I can't tell you yet." He lifted the bottle into the light, slowly turning it from side to side, admiring it. "There's something like twelve generations' worth of Quinlan-men's blood in here." He looked straight at her.

"You're now the only Quinlan woman left who can willingly carry on the family's bloodline, so it's your time now."

Of all the things that raced through her mind at that moment, Marian found herself focusing on one word: *willingly*.

Alan took hold of her arms and pulled her to her feet. Jack reached up and—like something out of a cartoon or a Washington Irving story—removed his head from his shoulders and held it in front of him, his twig-fingers grasping the stem and removing it from the top of his head.

"Not yet," said Alan to Jack as he took hold of Marian's injured wrist, removed the dressing, and pushed on her wound until it burst open, dripping blood into the stone bottle.

Jack guided his head under the flow, trying to ignite his flame with Marian's blood.

"*Stop it*," she said through clenched teeth, wriggling against her brother's grip but he was stronger than she remembered. He increased the pressure on her arm, pulling it toward the pumpkin while Jack loomed closer, his glow dimming, his form somehow larger and more powerful.

"We need to do it this way," said Alan. "Just a little more blood, please."

"Jack Pumpkinhead's lonely, hon," said the thing holding its own pumpkin head. "I want our family together again."

Marian took a deep breath, twisting her wrist as some of her blood slopped into the jack o' lantern, then kicked back, the heel of her shoe connecting solidly with Alan's shin. He howled and released her and Marian made a beeline for the back door because there was no way in hell she'd make it past both of them to the front door. Ignoring Alan's calling her name, she made her way into the kitchen and toward the back porch when she was struck in the face by a tree limb and fell backward against the sink counter.

Jack Pumpkinhead help to right her, then stroked her hair. "I'm sorry," he said. "I didn't mean to hurt you like that, but you just *have* to understand."

Alan was next to her now. "Look, Sis, I don't mean to go all Sleepy Hollow on you or anything, but you need to understand that . . . I'm sick. Just like Dad and Grampa and every other man in the Quinlan line going back for . . . I don't know how long."

Her face was throbbing and it hurt too much to move. "Wh-what's wrong?"

"Colon cancer. It runs in the men in the family."

"Have you seen a doctor?"

"No need to."

"Then h-how do you *know*?"

"The man I killed last night came here and told me."

Marian felt her shoulders tense.

"It'll all make sense soon," he said, and kissed her cheek. For some reason Marian then remembered that both Grandma, Grampa, Mom, and Dad had all died in this house, and all were buried in the Quinlan area of Cedar Hill Cemetery, along with their direct and distant ancestors.

Alan looked at the blood on his fingertips—whether it was his blood, Marian's, or some of that from the bottle, there was no way to tell. He turned toward one of the upper cupboards and began drawing faces on them. "I know," he said, "that there's nothing we can do about the dying, you're right there. But there is something we can do about the part that comes *after* the dying, I found that out last night." He finished the first face—it looked a lot like Grampa's—then started another. "I suspected for a long while that there might be ways to do it, I even tried a few—but I imagine Laura or Boots told you all about that."

Marian offered no response. There was no need.

"Okay," he said. "The first thing you've got to ask yourself is this: what kind of tapestry, quilt, whatever, are you supposed to offer up to the Divine Art Critic when you reach the great Gates? Answer: a beautiful one. Because if it's not beautiful, that means it's not finished." He stopped drawing Mom's face and leaned toward Marian. "But what happens if—regardless of how much you try to make it otherwise—your tapestry doesn't turn out to be so beautiful? What happens when you offer it up after death and the big Somebody shakes Its omnipotent head. 'But it's the best I can do!' you cry. 'I really tried, but I just didn't have all that much nice stuff to work with!' What happens then? Easy; you and your tapestry are thrown out to wander around all-blessed Night."

"I love you, Alan, but you're not making sense."

"Stay with me, Sis, you always were the best listener in this house."

Marian stared. "Please let me go, Alan."

He wasn't listening. "Families talk about 'the ties that bind' a lot, you ever notice that? You know how that phrase originated? From Story-Quilt

makers. I kid you not. See, there's a method of quilting called 'tessellation,' which means 'to form into or adorn with mosaic, a careful juxtaposition of elements into a final, coherent pattern.' Since the quilt-makers had to employ endless tessellations in order to join the various patches together in order to form the story of their family, the threads they used were referred to as the 'ties that bind.' Don't say I never taught you anything.

"Well, care to guess what those 'ties' are in our family, Sis? Love? Loyalty? Personal integrity? Think about. What is it, above all else, that ties you to your family?"

Marian looked down at her legs; they were shaking. She looked at the bloody faces on the cupboards; they were drying. She looked in her brother's eyes; they told her nothing.

"I don't know," she finally said.

"Guilt," replied Alan. "Guilt is what ties us all together, whether we admit it or not. Oh, sure, it's easy to dismiss that idea. 'I do it because I love you.' 'I do it because she's been so good to me.' ' I don't care how sick or senile he is, I'm going to see him because I love him.' "

Alan laughed; it was breaking glass. "What a fucking bill of goods! You don't do it because you love someone, you do it because your conscience won't leave you alone if you *don't*. It's not so much that you love that senile, oatmeal-drooling caricature of a human being in the nursing home bed, you do it so you can *clear your conscience*. 'Well, at least I came to see him. At least I did that.' It's all such *shit*. I'm not saying that love doesn't have a small part in there, it's just that we tend to ennoble our actions by saying they're done out of love, when in reality they're done because we're scared to death of never being able to forgive ourselves if we don't at least make the gesture!"

"God, Alan, that's a horrible way to think." Marian was so terrified she was on the verge tears, and the last thing she wanted to do now was give into it.

"Is it?" replied her brother. "Think about it. It's what drove Grampa to us, isn't it? His last-ditch attempt to clear the slate, to beautify *his* tapestry. There's so much that gets buried under the weight of compiling years, so many memories that can find a dark, dusty little corner to hide in, so much unresolved guilt that builds up unnoticed that we can never be sure if we have really made our tapestries whole, beautiful, acceptable, cha-cha-cha. What if Mom, Dad, Grandma, Grampa, all of them, what if when they got to wherever it is we go they pulled out their tapestries and—*voila!*—right smack in the middle of it was all this shit they'd forgotten about, all these disfiguring little unremembered guilts that crept into to the artwork, huh? Easy—they get banished to ever-blessed Night. But what if there was a way to *fix* those tapestries? What if there was a way to remove the ugliness from them? They'd *have* to be accepted then, wouldn't they? *Wouldn't they?*" He was almost right in her face now, and Marian, for the first time she could remember, was very much in fear of her brother.

"G-Given what you've s-s-said," she whispered, "I s-s-suppose they would almost h-have to be. Yes."

Alan's body suddenly released all its tension. His eyes grew less intense, his shaking stopped, and he smiled his crooked grin. "Good," he said, taking her hand. His touch was almost too gentle, and Marian noticed with a numb horror that the moist blood squishing between the flesh of their hands was not . . . was not at all that unpleasant.

She closed her eyes and swallowed.

"Marian?"

"Yes?"

"I'm going to tell you how we can do it. I'm going to tell you how we can make their tapestries beautiful once again."

" . . . all right."

He leaned over and kissed her cheek. She stared at the faces he'd sketched on the wall, wondering why none of them were dripping because his blood was so fresh.

"Last night, around six or six-thirty—I wasn't paying that much attention—I was sitting in the front room, just . . . just sitting, I guess. I kept thinking about all that had gone wrong between Laura and me, and try as I did I couldn't find the reason for us breaking up like we did.

"You have to understand that the nights were terrible for me, have been for the last eight months since she left, and I . . . I can't stand sleeping alone. The fact that everything in our house had her smell on it didn't help matters any. The chairs, the curtains, our bed—God, especially our bed! She took everything with her when she left, except her smell. It's the sweetest smell I ever knew. Everything about her was the sweetest I'd ever known.

"Anyhoo, I started going through the closet one day and I found her old black robe and a bra and panty set she'd left behind. They were covered with her scent. It was incredible. I'd hold them next to me and lie on the bed and just . . . just *breathe* it in.

"It was so overpowering that I could almost feel her there with me. So I tried laying all the things out like she'd be wearing them if she were still there, and I'd lay there and close my eyes and smell here, so near, so full and ready, and I could sense her body, every *part* of her body, there in the bed next to me. So one night I didn't open my eyes, I let her scent carry me as far as it could, and when I reached out to touch her I could *feel* her skin, and it was so warm, so near, so *ready* . . . it was like we'd never been apart. I made love to her that night like I'd never done it before.

"Afterward, I closed my eyes and let the scent cover me. And then I sensed him in the room with me. I looked up and he was just standing there, shaking his head at me."

Marian shuddered. "Wh-who?"

"He said his name was Joseph-Something-or-Other, I don't quite remember."

Marian swallowed. Once. Very loudly. "Comstock?"

"What?"

"Comstock. Was his last name 'Comstock'?"

"How'd you know that?" Alan didn't wait for an answer. "So Joseph says to me, 'You should turn the gas off.' So I did. I even opened all the doors and windows so nothing would go wrong. Then he told me what he'd come for, and asked me if I'd lead him to where he needed to go.

"I led him to the spot in the front room, under that hanging of *The Last Supper*, the spot where Grampa died. He stood there a long time, like he was searching for something, then he turned around and said there'd been a lot Grampa had forgotten about.

"I took him upstairs next, to the guest room where Grandma died. The first thing he did was ask me how she died, and I told him about how Grandma moved in with us after Grampa's funeral because she felt so bad about things, and I told him about how I'd bring her an orange soda every night so she could read and take her pills, then about that last night when I brought her the soda and she hugged me so hard and kissed me and told me I didn't have to sit with her if I didn't want to, she'd understand. I told him about how I left her and how, the next morning, we found her dead because she'd taken all her pills. He just nodded at me and then sat on the bed and then found the things she'd forgotten about, as well. Then I brought him down here and he went right to the spot Dad died—I didn't even have to show him where. He stumbled a little bit because of all the guilt and regret Dad had inside him when he died.

"The hardest part was finding Mom. I knew she had her stroke at the market and that she DOA at the hospital, but the hard part was going to be finding the *exact spot* where she died. We wandered through the store for a while—they're open all night now, isn't that nice?—until we hit the 'Miscellaneous' aisle. She'd gone into that aisle to get some more thread to use on her story quilt because she was almost finished with it. Joseph turned around and told me it started there, the first waves of dizziness and pain and breathing problems.

"Mom always checked-out through Lane 7 because it was closest to the pay phone so she could call a cab. And she *had* to call a cab—I'm sure we all know—because all my life I've been too chickenshit to drive. If I did drive then maybe—

"—but that's nothing. We walked outside and he found the spot where it really hit her.

"Then he looked at me.

"Took three steps.

"And found her.

"Those fuckers at the hospital *lied* to us when they said she died on the way! She was dead before they even *got* there. He even told me what it was she whispered to some woman who was near.

"She was worried that no one would remember to feed the dog, Midnight. Our dog that's been dead for six goddamn years!

"By then Joseph had everything that he came for, so we went back to the house and down to the basement. He found Dad's old toolbox and took out the hammer.

" 'It's the only way you can find out,' " he said to me. I knew he was right. I took the hammer from him and turned it around so the claw was facing out. He turned and knelt down in front of me like he was praying. I put my free hand on the back of his head to steady myself because I was so scared, but he said, 'Don't be afraid,' and I wasn't. It was all there waiting for me, all the ugly little guilts that had found there way into the tapestries.

"I took a breath, pulled back with the hammer, started crying, and swung down at the back of his skull. I remember thinking his head made an interesting sound when it split open. You know the sound a watermelon makes after you cut it down the center and then pry the halves apart? It's not really a pop or a crunch, but something wet *in between* the two? That's what it sounded like when I opened his skull. Then I had to put the hammer down and pry the halves apart with my hands.

"God, it was a *mess*, but it was worth it. They all spread out before me; all their tapestries with all that unremembered, disfiguring guilt. And I fixed them, Marian, I did it. I wallowed in the ugliness, then took it away, removed it from all of their tapestries until all that was left were the whole, finished, beautiful tessellations of love and memory and happiness. And the things I *found out!* Did you know Mom once had an affair she never told anyone about? It was with some old friend from her days in the Childrens' Home. It lasted three weeks and then the guy moved away. Afterward she had these little fantasies about him, which is why she and Dad seemed to have such a new marriage after their twenty-fifth anniversary. Dad never suspected, and wherever he is now, he'll never know because *I've* got that memory, that guilt, right up here in my mind and in my heart. It's part of my tapestry now and can't touch them where they are.

"Oh, and Dad. You know why he always had a problem with his mother? Bitch used to beat him with her shoes when he was a little boy. High-heeled shoes. Just take them off and pound at his back until it looked like Swiss cheese. Poor Aunt Boots used to stick him back together afterward and then they'd hug each other and hide in their room, scared to death she'd bust in with a ball bat and kill them both. And everyone wondered why he didn't cry at her funeral. But the thing is, he never blamed her—he always felt guilty because he was such a bad boy and got his mother mad enough to do that to him! Well, he doesn't have that anymore, *I've got it!* And I hope his mother is burning in Hell right now, I really do.

"I can't tell you what it felt like, taking it away like that. It feels awful now—the worst thing I've ever felt—but at that moment, up to my eyes in it, it was the greatest sensation I've ever known. But when it was over, Joseph's body flopped over onto its back and spoke to me. The two halves of his face kind of squirmed like worms, but I could understand him just fine, and he told me about you, about how it had to be like this. Then he fell back down and stopped moving.

"I wanted to call someone and tell them all about, how miraculous the whole thing was, but I knew if I called Aunt Boots or Laura they'd have the Twinkie Mobile over here in no time flat, so I did the next best thing; ;I walked over to the Western Union office and sent you a telegram. I knew where your show was so it was easy. It was always great of you to send us your schedule, really it was.

"And here you are. It's great to see you, Marian. I knew this would just bring us closer together. I just knew it."

Marian stared the man standing across from her. *Closer together*? She'd never felt so distanced from anyone or anything in her life. Or afraid. So afraid.

"So," Alan said in calm, conversational tone. "How's the show going?"

Marian blinked. Small talk? How-are-you?-chit-chat? Now? *Hey, Sis, there's a mangled body in the basement and by the way how are things with your career?*

"Okay," said Alan, "since you don't feel like playing catch-up, what say you go find out for yourself." He nodded at Jack, who began moving Marian toward the basement door.

"Turn on the light, and go down there. What do you say, Sis? If you really want to know if I've gone the Permanent Bye-Bye, that's all you have to do."

There was no threat in his eyes.

"I love you, Alan."

"You keep saying that. Look, no one's going to hurt you, I swear. You'll walk out that front door as alive as you came in. I'd never let anything happen to you. Never."

By now they were in front of the basement door. Alan opened it and Jack eased Marian forward. She took a deep breath and turned on the light.

"Want me to come with you?" said Alan.

Marian swallowed. Her mouth tasted of bile and fear.

"If you'd like." Strange, that even now he wanted to look after her, take care of her.

He put a warm and reassuring hand on her shoulder. "Don't be afraid. I'm not. Not anymore."

She looked at him and wondered why in the hell she hadn't gone over to Aunt Boots's house first.

Then she tried to smile.

And they started down the steps.

Marian was only aware of time passing. She held her breath as she descended the stairs, trying to keep herself from shaking. She became aware of all the underneath-sounds you never hear during the day because you're too busy to notice them; the faint, irregular drip of water as condensation fell from the pipes, her own breathing, the creak of a house still settling. She wet her lips, then squeezed the wooden railing for reassurance. No good; she was still petrified.

The stairs groaned and rasped with her every step; it would not have surprised her had the damn things simply splintered in half and sent her falling straight down, Alice in the Rabbit's Hole.

Then came a sound from somewhere behind him.

A soft sound.

But close.

"Doing fine," said Jack.

The doorbell rang upstairs. Alan grabbed Marian's shoulder, halting her, then turned to Jack and said, "You'd better stay up there and take care of the beggars. Make sure you tell all of them about tonight."

Wordlessly, Jack did as he was told.

Every muscle in Marian's body seemed to knot up all at once; her skin broke out in gooseflesh and her breath suddenly caught in her throat. She briefly flashed on an incident from her childhood when Dad had bagged a deer while hunting and split it open from its neck down to its hind legs, then hung it upside-down in the basement to drain. She hadn't know it was there when she went down to get something for Mom, and it was dark and she didn't want to go because the light switch wasn't working and that meant she had to go down the stairs and then walk all the way over on the other wall, which meant going across the basement in order to turn it on, which always seemed like a twenty-mile hike through the darkest woods to her, but she managed to get to the bottom of the stairs and took a deep breath and start hiking through the forest, then slipped in a puddle of something and fell on her stomach. She yelled because she was having trouble getting up, so Mom came down and walked over and turned on the light and there was so much blood everywhere because the deer was hanging right over her, its eyes wide, staring at her as a steady flow of blood and pieces of guts spattered down on her face and arms and she just *knew* that if Mom didn't pull her away the light would go out again and she'd die there with the deer in the dark forest . . . .

That same feeling returned to her as she came off the last step and found herself in the basement.

In the center of the floor, illuminated by the single bulb which hung from the center of the ceiling, was a pond of blood; there was no mistaking its color of its sharp, coppery scent. Though it had not turned the shade of rust as that in the bathroom, it was old enough to have begun coagulating.

Just a deer, she forced herself to think. *It's just the blood from Dad's deer.*

Her eyes followed the path of the arterial spray on the wall to the left of the blood, as well as the one directly behind it. She saw clumped bits of viscera and small chunks of shattered bone.

"Look at it," said Alan, pushing her toward the pond. "See how it glimmers? Isn't it beautiful?"

Deer blood, remember. Has to be deer blood.

Even though she knew that wasn't the case, Marian called on her training as an actress to make herself believe it; as long as she could do that, she might get out of her in one living piece.

"This is where you killed Joseph?"

"Yes," whispered Alan, staring into his reflection as he knelt by the edge of the pond.

"Joseph Comstock?" Marian asked once again.

"Yes."

"Then where's his body, Alan?"

"It's here."

"Joseph Comstock's body is here?"

"Yes. Our great-great-great-great-grandfather."

A layer of ice formed in the pit of Marian's stomach. "What?"

Alan looked at her. "Joseph Comstock was our ancestor, only he used to call himself Josiah. Came over here in the early 1800s and helped settled Cedar Hill. During the cholera epidemic he came down with a fever that drove him mad, picked up a scythe, and murdered his entire family. They hanged him for that, but when they went to cut down his body, it wasn't there. He couldn't be allowed to die, you see, because if he had, the bloodline which eventually led to you and me being born . . . it wouldn't have survived. We never would have been. So he's been hanging around, you see, in the cemetery, and can only move around during the month of October because it's the month for ghosts, you see?" He stared back into the pond.

Marian shook her head, but only slightly. *I did not fuck the ghost of my great-great-great-great-grandfather. I. Did. Not.*

"The bloodline has to be kept strong," Alan continued, "so it was up to us—you and me—to accept him."

Marian looked around for something heavy—but not too heavy. Something just weighty enough with which to knock him unconscious; then she could sneak back up the stairs and get out through the back door.

She saw a pile of old pipes in one corner and started edging her way toward them.

"So beautiful," Alan repeated. "Come look."

Marian passed close enough to her brother to look over Alan's shoulders and see his reflection in the blood—

—only his was not alone; on either side of him were the faces of Mom and Dad, with Grandma and Grampa behind them, as well as countless others whose faces she did not recognize but knew they were Quinlan ancestors, be it from the shape of the jaw or the set of the eyes or the fullness of the lips, they were the rest of the family bloodline, going all the way back to—

—Josiah Comstock, whom she had known as Joseph, who stood at the very back in the puddle of faces, slightly higher than the rest, the original patriarch smiling down at his lineage.

Marian, dizzy, reached out and placed one hand on her brother's shoulder to steady her balance.

"I knew you'd come around, Sis," Alan said. "Do you want to see the body?"

Marian said nothing.

Alan straightened himself, still kneeling, and removed his baseball cap.

The back of his head was clump of raw, seeping meat speckled with strands of bloodied hair, bone slivers, and brain matter, covered with maggots. Both the skull and the brain had been split in half and pried apart, leaving a jagged, black horizontal gap where blood trickled down and out, drawing a straight line of crimson down his neck that disappeared into the collar of his shirt.

Before she could pull away, Alan's right hand snapped up and gripped her wrist, pulling her hand closer to the ruins of his skull.

"You have to touch them now, Sis, you have to know what I know—"

She kicked out at his back but it did not good; his grip was iron, and before Marian could pull in enough breath to shout or scream or laugh, Alan was shoving her fingertips deep into the bloodied chasm, and it was wet and crumbly and thick and cold, sucking her fingers in deeper as the pupa swarmed over her skin.

"Feel them now?"

" . . . *ohgod*," she chocked, on the brink of vomiting.

"Give in to it, Sis, it's the only way."

The basement spun, the blood mixing with the light and the stench. Marian went down on one knee, her chest pounding, and felt a small part of her mind start to shut down—

—and then heard herself speak:

" . . . my goddamn prom dress . . . Mom spent months working on it in secret because she wanted to surprise me with it, she lost sleep staying up nights after we'd gone to sleep, and when she finally gave it to me I threw . . . *oh, fuck!* . . . I threw a fit because it was the wrong color, it didn't match my shoes, and she felt so stupid because she'd never thought to ask me what color my shoes were, but I wasn't about to wear any other shoes, so Dad had to dig into the savings to give me the money for a prom dress . . . "

Alan continued: " . . . and Mom felt like she'd failed you again."

Marian felt one tear slip from her eye and slide down her cheek. "I never apologized for that. All these years, and I never apologized."

"Know what she did with the dress?"

Marian shook her head and began to reach out with her left arm toward the stack of old pipes. " . . . no . . . ."

"She cut it up and used the material to start her Story Quilt. She's got your prom dress, my Cub Scout uniform, a bunch of stuff from her and Dad, our grandparents and great-grandparents, a bunch of stuff. I even made a new patch from the top of the pajamas Dad was wearing the night he died. Now the time's come for you to complete it; one Story Patch, and it's done."

"Let go of me." The strain of reaching was beginning to rip her shoulder apart, but she would not stop trying.

"Just one, tonight, at the bonfire, just one and . . . you'll see."

The rest happened quickly; she managed to grab onto one of the smaller pipes, swing it up, then down in a smooth arc, and connected solidly with the side of what was left of her brother's head; he released his grip on her and tumbled forward. Her hand pulled from the grisly chasm with the sound of a plastic bag melting on a fire. She rose to her feet and staggered toward the stairs, made her up to the kitchen, and thought she saw Jack coming toward her from the corner of her eye; not bothering to check if he was indeed there or if she were imagining it, Marian pulled in a deep breath and ran out the back door, leaving behind her coat and car keys, sprinting through the yard, over the neighbors' fence, and into the street, racing past dozens of goblins and witches and vampires and ghosts, all of them drawn toward the house of her childhood by the hypnotic figure of Jack Pumpkinhead.

Candy and shivers.

I want our family again.

Giggles and whispers.

Come to the shortcut tonight. We're gonna build a bonfire and tell ghosts stories.

She stumbled through the night.

Make sure to bring your pumpkins and your magic seeds.

She rounded a corner, clutching at her bleeding wrist, and nearly collided with a group of tiny clowns. She mumbled some apology, then took off again, not noticing the small spatters of blood that fell behind her like a trail of breadcrumbs through a fairy-tale forest.

An unseen group of children chanted: *"Who blows at my candle? Whose fiery grin and eyes/Behind me pass in the looking glass/And make my gooseflesh rise?"*

She looked back over her shoulder only once, and saw many figures behind her but couldn't tell if any of them were following her.

His head, you saw the back of his head, you felt it, it was real, it was real, it was REAL!

The sound of leaves skittering along the darkened streets became the blacked fingernails of a corpse in its coffin scratching at the lid, serenaded by the trick or treaters.

"Who moved in the shadow? Who rustled past unseen? With the dark so deep I dare not sleep/All night on Hallowe'en."

Gulping down air and panic, Marian ran on . . . .

6

If you failed to place strip sets together before cutting, place two segments right sides together, checking to be sure the colors and seam allowances oppose each other, and sew into a four-patch.

Boots opened her front door and Marian, without saying a word, dashed past her and into the safety of the bright living room.

"Marian, honey . . . what is it?"

It all came out in a rapid, deadly cadence (except for the part about the back of Alan's skull; Marian still couldn't bring herself to believe it and didn't want to sound crazy), broken only by a swallow here or a breath there to steady the beating of her heart.

Boots put her arm around Marian's shoulder and guided her to a chair. "You sit right here and calm yourself down some more. I'll go fetch some stuff to take care of that wrist of yours."

Marian leaned forward and pressed her head against her knees, breathing deeply. Boots returned with a legion of medical supplies and two cups of cinnamon tea sprinkled with peppermint schnapps. Marian took three swallows, not minding that it burned her throat, then sat in silence as Boots cleaned and bandaged her wound.

Afterward, she began to cry. God, how she hated crying in front of someone else! "I'm sorry, Aunt Boots."

"No need to apologize, honey. I had a nice crying jag myself after I saw your brother a couple of days ago. He and that house just seem to have that effect on people."

Marian smiled at her. Good old Boots. It seemed like everyone eventually turned to her. Fifty-seven and didn't look a day over forty-five, provided you didn't stare too closely at the amount of pancake she wore to cover the thin, jagged scar that ran from the left corner of her mouth and down her chin, only to curve back and go halfway up her jaw. Marian never knew how Boots had come by that scar, but she suspected that, like the marks on Dad's back, it was courtesy of their mother.

As she let go of her aunt's hands, it occurred to Marian there was a lot about Boots she didn't know, save that she used to play the organ at her church every Christmas, had never married, and always made sure no visitor to her home left without something hot in their stomach.

"Now," said Boots, brushing back a strand of her brilliant white hair, "tell me the whole thing one more time, from the beginning. I want to make sure I got it right."

"This is going to sound silly," whispered Marian, "but could you answer a question for me?"

"If I can, hon, sure."

"Why do we call you 'Boots,' Lucille?"

She laughed rather loudly at first, the quickly silenced herself. "I shouldn't make so much noise. I don't want to wake Laura—"

"Laura's here?"

"Uh-huh. Said she talked to you on the phone last week."

"Can I see her?"

"When she wakes up. Now, take another sip of tea and tell me everything again, just a bit slower this time, okay?"

Marian did, hitting on more details. Boots considered everything with an even, unreadable expression, her eyes never looking away, tilting her head to hear better, and asking all the right questions when Marian fell into confused and frightened silence.

When she saw that her niece was finished, Boots half-smiled, rose to her feet, and walked to her front window; pulling back the curtain, she watched as a few costumed children ran down the street, then let the curtain drop back into place. "Honey, I think your brother has made you a part of his craziness. Don't get me wrong, I don't doubt for a minute that he's made himself some kinda scarecrow and is calling it 'Jack'; I don't doubt that for a second. He's alone there with some pretty powerful grief."

"I know," whispered Marian. "And I feel awful about it. I know that I should've come back the minute I received the telegram, but—"

Boots raised a hand. "You don't owe me any explanation. I don't blame you at all for not wanting to be here. I saw your father during that last week. He wasn't nothing more than a skeleton with a bit of skin on him. Scared me so much I could hardly look at him. I've been having bad dreams ever since. A death like that isn't something a parent would want their child to see, so don't feel guilty about not getting back here. A human being's expected to take only so much."

"But Jack . . . that thing . . . it *spoke* to me! I saw it at the cemetery!" She held out her bandaged wrist. "It cut me."

"I'll say it again, Marian. Grief can do things to a person, make them see things that aren't there. Maybe you cut yourself on a busted pop bottle or something that was on the ground near your parents' graves and didn't notice. You said yourself that you'd been thinking about how your mom used to read to you when you was a kid, how you used to think Jack Pumpkinhead was your secret friend. Please don't look at me like that. I know something terrible's happened to you, I'm just trying to make some sense of things. Come on in the kitchen with me. I got a craving for some more of this nasty-ass tea."

When they were both seated at the kitchen table with a fresh hot cup, Boots lit a cigarette and watched the smoke curl around her. Her face tensed as she thought of something, then she spoke up. "When the funeral was over, a bunch of folks came to the house with food and stuff for Alan. I hung around to help him clean up after they all left. He wasn't in no condition to do housework, so I told him to go take a nap. 'Bout twenty minutes later I'm in the front room emptying ashtrays and hear Alan upstairs talking to himself. It was the damnedest thing. I swear that I could feel his heartbreak all around me, like it was as real as I was; I half-expected it to come through the front door and ask me where its supper was.

"Then I heard another voice—sounded enough like your dad's to give me the heebie-jeebies. So I left. Didn't bother to say good-bye or put away the cleaning supplies or nothing. I just wanted to get away from your brother and his grief and that house as fast as I could. I think there's a kind of sadness that gets to be so terrible a person can't be around it for too long without going a little crazy themselves. I got enough people who think I'm batty. I don't need to go hearing a dead man's voice."

Marian inhaled the peppermint fumes from her fresh cup of tea. "How bad was it for Dad near the end? Did he really feel that . . . forgotten?"

Boots took a deep drag from her cigarette, coughed, then sipped her tea. "Let me tell you something about your dad. When him and me were growing up, he was always made to feel like a failure by the other kids in the family. Our parents weren't the kindest folks in the world, they never had much money and even less patience. Pop wasn't too bad but our mama was one mean-tempered gal. She used to take off her one of her high-heeled shoes whenever she got mad and beat your dad on the back with it, making little holes until you couldn't see his skin for the blood. Well, I saved up a bunch of money from collecting pop bottles and scrap metal and newspapers and such, and I bought Mama a new pair of boots. They fit her just right and she said they were comfortable. She took to wearing them quite a lot. So I either hid or threw away all her high-heeled shoes, that way, when she got the hankering to pound on your dad, she never made him bleed. Oh, she left some nasty bruises, but never again did she leave him scarred and bleeding. He was so grateful that he hugged me and said, 'Thanks for the boots.' That's how I got my nickname."

Marian remembered how she used to giggle at those marks on her father's back when she was a child: *What's all them funny things, Daddy?—Why, those're dots, honey, so you can play at connect-the-dots and see what kind of picture they make.*

"The one thing he kept saying to me," whispered Boots, wiping something from her eye, "was that someday he was gonna do something great, something that would make Mama and the rest of the kids who used to call him a dummy feel sorry they'd ever been bad to him and me.

"He used to ask me if he bored me with all of his talking, his out-loud daydreaming. I thought he was the greatest thing since Errol Flynn. He'd always stand in front of me when mama would go off on one of her pounding fits. Most of the time, he wound up taking my beatings for me." She touched the scar on her chin. "When he was there, that is. He was a fine boy and an even better man, your dad. You should've known him back then, back when you could see his greatness instead of just hearing about it the way others remembered it. I'm gonna miss him so much—oh, goddammit!" She turned away and wept quietly.

Marian reached over and took Boots's hand. "Please tell me?"

"Oh, honey . . . it was terrible for him at the end. I wish I had it in me to lie and spare your feelings but I can't and I'm sorry. He kept . . . crying all the time, going on about how he'd never get to build his masterpiece. He figured that his life had been one big waste. There was no feeling sorry for himself, though. He had no sympathy for himself at all—he even said it'd make more sense if he *did* feel sorry for himself, 'cause that'd at least explain why he couldn't stop crying. He never got to do any of the things he wanted to do, only the things he *had* to do. I just couldn't stand it. He was so miserable. The cancer pain was too much. He needed . . . I don't know . . . *something* so much and none of us could give it to him. It was terrible. He started drinking, to help kill some of the pain, he said. I knew that he shouldn't have been pouring booze down his throat but when I said something to Alan, he only said—"

"'I can't deny him a drink when he needs one.'"

"That's right."

Marian got up and put her arms around Boots, holding her as tightly as she could.

"I'm fine, honey," said Boots, "thank you. I'm always fine. Don't know why I had to go and blubber like this. Not my way. Let's put ourselves back together now, whatta you say?"

Marain kissed Boots's cheek. "You were always my favorite aunt."

"Glad to know someone in this family was born with good taste. Listen, now; I'm gonna get myself freshened up. Why don't you go on and stick your head in the guest room down here and wake Laura? She'd throw a fit if she knew you'd been here and I didn't let you wake her to say hello. You go do that, I'll make myself presentable, then I'll drive us back over to the house. I want to see this thing your brother made."

Boots went upstairs and Marian—after another shot of doctored tea—went to the door of the guest room and knocked. "Laura? Laura, it's me. Can I come in?"

"M-Marian?" She sounded half-asleep still. "Hell, yes . . . come in."

For a while there were no words exchanged between them, there was no need. Marian sat next to her ex-sister-in-law's bed, holding her hand

and trying not to give in to the fear that was clawing at the lining of her stomach.

Laura was pregnant and—judging from her size—in the last month.

Marian wished she could smile and make herself believe that Laura had found someone new, a man who loved and cared for her and wanted a family, but the look of helplessness on Laura's face, one composed of fear and more than a little hatred, kept her nailed in the moment.

"I don't feel very good," said Laura, her voice thin, hollow, "so please j-just listen to what I have to say." As she spoke the color drained from her face until she looked ashen, a bloated graying corpse. Marian felt herself shaking as she watched the sweat pour down Laura's face.

"I left your brother over nine months ago, and I haven't slept with any man since then. I've been tested, Marian, and I there's a . . . baby in me. I feel it kicking, I feel its hunger . . . it's there. And its Alan's. I don't know how or why he did this to me, but I know.

"Early on, I tried three times to have an abortion, but when they got inside me there was . . . there was *nothing there.*"

The sweating was worse now and she was shaking badly—as was Marian.

"I never really wanted kids," said Laura. "All I ever wanted was a man who would love me, who would support me, and who knew that I came first once he'd left the family. But Alan could never leave your family behind. Was that so much to ask? Was it? To have a home all my own? A home that had no trace of whatever it was that happened to him when you guys were kids? I still love him, Marian, but this thing in me is moving and *I don't want it!* I just want to . . . to have my job and my husband back, I want to read in bed at night and feel him beside me, I want to go to movies and drive him crazy because I insist on sitting through all the credits, I want him to wake me up and send me to bed because I feel asleep watching some late night talk show again, I want him to crack bad jokes when our friends come over . . . ." She leaned back and started taking deep breaths.

Marian looked at Laura's middle.

It rippled.

A quick movement, a thin hissing sound, and Laura's water broke.

Marian jumped to her feet and called out for Boots.

"Press the 'O' key on the phone," called her aunt from upstairs. "That's 911."

Marian snatched up the phone and made the call. Four minutes later she and Boots watched as the EMTs loaded Laura into the ambulance.

Boots kissed Laura's forehead and told her they'd follow in her car. The ambulance pulled away and Marian followed her aunt into the garage.

The garage was dark but Boots was able to guide Marian to the car without either of them banging a shin. Once inside the car, under the harsh glow of the dome light, the strain on Boots was evident; she suddenly looked much older than her years. She caught Marian staring at her and smiled. "You are a pretty thing. Won't be much longer now and I'll be paying good money to see your face up on a movie screen."

"That's right. You're sharing space with the next Katherine Hepburn, so show the proper respect."

"And humble, to boot," said Boots, laughing, then closed the car door, plunging them both into darkness. "Lord, I hope they take 21st Street to the hospital, it's the quickest way."

Marian suddenly did not want to leave. Out there, Alan was waiting. And maybe something else. But behind her, just through the door, was a warm and bright house, a place of safety where two women could sit down with a cup of nasty-ass tea and have a good cry over a death in the family, a place where grief would eventually ease, not grow to become so strong it walked on two spindly legs and spoke in a voice teeming with coffin beetles.

" . . . all right," said Boots.

"H-huh?"

"I said you shouldn't worry, things'll be all right. One disaster at a time. Laura and the baby first, then your brother."

"Laura told me—"

"I *know* what she told you. She's been telling me the same thing for weeks."

"Do you believe her?"

"I don't know what to believe half the time anymore." Boots started the car, raised the garage door, turned on the headlights, and slowly backed out into the street. "Can't say I'm much looking forward to this."

"I don't think Alan's really dangerous. Besides, he cut himself worse than I did. He must be pretty weak by now and there's *two* of us."

"That's not what I meant," said Boots. "I'm probably gonna come back to find that the neighborhood kids have soaped every last one of my goddamn windows."

The two women looked at each other and laughed. Marian promised herself to take the time to get to know Aunt Boots better.

Wasted time. Lost opportunities. Regrets.

Nothing was ever accomplished by dwelling on them.

"You know, don't you, that we're gonna have to drive by the cemetery on the way from the hospital back to your folks's house, right? It's the quickest way."

Marian glanced in the rearview mirror to make sure nothing was following them. *Going paranoid's good.*

Nothing but shadows and the glowing faces of pumpkins in windows, a few groups of costumed children heading home, stomachs ready for sweet treats.

Only these things.

And the wind. Blowing harder. Whistling. Drawing the tree branches down like arms reaching—

She blinked, forcing the chill away. Boots reached over and snapped on the heat. "Not gonna have you catch your death on top of everything else."

"Thanks. I guess I'm just tired."

They rounded a corner. Then another. And one more.

The taillights of the ambulance—as well as its whirling visibar lights— came into view. Boots accelerated slightly in order to keep it in sight. Marian sat up straight, her heart suddenly pounding so hard and fast she expected to blink and see it lying there on the dashboard, pumping blood all over the windshield, blinding her, panicking her, sending her off the road and into a guardrail, over the side and—

—the ambulance's siren cut off as it began to weave; only slightly at first, then much more erratic and violently.

Dear God, thought Marian.

It's happening.

Though the car was a good quarter-mile from the ambulance, Marian could clearly see what was going on. The ambulance tried slowing to a normal speed, couldn't, then veered right and ran up on the curve, crashing into and then plowing over a mailbox before slamming into the side of brick building, shattering the windshield and popping open one of the rear doors, fumes from the engine obscuring everything in smoke and steam.

Boots yelled, "Oh, Holy Mother!" and braked quickly, throwing both herself and Marian forward into the dash. Once they'd recovered, Marian pushed open her door and jumped out of the car just as one of the attendants came out of the back, his uniform covered in blood, and collapsed to the ground.

Marian felt her legs go weak as she ran toward the ambulance.

The windows were smeared with dripping darkness from inside.

The driver scrambled out, his back drenched in blood, and dropped to his knees, softly laughing.

Boots was now beside Marian. "Oh, Dear God—*Laura!*" She ran from Marian, who quickly followed her aunt to the opened door in back and looked inside and saw—

—blood, a lot of blood and tissue, but no Laura and no baby, only the blood and tissue and something that looked like deep scratch marks on the inside roof—

"—do now?" shouted Boots.

Marian ran over to the driver and tried to bring him back, but his laugh and the hollowed look of his eyes told her in no uncertain terms that he wasn't coming home for a while, so she ran to the other EMT and rolled him over—

—a deep gash along the side of neck was still spurting blood, albeit slowly now, the artery severed, his life gone, gone, gone.

Keep it together, for chrissakes!

She jumped in the front seat of the ambulance and grabbed the mic from the radio unit, pressed down on the button, and said, "Hello? Hello? Listen, I'm calling from inside the ambulance that was dispatched about ten minutes ago. There's been a wreck and—" Her thumb slipped off the button. "—*shit!*"

The radio hissed and crackled, and buried somewhere in the noise she heard the sound of singing: *"A goblin lives in OUR house, in OUR house, in OUR house . . . "*

"Hello!" she shouted into the mic once again.

" . . . goblin lives in OUR house, all the year 'round!"

Then Boots was there, grabbing her arm and pulling her from the ambulance. "C'mon, hon, let's get back in the car and get to a phone, okay? There's nothing we can do here."

She didn't so much guide as almost *toss* Marian toward the car. In moments both were in and doors were closed and Boots was turning around and then they were moving again.

Too much, Marian thought, pressing closed her eyes as if wishing alone would make it all a dream. *Too much, too fast, dearGod make it slow down, make it stop,* anything!

"Hang in there with me, hon," said Boots, reaching over and squeezing her hand. "We'll get through this somehow."

Marian opened her eyes as Boots tore around the next corner and accelerated.

Marian saw it first. The street was blocked, filled with dozens, maybe hundreds of people; children, adults, old folks, all of them carrying pumpkins that glowed with a deep, otherwordly light.

Boots jerked the steering wheel to the left and stood on the brake but it was too late; the car fishtailed over the curb, spun sideways, and smashed into a section of Cedar Hill Cemetery's iron gate, slamming Marian against the dashboard as the windshield exploded.

It took less than five seconds.

Later—she had no idea how much later, but it was later, nonetheless—Marian pulled herself up and wiped the blood out of her eyes. A low pressure in the back of her head swam forward. She felt like she was going to pass out again. She hoped she didn't have a concussion.

Her door was wrenched open.

She turned and saw Jack Pumpkinhead.

And next to him, wearing her favorite old housecoat, his pumpkinhead wife.

Marian began tumbling back toward darkness.

"Everything's going to be fine," said Jack, reaching for her.

"Just fine," said Mom.

Then darkness took her.

7

You still need to go back and cut off the corners to eliminate bulk!

"I'm so glad you came home."

Mom's voice. So near, so warm. For a moment, Marian thought she was back home in bed, eight years old again, with a fever. She grinned, hoping that Mom would fix her a cup of hot cocoa and read to her from her favorite book.

The touch of brittle twig-fingers against her cheek tore her from her reverie. She opened her eyes and saw, at first, only the bright harvest moon above, then a twig-finger touched her face again and a pumpkinhead eclipsed the moon.

"I missed you, hon," said the thing with her mother's voice.

Marian swallowed a shriek and kicked back, trying to get away. A sharp pain stabbed her in the ribs as something inside of her shifted. Her chest hitched and she fell backwards, realizing that some of her ribs were broken.

The Mom-thing was next to her then, cradling her head in dry branch-arms. "You'll be all better soon, hon. I promise."

"Get a-w-w-way from me."

The thing froze, then lowered its face. A thin trickle of blood ran out of its rounded, glowing eye. "I'm so sorry I made you ashamed of me," it said, its voice cracking just like Mom's used to. Before Marian could try to move again, Alan was next to the Mom-thing, laying a hand on its shoulder. He'd put his baseball cap back on.

"She's just scared, Mom, that's all. She loves you, she told me so. Isn't that right, Sis?" He looked at Marian with pleading in his eyes.

Marian said, "Where's Aunt Boots?"

Alan pointed toward the church. "She's over there, talking to Dad."

Boots, her blouse torn and bloodied, her hair matted with dark splotches, was standing next to Jack Pumpkinhead. He had one of his arms around her shoulders and was leading her toward one of the church's collapsed walls. Marian could see a staircase inside the church, through the rubble. Jack leaned over and covered Boots's lips with his crescent mouth, then sent her on her way.

Limping and shuddering, Boots began climbing the stairs which, Marian now saw, led to the exposed organ loft.

"Isn't that sweet?" said the Mom-thing. "He's gonna have her play a song for our anniversary." It leaned close to Marian, its breath the reek of rotting vegetables mixed with dirt. "I always used to kid your daddy about how I knew he was gonna forget our anniversary, but he never did. He's a charmer. And he invited the *whole* family, did you know that? What a thoughtful fellow."

"That's why you married me," said Jack Pumpkinhead, taking one of Mom-thing's hands and pulling her to her feet. Two corners of the Story Quilt were tied together under his neck, the rest of it flowing behind him like a grand cape. Jack pulled the Mom-thing toward an open patch in the cemetery. They stared at one another for a moment, then embraced. The brittle sound of wood scraping against wood filled the air. They pulled back, still looking at one another, as a low, deep, throbbing hum crept from the organ loft and unfurled over the cemetery; softly, at first, then steadily louder, the pained cacophony became progressively more structured and only slightly prettier as a tune struggled to break the surface of the chaos.

A tune that Marian recognized.

"The Anniversary Waltz."

Jack Pumpkinhead and the Mom-thing tossed back their heads and laughed the laughter of Marian's parents; younger, happier, stronger, a couple in love long before the world had beaten them down. They danced away, gliding and twirling through the tombstones. Mom-thing's housecoat flowed in the night breeze like the grandest and most elegant of gowns; Jack's Story-Quilt cape flew up and out like the wings of some giant, majestic nightbird. Their laughter cut through the whistling wind.

A black mass the size of a truck bled out from the ruins of the organ loft, then exploded into dozens of bats who squealed, screeched, and swooped down toward the dancers, not to attack, but to join in the celebration, encircling them in a fluttering wind-ballet that flowed up and down, round and round, rippling in time with the music.

Marian looked around, trying not to meet her brother's stare. The smashed heap that once had been Boots's car sat under a section of fallen gate. Someone must have seen the accident, so where in hell were the police and ambulance and fire trucks?

"Everyone's already here," said Alan. "Look around."

The cemetery was filled with people, each standing at a grave, either alone or with others, holding their jack o' lanterns, looking at the headstone that bore the name of a lost loved one.

It was overpowering.

Though she could not say what exactly *it* was, Marian could nonetheless *feel* it all around her; above and under, in the air, in the trees and soil, in the beams of moonlight: thick, sentient, and all-powerful.

The music played on, the organ rasping, crackling, and singing.

Alan removed the stone bottle from his pocket and pulled out the cork. "Party time." He tilted the neck of the bottle and a thin slow stream of blood dribbled from it onto the soil of the cemetery. He emptied the bottle and then knelt down, using his hands to spread the blood right to left, forward and back, regulating the stream to flow. Marian could almost see the blood mixing down into the soil and mud beneath, blending in, spreading wider, then breaking through the last layer and staining the lids of all the coffins underneath.

The throbbing in Marian's ribs gave way to something stronger. At first she thought the pounding was only in her head but as she pulled herself to her feet she realized that the noise, the thumping—

—*deargod*—

—was coming from underneath the ground.

The little girl in her drew a picture of the dead beating their fists against the inside of their coffin lids.

(*Let-Us-OUT! . . . Let-Us-OUT!*)

From the grave nearest her the pounding increased, its desperate strength spreading to the grave next to it, then to the next grave, then on and on across the grounds, the rhythmic beating of a thousand dead hearts becoming one.

Jack Pumpkinhead and the Mom-thing stopped dancing and began to stroll among the mourners, stopping to talk with each in turn. Only after they had been spoken to did the mourners move, kneeling at the foot of their chosen grave, taking the magic seeds given to them by Jack and burying them in the soil. Then each mourner placed their jack o' lantern atop the spot where they had buried their seeds.

The pounding grew frantic though no less rhythmic.

—*thumpity-whump-thump!* . . . *(Let)* . . . *thumpity-whump-thump!* . . . *(Us)* . . . *thumpity-whump-thump* . . . *(OUT)!*

Marian turned toward her brother. "W-what are they going to d-do?"

Alan, took her hands. "This is their night. The important thing is, we're here for Jack and the whole family tonight. This is the least we can do." He put his arm around her and began leading her toward the church.

Marian struggled to get free of him but any movement only doubled the pain in her ribs. After a few seconds more of futile struggle she slumped against her brother and let him guide her.

As the last jack o' lantern was placed atop the last grave, Alan set Marian by the sealed oak doors of the church, kissing her bloodied forehead and smiling.

"I love you, Sis. Please try to remember that. In the end, it's the only thing that counts, though fuck only knows why."

Marian pressed her back against the doors and said nothing as she let herself slide down onto her knees.

The mourners remained still, eyes fixed on Jack and his wife as they stood at the bottom of the church steps. After giving Marian one last look, Alan moved down to join them, leaving his sister in the shadows.

From the organ loft above came the powerful opening chords of "A Mighty Fortress Is Our God."

From the soil below came the answer of the dead.

—thumpity-whump-thump! . . . *(Let)* . . . *thumpity-whump-thump!* . . . *(Us)* . . . *thumpity-whump-thump* . . . *(OUT)!*

Marian thought she saw movement beneath the soil at one of the now-deserted graves. Her breath came up short as the pain in her body increased.

Children broke away from their parents and started building the bonfire, clapping their hands and squealing with joy. A few small flames at first, growing higher, then a *whoosh!* as the fire roared to life, the children dancing in a circle as each tossed in more wood and branches. From the center of their dance came young, giggling voices: "*Beasties on the doorstep, Phantoms in the air/Owls on witches' gateposts, Giving stare for stare/Jack o' lanterns grinning, Shadows on a screen/Shrieks and starts and laughter, This is Hallowe'en!*"

The organ music rose beyond a scream, its music of praise becoming the howl of a wolf raging at the moon, shaking loose a few stones from over the doorway.

The moon seemed to move closer to the Earth, its light so brilliant and silver Marian winced.

And Jack said: "Ol' Jack Pumpkinhead lived on a vine . . . "

The dancing children answered: "A goblin lives in OUR house, in OUR house, in *OUR* house . . . "

" . . . Ol' Jack Pumpkinhead thought it was fine . . . "

" . . . a goblin lives in *OUR* house, all the year round . . . "

—thumpity (Let)-whump (Us)-thump (OUT)!—

Marian saw that she hadn't imagined it—something *was* moving under the graves . . . under the soil . . . shifting, rolling like small waves, rocking the jack o' lanterns back and forth as each mound rose and fell with ease.

It's breathing. The whole goddamn cemetery is breathing.

The bonfire grew higher and wider, its roar almost equal to that of the church organ, the flames spreading and raging, hissing and popping, scattering sparks that were caught by the nightbreeze and flung across the grounds.

" . . . First he was small and green," said Jack.

" . . . He bumps and he jumps and he *thumps* around midnight . . . "

" . . . Then big and yellow . . . "

—thumpity (Let)-whump (Us)-thump (OUT)!—

" . . . a goblin lives in *OUR* house, all the year round!"

" . . . Ol' Jack Pumpkinhead is a very fine fellow," all sang as one.

Marian struggled to stand again, letting the pain compel her, readying herself to make a run for it—

—and the organ music grew even louder, tinged at the edges with a dark majesty that soon gave it richer form and deeper feeling as it began "Let There Be Peace On Earth"—

—and Marian watched as a scene right out of her grainy childhood nightmares unfolded before her.

As the fiery sparks bounced against the soil, each grave split open and the thin, pale, rotted hands of its tenant reached up to touch the night air.

Marian felt her legs starting to buckle but she did not—*would not*—fall. She slowly pushed herself up, the pain pushing her forward, moving along the smooth oak doors, covering her head as bits and pieces of stone and plaster fell from above, steady, old girl, steady, that's it, keep moving, no one's looking at you, they all think you're down for the count so don't you dare stop moving, that's good, just . . . a little . . . farther . . . and . . . you . . . can . . . *there!* You can get through that gap in the gate and sneak back to the house, grab your car keys and drive away from here and—

—*Boots.*

She couldn't leave Boots, not here, not now.

She looked over her shoulder and saw the hands from each grave grip the jack o' lantern left for them and pull it beneath the soil.

Then came the sounds of tearing and snapping.

She tried not to imagine what those sounds might mean.

She pushed away from the doors and edged herself over a section of crumbling wall into the ruins of the church, fell on her chest, and choked as the paroxyms of pain doubled her into a tight ball. She gulped down air and tried to stand, fell on her knees, rose again, half-crouching, and slowly struggled forward. The organ loft stairs were only a few yards away.

It was the longest trip of her life. Every movement seemed to jar something loose inside. Once, gripping the edge of a pew, she thought she felt a rib dislodge and puncture a lung.

Outside, the flames were growing so bright it looked like mid-afternoon. She caught glimpses of children running back and forth, carrying more twigs and dried leaves.

"Marian!" came her Jack's voice.

She turned, balancing herself against a marble holy water font, expecting to see him standing behind her.

Nothing.

So don't wait around, she warned herself, moving toward the stairs. Where she was finding the strength to do this, she didn't know. One slip and she'd collapse, she knew it, she'd fall and be poured from herself like water, all of her bones out of joint and clacking against one another as they were swept away in the stream of her fluids.

From the loft high above, the organ howled in ecstatic agony.

An owl perched atop a rotting crucifix spread its wings and soared past Marian. She gripped the railing and pulled herself onto the first stair.

"Honey?" called Mom-thing's voice from outside.

Marian pushed herself up another stair, then two more, finally getting a delayed rush of adrenaline and taking them two at a time, blood dripping into her eyes, the pain spreading from her chest and ribs down to her pelvis. She kept climbing, thinking, *Use the pain, use it, use it!* She labored to breathe as smoke from the bonfire began rolling into the church and up the stairs, following her, nipping at her heels, then encircling her ankles and slithering up her legs, but then she rounded the first landing and found herself one flight away from the organ loft. The collapsed wall next to her allowed a harsh, cold breeze to cut through, holding back some the curling smoke. She filled her lungs with crisp air, blinking until her eyes cleared—

—and looked down on the cemetery below.

The glow from the fire illuminated the grounds, casting everything is a sickly pall of burnt orange.

From every grave (except her parents', some part of her brain noted) came its occupant; many were old and feeble with little flesh left on their bones—what skin remained was shriveled, torn, and discolored; some were younger, perhaps her own age, housewives who'd died in accidents or factory workers killed in the riots or by their machines; a few were teenagers, buried in their favorite clothes, nice clothes, trendy clothes, who'd perhaps died drunk behind the wheel of a car or at the prick of a needle; and, worst of all, there were babies, the small ones, slowly crawling up through the dirt that had lain upon their fragile bodies for so long. Behind them came the descendants, the settlers, the founding citizens of Cedar Hill, all of them only bones now, only bones, clicking, clacking, shuddering. She wondered if the remains of Josiah Comstock were walking amongst them.

Marian felt the tears in her eyes as she looked straight down and saw one baby that crawled on its arms because where its legs should have been hung a twisted, stumpy tangle of cartilage and skin, a sad trophy from Thalidomide days. Her heart broke at the sight of it; to have been born so horribly misshapen, to die so early, only to be called back like this.

The sight of the awakened dead was horrible enough; the Thalidomide baby made it worse.

Who moves in the shadow?

But what terrified Marian the most, what caused the blood to coagulate in her veins and her throat to contract and her bowls to twist into one excruciating knot of sick, was the sight of what each of these dead carried—

Who rustles past unseen?

—their own heads, the ones they had been died with. Some had eyes, others only dark chasms, but all of their mouths were locked in death's eternal rictus grin.

With the dark so deep . . .

And on every set of shoulders sat a new head, one with carved eyes, a three-cornered nose, and a crescent moon mouth, all glowing brightly inside.

. . . I dare not sleep . . .

She watched as every member of Jack Pumpkinhead's lineage was greeted by those who had mourned at their graveside with calls of *Mom* or *Darlin'* or *Grampa,* then with open arms and loving embraces in the light of the gigantic fire—

. . . all night this Hallowe'en!

—the organ stopped screaming.

Marian turned and saw Boots standing at the top of the stairs. Her eyes were wide and glazed, her hair hung around her face in clumps, caked with blood, and her hands were shaking uncontrollably.

"He told me he wouldn't let Mama beat us anymore," she said to her niece. "He told me that he'd make it better, that I wasn't ugly because of my scar. That's why Burt wouldn't marry me, you know. He said he couldn't look at my scar, it was too ugly."

"Oh Boots . . . ."

"Don't worry about them folks down there. Jack's gonna make every-thing fine again. All of 'em, see, all of 'em missed someone who was buried here. There ain't a person in this town who don't cry inside every day from some kinda loneliness. Even the spirits who live here, they cry, too. Loneliness follows you, hon, it follows you forever. But maybe that's all over now. You should feel good, having all the family back like this. They all think the world of you. Shame on you for not letting them know their love meant something."

"I'll not have you speaking to her that way, Boots," came the voice of Jack Pumpkinhead.

He was only a few feet away from Marian on the stairs. She had nowhere to go, except through the hole in the crumbled wall, and the drop was at least twenty feet. She bit her lower lip and cursed herself for getting trapped like this.

"I didn't mean anything," said Boots to Jack. "I only wanted her to know that—"

Jack raised a twig-finger as if to scold, then shook his head. "Don't apologize for anything. We've all spent way too much time being sorry for one thing or another."

Marian stared at him.

Something was wrong. He seemed . . . weaker now. The fire behind his eyes was growing dim.

I can't deny him a drink when he needs one.

Her fear suddenly vanished as Jack came up and joined her on the landing.

"Come along with me," he said, his voice soft and loving, no longer the horrid croak of before. He held out one of his twig-hands.

Deep within the human heart there lies a point at which there is no room for fear, no use for pity, and little consequence if old resentments are present or not; it is a place where failures are forgotten and past sins forgiven.

Looking at the thing she now, at last, recognized, Marian felt something in her change.

Grow stronger.

"D-dad?"

"Present and accounted for," said Jack. "I hope you can forgive me for all this, honey. I just needed to see you one more time."

She took her his hand. He led her down the stairs and through the pews, then across an aisle to a spot on the south side of the church where he pointed toward a small mosaic carved into the wall.

The Marvelous Land of Oz.

There was the Scarecrow and the Lion and the Tin Woodsman, along with Tip and the Gump and the Woggle-Bug and the Saw-Horse . . . and

Jack Pumpkinhead, his arms spread wide like an old friend who was about to give you the biggest hug you could imagine.

"It's beautiful," she said.

"When I was overseas during the war," said her father, "it seemed like every church my unit found had been destroyed by the fighting. I thought it was awful. Those places had been so *beautiful* once. One day we came into this town where the church hadn't been blown to shit and I decided to go in and light a penny candle, say a prayer that all of us'd get home all right. There was a sniper hiding in the organ loft. I guess he'd completely lost his mind. He shot me twice in the leg and once in my shoulder, then blew his own head off. I laid in there for almost an hour before somebody from my unit found me. I almost died from all the blood I lost.

"I promised myself that if I made it home alive, I was gonna spend the rest of my life building churches. I know it was that church that kept me alive. It was telling me I had to go on living because my life had a purpose. So I decided I was gonna be a great architect who'd go around the world fixing beautiful churches. I'd maybe even design a couple of them myself. The most beautiful thing I ever built was a tree house for your brother when he was seven." He doubled over in pain, then fell to the floor. Ignoring her own pain, Marian ran over to him and knelt by his side.

Marian cradled his head in her arms. "You're back now. You can build them. You can do anything you want. This place is yours. And you've got all those . . . people who have come to help you."

Jack's body hitched. His light was almost gone.

"You need a drink," said Marian, exposing her bandaged wrist and starting to tear at it with her teeth.

He gripped her hand, stopping her. "No. You listen to me. No matter what you think, I never blamed you for anything. You always made me happy. I really enjoyed seeing your commercials and shows on television. I'm sorry I never told what a good actress I think you are. I'll bet you'll be famous someday."

"I won't let it end like this," she whispered, her voice cracking.

"C'mon, Marian—you're an actress. You should know that when it's time to get off stage, you go. And don't milk your exit."

"Yeah," she said, ripping the remaining dressing from her wounded wrist, "but I've been known to demand re-writes."

She bit into the tender flesh of her wrist and tore away what little scabbing was there, then removed the stem from Jack's head and gave him a drink.

A good, long one.

And then he told exactly, precisely what needed to be done.

8

Once you have reached this step in the process, the base-patches should reveal to you the overall pattern you need to follow in order to complete your quilt. How wide to make it and how many patches should be included is up to you. You're on your way to having a patchwork quilt! Congratulations! Now, go back, and repeat steps 1-7 as needed.

Marian and Jack came out with Boots by their side. Alan stood by the Mom-thing's along with everyone else. Marian walked over and embraced her brother.

"Okay, Alan. I know the rest of it."

"You'll have to stay here now, you know?"

"I know."

"Can you accept that?"

"Someday, I think." Marian then caught sight of a new figure entering the cemetery, and smiled when she saw Laura walking toward her. Her sister-in-law's skin was cadaverous, her eyes blank. She had been torn open from the center of her chest on down. Her stomach, liver, and uterus dangled within shiny loops of gray intestine, caught there as if in a spider's web. Everything drooped so low it nearly touched the ground.

She was carrying something that was almost too big for her to handle.

Walking up to Marian, Laura handed over her Story-Quilt-wrapped burden, then took her place by her husband's side, draping one cold-dead arm around his waist, resting her head on his shoulder. Alan kissed her cheek and pointed to the spot where they would rest come morning.

Marian pulled back a corner of the quilt and looked into the baby's face.

Its head was so much larger than the rest of its body, semi-round with deep horizontal grooves in the flesh as well as the skull beneath. Its eyes were so abnormally large and round, its mouth deformed, its nose misshapen and dwarfed by the rest of its features.

Marian wept joy for its hideousness and blessed the night for the pain it was in, a pain that she was now more than willing to share, to savor along with this creature, her nephew, her son, her lover-to-be.

The Quinlan bloodline would remain pure. She could almost see the faces of the children she would have with this after it grew up. How glorious they would be.

She checked her watch. It was nearly midnight. At sunrise on All Saints Day the dead would have to return to their graves and wait for next Hallowe'en to come around before they could rise again.

She studied the pile of stones and human heads.

"A family cathedral," she said.

The thing in her arms cooed and coughed in approval.

There was a stone quarry not too far away. The lumber mill was even closer. She had the whole town here; young and old, the living and the dead.

They had until dawn.

Plenty of time for a good enough start.

She faced the crowd. "We all know what has to be done. If we don't finish tonight, we'll meet here again next year, and the year after that, and the year after that. However long it takes." She stroked the surface of the Story Quilt, knowing what illustration she'd use for the final patch once this project was completed. She could be patient. She was not alone.

She never would be again. She lifted her head and faced the crowd once again. "Let's get to it."

Everyone smiled, the Hallowe'en moon grew brighter as the church bell gave a triumphant ring, and, as a family, they began to raise a dream from the silent, ancient dust of death.

In Loving Memory of My Father,
Frank Henry Braunbeck
May 22, 1926–June 15, 2001

"No, good sir; the privilege was mine."

ABOUT THE AUTHORS

Ray Bradbury's first short stories were published in fanzines during the 1930s. He became a full-time writer by the end of 1942. Known primarily for his short work, Bradbury has also written, among others, the novels *Fahrenheit 451*, *Something Wicked This Way Comes*, and *Dandelion Wine*. He wrote episodes of T*he Twilight Zone* and *The Alfred Hitchcock Hour*, and from 1985-92 his stories were retold in the cable TV series *The Ray Bradbury Theater*. Many of Bradbury's works have been adapted into television shows or films. He received an Emmy Award for his work on animated television movie *The Halloween Tree*, based on his 1972 novel of the same name. Bradbury is one of the most celebrated writers of speculative fiction and the recipient of innumerable awards and honors including the French Commandeur Ordre des Arts et des Lettres and the U.S. National Medal of Arts.

Gary A. Braunbeck is the author of the acclaimed Cedar Hill series of stories and novels, which includes I*n Silent Graves*, *Coffin County*, *Far Dark Fields*, and the forthcoming *A Cracked and Broken Path*. His work had garnered five Bram Stoker Awards, as well as an International Horror Guild Award. He lives in Worthington, Ohio with his wife, author Lucy A. Snyder, and five cats that do hesitate to draw blood if he fails to feed them in time. He has been rumored to sing along with Broadway show tunes, but no recorded evidence of this exists or has yet to be found.

Peter Crowther is the recipient of numerous awards for his writing, his editing and, as publisher, for the hugely successful PS Publishing (now including the Stanza Press poetry subsidiary and PS Artbooks, a specialist imprint dedicated to the comics field). As well as being widely translated, his short stories have been adapted for TV on both sides of the Atlantic and collected in *The Longest Single Note*, *Lonesome Roads*, *Songs of Leaving*, *Cold Comforts*, *The Spaces Between the Lines*, *The Land at the End of the Working Day*, and the upcoming *Jewels In The Dust*. He is the co-author (with James Lovegrove) of *Escardy Gap* and *The Hand That Feeds*, and author of the Forever Twilight SF/horror cycle and *By Wizard Oak*. He lives and works with his wife and business partner, Nicky on the Yorkshire coast of England.

Charles de Lint is a full-time writer and musician who lives in Ottawa, Canada. With thirty-six novels and thirty-five books of short fiction published, he is known as a pioneer and master of the contemporary fantasy genre. Recent books include his young adult novel, *The Painted Boy*, published by Viking Books in November 2010; a short story collection, *The Very Best of Charles de Lint* from Tachyon Press (also 2010); and *The Mystery of Grace*, an adult novel published in 2009. Charles is currently at work on a new young adult series, and recently released *Old Blue Truck*, an album of his original Americana story songs.

Nebula Award winner **Esther Friesner** is the author of thirty-seven novels and over 185 short stories, in addition to being the editor of ten popular anthologies. Her latest novels include *Nobody's Princess* and *Nobody's Prize* (about young Helen of Troy), *Sphinx's Princess* and *Sphinx's Queen* (about young Nefertiti), from Random House, and *Threads and Flames*, from Viking/Penguin. She is presently working on a two-book series about Japan's Queen Himiko—*Spirit's Princess* and *Spirit's Bride*—for Random House. On the editorial front, her most recent publications include Witch Way To The Mall?, Strip Mauled, and Fangs for the Mammaries, an anthology series about witches, werewolves, and vampires in Suburbia. She is married, the mother of two, and lives in Connecticut.

The story reprinted in this volume (first published in 1924 in *Weird Tales*) is the only known fiction by **Lyllian Huntley Harris** (1885-1939).

Glen Hirshberg's novelette, "The Janus Tree," won the 2008 Shirley Jackson Award, and both of his collections, *American Morons* and *The Two Sams*, won the International Horror Guild Award. He is also the author of two novels, *The Book of Bunk* and *The Snowman's Children*. His new collection, *The Janus Tree and Other Stories*, will be published in late 2011. He co-founded, with Dennis Etchison and Peter Atkins, the Rolling Darkness Revue, a traveling ghost story performance troupe that tours the west coast of the United States and elsewhere each October. His fiction has been published in numerous magazines and anthologies, including *Inferno*, *Dark Terrors 6*, *Trampoline*, and *Cemetery Dance*, and has appeared frequently in *The Year's Best Fantasy and Horror*, *The Mammoth Book of Best New Horror*, and *Best Horror of the Year*.

Over the past twenty-some years, **Nina Kiriki Hoffman** has sold adult, tie-in, middle-school, and YA novels and more than 250 short stories. Her works have been finalists for the World Fantasy, Mythopoeic, Sturgeon, Philip K. Dick, and Endeavour awards. Her first novel, *The Thread that Binds the Bones*, won a Stoker award, and her short story, "Trophy Wives," won a Nebula Award in 2009. Novel *Fall of Light* was published by Ace in 2009. Her latest series is Magic Next Door: *Thresholds* was published in 2010, *Meeting*, was released in 2011 by Viking. Hoffman lives in Eugene, Oregon, with several cats and many strange toys and imaginary friends. For a list of her publications, see: ofearna.us/books/hoffman.html.

Four-time Bram Stoker Award-winner **Nancy Holder** has published seventy-five books and more than two hundred short stories and essays. She has written or co-written dozens of Buffy the Vampire Slayer, Smallville, Saving Grace, and Angel projects. Novels from her series, Wicked, appeared on the *New York Times* bestseller list, and she is writing two more young adult dark fantasy series, Crusade and The Wolf Springs Chronicles, both with Debbie Viguié. She teaches in the Stonecoast MFA in Creative Writing Program, offered through the University of Southern Maine. She lives in San Diego with her daughter, Belle, and their growing assortment of pets. Visit her at nancyholder.com.

Charlee Jacob has been a digger for dinosaur bones, a seller of designer rags, and a cook—to mention only a few things. With more than 950 publishing credits, Charlee has been writing dark poetry and prose for more than twenty-five years. Some of her recent publishing events include the novel *Still*, the poetry collection *Heresy*, and the novel *Dark Moods*. She is a three-time Bram Stoker Award winner, two of those awards for her novel *Dread In The Beast* and the poetry collection *Sineater*; the third award for collaborative poetry collection, *Vectors*, with Marge Simon. Permanently disabled, Jacob has begun to paint as one of her forms of phsycial therapy. To see some of Charlee's paintings visit www.charleejacob.com. She lives in Irving, Texas with her husband Jim and a plethora of felines.

K.W. Jeter is widely credited as having coined in 1987 the term "steampunk," and is the author of *Morlock Night* and *Infernal Devices*, two of the earliest novels in the genre. Both have recently been reprinted by Angry Robot. *Fiendish Schemes*, his long-awaited sequel to *Infernal Devices*, will be available soon from Tor. In addition, he has written many other novels, including *Dr. Adder, Farewell Horizontal, Soul Eater,* and *In the Land of the Dead.* In addition to his writing career, he has worked as a researcher for the University of California Medical Center on AIDS-related bereavement issues with heroin addicts, and as a creative writing instructor for Portland State University in Oregon. After residences in England and Spain, he currently lives with his wife Geri in San Francisco, California. For more information see: www.kwjeter.com.

Caitlín R. Kiernan is the author of several novels, including *Low Red Moon, Daughter of Hounds,* and *The Red Tree,* which was nominated for both the Shirley Jackson and World Fantasy awards. Her next novel, *The Drowning Girl: A Memoir,* will be released by Penguin in 2012. Since 2000, her shorter tales of the weird, fantastic, and macabre have been collected in several volumes, including *Tales of Pain and Wonder; From Weird and Distant Shores; To Charles Fort, With Love; Alabaster; A is for Alien;* and *The Ammonite Violin & Others.* In 2012, Subterranean Press will release a retrospective of her early writing, *Two Worlds and In Between: The Best of Caitlín R. Kiernan (Volume One).* She lives in Providence, RI, with her partner Kathryn.

Nancy Kilpatrick (and her noms de plume Amarantha Knight and Desirée Knight) has published eighteen novels, a nonfiction book, over 200 short stories, and five collections. (A sixth collection, *Vampire Variations,* is forthcoming.) She has also has edited twelve anthologies, the most recent of which are *Evolve: Vampire Stories of the Undead* and *Evolve Two: Vampire Stories of the Future Undead.* An new anthology, *Danse Macabre: Close Encounters with the Reaper,* will be published in 2012. A Bram Stoker finalist three times, a finalist for the Aurora Award five times, and winner of the Arthur Ellis Award for best mystery, she lives with her calico cat Fedex in lovely Montréal. As with previous dwellings, this one features Gothic decor, which suits the sensibilities of both residents.

Sarah Langan is a three-time winner of the Bram Stoker Award. She is the author of the novels *The Keeper* and *The Missing,* and her most recent novel, *Audrey's Door,* won the 2009 Stoker for best novel. Her short fiction has appeared in the magazines *Cemetery Dance, Phantom,* and *Chiaroscuro,* and in the anthologies *Darkness on the Edge* and *Unspeakable Horror.* She is currently working on a post-apocalyptic young adult series called Kids and two adult novels: *Empty Houses*, which was inspired by *The Twilight Zone*, and *My Father's Ghost*, which was inspired by *Hamlet*.

Joe R. Lansdale is the author of over thirty novels and numerous short stories. His novella, *Bubba Hotep*, was made into an award-winning film of the same name, as was *Incident On and Off a Mountain Road*. Both were directed by Don Coscarelli. His works have received numerous recognitions, including the Edgar, eight Bram Stoker awards, the Grinizani Prize for Literature, American Mystery Award, the International Horror Award, British Fantasy Award, and many others. His most recent novel is *Devil Red*, the eighth featuring Hap and Leonard. *All the Earth, Thrown to the Sky*, his first novel for young adults has just been published.

Thomas Ligotti's fiction has been collected in a dozen books. He also has a collection of poetry and one of nonfiction to his credit. The winner of the Small Press Writers and Artists Organization, three Bram Stoker Awards, and an International Horror Guild Award, Ligotti has collaborated with the musical group Current 93 on four albums. Fox Atomic Comics published two graphic titles—*The Nightmare Factory* and T*he Nightmare Factory: Volume 2*—based on the author's stories. Wonder Entertainment has released *The Frolic Collector's Edition DVD and Book* set, which contains a short film adaptation of Thomas Ligotti's short story "The Frolic."

H.P. Lovecraft (1890-1937) was an American author of weird fiction and what he termed "cosmic horror." According to Joyce Carol Oates, Lovecraft "an incalculable influence on succeeding generations of writers of horror fiction," comparable to Edgar Allan Poe. Stephen King has called Lovecraft "the twentieth century's greatest practitioner of the classic horror tale."

Gary McMahon's fiction has appeared in magazines and anthologies in the U.K. and U.S and has been reprinted in both *The Mammoth Book of Best New Horror* and *The Year's Best Fantasy & Horror*. He is the British-Fantasy-Award-nominated author of *Rough Cut, All Your Gods Are Dead, Dirty Prayers, How to Make Monsters, Rain Dogs, Different Skins, Pieces of Midnight, The Harm*, and *Hungry Hearts*. He has also edited an anthology of original novelettes titled *We Fade to Grey*. Current and forthcoming projects include anthology *The End of the Line*, novels *Pretty Little Dead*

Things, and *Dead Bad Things* from Angry Robot, and The Concrete Grove trilogy from Solaris. His website: www.garymcmahon.com.

Best known as the author of such children's novels as *The Railway Children* and *The Story of the Treasure-Seekers,* the English writer **E. Nesbit** (1858-1924) also authored fiction, drama, and poetry for adults. According to Gore Vidal: "After Lewis Carroll, E. Nesbit is the best of the English fabulists who wrote about children (neither wrote for children) and like Carroll she was able to create a world of magic and inverted logic that was entirely her own." In addition she was active in political causes and together with her husband, Hubert Bland, the playwright Bernard Shaw, and others, founded the Fabian Society in England to further socialist aims.

William F. Nolan is best known for co-authoring the novel *Logan's Run,* with George Clayton Johnson. The novel has been adapted to film, a television series, comic books, and an alternative reality game. Nolan co-wrote the screenplay for the 1976 horror film *Burnt Offerings* and has scripted fourteen teleplays. The author of more than 150 short stories, a dozen novels, and editor or co-editor of a dozen anthologies, Nolan had been named as a Living Legend by the International Horror Guild, received the honorary title of Author Emeritus from the Science Fiction and Fantasy Writers of America, Inc., and is a Horror Writers of America's Lifetime Achievement Award recipient.

Stewart O'Nan's dozen novels include *Snow Angels, The Speed Queen, The Night Country* (set on Halloween!), and cult favorite and International Horror Guild winner *A Prayer for the Dying.* He was born in Pittsburgh on George A. Romero's birthday.

Norman Partridge's fiction includes horror, suspense, and the fantastic—"sometimes all in one story" according to Joe R. Lansdale. Partridge's novel *Dark Harvest* was chosen by *Publishers Weekly* as one of the 100 Best Books of 2006, and two short story collections were published in 2010—*Lesser Demons* from Subterranean Press and *Johnny Halloween* from Cemetery Dance. Other work includes the Jack Baddalach mysteries *Saguaro Riptide* and *The Ten-Ounce Siesta,* plus *The Crow: Wicked Prayer,* which was adapted for film. Partridge's compact, thrill-a-minute style has been praised by Stephen King and Peter Straub, and his work has received multiple Bram Stoker awards. He can be found on the web at NormanPartridge.com and americanfrankenstein.blogspot.com.

Edgar Allan Poe (1809–1849) was an author, poet, editor, and literary critic. Poe, one of the earliest American practitioners of the short story, is considered the inventor of the genre of detective fiction and credited with contributing to the then-emerging genre of science fiction. A master of the macabre, his influence on horror and dark fantasy is incalculable.

Tina Rath has made radio and television appearances and lectured on vampires and other aspects of Gothic literature for various groups and societies. Her fiction has been published in periodicals such as *All Hallows, Ghosts and Scholars, The Magazine of Fantasy & Science Fiction, Supernatural Tales 16, Visionary Tongue,* and *Weird Tales.* Anthology appearances include *Strange Tales, Exotic Gothic 3,* and *The Mammoth Book of Vampires.* She edited the anthology *Conventional Vampires.*

Al Sarrantonio is the author of forty-five books. He is a winner of the Bram Stoker Award and has been a finalist for the World Fantasy Award, the British Fantasy Award, the International Horror Guild Award, the Locus Award, and the Shamus Award. His novels include *Orangefield* and *Hallows Eve.* He has edited numerous anthologies including *Halloween: New Poems, Portents,* and, with Neil Gaiman, *Stories.* His short stories have appeared in numerous magazines and anthologies. His best horror stories have been collected in *Toybox, Hornets and Others,* and *Halloween and Other Seasons.*

Sir Walter Scott (1771–1832) was a Scottish historical novelist, playwright, and poet and the first English-language author to have a truly international career in his lifetime. Many of his works remain classics of English-language literature.

John Shirley's many novels include *City Come A-Walkin', Eclipse, Demons, Crawlers, Cellars, In Darkness Waiting, Black Glass, Bleak History,* and the forthcoming *Everything Is Broken.* His numerous short stories have been collected in eight volumes including the Stoker and International Horror Guild Award-winning *Black Butterflies* (chosen by *Publishers Weekly* as one of the Best Books of the Year) and, most recently, *In Extremis: The Most Extreme Short Stories of John Shirley*. Considered seminal to the cyberpunk genre, he has been termed "the post-modern Poe." His dark fiction has been called "astonishingly consistent and rigorously horrifying" by *The New York Times Review of Books*. Co-screenwriter of the film *The Crow*, he has written scripts for television. His website is: www.john-shirley.com.

Peter Straub is the author of seventeen novels which have been translated into more than twenty languages. They include *Ghost Story*, *Koko*, *Mr. X*, *In the Night Room*, *A Dark Matter*, and two collaborations with Stephen King, *The Talisman* and *Black House*. He has written two volumes of poetry and two collections of short fiction. Straub edited the Library of America's edition of *H.P. Lovecraft's Tales* and the forthcoming Library of America's two-volume anthology, *American Fantastic Tales*. He has won the British Fantasy Award, nine Bram Stoker Awards, two International Horror Guild Awards, and two World Fantasy Awards. In 1998, he was named Grand Master at the World Horror Convention. In 2006, he was given the HWA's Life Achievement Award and, in 2008, both the International Horror Guild's Living Legend Award and the Barnes & Noble Writers for Writers Award by Poets & Writers.

The author of about 250 short stories, **Steve Rasnic Tem** is the recipient of British Fantasy, World Fantasy, and International Horror Guild Awards. His new novel *Deadfall Hotel* will come out in the spring of 2012 from Solaris Books, with simultaneous US and UK editions. A limited hardcover will appear in late 2011 from Centipede Press. In August 2012, New Pulp Press will publish his dark noir story collection, *Ugly Behavior*. He lives in Colorado with his wife, author Melanie Tem. Their website: http://www.m-s-tem.com.

F. Paul Wilson is the *New York Times* bestselling author of horror, adventure, medical thrillers, science fiction, and virtually everything in between. His books include the Repairman Jack novels—including *Ground Zero*, *Fatal Error*, and *The Dark at the End*—the Adversary cycle—including *The Keep*, and *The Tomb*—and a young adult series featuring the teenage Jack. Wilson has won the Prometheus Award, the Bram Stoker Award, the Inkpot Award from the San Diego ComiCon, and the Lifetime Achievement Award of the Horror Writers of America, among other honors.

Chelsea Quinn Yarbro is the first woman to be named a Living Legend by the International Horror Guild (2006). She was honored in 2009 with a Bram Stoker Lifetime Achievement Award by the Horror Writers Association. Yarbro was named as Grand Master of the World Horror Convention in 2003. She is the recipient of the Fine Foundation Award for Literary Achievement (1993) and (along with Fred Saberhagen) was awarded the Knightly Order of the Brasov Citadel by the Transylvanian Society of Dracula in 1997. She has been nominated for the Edgar, World Fantasy, and Bram Stoker Awards and was the first female president of the Horror Writers Association. Best known for her Saint-Germain Cycle of twenty-four (and still counting) books, she is the author of numerous short stories and scores of novels in many genres.

ABOUT THE EDITOR

Paula Guran is the editor of Pocket Book's Juno fantasy imprint, Senior Editor for Prime Books, and nonfiction editor for *Weird Tales*. In an earlier life she produced weekly email newsletter *DarkEcho* (winning two Bram Stoker Awards, an International Horror Guild Award award, and a World Fantasy Award nomination), edited *Horror Garage* magazine (earning another IHG and a second World Fantasy nomination), and has contributed reviews, interviews, and articles to numerous professional publications. She's also done a great deal of other various and sundry work in sf/f/h publishing. Anthologies Guran has edited include *Embraces, Best New Paranormal Romance, Best New Romantic Fantasy 2, Zombies: The Recent Dead, The Year's Best Dark Fantasy & Horror: 2010, Vampires: The Recent Undead, The Year's Best Dark Fantasy & Horror: 2011*, and *New Cthulhu: The Recent Weird*.

COPYRIGHTS & FIRST PUBLICATION

"The October Game" © 1948 (renewed 1975) by Ray Bradbury. First publication: *Weird Tales, Vol. 40, No. 3*, March 1948.

Tessellations © 2001 by Gary Braunbeck. First publication: *Trick or Treat: A Collection of Halloween Novellas*, ed. Richard Chizmar (Cemetery Dance).

"Memories" © 2010 by Peter Crowther. First publication: *Cemetery Dance, # 63*.

"Universal Soldier" © 2006 by Charles de Lint. First publication: *Mythspring*, eds. Julie E. Czeneda & Genevieve Kierans (Red Deer Press).

"Auntie Elspeth's Halloween Story or The Gourd, The Bad, And The Ugly" © 2001 by Esther M. Friesner. First publication: *The Ultimate Halloween*, ed. Marvin Kaye (iBooks).

"Struwwelpeter" © 2001 by Glen Hirshberg. First publication: *SciFiction* (SciFi. com), November 28, 2001.

"Pranks" © 2009 by Nina Kiriki Hoffman. First publication: *Lone Star Stories Issue # 33*, June 1, 2009.

"The Vow on Halloween" by Lyllian Huntley Harris. First publication: *Weird Tales, Vol. 4, No. 2*, May-June 1924.

"By the Book" © 2010 by Nancy Holder. First publication: *More Stories from the Twilight Zone*, ed. Carol Sterling (Tor).

"The Sticks" © 2007 by Charlee Jacob. First publication: *Cemetery Dance #57*.

"Riding Bitch" © 2007 by K.W. Jeter. First publication: *Inferno*, ed. Ellen Datlow (Tor).

"On the Reef" © 2010 by Caitlín R. Kiernan. First publication: *Sirenia Digest #59*.

"Memories of El Día De Los Muertos" © 2000 by Nancy Kilpatrick. First publication: *Dead of Night Magazine #8/The Vampire Stories of Nancy Kilpatrick* (Mosaic Press).

"The Great Pumpkin Arrives at Last" © 2008 by Sarah Langan. First publication: *Doorways #7*.

"On a Dark October" © 1984 by Joe R. Lansdale. First publication: *The Horror Show*, Spring 1984.

"Conversations in a Dead Language" © 1989 by Thomas Ligotti. *Deathrealm #8*, Spring 1989.

"Pumpkin Night" © 2007 by Gary McMahon. First publication: *Estronomicon*, October 2007.

"Hallowe'en in a Suburb" by H.P. Lovecraft. First publication: *The National Amateur, 48, No. 4*, March 1926 (as "In a Suburb").

"Man-Size in Marble" by E. Nesbit. First publication: *Grim Tales* (A.D. Innes, 1893).

"The Halloween Man" by William F. Nolan © 1986 by TZ Publications. First publication: *Night Cry*, Summer 1986.

"Monsters" © 2010 by Stewart O'Nan. First publication: *Cemetery Dance #65*.

"Three Doors" © 2006 by Norman Partridge. First publication: *At the Sign of the Snow Man's Skull* (Earthling).

"Ulalume: A Ballad" by Edgar Allan Poe. First publication (anonymously): *American Review: A Whig Journal No. XXXVI*, December 1847.

"Night Out" © 1985 by Tina Rath. First publication: *Woman's Realm*, 1985.

"Hornets" © 2001 by Al Sarrantonio. First publication: *Trick or Treat: A Collection of Halloween Novellas*, ed. Richard Chizmar (Cemetery Dance).

"The Young Tamlane" by Sir Walter Scott. First publication (this version): *Minstrelsy of the Scottish Border Consisting of Historical and Romantic Ballads, Collected in the Southern Counties of Scotland; With a Few of Modern Date, Founded Upon Local Tradition, Volume II*, 2nd Edition, 1803 (Longman and Rees).

"Mask Game" © 2000 by John Shirley. First publication: *October Dreams: A Celebration of Halloween*, ed. Richard Chizmar (Cemetery Dance).

Pork Pie Hat by Peter Straub © 1994 Seafront Corporation. First publication: *Murder for Halloween: Tales of Suspense*, eds. Michele Slung & Roland Hartman (The Mysterious Press).

"Halloween Street" © 1999 by Steve Rasnic Tem. First publication: *The Magazine of Fantasy and Science Fiction*, July 1999.

"Tricks & Treats: One Night on Halloween Street" © 1999 by Steve Rasnic Tem. First publication: *The Magazine of Fantasy and Science Fiction*, December 1999.

"The November Game" © 1991 by F. Paul Wilson. First publication: *The Bradbury Chronicles*, eds. William F. Nolan & Martin H. Greenberg (Penguin/ROC).

"Sugar Skulls" © 2005 by Chelsea Quinn Yarbro. First publication: *H.P. Lovecraft's Magazine of Horror #3*.